L'AFFAIRES NON FINI

V. J. NICHOLAS

Paperback: 978-1-964744-00-1
eBook: 978-1-964744-01-8
Library of Congress Control Number: 2024911180

Ordering Information:

Prime Seven Media
518 Landmann St.
Tomah City, WI 54660

Printed in the United States of America

"Ladies and Gentlemen, let us come to order please", said Senator Hiram Mulvahill, the US Senates President Pro tempore and Acting President of the United States. "Time is of the utmost essence", he said as he entered the crowded cabinet assembly room and took his seat.

"I've asked the cabinet from the previous presidency to hold over temporarily in the current positions, until Vice President Magnusson recovers from the wounds he suffered during the attack earlier this afternoon, during the inauguration day parade"!

As he adjusted his readsing glasses he stated, "Reports are in front of me indicating the Speaker of the House, is dire condition at Walter Reed Hospital and is not expected to make it through the night. Is this correct", Mulvahill asked the Surgeon General?

"Yes sir it is", answered Dr. Mace Greenlee!

"What's the rest of the bad news, Dr. Greenlee"?

"Bad news sir"?

"The damned body count Sir. Who's dead? Who's hurt? Who's gonna make it and who is not likely to"?

"Starting with President Dobbins and his family, they're all gone. The four RPG's, if I may call them that for the lack of a better word, eviscerated the Presidential Limousine and all it contained. Not even enough left to bury properly, but forensic teams from Quantico are at it sorting out the remains as best they can"!

"As to the Vice President Magnusson, He's at Bethesda Naval Hospital, and is poor but stable condition, suffering broken bones, a punctured lung, a severe concussion and an assortment of other injuries as well as one to one of his kidneys. Given that as of this hour of ten PM, the doctors completed their prolonged surgery an hour ago and induced a coma to the Vice President in order to aid in the healing process"!

"An, uh, what's the medical term Doctor, for his recoverability"?

"Oh, you mean prognosis"?

"Yes"!

"Prognosis seems as good as could be expected given the seriousness and amount of his injuries. All the myriad of known complications to his bodily functions have been seen to effectively, but what's unknown is the status of his concussion. The plan is to round the clock monitor his progress, never a moment when a pair of eyes will not be on his person. Top notch people, nobody going home for the duration Sir. In about two weeks, his status will be reviewed and if he appears to be making sufficient recovery, he'll most likely that he'll be gently be brought out of his coma"!

"So it's safe to assume that he has no cognition of what's befallen him Doctor"?

"No sir, which is why he's been placed in a coma, for the added psychological stress of knowing that his wife and two children are laying in the mortuary several levels below him, at this perilous time most likely can tip the scales in the negative"!

"Please continue Doctor"!

The Surgeon General hurriedly ran through the list of important personages that had died and those who were on the mend in one fashion or the other.

"So if I understand, the most recent report correctly there is slightly over three hundred dead and counting sir, inclusive of the civilian visitors"!

"Thus far subject to change as reports arrive"1

"General Ottenger, as Commanding General of the Joint Chiefs of Staff, where are we militarily"? "As of 1500 hrs. this day, all Branches of the military are on full alert, until otherwise directed. As of the same time, the District of Columbia has been under full military lockdown and control and the adjoining states of Maryland and Virginia are have called out the National Guard on full alert status awaiting further directives and or developments"! "Has anyone gone over the killing grounds and done the usual after action investigation General"?

"The Director of the FBI could better answer that question Mr.

President, but I can say that elements of the military are available for the director at any time and all he has to do is give a verbal heads up"!

"We'll talk to Director Hanley, in a moment. But what I want to do is hear from the Director of the Secret Service, Porter Ealing. Porter, you were in charge of the security for the entire event. Scores are dead and seriouslywounded. Right now all of this falls squarely on your shoulders. So tell us all how this could've happened"?

"Well, Mr. President", the…."Just how could this have happened", growled President Mulvahill angrily, interrupting the Director, "When the Secret Service puts everyone through metal detection devices and I mean everyone, no exceptions, or were there exceptions? When the Secret Service inspects the underground and tack welds shut all the manhole covers. When we have roving K-9 units, the sniffer dogs, sticking their snoots up everything trying to detect explosives or ordinance, when we have counter snipers on surrounding roof tops and a bunch of choppers discretely orbiting," pointed out an angry Mulvahill.

"If I may continue sir," offered Ealing, trying to compose himself. "We believe, for the moment that there were about seven females, with AP-4 Rocket launchers in amongst those attending the inauguration, with the sole purpose of beheading our government. After they had launched their rockets all but one blew themselves up. The one that didn't blow herself up, also luckily, was unable to ignite the AP-4 launcher and subsequently unable to ignite the explosive vest she wore and after shooting several people turned her pistol on herself and dies on the spot. A visual inspection of the body is indicative of that of Middle Eastern origin, but that will be confirmed or denied after a forensic autopsy that is taking place as we speak"!

In addition, there appeared from outside the perimeter, two Federal Express trucks from opposite ends of the parade route in front of the Capitol complex. Both trucks were stopped and directed to turn around, which they did. Now upon completion of the action and simultaneously acting just as the executive vehicles were being attacked, both rear doors of the trucks flew open and the nearby roadblocks were eviscerated, by quad fifty caliber browning anti-aircraft guns, of world war two vintage, that were assembled and fitted into each truck. Now both vehicles were several miles apart, but each weapon has a lethal range in excess of two miles. With the crush of the crowds and in all the excitement of the moment, the bands playing, the crowds cheering, all they had to do was point and shoot and massive damage would occur"!

Continuing his narration, Director Ealing said, "In the subsequent chase that occurred, that was televised by the overhead helicopters, the DC police cars that chased them were soon destroyed by the firepower of each vehicle and eventually one of the fleeing trucks was destroyed by one of the overhead military helicopters, while the other simply blew itself up after running out of ammunition. Each vehicle was blown apart to such a degree that only body parts remain. Once again forensic teams are examining the remains as to ascertain ethnic origin. We have some fingers which have been printed and are being scanned worldwide for any signs of identification"!

"All well and good Director Ealing, but that doesn't answer just how, some women could elude, your metal detectors and sniffer dogs and gain entrance into the ceremonies, with explosives strapped to their persons, be armed with hand guns and have an AP-4 rocket launcher, now does it", said the Acting President angrily!

"The very last thing you'd ever want to do is appear on 'Meet the Press', and have that lame story to tell, the moderator"! One wouldn't have to be a genius to conclude one of two possibilities, the first of which is that you are either stupid or complicit"!

"How could any of us in this room, trust the Secret Services Security Detail, given what you've just shared with us? Clearly there's something amiss somewhere in your organization. One doesn't have to be a TV lawyer to figure that out Director Ealing"!

"Sir, you're convicting an entire branch of Government, without a shred of proof and I find that unconscionable", said Ealing getting up from his chair.

"Sit right down Ealing, we're not done with you yet", said President Mulvahill. "This is not a court of law and we are not bound by the presumption of innocence. That only occurs when criminal charges are about to be brought"! "Anyone have any other questions", asked Mulvahill looking around to the others?

"What, Director Ealing, are you doing with each member of the Security Detail of an investigative nature", asked General Ottenger?

"We are going to polygraph each member of everyone on the ground, especially those responsible for manning the entrance points and the metal detectors", said Ealing his voice starting to wilt with the pressure he felt.

"Odd how no mention of the K-9's in attendance, comes up", said General Ottenger, "but I've no bona fides in the veterinary sciences, but it seems to me what with all the bomb and ordinance sniffing dogs about, not one of them seemed to sniff out a single piece of ordinance. So the question is, have the dogs involved with the event been examined for any evidence of tampering along with, or by their handlers"?

At that very moment the last light bulb in each of their heads, went on full light. Not a single report of any of the dogs, revealed any sign of the obvious. Somehow, the dogs had been gotten to along with something horribly amiss in the entry checkpoints.

"Mr. President, may I make a suggestion" asked General Ottenger?

"Please speak your mind General"!

"Since a cloud of suspicion has been placed on the head of the Director of the Secret Service, seems that a full investigation by the Justice Department and the FBI is in order along with some assistance in the area of security for the office of the President and the incumbent Vice President. So perhaps, the secretary of the Navy might suggest to the Naval Chief of Staff, that a contingent of SEALS be attached on a TDY basis to the Security Detail of the Secret Service and that the security be expanded to include various key members of both Houses of Congress on an 'Ad Hoc' basis"!

The Secretary of the Navy nodded his head in agreement saying "I agree", then looked at the Naval Chief, who said, "Aye sir! We'll make it so"!

"To include a joint round the clock detail to see to the security of the Vice President, until its determined that he can take the oath of office, or not", added Hiram Mulvahill, with all in concurrence as he looked around the table. The meeting concluded with the agenda for the next week being a daily meeting of the key members to exchange information and for the political transparency it conveyed.

As Mulvahill entered the oval office, he asked Orval Goodwin the current White House, Chief of Staff, to give him a half hour of solitude, prior to the round robin of meetings for the rest of the night.

With all of the security agencies on full alert, chasing down leads as to the probable perpetrators, there was little that he could do until more was known. Navy SEALS would be attached to the security detail for the current White House and key congressional members, thus eliminating a potential manpower problem. The government would keep running and the world would keep turning, at least for a little while.

As he stood behind the President's desk, he looked out of the bullet proof glass and wondered. For a number of years ago when he first entered the Senate, he had to admit that he briefly toyed around with the notion of running for the Presidency as did many other Senators, from time to time. Then with the arrival and departure of several presidents over the years, that thought fought its way back into his consciousness, but for only a brief while. He knew his limits and neither did he look Presidential, but he didn't sound Presidential.

His eastern Kentucky twang, always coming off to those who mattered as a common Hill Jack, sadly misplaced. But he fit right in with his fellow Kentuckians, who continually returned him to Congress and he never failed to remind those who mattered in the State, just who they were beholdin' to, distributing favors and earmarks to those who were responsible for returning him to office, one way or the other. After all, money was just one of many mediums of exchange. His unspoken mantra was first last and always, "Kentuckians First"!

Yet now, it was necessary to alter his thinking, at least for a little while. Then as a bird crossed his view and landed on a tree branch, a shudder went up his aging spine, causing him to wonder, 'Am I up to it'?

For years, both political friends and opponents heaped praise upon him as the great compromiser, the one person that could find the middle ground in any issue. But this responsibility that was heaped upon him by circumstance was one that could test his decision making ability, for after all, the Buck stopped right at this desk. No longer could he have the luxury of avoiding the black and white of a situation, thus embracing the gray.

Now he would have to summon something deep within and he would need help, a great deal of help.

Not being an overtly religious man, yet able to roll with any of the Pentecostals and Baptists in Kentucky for the political show, he slowly got down on one knee, his bones creaking with the arthritis he was afflicted with and whispered the Lord's Prayer and then the Psalm of David, "The Lord is my Shepard, I shall not want", he droned on. As he recited the prayers, a bead of sweat rolled down his weathered brow, hanging by a thread over his eyebrow.

When he finished, he grabbed the desk and sat in the Presidents chair, feeling a bit flush and asked the eternal, "Please show me the way"!

His reverie was interrupted by the buzzing of the intercom. He pushed the button saying "Yes"? "Mr. President, this is Peggy Myers, the Presidents secretary. May I have a brief moment with you"?

"Come right in Mrs. Myers", said Mulvahill! As the door opened into the Oval Office in walked Peggy Myers, the previous Presidents Secretary.

"Thank you Mr. President, I won't take but a few moments of your time. As you may or may not be aware, When President Dobbins was still alive, his transition team came with a new secretary and her name is Melanie O'Bannon. She'd been with President Dobbins when he was the Governor of Texas as his personal secretary and he thought to bring her along. My husband is suffering from Alzheimer's and I need to be with him as soon as possible and I'd planned on being with him in two weeks. Now I've been working with Mrs. O'Bannon for the last week, familiarizing her with the normal routine of the Presidential Office and the various procedures and I find her to be well experienced and a very quick study. So the reason I'm here is to verbally inform you of my departure, by the end of the week.

Now Mrs. O'Bannon has already been completely vetted, by the appropriate agencies. So if you'll allow me I'd like to briefly introduce you to Melanie"!

"I'm so sorry to hear about your husband Mrs. Myers and as long as we'll have your presence for a little while longer around here, I'm certain Mrs. O'Bannon will work out just fine so bring her on in"!

Peggy then arose from her seat and crossed over to the door and opened it saying, "Melanie, the President will see you now"!

Into the office walked a tall stately woman, with long well-coiffed Chestnut hair, and a long legged graceful stride, elegantly attired in a gray business suit.

As she stood before Hiram Muvahill, he was almost dumb struck by her beauty as she said, "Mr. President, I'm so sorry to meet you under these horrible circumstances, but I promise to do all that I can to be of service in these trying times"!

"Mrs. O'Bannon, you come highly recommended and I'm sure that if you met the criterion of President Dobbins, you'll do just fine"!

"Just one question if I may", said Melanie! "Fire away young lady"!

"How do you take your coffee"?

"Cream and sugar three cubes and how do you wish to be addressed? Mrs. O'Bannon or by Melanie"

"Melanie will do just fine sir, but I'm trained to respond either way", she said with a brief wink"!

As both made to leave the Oval office, Mulvahill said, "Oh Mrs. Myers would you hang back for just a moment"? As the door closed and Peggy approached the desk Mulvahill said, "I think this woman will work out just fine, so I want you to direct Orval Goodwin to make certain that she knows everything he knows. She is to be brought up to speed on everything soonest, before your departure"!

"A bit of departure from the normal procedure isn't it Mr. President", asked Peggy!

"Probably so, but these are trying times and never the less, there's a method to my thinking, so please tell Orval of my wishes"!

The rest of the night was spent in brief meetings with important personages from the various countries sending their condolences and promising full cooperation with the appropriate governmental entities. Yet since none of the attackers survived, there were no overt trails to pursue. It was understood by all appropriate governmental investigative agencies, of this being a full court press operation and that many people would lose a great deal of sleep, before many days went by. The daily meetings of the governmental heads were conducted at noon each day in the White House, each day with a gaggle of news reporters held at bay each day upon their departure, with only scant information being announced to the media each day, by way of the press secretary's daily televised meetings.

"Gentleman and Ladies, what do we know and what do we suspect", asked Acting President Mulvahill? "Director Ealing, you're up first"!

"Mr. President, we believe that we know of the origin of the fifty caliber anti-aircraft weapons that were used. The serial numbers were traced to weapons thought rendered unusable, that were housed in a World War Two exhibition warehouse, that was broken into some months ago, near a National Guard Armory in Colorado. The FBI is on it and Director Hanley can speak to that better than I"!

"Are the Navy SEALS in place yet, Director Hanley", asked Mulvahill? "Half of them are and the other half en route. By noon tomorrow all the additional manpower you've directed will be in place, Mr. President"!

"What about the forensic examination of the remains of the attackers, Dr. Greenlee"?

"Thus far, we've concluded that three of the female attackers were of Middle Eastern origin, while the rest are of eastern European origin. We conclude they're of Circassian or Caucasian origin most likely from a Muslim region north of The Republic of Georgia. As to the remains of the Federal Express truck attackers, forensic examinations of their remains indicate that they were all male and of various national origins, African's, Oriental, and Northern European.

"Director Latham, can you tell us what if anything the NSA has picked up"?

"Sir, nothing but useless chatter so far on the airwaves, but on a hunch I directed my people to go back some six months on operational reports and see if there were anything that was swept under the rug and given short shrift as it were. Well, I'm sorry to say that there was a lone report by one of our technicians, that was pigeon holed by one of the supervisors, that was rather revealing, when paid proper attention to. When all of the dots were connected, it revealed the attack on Washington in vague and unspecific terms, never mentioning the Inauguration, yet even of greater concern, is a multi-pronged assault on our homeland, set in place by foreign assets placed in country long ago. The attacks will be of both a high tech and low tech status and will be spread out during the course of the year"!

"And Director, what do you make of this", asked Mulvahill?

"As to the High Tech attacks, I can only speculate that some sort of Cyber-attack on our Cyber Infrastructure, that if successful can render the entire country deaf, dumb and blind. I've already taken it upon myself to set in place defensive measures that can at the very least partially deflect the attack and in some cases reflect the attack back upon the attackers electronically. We've run continuous models and exercises with the National Cyber Center and are but awaiting your approval to put them in place"!

"Do it", said Mulvahill! "Further, I'm directing on my verbal orders, the CIA and the FBI, to act jointly for the duration of this emergency. Tear down any walls that exist between you gentlemen and cooperate completely. The first indication of interagency non-cooperation will find the both of you gentlemen out on your ears immediately. There's way too much at stake and that goes for any agency of the Federal Government. Y'all have a lot of talent under your respective commands, so loosen the reins on the livestock. What is required here is complete cooperation. If one of your contemporaries asks for something, provide it immediately. As of now, the so called 'Rules of Engagement' are to be considered relaxed until further notice by this office by my verbal directive. No doubt there will be some political fallout from all this, by the civil libertarians. So be it, for the buck stops at this desk. It's clear to me that we're in an undeclared war by a host of the unseen and it's your collective jobs to shed the light of day upon these cretins. Now if there's anyone in this room that has a problem with this, or feels that they cannot fully cooperate with their contemporaries as directed, please speak now and I'll gladly accept your resignations as of immediately"! Mulvahill slowly scanned the room and no one sad a word. "Good, now that our team is in place, I want to add one more thing. No leaks to the press will be tolerated. Not a single one by any of your agencies or departments. Loose lips sink ships people. America cannot afford it.

When Vice President Magnusson recovers, god willing, he can modify or rescind these directives as he sees fit, in the event he assumes the mantle of the Presidency, but until then, please do what we all agree needs to be done, for time is of the essence. There's going to be a lot of lost sleep, by all of us, so please alert your families that any vacations planned will be put on the back burner, for the foreseeable future"!

In the coming days Hiram Mulvahill, met with various selected Presidents of Unions, the Banking community, key Governors, Mayors and a few trusted members of Congress, to tell them selectively of the overall peril that was about to descend upon the land. In each and every case, he told a variation of what was known sufficient to moderate any concerns or political agenda they may have harbored. In each case, the meeting was held at night away from the prying eyes of the press and in each case, the meeting was one on one, with a pledge of complete cooperation for the duration of the crises.

Every day he read a progress report on Larson Magnusson from the hospital as the very first thing on his agenda, praying each day for his full and complete recovery. This prayer was not altogether altruistic in nature, for each day of his interim duty he grew weary of the weight of the responsibility that had been placed upon his old back. He longed for the days when he could be simply the President Pro Tempore of the US Senate. The Grand Old Man. There, one only had to pontificate and have eager Young Turk lawyers do the heavy lifting. As acting President, during a period of crisis, one had to manage a horde of professional people effectively and that was the province of a much younger man, with zeal and energy.

Yet even if Magnusson recovered, in part or in full, would he have the right stuff to shoulder this heavy load, Hiram wondered privately? His family savagely obliterated and he being completely alone. How would he react? His entire political career had been pretty well undistinguished, voting pretty much along party lines as directed. He had been selected by President Dobbins, because he appeared and sounded Presidential. He had made no political enemies that were of any consequence and it was clear that he was being groomed for greater things. Was this the fine hand of the unseen working its will upon the world? Only time would tell.

There he lay in a hospital bed, where he didn't know. Lars Magnusson lay there inert, with tubes and sensors connected to machines that worked non-stop in a sterile environment. He felt no pain and had already experienced the trip. That pristine trip, down the long alabaster tunnel. At the tunnels termination, he saw an image of his wife smiling along with his young daughter and son. Then he knew they were in the hands of the almighty. Part of him wanted to cry, yet in the fields of Elysium there were no tears, no sadness. He heard no sound, yet he could somehow understand that they were in a better place. The children would never age, nor would his wife. When he caught up with them later, they would be exactly as he'd last seen them. Their message was simply for him not to worry, that time had little meaning where they were and that all of their wants and needs would be provided for. In his mind he tried to reach out for them, but they had no real form as he'd come to understand earthly substance, but they were real enough in this plane of existence. Then one by one, all of his ancestors and that of his wife, paraded past his view, for what seemed like the longest time, introducing themselves. People he'd never even heard of, paraded past, then drifted out of view leaving only his wife and children. He saw his wife move her lips as if to speak, but like in a Chinese movie, the English translation didn't match the movement of the lips, yet the message was clear, for him not to worry about them but concern himself with what lay ahead in his mortal form. He was going back down the tunnel for a while, to tend to unfinished business and that he would be needed. They would await his arrival directly, for a thousand years in the time of man, was but a brief eye blink in the time of the eternal. Eventually their smiling faces faded from view as he drifted back down the long alabaster tunnel, with a voice echoing over and over, 'Not yet, not yet'!

His eyelids began to slightly flutter, as the nurse on duty noted the flutter and summoned the Doctor assigned to his care.

"Is he coming out of his coma Doctor"?

The doctor noted the machines and then said, "Not yet, but perhaps it would be best to notify the others and make them aware of his condition"!

Within the hour, several of the finest neurologists the military had were clustered around the body of Larson Magnusson and after significant consultation, agreed that he'd somehow crossed the threshold and was on his way to recovery and in a few days they would take the necessary steps to bring the future President out of the coma and back to consciousness and eventual recovery.

The following day Hiram Mulvahill was visited at the White House, during the evening by Dr. Mace Greenlee, the Surgeon General.

"Mr., President I think I've good news. In a few days we will bring Vice President Magnusson out of his coma, for he's progressed sufficiently to affect this. If all goes well and we expect it to, he should be well enough to assume the Presidency. But it will take an extended time of physical therapy for him to be able to sit in that chair and afterwards he will still have to undergo daily therapy here at the White House and a weekly examination at Bethesda to monitor his physical progress. You can understand that his muscle mass has diminished somewhat during the healing process, but his brain scans reveal nothing abnormal"!

"Alert me directly after he emerges from his coma, as to his condition then allow me time, to let our Press Secretary break the news to the media for they have been foaming at the mouth"!

"Almost three months in a coma and another one or two in physical therapy before he can join the rest of us. Well thank you doctor, for your vigilance", said Mulvahill!

As the Surgeon General departed. He then closed his eyes and thanked the eternal, for if all went well, in a few months he could transfer his burden to a younger man.

2

The week had been exhausting for Mike Montero as he went to his apartment. The addition of a new water tower atop one of Houston's older High Rise buildings had been risky, having been flown in by helicopter, but all had gone well and the owners along with his employers would be pleased.

On the way home, he stopped by his private postal box to see if there was any mail and finding a single envelope, with yet another private postal return address and post marked from St. Louis, he immediately knew it was a message from his private contact. He then stopped by the corner Kroger store to get some food for the weekend. The envelope was of a size usually containing a greeting card of some sort. That was the way his intermittent contact had always communicated with him. Yet he knew that the origin of the communication wasn't from St. Louis, but from somewhere in Europe. St. Louis only being a drop off point. For over twenty years this was the way it was. A bit cumbersome, but with millions of pieces of mail, daily making their way hither and yon, a single innocuous greeting card, especially one sent just prior to a holiday, would gather no notice.

The brief written message on the card was always in code and easily deciphered by Miguel. In the early days some twenty years ago, when he was just getting started, seed money was wired into his account, through various banking sources, usually originating from some Caribbean banking entity, in amounts never exceeding five thousand dollars, in order to elude scrutiny.

Once he got home and put away the groceries, he turned on the Television, to watch the evening news, interested in how the Federal Government was fending off the legion of cyber-attacks by as of yet unknown local and foreign points of origin. 'Phase two, in the overthrow of America', he thought.

The card once opened, was a belated Easter Card, sent by his mythical Uncle Pedro and the message read, "Best wishes, from your favorite Uncle and onward and upward". Upon deciphering the message read, "Proceed as planned at your own pace, peace be upon you Beslan"! An acknowledgment that fifteen years of work and planning now received the green light.

It had been a very long time since Miguel heard himself addressed by his real name Beslan. Beslan Bujovic from Bosnia. He turned off the TV set and allowed his mind to drift back and remember the past.

The late eighties and life in Sarajevo, was intolerable, for the Serbians were in the midst of their quest to rid what was left of Yugoslavia of any remnants of Muslim influence, by the campaign of ethnic cleansing and Bosnia/Herzegovina was where the Muslims were to be found. He'd graduated from the finest school in Belgrade, with high marks, gaining dual Masters Degrees in Architecture and Mechanical Engineering, yet could find no work in his field, given the ongoing conflict in Bosnia.

His entire family was murdered by the Serbian forces, who hunted them down like rabid dogs, along with many others, while the rest of the world stood by and shrugged their collective shoulders as if to say, "Schadenfreude"! This was far more than a simple traffic accident on the Autobahn. This was murder on a grand scale, genocide and even the oil rich Arab nations stood by and appeared as if they couldn't care less about the plight of their fellow Muslims.

This is why he took up arms with the Bosnian irregulars and became a sniper armed with the latest long range Soviet Dragunov rifle with all of the accoutrements. He'd sit patiently in the upper floors of the bombed out ruins of buildings in Sarajevo, deep in the shadows and wait until one of the aggressors, got careless, then with great care he'd send that cretin a final message. He never missed. The bullet always arrived ahead of the rifles report and he never shot twice from the same position always having a series of hides, propositioned ahead of time. He disciplined himself, never to get in a hurry, for then mistakes were a high probability. He usually took either the head shot, or that of the lower torso, given the plethora of bullet resistant vestments the Serbian invaders wore, but his favorite target was the throat, that small window of opportunity, given whenever Serbian Commanders sat down for a meal.

The Commanders were his favorite targets, for they were the ones who directed the stupid peasants to usually do the dirty work while their hands remained relatively clean. Within a year and a half, he accounted for just under three hundred Serbian deaths and yet another two dozen Croatian soldiers, who tried to join in the fun.

But his absolute favorite activity was patiently hunting down Serbian snipers, who indiscriminately shot civilians, women and children as they ran to the streets. It pained him greatly when he saw a Bosnian civilian go down in mid stride, especially the few times they had children with them. As he searched the burnt out structures for the shooter, the Serbian sniper would then take aim on the helpless children that would always sit and cry for their fallen parent and in seconds themselves succumb to a bullet.

But Beslan had to steel himself for the grief he felt, searching for the other sniper. Often it took hours of patient waiting but eventually the other one would reveal himself in one manner or another, before Beslan would take his shot. In the aftermath, he would always make his way to the other snipers position and strip the body of all valuables and leave his name etched into the naked corpse, etched across his chest by his survival knife.

He always brought back souvenirs back and distributed them amongst his comrades. The day the Americans began their bombing of Belgrade, Beslan was visited by his Commander and another who would not give his name but simply said, "Please call me Salaam"!

"My son, we have been watching your progress and are delighted with the zeal and prudence with which you carry out Allah's work against the infidels. With one of your many talents there is however greater work to be done in the name of Allah, against the infidels. A life's work if you're interested.

"I'm listening", said Beslan!

"Our organization has no name, yet is well funded by wealthy and beneficial benefactors. We will allow others to take the lime light while we can be more effective in a more Sub Rosa capacity, do you understand my son"?

Beslan nodded saying, "I'm still listening"!

"The eyes of those who matter have been upon you ever since you joined the cause against the Serb infidels. You come from a Sunni family and have, by all reports, been well educated in the word of the Quran and the words of the Prophet. You are a highly moral man, observing all of the aspects of the Sharia, praying faithfully whenever possible. Your education attainments are well recognized as well as your facility with linguistics. By all reports you bring to the Jihad, all of the necessary elements that are needed to make the infidels pay dearly for their insult of Islam. So we have an offer of celestial employment that I hope you will accept, in the name of the Prophet"!

As Beslan listened on, he passively listened to every word, while sizing up the man before him. He spoke in English, but with a well-educated British upper crust accent. He was small in stature, no more than five feet six inches, and was attired in apparently newly tailored military fatigues, no doubt purchased at some toffy upscale Euro store. As he heard himself say, "I'm still listening"!

He then roughly outlined a plan where Beslan would be taken from Sarajevo to Athens, board a plane destined for Tripoli, where he would be met by a member of the Islamic Brotherhood. There he was to be taken under their wing and taught all of the skills and trade craft, one needed with which to become an agent for the cause.

After some six months or so, he would be provided credentials sufficient for him to emigrate into Mexico, where he would be provided significant employment in the field of mechanical engineering in the Mexican Oil fields during the day, and taught Castilian Spanish in the classical dialect of the Hidalgos and also in the dialect of the Texan braceros in America, along with an upgrading in the English language as it is spoken in colloquial Texan.

Along with a crash course in American and Texas history all gauged in allowing a new person to emerge, to extend the work of the world wide Jihad.

"You will be provided with a new official Mexican identity and all the official bona fides, courtesy of one of our people in the Mexican Government. You will then resign your position with PEMEX and immigrate legally into the United States, and will settle in Houston Texas, the heart of the American Oil Business. You will gain employment as will be directed in later communiqués and will be provided funds from time to time, with which to accomplish your task. That is all that I can tell you at this time my son, but we need someone of your talent and zeal"!

Then the visitor was silent awaiting Beslan's response. All through the visitors dialog Beslan sported that serious look, his attention riveted on the visitor and now it was time for commitment and he suddenly broke into a smile and said, "Well, since I've nothing to do at the present, a grand adventure awaits me in the name of Jihad"!

The following morning, both Beslan and the man called Saalam, crossed the Macedonian Greek frontier, with well forged documents and made their way to Athens where they boarded a plane for Tripoli.

His masters in Tripoli were impressed with his knowledge of the Quran and his zeal in mastering the tradecraft of spy's more quickly than any in the past had shown. His Syrian mentors, while very stern and exacting continually gave him high marks in his accomplishments in the field, commenting amongst themselves that he had all of the possibilities to become a 'Ghost', the highest compliment one could pay another in that field of endeavor. In his every spare moment he studied both Spanish and English tapes in an attempt to gain a running start in his linguistic skills, upon his arrival in Mexico. In every stage of his Libyan training, his adherence to proper and rigorous Islamic religious observances, was under keen scrutiny and he was found to be without fault of any kind, even to the point of periodic examination of the Sharia, with his recitation to be without fault to such a degree, that he even took his masters to task when they misspoke, in an effort to trip him up.

They all agreed that Beslan Bujovic was a true believer and a magnificent Soldier of Islam upon his departure from Tripoli some six months later. As his jet descended from the clouds to land at Mexico City, he reviewed what he'd accomplished in Tripoli, a mastery of disguises, penetration of locks of many kinds, urban escape and evasion, desert survival, codes and deciphering, munitions manufacture from scratch and the various attendant electronics that triggered munitions.

In short order, he became adept at the discrete purchase of various and unrelated supplies at Tripoli's markets and apothecary's, preparing up batches of Semtex and C-4 in the small apartment kitchen and assembling the munitions, then taking them far out into the desert un noticed where they exploded as expected. He'd thought about improving the triggering devices his instructors taught him, but that was not his mandate. He was there to learn, not to teach.

After some six months on and off the oil rigs in the Gulf of Mexico, he quickly mastered the tasks assigned him, suggesting some changes in procedure that were well received by his supervisors, that saved time and money and were quickly assimilated into the normal scope of operation.

Within that very same time frame, he mastered the Spanish Language, able to pass himself off as either a Hidalgo, or a Compesino at will. Away for the most part from his Islamic mentors, he even allowed himself to indulge himself with women of significant means from time to time. After all, he was well educated, affable and well spoken, with never a verbal misstep. Careful never to spend the night, with a chulita, be she high born or of common blood. His discrete dalliances were just that and nothing more, away from the prying eyes of the faithful.

Beslan Bujovic was now someone in the distant past and Miguel (Mike) Montero was the new reality. As his papers, his degrees, his birth certificate and his academic transcripts attested to as his second year in the employ of PEMEX came to a close.

His colloquial English became more and more adept as he spent time on the oil rigs, conversing with the few expatriate Americans that manned the rigs, along with the tan and the natural lightening of his dark brown hair, to light brown, from the effects of the elements while at sea.

His Mexican masters, eventually told him that his time in Mexico was soon to come to an end and that as soon as his American bona fides, were ready that he was soon to depart to the US. Birth Certificate, passport, Texas Driver's License, Degrees from Texas Tech University along with the bona fide transcripts and a letter of recommendation from his employers at PEMEX.

Mike Montero was now ready to become an American.

Armed with ten thousand dollars in seed money from his benefactors and the remnants of money earned from PEMEX, he settled into American life. Within thirty days from his arrival, he gained employment as a low level maintenance supervisor, working for Alamo Mechanical Contractors, deeply in need of experienced HVAC engineers with a construction and maintenance background that could hit the ground running, to take advantage of the construction boom Houston was experiencing.

Working often fifty plus hour weeks, Mike still found time to purchase some ten acres of heavily wooded land in the far northwest part of Harris County and in time drew up plans to subcontract out the construction of his home, some thirty miles from downtown Houston.

During his weekly shopping trips for groceries, no one took notice, of his weekly purchase of various extra supplies, from the grocery and drug stores stored in a small monthly storage warehouse, not ten miles from his newly constructed home in the county.

As many of his initial tasks included new high rise building construction around town, it was a simple matter to peruse the structural construction plans of each building as they came out of the ground and devise and install a pound of Semtex explosive and the attendant battery powered triggering electronics, on each support structure. As for day to day security, it was virtually non-existent and once, the building was up and running, all three of the four sides of a given building were primed for ignition. Simply push a single button on a given day, from the street as one drove by and a multiple series of explosions would occur in the sub- basement level of a high rise structure where the HVAC chillers and boilers were located, and a foot wide section of a buildings support beams would be blown out, causing the building to keel over in a massive crash.

When the new construction phase of the local economy began to eventually slow down given the propensity of real estate developers to overbuild, Mike found very little difficulty in converting his talents to maintenance of Downtown High Rise Office buildings, speaking at various luncheons to office property developers and managers, selling Alamo Mechanical Contractors, methods of ongoing cost effective maintenance programs to these potential clients, always ending with the catch phrase, "You can either pay pennies on the dollar now, in proper maintenance of your facilities, or pay the big bucks later and allow your reputation to suffer, along with the slew of lawsuits, that will claim constructive eviction"!

Mikes, hitherto unknown capacities as a salesman, came as a great pleasure to the executives at Alamo Mechanical Contractors, as they bid on maintenance contracts on downtown office high rise buildings and were awarded contracts on half of those buildings bid on. This served Mikes purposes rather well in the coming years ahead, with the close proximity of the structures to each other, guaranteed maximum impact on the day of days ahead.

Promoted to an upper management position in his organization and with Alamo having the management of the HVAC (heating, ventilating and air conditioning) maintenance contracts in fifteen of the High Rise office buildings in Houston's Central Business District, and Michael Montero as Senior Manager in charge of operations, gave him complete access to every property under his control, at any time day or night. Over time, they gained contracts and lost contracts, but in the span of nine years, eighteen buildings in the downtown area, were primed to explode, the munitions well placed to have each building keel over at the push of a button.

Tomorrow was Saturday and Michael would spend the day in preparation in assembling the high frequency transmitting triggering device, to be placed in his car, early Sunday morning for a leisurely drive through Houston's city streets. He briefly toyed with the idea of setting things off during rush hour, or the noon day lunch rush, but a myriad of operational problems came to mind, not to mention the unnecessary collateral damage to innocent civilians that would occur, bringing to mind the ruthless killers the Serbians employed long ago. So he settled upon an early Sunday morning when the street traffic was certain to be almost non-existent. He was glad that his employers had moved their office to the suburbs, for they had been good to him and didn't deserve what was about to occur.

The following evening, Sunday, he would hit the uptown and

suburban buildings. The following Monday evening he would trigger the two Hotels on his list. He hoped that management of these facilities, had sense enough to vacate the Hotels, if not, the culpability was squarely on their shoulders.

With all in readiness, Mike started the engine of his car and backed out of his garage, deep in the woods of his home in far northwest Harris County and started in towards the downtown Central Business District. On the Northwest freeway coming into the loop, he was careful to watch his speed and have his seatbelt buckled, for it seemed that every mile he drove had a patrol vehicle of some kind out on the street. As he glanced at his cars clock, it read at one fifteen in the morning. All was going according to plan, for he had tested the electronic triggers over and over repeatedly and the fact that they'd never failed yet, was his only real concern.

Passing into the Loop 610 complex that ringed the inner city, he briefly wondered if all of the buildings that were soon to be either rubble or inhabitable had considered "Terrorist Insurance" riders for their properties. Considering how 'thrifty', building property owners and managers tended to be, he concluded they probably didn't. Mores the pity, for soon most of them would be 'belly up' financially, along with many of the banks that financed their loans. Then the financial hit on the City Government with all of the lucrative tax revenue to be wiped out along with the myriad of business's, was due to maximize the financial impact in ways he had as of yet to consider.

In a way it was a shame that there were not more properties that couldn't be affected, but there was simply no way, a single man could do more. Were there more operatives involved, the risk of discovery by the authorities escalated.

As the Loop 610 exit ramp turned into the Katy Freeway, he smoothly made the transition, as several police cars passed him at flat out speed, with their lights and sirens on full blast, they were no doubt responding to a robbery of some kind and sure enough as he passed the Studemont exit, he saw the flashing lights of a host squad cars, somewhere off to the left, surrounding a small building.

Taking the Smith Street. exit ramp into the downtown area, he recalled his repeated rehearsal of the drive through at this hour. Driving at a modest speed of twenty five miles per hour, he was certain to catch every green light on his first pass through town. Then turning left on Leeland Street, he would proceed several blocks, before turning left again on San Jacinto Street and complete his pass through the Central Business District.

As he passed, the underpass into the Downtown Area, he reached for the console with the buttons that identified, the buildings, plugging it into the cigarette lighter receptacle, he pressed the 'On' button and saw the initial light wink on, indicating that all was in readiness.

Making certain his car traveled at exactly twenty five miles per hour, he came upon his first building and pressed the button. The light came on as designed, indicating full ignition.

Those pedestrians on the street felt a shudder under foot and stopped to look around, eventually seeing a building starting to teeter slowly, then another shudder under foot, and then another and another. All up the full length of Smith Street. As Mike approached Leeland Street, he turned left as drove a few blocks at the proscribed speed and then turned left again, on San Jacinto, driving slowly and steadily pushing buttons attending to the business at hand. He could view the carnage on TV tonight when he returned and all through, the weekend.

One by one, the combination of strategically placed Semtex, C-4 and the variety of plastique explosives, did their job as designed, undermining the sub structure of the buildings, causing them to fall over, collapsing into neighboring buildings, in many cases, rendering them inhabitable. The combination of the various explosives were sure to confuse the forensic examiners that were sure to follow in the aftermath, causing them to conclude that teams of different people were culpable for the disaster.

Of course, no doubt some intelligent investigator might conclude otherwise, eventually but not one single thing pointed in the direction of Mike Montero. Oh perhaps an investigation of the vendors that serviced the properties may conclude that Alamo Mechanical Contractors, had security access to the properties on the continuum, but so what? What was the inherent motive? He concluded, as he pushed the very last button, on the console.

As he drove past the University of Houston's, downtown campus on his way out of town north on Interstate 45, he noted his dash board clock, indicating the entire downtown adventure took just nine minutes from beginning to completion and had apparently worked out as planned.

Driving home, he went over his plans for the various other contingencies. All of his formal mail was delivered to the small apartment he rented, on the north side of town, which he visited once a week, without fail. As far as his employers were concerned and the various local and state agencies were concerned, Michael Montero lived at that apartment. His driver's license, his social security number, etc, etc.

Of course, he really lived in his multi acre well wooded home in far North Harris County, and the county tax records reflected that Miguel Montero resided there and nothing else.

So he concluded that it would take a good while and some pretty brilliant detective work for the authorities to connect the dots. Tonight when he returned to his home in the woods, he would turn on the tube and see what the early morning people had to report. Then tomorrow he would call the office and no doubt the managers and owners were there and he would join them in watching a significant portion of their business go up in smoke. Of course during the course of time, other Mechanical Contractors came after Alamo and were the current mechanical contractors on record, which clouded the issues for the investigative authorities.

'The nice thing about driving a ten year old Chevy Citation', Mike thought, 'was that looked that it had seen better days was that no one ever took notice, as he pulled into his garage'.

He made himself a drink and sat down on his couch, turning on the television. As he swirled his twelve year old Scotch around in his glass, with the ice cubes, the visual display of his handiwork set his mind to reeling. With but a number of exceptions a significant portion of the Downtown section of Houston a mass of rubble. Tall buildings having collapsed upon each other, every building that collapsed had fallen onto another.

The word would eventually work its way back to Tripoli the following day and his mentors would no doubt be pleased. They had trained him, gave him a mission, provided initial funding then left him alone. Allah be praised.

He then went to a closet and pulled out his prayer rug and turned the TV set on mute, and kneeled down and went through his litany of prayers, thanking Allah for the opportunity to hit the infidels were it would do the most good for the world-wide struggle to establish the universal Caliphate. He'd neglected his proscribed ritual in the past praying only whenever convenient. He would soon have the time tend to the things most essential.

The initial plan long ago was to cripple the big American Oil Companies in one fell swoop, by destroying their Houston headquarters. Over the span of time, many of the Oil Giant's moved their operations elsewhere. Conoco, Texaco, Exxon and others, yet there were stilla significant number of oil companies downtown and on his list tomorrow to make a significant dent in their operations. In a few days by the close of business, his work would be completed, with this phase of the Jihad writ large in the sands of time.

As he drifted off to sleep, his last thoughts were that his time at the rifle range was long overdue to maintain his skills, for there was more to come, somewhere.

By noon Sunday he arrived at Alamo's office, joining the other management people in their commiserations, as they watched the round the clock news coverage. The entire downtown area was in police lockdown, with only fire, police and medical personnel permitted entry. The Governor and various federal officials were escorted by the local officials to view the carnage and the Federal Government was in the slow process of declaring Houston a disaster area, allowing a slew of Federal entities to arrive the following day.

Mike's boss drew him aside, telling him of the need for laying off some of the employees and technicians until further notice and assuring Mike that he still had the responsibilities of the three large buildings, that he brought in under contract a few months ago.

'Too bad', Mike thought, 'He hadn't the time to plant the seeds of

Allah deep into their bowels. No use crying over spilt milk, for tonight and tomorrow more structures would fall. For the seeds had been planted in these fields, some years past and Alamo had been out bid by others anyway and now it was their problem.

By midnight Mike had driven home, with five more buildings near adjacent to the Loop 610 area, on the ground.

As he drove to his various meetings the following day, several High Rise Hotels in the crowded Galleria and mid-town areas plunged down upon pedestrians and motorists alike, raising an eternal cloud of dust and smoke, spreading even more fear amongst the populace.

The following day few if any people, that worked in a building more than three stories in height bothered to go to work, calling in sick to their employers. Causing certain news commentators to say the good news was that rush hour traffic seemed to be a bit more manageable, for the time being.

By the close of the following week, Mike had completely sanitized his home in the deep woods and disposed of any and all evidence of munitions manufacture along with the equipment.

His work load diminished at work, he finally allowed himself to un-wind for the first time in years. Watching all of the news channels on the TV and relishing in what he had wrought. He ticked off the various things he might have forgotten, his show apartment had been cleaned to an operation room quality, not a hair in the brush, no fingerprints anywhere, tub drains sanitized and filled with Clorox, baseboards cleaned and the floors triple vacuumed and the vacuum cleaner disposed of in a dumpster far away.

While he still kept up appearances, he decided not to visit the apartment for some months to come, paying the bills, and the rental out of one of his several accounts locally. Perhaps in six months, if he was still in town.

Mike had prepared well in the event of a sudden and necessary departure, his home in the deep woods north west of Houston. He bought the property right, by being on the Courthouse steps and paying cash for some financially distressed land one of the local banks had to take back.

Upon gaining full title for the property he hired some local contractors to cut selected trees on the land, and then contracting with others had the trees cut into the variety of sections of lumber stacked and categorized to conform to the building plans he'd drawn up. Then he subcontracted out the construction of the main house, the connected multi vehicle metal garage that he turned into a workshop. Glaziers for the windows, carpenters for construction, plumbers for the plumbing and septic tank system, electricians for the electrical connections, roofers, a water well and its above ground storage facility, a wind power generator and solar panels on his roof to provide ample electricity, a Satellite TV set up and a long winding gravel driveway all the way to the farm road, his nearest neighbor a mile away. As an afterthought, he designed a series of several escape tunnels that were above the water table and followed the slope of three ridges perfectly, joining right under his home, via a trap door located under a bed in the garage. The terminus of the tunnels ended right above a small creek that meandered around the edge of his property. He planted a few bushes randomly in front of the tunnel entrance and erected a small heavily screened door, to keep out the curious critters and there you have it, total self-sufficiency.

As he completed his home years ago, he wondered, 'Isn't America Great"? In Bosnia/Herzegovina, this could never have been accomplished except for the very rich and once people knew what was there, they would tell others and eventually one's security would be compromised.

The monthly stipends from abroad ceased after his fourth year, but by then he was doing well enough at Alamo financially that he just didn't need it, yet it virtually paid for his little place in the country. He lived modestly in the country, mostly keeping to himself, doing all of his shopping miles away closer to the city. Of course, in the event the authorities found their way to his homestead, they would have to confront themselves with three strands of razor wire, he skillfully erected between the trees on his properties perimeter that allowed the animals to come and go, but provide a nasty surprise, for anyone else.

Of course, he had a getaway plan and sufficient cash funds, deep into the six figures readily available, with which to make a quick as a blink exit, should it be necessary.

A month later, he went to his local firing range, to keep his skills current. He thought about building one at his home in the woods. There was sufficient land to construct a simple affair that could accommodate a hundred, two hundred and three hundred yard long range. He could construct a ten foot tall ground berm, in order to deflect the sound upward, trusting the plethora of surrounding trees in the long summer season to absorb the rest, but thought better of it, trusting to the old adage, "Do nothing to draw attention to yourself, nothing"! So he had to visit his local rustic firing range, some ten miles away towards town with which to maintain his steady eye, bringing along a simple Remington bolt action hunting rifle, in the 30.06 caliber, since the range had a firing distance of a hundred yards only it would have to suffice.

Arriving at the firing range at about ten in the morning, he paid his fee and then set up his rifle at his appointed firing bench under the metal canopy. His plan was to spend an hour sighting in his rifle, then spend another hour at the pistol range, then grab some lunch at one of the local burger placed that specialized in 'Heart attack Grub', guaranteed to clog your arteries, if ya let it.

Sitting next to him was a large man, with sandy colored medium cut hair, who nodded his head as Mike set his gear up on the firing bench, then got up and stepped away from the bench area, firing up a cigarette awaiting the range masters approval to commence firing.

Having set his rifle up and positioned his ammunition, Mike decided to have a cigarette and stepped away from the firing bench, joining several others in waiting. He reached into his firing jackets pocket for a smoke, but discovered that his remaining cigarette had been crushed.

"Damn", he muttered in exasperation.

"Here, try one of mine", said the stranger who was slated to fire on the bench next to him. After he lit up and took a long puff, he asked "What brand is this? It has a unique taste"!

"No brand at all, for I roll my own smokes. Mix in a tad bit of aromatic pipe tobacco in with the cigarette tobacco and through some trial and error, come up with something I like"!

"Well it seems you've hit a home run with your special blend", said Mike as he drew in another lung full of smoke.

"And thank you for the smoke. By the way I'm Mike Montero", he said offering his hand to shake in greeting.

"My friends call me Jaeger and you're welcome", said the stranger taking up the proffered hand in greeting.

"So Jaeger, how do you like this firing range"?

"It's ok, for its purpose, but it's too bad they only have a hundred yard long target distance. Good for sighting in purposes, but no one in town has a longer distance range. Ya gotta drive way out in the boonies and set up your own longer situation and I just don't have that kind of time on my hands, but for its purpose it'll do in a pinch", said Jaeger!

"So what are you firing today"!

"An old Winchester 44/40 lever action. Good for out to about three hundred yards only but whatever it hits it brings down. And you"?

"A standard Remington bolt action, 30/06. Good out to eight hundred yards or so, depending on who is the shooter"!

"You got that right friend, it depends on the shooter, first last and always", said Jaeger with a chuckle!

At that, the loud speaker erupted, "Shooters take your positions"! At that, both men snuffed out their smokes, then took up the respective positions at their assigned firing benches, their weapons already loaded and on standby.

The range master then announced, "The range is now closed until the Cease Fire order in given. 'Ready on the right', he announced. 'Ready on the left', all-ready on the firing line. Commence firing"!

Mikes rifle was equipped with a modest ten power scope, while Jaeger's Winchester was not, as both adjusted the sound suppressors on their ears, for the decibel level of the sound of eighteen rifles firing at the same time was sufficient to permanently damage ones hearing.

Both took careful aim at their respective targets and began their shooting. Several reloads later, and after some fifteen minutes of intermittent firing, the "Cease Fire", order came over the loud speaker. "Stand clear of your weapons please, while the targets are retrieved", came the secondary order. Prompting several of the ranges employees to walk to the targets and bring back the used targets putting each paper target on its assigned firing bench.

As Mike and Jaeger picked up their respective targets and compared them it was clear that the vast majority of the six inch diameter center section of the target was obliterated, with only scant patches of red still visible. "Good shooting", commented Mike as he viewed Jaegers target, noticing that there was little difference between the two as to the spread of their impacts, both being nearly identical, especially since Jaeger was shooting without benefit of a scope.

"Not so bad yourself", commented Jaeger. "What do you say we have a second round of shooting"? Mike readily agreed and they both went back inside and paid their five dollars and resumed their same positions at the same firing benches. While they were waiting for yet another group of shooters to assume positions, Mike asked, "Where did you learn how to shoot"? "My Dad was in the Marine Corps., then a Texas Ranger for a spell and he taught me how to shoot. I suppose the Marine Corps. Polished off the remaining rough edges. And you? Where did you learn your marksmanship skills"?

"Self-taught mostly I suppose and I read a lot", said Mike after a brief pause to effect the appropriate response. After all that indeed wasn't a lie, for he became a superior marksman out of sheer necessity, back during the Balkan conflict, some years ago.

"So what do you do, to put food on the table", asked Jaeger offering Mike another of his cigarettes"?

"HVAC contracting", said Mike pointing at his company pickup truck, with the big 'Alamo' logo emblazoned on the side doors. "And You Jaeger", Mike asked?

After a moment he said, "Let's just say that I'm an entrepreneur. I see an opportunity where bad management exists, I study the lay of the land, and if I think I can make a buck or two, I acquire the business. Build it up and sell it at a profit, then move on to the next opportunity"! Not entirely truthful, but appropriately vague, he thought.

"Ya doin OK"?

"It's a living and my heads above water", said Jaeger.

Just then the Range Master went through his standard routine regarding the firing range, before all hell broke loose. This time, both Jaeger and Mike, took things up a notch, firing much tighter groupings at their respective nine inch red targets, a hundred yards away. When the "Cease Fire" order was given and both men stood away from their firing benches, waiting for their respective targets to return, they enjoyed another of Jaegers special blend of self-rolled cigarettes, their sound suppressors hanging about their necks.

When the targets returned, and they compared shots, once again it was difficult to tell just who was the better shot, with both men's target spread showing much more red, because of their tighter groupings, neither of which exceeding three inches from dead center.

"I don't see how you do it", said Mike. I'm shooting with a scope and have perhaps a few more rounds on target, but you're firing without a scope and have identical groupings"?

"My distant visual acuity is rated at twenty/twelve, when most normal folks are at the norm of twenty/twenty. A gift I suppose"!

"Ah, I see", said Mike! "What do you say we go over to the pistol range and try our luck"?

"Sounds like a plan to me, Mike". They went to their respective vehicles and exchanged their rifles, with a pair of hand guns, in their zippered leather carriers and met at the Range Masters office and bout two targets each, one for each weapon.

As they unzipped their weapons pouches, Jaeger revealed an ancient single action Colt forty five revolver with a five inch barrel and his favorite the Ruger Police Six revolver, Caliber three fifty seven double action, with a three inch barrel, accompanied by a half dozen speed loaders, for its swing out cylinder. While Mike revealed a nine millimeter SovietMakarov Automatic and the Standard nine millimeter Browning High Power, with severalfifteen round magazines at the ready.

"Ah, the ever standard argument, revolvers or automatics, with the automatics having the greater firepower, or rounds on target", said Mike proudly.

"Then there the fact that revolvers, never jam up when ya need them, while some automatics will", said Jaeger!

"There is that", said Mike! But as if on the same beam, both said, "But it all depends on the shooter", they said with a laugh!

Weapons loaded, their sound suppressors ready to be placed on their ears, both awaited the instructions from the range master to come over the loud speaker. As the orders were given, both men adjusted their sound suppressors over their ears, picked up their weapons and assumed a standing firing position. When the order was given to "Commence Firing", Jaeger held the ancient Colt peace maker and assumed the classic one armed stance, firing singly from his right hand fully extended while his left rested on his hip. Every round fired coming singly while he had to cock the hammer with his thumb each time.

The bulls eye on target for the shortened twenty yard pistol range, had shrunk down to a scant three inches, from the standard almost hand span of the rifle range. It was a cumbersome procedure reloading the Colt, extracting each spent shell one by one, and then reloading each cylinder one by one. But he recalled a time when his ancestors swore by the Colt during their time in service of the Rangers and it was a sentimental favorite of Jaegers father.

After completing his forth reload, Jaeger put the Peacemaker down and picked up his Ruger revolver. It felt as one with his hand as he assumed the standard two handed grip and brought the second target into view and entered into the routine of squeeze and counter pull with the opposite hand. Soon he got into the routine of getting a round off ever second and on target, swiftly reloading via his speed loaders and repeating, until he was completely out.

A minute later the Range Master ordered, "Cease Fire", as everyone completed their discharge and stepped away from their weapons, so the range employees could retrieve the assigned targets.

"I noticed, you prefer the single handed grip on your Colt, while you revert to the classical dual handed firing grip taught at most police academies, said Mike!

"Seems, like the proper thing to do", said Jaeger, while offering Mike another cigarette.

When each man's target was returned, not much of a surprise came to Jaeger, for Mike had clearly more rounds on target and all within the three inch bulls eye, most of which passed into previously made holes, with not a bit of the black ink visible in both of his targets. Jaeger had most of his rounds, in the black with the Colt, but there were simply too few on target, with his Ruger simply holding its own…

It was clear that both men were superb marksmen, yet the automatics ruled this session, with their superior firepower, which prompted Mike to offer, "Automatics won't jam if one takes meticulous care of them"! With both of them saying in unison, "All depending on who the shooter is", with Jaeger adding, "And the situation"!

Both men gathered their weapons and walked to their vehicles, agreeing that this was indeed an enjoyable morning. As Jaeger was the first to drive away, Mike followed his car with his eyes, wondering if the two would ever meet again.

I n the following days, Mike found his workload vastly diminished, settling in to mostly administrative functions of manpower dissolution and redistribution on the projects that remained under his responsibility. Many good men had to be let go, for there was no work for them to do. Their buildings now lying in rubble. All over town what used to be a tight market in qualified building operational engineers, was now awash in qualified talent. Mike was busy drafting a slew of letters of recommendation for the employees he had to let go.

Eventually things began to slow down, with the exception, of the city being the epicenter of Federal and investigative personnel that flooded the city and county. All the current reports that found their way into the media and out into the public, indicated the theory that apparently several different groups of terrorist's, had defeated the security of the affected properties and planted explosives, then coordinated the ignition to a certain time.

What set this theory in motion was the fact that, three separate sets of explosions, went off at three different times, the last of which not only destroyed property, but took human lives in great abundance. That being the Hotels, destroyed with guests and employees crushed in the rubble.

Like the Twin Towers affecting the City of New York, Houston was now placed as historical evidence, of the heart of darkness that lay deep in the breast of man. It would be weeks and perhaps even months, before the complete list of the dead and the survivors was compiled, while on the other side of the world, people danced in the streets, rejoicing at the bloody nose the "Great Satan" had received.

As Mike drove to his home, deep in the piney woods, he made a brief detour to his private postal box, and was surprised to see a Greeting Card envelope along with a small package, both sent at different intervals, but recently and both bearing the same postal box address, without a name, originating in St. Louis.

He then pulled into one of the grocery stores, to pick up needed supplies and drove on; listening to one of the drive time, call in listener AM radio stations that allow the conservative points of view, to be exchanged.

While he had but scant interest in what was said, to stay abreast of their points of view, stood him well, during his daily interaction with those at Alamo Engineering.

Yet something that was said on the radio, triggered Mikes mind to reconsider his chance encounter, with the big Texan shooter called Jaeger a few days ago. Something just wasn't right. All his life, what drove Mike, was his caution and great attention to detail. His discipline of Mechanical Engineering demanded it. The events of the recent past gave evidence to that.

By all that was holy, his encounter had all the hallmarks of a random encounter. A serendipitous event, temporary in its very nature and then gone. As he relived the encounter, he viewed Jaeger of being an excellent marksman with previous military training as their rifle scores were virtually identical. Mike briefly envied his superior visual acuity at long range and yet when the hand gun results were compared, Mike held an edge with more shots on target. Yet, something about this man wasn't quite right.

Then it came to him, when asked what he did for a living, Jaeger responded in a rather oblique way, that he was an 'entrepreneur'. Mike had been in the company of many entrepreneurs during his time in the states and with Alamo, for that was what commercial real estate developers were. entrepreneurs and risk takers. He bore no resemblance to any entrepreneur that he's ever encountered, for they didn't have calloused hands. They had the best haircuts, manicures, drove expensive cars and apart from a very few that strove to hunt Bambi in the wilds of south and west Texas, most of them hand either a legal, accounting or financial background. No, this man bore all the marks of one that was possibility a former aging NFL lineman, with a plethora of scars and a history of past violence. Hardly the entrepreneurial type by the looks of it.

Still the man apparently was one of substance, driving away in a fully restored forty year old Ford Galaxie that looked as if it just came off the show room floor. As he drove onto the gravel road that approached his property, he started to shrug his concerns off as inconsequential, eager to see what Salaam had sent him.

After a brief dinner and having the news channels on reporting on the carnage in Houston, Mike opened the package from Salaam, discovering a brand new passport with the name Beslan Bujovic, giving him Diplomatic status. Along with that were documents stating that Beslan Bujovic was a long standing member of the Bosnian trade mission to the United Nation's. A second new Mexican passport in the name Miguel Montero along with a new Mexican driver's license was included. Whereas his old Mexican passport, was about to expire.

Then he noticed a separate fat envelope full of hundred dollar bills totaling some ten thousand dollars and a note affixed that said, "For expenses".

Opening the Greeting card envelope, he noticed a folded two page letter that of course was in their standard code. An hour later after he'd deciphered the unusually long missive, he gleaned that the Muslim Brotherhood, in Cairo was extremely pleased with the results of recent weeks in Houston and the cash stipend was but a small down payment for services rendered, for this phase of Beslan's personal Jihad. In addition he was provided with a new account number and password, for an account established in the name of Miguel Montero, in a bank on the island of Aruba, with an amount in the low six figures that he could draw funds from as he saw fit for future endeavors.

He was assured that all of the new documents were indeed genuine and would pass the most intense scrutiny. In closing he was asked if his shooting skills were still current and that in the coming days they would be called into use.

As he copied the account number, name of the bank and the pass word on a separate sheet of paper, then shredded the letter, card and envelope in his shredder, he settled back on his couch pleased.

At that very same time somewhere in Houston's suburbs, something brought to mind Jaegers encounter with the sandy haired engineer, who shot so well last weekend. Clearly something was not right, but Jaeger was damned if he knew why. The guy shot like a pro and that took extensive training and practice. Not that he'd met many engineers during his travels, but his view of that discipline was that of very cerebral types, not much akin to that of bankers and perhaps economists. While smaller in stature than Jaeger, there seemed to be a tad bit of that look in the man's eyes, the look that was reminiscent of one that could easily snuff out another's light and not ever loose a bit of sleep. He'd seen that very same look in the eyes of many hardened criminals during his vacation at Huntsville some years ago. A look that defied literal description, but the look was there none the less. Once a man saw it he usually never forgot it. The look of a Predator.

The singer Johnny Cash best described it in one of his songs, "I shot a man in Reno, just to watch him die"! Jaeger then wondered if he had the very same look and concluded that maybe he did.

Then he thought back to the time, not so long ago, up near the summit of the small mountain in the Texas Big Bend country looking out on the Rio Grande River, when he just sat there, watching three men slowly impaling themselves to their death. To this day apparently not a peep, from anyone, which probably meant the vulture's had done their work well. He felt no joy or elation at their slow and painful death, nor had he felt any remorse or guilt. What he felt was nothing.

Yes, he sat there, in attendance until they slid completely to the ground. He took lives, not out a sense of curiosity or glee, but out of the necessity of the moment. And in looking back, he felt not a shred of remorse, just one more rabid animal gone from God's green earth. Yet perhaps there were a few similarities and it was, he supposed, the way it should be. In his line of business, a business that had proved very lucrative as of late, it's what kept him sharp. The Heart of Darkness, the Reptilian Response, simply "Thinnin' out the herd"!

He then consciously returned to the book he was reading, and reminded himself to take all of his pistols, to the gunsmith and soon, to install a lighter spring on the triggers. An old trick used by professional hand gun shooters, to get more rounds out of the barrel and on target accurately, yet not so light a pull as to be considered as a 'hair trigger'"!

O rval Goodwin, the Presidents Chief of Staff, dialed the White House and was put through to Melanie O'Bannon immediately, as he heard, "O'Bannon here, may I help you"?

"Melanie, it's Orval! Is President Mulvahill, still in the meetings the congressional committee chairmen"?

"Yes he is Oval"?

"Still? They're running an hour over schedule"!

"I've buzzed him twice on the intercom to signal as such, but he's ignoring the 'heads up' Orval"!

"Well then I suppose you've done all that can be done, which must mean that the meetings are becoming acrimonious in nature"!

"He's just in an interim situation Orval and trying to get things off dead center, in congress, but apparently no one is willing to listen, viewing him as an interloper"!

"Yeah Mel, a Republican, trying to find the center in issues and being viewed suspiciously by the Democrats, while a number of the Republicans are seeing him as nothing less as a traitor to their legislative programs"!

"He just can't wait to get back to the Senate Orval"!

"Well then, we may have some good news. As you know I'm at the Bethesda Naval Hospital and the doctors have just brought Vice President Magnusson out of his coma successfully by the looks of things. He's off the IV's and is taking nourishment by mouth. I've spoken to him and he seems to have all of his mental faculties intact. But an interesting thing occurred. When I mentioned to him that his family didn't make it and that of the entire family of President Dobbins including the President, he simply said, "Yes, I know", with no apparent emotion of any kind. What I want you to do is wait until Mulvahill gets out of his meeting with the circular firing squad then let him know quietly. Then with his approval, give the Press Secretary a heads up on the situation, so he, and or Mulvahill can announce the news at the One PM Press grilling"!

"Will do Orval, but should any mention of the three visiting doctors, from Cal Tech, be mentioned"?

"Now how on earth did you find out about that Mel"? "Quite by accident I can assure you"!

"Christ, now that makes eight people who know about them. How completely do you know of their involvement in this matter"?

"What their attempt at doing and the hoped results, but as to the details nothing, I can go over it later with you when you return if you want"!

"Yeah we can do that later, just try your best to keep Mulvahill on schedule till I return"!

"Will do Orval"!

A half hour later, the Presidents meeting with the Congressional Leaders from both parties concluded, with all the members filing out of the conference room with glum faces. As he came back to the Oval offices he passed Melanie's desk saying, "Well, anything to report Mel"?

"Yes Mr. President, Orval called a little while ago and said Vice President Magnusson was successfully brought of his coma and is talking coherently and taking nourishment by mouth"!

"Praise the Lord. Any word of when he'll be able to assume the office"? "You'll have to ask Orval that upon his return. But he wanted me to give the Press Secretary a 'heads up' for his news conference, in a couple of hours and suggested that it would probably be appropriate if you were the one to break the news"!

"Call the Press Secretary and tell him the news and then tell him I'm coming to his office, right away. Then back up my other commitments and simply say, well, you'll know what to say Mel"!

Miraculously, no news leaks of Magnusson's recovery came from the hospital and the White House Press room erupted with a round of cheering and applause, being cut short when the press corps. ran for the nearest phones almost en masse', in order to be the first to announce the news.

At around dinner time, President Mulvahill, paid a visit to Magnusson's hospital room at Bethesda.

During the afternoon, Magnusson was eager to catch up on the events that passed when he was in his coma, badgering his secret service guards and several of the doctors at will, between his medical tests and hour naps along the way.

As Mulvahill entered his room Lars Magnusson had just awakened from his nap and was eating his evening meal, the second of the day.

"The Presidents burial and that of his family occurred a month ago and they were interred in Arlington with all of the pomp and circumstance that was appropriate", said Mulvahill continuing on. "We waited for your recovery to know your wishes upon the burial of your loved ones and the location as you deemed fit, Mr. President"!

"If there's a suitable plot available at Arlington, then that will suit me just fine"!

"We've reserved the appropriate plots next to the family of President Dobbins in anticipation of your wishes"!

"I assume that it will be a closed casket affair"?

For several moments Hiram Mulvahill was stunned as how to respond before saying, "Yes Mr. President, it should be a closed casket affair. But I can assure you their remains have been treated with all the dignity that human beings can offer in such a situation".

"I thank you for that Hiram and now I'm about to ask you for several favors, while I'm able"!

"Set up the funeral for about thirty days from today. The docs will no doubt have me on a program of physical therapy for the foreseeable future and thirty days should give me a goal to shoot for"!

"Yes Mr. President"!

"Next, try and set up a joint meeting of the Congress for about two weeks after I take the oath of office and relieve you of your responsibility, then try and fit in the funeral at Arlington the very same day if possible"! Mulvahill quietly nodded his head in agreement.

"Next, I'm going to ask you to hang around for a while as the interim Vice President until I get my feet firmly on the ground, before I can return you to the Senate and select another Vice President"!

"A Democratic President and a Republican Vice President", asked Mulvahill? Has there ever been a precedent for that"?

"If I recall my high school civics correctly, yes. Probably early in the nineteenth century, but never the less, you are a capable and more important, a moral man, that knows the inner machinations better than almost anyone alive, plus you've an open ear from those on both sides of the aisle. In addition, you'll be put in charge of several initiatives that I'm certain you'll agree with that are long overdue"!

"Well Lars, as you'll soon discover, if you already have, I just might have worn out my welcome on both side of the aisle, especially if my meeting with the congressional leaders this morning might prove out. But if you want this old codger to stand by your side a little longer, how can one say no? But I have to warn you, there will be talk in the neighborhood", Mulvahill offered with a slight wink!

"Fine, now there is one last task I have for you, while I regain my strength and I've an inkling that you just might agree"!

"And that is"?

"Is the situation on our Southern Borders, still in such a mess Hiram"?

"A nightmare with no light at the end of the tunnel in sight. In fact that was one of the things we all knocked heads over in the conference room this morning"!

"Good. Perhaps you can do some good and help out the Border Patrol with additional manpower".

"The very thing we discussed this morning that brought your people to the stage of foaming at the mouth, Lars"?

"Then you won't mind, I take it by instituting an Executive Order, by calling out either the Army Reserve Units, or the National Guard, whichever is appropriate, to lend a hand, on an Ad Hoc basis, to the Border Patrol on a rotating basis of ninety days, on our southern border for, say, about a year. Attach a squad of armed riflemen to a Border Agent, making certain they take his or her direction for the duration and the manpower problem is solved. At the same time you direct the ICE personnel to pursue any employers that are found to be hiring illegals, to the fullest extent of the law. Next you hang the sword of Damocles over the various local governmental entities that are sanctuary cities. Should they persist in ignoring Federal Laws already on the books, then they will see all Federal funding that flows through the executive branch of government to dry up to the last dime until they do and they have thirty days in which to comply, by reversing any local ordinances to that effect, before action is taken. Now it seems to me that certain people shout from the rooftops, about adherence to the "Rule of Law" until and unless that law doesn't agree with their point of view, don't you think Hiram"?

Once again Hiram Mulvahill sat there in stunned silence. He didn't know whether to cheer or cry, for such a pronouncement to come from the mind of someone of opposing political philosophy, especially from one who made a living as being a go along to get along guy, always voting the party line, never making waves, Mr. Rubber Stamp, a Lickspittle extraordinaire, was indeed, beyond words.

"Hiram, are you all right", Magnusson asked?

"You realize the shit storm that will envelope the country? Your party will call you a traitor, while ours will embrace you as one of their own making you a pariah amongst the Democrats"!

"The question still remains, can you, no, will you do this thing"?

"The question is answered by a simple Yes, Mr. President"?

"Thank you Hiram", said Magnusson!

"But I just have to ask you, what brought your conversion? Your moment of epiphany"?

"Let's just say that all that I've held sacred has been taken from me, except one thing. My duty towards our American way of life. Further we can say that perhaps I've finally grown a pair, no longer needed to propagate the species, or to satisfy my prurient interests. I'm going to have other occasions to exert myself. While I'm thinking about it, how are things going in Houston"?

"The day after tomorrow, I'm flying down there, to meet with the State and Local heads of Government, the FEMA and the local FBI Special Agent in Charge to assess what can be done at the Federal Level. But the current thinking and theory is that a number of teams of specially trained sappers were successful of the simultaneous ignition of explosives, of the multiple of buildings in the downtown area and the fact that it all happened in a relatively short span of time suggests precision timing by several groups. Then the following day the same thing in the suburbs. Then the day after that at the Hotels, suggests a departure from previous methods of operation. In addition, our forensic explosive expert's, see several different combinations of explosives, that point the investigators in the direction of several groups or governments working in unison unseen in modern times. It's a mess down there, but after I've assessed the situation I'll sit down with you to give you a full report. But until then, I'll have Orval Goodwin bring over to you, our library of the news reports video tapes for you to review as you see fit"!

As he rose, Muvahill said, "Just you hurry and get better Lars. I'm in your corner all the way and you might want to stay glued to the news channels to see just what is coming your way"!

As he left the hospital room, Mulvahill was met by the Navy Commander in charge of overseeing the team of specialists, responsible for his care. As they slowly walked down the hall Hiram asked, "Gloves off Commander, how is he doing"?

"When he was initially brought in here, few of us gave him any reasonable chance of recovery. The brain concussion, punctured lung, spleen, kidney, broken bones, kept us all on full out, rotating duty to just keep him alive. But those folks brought in under the cover of darkness, from parts unknown, knew just what they were doing and whatever they inserted into the future President went a very long way in contributing to his, what I'm going to say is a miraculous recovery. His cranial problems seem to be entirely abated. His other wounds are readily on the mend and his various casts, should be able to be removed sometime by the end of the week. In short, he should be dead by now, but he won't be. He's alert and given what he's gone through physically and emotionally, one wonders how he does it"!

"Good Commander, I'm glad to hear that. How soon will he start physical rehab"?

"The very day after his casts are removed, we'll conduct tests and if everything holds up, he'll start a regime of rehabilitation the following day, for about a month, then we'll release him to the White House, but he'll still be on what I'll call light duty for the next ninety days, then if he's up to it we'll leave him to his own devices, with a check up on a monthly basis after that "!

"Very good Commander, just one thing, you are to refer all comments about his health to the White House Press Secretary and impress that upon your team that has worked upon him, especially the activities of the three wise men that came out of the west. Top Secret stuff, do you understand Commander"!

"I understand completely, for the Presidents Chief of Staff has continually reminded us of this, every time he visits"!

Five weeks later, Lars Magnusson was quietly sworn in as President of the United States and Hiram Mulvahill stepped aside to become the Acting Vice President, as the event was held, en camera in the Oval office.

Magnusson started each day with his Naval physical therapist, on assignment from Bethesda Naval hospital for an hour before breakfast at six in the morning, then jumped into a full day of meetings with each member of his cabinet, asking them to stay in place for a while, while accepting their letters of resignation in advance, to hold in stasis, until such time that he may choose to replace them, or they verbally choose to move on.

Each meeting was slated to last an hour on a one on one basis, to hear the Presidents vision for his term and to see if each member of his cabinet would pursue the Presidents desires as to the direction he wanted to take the country. He expected some push back from a few of the cabinet, but surprisingly all eagerly came aboard with his vision.

In successive days he met with all of the Generals and Admirals of the Joint Chiefs of Staff, jointly and severally, to get their views on things germane to the military. While comfortable in delegating authority and responsibility, he was none the less, intent on being every bit the "Hands On" President, inserting his authority when deemed necessary, to take preemptory action if necessary to minimize problems, quietly and effectively.

Several weeks later, as soon as he was able to get around on crutches, President Magnusson, quietly held a Sunday Morning burial service for his slain family, attended only by a few key White House staffers and the immediate surviving members his and his wife's family.

Before the sun went down, a United Press staffer discovered the deception and upon investigation the following day, the UP issued a news release of the secret funeral, to the World Media at large.

A storm of venal criticism ensued from all sides of the political spectrum, centering on the fact that the Nation as a whole, should be allowed to grieve alongside the President. Of course there are always elements from every side of the political spectrum, keen on making an issue out of thin air and claim insult at the drop of a hat.

A decision was made several days later to hold a brief Press Conference in the White House Press Room, to clear the air.

As they waited in the Oval office for the White House Press Corps, to assemble, Vannevar Harvanian, the newly appointed Press Secretary went over the strategy of the meeting just minutes away then said, "Mr.

President, this will be your very first exposure to the Jackals in the press room. The very fact that you will enter on crutches and will politely assert your rights to bury your loved ones in the manner you see fit, will go far in extending your political honeymoon for however long it takes, to gain public sympathy and support and keep the wolves at bay, so you can get a running start on implementing the directives to redirect the country back to sanity. Just in and out politely, but forcibly and no questions for your plate is full for the day. Remember, give them an inch and they will make you regret it! Give me a few minutes, then enter and I'll look surprised and relinquish the podium to you"!

Just then the door to the Oval office, opened and Orval Goodwin stuck his head inside saying, "Mr. President, it's show time"! At that Van Harvanian got up from his chair and went to the door saying, "Wait about three minutes, then come on, after all this is your house for the foreseeable future". Three minutes later Lars Magnusson struggled to rise from his chair and grabbed hold of the crutches from Orval Goodwin who asked, "Mr. President are you ready to hypnotize the Chickens"? Magnusson nodded as he lumbered down the hallway on his crutches. He was feeling rather good about this ploy of Presidential insertion into a press conference, for it will set forth the agenda, indicative of this man's refusal to accept certain societal norms as he saw fit. Early assertion by this President and he was adjusting to the office wasn't a bad thing and with each passing day he was starting to appreciate his men.

As Van was in the process of tidying up some news from recent minor events, Orval opened the door to the press room and in hobbled Lars Magnusson on his crutches and ascended the podium. Upon his entry the entire room of well-seasoned reporters rose to their feet in surprise upon sight of the President, Van Harvanian was heard to say in mock surprise, "Why Mr. President"?

"Van, I don't want to take away any of your thunder, but I figured it was time to meet the fifth estate up close and personal and to clear up any misconceptions about recent events concerning the burial of my family", then he handed Van his crutches to hold while grabbing onto the podium.

"Mr. President, I'm only the hired help. The podium is yours", said Harvanian as he relinquished the microphone.

"Please be seated everybody, please be seated. The meeting in my office can keep for a few minutes", he said.

"Now it appears that some folks with apparently nothing better to do are raising up some dust in newspaper editorials and on the talk programs on what is a private affair, the burial of my family. I decided to exclude the press and the public from the affair and dispense with any of the official pomp and circumstance, for a number of reasons. Chief of which, this is a strictly family affair, just a few friends and close family members. Now if my wife had become first lady and all of you had gotten to make her acquaintance over time, growing to respect and perhaps love her that would be one thing. But that was not permitted to happen.

My grief, is mine alone and I ask no one to share in my grief. This nation is beset by a host of problems and by enemies both inside our borders and abroad. So my wife and our family can rest in quiet repose and await my arrival whenever the almighty deems fit. I wanted to make as little a disturbance as possible by this private burial, but it seems that some will make an issue of something that is none of their business. So what I'm asking everyone to do is stop this bickering and move on to something else.

Thank you and I'm sure I'll see you all at the Presidential Congressional address next week"!

At that, he accepted the crutches form his press secretary and hobbled out of the press room. As they walked back to the Oval office, Orval Goodwin said, "Nice touch there Mr. President. Returning to a phantom meeting. You're catching on fast. The chickens are mesmerized, in case you didn't notice"!

"I noticed Orval, I noticed", said the President. What was left unsaid about the early Sunday morning service at Arlington was the fact that Lars Magnusson had bid his final goodbye to a beloved family that lay in their caskets, literally in pieces and those were the pieces that were not vaporized at the inauguration parade some months previously. All that he'd cherished was gone. One wondered what kept him going. The real and unspoken reason that the burial was not a public affair was that Lars had completely broken down in tears. Not simply crying but bordering on a complete breakdown, as the caskets were lowered into the ground. For the public to see this in the President, would no doubt garner sympathy from some, but far more important, it would show mortal weakness to the enemies of the Ship of State. He'd had difficulty falling asleep as of late, and his pain medications were closely monitored. His daily exercise regime was designed to help him rebuild the muscle mass lost while in recovery, but his daily exertions were painful, yet physically he was apparently on target.

Every day he was expected to be of keen mind and spirit and his grief had to be buried for the good of the country. No, it would not do for the country and others to see a grown man cry.

The few times Orval attended the Presidents daily physical therapy and exercise sessions, Orval noticed the President was in great pain, in spite of his pain medications, with the therapist repeating the Mantra, "No pain no gain, Mr. President and Magnusson saying back through clinched teeth, "I love pain. It's my best friend. Someone you always can depend on. I love pain"!

This was the man who was the Nations head of state. 'If others only knew', Goodwin asked himself? 'But that would have to wait for the man's memoirs sometime down the road. Far down the road', thought Goodwin.

The President had quietly dismissed his staff speechwriters, in the view that they were an unnecessary extravagance, designed to make the Presidential appear more Presidential and regal. It was time for plain talk, without the lofty rhetoric, in simple words that appealed to the common man. Yes it put a greater burden on the White House staff, principally the Chief of Staff and the Press Secretary in helping him assemble his thoughts in a cogent manner on his legal pad, but the words that were conveyed were those of Lars Magnusson, the farm boy from far western Minnesota.

The good news was that Lars Magnusson was a man quickly on the mend physically. His daily physical regimen became gradually less onerous more rapidly than expected and a few days prior to his first and long overdue, State of the Union speech he didn't need the crutches anymore, having a simple wooden cane, to get around on and by summers end he would probably be jogging. But for the sake of effect and not need, he would cling to his crutches just a little while longer, to maintain a certain image.

After secretly meeting with the USAF's Cyber Command and their counterparts of NSA, he determined to bring to an end the relentless cyber- attacks from those foreign and domestic entities that were determined to bring America's infrastructure to its knees.

"So if I understand you correctly General, we have finally the capability to counterattack, those who would do us great harm"?

"Mr. President we have had that ability since last fall, but the outgoing President and President Dobbins were reluctant to cut us loose. Citing international diplomatic concerns originating from the State Department as the chief obstacle"!

"And general, you can accomplish this in such a way that leaves no cyber trail of point of origin"!

"Yes sir we can"!

"Then you can understand, that when I give you a strictly verbal directive along with the Director of the NSA, that only those present in this room and those you carefully select to engage in this activity, we will be engaging in an undeclared war on the cyber eggheads"!

"We only await your verbal directive Sir", said the Director of NSA! "And your targets Director"?

"As we've indicated, we've run extensive testing on our approach, to the degree of completely obliteration a million dollar state of the art server, that we set up in northern Nevada. We set up two teams of Wizards, one to go on offence and one on defense. The event took just five hours to complete and the server in question was completely fried. I'm talking ready for the junk pile. It imploded upon itself. Now, out of the dozen or so targets we've positively identified as originators, we've decided that the "Black Hole" located in a unused warehouse in Helsinki Finland should be our first target, since the Russian Mafia, uses that as a routing point for all of their illegal activities in Europe and elsewhere. Once that's accomplished, there's a rotating group of servers in San Jose, California that's driving our banking system up the wall. Finally in Shanghai and Canton China, lay a series of computers and servers derived from the Chinese Government but they deny their existence, that need to go bye, bye and again, we only await your verbal directive"!

"And there is no way that it can be traced back to a point of origin", asked Magnusson?

"How can it when everything in the circuitry will be fried to a crisp"?

"Well then, make it so", said Magnusson. "But as the Brits always say, on the hush, hush"!

"You'll keep me personally aware of your progress, gentlemen"!

"Just buy us a late supper in White House kitchen from time to time, Mr. President"!

As they left the Oval office, Orval Goodwin walked over to the President's desk and asked, "Well, what do you think"?

"It seems that it'll work Orval"!

"Are you sufficiently up on your old College English literature", he asked?

"Never took English lit in school, the law books had no room for that stuff"!

"I believe it was in Shakespeare's 'Henry the Fifth', when he said to his troops, "Cry Havoc and let loose the dogs of Cyber War', or words to that effect", he said with a grin!

In the time running up to the State of the Union speech, the White House staff was relentlessly busy day and far into the night, answering letters and emails from the hoard of well-wishers and categorizing gifts sent by foreign countries and holding them in stasis, to be returned at a later date as the President saw fit. Then there was the significant time management problems given the almost round the clock meetings with various political and business entities, as he tried to position them for solid commitments well in advance for his planned agenda. Work, eat, rest, and then work some more, physical therapy, rest, and then work some more, was Lars Magnusson's way of existence. Yet bit by bit he was growing stronger.

Management is the art of effective direction of an organization's resources and sitting right on top of the food chain is the time of the executives and their respective staffs. Time is money was the mantra. Much of the existing staff was held over from the previous administration, many of which had jobs awaiting them at the end of their government service. But with few exceptions, the majority of personnel stayed over, after talking with Orval Goodwin, the glue that held everything in place. As Chief of Staff, he was the puppet master, who sub directed activities in a precise manner, via moral suasion.

As the previous Presidents Chief of Staff, he usually worked a standard twelve to fourteen hour day, six and often seven days a week. His family visited him often at work delivering whatever he needed to extend his workday, catching often fleeting glimpses of him running from meeting to meeting. Most other families would have bolted or broken, but Goodwin's wife was made of sterner stuff, offering appropriate direction and love to his children.

Prior to the inauguration Orval Goodwin was looking forward to a long vacation, where he could actually sleep late in the mornings, instead of being up well before sunrise and driving home well after rush hour traffic. He knew of a half dozen law firms in DC, that would offer A partnership in a heartbeat after his White House service, but after the debacle and the confusion that took place, he simply stayed in place, with no one asking him to either leave or stay.

Several nights later when he finally did arrive home just short of Ten PM, his wife sat beside him on their couch as she handed him his standard Scotch and water and said, "Looks like that vacation is going to take a back seat for a while, isn't it"!

"It all depends on the circumstances Meg and most important, you"! As she hugged him, she then got up and said, "Drink your drink, then come up to bed. Disney Land will have to keep for a while. You're going to have another long day tomorrow"!

The following evening as Orval Goodwin, Van Harvanian and the President sat in the conference room, eating their sandwiches while working on the format of the Presidents first address to the nation, Van Harvanian said in utter exasperation; "Mr. President, this subject is far too toxic to bring up to the Nation at this time. Term Limits of our legislators? Of course it's time! It's long past time. It's ridiculous that ninety year old men, who've held office as long as thirty years, claim to be the servant of the people. It's pure bullshit. They have seniority. They have power and influence. They have perks that are off the charts. They can pick up the phone and fly anywhere they want, first class at the taxpayer's expense. They can shower their constituents with pork barrel projects, have their names put on public buildings and boulevards galore and the sheep that form their constituency will reelect them again and again, like that old coot from Alaska with the bridge to nowhere, or the old curmudgeon from South Carolina, who had to be wheeled into the Senate and have an aide help him raise his hand on a vote, then wheeled back out. Not to forget the old Geezer from West Virginia, ex clan member as he may be, having his name emblazoned on Schools, Streets, Universities and Federal Buildings. There is no way you can reason with these people of honor, when it comes to limiting their tenure. Once you have power, you cling to it like mothers milk"!

Remember Lord Acton who once said, "Power tends to corrupt and Absolute Power corrupts absolutely"! "To ask any politician to limit his power is to literally piss against the wind. Ain't gonna happen"!

"But Van", asked Magnusson, "What about Washington, getting out after his second term, then the Roman wartime Consul Cincinnatus, in the days of the old Roman Republic, returning to his villa and ignoring the Senate's pleas to stay on"?

"Mr. President, two examples of apparently righteous men in some twenty five hundred years? Please! What about Caesar, after the Senate proclaimed him Dictator? How well did that work out? Then FDR and his four terms as President? Then the Romanov's and every king that ever lived in the history of man. Once one gets power and influence he will move heaven and earth to retain it! No sir mere words and logic will not persuade enough people to relinquish their hold on their Congressional power. Like Mel Brooks once said, 'It's good to be the King'! Something other than words is needed. Something that will compel those it power to give it up willingly. What that is for the moment eludes me"?

"Point made Van, so I suppose that 'Line Item Veto' is off the list"? "Different thing, for different reasons. Mid-eighties, President Reagan gave it a shot. It was a weak sell, for the poor man was starting to exhibit Alzheimer's at the time and he was delegating most of his agenda to others. Now his people were capable men. It was the Supreme Court that shot that down, if you'll recall. To get the line item veto through Congress, would be a heavy lift, but just barely possible. But then you'd have to have a sympathetic court to approve the law, once the other side got through with all their Lawsuits and I just don't see that happening. The courts will look back to the previous ruling and via Stare Decisis that will influence their thinking, most likely in the negative"!

"Then what about, the President vowing to Veto any bill of particulars, that has amendments attached, not germane to the bill at hand", asked Magnusson?

"It's doable, but no one has had the guts to get it done. It would be like declaring war on various elements of both houses of congress. Oh you would get a few true believers to come along for the ride, but for how long. Some would holler for impeachment", said Goodwin continuing. "At the very best it would make headlines for a very long time and even if you did win the battle, the next President could come in and do things the way they've always been done and your time in office would go for naught"! "But you think it's doable, right Orval"?

"Oh it's probably doable, but don't expect any applause over that line of your speech and your honeymoon would be instantly being over before you ever got kissed! The boys and girls in both houses of congress, just have to have their earmarks. It's their mother's milk. Insertion of earmarks for their constituents in the dark of night, go far to reinsure their reelection, so they can go back and claim, 'See folks I brought home the bacon"!

"What about our recent meeting with all the White House staff, that they called up"?

"That's where you hit it out of the park", said Harvanian. "Leadership through personal example. The country is in precarious fiscal shape, the government is bloated and since you've cut your remuneration in half, the entire White House staff came to you of their own free will and offered to do the same. You politely refused and they politely insisted. You gave in on the proviso that the new policy gets modified upward on a sliding scale.

Those at the top take the greater cut in pay while those on the bottom take the least, for the duration of the economic crisis. Still won't get much if any applause by the congress, but it'll play well in the boonies"!

"The rest of your agenda will be a winner in the heartland and in the TV audience, guaranteeing you front page mention for weeks to come and will keep the political talk programs with something to talk about for weeks to come. No previous President in memory has reduced his regality and rolled up his sleeves and jumped right into the pile like you have. No previous President has both talked the talk and walked the walk. We both like your mention of old Teddy and his speak softly, but carry a big Barzong comment. Both quaint and unique and with a wee wink of the eye"!

"It's almost Eleven PM guys and time for the both of you to get home to your families" said Magnusson"!

"We will on one condition Mr. President", said Goodwin!

"And that is"?

"That you do go upstairs and hit the rack also and do it now. You've been hard at it since five in the morning and we need you in top form"! Goodwin then took the Presidents work papers and said, "These will be in your upper right hand drawer first thing in the morning", then went to the Oval office before going home, while Harvanian escorted the President upstairs, both making small talk, before turning him over to the Presidents Valet for the evening.

54

5

The run up to the Presidents first State of the Union speech, was the subject great angst, curiosity, speculation, consternation, sympathy, empathy and anything but apathy, not only in America, but the world over. Some media headlines implied that, "Lazarus had come back from the dead", while others answered with the question, "Yes but how long did he last afterwards"? While one stated, "Welcome to the Meat grinder"!

The White House had all rallied around the office of the Presidency, throughout Lars Magnusson's hospitalization and ongoing convalescence, managing well the information that it allowed the media to know. Vannevar Harvaninan, was brought onboard just days after, the debacle of the inauguration by Hiram Mulvahill, coming seemingly out of nowhere as a Liberal Canadian political television commentator from the wilds of Vancouver Canada. From the very onset, he and the conservative Orval Goodwin hit it off, forming an impenetrable phalanx around the office of the Presidency, managing his hectic schedule and the news releases that emanated from the Oval office.

All during the caretaker Presidency of Hiram Mulvahill, many in the media conducted a White House watch from a distance, reporting mainly on when the lights went out in the Oval office, which usually was somewhere between Seven and Nine PM. But as soon as Lars Magnusson assumed the Presidency, often was the time when the lights in the Oval office stayed on till midnight and beyond. Clearly the new President, on the mend in a host of ways, was only getting from four to six hours of sleep each night.

Members of various aspects of the Government and the Military were seen streaming in and out of the White House, indicative that Magnusson and his team, were fully engaged in the ship of state. While Van Harvanian was delicately releasing cleansed versions of the results of the meetings that occurred, no one really had a handle of where the country was going.

The nation and the world at large, was eager and curious to see, the newly recovering President speak. While his back ground was thoroughly investigated and rehashed, most of the intellectual class gave him scant credit as being a charismatic and transformational head of state. At best a caretaker President, for the interim. An intellectual light weight that never took an adverse position politically. Yet clearly something was happening at 1600 Pennsylvania Avenue and what it was, the nation and the world would soon discover.

Much like the debacle of 9/11, the nation was once again brought to its knees, by a series of devastating body blows. Yet as it lifted itself off the canvass, it turned to a wounded leader also on the mend, for some comfort and direction.

Although he probably could've ambled along on a cane alone, his doctor and Van Harvanian, insisted that Lars Magnusson enter the Capitol rotunda via a wheelchair and just before entering the packed to overflowing House chamber for his first State of the Union presentation to the nation, the President rose up from the wheelchair and stood by on a pair of crutches, while the Sergeant at Arms announced his presence by saying, "Mr. Speaker, the President of the United States"!

The nation viewed in wonder, via the nationwide television feed to all channels, Lars Magnusson, hobbling down the aisle, smiling weakly as all leaned over the railing, acknowledging his presence and wishing him well, preceded by his Press Secretary and Chief of Staff.

As the President ascended the podium unaided, to the cheers and applause by thosedignitaries assembled, Harvanian opened the Presidential briefing folder, to the beginning of his bullet pointed previously prepared notes, then took the crutches from the President and joined Orval Goodwin in the background and said a brief prayer to whatever unseen entity was at hand as the President looked up at his invisible parents sitting in the unseen visitors section, for some inspiration.

He raised his hand and asked those assembled to be seated as the applause began to gradually diminish, entering into his acknowledgement of the important personages in government on hand.

"Ladies and gentlemen, before I begin I'm going to ask everyone to forgive me, for I'm going to speak to the Nation from prepared notes, without the benefit of a prepared speech or teleprompter's. During my term as President I'm going to do without speechwriters and work from notes only, so while the lofty rhetoric will gone, I think it's time for some straight talk, to the American people. I speak to you from both the mind and the heart"!

As he looked down nervously at his notes, he again briefly glanced up at his unseen parents in the gallery for inspiration, seeing tears in their eyes, then stood erect saying haltingly, "Our nation has recently suffered a series of tragedies, on top of the tragedies of ongoing military conflicts overseas, a national economic recession, along with all of the other standard conflicts that confront us as a nation. We are all aware of them every time we pick up the paper, or watch the evening newscasts"!

"Quite apart, but included in the mix of what ails us, is the fact that when one looks at the accounts, our fiscal health, we have seem to have bitten off far more than we can chew. "Service to all, is service to none", some wise old North Dakota farmer once told me long ago. Our nation has seemed to have made more commitments than we can reasonably fulfill to not only our citizens, but to the rest of the world at large"!

"Our government has become so bloated and bureaucratically top heavy, by those sworn to enhance and direct our daily lives, that nothing can get done anymore and the American taxpayer has the burden of shouldering this heavy load with the diminishing resources of massive unemployment"!

"Visited we all are, by a legion of lobbyists, hired by American business interests, along with others, exhorting one and all to carve exceptions out of pending legislation, (we usually call them loopholes) to gain advantage for their clients at the expense of another and that other usually end up being the American taxpayer. One really can't have any expectation of that ever changing, for that has become part of our American tapestry, hasn't it"?

"Our political parties divided so widely by chasm of special interests and secret deals that never see the light of day, coupled with arcane procedural rules that have evolved gradually over time, claiming to enhance the checks and balances of our legislative process, that little of any importance ever gets accomplished and yet we are the most stable of all governments on the planet. However, 'How long can this set of circumstances last', is the unasked question on everyone's mind"?

"We have a host of untouched resources readily available and a highly intelligent and educated population ready to be put to work, to craft these resources into a finished product for the common good, by private enterprise, if we will only get out of the way of progress, again for the common good"!

"For, the common good. Four words, that seem to have been overlooked by all of us in this August assemblage. For the common good"!

"All of my professional life, I've been taught and have seen many examples of the fact that effective leadership starts at the top. Every great leader in history has lead by positive personal example, leading from the front. Getting his hands dirty if need be and that is what I intend to do during my term in office"!

As Magnusson spoke, the entire assemblage remained silent for there was little to cheer about. Gone were the periodic interruptions from one side of the aisle or the other, cheering on some initiative or the other while the opposite side sat on their hands. The President was holding a mirror up to the body politic and they didn't like what they were seeing or hearing.

President Magnusson put down his glass of water, continuing on. "The other morning, while at breakfast, I was reading the paper and a comment by a citizen planted itself deep in my head. After all aren't these the very people that employ us? The citizen, the taxpayer, was commenting on that fact that some important personage in the news stated that every one of us just might have to take an economic haircut for a while, while no one was willing to step up and be the first. Seems it was every one waiting for someone else to make a move and of course that move would never arrive.

So taken was I with that, I called in my Chief of Staff and directed him to initiate the appropriate paperwork to diminish the Presidential remuneration by fifty percent for the duration of my term in office. Now somehow the news leaked out and the following day, the entire White House staff offered to follow suit, starting at a fifty percent diminishment of their earnings, during their term at the White House"!

"Of course, this was madness, for the greater Washington DC area is an expensive place to live, so after some negotiation, lest I have a revolt on my hands I relented to the White House staff and allow a far less Draconian reduction in their remuneration"!

"After all, I can afford it and most of them cannot. I have no immediate family to take care of. The people provide a roof over my head, a place to work, eat and sleep, so I can afford the cut in pay and they cannot"!

"At the last meeting of the Cabinet, I asked each Cabinet Secretary to draft a voluntary set of proposals to reach a remunerative target of ten percent in expenditure reductions for the next fiscal year. In addition I've issued directives for a spending freeze across the board and a travel ban for all personnel germane to meetings, with but a few exceptions for the very senior officers, which must be approved by the appropriate Cabinet Secretary"!

"Their recommendations will be on my desk early next week for approval. This will in no way hinder the operations of the Executive Branch of our Government; simply minimize the fat and waste that's been going on for far too long"!

"It is my sincere hope the Unions that have contracts with the Government will partner with us, to reach some accommodation during this time of our fiscal crisis. I have directed all Cabinet members to enter into negations with the appropriate Union entities where appropriate"!

"In addition, I've asked the Defense Department, to take a long look at paring down the costs of the entire military structure with the ten percentile cost reduction target in mind, with the only proviso, being the remunerative structure of our enlisted and noncommissioned personnel and that all quantitative and qualitative levels of logistic materiel be maintained at current levels"!

"That takes care of the Executive branch of the government for the present, with the goal of minimizing the layoffs of essential personnel. Now as for the Legislative and the Judicial Branches of Government are concerned, all one can legally ask is that they consider what the Executive Branch is endeavoring to accomplish and do what they can to follow our lead, mindful of the fact that America is watching"!

"All over this great land of our, exists pockets of uncertainty as far as how long will my current job last and of course, when can I get another job and get income once again flowing, into my family unit? It all gets down to 'wants' and 'needs' and the 'wants' are having to take a backseat, for a great many people"!

"My time in the Senate has revealed that many great cost cutting initiatives can occur if the members of both houses wish it to be so and that is the province of the Legislative Branch of government and all I can do is try and exert as much moral suasion as possible, from the bully pulpit. Now I would ask each of you to keep in mind, the following question. What is essential? Just three simple words as you enter into deliberations."!

"I would submit that nothing is of greater importance than the fiscal integrity of our Sovereign Nation, for the foreseeable future. Now of course other aspects of legislation are in the pipeline for consideration and they could and should proceed in the normal course of affairs. We all can walk and chew gum at the same time, can we not"?

Magnusson took a brief pause as he picked up the glass of water and briefly scanned the crowded assembly before continuing, noting that since his opening statement, the assembly had remained silent. Clearly no one wanted to hear his message, for grim faces greeted him wherever he looked yet, 'In for a penny', he thought before continuing.

"Yet after much thought and reflection on the matter of unnecessary and wasteful spending that lands on every Presidents desk, there is but one elegantly simple solution to the problem at hand. Thus the solution is this.

Any bill that passes through the scrutiny and approval of both houses of Congress and is presented for the Presidential signature, that contains amendments of any kind not directly germane to the bill, will not be approved"!

Magnusson stopped for a moment to allow that message to sink in as he noted a sudden restlessness occur amongst the legislative members on both sides of the aisle before continuing, "Should a member of Congress have a need in his or her District or State that is in need of attention and thus funding, it should be given the appropriate objective consideration from each member of Congress, regardless of party affiliation, after the appropriate due diligence has occurred. Ladies and Gentlemen, this is called fiscal discipline and those of us that derive our positions from the American people, owe them the wisdom of that apportionment, for the common good"!

"For isn't that what the American people expect of us in government? Wisdom? Wisdom for the Common Good? To be the effective stewards of our society? Would they knowingly elect a legislator, that was of low moral character, or have the reasonable expectation to be guided by those who lead by positive personal example all of the time, always"!

"Much has happened as of late and that is behind us as a guide post and much will happen that is ahead of us, but none of that is as important, as that which is in deep within us! If we all work together, then we can work our way through these perilous times, for the common good. I'm reminded of the time in the early days of our society, during the dark days of the Continental Congress, when it was a very close run thing and bounties were placed on the heads of our forefathers by the King. Congress was at odds whether to throw in the towel, or put their collective heads together and come to a common accord, when old Ben Franklin was purported to say and I may be paraphrasing here, but I believe he said, "Gentlemen, let us all hang together, lest we hang separately", or words to that effect"!

"I would ask every legislator, to consider the common good, not just your State or legislative District, when you consider the apportionment of expenditures annually. I would also ask the various State, County and Municipal Districts, to set the appropriate example when considering their appropriate legislation. Strive to obtain the most cost effective bid price on every contract and monitor the progress to completion, so the American tax payer can achieve value for every dollar spent, rather than award contracts as a result of crass favoritism. Now this may not be humanly possible, given the frailties of the human condition, even though that's what you're there for, so now enters the fifth estate. Yes the Media in all of its various forms. You have a target rich environment in which to choose from. Possibilities of governmental malfeasance and hypocrisy are everywhere, regardless of political affiliation. Should you see something, and then feel free to shed the light of day and inform the nation as a whole. Then perhaps the word, 'Accountability' will again recapture some literal meaning to America and the public at large will start to regain the appropriate respect for those people of Wisdom, and Character, who will provide for the Common Good"!

"Next week I will be meeting with the much maligned Wizards of Wall Street, to see if they can regain the respect of the American people and privately fund some ideas I have in mind, to bring America's economy back to the forefront. Companies will be formed, people will be employed at a rapid rate, for occupations that will be long lasting and we will all profit at every stage of its progress. With only slide rules, hard work and collective brains, our nation jumped right into the nuclear age years ago, in just about three years. Now days we have even smarter people at the ready and mega computers, if we only exhibit the collective will to succeed for the common good. Now the Captains of industry will only act if there is a profit incentive for them. My job is to see that there is that incentive, but also for the incentive that provides for the common good. The White House Press Secretary will keep America well aware of all developments. Politics, the economy and business, doesn't have to be a zero sum game, with winners and losers. America deserves a win, win solution wherever possible.

"Mr. and Mrs. America, I thank you for listening and to all out there, who have inundated the White House with your expressions of sympathy and good will, I humbly thank you again"!

Magnusson then closed his folder, signaling the end of his State of the Union speech as the entire assemblage rose to politely applaud and in some cases cheer. The entire speech was the shortest in known memory and quite to the point as to the State of the Union. As Magnusson exchanged his folder for the crutches, he hobbled down from the podium as Orval Goodwin whispered in his ear, "You draw a great line in the sand Mr.

President" as Magnusson nodded his head and lurched up the aisle with far less people eager to congratulate, him for his speech than were there at his entrance. Still the tradeoff seemed appropriate with a speedier exit from the hall and less hangers on eager for their photo op at hand. Once in the hall way, he relinquished his crutches for the wheelchair and was wheeled to the Presidential Limo.

On the short drive back to the White House, Van Harvanian commented, "Well, that went over like a fart in church, but that was expected wasn't it"?

"As we all know Van, the message was more for the people than the Congress and their acceptance, or lack thereof was expected. We'll follow the polls for the next few weeks and Peek in on the political talk shows to see, just who is on what side of the political fence"! "Well gentlemen, we all will see just what comes out of this in the days and weeks ahead and we shouldn't be surprised if we see some push back in certain quarters, given the President diminishing some of the congressional prerogatives", said Goodwin!

"Finally Mommy has said a quiet 'No', to Junior's candy for a while", said Harvanian with a wink and a nod"!

As the smooth riding Presidential Limo went out into the misty night, Lars Magnusson looked out of the rain drops clinging to the window and said wearily, "Gents, as Betty Davis once said in a movie long ago, 'Fasten your seatbelts, we're all gonna be in for a bumpy ride'"!

Tyler Montag, stood atop his palatial thirtieth floor penthouse, in one of the Trump emporiums looking out at the glittering New York skyline.

Thirty year old scotch in one hand and a thin Cuban cheroot in the other mulling around in his mind what he'd just witnessed. He was joined by several others out on the white marble patio by several other venture capitalists he periodically partnered with as they stood there looking westward into the depths of New Jersey.

"Any thoughts Tyler", asked one of his associates?

"This guy just might be someone we can do business with, maybe"! "But he's going into it clearly overmatched, isn't he? I mean you vetted him back to the day he was born right"?

"The guy is squeaky clean alright. You could change his name to Jack

Armstrong, All American Boy tomorrow and he wouldn't miss a beat. He'd have been playing pro ball years ago when he was at Minnesota, except for some freak accident on the gridiron. Now he has the sympathy of America on his side and depending on how skillfully he plays things and how well his handlers direct his activities"!

"Goodwin and Harvanian are about as fine a duo as can be found Tyler. Goodwin knows where all the bodies are buried in both houses of congress, while Van Harvanian is the Saint Paul of spin doctors"!

"Pierre, your correct in that assessment, but with what that guy is facing and even though both of his handlers are excellent street fighters politically, I just don't like the odds of him succeeding", said Montag looking up at the stars!

"So if I hear you right, Magnusson is going to need help"!

"Yes and lots of it. The nasty and dirty kind of help. See you have to convince people in power to relinquish their power and be reasonable. Now these people fall into two distinct categories, those that are irredeemably corrupt and those that are true believers. Of the two, it's the true believers that are the most intractable. It's their way or the highway. Now Magnusson falls into the latter category, while a number of influential people in his party fall into the very same category. Neither one budging on an issue for love or money. Now Magnusson is squeaky clean and his family is gone, so what is one going to do to him that hasn't been done already? Nothing"!

While he was talking, several other venture capital associates joined them on the penthouse patio, drinks in hand to see what Tyler Montag had to say.

"The question Tyler, is should we help him or even more can we help him", asked another?

"The answer to the first question is simply, It depends on what he has in mind for our little chat next week. If we can make a buck then we help him. If not, the answer to the second question is, sure we can help him, and in the very same manner we persuade some influential weak sisters on various boards in companies we decide to take over. By any means possible. We can't kill them, we can't eat them it's against the law and the probability of culpability is far too great. But most everyone has a skeleton in their closet. We discover what it is, and then we turn the screws, but always from a distance. No comebacks at any cost. Low risk, high yield concept of moral influence. We discover the weakness, we exploit the weakness, we promise anything in return to walk away, then once things are cast in stone we destroy the object of our attention, then we walk away. Gentlemen that is how we work is it not? We never relinquish the high ground completely, only appear to"!

"But the question remains, is he worth it, Tyler" asked another associate?

"It'll all depend on the meeting next week. The guy is nuts about solar and wind power and he sees Mag Lev Trains self-powered by wind and solar power all over America, whisking people from hither to yon within a relatively short time frame. The financing can be had and the terms can be had, but the bureaucratic hurdles are monumental. If this guy can play blocking back and eliminate the red tape, with a wee bit of help here and there, then there might be some possibilities to back his play and make a bundle in the process. If not, then we take our toys into another sand box"! "We all know some off the books people Tyler, that can be brought into play", said another associate!

"Pierre and I will attend the meeting next week along with a slew of others no doubt. If Magnusson has in mind what I think he does, then there may be some possibilities, we will just have to see. But never fear all of you will be summoned to hear our assessment, the next evening. One good thing though, the book on Magnusson reads that he is a man of his word, unlike many of us and those we deal with"!

As the President's Limo came to a halt underneath the large portico at the entrance to the White House, a wheelchair was provided for his visible entrance. Once inside and away from the prying eyes of the public, he arose from the wheelchair and took the proffered cane and limped towards the Oval office followed by Goodwin and Harvanian. As the trio entered the office, Harvanian said I'll break out the brews and went to the connecting area where the small office refrigerator was located and returned with three bottles of ice cold beer saying, "Orval, have you told him the news yet"?

"News, news", exclaimed Magnusson!

"Orval has been sitting on some very good news, for about an hour"!

"The news came in from the USAF Cyber Command and the NSA Mr. President, just before you were to speak to congress. Since you had a lot on your plate I decided that it could wait until afterward. If you'll recall our meeting with the Air Force and the NSA Cyber people in discussing the pros and cons of the cyber operation to silence the world wide hackers that are trying to infiltrate our financial, defense and logistics systems"?

"Yes I do and I hope you have good news Orval"!

"Well its good news depending on one's point of view", said Goodwin sneaking a quick glance at a grinning Harvanian. "Last evening the first target of target 'Cockroach' was hit in Helsinki Finland and if you'll recall it was suspected that target was used by the Russian Mafia, in the main and possibly elements of the Russian Government. The entire computer network and the attendant servers all imploded, causing a large fire in an industrial area. Now since no loss of life was detected and the locus of the fire was in an industrialwarehouse area, the media in that part of the country gave it short shrift, accepting the general opinion the fire was caused by a wiring overload of an older building with substandard wiring. At least that's the reports that are coming in thus far. Several hours later, a similar building located in San Jose California, went the very same way as the building in Helsinki. Finally the locations in Shanghai, Canton and Wuhan China suffered a similar fate, with the computer hardware literally igniting and thus causing a fire. Now what we didn't expect was that the Chinese were sending much of their hacker attacks via their Satellite that's in orbit. The Wizards at the NSA somehow figured out a way to route their counter programs called, 'Cockroach', through the Chinese Satellites and when the ground targets were destroyed, the signals from the ground would cease, signaling the Satellites entire circuitry into an overload situation and fry all of its circuits automatically. So currently the Chinese have a Satellite that's space junk."!

As Goodwin spoke, he could see a smile grow on the Presidents face, then he continued. "If you'll recall, the reason the Wizards called the entire program Project Cock Roach, was that unlike any other hacking program that literally bangs against an objects firewall, thus alerting the target that an intruder is trying to gain entry, this program is subtle. Its originator, a chap from Quebec, insists on its 'Delicatesse' as its weapon insisting on cyber finesse as the way in. It arrives in silence, lingers, subtly probing for an entry past the firewall, and once it's found, no matter how small, like a Cock Roach, flattens itself and squeezes its way in. Imagine a thousand binary Cock Roaches trying to gain entry into a dozen small entry points of a cyber-target. The defenses tighten up and some binary re enforcements are redirected from point A, to point C. But then point A becomes vulnerable at the very time the Cock Roach then flattens itself and gains entry. Once entry is achieved all is lost for the forts cannons are all pointed seaward and that is how a Wizard thinks"!

"There must be a way we can show our thanks to this guy Oval"!

"Perhaps someday in the future perhaps, someone will write a book. Maybe several months down the road you can quietly fly him in to have lunch or dinner, but then there are at least several dozen techs that went along for that ride and the logistics of reward become untenable. My bet is that right about now, these guys wherever they are breaking out the thirty year old Jack Daniels and celebrating"!

"Even better", offered Van Harvanian, "Is that the whole event appeared out of nowhere and disappeared into nowhere, leaving no trail. All one can ever do is speculate and there's nothing there to speculate. No speeches. No comments. Nothing. The binary Ninjas came, saw, conquered, then poof, they're gone"!

"Which reinforces what you've been saying all along Mr. President?

Never give a warning of your intentions. Never rattle your sword. Take your lumps if need be, let time pass, then act"!

6

"By special invitation only", was the header on the special email that was sent to the Captains of Industry and the Movers and Shakers of the Investment Community. One had to have very deep financial pockets or the fiscal influence to pick up a phone, utter a directive and make things happen, to have a seat at this particular table.

The White House ball room was the only venue possible, to be able to seat, the various cabinet secretaries, the Head of the Federal Reserve, the CEO's of all the investment banking houses and various key investors, heretofore sitting on the sidelines awaiting the right opportunity.

Melanie O'Bannon had been tasked in pulling this event off logistically.

Since the White House had done away with the frills of office, Mel had called in some markers from the Washington elite to help her in pulling this off logistically. It was to be a daylong event, starting at eight in the morning, through lunch and dinner and break up whenever it was over.

Working in the background, flitting from place to place in the ballroom, checking on the seating arrangements and coordinating the staff, she was her elegant self as she marshaled her volunteer forces of the Washington mavens, to bring this event off without as much as a whimper.

At five in the morning, the remote media vehicles were well in place along with their technicians and on site news reporters, awaiting the arrival of the "Cavalcade de Money", soon to spend a day deciding whether it was worth it, or not.

Starting at seven thirty, the Limousines arrived, disgorging well-dressed personages, who were swiftly and politely moved along to the innards of the Nation's home. Each guest was deftly handed off to one of Melanie's societal helpers and politely guided to their appointed seat at the overly large rectangular box like table setup, with seating chosen alphabetically as not to give preference to one or the other. Coffee, fruit juice and croissants were to suffice, until noon.

The wives of the nation's capital elite were at hand to serve the needs of those at hand, some said as their way of 'paying things forward'. By Seven Fifty Five, the last guest had arrived and was seated. At precisely the stroke of Eight AM, the main door opened and in walked Lars Magnusson, with the assistance of an old, gnarled looking cane, as Mel O'Bannon announced, "Gentlemen, the President of the United States"! As Magnusson made his way around the assemblage of tables, he briefly stopped by each person to say a brief hello, before coming to his place, flanked by his press secretary and his chief of staff. As he took his seat, he was handed his portfolio with his bullet pointed notes of interest to speak from.

He signaled for everyone to be seated, Melanie, having followed the President around the table, picked up an empty water goblet and a fork, and gave the goblet several taps and said, "Please be seated so we can commence", then retired away to a seat and a small table behind the President and near a window. In doing so, she discretely pushed a button inside of her dark French Tweed business suit, thus activating the White House video recorders. Every twitch, every whisper was to be recorded at this event, by a state of the art system hidden from view. She briefly thought before the President began, 'The Russians would be proud'.

"I want to thank each and every one of you for coming today. For I have a modest proposal to offer and I come to you asking in behalf of the nation for help. As I need not remind you, financially our nation is in a bit of a pickle financially. The cumulative effects of reckless fiscal over commitment's that over time threatens to sink our ship of state and therefore all of us. This has been known for every election cycle going back years and years. Yet each election cycle the can effective decision making gets put off for another time and we keep sinking deeper in debt. There are those in my party that if they had their druthers, would tax every one of you deep into the ninety percentile and quickly the Islands of the Caribbean would experience a rapid upsurge in population"!

This brought a nervous chuckle from all in the room, but Magnusson continued on saying, "Now most of you are businessmen and not social workers and could clearly care little for the day to day maladies of the great unwashed, but you do care about retained earnings. For this is your mother's milk. It's the air you breathe, is it not"? Yet again a gradual slightly perceptual nodding of the heads occurred by those assembled.

"We still are a nation of vast resources and yet are restrained almost at every turn by our governments by employing these resources for the common good and thus are at war with ourselves. To get a business up and running these days is a monumental task for an individual who has a better mousetrap. One has to obtain the financing, then depending on where he sets up shop, has a plethora of governmental and or environmental entities to surmount. Then hire a competent and cohesive staff, then obtain equipment and so one and so on. All of you are way past that stage and are of the investor class. Which is why all of you are here.

In the latter part of the nineteenth the Federal Government was on the verge of bankruptcy and JP Morgan himself was called in to help bail out the country, which history tells us, he did. Now the man was hardly a social worker, but acting in his own best interests, he worked a deal and saved the nation from bankruptcy and I'm told made more than a few dollars in the process"!

"People need to be put to work at every level of our society, but not by special make work projects, funded by the government, but by private enterprise, creating lasting jobs that create wealth not consume wealth. As we all know, government at every level consumes, not creates wealth. Thus as the Federal government shrinks, which I have every intention of accomplishing gradually, these very same people of skills will need employment in the creation and expansion of the companies of the future. Engineers, technicians, and yes even lawyers will be available for employment, but by whom and to do what"?

"And now to my modest proposal. For many years, solar and wind power generation have been available, but for the wealthy only. Currently there are several companies that are in that business, yet are hitting repeated obstacles, via environmental concerns and various NIMBY entities that get in the way of progress. So I ask each of you to consider this. If these obstacles were to disappear and these companies were to be allowed to grow unhindered by the activities of various political concerns, would not any investment grow rapidly in value. Further, if each of you had on your very own homes self-sufficiency power wise, would not that send a strong signal to other investors that this was a worthy investment"?

One of the basic precepts of salesmanship was to sell ones product to a given point then shut up and allow the buyer to roll around in their mind the value of your point of view. Magnusson kept that well in mind as he picked up his water glass and took a drink, cleansing his mouth and reviewing those assembled, before continuing.

"Some years ago the German Government made a massive commitment towards wind power and to a lesser degree solar power, that when completed will supply a quarter of their country's energy requirements for the foreseeable future. China is already headed in that direction and I'm told is on a fast track. It takes no imagination for one to see wind farms rimming the Great Lakes, in partnership with Canada. Or wind power generators that start from Seattle to San Diego, or from Maine all the way down the Atlantic Coast to and around Florida and all around the Gulf Coast. In the Deserts of California, Nevada and Arizona are Solar Electric farms on the drawing boards, blocked by environmentalists and Unions, awaiting their cut of the pie. We are already moving to eliminate these obstacles."

"With the cooperation of the Secretary of Energy and the Secretary of the Interior, we are quietly moving full speed ahead in relaxing any environmental constraints that may impede rapid growth of any energy generating organization. We are going to open up the nuclear waste storage facility in Nevada and plan for Nuclear power plants. We are going to invite the infant Coal Gasification crowd to do whatever can be done to grow that aspect of the energy producing business. It would help a great deal if they could make the process cleaner and more cost effective and if our members of the oil industry were far seeing they could partner up where practicable, with the coal people to produce fuel that can be sold. The Secretary of the Air Force can be of assistance in this regard, for they have a pilot program in place to provide fuel for our aircraft. I'm certain our air carriers would have an interest in this, for jet aircraft consume a great deal of fuel. The supply would be at the ready, all we would have to do would get the costs more competitive."

"There will always be a need for oil products far into the future, if for no other reason than the production of plastic products far into the future and I've directed the Secretaries of Energy and the Interior, to be instrumental to remove any obstacles that may exist for the development of oil shale on Federal Lands. In this I have there complete commitment". As he made that statement Magnusson again paused as both Secretaries' nodded their heads in agreement.

"And now to the discussion of Mass Transportation. Japan has developed high speed mass rail transportation ever since the mid-sixties and it works very well. Europe has it and China is embarking in the latest concept of mass rail high speed passenger transport in the form of Mag Lev, or Magnetic Levitation transport. Extensive testing has shown that Mag Lev transport systems can safely transport people at speeds exceeding two hundred and fifty miles per hour. Which means that if you're in the DC area and you need to be in New York in about an hour and a half and the flying weather will not permit this you can still be in New York on time. Given the security constraints that exist these days, a Mag Lev ride just may get you there faster"!

"Now one of the many problems in already heavily populated areas is the acquisition of the right of ways, in which to place the Mag Lev pathways, if that form of transport proves cost effective and I suggest that it does. Everyone tells me that massive expenditures will be required by the governing entity in land acquisition and normally they would be correct in that assumption, except for the fact that enforcing Eminent Domain will be completely unnecessary, for we intend to utilize the space above the existing rail tight of ways for the proposed Mag Lev people movers. No doubt some before must've thought of this and some managing bureaucrat gave either him or her back of his hand. Happens all the time in any bureaucracy, but not this time if I can help it for gentlemen, time is of the essence and in this, our joint interests coincide. You wish investment possibilities with minimal governmental interference and the people and the government needs your brains and capital."!

"You will note the attendance of the Director of the IRS, who can answer any questions Regarding the tax status of any emerging or existing entities that are involved in these 'Special Privately Funded Initiatives', that serve the common good. They have been well considered by people that are after progress first and tax revenue only after we all know we have a winner. Your original investments must be recoverable. The Federal Government will have ample time to gradually apply remunerative taxation, on the beneficiaries of these initiatives and I can say with certainty that during the initial construction phases and for ten years thereafter the completion of each phase coming on line, the clock will be held in abeyance on any corporate taxes derived from income on these projects."

"The Director of the IRS as well as the Secretaries of the Interior and Energy are available to provide the appropriate details."

"Now, I'm certain there are a number of questions you have gentlemen".

Pierre Duquesne stood up and said "Mr. President, If you please"!

Magnusson looked to his left and seeing his name on the placard in front of his seat said, "Yes Mr. Duquesne"!

"Mr. President. In Death Valley California, there is a startup company intent on providing a vast Solar Energy array to provide clean competitively priced energy for the people of Southern California. Now a coalition between the Unions and the Environmentalists have joined in a lawsuit that has brought an injunction against any further construction activity. The Unions have their own reasons for this action for they want a slice of the action and the environmentalists want to save from extinction, some obscure worm that is claimed to exist nowhere else but in Death Valley. The Unions insistence on using their labor during construction and beyond, throw the projected construction cost through the roof while the Environmental Groups wish us to move the project into someone else's back yard. Should this Judicial Injunction continue the project will have to be abandoned. So I ask Mr. President, what can be done"?

"Odd you should ask about that very project, because early last week I called in the Secretaries of Energy, Interior and the Attorney General to look into that very matter. The very next day they formed an Ad Hoc task force and took off westward to see what could be done. Apparently they did some good, for late last night the very Judge that initiated the injunction against the company, lifted that injunction and dismissed the case completely. So, as of dawn in California, construction can continue, unabated for the time being. I'm told the task force will be out in Southern California for a few more days wrapping up loose ends before returning to DC, but when they return we want them over for lunch so we can find out how they did it"!

"Does that answer your question Mr. Duquesne"? Duquesne, nodded his head before taking his seat. As the President fielded another question, Tyler Montag, scribbled on a small memo pad, "I'm cautiously starting to like this guy"! As both men glanced at each other, each gave a brief shrug of acceptance.

As everyone broke for lunch, Mel O'Bannon directed the staff to enter the ball room and start the luncheon procedure, drinks, salad, main course, dessert and then a swift clean up and back to the conference at hand, with a precision that would do a Prussian General proud.

"How are you holding up Mel", asked Marge Corcoran, wife of Virginia's largest Commercial Real Estate Developer and Mel's closest friend.

"I can sleep another time, until then its coffee and more coffee. This has to go off without a hitch for the President"! Then she turned towards Marge and said, 'I couldn't have pulled this off without you Marge, getting into your rolodex and inviting all these women in to wait tables, along with the normal White House Staff"!

"Many of those same women you've met somewhere along the way and the feedback I'm getting from all of them is that you're simply marvelous.

They've all tossed big soiree's a time or two, so they all know what's to be done. And they all know what's at stake, so this is their way of paying it forward. Besides, many of them have already been recognized by the guests and that alone makes a point"!

Every one of the venture capitalists that attended, the days event were men that were not only highly intelligent, but devious and crafty in nature, surrounding themselves with highly skilled and equally devious lawyers on hefty retainers. Yet as the clock worked its way towards the four in the afternoon hour, the conference started to wind down, with each question asked was fielded skillfully and precisely by the President and his staff.

Lars Magnusson rose and addressed those assembled saying, "Gentlemen, it seems we've covered a lot of ground this day. So it's down to this, are you all on board? Can we make America great once again?"

At the far end of the long table facing the President and his staff, rose an old man, perhaps the wealthiest of all of them in the room who said, "Mr. President, my name is August Merrimac, perhaps you've heard of me"!

"Mr. Merrimac, everyone who matters financially has heard of August Merrimac"!

"Good Mr. President. So I believe I can say with little reservation, that most here are on board with you, in this wee bit of a project you have on your plate. However, 'Caveat Emptor', Mr. President, 'Caveat Emptor', for none of us can be trusted as far as you can toss us Mr. President, not a one"!

As the old and crusty August Merrimac sat down, there was a nervous laughter that echoed through the hall, as the President replied, "I thank you for that heads up Mr. Merrimac and to that I say, 'Caveat Vendor', Mr.

Merrimac, 'Caveat Vendor'. What I'm counting on is the need for profit from each and every one of you. In that we will be partnered. Should that ever turn into unbridled greed at any time along the way, then the structure we build together will fall of its own weight affecting us all. See to your own reasonable expenditures at every step along the way, mindful that someone will be constantly peering over your shoulders demanding quality of product, and see therefore to your profits, but be mindful of the profits of others. Should another partner suspect he's getting the short end of the stick, then outcome the lawyers and it all comes crashing down. Are we all in agreement"?

Everyone stood in agreement and said a resounding "Yes"! As the meeting came to an end point the Limo drivers were all alerted and filed slowly forward. As the guests filed out of the White House, cards were traded between all concerned and Magnusson shook hands with many of those he failed to meet earlier in the day.

A half hour later, Melanie and Maggie, ushered the phalanx of Washington matrons into the Oval office to meet the President. After they all had a chance to be 'hands on', with the Commander in Chief, he insisted that they all take a seat, while he, Harvanian and Goodwin took each ladies order and personally fashioned them a mixed drink of their choice. After each of the ladies were served Magnusson said, "Ladies, I am forever in your debt, for each of you were marvelous. Perhaps, should the occasion yet again arise, we can start a trend of sorts, perhaps even a custom amongst the elite women of the Nations Capital. Should that ever come to pass, it will be my pleasure to serve each and every one of you afterwards"! An hour later as the women of Washington gradually filed out of the Oval office, never having dreamt of spending time in the Oval Office with the President, each had a story to tell, when they got home tonight.

As Melanie was about to wrap things up at her desk with Marge Corcoran, Magnusson came by her desk and said, "Ladies, I just can't thank you enough, you pulled it off. And Marge, your rolodex was just what was needed, the women were perfect"!

"Well, Mr. President seems you've already recruited a workforce for your next Presidential soiree, whenever it's to occur, the ladies have become smitten"! At that Magnusson gave her a brief hug then asked, "Mel, by the way how is your son doing? He's down at Annapolis isn't he"?

"Yes sir, just down the road. He's just completed his sophomore year and will spend the summer helping the upper classmen break in the freshmen when they start to arrive next month"!

"He's well"?

"Very well thank you"!

"It's been a long day ladies so why don't you all punch out and go home and get some well-earned rest"!

After they departed, Magnusson joined Harvanian and Goodwin on the Oval offices couches, each with a stiff drink in hand.

"Well, guys how did we do"?

"Hard to read these guys", said Harvanian, "but from the looks of things body lingo wise, it seems like most all of them will get on board. They'll try and grind out the very best deal for each of them, but I've got good vibes. Anyway, Orval has invited this female body language expert in tomorrow to scan the day's tapes and give us a report as to how she sees each invitee. She's got a damn good track record. So god in fact that the boys at Langley bring her in from time to time for High Value interrogations. They call her the "Truth Teller" and with good reason"!

The trio spent another hour together, going over his long overdue trip to Houston. Boots on the ground to get an eye's on view of the carnage. He'd already declared the city a federal disaster area, and considering most everything that was destroyed, the city was coping amazingly well. The entire downtown area was of course in shambles, with the cleanup of the wreckage estimated to take every bit as long as that of lower Manhattan some years ago. The investigative agencies were all on board and cooperating like never before, but it was still too early in the process to solidify clues as to who was responsible.

His daily presidential briefings were a simple rehash of the previous day's briefings, with nothing tangible to report. Air Force One, would fly into Ellington AFB, the Presidential entourage would spend a few days with the locals, photo ops would be plentiful, face to face discussions would take place, then Lars Magnusson would get out of their hair and fly back to Washington.

Already there were rumblings from his own party of his being a traitor to the Democratic Party's political philosophy of highly centralized governmental authority. The entire country was in an undeclared war with religious and political radicals, at war with the financial markets, at war with each other politically, morally, philosophically and spiritually. The country was all but broke financially, with revenues chronically falling short of legislative commitments. George Orwell's look into the future in his book "1984", written in the early days of the last century was looking more and more like a worldwide reality, with unseen enemies of mankind and the state everywhere along with a burgeoning plethora of camera's and recording devices at the ready. Next, would be everyone informing on their neighbors and then their family, for reasons real or imagined.

Magnusson's greatest concern was the entire legislative branch of the government. In his brief experience at the Federal level, there were perhaps two dozen members, in both political parties that were worth retention, as for the rest, they should be somewhere else and not in any legislative process at any level of government.

He was on a fool's errand and he knew it. Suddenly he felt a chill run down his spine. He turned out all of the lights in the Oval office and sat in his chair. Washington's rush hour traffic was on the back side, with most people sitting down to supper with their families.

Here sat Lars Magnusson, returned from the dead, saddled with more to accomplish, to put right than many others that sat in that chair. Did Lincoln, the Roosevelt's, Eisenhower, Kennedy and all those that came before have these doubts in their abilities to get the job done? No doubt they did! Somewhere, he must find the inner strength. Somewhere he must find the wisdom to persuade and endure.

One of the reasons he hated these private times, was that invariably his thoughts would drift to memories of better times, with his wife and children. Of course, they were no more, than a painful memory. Breathing became labored in his private times and incidents almost forgotten flooded back into his consciousness. Times with his children, the look of his parents as they enjoyed family get togethers during holidays. Finally the very first time he met his wife at a college party. It was a disaster. The entire football team in a typical frat boy event. He was smelling like beer and sweat, while she was demure and drop dead gorgeous. It went badly at first and he initially viewed her as a pseudo member of the campus egalitarian elite, for too good to be seen with a Neanderthal like the All American BMOC, Lars Magnusson. Of course his assessment of her was spot on. But from her perspective, handsome he may be, but certainly exhibiting little between the ears that could be construed as intellect.

But as time rolled on and they kept running into each other at one campus event after the other, their attitudes gradually softened towards each other, with the eventual force of gravity two orbiting bodies have on each other joining them inextricably as one. He recalled the very moment of their first kiss. The kiss that lasted the better part of an hour. As they withdrew a bit breathless, she surprised him by caressing his swollen member saying, "Ya know, eventually we're going to have to do something about that! But not just yet"!

At that moment he knew, that she was the one. But deep down he knew far before that. When he got hurt in that terrible collision on the gridiron weeks later, she was inseparable, spending every hour not in class, but at his side as he lay in pain in the University Hospital, his football days over. No longer the campus BMOC, just a cripple on the mend, their bond became as one.

As the sun went down, his eyes closed and the cavalcade of memories gently flooded back into his consciousness and his dour face gave way to a smile.

Wilson (Willie) Jackson, came to an early maturity in Gary Indiana. There was never a time when he experienced, the 'Good Times'. Never knowing his father, whenever he asked who his father was his drug laden mother would only shrug her shoulders, for even she hadn't a clue. For all she ever knew, from her earliest memory was whoring. Pretty yourself up as much as possible, then open either your legs or your mouth. Since she was only fifteen years older than Willie and sported a bulb that burned rather dimly even during those fleeting minutes of sobriety, it was a miracle that Willie ever made it past childhood.

One his mother's thirtieth birthday, she was murdered by her pimp and cast into a dumpster. Were it not for the pimps stupidity during a 'Chicago Wilding', bragging about the fact that he was laden with one less headache, Willie would've never have discovered about the source of her disappearance and subsequent murder. Just hours before the trash truck was to arrive at the dumpster where his mother lay, Willie climbed into the dumpster and after some messy sorting he discovered her cold and beaten body.

He just sat there on that cold and windy day in the dumpster, his mind full of mixed emotions, looking at what forced him into the land of the living, if one could call this living. A few good memories, but far overshadowed by the bad. The many nights he went to bed hungry, the periodic beatings by his mother. He was in it now, all the way up to his neck. Still, he owed her something. Not much, but something.

He sorted through her hand bag hoping to find some money, but finding none, figured what little there was, was now being spent by her pimp. Some hours past as he sat there not quite knowing what to do, looking at his dead mother covered in blood, mouth opened and lifeless eyes staring straight ahead. He had not a single dime in his pockets, much less anything to bury her with. Soon she would join whatever lay in the county landfill. It was then that a glint of something caught his eye and as he sorted through the rubbish out of curiosity, his hands came upon a nickel plated .32 caliber revolver. He swung open the cylinder and saw that five bullets were still in the cylinder. Then something else caught his eye and there within reach was an open switch blade knife, the blade still containing some partially congealed blood and was no doubt recently used. Used on his mother? He refused to think about it. As he climbed out of the dumpster he briefly thought about a final goodbye to his mother, but wasn't that what he'd just spent the last few hours doing?

Just then the sounds of the trash truck entering the alleyway came to his ears as he turned on a dime and made his way through the myriad of old alleyways back to their cold water flat. The rent was due in just a few days and the land lord wasn't one who exhibited patience, so it was just a matter of time until Willie would have to vacate. But before he did, he had a little unfinished business to conduct with his mother's murderer. He knew where 'Big Mac', cruised and he knew all his whores and he had some time, not much, but some time.

He was the Prince of scurrying around alleyways ever since he could remember. He never made it past the eighth grade being a part time attendee and even in the best of times an indifferent student. Yet he knew how to read, write and know standard arithmetic well enough to get by in the world. When not at school, he usually was busy as a runner or as a lookout for several of the street gangs. Whoever had paid him. The clothes and shoes he wore usually were a result of his petty larceny and smartly enough, never in the neighborhood where he resided in.

Whether in the winter or in the summer, he was smart enough to never give someone the chance to get a good look at him and as a swift and shifty runner, he always was able to outsmart and out run his pursuers. Police report after report simply listed him as the "runner". So in many respects the death of the person who bore him into this world was a blessing for she only slowed him down.

He went back to the flat and cleaned himself up, changing into relatively clean clothes and set to cleaning his newfound weapons. He turned on the twelve inch black and white TV his mother scored a year ago in lieu of a payment for a neighborhood blow job. The weather report said that yet another cold front was to arrive in two days, from the wilds of Canada and it promised to be a sheer "Wooly Booger and for the viewers to stock up on their groceries and necessaries.

Out of cash, he had two things to accomplish. Score some loot, then hunt down, 'Big Mac'. his Mom's former Pimp and apparent killer and send him on his way.

The word was that his Mom, a woman who never knew how to shut up and always spoke her mind, right or wrong, had given "Big Mac" some back talk and held out some money. Two things 'Big Mac' never put up with, Any of his bitches holding out on him for any reason and anyone what raised their voice at him, especially if it were one of his bitches. It was not in Willie's mom to know when to be silent and if was not in 'Big Mac', to put up with backtalk from anyone. Willie understood that simple fact. Never the less, 'Big Mac' had to go.

First things first. He walked some twenty blocks to a late night convenience store, he knew closed at midnight. It was operated by an old Indian man who wore a turban and a beard. He entered and quickly went down the aisles, selecting several items and went to the cash register, as he presented the items to the clerk for checkout, he made as if he were going for his wallet and just as the cash register opened, he produced a small wooden club he picked up from the street and clubbed the clerk over the head, knocking him to the ground. He quickly jumped over the counter and scooped the cash and coin from the register, amounting to some eighty dollars, scooped his foodstuffs into a plastic bag. Then he ducked into the closet behind the checkout counter and removed the currently recording security tape, putting it into his plastic bag. As he went back to the counter area, he noticed the sawed off double barreled shot gun under the counter. He scooped it up, stashing it into his belt. Then he turned off the lights, locked the door from the inside and went out the back door into the night.

Over time he'd cased the old mans' place at various times, keeping it in mind for just such an occasion.

The shot gun was just a handle grip behind two big short barrels. Easily concealable and several blocks later, when he stopped in an alley way to inspect his unexpected bonus, he smiled. It was loaded. Now he had what he needed to go hunting.

Now the reason he was called 'Big Mac' was because this man was big. Drove a flashy late model Cadillac, wore gold chains, gold Rolex watches, gold rings on his corpulent fingers and of course he had gold teeth everywhere. His three hundred pound plus girth on a six foot five frame was such that few people dared to cross his path, even the cops gave him a wide berth. He policed his own business and that was 'Jake' with them.

Willie knew Big Mac's routine as well as anyone. The winter storm was coming and promised a whole lotta snow. Big Mac was eager to make his collections, before his bitches hunkered down for however long the bad weather lasted. His favorite girl and his best earner was usually his last stop. Blind alleys at night were Big Mac's favorite collection point away from prying eyes. Big Mac was afraid of nothing and no man, so a dark alley held no mysteries in his mind. So Willie waited, in the alley. Deep in the shadows he just waited, patiently, enduring the cold front that promised a great deal of snow. Eventually his patience was rewarded, as the big gaudy Cadillac turned into the alley and stopped not ten yards in front of him. He could see that Big Mac was after a something little extra, from his favorite earner. Not content to take most of her hard earned money, he additionally insisted, as he thought it was his rights, to have her milk his snake.

Willie could see it all unfold from the shadows near the Caddy, lit as it was from the dash board lights, he saw Big Macs favorite bitch pull away as he grabbed her hair, pulling the bright red wig from her head, allowing her to break free and bolt out of the passenger's side of the front seat, just out of her tormentors grasp. As she took the first few steps towards freedom, she fell just a few yards in front of Willie still in the shadows, for platform shoes are just not proper foot ware when one has to escape.

Now Big Mac may have been big and fat, but he was not slow off the mark, as he slid out the passengers door, just missing his bitches skirt, but regaining his balance, he caught up with her in two steps, grabbing her by her blouse and ripped it from her body, then forced her down into a kneeling position and then struggled to free his now throbbing member from the confines of his voluminous pants.

He forced himself inside her mouth and held her there thrusting his hips forward and back, as his eyes gradually began to roll upward in ecstasy.

Looking skyward through half lidded eyes did him little good, as he failed to see Willie emerge from the shadows.

Willie took little notice of the head of the whore just below Big Mac's midsection as he brought the shotgun to bear on that very spot and pulled one of the triggers. The blast of the twelve gauge short barrel, tore apart Big Mac's left hand which was holding the whores head in position and the pellets kept going through her head and ended up in Big Mac's, belly knocking him backward, flat on his back, illuminated by his cars headlights. He tried to move, the pain not yet reaching his brain, for as he was in the bitches mouth, it slammed shut, severing his manhood from his body. He saw her lying face down on the ground a few yards away and before he could react, out of the shadows came a familiar young face holding a smoking sawed off shotgun. His last thoughts came from the sight of a nickel plated barrel pistol, as the barrel quickly came to his temple and then a searing pain and then nothing....

Willie quickly rifled through Big Mac's pockets, then removed all of his jewelry, rings, Rolex watch, shoes, then opening his massive jacket saw the bulging money belt around his waist. A few minutes later he put the big warm Cadillac in reverse and carefully backed out of the dead end alley, then drove slowly down the street as the snowflakes started to swirl.

He put the Caddy into a multistory parking garage, within walking distance from his apartment and by the time he climbed the steps to the fourth floor, the snow was already an inch deep on the ground.

As he counted his take, he saw on the Television, the weather report which bode ill for Chicago land. A foot of snow at the very least which guaranteed that everything would come to a halt for at least a week. The Expressways would be the very first thing the snow removal crews would attack, then the principal streets and avenues. Side streets would perhaps be attended to in a week, maybe. No mention of alleys at all.

'Not bad for a kid just short of his sixteenth birthday', Willie thought. His mother's death had proven a blessing in a host of ways. He was now a man of modest means, with some eight thousand dollars in cash, firepower, jewelry and freedom to go anywhere. He briefly thought about going back and cutting out the gold teeth in Big Mac's mouth but considered it too gruesome. Besides best to let the dead stay comfy in the snow. With any luck it would be a week or so before the bodies were discovered. Then he saw the wallet, fishing out the driver's license wrote down the address. A couple of miles walking distance, but no telling what treasures the man's place would bring. After a few seconds, he decided that tomorrow would be a good time to find out.

The following morning the City of Gary Indiana was shut down. No cars or trucks were out on the streets. Public transportation was nonexistent; no one was even walking except the few children playing in the snow, but as the temperature plummeted steadily through the day even children went inside content to wait things out.

As Willie trudged his way through the snow, the city was strangely quiet for a Friday. The sounds of the city gone. Just a few stray dogs wandering around. He wondered how many of them would be around a week from today. An hour later, he came upon the dilapidated house of Big Mac. He already knew the man lived alone, but he was cautious as he inserted the key into the lock of the kitchen door in the rear of the house.

If all went well, he had all day to toss the place, for few people had any inclination to go anywhere, except Willie. He methodically went through everything using a sharp kitchen knife to cut up pillows, mattresses, rip up the shag carpet, empty drawers, remove them looking for secret places to stash things. By noon he gleaned only a few baubles of jewelry and then opened the refrigerator door and examined the contents. He removed a few things to eat, then opened the freezer door and was astonished to find nothing but a freezer full of ice trays. He curiously removed a few trays and then ran some warm water over them, finding they started to yield trays full jewelry and precious gems.

With a renewed vigor, Willie redoubled his efforts, removing the backs from TV sets, stereos, finding even more valuables. Then he went up into the attic and scoured every inch of that cold and musty place.

Removing some junk he noticed a place where the accumulated dust had been disturbed and after some prying up of loose boards, he hit the mother lode. Five shoe boxes full of one hundred and fifty dollar bills along with fifteen other shoe boxes full of small glassine bags, full of a white powdery substance. Within minutes he had it all removed and set down on the kitchen table.

An hour and a half later, he closed the door to his apartment, exhausted from carrying the entire haul back to his place. The sun had set and the snow was beginning to fall once again as night fell upon the greater Chicago area. Somebody up there had been very good to Willie Jackson.

Just one thing though. Those poor whores would now either have to find another pimp to steal from them, or fend for themselves. 'Hey, they could always form a Union', he thought.

Big Mac had been the very first man he'd ever killed. It should've been a big deal, sorta like, bustin' your cherry. But he didn't feel very different. The guy needed killing. He was long overdue for killing. He didn't feel sad or happy about it. He'd no attitude about it either way. From this point onward it would be easy. One just had to take ones time and pick your spot.

The lesson he learned, from this all was 'patience' and oh just one thing more, 'never play fair'. That was for punks. After all was said and done, the shoe boxes yielded over a hundred thousand dollars in cold cash. He would have to be careful about the hundred large of the shoe box cash, just in case it was funny money. He had to be careful about a lotta things. He was too young for a driver's license, but he had a birth certificate, a social security card and perhaps in Chicago he could find someone to forge a driver's license. For that he'd use the shoe box cash. Something that indicated he was of legal age. Then he'd go to a bank open a small account and rent a safety deposit box to put his stash in. For the first time in his life he had to rethink things very carefully, every time, all the time.

A week later, the streets had been cleared to a level where people could get around without getting stranded. Willie had abandoned his crib and had taken his stash to Big Mac's Cadillac. He was on the road to Chicago.

The following day, his mother's landlord came knocking on the door to collect the overdue rent only to discover, his flat empty and available to rent, after he cleaned it up. The following day, two car-loads of thugs, drove over the state line from Chicago to Gary Indiana, to pay Big Mac a visit, for some long overdue cash they were due. As they entered what used to be his crib, which was easy to find since it was the only house on the street not abandoned, they discovered that someone had beaten them to it. Unaware of Big Mac's death they concluded, that he cashed everything out and had beat feet for parts unknown.

Within two days of arriving in Chicago, Willie had a driver's license that indicated he was twenty one years of age. It certainly looked like the real thing, given that it was from the Illinois Bureau of Motor Vehicles and had cost a thousand dollars. He'd considered trying to sell the Cadillac, but parked it in a parking garage, then wiped the vehicle clean of any sign of his presence and walked away. He didn't need the aggro. For watching the detective shows on the TV, had taught him a great deal.

By the days end, he'd bought a late model Ford from a used car lot and drove that back to his crib. Living in a furnished apartment in Cicero, he was close enough to the action. Every day he went into the city, scouting out opportunities wherever they may be. He was in no hurry to get into the action, for his basic wants and needs were provided for. He opened an account in a bank using his driver's license and started to make small cash deposits thus drawing little attention. Some months later he rented a safety deposit box and began to put the rest of his stash there for safe keeping.

Working around the fringes of a few of the gangs, running errands and doing what any normal sixteen year old skinny black kid might do, he gradually earned the confidence of the those who gave him the crumbs.

Late one evening, he saved one of the gang captain's skin by taking his gun moments before he was arrested on an assault charge. Several days later after the guy made bail, he returned the gun to him with the words, "Yo gonna need this"!

The thug turned to his posse and said, "This lil nigger just might be aright"! A week later, Willie overheard the gang discussing just how one of the rival gang leaders, might be offed"! The discussion soon broke into a scuffle when some of the members thought better of it, in direct opposition to their leader. In a huff, the leader stormed from the room, going back to his apartment for his "piece". Willie ran after him and pleaded for the contract saying, "Lookie hear. No one over there knows I do work for you. I've done some runnin', for them. Gimme da contract and I'll get the job done. Just one thing. I do it in my own way and in my own time. Now ya doan want no mistakes do ya"!

Viewing little Willie as nothing more than cannon fodder, the leader said, "Ya do this for nothing and you're in the gang". Willie thought for a moment then agreed, with just one thing. "Ya go back in there and make nice with the ones you argued with. After it's done, ya want those what stood up against ya offed, I'll do it. Then it'll cost ya money"! A month later, the opposing gang leader was found in an alley, his throat cut from ear to ear. Weeks later two of the gangs' captains were found shot while in bed with their girlfriends, in the dead of night. Shot guns are terrible things, even for the girlfriends who crossed over the bridge the very same moment as their 'daddies'.

'Fat Jack', now had a protégé and a trusted confidant. The serendipitous thing was that it was that very gang that Big Mac from the wilds of Gary Indiana owed all that money to. For a cautious yet aggressive teenager on his way up, the very fact that he knew something that no one else did gave Willie no end of quiet satisfaction. Whatever he did from here on out would always be with "OPM" (Other People's Money).

Fat Jack was nobody's fool. Barely able to read and write, he none the less learned the Draconian lessons of the streets well. Never do business with someone you didn't really know. Trust no one, especially your best friends. Treat everyone with suspicion. Yet there was something about this little skinny teenager that drew Fat Jack to him. Therefore, over time, Willie gained both in knowledge and in expertise the ways of the ghetto gangster. Never exhibiting a desire to become part of Fat Jacks inner circle, never engaging in the play time activities of the others, never showing any more ambition other than to be a loyal street soldier and always bringin' home the bacon. All that went far in keeping Willie off the radar of the other gangs and that of the local police.

Just like Fat Jack, always being distant from large transactions and leaving the grunt work to others, Willie usually served as either a courier, or as security for transactions, careful to change his appearance every single time. Every gang usually has some hard ass that was known as an "Enforcer" and the Enforcer usually made it a point to keep a high profile. Fat Jack was no different except in one respect. His Enforcer had a backup and that unknown backup was the very last one that anyone would expect. A skinny teenage kid that kept to the shadows as a part time gunman and full time runner.

Drugs, counterfeit money, guns, and stolen property all passed through Willie's hands on their way to Fat Jack. His stash provided for his basic needs, which Willie kept modest. Whenever it was asked why he didn't adorn himself with 'Bling'? He simply said, "Can't afford it! Besides it makes too good a target"! While that basic wisdom rang true to many, it was quickly forgotten, in seconds.

Four years had quickly passed and Willie was just living each day as it came, making no overt plans, taking the occasional contract on some other poor soul, another gang member, someone who insulted Fat Jack, a witness for the prosecution, or even the odd police officer, now and then who came way too close. In the case of the latter two categories, the people simply disappeared. Vanished without a trace.

Often Willie would disappear for weeks at a time, only to return with some lame story about a sick Aunt in Alabama.

He stayed clear of other gang's territories, except at night when the shadows came to his ready assistance. His manner of clothing was not that of the street gangs usually unless he was 'Working'. Prior to his twenty first birthday his periodic need for ammunition, was satisfied by one of the older gang members at the insistence of Fat Jack.

Whenever Fat Jack shorted him, on a contracted price as agreed, which was frequently, Willie never complained and always accepted what was offered, placing the transgression in his memory for the eventual judgment day. Several times Willie came uncomfortably close to being arrested, during a transaction, as "Rat" who turned State's evidence provided the law with the "Who, What, Where and When", turning a deal into a trap. Each time Wille barely escaped eventually finding the "Rat" and making him disappear into a dumpster. No one knew where Willie lived, for each day he suddenly appeared, then when business was concluded he disappeared.

One day one of the members of the gang, who always peppered Willie with far too personal questions, decided to follow Willie, to see where he went each night.

The following day he was discovered by the police, dead in the middle of the street early one cold Chicago morning with his throat cut, in a rival gang's territory. Retribution was quick to occur prompting a week long war between the rival gangs that thinned their ranks considerably. With the arrival of Chicago police anti-gang task force units. The shooting eventually calmed down, yet no truce was entered into by either gang. The rats had gone underground for a while.

Angry with Willie, who wisely decided to sit this one out. Willie arrived in the hood several days later knowing what to expect. Attired in a black leather full length car coat, he walked into the gangs crib to see if there was anything happening.

"Where da fuck you been Nigger", asked Fat Jack angrily as his two captains that flanked him sitting at the poker table with their guns just inches from their hands, chimed in "Yeah Niggah, where ya been"?

"I hadda cold and was in bed all the time", said Willie, shivering from the cold outside, both of his hands in the pocket of his now opened black leather coat. Knowing what was coming next, he readied himself as Fat Jack was about to speak.

"Before the next word left his mouth, Willies coat flew open and two quick blasts from his double barreled sawed off shot gun, caught both Fat Jack and one of his captains full in the chest driving them back over the chairs they were sitting in, while with the other hand, the old .32 caliber revolver spoke twice into the face of the other captain, before anyone could reach their weapons.

The gang was beheaded. Without the leadership the gang was no more.

He quickly went to the door and locked it, then removed his coat to see if any blood splatter came onto his coat. Finding none he put his coat back on and went over to the dying bodies bleeding out and grabbed a bar towel and put it over the barrel and administered the coupe de grass. One bullet to each man's head.

He quickly rifled through each of their pockets removing valuables and weapons, then gradually explored the crib, just as he had Big Mac's years earlier. Within the hour he located where the money and the drugs were kept. Then just as he was bout to bundle everything up, he had one more place to search and there between the floorboards, were a small cache of hand guns and ammunition, still in their boxes and never used. He took the weapons and placed them in a trash can out back piling trash over them, then piled everything else onto a table cloth and sat down waiting for sundown. Then he turned off the heat. Several times during the day, he heard knocking at the doors, presumably gang members coming by, but eventually the knocking stopped as others went away.

By Six PM, the sun had gone down, the building was so cold that one could see the mist escape from his mouth every time he exhaled, so Willie took the folded table cloth full of the stash and peered out the back door and disappeared into the night, staying in the shadows all the way back to his car parked blocks away. Emptying everything back into floor boards of his car, he bundled the sheet up and went back to the trash can to retrieve the weapons. The car now warm, he made his way back to his crib in Cicero, his gang days now only a memory. He would spend the rest of the night sorting out the new weapons, the cash and the drugs. he would now have a reason to revisit his safety deposit box.

He'd grown accustomed to his cheap pistol and the shotgun over the years, but the sight of several new Mac-10 machine pistols made him giddy in anticipation. He would spend some time learning about his newly acquired firepower, but then he thought what was he to do with the rest of his life?

Willie Jackson always likened himself to that of a shark. Something deep inside kept him swimming at all times. Always having to be on the move. Working on some scheme or another. Always plotting or planning. Once he got the hang of killing another human being, he regarded that as a target of prey. The hunt, the patience of planning the method of another person's death was the thing that deeply fired him up. The whole thing was regarded as a sporting exercise, yet there was nothing sporting about it. The target had to meet its end in the manner Willie chose. Once Willie fixated and set to a plan, there was no escape.

So now that he was out of the gang banging business, he was at odds at what he was to do next. He could sit around for a good long while, wasting away like all the others, victims of their own excesses, or do something significant. He had several assets those of his kind lacked. A fertile and quick mind, an inner sense of self-discipline and patience. Thin of frame, he wasn't going to out muscle many people, but in today's world with so many different forms of weapons at his disposal, he didn't need muscle, only brains and self-taught skills.

Willie relished in the fact that, through simple but effective means, he could change his appearance, either subtly or radically to fool even those who'd known him for a good while.

After several months of self-imposed indolence, he found himself standing in front of the Mosque of Maryam, on a Friday watching a stream of Negro's entering into the building located on Chicago's South Side.

Willie had never entered a church of any kind in his entire life, so without quite knowing why, he felt drawn to this particular place. More of a curiosity thing if anything. Anything to fill this unconscious hole that lay deep within.

Good at blending in to most surroundings, Willie just walked into the Temple, paying keen attention to what others were doing and did just the same. Eventually a bespectacled, bow tied and well-dressed man ascended to the podium to give his fiery sermon, mostly against the white infidels, at some length. While Willie had no special love for 'Whitey', he held no great animosity for them. What he grew to dislike, were the lying, cheating 'Niggers' of his own race, deep in the ghettos who took every advantage of their own kind. He'd heard the word 'Nigger' used so many times in the ghetto; it had little meaning for him.

While he was experienced in the life of the inner city, Willies experience of the word at large was non-existent. As everyone filed out of the Mosque, a well-dressed man approached Willie and introduced himself. "It seems that this is your first time in a Mosque young man. My name is Selem X and should you want to learn more about Islam, please accept my card and feel free to call me at any time, so I can answer any questions you may have", as he handed his card to Willie.

The whole encounter took but a few precious seconds and was so low key that Willie had little time to be concerned, for the inner city taught a painful lesson to be wary of strangers that come on you all sudden like. Yet the man was well dressed, snappy suit of clothes and bow tie on a white shirt. Well polished shoes and soft hands. Clearly this man didn't use his hands to earn his daily bread. When he returned to his crib in Cicero he took a good look at the man's card and thought about all the blacks that attended the Mosque. He wondered why? Eventually he knew his sense of curiosity would get the better of him and later in the day decided to call the man up and see what was up, with Islam.

Willie met with Selem X later on in the afternoon of the next day.

Meeting at Momma's Ribs, which touted themselves as serving the beast smoked 'Southern Style Ribs' in the World. Willie of course ordered the premier dish of smoked pork ribs with all the trimmings, while Selem ordered a salad and coffee.

"How come ya don't order the pork ribs? They're the best"!

"The Quran says that pork is unclean, therefore forbidden to eat. The pig roots around on the ground, eating the unclean offal! Therefore it is bad, or unhealthy, for all believers, to consume anything that derives from an unclean source"!

"Well sir I been eatin' pork ever since I can remember. I eat it every chance I get and I'm healthy enough", Willie shot back!

"Yes, my son but for how long? People smoke, drink alcohol, get addicted to illicit drugs, do all kids of unsavory things to their fellow man"!

"And you're blamin' it all on Pork", Willie interrupted?

"The Quran infers that one clean the mind as well as the body to remove any impediments to the word of Allah, the merciful", replied Selem as the food arrived.

'Well I hope you don't mind, while I dive into these tasty ribs! It would be a shame for these to go to waste", said Willie eagerly.

"Do what you must my son"!

"Why do ya keep callin' me your son", asked Willie?

"Simply a manner of speaking, not necessarily to be taken to heart, but as a sign of dignity and respect"!

As they continued eating, they engaged in light banter, while Selem watched Willie consume his food, he made it a point to pay close attention to his every mannerism, starting with his choice of the seating selecting a booth in the corner with the blinds drawn down from the windows, with his facing the front entrance. This young man was street savvy sure enough, yet not attired as the typical black street thug. Perhaps there was indeed something there, which was worth spending time with.

Eventually the subject came down to Islam and what it represented, with Selem fielding every question in a very pedestrian manner. Entering into their third hour of conversation, and having to get back to the Mosque Selem asked, "Do you read much Willie"?

"Only the newspapers"!

"Do you have a library card"?

"No"!

"That's all right for their easy enough to get. May I suggest that you go to a library, obtain a card, they're free and then I'll give you a list of books to check out one at a time. Feel free to attend prayers every Friday, and then as you read, the books, you'll no doubt have questions about what was read. Write them down and we can get together as we are doing now and I'll be happy to explain the joys and ecstasy of Islam to you"!

After they'd parted, Willie made his way to the nearest Library and obtained a card, then after some help checked out two books explaining the religion of Islam. The following week and every Friday thereafter, Willie attended Friday prayers and nodded at Selem when prayers were concluded. They met for ribs and a salad the following week and Selem, surprised Willie by reaching in his jacket pocket and removing a paperback book titled, "The Koran". "This for you Willie! The teachings of Mohammad the merciful. As you continue with your studies at your pace, feel free to go back into the Qur'an as needed"! The next several hours we're spent answering a slew of questions, Willie had written down from his reading, with Selem patiently answering each and every one, in a manner readily understandable to Willie's mind at the time.

Several months later Willie inquired about joining the bi weekly Madrasa sessions, held at The Mosque of Maryam, joining in at an entry level with several others, chanting portions of the Koran in both English and Arabic. He then bought a tape player and some books and tapes to learn Arabic as soon as possible, to gain at least a working knowledge of Arabic, to help in his learning.

As he entered his twenty second year, doing little with his life but devoting himself almost day and night to learning all about Islam and its language of origin, he grew in confidence as he quickly mastered and understood the intricacies and subtleties in his mind, what the religion of Islam was about. As he performed his multiple daily prayers, his mind achieved a state of peace he'd never known.

He secretly visited a variety of Christian services, from time to time, to compare their view of the Almighty, with that of Islam. With the possible exception of the hard sell, Pentecostal form of Christianity, he had scant argument with their point of view, from the look of things on the surface.

Yet he felt bound to explore Islam and all of its manifestations. Willie's weekly discussions with Selem, grew more complex and as time went on and his knowledge of Islam grew.

One day he suggested they meet at a salad bar, rather than at Momma's Ribs and that told Selem, that Willie was perhaps ready for the next step on his journey towards celestial enlightenment.

His weekly studies at the Madrasa bore fruit quickly as his knowledge of Arabic grew towards fluency, he gradually grew able to recite entire passages of the Koran, both in his native tongue, English, but also in Arabic. Soon the Imam Louis of the Mosque began to take notice of his intellectual progress, given that Willie consistently progressed far past the other students, in intellectual acumen, while remaining seemingly humble.

Within the time frame of slightly less than three years, Willie had progressed to a point where he seemed to be an exact clone of his mentor

Selem X. He dressed well, spoke well, and had table and social manners, a mirror image of his guiding hand. Gone was any apparent trace of the boy that emerged from the depths of the inner city, the motivation arriving from somewhere deep within. All Selem X did was answer questions and point him in the direction he was seeking.

The Imam however, suspicious of anyone so talented, hired a private investigator to look into Willies background, from secret funds the Mosque ferreted away from the peering eyes. The initial report came back negative. Somehow Willie Jackson just seemed to appear, a few years ago. Of course Selem was made aware of this, for the government had an eye on Imam Louis, for years ever since the death of Malcolm X. All indicators indicated that Willie was a government spy inserted to gain access into the Nation of Islam. Selem had an idea that why not expand the search slightly and expend a few more dollars, to discover the truth about Willie Jackson and who he really was. He hammered that fact home with the Imam, for he just couldn't believe that his judgment could be so off base. The Imam agreed to fund an expanded search of the surrounding states. Two weeks later the private investigators report came in and Imam Louis called in Selem to discuss the two possibilities that surfaced. Although there were a great deal of people named Willie Jackson in the surrounding states of Wisconsin, Iowa, Missouri and Indiana, just two possibilities came to light.

The first was serving a life term in Joliet State Prison for murder, convicted just eighteen months ago. The second possibility was born in Gary Indiana, of a prostitute mother and a father of unknown origins. The last known sightings of Willie Jackson were during the great snow storm of a few years ago. Willies mother had disappeared just a few days before the storm as well as her pimp and one of his girls. The bodies of the latter being discovered a week later, as the snow began to melt. A look at Willie Jackson's Illinois DMV information and some simple math pointed Selem and the Imam in the direction they were seeking.

A footnote on the report reported, that although the was no proof, and only scant suspicion, one of Chicago's major black gangs disintegrated about two years ago and someone bearing a scant resemblance to Willie Jackson was reported to be a runner and part time 'Hitter' for the gang.

But other than rumor and speculation by someone of questionable reputation, it should just be considered as random gossip.

"What do you think of the report Selem", asked the Minister?

Considering his response with great care, Selem said, "It would seem that our search for the truth is over. The few known facts, along with the suppositions, appear to fit time wise. When I first discovered that young man in our Mosque, he seemed to be searching for something greater than him. A direction in which to take his life. Some years ago he was just like others of the streets, yet there was something of him that spoke of a rare intelligence. In the time he's spent with us, he's grown remarkably in every conceivable way, leaving all the traces of his origin strictly behind him, concerning himself only with the study of Islam and nothing else".

"Now from time to time, the authorities, have tried to penetrate the sanctity of our Mosque as you well know, participating somewhat haphazardly into our educational programs and leaving the impression as indifferent students, eventually attempting to insert themselves into other aspects of our operations. They were all eventually discovered for what they were and dealt with accordingly. Here, none of what has gone before applies. For I say that few in the entire city can surpass his fluency in the Arabic language or his extensive knowledge of the Koran".

"I suggest that should there be any further question of his competence of loyalty, and then summon him for a questioning or perhaps a polygraph examination"!

The Imam, looked at Selem deeply then said, "No one is questioning your judgment Selem, for no one had proven their service with greater dedication than you. Yet you can understand that we must protect ourselves from the infidels that surround us. With that in mind, I suggest that we find another way to prove his loyalty rather than resort to the white man's technical expertise and I have a plan in mind"!

"As you know one of the Mosques on the North side of town is threatening to break away from the Nation of Islam and we just cannot have that happen. Now if the one who keeps up with that blasphemy were to disappear forever, then we could perhaps find a person to replace that person with another more responsible person and the person I've in mind is you Selem as a reward for your loyal service. Now as you know, every year we fund a single pilgrimage to Mecca, for the most deserving individual in the congregation. We invite Willie Randolph in for a simple meeting; we want him with a metal detector prior to entering, which would reveal any listening device. Then after the preliminaries we offer him the trip of a lifetime, if he will perform this task for us. Of course he'll require a passport, but he's no criminal record so that shouldn't present a problem.

Now should he decline or be hesitant in Any reasonable way, that will tell us a simple fact that he is not with us and with someone else, or hasn't the talents that we suspect he has. Then he can be dealt with accordingly at that time. But should he agree and accomplish his goal, and then we know that he is the genuine article and a true believer. One to clasp to our breast as a brother. Your thoughts Selem"?

Selem simply nodded his head in agreement with the Imam saying, "Your plan is a viable plan Minister and yet another example as to why it is you that lead the flock"!

As he left the meeting, Selem felt as if he had just wallowed in shit. Of course he could see the logic of the Imam's point of view, but he'd now just sold his soul for the sake of acquiring his very own flock to lead. He'd hoped that he'd left the land of the Draconian decision years ago, but perhaps not. As before, he'd rationalize rather than take a more spiritual view of things, and when the sun rose the following day, he'd take yet another good long shower. Perhaps that would cleanse him of his many past sins.

The following day Willie, eagerly accepted his invitation to meet the Minister, from Selem. As he arrived on time at the Mosque he was ushered into the Imam's presence by his bodyguards. Prior to entering, he was commanded to empty his pockets, frisked, then slowly wanded with a portable metal detector. Leaving his inexpensive watch and valuables in the basket he was bidden to enter.

As he entered, he saw Selem sitting down with the Minister, in one of his expensively clad easy chairs as they both rose to greet him.

Approaching the smiling duo, Willie kept his smile in place, yet something deep within told him that his life was about to change in the minutes ahead, forever.

"Minister Louis, I wish to formally present Willie Jackson, our most gifted student by far in the Madrasa"!

Clasping his hand softly and speaking in the same manner the Minister said, "I've seen you before and have been following your remarkable progress young man with great interest. It seems the confidence that Selem has in you has borne fruit. Please be seated"!

For the next hour, the Minister examined Willie's knowledge of Islam in a casual way via indirect questioning; coming to a conclusion that this young man before him was remarkable in every way and either was the world's greatest natural actor or the real thing. Nodding knowingly towards Selem, each time Willie produced the desired answer to the questions of religious doctrine or Islamic history.

"Now I'd like to change the subject young man if you don't mind and tell you that each year we select just one most deserving individual to make a fully funded pilgrimage to Mecca. You have been recommended as the most deserving my son. Yet there is one little service that you must perform to prove to us that you are most worthy"!

The Minister then nodded to Selem, to hand Willie the file folder and as Willie opened the file he saw a picture attached to a single sheet of paper with typed information. As a service to Allah, most beneficent, you must bring this infidels head to me in a shoe box. His body must disappear completely. I am only concerned with the head. Will you do this"?

This had come completely unexpected to Willie, as he sat there knowing not what to say for a moment. His mind raced, then as his eyes went back and forth between the Imam and Selem, he realized there was only one course of action he could take as he took a deep breath. His entire countenance slowly changed. His eyes told the entire story, changing from the eager young student, to the stone cold unemotional killer he thought was left behind, saying, "If it is what you want, then the head it shall be and the body disappearing. Just one thing, I will not be hurried or rushed in any way. Are we agreed"?

The Minister nodded his head saying, "Young man, we are agreed"!

Willie rose up from his chair saying, "Neither of you will see me for a while. When next you see me the task will be completed. Should I see anyone I recognize in my wake then don't expect to see them ever again"!

Then he nodded towards them both, picked up the subjects file turned and left. As he left the room the Minister said, "Selem, we shall see what we shall see"!

Three weeks later the morning papers held forth a front page story of the disappearance of a much beloved 'Minister of the Nation of Islam', with a missing persons report having been filed with the Chicago PD.

At noon of the following day Willie called Selem telling him that the Minister would be wanting to see him and that he would call back in an hour.

Later on in the evening Willie entered the Minister's presence accompanied by a silent Selem. Willie was carrying a plastic lined hat box that he placed on the side table next to the sitting Imam, then took a seat without a word.

For the better part of a minute no one said a word, and then the Minister, gently picked up the hat box, untied the ribbon, then unfolded the clear plastic liner and gazed into the box at what had been presented. There, lay the head of his antagonist, as to where the body lay, he was about to inquire, but after looking deeply into Willie' expressionless eyes, thought better of it and placed the lid on the box, then put the box on the floor beside him.

Then he said, "Thank you my son, thank you"! Then he turned to Selem saying, "Next week will be a busy time for this young man. We will have a special occasion to accept 'Salaam X' into our midst. A pass port and visa must be obtained in his old name, before he can depart on his pilgrimage.

Upon his return we can formally have our lawyers change his name from the old name into the new. Then we must book round trip air passage and alert our counterparts in Riyadh of his arrival with the appropriate lodging"!

As he rose, the Minister signaled for Willie to rise, walking over to embrace him and formally welcome him into the inner sanctum of Islam as a man who is to be trusted. As Willie departed past the Ministers body guards, he stopped him in front of the rest and said, "This man is now one of us forever. He is to be considered as each of you as a trusted brother. Are we understood"? The protectors all nodded their heads and took turns embracing Willie as one of their own.

After he had departed Selem said, "When do you wish for me to depart for the North Side"?

"I think sometime tomorrow morning. Of course you'll have to make the standard provisions for his family, but that will come out of your new flocks offerings. Then move them to a suitable place of your choosing.

Should they ever prove to be a problem in any way, we then have the services of one who can eliminate them, upon his return.

True to his word, the following week was a whirlwind of activity, with Willie being hand carried to the Federal passport office by one of the Mosques attorneys and in a single day receiving his passport. It helps a great deal when one of the Mosques flock works in a key position at the Federal Passport Office. Airline tickets obtained several overseas phone calls to make to appropriate connections and Willie was all set to depart, on his journey of a lifetime. The following Friday, Willie was formally inducted into the congregation as "Salaam X" and the congregation was told exactly why Willie's superior intellect and his rapid absorption of the precepts of Islam was why he was selected to make the pilgrimage to Embrace the Center of the World.

Willie took a cab to the Mosque on the day of his departure. He received two thousand dollars in Travelers Cheques for expenses, and held onto his luggage as he was driven to O'Hare Airport for his departure to New York's Kennedy Airport. Once at Kennedy he changed his tickets to a different flight schedule to arrive at Riyadh at a different time.

He was now a Muslim, but his passport did not reflect that for the obvious reasons.

He was on pilgrimage he would blend fin with all the others. The result of his caution was that the Nation of Islam, at least what they called themselves, seemed to depart so radically from what was taught by the Prophet, long ago. He was now conversant in the language of the land, so he should be able to get by without any assistance from anyone. He would meet people and who knows what the future may bring. Besides, he knew one thing, he must be very wary of anyone connected with the Nation of Islam, including Selem and especially Minister Louis. All the speculation that bubbled up through the cracks about the man was true, for Willie, now Salaam, had experienced it first hand and had done the man's bidding. As long as Salaam was alive, there was always the scant possibility that he would pose a threat to the Minister. Should Salaam cease to exist the threat would disappear, with the exception of Selem.

As he flew into Cairo, he had a change of mind and decided to proceed and meet his provided connection in Riyadh. He called his counterpart and explained the different flight time by blaming the airlines.

He was greeted in Riyadh by a seemingly friendly man upon his arrival who introduced himself as Hassan.

"I am to be your guide wherever you go at no expense to you Salaam.

All has been taken care of and my directions have not come from that apostate the Chicago Imam, but from Selem. I will explain everything to you over dinner. Then tomorrow we will depart for Medina, for a short stop so you can experience firsthand the Prophet's experience, then on to Mecca.

During dinner, Hassan explained the various divisions of Islamic religious doctrine, indicating that Islam was just as divided as the western religions.

"For example, we in Saudi Arabia are Sunni and we practice what we perceive as the purest form of the religion, untainted by corruption or any hierarchy, while in Iran and in parts of Iraq, for instance, there exists an upper class of Imams, who dictate to the masses what to believe as if they were the right hand of God. We Sunni consider that as apostasy and an outrage, considering them as infidels, no different than those of the various Christian and Jewish forms that have gone astray from Gods original intent. So what is it that you seek Salaam X"?

"I seek purity Hassan, purity", said Salaam as he looked deeply into Hassan's eyes with the intent of a true believer. "I believe that you do my brother", replied Hassan continuing. "Be prepared to shed some of what you've been taught. Some of what you've been introduced to. For the western influences have seeped into the very soul of Islam and what I am prepared to introduce you to is purity of thought. Now the reasons are many starting with you are a willing convert and according to Selem, your journey has come a long way very quickly. You are a convert seeking revelation of your own free will. Out of curiosity for a way to rise from the corruption and the perversion that is everywhere in the world we live in. So it was with Mohammad, may he be merciful, back in the time when God opened his eyes and ears and mind. From the soul of a simple goat herder, ignorant of the ways of education and untainted by so called intellect, came the truth. So if you will allow me and others to be your Guide and mentor, we will be happy to introduce you to truth. On your journey you will experience, many things and meet a number of important people that are looking exactly for someone with your talents and more important dedication"!

"I'm eagerly looking forward to this Hassan"!

"Just one thing my friend. What you should fear is not Selem, but that apostate Imam who holds power in your city. The man is a strutting buffoon, who speaks with a soft voice, seducing the masses and perverting the truth no different than Lucifer the light bearer. Selem is doing what is necessary in preparation of the coming"!

True to his word Hassan took Salaam on a whirlwind tour of Medina and all the points in between to Mecca, pointing out various places mentioned in the Prophets flight from Mecca to Medina and subsequent return in triumph. Along the way he was introduced to a number of wise men or Sharif's, who each in turn after some conversation said that Salaam had the look of a true believer.

As they drove their hired car to a certain spot, on the periphery of Mecca, Hassan parked the vehicle on the side of the road with a host of others. Busses laden with pilgrims passed them by, on its way to a tent city erected by the Saudi Government, to house the pilgrims who had not been able to arrange for lodging in the sacred city.

"Now, my brother, we join the others and walk", said Hassan as he emptied the car's trunk of the few things they would need to complete their journey.

"We have approximately a ten kilometer walk before we reach the place of assembly, where we can will be assigned temporary quarters we will share with others. Fortunately we are several days early, for the Saudi government always misjudges the needs of the pilgrims, falling short every year for the tents and sanitary facilities required. The tents will fill up quickly and those who come after will have to fend for themselves as best they can. But rejoice my brother, that we live in modern times, for before the time of oil, there was no money, except for the very rich to provide transportation, much less than temporary facilities of any kind for the pilgrims that arrive each year. In olden times, people either walked or rode a camel and riding a camel takes some getting used to, wretched but necessary creatures that they are. They even slept under the stars, with nothing but Allah's benevolence, to keep them from harm. In the olden days, the rich were intercepted and held for ransom, by bandits. Thankfully those events are rare indeed these days"!

"But it still happens, right", asked Salaam? "Yes my brother"!

"So what happens if the kidnappers get caught"? "They are punished under the precepts of Sharia Law"!

"So they get a hand or limb hacked off as punishment", asked Salaam? "It depends on a great many things, starting with the testimony, the Sharif that sits in judgment, his understanding and interpretation of Sharia Law and finally, just how he feels on a particular day"! Several hours later, as they crested a hill amongst a growing number of weary pilgrims, they looked upon a vast tent city, with the tents arrayed in linear formation and descended, into the valley, as the sounds of the Muezzin echoed forth from the valley calling all pilgrims to prayer. Every one along the line stopped at the sound of the summons and dropped to their knees, removing their prayer rugs to kneel upon and the prayer shawls to cast over their heads as a sign of true faith and respect.

As they uttered their formulaic prayers in Hassan marveled that this American was so fluent in Arabic and as he had previously witnessed on their journey, his charge was well versed in the Quran and its precepts, exhibiting an understanding that matched even some Islamic scholars he'd escorted in the past. Sometimes his time with some pilgrims was less than pleasant in a host of ways, but his time spent with this American thus far ranked right near the top of his annual tasks. His intelligence was keen, he was indeed both quick witted, yet thoughtful and reflective, depending on the occasion, his attention span was long indeed, he was a polite man and soft spoken, yet the other Hetmen and Sharif's comments about his having the eyes of a true believer we're spot on, with one more observance. His eyes were that of a killer of men, completely without feeling or remorse.

Perhaps those who would meet him later would see that and make appropriate use of that part of his being. His future lay in the hands of Allah. For as the Prophet Muhammad, peace and blessings be upon him, was purported to have said, "Each man's fate is writ large in the sands, at his moment of birth"! Hassan wondered what the fate of this believer would be, after his ultimate task was completed?

It was a whirlwind of events that surrounded both Hassan and Salaam during the week of the Hajj. There was the myriad of events and the people that Hassan knew by sight and introduced to Salaam. A smorgasbord of diverse peoples from all over the world swirling around the Kaaba. The cubic shaped structure in the center of the 'Masjid al Haram', the Grand Mosque of Mecca responding to the exhortations of the Muezzins that bellowed forth from the tall minarets that surrounded the surging throng.

Of all those he met the most interested in Salaam, was Ibrahim al Majid, a Sunni Sharif living in Riyadh. In his middle forties and of mixed heritage, he nevertheless had gained in stature over the years in the resurgence of Wahabism, a very conservative form of Islam that viewed all modernism to be an affront to the true purpose of Islam. Secretly a true and devout believer in Wahabism, he nevertheless moved easily in the Sunni and Shiite camps of religious belief as well.

Upon meeting Salaam, Ibrahim invited them both to join him for tea, in the shade of a storefront canopy. Upon meeting and conversing in Arabic, he was taken with Salaams grasp of a language not native to his own and recently acquired. As they conversed, mostly about the precepts of the various forms of Islam, Ibrahim was impressed with the man's understanding of Islam by the questions he asked and the comments that were made. As the time raced on from afternoon to evening they immersed themselves in religious ideology, with Ibrahim and Hassan trading periodic knowing glances at each other furtively. As the dinner hour passed them by no one seemed to notice or be hungry. As the evening passed, they all acknowledged a physical hunger as Ibrahim invited them to the home of a wealthy Meccan merchant whose lineage traced back to before the days of Islam. As the evening progressed, and the wealthy merchant came to know Salaam, he became impressed that any American could possess the knowledge and understanding of Islam as well as the language mastery in such a short time as well as be so young.

Wellfed and entertained, the hour was late, far past midnight and it was time to leave and not test the generosity of their host too much. As Hassan and Salaam departed Ibrahim asked them to wait a minute as he hung back to speak to the merchant.

"He has been tested, my brother", asked the merchant?

"Before his arrival he passed the most stringent of tests"!

"And your thoughts Ibrahim"?

"I'm ready to bring him back, to complete his education, god willing. Will you join me in this"?

The merchant, not a fool when it came to the parting with his money, looked carefully in Ibrahim's eyes and said, "I sense no deception and great intelligence and dedication in the young man, so in this we are partners and will jointly fund whatever is necessary in his further education. As is possible I will carefully recruit others towards that end my brother"!

The embraced as Ibrahim joined the others to talk as they walked through the dark streets of Mecca in the early hours of the morning. The following morning, the events of the Hajj concluded for this year, the faithful all made their separate ways back to the lands they came from, while Ibrahim persuaded Hassan and Salaam to journey back to Riyadh with him on his private Jet.

As Salaam drifted off into a deep slumber, thinking that at long last he was in the embrace of a loving and welcoming family he'd never known, he came accustomed to the fact that this journey was indeed Gods will. He was determined to surrender his fate to Allah the divine and do whatever could be done to further the cause of Jihad and a worldwide Caliphate.

A day in Riyadh and yet even more closely held introductions to those who's hatred towards the House of Saud, the ruling family of Arabia, revealed not a single dissenting comment, regarding his dedication or competency. Yet one revealing comment to Ibrahim, by one of the faithful shed further light on the inner workings of Salaam. "The young man had been in the intimate company of the 'Jin' and is searching for the truth. We shall take full advantage in nurturing him at every step of his journey where necessary, while using his natural inclinations towards the progress of the Jihad"!

Thus it was agreed that Salaam would travel back to the States, settle his affairs, staying far away from the apostates in Chicago and return to Riyadh within the month to further his studies in not only Islam, but in a host of other activities, for several years of more, before returning to the United States to settle in an area in which he could recruit and train more true believers to the cause, deep within the bowels of the 'Great Whore'.

Thirty five days later, he landed in Riyadh, where he was met by both Hassan and Ibrahim, taking up residence in one of the many houses owned by Ibrahim. Being a city block from the neighborhood Mosque, Salaam quickly dove into all the local customs and observances, joining a special senior Madrasa that guided the most gifted believers in the true interpretation of Islam. The daily classes were small, never having more than a dozen students, all of which were carefully selected, mostly from all over the Arabian Peninsula, but also traveling from other parts of the Islamic world. Yet no matter where they came from, most had in common basic requirements essential for further development. A deep and profound understanding of the precepts of the Sunni aspect of Islam, a long and uninterrupted blood-line, of Sunni heritage, a religious zeal to achieve a worldwide Jihad against all infidels and finally certain skills, required to achieve that end. Salaam (Willie) was one of a rare duo in this class, that possessed none of the birth lines of Sunni purity, but his superior knowledge and intellect was more than sufficient to overcome such impediments, as well as his ability to effectively communicate in the language of the land. Able to verbally communicate in Arabic was a help, but his working knowledge of the written form of Arabic was not up to contemporary standards. But within six months of daily emersion, building upon what he'd learned in the states, he was able to read and comprehend the often complex subtleties of the language. The selected students of this secret school lived almost a monkish existence, being instructed, from sunup to past sundown, each day by Wahabi religious scholars, with the only exception of Friday prayers at the Mosque. They wanted for nothing, food, clothing, or shelter, dedicating themselves to the furtherance of knowledge.

After their first year of studies, a senior scholar was brought in to verbally test the students, on a pass fail basis, with the acceptance bar placed especially high for all. Should they pass, they were to be advanced to a point where they would be permitted to preach to the faithful every Friday at the Mosque during prayers. Should they be found wanting in either religious zeal or knowledge, even of the most obscure precepts of religious thought, they would be seconded to other important duties, with all further religious studies coming to an abrupt halt.

When it came Salaam's turn to undergo the testing, he was somewhat nervous, for much of what he was taught was of a subjective nature, so foreign to what he'd come to know. But as the year went on, he grew to understand Sharia Law as it was practiced by the Wahabi, and its varied and different interpretations in the rest of the Islamic world.

The test is conducted verbally, with the scholar asking questions and the student answering. But once into the testing, Salaam gradually began to challenge the scholar on certain points of the Sharia, insisting the already radically conservative views, were insufficient in many cases and always verbally quoting passages in the Quran to buttress his arguments, thus quoting long passages from the holy book from memory, correctly.

Normally these tests took two hours, but after the third hour, the scholar could find no fault in Salaams knowledge or reasoning, acknowledging a wonderment of his progress, considering his origin.

With the war in Afghanistan against the Soviet infidels at its midpoint, Salaam was then sent forth to join in with the warring tribes. After the better part of a year, he was summoned to return to Riyadh to resume his studies. During the course of his activities in the mountains of Afghanistan, he was known as the fighting Imam, leading raids against the Soviets, always returning successfully and then leading the daily prayers amongst the faithful.

The reports of his activities preceded Salaams return and he was accorded a modest welcome home by those who prayed daily for his return. Had such a man perished on this dangerous segment on his life's pilgrimage, it would be considered his destiny and therefore God's will. Of course a great deal of time and effort would've been lost in his education and molding as a 'Soldier of God', but so be it. The will of Allah was always supreme and past all mortal understanding.

However Salaam had indeed returned, with reports of his bravery and resourcefulness preceding him. At every station along his journey Salaam had won over the most severe skeptics and had proven his worth many times over.

Over dinner one evening, with Hassan, Ibrahim and another stranger, Salaam was introduced to a moribund individual from Cairo, known only as the 'Doctor'. As the meal worked its way forward through its many courses, the 'Doctor' said little, yet kept a wary and constant eye on Salaam, noting his every movement.

During the course of casual and relaxed conversation, Salaam grew uneasy of the half lidded scrutiny of the 'Doctor' and finally asked of him, "So I am being tested still am I, Doctor", in his finest Arabic?

The Egyptian taken aback by this dark one, put down his tea cup and looked deeply into the eyes of Salaam saying, "You are not of our kind"!

"And you're wondering if I can be completely trusted, or not. Are you not"?

The Egyptians lack of response spoke volumes, with Salaam eventually continuing, "If the world wide Caliphate is to succeed, the cause will require many true believers that can travel freely in the west, will it not? A person like you will be immediately spotted by the infidel authorities and be subject to torture and in the end will give up his compatriots. I have seen this many times in the past year, by the periodically brave Mujahedeen, when they've been captured by the Soviets. Their faith almost non-existent. Their gross ignorance about most things, an affront to Allah. Each and every time I've acquitted myself well and have passed every test placed before me. Further, your presence here says that you know it to be so. Yet there still is a question in your mind. Is it not"?

Still not breaking eye contact with Salaam, the Egyptian Doctor remained silent, prompting Salaam to continue, "Your parochial view of the Jihad will never be achieved until and unless, those of you change your thinking and soon. You were raised in a world that even your closest friends and family will lie and sell you short at a moment's notice, for profit and even though the Prophet, peace and blessings be upon him, teaches truth, you haven't the slightest notion as to what truth is. At this very moment Egyptian, your life is at a crossroads, for the next words that come forth will determine your longevity", Salaam whispered with a tone of certainty.

A gradual smile formed on the Egyptians face as he then said, "You are correct my brother. We will need more like you to carry forth the message of the Prophet into the world as it exists and I apologize for my rudeness.

There is no doubt that you are a man to be feared and respected. More important, trusted. There is no doubt that you are one to be reckoned with and deserving of great responsibility and authority. Your achievements in the Madrasa and against the Infidel will be used as a standard to evaluate those who come to Jihad in the later days. If you will permit me to live a little while longer, I will be happy to guide you to the right people who can supply you with what will be needed for your journey ahead"!

Hassasn and Ibrahim began to be relieved as Salaam's scowl slowly evaporated and he nodded his head in acceptance. For this was the very first time either of them had seen him angry. So the legends that preceded him from America and those of the mountains of Afghanistan rang true. This was indeed a formidable man in many ways, who spoke softly, but struck swiftly, with a smile gradually forming on each their faces.

"Your life also is at a crossroads", continued the Egyptian. "You can stay in Riyadh and continue your studies and end up being a superb Imam at some Mosque, or go back to America as the perfect example of a new wave of true believers to carry on Jihad. A letter of introduction from me is yours for the asking, my brother, to a number of us in the world that are eager to make the acquaintance of someone like you"!

The key words and the very ones that paved the way, were the words of acceptance, "My brother", coming from the mouth of the Egyptian. Thus Salaam, slowly nodded his head in agreement, his guarded eyes never leaving that of the spectacled Egyptian.

"In several days I must depart for Khartoum for an extended stay, but before then I will alert friends of the Muslim Brotherhood, in Cairo to prepare for your arrival. You will spend a month there learning things you will need to know to advance Jihad. Then you will be taken to Tripoli to learn other things then to Madrid and then funded well for your journey Back to America where you will be provided credentials to initiate at your own pace, cells of men who you will train to your own high standards then to wait, for an opportunity to strike at the heart of the Great Satan. There will be others in America, who will be similarly funded by you in the course of time. Others well trained will come your way and you will assist them but neither of you will ever meet. Still others, will be used as cannon fodder, for the authorities to discover. Their feeble attempts at instilling terror will be useful for your purposes, deflecting any possible attention to your existence.

In those we expect them to visibly fail, should they succeed, much the better, but in failure, they will serve Allah's purpose"!

The Egyptian then rose up as well as Salaam and both embraced. Then the Egyptian nodded to his hosts and departed into the night.

The trio then sat back down as the remainder of their meal had grown cold and had to be replaced. Then the smiles resumed all around as Salaam's future was now seen to. Days later Salaam departed from his hosts, on a journey back to America, stopping in Cairo, then Tripoli, then Tunis, then on to Madrid and then to Mexico City, learning a host of things from those true believers determined to help him on his journey. As he flew, back to Chicago, he pondered the phone number given him regarding a brother in arms awaiting his call in St. Louis.

The connection made, he drove down to St. Louis and met his connection, who lay on his death bed, dying of old age. In the space of two ever so brief days, the old black man had given him just what Salaam needed to set up shop, deep in the bowels of the Great Satan America.

Salaam assumed the responsibility of placing the old man in the ground after his passing, in a suitable final resting place. Then drove back to Chicago and to settle his affairs, before driving back to St. Louis to reside.

Salaam was finally his own man. Now more than ever was a time to be careful in all things, for he had much to prepare.

8

The months after his taking office as President proved increasingly difficult for Lars Magnusson. The honeymoon was clearly over and the once seemingly loyal Democrat was viewed with increasing levels of distaste as he inserted himself as the role of micromanager of the Executive Branch of government, prodding cabinet officials at every turn when they appeared to drag their feet regarding the efficiency of their departments.

In a few cases, he accepted their previously tendered letters of resignation, at the weekly cabinet meetings reluctantly, immediately promoting their Deputies to rank of Cabinet Secretary, in an interim appointment, prior to the full approval of the Senate. Normally party loyalists and political hacks achieve the rank of cabinet appointee, yet Lars Magnusson, broke with tradition and reached into the ranks of those accomplished in the world of business and academia to fill the vacant cabinet leadership roles. He insisted on several things, loyalty to the constitution, efficiency at all reasonable costs thus getting the biggest bang for the taxpayers buck and a tightly run ship.

The problems he was having with some of the cabinet secretary's was that, besides their earlier promises of loyalty to the people, some of the more recalcitrant members had their own paths to pursue, thus giving mere lip service to the President's vision. Often reports of malfeasance of a Federal official would reach his office and rather than send a letter to the appropriate cabinet official, he would pick up the phone and talk to the Cabinet Secretary first hand, following up their conversation with a letter, placing a short time frame for resolution. In the event the problem wasn't resolved within the agreed upon time frame, the offending Cabinet Secretary and the problematic official were immediately removed from office.

Once word got around about the Presidents micromanaging forays and Draconian actions, the press immediately labeled him, "The Sword of Damocles" and political cartoonists tended to portray Lars Magnusson as akin to "Henry the VIII", lopping off the heads of those who offended him.

As the months went by, he spent more and more time flying around America, visiting first hand, distressed areas, whether man made or by nature, cutting through red tape, demanding immediate action by the authorities, be they federal, state or local, followed at every turn by the media, with cameras ever at the ready. Slow moving officials grew to dread his arrival, while those ahead of the events at hand found him supportive and a great publicist. President Magnusson made great press as he appeared sometimes seemingly out of nowhere, with his small quick moving entourage of secret service operatives, reporters and cabinet officials.

He decided to press into service several smaller executive jet aircraft rather than the large 747 normally employed in the course of his travels, because it was cheaper and faster.

On one of his several trips back from the devastation visited on Houston months ago, he publicly berated several of the state and local officials, for holding up reconstruction grant money, due to local and state bureaucratic red tape. Contractors hadn't been paid and no one seemed to know why, thus everything came to a halt.

In the space of one afternoon, in the company of three cabinet secretaries and their state and local counterparts, a televised meeting was set up chaired by the President. The source of the logjam was quickly ascertained and quickly, the funds were released, with the President saying before he left for Ellington AFB, in front of the media and the entire nation to embarrassed state and local officials, "Please don't give meany reason to return in the near future, other than a ribbon cutting ceremony"! As he entered his locally supplied transportation, a roaring cheer went up from the crowd. The Presidents secret service handlers were presented with security problems, whereas the Presidents movements are usually heavily scripted, and timed to the minute. But Lars Magnusson was a man on a mission, moving swiftly with scant notice to local officials and none to the media which made for a hectic scramble for all to keep up with him.

As he the FBI's Gulf Stream Executive jet climbed to gain altitude from Ellington Field on its way back to Andrews AFB, Magnusson looked at Orval Goodwin and Vannevar Harvanian, both exhausted from his twelve hour tour of Houston.

"The locals are pissed", said Goodwin!

"But the press is ecstatic", interrupted Harvanian. "You really kicked some local butt, yet in the process made few local party friends"!

"Screw them", said Magnusson emphatically. "We bust our butts and twist arms to get them financial help and they stand around with one finger up their ass trying to appear important. Screw em. We have to hustle, they have to hustle"!

"We're due back at Andrews at around 2200 hrs. Eastern time", said Goodwin. So you need to get some rack time for your 8AM meeting with the Congressional Committee Chairmen. Need you to be bright eyed and on the ball for these guys. You might want to go a little easy on them, for they're holding the purse strings for your initiatives and cabinet appointments. Another public butt whipping like you gave the party hacks in Houston, just might get their hackles up"!

"Orval, you're the best politician I know, so I'm asking you if there is any way that I can carry some baby wipes into the meeting room with these people, so I can wipe the slime off my hands after coming in contact with them, without being obvious", asked the President?

"Unknown, Mr. President, unknown. However I might remind you of the importance of Willie Shakespeare, to tomorrow's meeting"!

"Shakespeare? What's he got to do with anything"?

"I believe he said something like, "All the world's a stage and we are the actors, playing many, many parts"! "Then comes the wisdom of Don Corleone', "Keep your friends close, but your enemies closer", etcetera ad nausiam, then finally 'always to own the high ground when in combat', translated in political terms to mean, if you want an assured outcome, you have to have complete leverage"!

"All great in principle, but how does one get recalcitrant people in power to do the right thing Orval"?

"Van and I are working on that solution, Mr. President. We're working on it"!

"Any progress on the investigation regarding the Secret Service screw up at the inauguration Orval, asked the President"?

"The FBI and the DOJ have been all over them, especially those manning the entry check points to the Capitol area. Revetment investigations almost back to the day they were born and of course a series of polygraph tests, both clothed and stripped down to their shorts and every one came up roses"!

"And any progress from the Houston FBI on what happened there, Orval"?

"Everyone local is sticking to the theory that several different groups were responsible for the explosions and the visible forensic evidence bears that out somewhat, but the localSpecial Agent in Charge, Corinne McKay, has a hunch and nothing more, that it just might be the act of a single highly skilled operative"!

"So why isn't she pursuing that line of investigation Orval"?

"One word, Manpower! Everyone is spread so thin that the various agencies would have to borrow from other ongoing investigations to man these investigations, is what everyone is telling me"!

"Orval, tomorrow evening after the meeting with the Senate and the House committee chairmen, summon all of the heads of the Federal Investigative agents, to see where we can reallocate personnel. Ninety days ago we got the National Guard to back up our Border Patrol people for the purpose of apprehension and its showing its worth isn't it. Everyone on a ninety day rotational duty time, then back to their normal civilian jobs. Last month we assigned certain units to the ICE people and apprehensions are up at the workplace, so it must be working effectively"!

"And the DOJ is at war with a flood of lawsuits, claiming a violation of 'Posse Comitatus', Mr., President", said Harvanian!

"And the DOJ's lawyers assure us that we're acting well within our Constitutional parameters as the Executive Branch, in the time of an undeclared war. The first rotation of Military personnel comes up in a few days and the troops will be rotated back to civilian live with a slew of stories to tell about life at the southern border and even more important, not one casualty or documented screw up. The ACLU can rail all they want, but they've a loser in this one"!

"I'll set the meeting up for tomorrow evening, Mr. President, replied Goodwin!

"While I'm thinking along those lines, sometime next week, the sooner the better, we need to round up the Union leaders that govern federal workers at every level, to have meeting of the minds. Time to exert some moral suasion, to see if these people will join the national haircut party.

Then perhaps the very next day the Unions that govern the various State Governmental employees. Not much we can do there, States rights being what they are, but at least we can identify just who the roadblocks are, for future national illumination"!

"Gonna shine the light on them Mr. President", asked Harvanian?

"Going to run a few concepts right up their flagpoles and see who, if any salute, Van"!

"And those that depart without a positive commitment"?

"Then we take the argument straight to the people, via the media and see if pure democracy has any chance of working! Either the average man will see just what America is up against and will themselves put the appropriate pressure on the right people, or the folks will be apathetic and all will be lost"!

"A huge gamble Mr. President. Never been done before. The Governor of California tried to go over the heads of his legislators a few years back and the Unions along with the legislature ate him up and spit him out like used chewing tobacco"!

"Should make for an exciting time the next several months, eh Van"?

Several days after they all returned from Washington, Van Harvanian was as everyone else in the White House, was putting in long hours, doing their bit to right the ship of state. A seemingly never ending round of meetings of important personages, each trying to gain advantage or at least minimalize the intrusions of what they perceived was their turf. The meetings with the Federal Union bosses, evolved into a marathon session of several days of sometimes acrimonious exchanges, with finally a visibly tired Lars Magnusson interrupting everyone into silence, by mentioning what a former president did to the Federal Air Traffic Control Union by Executive Order. "Ladies and Gentlemen, we've been in this room for some thirty odd hours, trying to work together to come to a common agreement.

Now I'm a lot younger than President Reagan was and in this time together, we've made absolutely no progress in reaching a common accord.

Therefore I'm going to take a break, go upstairs and take a nap. When I come back I expect to see everyone in agreement on each and every one of my proposals. Failure to do that will find you all out of a job, by Presidential Executive Order, thus terminating the Unions. When I return I expect each and every one of your signatures on this renegotiated agreement. Any attempt at a strike, will be met with Draconian measures, such as immediate termination by all those involved, inclusive of present company."!

"Mr. President you are, holding us all hostage to your Imperial thought processes", yelled one of the Union Presidents! "Holding a gun to our collective heads, in order to bully us to signing this egregious document and I for one will not have it"!

"Mr. Lee isn't it", asked Magnusson as he glanced at the man standing as if he were an icon? "You've been invited into the people's house and fed rather well at the people's expense, for the purpose of coming to a common accord in behalf of the common good. You've made not a single recommendation and have arbitrarily refused to see the problem at hand.

Clearly you are not acting in behalf of those who you represent. Better they take a cut in pay and benefits, than risk being laid off, or even worse, terminated with no possible chance of rehire in any branch of the Federal Government, with prejudice. This office has attempted to reach an accord with all of you. Perhaps, given the present company, this is not possible.

I'm going upstairs and will return in a few hours. Either your signatures will be on the agreement, unchanged in any manner or they will not. These are the government's terms. Ignore them or accept them"!

Two hours later Lars Magnusson came downstairs refreshed after a shower and a fresh suit of clothes and peeked into the ballroom, only to find it emptied, with but Orval Goodwin and Van Harvanian asleep in their chairs, with a neatly stacked pile of Federal Union Contracts, in front of them. He shook each of them awake as gently as he could, with Van saying, "It's done Mr. President, all signed sealed and as soon as their respective rank and files ratify these agreements, which should be in a few days, it'll be fait accompli. But I gotta tell ya, there were a lot of tired and very pissed off Union Bosses and not a single one a friend of the White House"!

"Well Van, its 0300 and its Saturday morning. Go get some rest. You've nothing to do until Monday, when you get to address the media, for your press conference. I'm going back upstairs and get some more shut eye"! On his way out he directed the Secret Service to drive an exhausted Orval Goodwin home.

As he drove home Harvanian made two phone calls, one to Tyler Montag, asking him to have one of his people to pick him up in New York for the Acela commuter train ride by midafternoon. The other call was to book the ticket. He could catch a few hours' sleep on the train.

With the overnight bag sitting at his feet, Van Harvanian slept fitfully as the Acela, sped along the eastern seaboard countryside. The fastest and smoothest train America had to offer, but far behind that of Japan, Europe and the Emerging Chinese technology. He could envision Lars Magnusson's vision of rapid Mag Lev people transport, on elevated platforms following existing rail right of ways, some thirty feet above grade, minimizing any concerns about eminent domain and warranting speedy construction at a given budgeted price. Trips between DC and New York could conceivably be accomplished at slightly over an hour.

Of course the Unions would prove to be a headache, but a simple proviso of cost effectiveness should be sufficient to slow them down. Any interaction with the Unions always brought to the fore, elevated construction costs and inflated budgets. This was especially rampant in the Eastern States where the Unions had a strangle hold on most everything that moved. Earlier in the morning after the President went upstairs, Van relished in silent joy as, one by one, the Federal Union leaders signed the agreements reluctantly, mumbling about signing under severe 'Duress', prior to their departure. He almost felt sorry for them, for like any Ponzi scheme, the only reason for their existence, was the continuous periodic achievements of greater and greater concessions by the employers, irrespective of the upward inflationary pressures that their efforts gleaned in the form of higher prices for goods and services. In the private sector that was one thing, but when it came to the best and highest use of the taxpayer's dollars it was entirely a different matter. Now the Federal Unions would have to spin a story to the rank and file that this contract was for the good of the country in these perilous economic times.

Magnusson had done well with the Federal Workers Unions, but the others would prove more of a problem. He had to help Magnusson find the high ground.

As he rode the elevator up to Tyler Montag's plush digs on the twenty first floor of the Trump Towers, Harvanian had second thoughts about summoning assistance from someone like Montag and his chief business associate Pierre Duquesne. Both of the same feather. The personification of the old adage, "How does a man like him get to be a man like him"? The answer was simple, "Be smarter than anyone else, be ruthless and move at the speed of light"! The only thing that concerned him was what he and Duquesne would want in return?

As the elevator doors opened into the marbled foyer of his apartment, he wondered just how someone could afford the cost of an entire floor of the Trump Towers, and then lavishly equip it with furniture, paintings, sculptures and the latest technical frivolities. The dozen times that Harvanian had encountered Montag, he always saw Duquesne at his side and this was no exception as they both greeted him warmly upon his arrival.

I hope you haven't eaten Van, for I had my chef whip up a few things I think you'll enjoy", said Montag. After drinks were served, they went into the dining area where upon being seated they were attended to by several well-choreographed waiters. "I trust you'll enjoy Prime Rib of Beef, done to a turn", said Montag.

While they ate their salads Duquesne asked, "How did things come out with the Federal Employees Unions"? Harvanian responded by giving them a thumbnail version of the almost thirty hours of negations with the Union bosses and the aftermath.

"Well done Van", said Montag. "Apparently we've inherited a man at the helm, with some smarts and staying power", in which Duquesne agreed. As the main course arrived, there was a period of silence where the men savored the finest cuisine known to man, with the strains of a Mozart sonata whispering in the background.

"In anticipation of your eventual arrival and following the adventures of the President, Pierre and I concluded that eventually you were going to require a helping hand. Therefore we took the liberty to invite into our little circle another individual that could be of help. Of course he doesn't run in the same social circles that either of us does, but he does have certain skills that will prove useful. His name is Bronko Lubetska and he's proven useful to Pierre and I from time to time"!

Their dinner concluded, the men retired to the spacious balcony looking down out over the Manhattan skyline as the after dinner aperitif's were served. A few minutes of small talk ensued, before the Butler announced, "Your other guest is on his way up on the elevator"!

A scant minute later, a short, heavily muscled man, walked out onto the balcony as Pierre joined him and brought him to Van Harvanian saying, Van, this is Bronko Lubetska and I believe that he can be of assistance to us all.

Lubetska reached his hand out and enveloped Harvanians much smaller hand with a surprisingly gentle hand shake, saying in a heavily accented eastern European accent, "Good to meet you Mr. Harvanian"!

"Bronko's Ukrainian and he has no great like for Russians", said Montag. But in the world he moves in he is a vital and quite necessary element to our success and we enjoy a mutually beneficial relationship"!

"Of course you've brought along the diskettes for our guests enjoyment this evening", said Duquesne!

"But of course", replied Lubetska, reaching into his coat pocket and handing them to Duquesne!

"Then let us all go inside and spend an evening at the movies", said Montag as one of the waiters brought Lubetska his drink.

As they sat down in their respective chairs, Pierre stood in front of the massive LCD television set and began, "The problem that our President is having and will continue to experience, is dealing with unapologetic recalcitrant people both inside the body politic and without. Key people for the most part that for a variety of reasons refuse to agree or even find a middle ground. In the world of business we have the same problems from time to time"!

"Now in Russia and the Ukraine the same problems exist, as Bronko will no doubt readily agree and are usually resolved by a sizeable bribe, or by the impediment simply disappearing, only to surface in a snow bank months later when spring arrives"!

"Here in the west, for a variety of reasons, that avenue of reasoning just will not do for reasons that are obvious. Thanks to our friend Bronko, we've discovered a far better manner of dealing with immovable objects. These objects invariably lead double lives and as we've discovered in several instances, are they are own worst enemies, a victim of their own hubris.

This malady is especially evident in the realm of politics. As Lord Acton is purported to have said, "Power tends to corrupt and absolute power corrupts absolutely"!

Pierre waited for a second before continuing, then said, 'What you are about to see may be distasteful in the extreme, but is but a small example of the corruption that exists today, not only in the Federal Government but in the lives of many you are currently dealing with and will deal with before our Presidents term is concluded"!

With that said, he inserted the CD, and provided a running commentary as to the ensuing novellas. "You will notice, this young woman, on a European sabbatical from her University, has decided to spend a rousing evening with her girlfriends at a certain club in Hamburg's infamous Reeperbahn District, specializing in purely feminine entertainment. Well- built blonde male dancers, along the lines of America's Chippendales, take things all the way and engaging in very public sexual intercourse in the most European manner. No doubt the young woman is drunk and may even be drugged to a given degree, but she was there of her own free will. You will notice how eagerly she grabs onto the male dancers phallus and swallows him completely while another dancer takes her from behind. Now normally this would be just another porn movie, except that this woman is the granddaughter of a sitting Senator in the United States Senate. A Senator is the Ways and Means Chairman that will prove a thorn in the Presidents side. In later novellas, we will see the Chairman have his way with young woman that he has exclusively retained on a long term basis. Still later we will see a Major Union official work his will on one of his secretaries, in the file room in Union Headquarters. She is still employed with that Union"!

Duquesne remained largely silent as the novellas played on, only inserting the characters in each new novella, as it began its edited five minute video run. Harvanian was torn between two emotions as the videos rolled on. The sheer stupidity and hubris of people in political power and the prurient interest that grabbed hold. After some forty five minutes of continual viewing of his government in action, Harvanian asked distastefully, "I think I've seen quite enough gentlemen"!

When it was over and the drinks refilled, Harvanian finally asked, "Is that all of it"! Lubenska then answered as the butler offered him a Dominican Cigar, "Oh no Mr. Harvanian. It's simply the tip of the iceberg! We could be sitting here for days on end, looking at the Rich and Powerful, worldwide"!

"Bronko, I think Mr. Harvanian is asking about the extent of videos concerning American Politicians, Union Bosses and various other key elements concerning America", said Montag!

"Including the American Military"? Montag nodded his head.

"Oh, well that would only take a morning and afternoon. A very long afternoon"!

Harvanian, thought a second, then said, "There are some who would call this potential blackmail"! Montag then stood up saying, "In certain other parts of this world, we have from time to time run into certain governmental bureaucrats that threaten to stall our operations at critical times. We could either pay them or have them liquidated. Both engender a certain degree of risk. If you pay a bribe, it's never the end of things, for there will always be someone who wants more and more, feeling that they're in an invincible position. Then the option of liquidation arises. Once again this engenders another set of problems depending upon the skill and the sanctity of those employed. No matter how skillful, no matter how well the plan is laid, there is always Murphy's Law to contend with. No, it is far better to use ones weaknesses against them. I believe Caesar once stated in his Gallic adventures, when he tried to parley with the Gallic Chieftain Vercingetorix and was insulted when the Chieftain reminded him that he was surrounded and that the gods had clearly deserted Caesar and his legions. Caesar calmly replied something to the effect, "The gods allow certain mortals the time to go about the world, wreaking havoc at will, for long periods of time, so that when the end does finally arrive, as it eventually does, the pain is more keenly felt"!

"Days later they did battle and Vercingetorix was defeated, captured, his family sold into slavery and he was transported to Rome and eventually strangled"!

"Now we have no intention of blackmailing anyone. You're President nor anyone other than you, can have any knowledge of this. No money or favors will transact at any time, either now or in the future. At no time will any funding be required. Everything begins and ends with us".

"Should any impediment to the President's plan arise, you will make our associate Mr. Lubetska aware of the impediment then go about your business. Bronko's funding will be of a private source and of no concern of yours. Of course neither the President, nor anyone else can ever know of this, for the obvious reasons"!

"Now Van", Montag continued, "You're probably wondering what we get out of all of this?

It's simple really. We intend to develop a consortium of private investors with the deepest of pockets, to fund a number of the Presidents initiatives and we must have a political certainty that no unforeseen impediment gets in the way. The Government is virtually broke and needs to direct its full attention politically to provide the eminent front. But even more important, America has provided the most stable of all the political entities in the entire world and has the strongest Defense capability the world has ever seen. That is why the wealthy park their cash here for the most part. We wish to maintain that status quo and nothing more. A stable society is what we must have if we are to prosper. An unstable society guarantees only chaos and disaster for all"!

Harvanian then said after a moment of reflection, "The argument is solid; you help us provide fiscal and political stability"!

"That and nothing more", said Montag. "The market plummets, we sell short and make money. The market expands, we buy and create wealth. The latter being more preferable"!

"So how does this work logistically", asked Harvanian?

"You will depart with a new cellular phone. You will text message the name of the subject or subjects for interdiction. Bronko will receive the text message. The phone you use will have an automatic code module in the phone itself. Then that's all you do. The phone cannot be traced back to its point of origin. You turn the phone on, you text the message, then you turn the phone off. You do not use it for anything else. The CIA is using this in Europe and it's been in use for several years with good results"!

"Once Bronko gets your message give things several days then see what happens"!

"I have several people in mind, that I'd like to start with", said Harvanian!

Lubetska then reached into his coat pocket and produced a ball point pen and a small note pad and pushed it in front of Harvanian, without a word"!

Then Duquesne inserted himself by saying, "I know you're on board Van but let me make you aware of a simple truth to put your mind at ease. No blackmail will occur at any time. For it infers a certain 'quid pro quo' and Bronko doesn't do that. Bronko destroys reputations at a distance. Once he receives a complete name in its appropriate context, he scans his data base which is extensive to correctly identify the object of his intentions. The weakness may be the subject, or his wife, or a member of his family, it makes no difference. The video will surface and it'll be fairly recent or not. Sins, be they recent or in the distant past are sins none the less. The video will be copied several times and sent anonymously to key elements of the media, which are always eager to get the goods on people in power. Some may run with the story while others may not at first, but in the end they all get on board because its headlines or ratings. Great care is taken by Bronko, to such a degree that there is no way on earth that it can be traced back to its source. Once something leaves Bronko's hands, it is past the point of no return and then we sit back and watch what happens. A man's reputation is his most precious thing. Once that is gone, he usually has no reason to continue. Thus nature corrects itself"!

"Bronko has earned our trust as we have earned his over the passage of time. It is in our mutual best interests that we take care of those who matter and this goes beyond the bounds of mere friendship. We sleep rather well at night with the full knowledge that those negatively affected deserve what they've received and all the while we make money"!

True to his word, Bronko Lubetska departed with five names written on a sheet of paper.

Within the next thirty days, three sudden resignations would occur, two in cabinet offices and one at the Department of Defense. Later on, two suicides took place, one of which was an influential big city mayor, while the other was an influential trade union official. All occurred after headlines appeared in the media, regarding their private lives.

The Acela took Harvanian back to Washington the following Sunday afternoon. Followed by his normal round of meetings the following Monday morning in advance of his weekly telecast press meeting. As he concluded his press meeting, he ran into Orval Goodwin on the way back to his office. "How did your train ride pan out Van?

"All is five by five and in the slot", Van mumbled as they walked down the hallway. "Just keep reading the newspapers for the news of the day. By the way, the press wants to know when the President will hold his next news conference, while one of the correspondents has noticed his physical appearance looking a bit peaked. So how did his latest physical work out"?

"The people from the coast flew in Sunday, and admonished him properly. He's down fifteen pounds in body weight and is getting by with only four hours of sleep each night. He's just got to slow down sometime soon or else he'll crash and burn, but the good news is that apparently the nanobots that were inserted months ago are doing the job and his wounds are just about all healed, far ahead of schedule"!

"He's in a lot better shape than we are Orval"!

"What did you think about Montag and Duquesne, Van"?

"Righteous they are not and each of them has both angels and demons on their shoulder, but what they propose and what the Presidents want's for the nation go hand and hand. It's just the whole 'ends justifying the means' thing that makes me uneasy"!

"Pure Democracy never worked well back in ancient Greece and the Roman Republic eventually crumbled thanks to Caesar. Seems mankind is still struggling to find its way forward, two steps forward and one step back. As long as the rest of the world chooses the US, to park the bulk of its money, we'll struggle forward. When that abates, then we're all in the deep six, Van"!

A month later, the President had his long awaited, televised news conference with the nation to announce, the formation of a new transportation company, for the purpose of construction of a nationwide Mag Lev Mass transportation system, that would be privately funded and not require the Nation's tax dollars to finance. The system would be built above existing rail corridor right of ways and acquisition of additional right of way properties would be minimal. After that announcement he opened the news conference to questions from the press, fielding all questions in detail, demonstrating a mastery of his subject.

"I apologize for not being as available to the press as I would've liked, but I've been a bit busy as of late, getting people together and ironing out the details of this monumental initiative. Oh, did I mention that this will put a lot of people to work and it will cost the taxpayer, not a single cent"?

"Ladies and gentlemen, it's late and I need to go upstairs and get a little shut eye or elseSurgeon General Greenlee, will be giving me six kinds of hell. So thank you and good night"!

The following day, all of the talk shows we're abuzz with conversations regarding the Presidents privately funded transportation initiative. Already complaints were coming forth regarding Presidential executive over reach and an unholy alliance with private enterprise. All the Federal Government had to do was get out of the way and in the process, pave the way for private enterprise to rapidly progress, by overriding any and all objections by any entity that would delay progress or escalate the startup costs past projections. Many state and local agencies weighed in on their opinions as well as many Unions that were eager to unionize. The most interesting aspect of the union objections was the complete computerization of the proposed transport system. Requiring no human operators of the overhead transportation system.

The most interesting aspect of the Magnetic Levitation system of transport was that while requiring a great deal of electrical service to be operational, it would all be completely self-sustaining, by a series of wind and solar power generators spaced along the existing right of ways, all over America, were privately funded Bill Boards located in Metropolitan areas proclaiming a Cartoon rendering of Pogo Possum addressing the swamp creatures, heralding the mantra, "We have met the enemy and he, . . is Us"! Gradually all over America, the messages were slowly getting through, Long lasting jobs, in construction, operations and ongoing maintenance, faster and safer inter and intra city transportation at a lower cost. Cost projections were finalized and engineering companies were engaged to quickly draw up plans. Contracts were quickly executed and duly challenged by a flurry of lawsuits by certain citizen groups that in reality were representing a host of private interests, allegedly representing the 'Common Good'.

Bronko Lubetska had never been so busy gleaning, wherever possible, the dirt on any group or individual that proved an impediment to progress.

To his prime benefactors, Messrs.' Montag and Duquesne, it was simply the private cost of doing business.

As the wheels of progress ground inexorably forward, everyone found profit to greater and lesser degrees, as the level of private and governmental scandals started to escalate. Key impediments to progress either retired, were terminated, divorced, prosecuted, or began to drop from sight.

At the end of his first year in office, President Magnusson had included yet another privately funded initiative, to accelerate the construction of a series solar and wind power generation farms, throughout the Continental US. It was an ambitious twenty year project that promised to provide wind power along the eastern, western and gulf coasts as well as the great lakes in partnership with Canadian enterprises. The majority of oil companies gradually entered into partnerships with the newly formed consortiums, reasoning the enterprise was a significant part of the business of energy.

Making the numbers work for the public at large, were the actuarial projections of the reasonable cost to each citizen of their monthly electrical power costs into the foreseeable future, which would retain stability at no additional cost.

What made this all work was the participation of Wall Street, with Initial Public Stock Offerings, raising the necessary capital from America. All the while, the media was ever watchful of the progress being made and the consequential impediments to progress, via the flurry of lawsuits that were initiated by a host of entities, both private and governmental. But America was being put to work in their own behalf, at a rate not seen in the last sixty years. The last time this level of activity occurred, America was fighting a declared war against two foreign aggressors. People were working at long last, at jobs that would be needed far into the future.

Prompting a series of headlined articles in the New York Times, proclaiming that "America is at War", with the subtext, 'With ourselves'! The Office of the President finally convinced a reluctant congress and his own State Department to engage in a radical reduction of foreign aid. The few countries that Continued to receive aid from the United States, did so on the provision that American aid would be administered by Americans, answerable to the American Government exclusively. As a result the roster of aid recipients abroad was cut by seventy percent, with funding going solely to nations where America had significant interests.

In a nationwide address President Magnusson went into great detail as to why, offering the United Nations as a place where those nations in need could seek help! While most of America cheered, much of the rest of the world, cried foul.

By the beginning of his second year in office President Magnusson started to see the economy stabilize and gradually recover, thanks in part to his governmental initiatives, but in reality, to the industry of the American experience.

To the American public, Lars Magnusson was a rock. Steady, sure and certain, but in his very private moments things were otherwise. Thanks to the very best medical practitioners in the world monitoring his daily progress and to micro technology his body had healed far ahead of expectations. Sure he had visible facial scars, a slight limp and a lower back problem that had limited his range of motion, but the energy in which he attacked problems and swept away bureaucratic log jams, went a long way to illustrate his viability.

In his meetings, be they public forums, or private meetings, he seemed to function as an "Ubermenchen", cutting to the core arguments swiftly and finding the optimal way forward.

He encouraged a diverse view of ideas, as long as an argument could be presented within the cooking time frame of a three minute egg, compelling presentations to be concise, with details to follow.

Yet in his private moments, given his standard eighteen hour day, he agonized at the private loss of his family. The long days sped by, while the nights portended the terrors of the deep. The doctors took notice of that during his initial hospitalization and during his periodic trips around the nation with his staff, he'd fall asleep always on the return trip, for a few hours. Since the small Gulf Stream Executive Jet afforded little privacy, his tossing and turning while asleep, revealed his private horrors to the select few.

The weight of the nation was on his shoulders, while the world looked on, wondering with everyone else, how long would he hold up? If ever in the history of man, this mans every word, every movement and mannerism was scrutinized like no other. Yet he had done the seemingly impossible, by getting private enterprise off their collective backsides and into the fight towards progress, surmounting every challenge quickly and in a variety of ways. Yet deep down inside he was a broken man, during his private moments.

He borrowed the mantra of a great man of not so long ago, "Lead, follow, or get the hell out of the way"

9

The ray of sun peeked thru the sparse curtains, alighting upon Salaam's eyes. It was Friday morning and he arose quickly to get ready to attend the prayer services at the small and struggling storefront Mosque that had started a year ago. It was located in a seedy looking strip shopping center, with a convenience store at one end and the twelve hundred square foot Mosque at the other. In between were a barber shop, a tailor, a beauty salon, a takeout Barbeque restaurant and a liquor store, with the rest being a series of long vacant spaces, with their signs still in place as if they were still in business. The neighborhood was in serious need of a wrecking ball at the beginning of the Korean War and was about as rundown as a neighborhood gets. A six month supply of trash starting to grow roots curb side, while two mongrel dogs lay dead in the streets, long past the stage where they were rat food, with cars having run over them repeatedly, so they were almost part of the pavement.

Inside the Mosque of Abraham, kneeled seventy five hardy souls at the hour of seven in the morning, trying to squeeze in the first of the days prayers, before hustling of to their various work places. Perhaps half of them would return for evening prayers, when the city streets would be alive with action of every kind.

Like some of the other tenants in the center, the Mosque always struggled to pay the rent and the utilities each month. The roof leaked and the air conditioner needed replacing and the land lord said abruptly, "You get caught up on your rent and start paying on time and I'll make the necessary repairs"!

The likelihood of that ever happening was slim and none. Salaam had spent the last month coming to weekly prayers, going thru the ritual, sitting silently in the rear and always leaving a twenty dollar bill in the offering box when he left, whereas most of the others scarcely gave more than a few dollars.

The Imam's flock was all black and most were out on parole or fresh out of prison. A few even came over from East St. Louis, across the Mississippi River. He could tell when six people piled out of a ten year old Chevy Nova, with Illinois license plates at a quarter of seven in the morning.

The sessions were a far cry from the boisterous sessions; he'd been indoctrinated long ago in Chicago, with the White Devil being the object of discussion on every occasion. This Imam's method of indoctrination was like a quiet drip, consistent and relentless. Yet his every word, spoke ill of the infidels that surrounded them all.

After thirty days of witnessing his new host, he discovered what his 'connection' had revealed about the duality of the Imam's existence. The so called Mosque was simply a transaction point for narcotics. Apparently the locals hadn't caught wind of it yet, but in time they would and that would put a kink in Salaams plans.

One day Salaam lingered after Friday evening prayers in the rear of Mosque after all had departed, silently kneeling in the rear of the hall in contemplation as the Imam approached saying, "Salaam Aleichem brother", as he kneeled down and joined Salaam. "I've noticed that your new to our gathering and have been meaning to welcome you but your usually out the door quickly"!"Didn't want to raise a fuss brother. Brother Morton sent for me to join the brotherhood before he died"!

"You knew Brother Morton", asked the Imam?

"I put him in the ground and held his hand when he died", said Salaam! "He said that I was to join you and do what I could to be of help"! "Brother Morton always said that someone would arrive to elevate our cause. Are you the one he was talking about"?

"I am the one, my brother and I'm here to do what I can to see you prosper", said Salaam!

"Just what can you do in my behalf", asked the Imam sensing a threat? "Brother Morton has told me everything, before he died and has told you often enough I understand, that someone is coming to further the cause of the brotherhood, did he not"?

"Why yes he did, my brother, but you arrive unannounced"!

"That is the way it was intended, said Salaam. He has told you of the name of the one, has he not"?

"Yes, my brother"!

"And that name is"?

"The name mentioned was Salaam", said the Imam nervously

"I am Salaam! And we are to prepare for the coming Jihad, my brother. Please understand this I am here not to replace you but to assist you. Were it not for brother Morton some years ago you might still be in Joliet Prison punching out license plates. He secured your release and parole, nurtured you and provided the financing for the continuance of your work in the name of the Prophet, peace and blessings be upon him, did he not? All that he was, I am. All that he had, I now have and I now am here to tell you the moment will soon be at hand when the oppressed will rise and you my brother are to be the one of the leaders"!

"But how can you help", asked the Imam feeling him out?

"We are to expand our mission, with the help of the brotherhood"!
"The Kansas City and Chicago brotherhood"!

"No, my brother not them. Anything but them. They are not kindly regarded by our friends abroad and they must know nothing of my existence if you are to receive my assistance. Are we understood"?

The Imam nodded his head saying, "You said prepare for Jihad"!

"I did, but that is for the near future. First your struggling efforts here must be rewarded and this Mosque must grow and then give birth to another, then another, then another and so on. When the time is right and we are strong, then we will make our intentions known to the world, from right here in the belly of the Great Satan"!

"You mentioned a reward", said the Imam!

"That I did", said Salaam, reaching into his coat pocket and removing a standard sized envelope and handing its bulging contents to the Imam, saying you needn't count it for it contains five thousand dollars, for the purpose of you getting brought current with all of your creditors. You will of course provide me with receipts of your transactions. Once this is done, you will introduce me to the congregation as your assistant and nothing more. Your assistant I will be in all things regarding the Mosque"!

Within six months the Imam or what was left of him was discovered floating down the Mississippi, without a head, hands or feet. His body having washed ashore downstream at Chester Illinois. All that formerly belonged to the Imam now belonged to Salaam.

Shortly after Salaam began to address the congregation it was readily apparent to all, That he was a man well learned in every aspect of Islam, able to answer every question calmly and give insight as to what the Prophet actually meant in his teachings. His insight as to the daily struggles of his flock and how the teaching of the Prophet can bring peace and hope to their common existence, gradually proved its worth, with everyone approaching him and contrasting his extensive knowledge with his predecessor. His original five thousand dollar investment was returned tenfold within months, the former Imam's sideline being transferred to another of the flock.

Within three years he had four small neighborhood Mosque's in the greater St. Louis Area, each keeping a low profile, gradually growing at a measured pace. Two years more brought into the fold a variety of other small secular retail enterprises, daycare centers, dry cleaners, car washes and others all catering to the needs of the community and employing members of the various Mosques.

All of this occurred quietly and out of scrutiny of the larger Nation of Islam. Precisely the way Salaam wanted it.

Every true believer that starts out in the world either receives a franchise of sorts from a central entity, and then if good fortune and hard work are with him, he will eventually grow and prosper. Some do, while others fall by the wayside. Salaam, was intelligent, wise in the ways of the world, extremely knowledgeable in his religious doctrine, a good organizer and relentless in his zeal for the common man, but always operating from the shadows and above all he was patient. His plan was coming together.

From time to time, it was noted and commented on that he had no wife or family and he was asked about it, which he would always reply that his purpose in life was to serve Allah and his people. This way it was the only thing than concerned him. To have a wife and a family would be to take away from his efforts in behalf of the community.

The simple truth was that the physical aspects of the feminine gender or any aspect of procreation held little interest for Salaam. In fact the physical aspects of the male gender, like wise held even less interest for Salaam. It wasn't as if Salaam was a virgin, he had experienced an erection from time to time and even had experienced the joys of physical climax upon occasion. The only difference between Salaam and normal people was that Salaam was only aroused to the point of climax by the physical reality of termination another person's life. The closer the contact with the subject, the greater the physical and emotional release. To peer deeply into the eyes of another as you pressed a blade deep into their heart and see the very life force ebbing away from the object of Salaams intentions, gave him a joy that was excelled by no other imaginable. That was Salaams normal. He simply regarded that as one would exterminate vermin and nothing more. He gave it not a moment's thought, until the next time.

That was not to say that from time to time he didn't get the urges. He did. However there was a greater goal in the offing, the ascension to heaven after his work was finished. When those primeval urges surged to the fore, it would usually be his conscious mind dictating an individual that he came in contact, worthy of his attentions. In his subconscious mind during his REM sleep, he would experience a series of dream scenarios over several days and work out several workable scenarios of the subject's demise, offering him several avenues of approach, each of which would give him the physical release his body demanded. Upon his awakening he would always have a clear memory of what occurred, along with evidence of his freshly soiled bedclothes.

Once he gave it some thought as to why this seemingly automatic set of circumstances occurred, concluding that this was the work of Allah, peace and blessings be upon him and that a 'Soldier of Allah' was never to question his masters will. As his work in St. Louis grew in volume, he had to train other Imam's in the tenants of the Wahhabi, or the traditional form of conservative Sunni Islam. Yet an overriding necessity was apparent. At all times were his disciples to behave in such a manner as to never draw attention to themselves. In several cases this required a radical change in his disciple's behavior, those who adhered to Salaams teachings prospered, while others became the objects of his dreams, eventually disappeared.

Of course, during the course of his holy expansion, Salaams other enterprises began to flourish, for somewhere in the greater St. Louis area, a source of heroin and cocaine was finding its way onto the streets, a constant supply at a consistent price. Always was Salaam a distant observer, while the drug profits fueled the expansion of each of his enterprises, with always a strict accounting, under the watchful eyes of Allah the eternal.

His local organization was small, but profitable and everyone modestly prospered. Whenever he gave private teachings of Islam to his key disciples, he always was quick to point out the hypocrisy of their illicit operations, reasoning that the scriptures gave a special dispensation to the faithful in the name of Jihad.

Still, with things going so well, and his guiding several key people into America, for special projects in other places, he still felt that a greater purpose lay ahead, but what was it to be? He shared his thoughts with his disciples and told them of his need to depart from them from time to time periodically, in search of the greater need. Never gone from their presence longer than a month at a time, he reminded them that Allah was always looking over their shoulders, casting his eyes on each and every one of his key followers. "Every waking hour of every single day, be watchful, be faithful, be loyal and blessings will be upon you"! His flock was faithful, acted modestly in all things and no one took notice.

During the attack of the Twin Towers and the Pentagon, while many cried and some around the world cheered, Salaams followers mirrored the sentiments of those around them, cheering silently with their brothers elsewhere.

It was shortly after this, that Salaam started his travels, to all the major cities in America. Always traveling alone and by car. Never away from St. Louis for more than a month. He was very careful in selecting those he wished to meet again, for they were usually the quiet ones that sat in the shadows. Quite unlike the charismatic firebrands that were clearly the cannon fodder for the struggle to soon be upon us all.

Salaam, by his very nature was not a very affable man and was a hard one to get to know, thus those he wished to associate with were of a similar nature. Yet given time, patience and the appropriate circumstances, the inevitability of it would come to pass. His chameleon like abilities, afforded him the ability to be all things, to all people.

Within the year, he was able to connect with people in Tampa, Dallas, Baltimore and Boston, all in search of one with wisdom and a purpose. All impressed with his knowledge of the prophet and the sacred tongue of the Kaaba. Still, his periodic trips offered him no relief from his search for the one thing that he could do, to bring death, destruction and chaos, to the infidels of the Great Satan.

As his travels drove him westward, he prayed to Allah to open his eyes and reveal the one thing that would humble those infidels around him. The news reports gave extensive reports of a great drought that ravaged the western states and of the wild fires that raged all over the land. The Federal Government was hard pressed. The Insurance Companies were Certain to suffer great losses, in the third quarter of this year and actuarial rates were certain to climb for those living in the drought afflicted states in Americas western states. All that was very good as it passed through Salaams mind registering little. Yet as he drove through Los Angeles, San Francisco and up to through Oregon a state similarly afflicted by the drought and heat, he suddenly pulled his car over onto a roadside park. Got out of his car and walked over to one of the picnic tables and observed the wonderful view of the miles and miles of verdant forests that were evident.

Then it came to him all at once. The elegance of simplicity. He recalled reading something about a certain nuclear physicist named Bronofsky, one of the slide rule genius's that worked on the Manhattan Project to develop the world's first nuclear weapon. He searched his mind for the exact quote, then smiled as he whispered the words to himself; "When confronted with a seemingly impossible task and you stumble across an elegantly simple solution, then and only then, can one hear God think"!

As he stared out over the lushly wooded mountains, Salaams eyes glazed over as the plan elegant in its simplicity gradually unfolded before him like a Rand McNally Map. It would take time, careful selection of people, planning and patience but unfold it would in due time.

It was time for prayers and Salaam looked around finding no one within sight and removed his prayer beads and knelt down to perform his daily ritual of prayers. Of course his prayer rug was in his car, but he was sure that Allah wouldn't mind this slight transgression.

When he arrived in Portland, he placed a brief call back to his Mosque in St. Louis and briefly talked with one of his disciples telling him that he'd found what he'd been seeking and that he would be away yet another thirty days or so, but to be of good cheer for he would reveal the plan in good time upon his return.

He spent a week in Portland, then drove up to Seattle and was introduced to some influential people. They of course, referred him on to Vancouver, then to Winnipeg then down to Minneapolis and back to St. Louis, whereupon he slept for an entire day, upon his return.

All during his trip, his plan began to take form, manifested incrementally while he slept, in his dreams. He would require several cadres of disciples, true believers conditioned to go forth without fear, certain as to their cause, to convert, subdue, or eliminate the infidels, to the will of Allah, by any means possible. To sweep the world clean of the corruption that surrounded them all, making way for the World Wide Caliphate. But first he had to identify and categorize those susceptible to further indoctrination.

Upon his return to St. Louis, the back seat of his car was full of books on hypnotism. Before the year was out he was determined to be an adept in the art of submitting others to his will. As the year wore on, he was able to identify, in his midst, those easily susceptible to hypnosis. At first planting various behavioral suggestions towards the elimination of habits, detrimental to their health or surroundings. With little fanfare, in time he noticed various behavioral improvements to the members of his flock.

Many lost weight, while others quit smoking and others suddenly lost their desire for drugs, other women, and even grew to desire their wives all over again, without giving it a second thought as to why. Salaam found a way into the realm of the human auto pilot.

As he practiced and mastered the craft of Mesmerism on members of his own flock, he deeply implanted in each and every one an irreversible desire, to follow the directives of their Master Salaam, without question, in the days ahead.

Of course, the acid test of his will over that of his subjects, was to conduct an act, so out of character with their persona, immediately and without hesitation, precisely as directed, then upon completion, have absolutely no memory of the act. The trigger to their activity, would be a single 'word', uttered by the voice of Salaam himself, or his any of his principals and none other. The 'word' being of such obscurity, there was little chance of it being triggered by random circumstance.

By the years end, he had what he needed. All four of his Junior Imams, were deeply indoctrinated and each of them had four acolytes, whose lives had miraculously turned for the better and would willingly plunge into the depths of hell, rejoicing if need be, thinking the blessings of heaven were close at hand.

Now for the series of grand tours spreading the doctrine quietly, without need for personal gratification, driving out, or overwhelming the evil 'Jin', from prospective acolytes.

Certainly no different from the Apostle Paul two millennia ago, Salaam traveled in a series of month long forays, to the nations metropolitan areas, casting his spell upon those susceptible, redirecting their lives for the better and asking for nothing more than their silent obedience. "Go forth and prosper", he would always whisper, "but prepare for the day when you will be called on to do Gods will".

Of course, the precise instructions and direction of Gods will, was now deeply ingrained in each and every one and they all had reason to be grateful for Salaams interdiction. For each of their lives were vastly improved by Salaam. In each city Salaam visited, there was a Mosque.

Within each Islamic community were those, whose lives could use improvement. Preaching in each Mosque, he was able to identify, those in need and more important, those who would willingly submit to the will of Allah. In many of those silent cadres he established, were those who formed close relationships with many of which they normally would not be associated, without knowing why.

The earth had made three circuits around the sun, in the interim, while markets ebbed and flowed. America was embroiled in two Middle Eastern conflicts. The nation was in an economic whirlpool, with a plethora of conflicts, political, pestilential, spiritual, physical, meteorological and emotional. The time was close at hand, for the Great Satan to be brought low, from within by a multi hydra cataclysm so vast the land would be laid waste for generations to come. All of the elements were in place for the coming Unveiling.

Far past the efforts of the faithful in bringing down the World Trade Center Buildings, in past years and the feeble misdirection's of those poorly prepared and subsequently discovered by the authorities, was the brilliant bringing low of one of Americas great cities, some months ago, by one who was deserving of masterful skill and deception. His successful efforts would no doubt not go unnoticed in the grand scheme of things, but the City of Houston would be years in recovery, with misery abounding. What astounded Salaam was that with all of the investigative sophistication the Federal Government proclaimed, they were chasing ghosts in their efforts to identify the several terrorist groups the media claimed. Just like his distant southern associate, soon the time would be at hand, where the nation would erupt in an inferno, that would overwhelm their resources and they would be just as helpless in identifying the causal effect. Then from the ashes of the Phoenix would rise the beginnings of the new Caliphate, for the Glory of Allah.

As Salaam, looked out of the window of his second floor apartment, the sun was melting the snowfall of the previous evening and winter would soon evolve into spring and then into the summer. In his mind Salaam thought that perhaps the month of August would be the time to get things started. Then again there was always September. It all depended upon the climate.

10

Senator Roland Stonecypher, stormed out of the Oval office followed by Senior Democratic members of the Senate Appropriations Committee. The meeting was a contentious affair, with the good Senator accusing the President of being a traitor to the Democratic Party. Well into the majority as well as the House of Representatives, the Senators were reluctant to relinquish their age old prerogatives of earmark insertions, germane to their pet projects in their home states.

Stonecypher, a crusty, aged, six term Senator was used to getting his way at all times, especially given his seniority. He was the textbook example of an old line politician, a chameleon, being all things to all people, breaking promises when expedient and getting away with it repeatedly. A master of the exertion of moral pressure upon anyone who got in his way, he was an unapologetic bully to some, a savior to others. The man had indeed paid his dues, coming up through the ranks of seniority long ago he evolving to a position of massive influence; he was cashing in his chips whenever he deemed it necessary. Considered the master of the unfunded mandate, he got bills passed time and again, leaving it to others to concern themselves about how to pay for the obligations. His State was rife with Schools, Highways, Library's and public buildings, emblazoned with his name.

The secrets of his success were clear. He knew of a great many influential people, having what they wanted and relinquishing just enough to get his way. He also knew of their weaknesses and exploited them at every turn. If the age old adage of the 'good dyeing young' held any truth, Senator Roland Stonecypher was guaranteed a very long life.

Of course, it was the people of his state, grateful for the largesse he always brought home, that always reelected him, by wide margins, to serve their interests. Political cartoonist's, had a field day, illustrating him as the Pied Piper, leading a hoard of lesser politicos and bureaucrats off the cliff, stopping just short of the precipice himself while piping a tune as they all fell into the abyss.

From time to time a challenger would arise, eager to topple the King of the Senate, only to end up cannon fodder, fading back into the obscurity from whence they came.

Which brought to the point the thrust of Senator Stonecyphers pique.

The Senate appropriations bill, which the good Senator worked and schemed so long and so hard for, was returned to the Congress after having passed both houses, not only Vetoed, but marked up like a schoolboys term paper. Entire amendments eliminated, with the reasons written in the margins. To add insult to injury the President gave the entire bill an "F", grade sending it back unacceptable. To add further salt on the Senators wounds, the President had pictures taken of the front page of the Appropriations Bill, with his remarks along with a video giving his reasoning for the veto, for the media.

The Presidents reasoning was simple. Here was a bill of particulars that had amendments added to it that had nothing to do with the subject of the bill. A clear contravention of the Presidents wishes months earlier. Thus provoking the confrontation between President Magnusson and Senator Stonecypher, in the Oval office.

Leading a few of the senior members of the House and Senate, into the President's office, the meeting quickly grew contentious, between a young President, come to office on the coat tails of his deceased benefactor and the Lion of the Senate, wise in the ways of duplicity. The bone of contention was simple, the President, noting the precarious fiscal situation the nation had found themselves in, and set forth a personal example for the government was to follow in behalf of the nation.

The executive branch of the government was slowly adhering to the Presidents example, while influential senior members of both houses of congress chose to employ their long held prerogatives as keepers of the National purse.

"Present no bill of particulars to this office, containing amendments that are not directly germane to the subject of the bill", said the President!

Senator Stonecypher and others chose to ignore the Presidents example, oblivious to the fiscal condition the nation found itself in, inserting costly amendments that inflated the cost of government and escalating the national debt.

"It is our prerogative as members of the Federal Legislature to invest the taxpayers money as we see fit", bellowed Stonecypher belligerently.

"And Senator it is my responsibility in behalf of the people to act as a steward and act as a backstop when Congress acts irresponsibly", said Magnusson calmly.

"Irresponsibly", bellowed Stonecypher! "Let us be clear Mr. President.

Your term in office is only possible as an accident of fate. You assumed office on the coat tails of a great man President Dobbins and I can assure you that he would never have acted in such an egregious and insulting manner towards Congress"!

"So this is all about hurt feelings and not about content", asked Magnusson calmly?

"It's not about that at all, it's about your unreasonable manner towards the American people and our rights as legislators to do as we see fit", spewed Stonecypher as the others nodded in agreement!

"Senator, I can see that you are truly all lathered up and at this very moment I'm concerned about your health, for the blood vessels on your bloated neck are almost at the point of bursting so I suggest that you take a load off your feet and listen for a while"!

"How dare you, you", at that point Magnusson rose up from behind his desk and shouted, "Senator, shut up and sit down. Do it now", as he walked from behind the desk, imposing his will upon all in the room!

"In case it has escaped any of your notice, the entire nation is in financial trouble, not seen in generations, but it seems that perhaps you've collectively been asleep or perhaps it's because the lot of you are corrupted beyond repair and beyond reasoning. Like thieves in the dark of night this August body of legislators skulks around practicing the arts of obfuscation at every turn rather than relying upon the strength and logic of your position to carry the day legislatively. I asked you all, months ago, to follow my lead to fiscal sanity in behalf of our nation. At the time I knew the high probability of coming events and as your presence here proves, I and others were right. Here you are like a pack of rabid dogs, foaming at the mouth and crying foul implying that a state of moral war exists between us"!

"Well gentlemen, it's down to this. You have my comments on the bill, feel free to return to commiserate amongst yourselves and return to this desk a clean bill. You've called me a traitor to the Democratic Party in the press and it's too bad you feel that way. But I'm standing up for the common good and as I look at my watch it's an hour prior to lunch and after the noon meal, I will be involved in hour long interviews, with representatives of all the major networks, for the rest of the day. I invite the hard questions and am ready with a plethora of facts and figures. No doubt this meeting between us will be the point of certain questions and I will give forthright answers to each inquiry. No doubt the media will assail each one of you to gain your perspective. In any event, the coming days will prove to be a target rich environment for the citizenry to make their judgments for the next election cycle. With any luck the voters will have a long memory. Before the weekend we will see just who emerges whole and who does not. This meeting is concluded", Magnusson announced as he pointed to the opening door!

As the Congressional entourage quickly filed out of the oval office, Orval Goodwin gave the President a slow wink and a below the waste OK sign, as he and Van Harvanian, filed out of the office after the congressmen hurrying to leave the hostile environs of the White House and back to their congressional confines.

"That was a short meeting Van", said Goodwin wincing! "Should make for great TV watching, in the coming days"!

"They never had it so good Van. But it seems that we have a problem in Stonecypher. The man is hard headed as a tired and hungry mule. It'll take Nukes to budge him"!

"Will not need Nukes, to budge him", said Harvanian as they rounded a corridor corner. Don't forget the secret weapon"!

"The secret, oh that. Seems that it's been quiet as of late, Van"! "Never go to the well, more often than you have to"!

"Stonecypher has been investigated up one side and down the other, by practically everybody for the last thirty years and has always turned up unscathed and clean as a snowflake"!

"Then nobody looked hard enough", winked Harvanian!

Goodwin stopped in mid stride and said, "You mean there's dirt on the guy"?

"A couple of things, starting with the guy has a serious heart condition, that's being hushed up by the folks at Walter Reed Hospital and is under medication. You noticed how flushed he looked as he ranted at the President and even he commented on it during the meeting. Now that's not even the best part, Stonecypher is as pure as the driven slush"!

"What, come again", asked Goodwin? "Stonecypher has a girlfriend, of sorts"!

Goodwin's eyes grew wide in surprise saying, "The moral icon of the Senate and the entire congress has a girlfriend?

"You better sit down Orval", said Harvanian as they passed one of the antique hallway chairs. As Goodwin took a seat, Harvanian took a quick look around before continuing, "I said the man had a girlfriend of sorts, didn't I"? Goodwin nodded his head.

"It's just that his girlfriend is blessed with, oh how can I put it? Extra parts"!

"Extra parts" silently mouthed Goodwin?

Harvanian nodded his head then continued, "The President will spend the afternoon selling his actions to all of the anchor media journalists. They will be loosely granted approximately hour long sessions each. He will make his points every single one and not be shy in mentioning names. No doubt the next day will be filled by two events, the TV anchors proudly exhibiting their exclusive interviews with El Presidente', while as a contretemps to their interviews, all of their networks will be airing videotapes, clearly showing Senator Stonecypher romancing a clearly attractive woman. The process of disrobing, fooling around, then entering into the realm of Sappho and Eros, with a woman endowed with, extra parts"!

"You've seen it", asked Goodwin?

Harvanian nodded his head saying, "It's about as revealing as an afternoon in a gynecologist's or should I say a proctologists office, except with soft music, candles and the trappings of red tapestry.

Goodwin normally a serious man, stifled a giggle as he stood up saying, "Pure as the driven slush, eh"? Turning his head and slowly walked back to his office.

After lunch Harvanian conducted his weekly press conference, fencing with the media, while the President started his afternoon, generous with his time with the network's news anchors. Directly answering all of the questions germane to the governance of the nation.

True to his word, the following day was filled with segmented interviews of all the major network TV anchors interviews with the President, while the cable news channels ran heavily edited excerpts of a video revealing a side of Senator Stonecypher, in one of his more private and revealing moments with an unadorned female endowed with, extra parts.

That evening after dinner, Senator Stonecypher and his wife were quietly watching one of the cable news casts about the Presidents previous days interview with that networks premier news anchor, when in the aftermath, a news bulletin interrupted the program during the nine PM hour, with a story regarding the very private life of a sitting US Senator titled, "The Apocalypse of a Senator"!

Some minutes into the telecast story, the Senator tried to turn off the TV set but his wife insisted that the program continue. Thus he just sat there, watching the program reveal his dark salacious lifestyle, known heretofore to a select tight lipped few. His wife just sat there, shocked at what she regarded as an abomination of a lifetime spent with a man she'd never really known. When the program was over, she silently climbed the stairs and near the top grew faint and tumbled down the stairs. Running over to her and seeing her body crumpled up at the foot of the stairs, he went to the phone and dialed 911. As the operator came on line, the Senators faulty heart gave out and he crumpled to the floor.

The following day's newscasts were filled with not only the revealing of the Senators private life, but the death of both he and his wife, by natural causes. The Lion of the Senate roared no more.

In the coming weeks, with no one left to lead them and with growing pressure from the media and the public at large, the obstructionists in both houses of congress, reluctantly relented, stripping out all of the unnecessary addenda to the joint House and Senate Appropriations Bill.

Two days later, in a private ceremony in the Oval office, Lars Magnusson signed the bill, with a single pen. No members of the legislature were invited. The world continued to turn and the sun still rose in the east.

As summer approached, the Caribbean Sea normally sent forth its annual tributes to Mother Nature, in the form of tropical storms. Surging forth from the bowels of the equatorial Atlantic Ocean, the yearly event of Hurricanes, developed in strength, surging either into the eastern seaboard of the United States, or the vast expanse of the Gulf of Mexico, where it would be often reenergized and surge northward deep into the midsection of the nation.

After years of trial and error, in dealing with the aftermath of high winds and excessive flooding, the Federal Government formed a system of emergency response organizations, to quickly respond to the needs and suffering of those afflicted. Reams of procedural documents were distributed by the Federal Government to various State and Local political entities, along with the prepositioning of supplies at key locations, for rapid access in case of a federally declared emergency.

The last week of May heralded a series of tropical depressions, in the Mid-Atlantic region that grew in strength into full blown Hurricanes, the first of which worked its way across the Yucatan peninsula and back out into the Gulf of Mexico working its way up the western shore of the Gulf, coming on land north of Corpus Christi and spent itself on the Central Texas landscape. On the heels of that the very next week came forth yet another hurricane, bursting forth some fifty miles east of the Florida peninsula and slowly worked its way northward along the Atlantic coastline, giving the eastern seaboard a broadside from Miami to the New Jersey shore before wandering out into the Mid-Atlantic to disburse.

By the middle of June, two additional Tropical storms emerged, the lesser of which followed its immediate predecessor once again up the Atlantic shoreline, this time coming ashore on Long Island and across the sound and smashing full force into Massachusetts and points north, while its greater cousin slowly worked its way northward along the western coast of Florida, ever so slowly, gaining strength and breaking itself upon the Florida panhandle and laying waste to the States of Alabama, Georgia and Tennessee, showering its blessings northward.

East of the Mississippi River the nation was hunkered down, just trying to survive its way through, the plethora of seemingly never ending high winds and rain.

Not receiving the appropriate responses from his people in the Department of Homeland Security or FEMA, after the very first Hurricane that struck southern Texas, Lars Magnusson, directed Orval Goodwin, his Chief of Staff to reschedule all of his appointments and events for the next week or so, while he rounded up several key members of the White House Staff and headed for Texas via Air Force One, unannounced. Landing in San Antonio and flying down to Corpus Christi Naval Air Station, he summoned the Texas Governor, his staff and the heads of the appropriate federal agencies, acting as an immediate catalyst directing aid and supplies to wherever it was needed. Each and every meeting was accompanied by a small pool of media reporters and cameras, recording every word, excuse and utterance, by all the parties. Where previous procedures and protocols were shown to be either slow or cumbersome to response to the events on the ground, the President immediately cut through the red tape, over any objections raised by Federal, State or Local bureaucrats.

While still on the Gulf Coast, the second hurricane worked its way up the eastern seaboard and the President and his entourage flew across the Gulf in its immediate aftermath, landing at Homestead AFB, west of Miami and went through the very same procedures with the Federal, State and Local governmental entities, moving things along and as he had done in Texas, leaving a Federal overseer behind to insure that all Federal expenditures were accounted for and that no price gouging occurred for the duration of the emergency.

As the President and his retinue worked their way up the eastern seaboard in the aftermath of the second hurricane, many of the very same problems developed, with bureaucratic bottlenecks occurring with repeated regularity. Key people were immediately replaced unceremoniously and publicly for the nation to witness.

The National newscasts were rife with those criticizing the President for his overuse of executive prerogative and in the Draconian manner of a benevolent dictator, while others shot back in the Presidents defense the fact the man, "Got things done and ran off the Scallywags"!

By time they everyone got back to Washington exhausted from ten solid days on the run, the third hurricane followed in the second's wake, affecting the already weary and suffering on the eastern seaboard, in the midst of cleaning up from the Hurricane of a week ago, to the arrival of yet another Hurricane. This time even the authorities were affected along with the weary inhabitants of the region.

The National Guards of every State east of the Mississippi River was placed on full military alert by the Office of the President along with all existing active duty military instillations.

Piling back into Air Force One, the President and his weary staff flew back down to Florida and acted as a mobile Command Post, following the third hurricane up the eastern seacoast, summoning assets along the way, from far and wide. As the third hurricane crossed Long Island on its way northward, its strength forged a path of destruction of the wealthy along with the common man, destroying the mansions of the fortunate few, along with the homes of the many.

One would've thought that with all of the publicity the previous two hurricanes had brought, that the Federal officials had learned the recent lessons of moving at a glacial pace, in the service of their fellow man. But in many cases they had not, with the President having to insert himself personally to resolve procedural conflicts and in some cases remove people on the spot and in a public manner.

By the time of the fourth and final Hurricane, yet again broad siding the western coast of Florida and working its way northward towards the Florida panhandle, the Secretary of Homeland Security prevailed upon the western states to remove all of the National Guard on duty on the Southern Border to be immediately transferred to the Eastern Seaboard for cleanup duty.

When Lars Magnusson learned of this he immediately countermanded that directive and summoned the Director of Homeland Security and the Director of FEMA, to his presence in the Air Force One Command Center, now located at Eglin AFB in Florida, for a brief conference.

Upon the termination of that conference, the President announced their immediate resignations and interim replacements to the nation at large.

He followed the rest of the storm up the midsection of the nation, but by now the Federal response was operating on all cylinders and those in authority were operating at flank speed.

One haggard reported commented to another, that he hadn't slept in several days and that the local politicians were complaining of battle fatigue. The response he received by another was, "The President has been on a dead run for a solid month now and here we are bitching about a few nights sleep"?

"When is this all going to be over", some of the reporters were heard to complain, while assembled on the flight line at Eglin awaiting refueling for the flight back to Washington?

The President wandered into their midst and grinned, "Folks, it'll be over when Mother Nature says it's over"!

One of the reporters drew the President aside and they walked towards the front of the Presidential aircraft as they looked as if they were inspecting the aircraft and the reporter asked, "Mr. President, never before in the history of this country, has a President insert himself so directly into a country's emergency. Just why did you do it at great risk to your person"?

"Why did I do it, you ask, right"? The reporter nodded his head as they stopped just Below the starboard wingtip of the great aircraft. "Well sir, I had a few examples of executive micromanagement in which to choose from, in the history of our great nation starting with James K. Polk, who presided over the War of 1847, in which America freed the fledgling Republic of Texas from the tyranny of Mexico and in the process, completed the quest of Manifest Destiny in the acquisition of land from Mexico. The History books are replete with examples of President Polk's incessant intervening and meddling to such a degree that he made an inefficient bureaucracy work. America won the war and the land. As a result America said thanks, by turning the rascal out of office the very next election cycle"!

"The next example was President Lincoln, who in the early days of the Civil War, discovered that Americas best Generals went with the

Secessionist's leaving him with a staff of Generals of lesser talents. Not only did he bone up on the Military Arts and Science as was known for his day, he was everywhere, unlike his predecessor President Buchanan, all the time, trying to hold the Union together. Seems like he succeeded in his task, wouldn't you say"?

"Now what did he receive for his efforts? He got himself shot! However the nation survived and eventually prospered. So it seems in retrospect, that I had a few good examples to draw from. But to directly answer your question, with all that was happening at a breakneck pace and Americans suffering from blow after blow and after all of the plans seemingly well placed, there was an egregious lack of coordination and execution of those plans. To sit hunkered down in the White House isn't the right thing to do.

To get well into the weeds was the right thing to do! People can't get a job done right, you replace the people"!

The reporter thought a second before asking his next question, "You've just lead us all through a wild ride Mr. President"!

"Yeah, but your all reporters aren't you? And what a juicy story you've all gotten, right"?

"That is correct, but more to the point, what do you expect will become your legacy after all of this is over"?

"John, I haven't a clue! Right now I'm just winging it. As for any expectations after all is said and done? I have none. The world will keep on turning, or not. There will be good people walking around as well as bad.

Am I trying to lead the nation by personal example? Yes I am, but look at how many are following? Doesn't seem like near enough to make a difference. I've come to believe the Office of the President, is nothing more than that of "Chief Arrow Catcher" and I imagine that I've made more than my share of enemies along the way. But all I can do is to keep my head up, my mind clear and press on regardless"!

After a moment of silence, the reporter said, "Mr. President I believe you've made more than a few friends along the way and those that aren't just don't matter"!

"Thanks John. Now can I have a moment alone"?

"Yes Mr. President", said the reporter and then he rejoined the others on the far side of the aircraft. As he approached the others they all gathered around and asked him what he and the President talked about? "I'll tell you later", said the reporter. Who then added, "But this I can tell you. The next person I hear bitching about that man will get a fist in the face, by god"!

As they all turned back to look at Lars Magnusson, they saw him kneeling in apparent prayer, under the wing tip of the Presidential Aircraft. What they didn't know, what they could never know, was that he had tears in his eyes as he had a very private conversation With his long lost wife and children. After some time Magnusson arose, wiped his eyes and rejoined the others bellowing, "All aboard folks. Let's get this bus going back to Washington. We've done enough damage around here. Captain, are we ready to take off"?

"We will be Mr. President whenever the Eglin control tower says we're good to go. We're on the back side of that Hurricane"!

Magnusson said, looking northward, "I see a break in the clouds over there, so why don't you ring up the control tower and inform them of that"!

Within a few minutes, the Aircraft captain summoned everyone up the stairs as the POTUS Aircraft cycled the massive engines, going through their take off procedures and taxied down the ramp, eventually turning, then took off finding that hole in the sky.

The following day, there appeared a long article, in the New York Times, titled, "Leadership from the Front", the beginning of a legend.

11

Jaeger lay doggo in his hide. The sun was high overhead and not even the scorpions would emerge in the heat of the day. Everything was set now and all he had to do was wait for the subject's arrival. It had been a long time since he'd been called upon for a snuff job. But the pay was good a smooth million in Swiss Francs deposited in his account in Bern, half upon agreement and the rest upon execution of the hit.

His bail enforcement career had grown in stature from the common criminal, over time, to the international fugitive. Usually the objects of his intentions were political in nature rather than criminal, but often both went hand in hand. In most cases the security of the subject was of the highest quality. Ex-military soldiers of fortune, that sold their skills dearly to the highest bidder.

Jaegers quarry this time was not political in nature, but the subject of a disagreement between two parties engaged in the narcotics business. A shipment was made as agreed, yet paid for in counterfeit American currency, of questionable quality. Had the quality been better, probably nothing would've been said, until the next transaction. But since the quality was marginal, it was considered little better than wall paper. Thus an example had to be made.

Everything was in place. The large caliber Soviet Dragunov sniper rifle, specially outfitted with the latest British accoutrements, such as the fifty power scope with day/night optics and a range finder, with a separate battery operated forward wind indicator, placed some two hundred meters from the target area. Push a button on the scope and one would receive a signal down range as to the wind speed and direction close to the target, vital in assessing the bullet trajectory calculations. Real state of the art stuff.

Of course, after the event the Dragunov would be left in place, to be discovered after the event to deflect culpability, as well as the other hardware to be abandoned in various places during Jaegers exit.

The range finder signaled a distance of some eight hundred fifty meters to the front door of the chalet, that Paco Rubirosa owned and the current wind speed down range was sliding off the steep jungle slopes at a gentle five miles per hour. Of course it was mid-morning and the fog was lifting on eastern slopes of the northern Andes Mountain range. The best Jaeger could hope for was an appearance early in the morning, when the wind was minimal yet even at that there was the ever present early cloud cover to consider.

There was a small stream, some seventy meters from his hide, that provided fresh mountain water and ten tins of Bovril beef on hand to provide nutrition and at the altitude of eight thousand feet above sea level, the mosquito repellant he brought along would not be needed until after the fact during his exfiltration. He would be moving fast carrying only what was necessary.

The insertion went well enough. The private émigré chopper pilot had dropped him off on a mountaintop some fifteen miles distant and he'd paid the pilot sufficiently to ensure that he'd be available when called for on the way out. Besides, the pilot had sufficient reason to see Paco Rubrirosa dead, since he raped and sodomized his sister long ago. If his talents weren't sufficient to see the man dead, the he would do whatever required to help another to act in his behalf regardless of the reason.

The hand drawn map through the mountains was accurate enough and tallied with the miniaturized GPS satellite direction finder. Two days of cutting a path through the thick mountainous terrain, brought Jaeger in sight of the Rubirosa's chalet.

Only one small seldom used winding dirt road lead into and out of the area, with most arrivals and departures occurring by helicopter. It took Jaeger an entire afternoon to find the right location for his hide partway up a steep mountainside, hidden by fresh jungle growth to such a degree, that Jaeger had to shinny up a tree and selectively remove some tree branches lower down the slope for a clear down slope view of the chalet.

The entire chalet was surrounded by a ten foot high wall, topped with broken glass and rusty nails embedded in concrete. From dusk till dawn the guard dogs were let out to patrol the grounds inside the perimeter. It took a few days until favorable winds were such that Jaeger could approach to within two hundred meters of the compound slowly and firmly secure his remote wind indicator on the lower branches of a tree and withdraw back to his hide, lest the guard dogs gain his scent. Now he had to be patient.

A man like Rubirosa would never adhere to an exact schedule, performing his tasks in a random sequence, consistently on a moment to moment basis. Yet here was his roosting place, known to only a chosen few. His women and all visitors were brought in and out blindfolded. He'd been gone for over a week now on business to Lima Peru and was due to return eventually at his own pace.

Jaeger estimated that supply wise, he was good for ten and if he conserved a bit, perhaps twenty days waiting time for Rubrirosa to return. Then upon his return it was unknown how long it would be for the man to emerge from his house and become a target. So much was in Jaegers control, yet so much more was in the hands of Dame Fortune.

His hide was well constructed, a small depression in the earth enlarged with his trenching tool and well covered with local branches and dead leaves that took him an afternoon to get right. His firing platform was a low slung affair cobbled together with local wood and placed into the earth and completely level with small vise like contraption that secured the Dragunov leaving it with a downrange traversing range of only one inch laterally and a half inch in elevation. Once the windage mechanism was in place, Jaeger took readings every other hour in order to try and find a pattern if, of wind direction and speed. His small portable radio was tuned in to sideband frequencies, and once settled in place Jaeger kept it on constantly, with the earplugs in place. He was a light sleeper anyway so any outgoing radio traffic from the chalet would immediately alert him to arrivals, day or night.

He'd taken the precaution to bring along several different kinds of hunting scents, to spray in his general area. A scent that indicated that of a predator and another to indicate that of a dead animal and finally a scent to eliminate his human body odors. Useful during a hurried exfiltration in case hunting dogs were hard on his trail. A dozen Dexedrine capsules to give him a boost of energy when needed, another two dozen caffeine pills to keep him awake and finally a dozen packets of sugared chewing gum to provide energy and to prevent dry mouth.

He wanted a cigarette badly, but in his line of work, cigarette smoke carried a long way and was indicative of human presence, so that luxury would just have to wait. There was about thirty yards of trees between his hide, in the line of site down slope and the canopy's edge, with only the selective clearing of branches to reveal the target area. He could see the chalet rather well, but they couldn't see him. In addition, the presence of the trees all around, would give some help in the sound suppression of his big bore rifle. He'd brought along two dozen rounds of carefully crafted and wiped ammunition for the big bore Dragunov, but he shouldn't need more than one to get the job done. For all else, there was theStreet Sweeper twelve gauge shotgun with the ten round drum clip, accompanied with fifty rounds and his Ruger magnum revolver and his old Marine K-bar knife.

The chalet occupied about an acre of space that was walled, and there was the main house, a large pool and cabana area for outside entertainment and a multicar garage separate from the main two level structure yet next to another building which apparently housed the on-site help. During the day some minimal maintenance activity occurred, the cutting of lawns the pool area maintenance and the third day out, four men emerged from the compound with large scythes to cut down the tall grass that surrounded the compound, out to a distance of almost seventy five meters. This along with the fact that the main house was never illuminated during the evening said two things. First, that the master of the house was not at home and second that he was expected soon.

Every evening the servants of the house would emerge from the compound with the dogs on the leash to walk the freshly cut exterior of the compound. The dogs straining at the leash, sniffing everywhere for a foreign scent charging off pulling their handlers periodically to the very edge of the freshly cut area, then halting, barking at some phantom in the brush, then pulling their handlers in another direction, until the entire area was investigated and found safe, before returning to the compound.

The entire place was apparently self-sustaining with a water well, solar energy collectors covering most of the roof space and two, hundred feet tall wind power generators, spinning constantly most of the time from the air constantly rising and falling off the mountain slopes. Inside the compound was an overly large dish antenna, no doubt Rubirosa's connection with the outside world. The man embraced his privacy and clearly had the cash with which so sustain it.

The worst thing about waiting was the act of waiting. All of the planning had been accomplished and now the boredom started to set in. One slept fitfully, taking a series of catnaps, no more than two hours at a stretch. Jaeger put himself in Rubirosa's situation, guessing that he would arrive after dark, by helicopter. A bit dangerous flying in the mountains after dark, but an experienced pilot who knew the in and out, could handle it readily, for Jaeger had flown before with such men, who somehow could find their way in the dark of night, in the air and at speed.

He recalled an event several years back, while performing an extraction in Nicaragua, flying into a hundred and fifty yard long landing strip carved out of the jungle in a heavily loaded pre WWII Curtis C46 aircraft, into the teeth of a Hurricane. The pilot had the flaps fully distended and the aircraft stopped within a scant hundred and twenty yards thanks to the head wind.

This was accomplished just as the eye of the hurricane began to pass over the landing strip. The plane was quickly unloaded within ten minutes and the only return visitors were Jaeger and his prisoner. The pilot stood the plane at idle at the far end of what passed for a runway as the eye passed over watching the wind direction of the trees at the far end of the dirt runway. Just when the wind changed blowing toward the aircraft was when he gunned the engines. It was a close run thing as the aircraft lumbered down the runway into the oncoming hurricane wind, but after a hundred yards the wheels left the runway and the plane just barely cleared the trees as it climbed skyward. Safely in the air for the moment and buffeted by the high winds lightning and rain, the plane made its way southward towards Panama City and the American authorities for Jaegers handover of the fugitive. During the return trip he stayed with his prisoner in the rear of the aircraft, for the pilot had all he could say grace over, flying a very old plane in the teeth of a hurricane. After they landed and the prisoner hand off had been accomplished, Jaeger just had to ask him how he'd done it and if he'd ever done that before?

"Done that before? Fuck no pal!!! It was down to this, I needed the money before I even agreed to the trip into a hurricane. Next, I was lucky that we flew into the eye of the hurricane just as it crossed over the landing field and caught the headwinds just right. Next I was lucky the plane was unloaded so quickly, making it a whole lot lighter. Next, I was lucky that I caught the tail end of the eye just as we took off into the wind"!

"So how did ya know it was possible", asked Jaeger?

"I SWAGGED it pal"!

"Scientific Wild Ass Guess", answered Jaeger recognizing the age old military acronym!

"Well ya, that experience and the fact that I'm a damn great pilot", bragged the pilot as he swaggered away. Jaeger figured he'd earned the swagger.

Over the years, Jaeger had tried not to think about that moment in time, for as the aircraft cleared the trees, for just a moment he felt as if the craft was motionless, hanging in the air by a thread, fighting to gain altitude as the engines screamed at the maximum RPM's, the aircraft shuddering and being buffeted by the airflow, then finally discovering a hole in the wind in which to gain speed and momentum. Once again, it was as if the 'Hand of Providence' was guiding the craft skyward. He didn't recall praying at that moment, for just too much was assaulting his senses at the time. But as the plane finally gathered sufficient altitude and distance into relatively clean air some twenty minutes later, emerging from the swirling clouds, Jaeger lifted his head and whispered a silent 'Thanks'!

His thoughts then drifted to his lawyer, Elizabeth Beavior, aka. Buffy.

Over time they'd drifted out of touch. He supposed that she was yet another of his guardian angels in a whole host of ways. First his lawyer, losing her very first case, causing him to spend many years in prison, then acting as his savior, springing him from the unjust captivity, welcoming him back into the family of mankind. Eventually they became lovers of a sort, coming together for a moment in time then drifting apart, without malice, eventually becoming friends. She had gone to the very edge for him and in the process, he'd reciprocated in kind.

Then his thoughts drifted to Melanie O'Bannon. He tried not to think about her. But every so often thoughts of their ever so brief six months together drifted back into his consciousness. Their time together was by far, the happiest he'd ever known. Time raced by when they were together and conversely dragged slowly when they were apart. He'd often wondered what things would've been like had they made a life together. She had a young boy from her previous marriage that had immediately connected with Jaeger, eagerly hanging on his every word when they were together. Glad by his every arrival and distraught by his departure. As for his mother, things couldn't be possibly better. Tall, well structured, with long flowing Chestnut colored hair and a face like an angel. Her distinct voice, with just a trace of a South Texas accent, was ever music to Jaegers ears. Apart from a few uncomfortable moments upon their first meeting, they drew together like a magnet, with similar likes and dislikes, enjoying every single moment together. Easy on the eyes, well read, highly intelligent and in love with him. So then why did Jaeger leave her in a lurch, breaking her heart, he wondered?

He couldn't directly answer that question, even to himself. Part of the answer was perhaps derived from that old axiom, "If something looks too good to be true, its isn't"!

Another possibility was that, with all that had happened in his life, perhaps he simply wasn't up to the task of being a good husband, lover, confidant and life partner with such a fine woman. Her first marriage was simply a disaster and Jaeger just didn't want a repeat of her first experience, for her to endure. On one level of thought, he felt somewhat comfortable with the axiom; "Loved by no one, in love with no one. Cared for no one and cared for by no one"! His life thus far was an endless series of peaks and valleys and the lot he either chose for himself or had chosen for him by Providence, was pretty much cast in stone.

No good woman should be expected to endure such a partnership.

Still, as the cavalcade of time went by he thought more and more of Melanie.

Even though there had been several women that briefly passed through his life, only one left her mark. Like Elsa and Rick back in Casablanca, she coursed through his heart and burned with an eternal flame. He'd provided her with a generous funding through the efforts of Boyd Parmalee in Houston, sufficient to provide her with a financial cushion for both her and her son.

Rumors surfaced that she'd become involved in Texas politics over time working for one of the political party functionaries and that her son didn't need the educational funding he provided, securing an appointment to the US Naval Academy. He knew the kid was smart, but with a mother like that, how could he not succeed?

He'd truly loved that woman with all his heart, but had to admit she was better off without him. He emerged from his reverie, feeling the effects of a full bladder and a lower intestine that was screaming for release, moving back the covering of his hide and making his way some twenty yards downhill to the latrine he'd previously dug. Just a hole in the ground, a foot wide, by three feet deep. Simple but effective. Squat down over the hole, take care of business, shovel several inches of dirt over the top, spray antiscent concentrate over the top, put the home made wicker top back on, then back to the hide, wiping ones tracks with a branch. Should be good for a month. But since Jaeger was on limited rations, he didn't anticipate a great deal of use.

He had an entire gallon of water from the mountain stream nearby, stored in the clear, plastic fold up container. Several trips to the stream were necessary, to fill his quart canteen, then back to the hide where he carefully poured the water into a fold up funnel that held several strips of cotton cloth as a filter. When the gallon container was filled, Jaeger held it up to the light and seeing nothing floating around inside the container, placed a single drop of chlorine bleach in the container and the water was drinkable. Each time he'd ever done this, he'd always remembered what his father had taught him on their periodic hunting trips down in the Rio Grande Valley saying, "Son, never drink the water downstream from the herd"! That thought alone never failed to bring a smile to his face.

Settled back in the hide, he quickly took a wind reading down range and made note in his small pocket sized notebook, trying to establish a pattern of wind activity over time. None yet developed that he could see. If a time and wind directional velocity pattern developed then he'd be better off selecting a time of day or evening to make the shot. It was seemingly minor details such as this that often made the difference between a hit, or miss, the latter offering up nothing but problems.

During the previous evening after he'd made yet another visual sweep of the chalet down below, he sensed, rather than heard, movement heading his way. The sounds of the jungle at night are such with all manner of animal and birds calling out to each other, that Jaeger often reckoned it to a rock concert for the critters. What he and the animals didn't want to hear, was absolute silence. Without fail it would indicate the presence of an intruder. If one listened very carefully, one could sense this for as an intruder approached, usually a predator, the sound level would escalate, then drop off to almost nothing for a period of time as the intruder passed through a certain territory. The critters would always tell you when the intruder had gone, by gradually calling out to each other. You just had to know what to listen for. But on this certain night, Jaeger failed to catch the escalating sound from the trees, but when it started to fall off to nothing, that's when the hair on his neck signaled alert. Minutes later he heard the scream of a male Jaguar not fall away to his right. On his many hunting trips with his father, when he was young, into Mexico and the Rio Grande Valley, they both brought down their share of game, stalking both predator and prey. On a certain occasion his dad, fired his Winchester .40/70 just as a large Jaguar leapt at him from a ledge. So had Jaeger at that moment hitting the big cat in the hind quarter while his father fired at the Jaguar at almost point blank range, the big bullet slamming into the Jaguar almost head on in the chest dropping it like a stone.

The Jaguar was significantly larger than the Cougars, Jaeger and his father hunted back home and would've made a magnificent trophy back at the house, but they had to leave it lay for the Mexican Government would've arrested them had they learned of the kill.

Jaegers thoughts came back to the Jaguar prowling about, as he slowly shifted in his hide. He slowly reached for his K-Bar knife in one hand and his Pistol in the other. He prayed that the Jaguar would pass him by, for the knife, while normally deadly was but small comfort when it came to defense from the Jaguars fangs and claws. The Ruger Magnum pistol would probably make short work of the animal, yet the sound of a gunshot at this time was likely to alert those down below and he just couldn't be certain of the muffling effect of the trees and surroundings. The single sound of a gunshot was certain to compromise his efforts as well as any injury suffered from the animal. Knowing what the Jaguar was capable of guaranteed that any injury, even should he survive the encounter, would be serious and be quite a challenge for the nanobots that lay within.

Now was the time when he'd find out whether or not the antiscent spray worked or not as he lay silent in the hide from the predator outside, glancing at the luminous dial of his watch, that indicated just shy of 0300 hours in the morning. His only rational option was for the Jaguar to pass him by and move on.

Minutes slowly passed, which seemed like hours as he both heard and sensed the ever so slow passage of the Jaguar across Jaegers hide site, with eventually the animal passing into his view from the right, stopping and sniffing the air all around, then slowly moving down slope, stopping once again in the vicinity of Jaegers makeshift latrine, sniffing all around the area as if something were there, finally squatting down slightly and urinating, marking his territory no doubt, before continuing on down slope and out of view.

Jaeger waited five minutes, then slowly approached the Dragunov rifle and turned on the night scope. Even though the moon was in its quarter phase, sufficient moonlight was available to light up the landscape below as if it were high noon. Jaeger heard yet another scream from the Jaguar as it almost came into view below, seeing nothing but movement in the tall grass for a while and then finally emerging the big cat, walking slowly around the edge of the freshly cut area surveying his domain, staying well clear of the settlements walls and disappearing a half hour later into the tall grass on the other side. Yet another close call, to his survival, he had to chalk up to Devine Providence. On this day, his thoughts drifted to that of a man named Lars Magnusson and the time, long ago when they met on a football field in Minnesota. Surrounded in a stadium full of rabid screaming fans, Jaeger and Magnusson came to briefly make each-others acquaintance.

The guy was as big as Jaeger and as an All American tight end was nothing short of magnificent. As a blocker on running plays, he was very good in the subtleties of blocking and had the brute strength in laying one flat on ones back, in advance of the ball carrier. On passing downs, the guy had the kind of soft hands that guaranteed a catch, with overall playing fundamentals that were flawless. Try as Jaeger might Magnusson had nine catches during the game; with each and every one just a hair ahead of Jaegers outstretched hands. On the few running plays that came Jaegers way, he held Magnusson to a draw, neither one gaining the advantage of the other, yet was just unable to match his ability as a pass catcher. Thus going into the game's final moments, by Jaegers reckoning, each man was fighting the battle to a draw. Yet the man drew Jaegers respect during the game, by not resorting to the dirtier elements of football that others often engaged in to gain advantage.

With but seconds left to go in the game, the final pass play and subsequent interception by a Longhorn player, then fumbled straight into Magnusson's hands then his sudden collision with Jaeger and resulting fumble straight up into the hands of a trailing Longhorn player who ran the ball in for a touchdown, ranked right up there as one of footballs all time freakiest plays. In the words of the faithful, "A real Bang, Bang play"!

Jaeger's memory of the play was feeble at best. His first memory was of the aftermath. A silent stadium, full of fans, with Jaeger at last getting shakily to his feet, then seeing a small crowd of med techs surrounding Magnusson, his helmet removed and a neck collar installed to immobilize his neck and his leg, spasmodically jerking as Jaeger was helped from the field, looking back from time to time at Magnusson. Clearly another example of providential intercession. In the later days to come Jaeger had recovered to play again, while Magnusson lay still in a Minnesota hospital, his neck broken and his days of ever engaging in a contact sport finished, 'Kaput', forever.

In the months ahead, while Lars Magnusson lay in a hospital bed, completely immobile, a certain career in professional football taken from him by sheer circumstance, Jaeger had scaled the heights in the Cotton Bowl as the "Uberballer Supremo". A hero for the moment in time, only to suffer ones most egregious fall from grace, by having his entire family murdered and then being successfully framed for their murder and spending what seemed like an eternity in Huntsville prison. From Hero to Zero in the space of a month.

Of course Magnusson had married an excellent woman, during that period of his convalescence, completed his undergraduate studies, then received a Law Degree, raised a family, gotten into politics, eventually ascending to the rank of US Senator, for a single term, riding the coat tails of Dobbins straight into the Vice Presidency.

Then for Magnusson, his ultimate sacrifice, the terrorist attack during the inauguration parade. The President and his immediate family gone.

Magnusson's family gone, with a host of other deaths and casualties. Jaeger had stayed glued to the media reports of the event and of Magnussons miraculous recovery. For here was a man of magnificent inner strength who also had everything of value torn from him by a malevolent entity. His only experience with the man, a chance meeting on a football field, and their common aftermath, gave Jaeger a sense of complete commonality with the man.

His sense of overall leadership, during his ascendancy to the Presidency, seemingly alone, fighting the enemies of America, both internal and external, saying and doing precisely the right thing at the right time, taking charge of a chaotic situation time and again drew Jaeger firmly in his camp, with the silent vow that if in the course of time, he ever could be of service to Lars Magnusson, regardless of the means or the end, he was there. Rather unlikely of course, but after all, he felt that he owed the man something after changing his course in life. Something. Several more days passed uneventfully for Jaeger fighting off the boredom, yet grateful that he was at elevation, for the summer days were indeed hot but relatively dry free from the constant humidity of lower climes. Of course the nights grew cold, but he could deal with that. On the eighth day out, his mini scanner sideband radio came alert, with an alert that a helicopter was coming up the valley and about to land inside the Rubirosa compound.

Twenty minutes later following the rudimentary dirt roadway up from the lowlands came a lone, black Bell 'Little Bird' chopper flying at tree top level, slowing as it approached and making one complete circuit of the chalets compound before descending to the landing pad. Out jumped his quarry Paco Rubirosa himself, all smiles standing erect under the idling blades of the 'Little Bird' and motioning something into the house, where upon several people brought out four boxes and secured them into the idling helicopter and then stepped aside as it rose up and dived back down the valley from where it came.

As it disappeared, it passed another slightly larger helicopter on its way to the chalet, which unloaded three more men, each carrying two aluminum suitcases into the main house and shortly thereafter came back out with several large boxes and placed them into the helicopter, that promptly gained altitude and went back down the valley, leaving the men at the chalet and taking only what was in the boxes.

Of course with all of that wind turbulence, any thought of taking a shot was out of the question, when yet another helicopter appeared, similar to the one that had just left. This time upon landing, it disgorged five rather attractive women and a small entourage of what appeared to be musicians by the looks of what emerged of their luggage. Jaeger could only conclude that with the musicians and the women, that in the subsequent days an ongoing celebration was to occur. Seems the pool was going to be of good use, with the girls working on their tans, either with or without their bikinis.

At long last the stage was set. Rubirosa had done his business, things were set in motion. His people were off doing his bidding, while he was engaging in some relaxation. That evening, they all came out on the patio, with the musicians playing and the girls cavorting both in and out of the pool. Jaeger keenly followed the activity all through the afternoon and the evening. During the evening hours, his night scope capabilities were useless, with the outside pool area lighting casting harsh glares and shadows. He had to be patient even though there he was, Mr. Paco

Rubirosa himself in all his glory having his way with anyone within the compound, at will and getting roaring drunk in the process.

Sometime around midnight, Jaeger toyed with the idea of firing on Rubirosa as his men carried his prostrate drunken body into the house after having fallen off the diving board into the pool partially clad. His finger was tightening on the trigger of the Dragunov, when a sudden gust of wind down range, caused him to abort.

As he watched them all fish Rubrirosa out of the pool, he was grateful for the electronic wind indicator, for when engaged it electronically sent in real time, the wind speed and direction straight to the scope. Had he fired with any other wind indicator, it wouldn't haveregistered the random and sudden wind gust and his shot would've missed the target at this distance. So the party over as far as the host was concerned, causing Jaeger to shut everything down for the evening. His target safely inside for the night, indicated that it was time for him to get some sleep. Tomorrow would no doubt supply other opportunities and random chance provided yet another day of life for Paco Rubirosa.

At 0600 hrs. in the morning, Jaegers eyes suddenly opened as he slowly emerged from his hide, surveying his immediate area then going down to the latrine to relieve himself then back to the confines of his hide. As he settled into the hide, he peered through the scope, to see that apparently every one was sleeping late, with two of Rubirosa's female guests still asleep on the chaise pool lounges in various stages of undress, as well as two of his men close at hand. One, still clutching a bottle of liquor still in his hand.

'Might as well party hard and often', Jaeger thought, 'for tomorrow we all might die', was a common thread. Clearly the host was asleep upstairs in his bedroom and would rise eventually with a monster of a hangover, no doubt needing sustenance and possibly relief of sorts. Jaeger didn't really care as long as the relief occurred outside the house near the pool area.

He readied his kit and his area, for a rapid departure, dumping the used tins of Bovril beef into the latrine and generally policed the area, before settling back into the hide and wait for the emergence of his quarry.

Around ten in the morning, the two girls finally came awake, adjusted their clothes and wandered inside the house, no doubt to eat breakfast of sorts and make themselves presentable for the next day's activities, however they shook out. The other two men came awake, one by one a half hour later and staggered inside. By noon the musicians emerged from the house and went to the pool, set up their equipment and began to play, followed one by one with all of the rest to resume the party and relax by the pool. Several servants then emerged and set up a buffet near the poolside cabanas in the shade, for the guests to help themselves to at their leisure.

Jaeger kept a steady eye on the wind indicator down range, making slight changes in his firing trajectory periodically, mostly to keep busy. At about one in the afternoon, the host himself came out onto the patio wearing a Caribbean styled shirt, loose slacks and sandals.

The shirt was not tucked into his waistband and as he wandered around the pool area, passing each of his female guests, he apparently bade them to remove their bikini tops and get a better tan, for each of them immediately complied as he made the rounds. Hell, he was paying for the party and all that it conveyed and after all he was Paco Rubirosa and to deny him a request would be an insult payable by death. To immediately and cheerfully obey his every request warranted a good payday for all, when they flew back to whence they came.

He stopped by the cabana partially shielded from view by the long rectangular canopy that provided shade. Finally he stopped by a particularly statuesque woman and gazed down at her, summoning one of his men to bring a video camera and start it rolling. He then made another slow circuit around the pool, chewing on what appeared to be a pork chop, with one hand and again stopped by each of the girls and in turn they removed their bikini bottoms and spread their legs moving suggestively as he had his video camera man circle the subject taking in all of their charms, before moving on to the next girl in line and repeating the activity. Each of the women had much to offer visually in a prurient sense, their appearance no doubt altered by skillful cosmetic surgeons, to appeal instantly to the manly pursuit of sex at all costs. As each was carefully revealed, Jaeger monitored the down range wind indicator, noticing that the wind was abating and hoping for a negative wind reading downrange, so he could dial that in and fire. As Rubirosa came back to the original statuesque beauty she slowly removed her bikini bottom suggestively like all the rest, opening her legs and inviting him to become one with her. As Rubirosa approached he opened the front of his trousers and the girl rose up to comply with his apparent desires. At that very instant the wind indicator registered calm and Jaeger made the appropriate adjustment in his scope, peering once again down range and seeing Rubirosa's back to him with only the girls form mostly blocked from view as the video cameraman circling around behind the busy girl trying for an artsy shot.

The time was right as Jaeger slowly exhaled, his finger exerting a steady pressure on the trigger until the Dragunov erupted in force, sending the big bullet down range at an eleven degree angle and two instants later, it crashed into Rubirosa's back, tearing right through his heart, straight out into and through the head of the hapless girl and into the kneeling cameraman, sending them all right into the ground.

Apparently the tree cover sufficiently masked the sound of the shot to such a degree that it didn't register immediately with the others around the pool, who were involved in other activities, to rhythm of the amplified sounds of the band.

Not often does a sniper get a two fer, much less than a three fer in one shot, but Jaeger immediately ejected the spent round and slammed in another as he watched for activity around the pool. It took a whole minute for someone to notice three dead bodies splayed out near the house, bleeding out onto the concrete poolside patio. One by one the men approached the dead trio and as they stood together staring at the dead bodies, the Dragunov, belched three times more, each round slamming into one of the men, standing with weapons drawn in place a perfect target, leaving a red splatter. As the big bullets tore into and through each target, it brought with it a significant amount of bodily tissue, to guarantee none survival of anything it hit. Especially since any medical help was at least a day away. Four bullets and six bodies. Not a bad days work, reasoned Jaeger. He stayed in place for a few moments longer to see the other girls apparently screaming and hurriedly putting on their bikinis as the house servants came slowly out of the house to view the carnage.

Since the house servants appeared to simply be the hired help as well as the other three girls, Jaeger decided to let them be. They would have stories to tell for generations to come. Plus who knows, perhaps they'd choose another line of work. But Jaeger put that option quickly out of mind, for clearly those girls had but one saleable commodity and it was the oldest skill known in the history of mankind. It's all they knew, or would ever know.

He emerged from his hide, looked around the area, wiped down the Dragunov, removing the scope set, picked up his kit and headed north along the trail he'd cut on his way in. Five miles along the trail, he disposed of the scope in the brush and as soon as he reached high ground, he dialed up his chopper pilot and informed him of his success and to meet him at the very same rendezvous site for exfiltration.

As Jaeger flew back to the States, in the private plane he'd hired, the chopper pilot phoned the local media with the exact coordinates of Rubirosa's chalet, which in turn quickly filtered up to the National Media, who beat the Peruvian National Authorities to the site of the massacre by several hours, good enough to take what pictures and videos of the massacre, necessary to develop a story of international implications. The following day, Malatesta Scaramanga sat in his twentieth floor penthouse in Paris, watching the International evening news. He'd received the coded message from Jaeger, earlier in the day informing him of the task being completed as agreed and as Scaramanga watched the newscast and there it was. The death of a drug smuggler. All considered things went remarkably well for Malatesta and his branch of the organization. For a number of years he'd done business with Paco Rubirosa, buying processed Peruvian Cocaine and smuggling it into Holland and Belgium, cutting its purity then dealing it out to wholesalers at a profits of staggering proportions. A million Swiss Francs worth of raw cocaine was skillfully cut into ten million worth at the street level. What ever happened to the product after it left his hands was of little concern. Of course the Poule's would dilute the product in addition, but that was their affair. Business was always done with the locals through a series of middlemen and cut outs. The Gendarmes having not a hint of Scaramanga's involvement.

Quite unlike the American Mafia, the various European branches of the loosely knit organization rarely if ever opened their mouths, if ever captured by the locals. For to talk, meant certain death, eventually. There was nowhere to run. Nowhere to hide. Besides Scaramanga paid those who mattered extremely well, while the others always ran the risk of betrayal.

Such it was in the elimination of Paco Rubirosa. Scaramanga came across Jaegers name through a chance encounter with one of Jaegers old associates. A certain Nestor Magellan.

Returning from America, some years ago, he started a Security Business in the European Commonwealth, called "Securetie' du Nord". He had learned of Magellan's checkered past as a former Legionnaire', who had associated himself with a Texan Drug Smuggler named Ortega, he invited Magellan to assess his electronic security setup for both his office and his Condo in Paris. Over dinner he made a delicate inquiry as to the availability of an individual, capable of a long distance elimination. The only caveat being that the man in question be capable, resourceful and not on anyone's radar.

While Magellan thought for several seconds, he recalled what he'd recently learned about Scaramanga. His coming up through the ranks of the Unione' Course, making his mark in the world, like his former employer Ortega, in the importation of South American Drugs. Oh, Scaramanga's Import Export Company imported and exported legal pharmaceuticals alright, but they made their off the books money from the jungles of South America. His Import Export Company was fronted by a French Citizen, highly educated and with impeccable credentials, but Scaramanga gave all the directives and wrote all the checks. His front man usually appeared once a week to sign anything that was placed before him. Take an envelope and depart.

He gave Scaramanga Jaegers name, last known whereabouts and a thumbnail break down of the man. Former US Marine, College Football star, Convicted Murderer and as far as was known, an International Recovery Operative. He'd heard some rumors along the way that Jaeger or someone like him had performed some wet work along the way, but those were rumors only. One thing he did pass along to Scaramanga, was that Jaeger always worked alone and that he was brutally efficient. Of course there were a host of other things Magellan could've revealed about Jaeger, but he wasn't a Library and he was trying to obtain a contract.

Two days later Scaramanga's man executed the contract with the Securetie' du Nord, for the upgrade in the office and Condo security system. Making certain that it was strictly state of the art and the best that money could buy. The terms, half up front upon execution of the contract, with the remaining upon full completion. The work went rapidly with Magellan contracting out most of the highly technical work to others, he repeatedly employed on the continuum. Within the time limit of thirty days, he completed the contract, tested the equipment and instructed the Scaramanga people in its use and was paid with certified funds drawn on a Parisian bank. He immediately went to that bank on the very same day and successfully converted the bank draft, to cash. With a man like Scaramanga one couldn't be too careful.

The following day, one of Scaramanga's lieutenants was successful in contracting Jaeger and made the first installment of the contract in Jaegers private off shore account. His account was set up as a Shell corporate account with no assets other than money to speak of. The following day, the bulk of those funds were wire transferred to yet another off shore Shell corporate account in the West Indies.

Jaeger was under the impression that the contract was for the reason, that Scaramanga was the aggrieved party, while the reality was that Paco Rubirosa had been steadily raising the price of his product to Scaramanga over time. While Scaramanga was paying with the product with a combination of real American currency, mixed in with rather high quality counterfeit currency. The last shipment that exchanged between the parties was paid for in rather moderate grade counterfeit American currency that had not been carefully examined at the point of exchange. Of course Rubirosa's point man in the exchange somehow leapt from a helicopter high above the Peruvian jungle to his death. When Rubirosa discovered this he contracted for a hit upon Scaramanga, with an individual sorely lacking in expertise. The whole affair was exposed on a boat in the middle of the River Seine and the would be assassin was worked over, eventually revealing that Paco Rubirosa was his employer before dying. Within the week, his remains were being consumed by Parisian's in the form of Big Macs all over the city, while his bones were anchored deep in the English Channel.

Malatesta Scaramanga had been secretly conniving with one of Rubirosa's lieutenants for a time, for him to eliminate Rubirosa and take over his operation deep in the Peruvian Jungle, whereas he had the relationship with the growers and the jungle processing plants, planning to pay them better thus painlessly making the transition of power easier.

However, that individual had been gunned down with all the others, by Jaeger, making all the plans he laid useless. Had Jaeger not exceeded his mandate, all would've been well and everyone would have benefited with greater margins of profit. Now Scaramanga had to start from scratch and search for another supplier of product. As the squat, thickly built, swarthy man paced his apartment, high above the Parisian skyline; he rolled over in his mind whether or not to contract someone to eliminate Jaeger. He decided against it. He hadn't intended to pay the man the remainder of his contract anyway, so in his mind all accounts were closed. He dreaded the prospect of having to deal with the Columbians, for they were even more untrustworthy than he was. Still and all, he was some twelve million Euros ahead of the game and this Jaeger business was behind him as far as he was concerned.

12

For three days in a row upon his return to Houston, Jaeger contacted his primary overseas bank in Bern. He'd notified his French contact in Paris of his completion of the agreement and awaited prompt payment for services rendered. The message was acknowledged as received on the other end, but after the third day and still no reaffirmation regarding a recent deposit in his shell account. Jaeger saw the writing on the wall. The skinny, sandy haired Frog was going to stiff him. Jaeger recalled upon their one and only meeting a name that was dropped when he asked Gaspard du Lesseps, just who precisely had recommended him. He was initially reluctant to reveal the name, saying only that it was someone highly reliable and that had worked with him in the past. Now this narrowed things down quite a bit since Jaeger usually worked alone and those that had worked with him in the past were mostly dead, for one reason or another. When Jaeger pressed the Frenchman further, he refused claiming that the security of his employer was utmost in these proceedings.

"Look here pal", said Jaeger calmly, "I don't do the pig inna poke dance. If you've done your homework you know that I've been around a time or two and I know what tight security means. Now I don't need to know who your boss is necessarily, because nothing is going to happen until the funds reach my account, but I do need to know, just how you guys found out about me and I need to know a name I recognize now! Failing that, I thank you for the dinner and bid you a fond adieu"! Jaeger sat there a moment to let that sink in, then seeing no response, put his knife and fork neatly upon his plate and started to get up from the table.

"The man's name is Nestor Magellan, whispered Du Lesseps nervously as if he betrayed a confidence, which he did. Jaeger resumed his seating and continued with his meal as he mused, "Well, well, Nestor Magellan. There's a name I hadn't heard of in a long time. Last I heard he went back to France and is now a businessman of sorts. He does have a business, doesn't he"?

"Oh yes, he's in the security business and I understand he's doing very well"!

"Security Business", asked Jaeger? "What's he in stocks and bonds? Seems that's unlike him as I recall"!

"Oh no, he's got a company that provides a wide variety of security products for banks, businesses and residences. Very upscale and expensive", whispered Du Lesseps.

Jaeger thought a moment taking a bite of his steak wondering whether or not to press things further, filing that fact away in his memory, should the need arise, then saying, "Well should you see old Nestor any time soon tell him I said hello and thanks for the work. Now tell be all about this Paco Rubirosa of the Peruvian Rubirosa's. I need to know details" and with that the deal was concluded. A hand drawn map of the man's location was provided, since it was deep in the eastern side of the Andes mountains, where the roads didn't go and were largely unmapped, but the GPS coordinates were provided along with a recent set of pictures taken in Panama City and the names of several places in cities he was known to frequent.

With that accomplished both men arose after the meal and departed, with Du Lesseps nervously saying, "I hope that you will keep secret the fact that I revealed the identity of Mssr. Magellan"!

"Consider it done Pal, ya did the right thing and said the right name.

For if ya hadn't we wouldn't be talking right now. Loose lips sink ships and all that kinda stuff. I'll check my account tomorrow and if you're a man of your word, by tomorrow afternoon everything begins"! Jaegers recalling of that meeting bore fruit as he readied himself for his trip to Europe. As he prepared, he thought, 'Well Nestor's in Paris and is in the Corporate and Personal security business, eh? He will know, Gaspard Du Lesseps and through Du Lesseps, I'll find out who the bastard is who stiffed me. He will either pay me the half million in cash he owes me, or not. He probably won't, Jaeger concluded, so he'll just have to join his ancestors, ahead of schedule'.

'Besides, Nestor owes me, his life and the million I gave him from

Ortega's stash'. So a trip to the city of lights was on. He had never been to Paris before, save a single occasion long ago on an escorting assignment. A simple hand off of an émigré to the boys at Langley. A drop and pop, then back from where he came. Never even leaving the airport.

These days one had to fly to Europe without hardware, trusting that either one could connect on the other end, or tend to business by your pluck and persistence alone. The trip over spanned the night time and the pass through Customs at Heathrow was uneventful. He took a London Cab through to the Train station and bought a ticket on the Chunnel train that went under the English Channel.

When he arrived in Paris, he searched for one of the lesser known Hostels off the beaten path and there spent the night. 'Keep a low profile', he thought, for after all he wasn't exactly James Bond. The following morning he sought out one of the Libraries and armed only with the name, "Nestor Magellan", he was hoping the man hadn't changed his name. After a bit of a struggle with the local computers, he got one of the librarians to instruct him, as to the procedure, to affect a changeover into English, which apparently was almost a second language in Paris. Scanning the Parisian Business directories, regarding any registered Corporate and Personal Security Companies, he punched in the name, "Nestor Magellan" as a possible corporate officer, UN 'Viola", there it was. 'Securitie' du Nord', listing the 'Directeur General' as one "Nestor Magellan".

He quickly wrote down the address and phone number, thinking, 'Just how many Nestor Magellan's can there be in Paris' and grateful, the bastard hadn't changed his name.

He then grabbed a cab and gave the driver the address on the Rue de Allemande', in the Parisian suburbs, a small industrial park. It was shortly before lunch when Jaeger walked through the front door and was greeted by the receptionist, with a cheery "Bonjour Monsieur"!

"Do you speak English", asked Jaeger?

"But of course Monsieur", she answered in a slightly accented manner. How may I help you?

"I'd like to speak to Nestor Magellan, your boss. My name is Jaeger, an old business acquaintance of his"!

"He is in a meeting currently and his schedule is rather busy this day"! "Your boss will want to see me and I'm sorry I've no appointment.

However it's of a matter of vital importance to him and I'm sure if you mention my name, he'll be happy to adjust his schedule", said Jaeger with a degree of calm certainty that would allow no objection.

"Of course Mister Jaeger. May I get you something? I'll write him a note and take it to him straight away for he is in a staff meeting that should last but another half an hour". She then got up and went down the hall, returning a minute later saying, "I slipped this note In front of him and he asked me to tell you that he indeed wants to see you and that he should be with you in just a few minutes"! Then she resumed her duties at the front desk answering the phones. True to her word, fifteen minutes later a group of technicians walked down the hall past the reception area, as the receptionist said, "Seems the meeting had concluded. Mr. Magellan should be with you directly". No sooner the words left her mouth around the corner came Magellan himself. Attired in shirt tie and dress pants saying, "Jaeger my friend, it's been quite a while", as he held his arms out in a gesture of embrace. "I apologize for keeping you waiting, but business must have precedence. Have you been waiting long"?

Jaeger got up and reciprocated Magellan's embrace saying, "No not long at all and your girl here is very efficient", nodding towards the receptionist"!

"Good my friend, come with me to my office for we've much to discuss and Madeleine will you bring us several coffee's when you can"?

As they entered Magellan's Spartan looking office, with work papers and engineering drawing's strewn on his work table, Magellan started off, "I think I know why you're here my friend, but let's wait until the refreshments arrive so we can talk uninterrupted". No sooner he said that, then his receptionist arrived with the coffee and the accoutrements and as she left, Magellan asked her "Please no calls until I instruct you otherwise"!

After the door closed Magellan started out, "I suspect the prime reason you are here, is regarding a certain Gaspard Du Lesseps am I correct"?

"A little unfinished business regarding that man, Nestor"!

"Then perhaps I can be of some help, for after all I owe you a great deal and I'm the one who originally vouched for you. Allow me to explain"!

Jaeger nodded his head as he reached for the cup of coffee saying, "Please continue"!

"Some months ago I and several other Security companies, were in a bidding contest to upgrade the security system of a sizeable Import and Export company based here in Paris.

The President of that company is listed as Gaspard Du Lesseps and that is who my prime contact was. That was who executed all of the contracts and signed the checks. At a certain point of the negotiations, a rather delicate proposition arose involving one of his supposed partners, in Peru. He required someone not normally known by Interpol or anyone else, but who was highly reliable. Since I had worked with you in the past and I suspected that this favor would be a significant part of the negotiations for the sizeable contract, as in fact it probably was, for a week later my company was awarded the contract for the upgrading, with state of the art hardware, of his personal homes security and that of his business. What made me suspicious of that fact, is that I expected severe price negotiation as the contract negotiations narrowed down to the last bidders, but to my surprise, he took the initial figures listed in my proposal and signed the contract without a single change. Highly irregular"!

"The work was performed on our end without a flaw and payment went according to the terms stated, half up front upon full execution of the contract and the remainder upon completion and full testing of the systems. What sent up signals to me was when we installed the upgrades in what seemed was Du Lesseps Condominium, my technicians who had seen Du Lesseps, reported to me of the clothes in the man's closet were not of the same type and size that the man wore. Indicating that someone else lived in that Condo other than Du Lesseps. At that point I decided to do a little digging into the man's business through some friends of mine. I discovered that he is involved in that organization as the President, but in name only and the real individual that pulls the strings is a Corsican named Malatesta Scaramanga. Now this Scaramanga is a really nasty piece of work. His organization has most of the Bordellos in France, Belgium and the Netherlands under his wing as well as the loan sharking, unions and of course the narcotics that flow into France".

"My guess is that his South American connection or partner ran afoul of him in some way and he directed Du Lesseps, his well-paid point man, to seek out someone, outside of his organization for the snuff job. Last week in the newspaper Le Monde', was an article regarding the elimination of a certain Paco Rubirosa and his lieutenants in the jungles of Peru and the simple man that I am, I can put two and two together and spell your name. Am I wrong"?

"Your Momma brought you up right Nestor"!

"Further, I'm guessing that there was probably some hitch of a kind regarding your remuneration, for services rendered"?

"Your Momma was a very smart woman"!

"That she was, may she rest in peace", said Magellan sadly.

"May I inquire of the terms of your contract with du Lesseps or Scaramanga"?

"Same as yours, half up front and half on completion. I got the front end, but not the back end".

"And in that business, no invoices are tendered for payment. So you indeed have, shall I say, 'L'Affaires Inachieve", with the man"!

"That I do Nestor. Need to tie up loose ends"!

"Then allow me to be of help if I may"!

"I'm all ears sport"!

"The man, Scaramanga I'm talking about, is not to be taken lightly. The Algerians steer a wide path around him and his organization as well as the Italian's and the Sicilians, which have almost presence in France and Northern Europe other than what scraps he allows them to have. He has a way of making people disappear, not unlike what Ortega practiced back in Houston, if you'll recall. He had surrounded himself with highly capable and hardened men and we both know and respect the type. Neither he nor his men are prone to negotiation of any sort, thus the only thing I can think of is his new security system that I installed"!

"I was hoping you'd bring that up Nestor", offered Jaeger.

Turning towards the wall, Magellan put his feet up upon the work table that flanked his desk and clasped both hands behind his head saying, "What is needed is access to du Lesseps and through him Scaramanga, for that is the only way that I can see. I have a junior technician available to run service tests on his security equipment as per the terms of our maintenance agreement. This may take a day or so to set up my friend. I hope that you have no expectations of seeing another dime of what's owed you"!

"Things are beyond that now Nestor, don't ya think"! "Knowing you and knowing of this Scaramanga, I would expect nothing less my friend". Then thinking some more, he surmised, "This Du Lesseps as a front man, I suspect has no office at Scaramanga's Import Export Company, for I've been there myself and they don't appear to employ more than twenty people. So the office I met him in for business, must belong to Scaramanga and he is conveniently away whenever there is official visible affairs requiring paperwork to be signed by Du Lesseps.

Since no Northern European looking people appear to work in that office, I presume that he either pays his people extremely well, or that they are family of sorts or both"!"This afternoon I will have my junior technician make an appointment with Du Lesseps for the first operational test of the newly installed security equipment at both the residence and the business.

They have seen him before and know him by sight and he wears horn rimmed glasses they joke about, except built into the glasses he wears will be tele lenses. A miniaturized TV camera that will record to a miniaturized video disk recorder. During the normal course of testing our equipment, we will get an update of the equipment and know whether or not the equipment is the same we installed or not for a possible over ride at a later date. He will be wearing our corporate uniform. With any luck, perhaps we can get a picture of Scaramanga, but don't expect it for the man hasn't had any recent photos taken of him in the last twenty years that anyone knows of, since he had facial reconstructive surgery performed from a skiing accident in Gstaad"!

"No our way to Scaramanga is through Du Lesseps. Right now I don't know how, but if we had a rough idea where the man would be at a given time, perhaps he can be gotten to"!

"You can get me in there can't you", asked Jaeger?

"Oh I can get you in both his residence and his business, but will he be there at a given time, then once you are there, can he be reached? My people installed a state of the art security system, with check points all along the way. The doors are all hard wood, thick and solidly installed. A card must be had upon entry to certain areas and to gain access during working hours, one must be expected. So a certain amount of guile must be employed to gain successful entry. At his office, there are several offices where people that do not appear to be your everyday office worker, staffed with men at a desk and one must presume they are well armed. You can be gained access, but I'd think you might want to get out in one piece, ma non"?

"This will take several days to set up", said Magellan reaching into his pocket and removing some keys and giving them to Jaeger continuing, these are the keys to my gray BMW, out back. In the car is a GPS directional system in English that will help you get around. In the glove compartment is a cell phone. Please keep the cell phone close at hand. Time to wait. Call me tomorrow afternoon and I'll let you know what the next step is"!

"One thing Nestor. Why are you so eager to help me", asked Jaeger? As the two men stood up, Magellan thought a moment and replied, "Several reasons that have little to do with friendship, starting with I owe you my life. You could've left me back in Texas, alone, penniless and ready to die. Then there's always the unspoken debt of honor, but if you'll recall your last words to me upon leaving Ortega's apartment long ago, "I just don't want to be looking over my shoulder wondering where you are, for the rest of my life"!

"That's good enough Nestor and thanks. I'll await your call".

"Enjoy Paris my friend, but be careful of the Parisian drivers. They're worse than the Romans".

Jaeger made his way back to Paris, well enough thanks to the GPS directional finder installed in the BMW 745i. As he drove, he marveled at the German engineering and quality of this road beast, almost making him want one and casting aside his old 63 Ford Galaxie fast back, that he resurrected from a San Antonio and restored back to far better than its original condition. The only thing that appeared as factory original was the body and the frame, all else being state of the art and costly. So as he drove back to Paris he was torn between his love for the old as well as the new.

Still as he drove, he was torn by several concerns. Would Magellan give him up to Scaramanga? He had every reason to, yet he was the quickest and surest way to his target. Next was the cell phone he was compelled to have close at hand. The BMW could easily be tracked by the GPS system as well as the cell phone and if he was of a mind, he could alert Scaramanga to his location, (no doubt he has a recent picture, thanks to Jaegers recent picture) so the man could send in a killer group to make him disappear. So the only thing Jaeger, could do was alter his appearance temporarily, stay on the move, park the Beemer several blocks away from the Hostel, and turn off the cell phone and remove the battery, periodically turning it on for messages. That should cut down the odds a tad against a nasty surprise.

He spent the rest of the afternoon taking in the sights. "See Paris and die", was a statement he recalled reading in a novel some time ago. How apt it seemed for the current circumstances. He wondered just why he was on this thankless quest. After all, he'd made a smooth half million on the deal and rid the world of some nasty vermin. Let time pass and memories fade a bit and then go after the guy at his leisure, rather than this headlong rush towards uncertainty. Letting time pass and memories to grow cold would've been the smart move, but sometimes Jaeger wasn't so prudent in his evaluation of a situation. Sometimes, when ya thought you were on a roll, ya just had to go for broke and roll the dice.

Someone up top was clearly watching after Jaeger for some time now, so he just had to go with the flow. After all, Magellan was still alive and apparently prospering. Perhaps he was a man of honor.

As he walked down the entire length of the Champs de Elyse and back, he marveled at the flow of the city, finishing up at the Tomb of Napoleon. A monument to one man's greatness and overblown hubris. Along the way he purchased a bamboo cane, several different pairs of sunglasses and a wide brimmed panama hat as part of the disguise he would use in the days ahead. After dark he drove over to the left bank to enjoy some of the fine food the Michelin touted, careful to park several blocks away from where he was to eat and sit with his back to the wall in the rear of the restaurant where he could see anything that came his way.

He returned back to the Hostel around two AM and was up by six AM and out the door. He would stay on the move until he heard from Magellan.

Every other hour he checked Magellan's cell phone for messages and at eleven in the morning; he had a message from Magellan.

"Hello my friend", said Magellan. "How did your sightseeing trip go"? "Paris is an interesting town Nestor. Any news"?

"Tomorrow our man will gain access to both the Condo and the entire office. He has been instructed precisely what to do and look for as he conducts his testing of the new equipment and will install some counter measures we've worked out if he's not being watched over. So stay on the move as you have and keep the cell phone turned off so no one can track your movements. By the way, how was the food on the Rive Gauche last evening?"

"So you were tracking my car yesterday" said Jaeger.

"Correction my friend, the car is mine and you only have its loan", said Magellan. "By the way how do you like German cars"?

"You may have ruined me for anything American"!

"I thought you'd like it, mon ami. Oh two things more. Please park more than two blocks from the Hostel you're staying at and the same goes for wherever you choose to visit or choose to dine. You are a guest in my city and should be treated accordingly"!

"I'll keep that in mind pal and thanks for the heads up"!

"I will call you tomorrow as soon as things firm up, my friend", then he hung up.

Jaeger thought a moment and then concluded that Magellan was probably OK. In just a few words, he let Jaeger know this was his turf and if he cared to he could probably find him no matter what Jaeger did, as long as he clung to his techie life support crutch. If the Beemer could be found then a bomb could be planted. Oh he could always get behind the dashboard and try to disconnect the GPS system, but his technical skills were wanting in that area. So yet another day of sightseeing and trusting ones luck.

Still, he would be on the move, see the sights, the Louvre', the Eiffel Tower and hide in plain sight.

This business of constantly looking over ones shoulder was starting to get old fast, even though he was having a reasonably good time merging with the hundreds of tourists many of which were with their families, sticking out wide eyed, in wonderment like a sore thumb, just blending in with the others. Boarding a sightseeing bus with others and touring the city, always keeping an eye out. Like any big city, Paris had more than its fair share of hustlers, posing as tour guides, when in reality they were gypsy thieves, ready to pick ones pocket and more if the opportunity presented.

The 'Flick's, or the Police Municipale' were seemingly out in force this day, putting the arm on any number of supposedly tour guides, asking for their papers and finding either that the tour guides had no papers and arresting them or engaging in a foot chase, often coming up empty when the suspects eluded them. Over in Paris, the concept of probable cause apparently was simple suspicion and with good reason.

Towards the end of the day, Jaeger checked his phone for messages, finding that Magellan had placed a call not minutes previously and hit the return call button. Madeleine, his secretary answered the call and immediately put Jaeger through.

"Bon jour Mon Ami", answered Nestor, "And how did your day go"? "Well enough. Any developments"?

"Yes indeed, my man has completed his inspection and is on his way back into the office and he sounds excited. With any luck we may just be able to see just what this Scaramanga fellow looks like. Care to join us"?

"Give me an hour, I'm on my way", said Jaeger.

As he pulled into the rear parking lot, of the Industrial Park that housed Magellan's Security Company he saw the rear metal door open and the smiling face of Magellan looking at him park the BMW.

"Pardon me for showing off, but we have been monitoring the position of the BMW as you made your way here", said Magellan as he greeted Jaeger. As they entered Magellan's office a technician was setting up a video loop for them as Magellan said, "Didier is my finest first year technician. The young man is brilliant. So Didier, impress us"!

"As you may know, this company covets their privacy and we have installed the finest digital video surveillance system available. The first concern was, has anything different been done to our system since we installed it? And the answer is no! The second question is was I able to install the countermeasures we discussed? The answer is yes! Did they watch me like a hawk? The answer is yes, but not all the time! There was just sufficient time to install the counter measures as you've directed, thanks to one of my minders had a case of intestinal problems. I didn't have sufficient time to test my installation, but I'm certain that it all will work"! As I entered Mr. Du Lesseps was not available, but apparently I was expected and another big tough looking man was to be my constant escort for my inspection".

Now the slender young man began to beam brightly as he said, "You asked me to keep my eyes out for someone who appeared to look like a Mediterranean type, small, powerfully built, in his sixties and who looks in charge and I may have found that man sitting behind Mr. Du Lesseps desk as we entered his office. No sooner than we entered and the man yelled at the minder and me, so I was quickly ushered out to begin my inspection at another location. But I'm certain I have the man on tape"!

As the video rolled on, it showed the technician entering the offices of Ajaccio Import Export Ltd. Greeted by a secretary and told to wait, then a very large man in an illfitting suit came out to greet him and leading him all the way down a long corridor and into a large well-appointed office, following his escort as they went through the opened door. Carrying his large work case Didier entered the room turned to his left and caught sight of a man clearly not Gaspard Du Lesseps, but a man in his shirtsleeves working at Mr. Du Lesseps desk.

And there he was a man who clearly didn't want to be seen, yelling obscenities at the duo to leave immediately. Jaeger and Magellan each looked at each other, then back at the video display then back at each other.

Magellan then hit play once again as the video clearly ran for a few minutes longer before he hit the stop button saying to his technician, "And all is in place just as we designed"! "Oui "!

"The day has been a long one for you Didier and you have done well.

We can take it from here young man. Oh, the 'initiator' if you please"! Promptly the technician reached into his work case and brought out what appeared to be a television channel changer at first glance, but in reality was a sophisticated on/off button that would electronically turn off and on the video surveillance system to both the office and the condominium as well as open any door to both places.

After he went through the sequence and the various buttons of the device with pride, he said, "Straight out of a James Bond flick, No"?

Jaeger then replied, "If it all works, your boss might just start calling you 'Q', if not then who knows"?

Didier smiled, picked up his case then left. After the door closed, Magellan then said, "What do you think now, my friend"?

"The guy looks the part. Got that Mediterranean look. Looks about the right age and looks like someone that would like to see someone die slowly just for the hell of it. But if it all works the odds just might have shifted"!

"Let us see if we can improve the odds even more. Pardon me while I call someone who just might have an interest in our enterprise". With that he picked up his office phone and made a call in Jaegers presence. After a few minutes on hold, he connected and for the next fifteen minutes he conducted a highly animated conversation in French with someone that he clearly had a positive relationship with. Jaegers knowledge of French was sketchy at best, but he did catch the name of Scaramanga and du Lesseps during the verbal exchange. After a half an hour some of which was with Magellan being put on hold, his friend came back on the line and after some minutes more Magellan hung up the phone with a smile.

"My friend in the Surete' of course cannot directly have anything to do with this enterprise of ours, but what is on tap, clearly aligns with what he'd like to see happen. Oh we could simply provide a current picture of Scaramanga and they might or might not be able to apprehend the man. If they did arrest him, he would be held and then no doubt a case would be brought against him. Scaramanga would hire a top notch lawyer and might or might not make bail. If he did make bail, then that would complicate things for the authorities. Now if he could be made to have an accident or disappear, difficult as it may be and they had complete access to his place of business, in the form of a timely and unexpected raid on his office, then it would save the state a great deal of time and money rolling up his lieutenants and doing what the system does best"!

"What Didier forgot to mention is that our man Du Lesseps is holed up in Montmartre' with one of his poule' girlfriends with the same intestinal problem that Didier's minder had and I know where he will be for the next several days, being nursed and hors de combat. So he can be gotten to and perhaps through him we can learn something of Scaramanga's schedule. Du Lesseps, as you've no doubt surmised is a fop, a dandy, fallen from the grace by a rich family, due to a gambling problem of long standing. He stays alive only because of the name and standing of his family politically and that he has and continues to be useful to Scaramanga as a front and nothing more. Should he fall upon misfortune few, if any will mourn his passing. He shouldn't be difficult. Finally should we need, we can probably obtain several retired members of the old Special Action Group, to run shotgun in our behalf. They may be old but I'm told they can still shoot straight. Now they can't be directly involved, given their status, but should they just be wandering by and see a disturbance…Finally, should we need it and we will, we can have access to a Ecurevil training helicopter, from the Academy Militaire' at St. Cyr just outside of the city along with a pilot I know of that can keep his mouth shut"!

"You lead and I'll follow sport, just as long as I get to meet this Scaramanga", said Jaeger. Magellan then got up and went to his wall closet and shoving aside an assortment of cold weather garments, went to a secret door and upon opening it revealed a mini armory saying, if I recall, you have this penchant for revolvers, so the only one I have is a well-used breakfront Webley .45 that's older than any of us, but is reliable", as he handed the short three inch barreled weapon to Jaeger along with a box of half-moon clips ready loaded. Then he returned with an old Browning Hi Power 9mm automatic and five clips ready loaded at fifteen rounds per clip, along with a screw on silencer, finally he emerged with a box of stun grenades, placing it on his desk, handing three to Jaeger and keeping three for himself, returning the remainder to his interior compartment and closing everything up.

"Your Webley is loaded with .45 expandables, I trust you don't mind.

Good only for close work, while I have armour piercing rounds and a select fire mechanism on the Browning that can fire at full auto if needed. But before we go out, I must reserve that helicopter", Magellan said as he picked up the office phone. As they left the building Magellan grabbed a small gym bag to bring along saying, "What's inside can get us through any locked door"!

Jaeger tossed the keys of the BMW, back to Magellan as they left the rear entrance saying, "Here, it's your car and your city"! As they drove across the City and over the Seine river towards Montmartre', Jaeger said, "I suppose that after this evening you'll be in like Flynn, with the Surete' "! "It's always good policy to have friends in high places, besides over the years I've missed the action. Before this night is through I may regret that sentiment, but there it is, the die is cast"! Once they arrived at the old building badly in need of refurbishment, Magellan pulled the BMW sedan over to the curb a block away, where a parking space was to be found.

Both men walked down the sidewalk of the seedy neighborhood with Magellan taking the lead, carrying his little dark gym bag, closest to the buildings and Jaeger following some five yards behind closest to the crumbling curbs. Running up the front stoop of the building, Magellan encountered an old woman struggling with unlocking the front door while holding a package. He said something to the woman, who smiled handed him the packages temporarily, fumbled with the key, eventually opening the front door, as Magellan handed back the packages and signaled for Jaeger to follow them inside.

The old woman continued on to the rear of the building on the first floor, while Jaeger and Magellan climbed the four flights of stairs to the top floor, where four apartments flanked the staircase. Moving quietly they stopped at the rear apartment. Magellan looked under the doorjamb and seeing light underneath, tried the door knob and as it turned free, he looked at Jaeger whispering, "I guarantee we will need 'Le Tool' later on my friend", motioning to the black gym bag. He placed the bag by the edge of the doorjamb and he reached for his Browning automatic and screwed the silencer into the barrel, nodded his head and opened the door. In a split second the door opened and both men were in the apartment, with Jaeger quickly closing the door as Magellan took two steps forward and turned to his left seeing a slender woman in the small kitchenette, dressed in a slip and washing some dishes. She quickly turned as the Browning coughed twice, while Jaeger quickly made for the bed, where du Lesseps lay watching the television, clearly in distress, wearing adult diapers. As Jaeger reached the bed, du Lesseps was reaching under his pillow, his face a mask of surprise, as Jaegers Webley crashed down upon his head. Jaeger reached under the pillow and pulled out a small caliber Biretta automatic.

Jaeger turned towards the kitchenette, to see Magellan gently laying the scantily clad woman down on the floor to die. As Magellan rose up and looked at Jaeger he said, "She was one of thousands of Poule's. She won't be missed"! Then he saw the small automatic in Jaegers hand saying, "Seems apropos. A small weapon for a smaller man"!

"Yeah, but one in the skull might change your thinking Pal", said Jaeger as he put the gun in his coat pocket.

They put a clean diaper on du Lesseps, rounded up his clothes and dressed him as Magellan said, "You bring him down and I'll get the car", as he left the apartment and grabbed his black bag. Jaeger then hoisted the limp body upon his shoulder and left the apartment, mindful of the key he spotted upon the dresser and with the television set on as well as the lights, he left the apartment and locked the door, mindful to twist his hands upon the doorknob several times, thus leaving no hand prints.

As he went out the front door and down the stoop, Magellan arrived opening the rear door as Jaeger wrestled his cargo into the back seat, joining him as the BMW sped off into the night. Magellan then dialed a number on his dashboard mobile phone and in French had a brief conversation then hung up saying, "Our air taxi will be on its way back to a place near my office"! Driving back across the Seine River at night Jaeger interrupted the silence by saying, "I can see why you chose Paris to make your home, for it's even more beautiful at night"!

"Yes it does my friend, but as you can see, like any big city it has its dark side. But who knows, perhaps someday under less onerous circumstances, you will return and allow me to be your guide. But be warned, in order to truly enjoy Paris, one must not be rushed or on a schedule of any kind"!

"Pal, I'll keep that in mind"! A half hour later they arrived as du Lesseps was starting to awaken struggling against his restraints and his gag, with the look of sheer terror in his eyes. Pulling into the deserted office warehouse complex, not a mile distant from Magellan's office, they stopped and waited. Not three minutes after the engine was shut off, the whizzing sound of a French Ecuevil helicopter signaled its approach with its lights out. As it touched the ground, Magellan entered the passenger compartment carrying his black bag as Jaeger followed, shouldering an inert and limp du Lesseps ahead of him none too gently and followed him into the chopper closing the door as the pilot ascended, up and away from the dark parking lot. As the pilot gained altitude away from the landing area, he turned the crafts red and amber running lights full on as the chopper made its way towards the English Channel.

Coming alert and feeling his hands secured behind his back, as well as his legs secured together by plastic restraints, Gaspard Du Lesseps found himself sitting between Magellan and Jaeger. Surprisingly the helicopter was well insulated, as the sound from the engines was minimal allowing for a normal speaking environment as du Lesseps looked to his right and exclaimed, "Magellan, why have I been abducted in this manner"?

Magellan turned to his captive saying, "Ask him, it's his party", nodding towards Jaeger, who removed his hat and glasses! Du Lesseps face filled with horror as he saw Jaeger and as he tried to speak, Jaeger silenced him with, "All we want to know pal is where this Scaramanga is and what time he's gonna be there.

Trying to muster the strength to speak, du Lesseps opted to try and brazen things out by saying, "I'm not my brother's keeper and what happened to my girlfriend"?

"She's didn't make it my friend and your only option is to tell us what we need to know", said Magellan as he looked out into the night!

"Where are you taking me", asked Du Lesseps?

"For a midnight sightseeing trip of the English Channel", answered Magellan, who then pushed a button on his intercom and asked the pilot about the arrival time at the channel.

"In about twenty minutes, more or less," answered the heavily accented pilot!

"So my friend, in about twenty minutes we will either know the whereabouts and time of Scaramanga, or else, you will go for a test flight. It's your choice", answered Magellan casually.

The next ten minutes was filled with the eerie silence of conversation, the only sound coming from the muffled sound of the engine as the helicopter sped towards the Channel.

Then over the compartment speaker came the sound of the pilot saying, "Radar indicates the Channel coming up in about ten minutes"!

The craft was flying at about five hundred feet altitude and during a quarter moon the channel was difficult to see at night, guided more by dead reckoning and the lights that shown down below. Then Magellan said casually, "Once we reach the Channel, Hector will ascend to a height of about three thousand feet. I certainly hope that you have special powers of flight, like the children read in comic books, for the human body is not suited for hitting a body of water from such a height. Survival is highly uncertain"!

Still, Du Lesseps remained silent and yet the perspiration that flooded his brow and the Odor that started to come from him indicated that he was weakening as he finally said, "I'm not a well man as you can see"!

Prompting Jaeger to say, "Tell us what we need to know and we'll see that you're taken care of. Other than that, we'll still get to Scaramanga; it'll just make things a little more difficult"!

Several minutes later, they felt the helicopter gain altitude as du Lesseps asked in a panic, "What is happening"?

Just then the pilot came on the speaker saying, "We've just crossed the frontier and are over the Channel"!

Still, Du Lesseps clung to silence as his mind raced in terror. If he told them what they wanted to know and they failed to kill Scaramanga, his life would be over and his death would be long in coming, slow in duration. If he remained silent a horrible death was certain. His decision made, his only apparent option was to tell them what they wanted to know and hope they succeeded, still at very best his life, or whatever remained would be altered forever.

"I didn't know that Scaramanga would not pay you the remainder of your remittance, Monsieur Jaeger. I had no party to that"!

"Well pal, you were the one who fronted for the man and you were the one who hired me to do a job. So you are the one we've got up here and you've got one mighty slim chance for survival and only one", said Jaeger.

Just then the aircraft seemed to level out having achieved its desired altitude and started to gradually slow in its speed, as the pilot announced, "We have arrived at the designated altitude"! A minute later the helicopter seemed to hang in the air as it hovered over the Channel waters below.

"Times up" said Jaeger! Followed by Magellan chanting, "The time has come", the Walrus said, "To talk of many things. Of shoes and ships and sealing wax, of cabbages and kings and why the sea is boiling hot and whether pigs have wings, or not"!

He let that statement hang in the air a moment, and then made to open the cabin door as Du Lesseps finally cried out, "I am due in his office tomorrow to sign checks and contracts and Scaramanga and his people will be in the office all night, in preparation. I should have been in the office today, to help but I was ill and Scaramanga had to arrive to sort things out which is why your technician saw Scaramanga today", the words came tumbling out in a rush.

"So he and his people will be there all night long", asked Magellan"?

"Yes, till dawn"!

As Jaeger looked at Magellan, they both nodded at each other, as Jaeger immediately opened the rear cabin door on his side and yanked the skinny Du Lesseps out of his seat and out of the helicopter without a word, shutting the door immediately. The pilot then pushed the crafts collective forward as the helicopter gained speed, turned and made its way back to land.

"My friend you lied to Monsieur Du Lesseps, did you not", grinned Magellan.

"Jesus Christ man, I think I said that if he fessed up, I'd see that he was taken care of. No one asked me how he'd be taken care of. Besides, he was starting to smell from his diaper and I don't think the pilot, who's doing a favor will like flying all the way back to Paris in a Shit Copter would he"?

Just then the pilot came on over the speaker saying, "Nestor, the man is right, so give him his due"!

"Well said Hector, well said! To the roof of Scaramanga's office building", said Nestor! Jaeger nodded saying, "Hector's doing a great job flying so why stop now"? Magellan picked up his cell phone and placed a call, speaking in French to others briefly then hung up saying, "The others on the ground have been alerted. While not able to assist us directly, in our assault, they will be in place to divert any untoward arrival by the local authorities in case things get out of hand"! "How so", asked Jaeger!

"During our initial upgrading of Scaramanga's security, we had to integrate his new system with the buildings existing security system. To accomplish that we had to gain access to the system. The buildings system is not state of the art, but sufficient enough under normal circumstances. On the roof is a helipad and their HVAC systems cooling towers. The helipad is wired with sensors that will alert the security guard downstairs in the lobby of any landing after hours. We don't want that so the chopper will deposit us on the roof elsewhere, while still in hover mode, and then depart back to St. Cyr for refueling. It will take the craft twelve minutes flying time back St. Cyr, another fifteen minutes to top off its tanks, then will be on standby, on the ground till Hector hears from us. It can be back on the roof top within fifteen minutes of hearing from us. We will enter the building through the rooftop metal door and down the fire stairs to Scaramanga's floor. Of course the fire door from the roof and Scaramanga's floor will be locked and engaged electronically to the buildings security system, which is why I brought the gym bag along. Inside a mechanical devise that will open and secure any locked door".

"Covered all bases have you", mused Jaeger.

"Not all my friend. We don't know how many Corsicans will be in the office with Scaramanga or how well they are armed. Assume the worst and the rest is up to us. Which reminds me, reach under your seat, for a little reassurance", said Magellan who pulled out a Kevlar vest and took off his coat and started to slip into the vest. "I hope I guessed your correctly size my friend", as they helped each other into their vests. "Latest in fashion militaire'. Should stop anything up to a magnum round, courtesy of the Academie Militare' at St. Cyr. Of course they'll have to be returned afterward and any penetrations will have to be accounted for, but that problem is assigned to Hector"!

Twenty minutes later, the French Ecurevil, approached the building hovering at a point just ten feet away from the helipad, its skids three feet off the ground, as Magellan and Jaeger, skipped off the skids, with Jaeger the last out securing the rear door and to the roof below. The pilot without a word moved the collective forward and flew off into the night, its lights periodically flashing.

"Now my friend is where the master enters" said Magellan who removed a small device as they stood before the metal roof top door, to the stairwell. "The good news is that there will be no cameras in the stairwell, thanks to the developer who built the building and none on any of the floors hallways". Within thirty seconds, Magellan's machine unlocked the door.

He put the device back into the bag then removed a thin rectangular piece of metal and a metal roll of aluminum tape as Jaeger slowly opened the door, the sliver of metal was deftly inserted, between the door and the metal sensor on the doorframe, in order not to break the circuit. Then Jaeger sliced a large section of the metal tape and handed it to Magellan, who said. "Once this tape is on, it's on for good, for the air activates a wonderful American invention called Super Glue. So we don't have to concern ourselves about a repeat of Watergate"! They entered the stairwell and descended to the floor containing Scaramanga's office, performing the very same procedure on the stairwell fire door to gain entry to the floor.

Now on the subject's floor, Jaeger followed Magellan to his right, avoiding the obvious front entry to Scaramanga's offices and to an unmarked door at the end of the hallway.

Our only concern may be the cleaning crew that works at night that we might run into. But Scaramanga's lease contract allows for his own people to perform that function, so once inside. He reached inside the bag and produced the hand device that looked like a TV channel changer, punching in a series of numbers and then seeing a green light, light up on the devise said, "The video system is now overridden and is not functioning anywhere in his offices. As we move through his office, allow me to go first since I have the silenced weap on and with this device I can electronically open any door in his office. Of course they will all have to be eliminated for you to do your work, agreed"?

Jaeger nodded his head in silence. They quickly entered the rear door of the office complex, moving down a short hallway that connected with another hallway that ran the entire length of the building. Flanking each other as Magellan peered quickly around the corner, he whispered, "Turn to your right and at the end of the hallway is Scaramanga's office, but wait until I've cleared the length of the hallway"! Jaeger nodded his head as Magellan rounded the corner, working his way down the main hallway, sticking his head in each office, his silenced automatic quickly spitting a quiet double tap, at each individual encountered. In Jaeger's mind it almost seemed too easy as Magellan was now almost halfway down the corridor, when two men appeared in the hallway as Magellan was dispatching another. Quickly recognizing that their security was compromised, one of the men tried to reach for his weapon while the other ducked back inside his office. As Magellan was partially hidden from the others in his victim's doorway, firing twice, he heard and felt three bullets fly just past his body, as Jaeger had fired on the duo down the hall, two of the bullets finding their mark in one of the workers as he lay crumpled in the hallway.

Magellan quickly looked at Jaeger who indicated that one other had ducked back into his office. Seizing the advantage, Magellan ran past the reception area, reaching for a stun grenade in his pocket and pulling the pin as he passed the office and tossing the grenade inside the man's office then ducking into another open door as the grenade exploded.

Jaeger fired three times more as several others emerged from other offices, with weapons drawn. Hitting one and grazing another, then quickly reloaded as he ducked back in his own hallway near Scaramanga's office.

Suddenly he heard automatic gunfire, from his end of the hallway, which could only mean that whoever was in Scaramanga's office, had decided to join the party and spray the hallway in hope of his bullets finding the right target. If it hit any of his people, well so be it for the fortunes of war.

Jaeger dropped down to floor level and allowed his Webley to peek around the corner and quickly fired off, all six rounds in rapid succession at knee top level in hope of just one finding its mark. The fifth round found its way luckily into a spot just above Scaramanga's knee, dropping him with a shout to the floor. Jaeger quickly peeked around the corner as he heard more firing down the other end of the hallway and ran towards Scaramanga as he was trying to insert another clip into his Uzi automatic. Quickly kicking the struggling figure in the head as he reached him, seeing the body go limp, he grabbed the Uzi and completed the reload, kicking the head once again a glancing blow and made his way down the hallway to see if Magellan needed any help. Just after he passed the main entrance, he saw a form stagger Out of one of the offices that received the stun grenade, through the smoke and fired a Short burst at point blank range, driving the man backwards into the smoke filled room. He quickly closed the door to that room, before too much smoke could drift out into the main hallway, triggering the fire alarm system, shortening their possibility of their visit.

Then he saw Magellan as he poked his head around the corner of one of the offices twenty feet away, as Magellan made a sign that two remained, down the hallway in two different offices, apparently it the hope of catching the invaders in a crossfire. Magellan indicated that he would go first as he slid a fresh clip into his automatic and flicking the small lever to Full Auto.

Although the office doors in the building were of solid wood, the office walls were, built of sheetrock fastened to aluminum wall studs, hardly any protection from any bullets no matter how small the caliber. As Magellan silently took a few steps towards one of the offices, he then broke into a run and started to fire into the wall as he passed an office.

As he passed that office, diving towards the hallway floor in a rolling maneuver another form ducked out of a doorway, taking two quick shots at Magellan, failing to look behind him as a loud short burst from Jaegers Uzi, dropped him like a stone.

Jaeger ran towards Magellan, firing a round into the man's head, just to make certain of no unpleasant surprises later on. Jaeger stopped in mid stride, then backed up peering into the room that had a string of bullet holes in the hallways wall. He saw a man clearly driven back across a desk, still, mouth agape and staring blindly at the ceiling, gun in hand and what appeared as an open safe strewn with papers. His attention quickly returned to Magellan, who was struggling to get up and ran to asking, "Were you hit"?

Magellan opened his coat and they both saw nothing. Then he removed his coat and it revealed two bullet holes in the coat and two more indentations in the Kevlar vest, in Magellan's back, prompting him to muse, "It only hurts for a little while", as he put the coat back on and said, "You did well by closing the door, to the smoke filled office. They shut off the air-conditioning system at midnight so I'm guessing that we've barely fifteen minutes available until the smoke sets off the fire alarm system. What about Scaramanga"?

"He's down at the other end"!

"Then I suggest you tend to him while I clean up at this end", said Magellan as Jaeger nodded and went back along the hallway placing a bullet from his reloaded Webley in each of the victims heads as he passed for insurance.

As he reached the end of the main hallway, he saw that Scaramanga had come to his senses and was struggling to rise. Without losing a step, Jaeger grabbed Scaramanga by his collar as he passed and dragged the man back into his spacious office, throwing the man onto a very expensive looking leather couch. As Jaeger glanced around the office, he said, "Nice digs you have Pal"!

Scaramanga looked up at his assailant with half lidded eyed, filled with pain and hatred as he asked, "Who are you"?

"Does it matter Pal", Jaeger replied letting that answer hang in the air a moment? "Well of course it must to you. As for my name, you know my name already, for you owe me a great deal of money for past services rendered"!

Thinking a moment then really looking at his enemy, his UZI hanging on Jaegers shoulder and a pistol in his hand he suddenly blurted out, wide eyed, "Jaeger"!

"Good for you, you still have a brain left, for the moment. Ya should have paid me Pal"!

"You exceeded your instructions, in Peru", yelled Scaramanga, "and ruined my business there. I'll never pay you"!

"Truth is, you were never gonna pay me anyway and its way past the point about being about mere money Pal. Your time on earth is soon to end", said Jaeger as he approached the couch. As he bent over the prostrate Scaramanga, suddenly the man lifted from the couch and a flash of metal caught Jaegers eye just in time as it came up suddenly towards Jaegers midsection, the blade caroming off his belt buckle and glancing up past his chest tearing past the Kevlar fabric and missing his eye by a fraction. Jaeger reacted quickly by trapping his arm and burying his elbow into Scaramanga's jaw, wrenching the flick blade from the man's hand and closing it, and putting it into his coat pocket.

"No more Boulliabaise for you Pal", said Jaeger as he looked around and saw one of Scaramanga's expensive leather clad smoking chairs, there next to the tall picture window. He walked over to the chair hoisting it up over his head and threw it through the window, quickly turning towards Scaramanga as he was recovering from Jaegers blow.

"Damn your some kinda tough, but it's now time for your flight test, as he drug a struggling Scaramanga towards the now open, floor to ceiling window space, hoisting him up over his head, leaving him hanging for a brief moment and pressing him forward through the jagged edges, towards the street down below.

He quickly turned around and left the office to join up with Magellan, placing his elbow on the light switch on his way out, turning out the office lights. As he came into the hallway, he saw Magellan walking towards him while on his cell phone.

As they made their way in silence up the fire stair well towards the roof, each knew the others business was concluded.

Once they reached the roof Magellan reached into his bag and removed the TV channel changer, punching a few buttons then saying,

"Right about now, the Security system will be reengaged and the devices inserted to interrupt them will dissolve into a blob of protoplasm"!

Jaeger then took notice of the large brown, thick looking leather briefcase sitting on the roof top next to Magellan's bag of tricks and meant to ask about it, but instead asked, "How about our ride"?

"That was the purpose of my cell phone call as I came down the hallway. Hector is en route and should be here, shortly after we conclude our cigarettes", said Magellan reaching into his coat pocket and producing his own private brand offering one to Jaeger.

In the distance after their cigarettes went out and both men field stripped each butt, tossing the remnants over the buildings parapet, approached a helicopter, from the northeast. Suddenly, a mile away, its running lights went dark as it gently lit down and hovered several feet above the building and took on its passengers, then lifted up quickly into the night sky, turning back on its running lights, after it was a mile away.

Minutes later it landed at the parking lot a mile away from Magellan's business, running lights again distinguished, disgorging its passengers, lifting off quickly into the night, again turning on its running lights as it achieved altitude and distance.

Magellan then drove Jaeger back to a block from his Hostel, in silence, his car radio on playing a Grace Jones lilting tango sung in French on the way. As the BMW idled by the curb, both men looked at each other, like brothers in arms, with a bond that was to last a lifetime. Each nodded his head to the other and smiled. Jaeger emerging from the car and looked around as Magellan drove off down the narrow street into the night. Jaeger looked at his watch and decided that it was time for an early breakfast, seeing an all-night Boulangerie open a block away, he decided upon croissants and some strong coffee.

He lingered for some time until eight in the morning when he went go to his room at the hostel, took a shower, dressed, packed to leave, paid his bill, retrieve his passport and grabbed a taxi to the Aerodrome.

As his flight over the Atlantic flew westward, he was sitting alone in first class, thinking about the grand adventure he'd just experienced. He looked at his watch and already considered that it must be midafternoon and glanced over the English language edition of Le Monde that he'd purchased just before boarding. The name of Scaramanga emblazoned across the front page caught his eye and he thought it would make good reading as he passed the long flight home. After lunch and with everything cleared away, he put on his reading glasses and started to read. The French Press apparently concluded that Scaramanga's flight through the buildings window and the after-hours massacre within his office was nothing more than an underworld turf battle, by professional operatives. Gone missing was the Director General of the Import Export Company, one Gaspard du Lesseps.

The Gendarmes were apparently combing the crime scene for evidence, coming up with only the gradual identities of known Corsican underworld operatives, with no known leads as to the identies of those who engineered and undertook the massacre. One of the crime reporters, in an opinion piece, came to the conclusion that, "Since no innocents came to any harm, although the Gendarmerie were apparently working diligently and with purpose, in a professional manner, that nothing of any consequence would come of the investigation. Thus it must be a thoroughly professional hit, designed to send a message that others had taken over"!

Suddenly as Jaeger put the paper down, he then thought of the brown briefcase that Magellan lugged out of Scaramanga's office. He'd meant to ask just what was in the briefcase, but with all that was occurring, it had simply slipped his mind. He'd gotten exactly what he'd come for.

Scaramanga's death and that was sufficient. Besides, there was one less bad guy in this world. Correction, the entire leadership of the Corsican Mob in France was kaput sending the European underworld reeling, for the time being, according to Le Monde.

It then reoccurred to him how close he'd come to death himself, allowing himself to get sloppy at the very last moment, with Scaramanga's blade coming out of nowhere and snagging on his belt buckle and missing his eye by a hairs breadth, then as he was just about to enter the airport he suddenly remembered Scaramanga's flick knife in his coat pocket, disposing of it in a trash receptacle prior to entering the building. He briefly wondered why, he eluded death in one instance and what jarred his memory in the other? What brought both occurrences about? As he gazed out the cabins porthole, he viewed the little fluffy clouds in a distance floating in the air and then he knew.

Several days later he received a Federal Express package, by messenger and upon opening it were several envelopes containing Swiss bearer bonds, redeemable in Swiss currency. Each bond was in the amount of two hundred thousand Swiss Francs. All he had to do was sign his name and produce his bona fides, as the bearer of record, at any banking house equipped to handle international transactions. A raft of clippings from the English language edition of Le Monde, gave a running account of the investigation the French authorities was conducting of their little adventure.

In a separate envelope was a small letter from Magellan, thanking him for "Le Grande' Adventure' ", and telling him not to be concerned about any of their associates, for they were all, to a man, well taken care of for their efforts. Also in the letter was Magellan's personal contact information, should he ever decide to visit the City of Lights, for a personal visit, as long as he didn't look the part of 'Le Touriste'.

Since nothing was on Jaegers schedule of immediate importance for the moment, he decided that a trip to the Bahamas Islands was in the offing.

There was a banker to visit and a tan to work on. 'So "that" what was in the heavy brown briefcase', thought Jaeger.

13

President Magnusson was now well into his second year in office, during the hottest and driest summer anyone could remember. America was still reeling from a massive recession, its national debt nudging the nation towards oblivion and the branches of congress bickering amongst themselves, none giving way to rational thinking.

Magnusson was busy almost around the clock, doing what he could to trim the sails of the executive branches of government, nudging cabinet secretaries at every turn to eliminate waste, maintain or trim their annual budget requests and lower the overall annual costs to the government. He ordered each branch of his cabinet to have their inspector general's turn over their annual reports directly to the oval office, thus bypassing the normal procedure and what was revealed was a massive editing of those reports by many of their bosses as to waste and corruption. One by one, a number of the cabinet secretaries, he inherited were asked to resign, eventually being replaced by others with congressional approval.

While the cost of governance was continuing to escalate overall, at least the executive branch of the government was leveling off cost wise and then starting to diminish, quarter by quarter.

In his every available moment, Lars Magnusson was flying to the various parts of the nation, directly inserting himself wherever Federal bottle necks occurred due to lax management by agency officials. It got to a point that his unexpected arrivals in an area, was about as welcome as a visit from the 'Sixty Minute' news crew, usually resulting in a rapid and sometimes long overdue, on the spot retirement or resignation. In due course, the various offices of inspector general of the various departments achieved almost carte' blanch status, reporting their findings, both to their respective cabinet secretaries and the Oval office, unedited.

The President was rapidly making friends amongst the rank and file of government employees that cared about efficient governance, earning their trust and confidence as a host of upper managerial policy makers were replaced. But simultaneously, The President and members of his staff were held with scant regard, by those who felt the verbal lash at their incompetence, finding themselves quickly out of government.

The White House began a series of revelations to selected members of the media that eagerly revealed the existing malfeasance and incompetence of those in government prompting some in the media of accusing the President of conducting something akin to a Stalinist purge of government officials. Therefore offering the media a plethora of news worthy reportage and the public at large, much to consider.

He'd not had a direct Presidential news conference since he'd been in office, speaking to the pubic officially on but two occasions since he'd taken office, via the annual State of the Union offerings.

Succumbing to pressure from the media, he adjusted his schedule to make his first official televised, Presidential News Conference from the White House.

All afternoon of the day of the televised news conference, he was occupied in the Oval Office, in a closed door meeting with Van Harvanian, his Press Secretary and Orval Goodwin, his Chief of Staff, ironing out his notes regarding likely subjects to comment on and more important, likely questions the reporters might ask. In keeping with his policy of reasonable openness and transparency, no prearranged schedule of reporters to select was adhered to.

Members of the media would raise their hands and the President would select those in random order. As the trio concluded their preparations for the evening's event, the President caught sight of Chief of Staff staring at his shoes with a worried look on his face, asking, "Orval, what's the matter now"?

Goodwin looked up and replied, "We just issued Oliver Hastings, his credentials for attendance this evening at the news conference"!

"Yes, I know. Van informed me when the request came through and I said yes. You will note that Van has him seated right in the middle of the pack of the White House scribes"!

"Then Mr. President why on earth would you ever dignify the man by accepting his request to attend your televised news conference, when you know damn well that he's been ripping you a new one for the last six months, every week in his national column. The son of a bitch is a yellow journalist of the first class, who deals in outright lies, unfounded gossip and innuendo. No good can come of this, none at all"!

"Orval, I insisted that our friend Mr. Hastings attend this evening, of all evenings and I knew that you would object just as you are now and for good reason. Yes I've read every word that elitist bastard has written about both me and my family, holding my water all the time. You'll note that we have refused an interview with him each time a request came through, so his invite will seem as if our overworked office had screwed up and he squeaked on through by mistake. What I'm counting on is his overconfidence and his overabundant hubris this evening. I plan on calling upon him this evening, at some point whether he raises his hand or not. In his parlance, "He will be laying doggo, in the tall grass, just waiting to pounce"!

"But thanks to Van here we have a bit of a surprise. Van being a student of Roman history reminded me of his understanding of Caesars Gallic Wars. When parleying with a Helvetian Chieftain, his legions severely outnumbered, he let the Chieftain, go on and on about how they were going to slay every Roman Legionnaire to the last man. When the man was finished with his diatribe, Caesar calmly said something akin to, "The gods allow some men to run amok for extended periods of time, so when the end arrives, as it always does, the pain is more keenly felt"! As for Caesar, the following day his Legions, severely outnumbered, did battle with the Barbarians, winning the day, due to superior generalship and the hard discipline of the Roman Legions, driving them from the field, capturing their Chieftain and his entire family as they tried to run. The family was sold into slavery upon his return to Rome in triumph and the Chieftain was held in a dungeon for a time then privately strangled"!

"Now should the man arrive, as we expect, he'll be walking into a very public trap, he'll regret for whatever is left of his miserable life. With any luck, this will take the wind out of the sails of the so called, Egalitarian Elitist's for a while and all I have to do is provide the bait and set the trap, letting Hastings do the rest"!

"Well I still don't like it Mr. President, for the guy is Satan personified, but since it seems that you're hell bent to destroy the man, what can I do to help if anything"?

"Light a candle Orval", said Harvanian! We can't be turning the other cheek anymore, because it's time to fight fire with fire"!

"This entire thing has your prints on it Van", said Goodwin!

"Not his idea, Orval. It's all mine. He also advised against it, but being the delightful cretin that he is, summoned his dark Machiavellian instincts, laying out a superb battle plan", answered Magnusson. The meeting broke up, Magnusson going to the White House kitchen directly to take his evening meal directly, peering over the shoulder of one of the cooks as he charbroiled a large T-bone to a turn, then nestled between two thick sliced of freshly baked sourdough bread replete with garlic butter. He went over to one of the stainless steel preparation tables, sliding a stool beneath him and took his first bite, giving the thumbs up signal to the cook with a wide smile. When a journeyman cook working in the Chief Executives kitchen personally prepares a meal for his ultimate boss and he receives the thumbs up, nothing in the world seems of greater importance.

After the meal, Magnusson walked upstairs, took a shower, shaved and dressed in the clothes that had been laid out for him by his private staff. He went over his pre rehearsed presentation to the nation at large, in his mind and the anticipated questions from the White House Press Corps. Try as he may a degree of nervousness started to set in, somewhat akin to what he felt long ago playing College football. The pregame jitters. As his success as a football player developed he learned gradually how to deal with it, usually fading away upon first contact with the opposing team, being replaced by personal resolve and concentration.

But this was quite different. Far more than a stadium full of screaming fanatics, he was addressing not only a room full of skillful and seasoned reporters, all far more clever than he. He would not have the release of physical combat to drive away the jitters, but he had to dig deep and engage them with his wit and mind. He must appear in command and certain at all times answering quickly and in a concise manner. He was the Commander in Chief of the most successful and powerful nation on the planet in known history and must be what America needed badly.

An effective leader of a society and a nation. He must attack problems, not ponder or shy away. He must run to the sound of conflict and win the day. For the time was now. As the lawyers would say, "Time is of the essence"!

Finally there was Oliver Hastings. An individual he'd never met, who somehow made it his personal crusade to verbally destroy the office of the Presidency. Magnusson vowed this must not happen, praying to whatever celestial entity that was at hand to provide the subtlety and finesse to verbally skewer the man.

As he put the final touches in crafting the double Windsor knot on his neck tie, fretting over it, in getting it just right, in walked the butler, with his brilliantly shined shoes. They glistened, for the man was a former Marine in his youth and insisted that those in his charge look the part. As Magnusson put on his dress jacket, the butler fretted over him, carefully tending to the lint that inevitably collected, then stepped back for a final critical inspection.

"Well, how do I look", asked Magnusson?

A man of few words, the butler answered, "Mr. President, you'll do"!

That was about as good as it got from the man, as they both nodded at each other and he made his way downstairs, followed by his butler.

Normally, the bulk of the White House staff, went to their homes at the end of their respective work day, but on this day, the entire staff, was on the premises, to cheer on the President, for the word went around this was a pivotal moment in his Presidency and during his time in office, he'd earned the loyalty and respect from each and every one. It was a source of never ending irritation for reporters, to question the staff about the most trivial matters concerning the President. His private tendencies and possible quirks in the never ending effort to create news worthy items of interest. But they always clammed up saying the standard, "I know nothing"! As he came to the foot of the stairs, he saw the entire staff assembled and was greeted by a modest round of applause, as he made his way through the crowd to the staging area. Followed by Orval Goodwin, Van Harvanian and his personal secretary Melanie O'Bannon, Magnusson suddenly turned and addressed those assembled, with a grin,

"I hope those of you who're off duty, punched out on your time clocks", followed by a slow wink!

Then a slew of comments came from those assembled as he passed, "Break a leg and Give em hell, Mr. President! As he stopped just short of the door that led to the hallway of the Grand Ballroom, He was joined by Goodwin, Harvanian and Melanie O'Bannon. It was his personal secretary that handed him his leather bound cover to his legal pad, containing the bullet pointed notes that she had typed, for him to refer to during his presentation. Everyone knew that he'd memorized what was written down and that he'd crammed endless facts and figures into his head, in preparation for the event.

"Well Mel, how do I look", he asked as his secretary was giving him one last once over, touching his tie just to confirm that his visuals were on the mark!

"Mr. President you're about as good as it gets"!

Then he asked, "Any thoughts or concerns Mel"?

"No thoughts, Mr. President. As for what's ahead of you out there, Screw them all and the horses they rode in on"! That prompted immediate laughter and appropriate surprise from the rest, especially since the Presidents Secretary was well known as an extremely polite and efficient individual, known to keep her linguistic acumen at a high level. All that came to know her, discovered she had scant tolerance for fools, serving her President well in the process.

That well timed comment served to break the ice and moderate the tension as Magnusson replied, "Spoken well, by a true Texan woman and thanks Mel"!

Harvanian then put his hand to his ear, getting instructions to approach from the media director, through his earpiece and went through the door and approached the podium to introduce the President. This was the signal that his appearance would commence within two minutes.

The trio stood quietly and calmly awaiting Harvanians summons, "Ladies and Gentlemen, the President of the United States! When he heard the introduction through the door, Magnusson took a deep breath and entered the hall way and proceed to the podium amidst a round of polite and restrained applause. He opened his leather folio and laid it in front of him as he put on his glasses and waited for those assembled to be seated.

"Ladies and Gentlemen, I must apologize for keeping the media at bay, for it was not my intent. Were we living in a different time, I'd be far more accessible, but as most everyone knows, I've been a little busy for the months since I assumed office. The conflicts in the middle east, the horrendous tragedy in Texas, namely the bombings of Houston's office structures, the slew of Hurricanes that mother nature chose to give a broadside to out Gulf States and both coasts of Florida in particular and in my spare time cleaning out the graft and inefficiencies in the Executive Branch of the Federal Government. As most of you have eagerly reported, my cabinet has been in the process of a complete overhaul, which required my delving past the cabinet level administrators, deep into the ranks of middle management of each agency, gaining access to unedited reports from each agencies Inspector General's office and discovering what and who is relevant to the efficient operation of the executive branch of the government. Now as most of you know, a number of people have departed from governmental service to the private sector. Most of these were of relatively high paying positions, where either the individual was, shall we say, found wanting in skills or motivation to be an effective manager of his resources, chief of which were his employees, while in other cases, people opted for retirement and we allowed attrition to take its normal course"!

"What is taking so agonizingly long is that the last thing anyone wants to happen is to engage in massive layoffs, thus tossing the baby out with the bathwater. Those who departed were either found incapable and in a number of instances, their departments were found to serve no useful purpose and should've been abolished by congress long ago. It would have been easy to slash Federal spending with an ax, but instead we opted to use a scalpel. Our work, in this regard still goes forward as I speak. The number of Federal Agencies created by congress over time and I might add, by both political parties, serve no useful purpose and stay on the books by appearing to be busy performing 'make work' functions is astounding. I can't tell you of the number of times, Inspector Generals, interested in efficiency, paid surprise visits to agencies regional and district offices, conducting audits to discover that little of any consequence was being done to justify their existence. Yet there they were, for years consuming taxpayer's dollars, in an infinite variety of ways, for no discernible purpose"!

"The entire country, in case it has escaped anyone's notice, is experiencing a crises of debt, never known since the end of the great depression suffered by our grandparent's. The causes are many, but chiefly self-generated. By government trying to be all things to all people, by engaging in costly wars, which were badly executed as a result of attempting the become the world's conscience and further as a result of the feckless inaction of the body politic of the United Nations, originally intended to put an end to International aggression.

"We have met the enemy and he is us", said the cartoon character Pogo Possum as he observed the machinations of his mythical swamp. Were truer words ever spoken? So it's time to reboot a bit and determine if we wish to follow a path of relative prosperity, or stay on that one way ticket into the abyss. The same journey that had been experienced by every great society in the long history of mankind"!

"At every juncture, we are experienced a reciprocal effort to resist change, mostly out of purely self-sustaining and political reasons. I recall one inspector general commenting to me, that he was amazed by the attitude of one of the regional directors, now currently out of government, who knew that his agency was ineffective and could've cared less. And he further stated the entire management of the agency was outright hostile to 'suggestions' at first, then later, 'directives' on how to streamline the agency to better serve the taxpayer".

"The entire agency, in question, is currently in the process of shrinking their operations nationally and will no doubt fade into memory within the next fifteen months. Now I know that a number of you will no doubt inquire as to whether or not the various inspector generals have been given carte' blanche' by the Oval office and the answer is no. For years, inspector general's reports have been either ignored or highly edited as to content prior to their release to either the executive or the legislative branches of the Federal Government. Those days are over"!

"What hasn't been anticipated was the overall attitude of those who have remained, led by capable management. They are now listened to by those who care about how to improve the effectiveness of their operations and they are happier for it because the dead wood has been cleared away.

Still, we are receiving a great deal of resistance by various members Of congress and certain unions that have a vested interest in maintaining a status quo for the purpose of continuance of their existence. They told me this wasn't going to be easy and they were correct"! "Now to shift to another subject, I again apologize to the International body politic at large, for again I've been busy righting the ship of state and have been remiss in my Presidential duties as receiving guest heads of state. Again the requirements of my office in these perilous time provide little or no time for socializing. Much of this has been transferred to my very capable Secretaries of Defense and State, by whose actions in the past year or so, has earned my confidence. We are in constant contact in circumstances germane to their departments and our thinking is generally following down the same path. I repeat generally following the same pathways, not always. We sometime have different ideas on how to achieve a desired result, but we get there none the less. Hopefully sometime in the next year things will calm down so the Oval office can be more hospitable"!

"Now to yet another of concern, the 'Illegal Alien' problem that our society and congress has been wrestling with for years to no reasonable conclusion. Many years ago, our country opened our doors, to populate our vast country as quickly as possible. 'Bring me your tired, your poor, your huddled masses yearning to breathe free'. Such are the words of Emma Lazarus in the nineteenth century. Even though those words attracted many from the world over, eager for a chance to be in a land to make your own way in the world, in a place relatively free of corruption experienced in their homeland, they came to our shore, many at great risk, some arrived too afflicted by disease to be absorbed and were sadly turned back, while others arrived, went to work eventually being assimilated into our society.

During that process of assimilation, not always were they treated with fairness and justice, but those they bore made their way in the world to greater and lesser degrees, with each generation proving the differences marginal, bit by bit"!

"Yet here we are in the twenty first century and I would argue a very different time, a more complicated time. We can no longer afford to absorb, the 'Wretched Refuse from the distant shores', regardless of whether or not we might wish it or not. The country is awash with illegal and thus undocumented aliens from both distant shores and nearby lands, many of them hardworking people, while others seek to find easier paths to prosperity. Our prisons are full to the brimming with the 'wretched refuse' that have made their way into our land and we let this happen. They fill our social service facilities to the breaking point as well as our medical facilities and we have no real handle on the problem. Of course we have no idea just how many illegal and undocumented people are here, only estimates by those who cannot justify their figures of those who live in the shadows"!

"Our Immigration system is broken, is a cry from those from the far left who desire either open borders or a so called 'Comprehensive Approach' to legalization. Pay your back taxes and pay a fine, then register and get in the back of the line and learn our ways and the English language', or not, is what we always hear. Well let's look at that for a moment. We say pay a fine, then your back taxes. They ask and they all know, 'even if they wanted to, which they don't, where are they going to get the money to accomplish this'? Many work at menial jobs, often day labor, living in sometimes wretched conditions, dealing with everything on a cash basis and sending money back to the old country, in the billions. So where are they going to get the money? The next thing to consider is that for many of these poor people, their country of origin is to varying degrees, corrupt. The people have an almost ingrained distrust for their former governments at every level.

To get them to do a thing a bribe, or "Mordida, the bite" must take place and without that nothing is possible at any level. So even though our citizenry has a growing mistrust of government it pales in comparison with our neighbors south of the Rio Grande River. Thus to expect any reasonable assistance in this regard is a pipe dream, for it is we who provide a safety valve for their failed policies and as long as we are willing to keep absorbing the wretches refuse from their lands, they can maintain their comfort level. Their status quo. If one looks about one can see that every country in Europe, for example, has a similar problem, to greater or lesser degrees, due to their own lack of due diligence, similar to ours"!

"As a result we need no further laws, only to have the will to enforce the existing laws we have on the books already. Therefore you will notice that I've approved of the appropriate changes in several of the agencies involved, regarding the immigration problem. We're in the process in setting up tent cities in the southern border areas, in order to process the repatriation of the illegal alien back to their homelands in a law full, decent yet expeditious manner. ICE has been instructed in investigating any company and we are starting with the largest and working our way down, to conduct investigations and subsequent detention of anyone in their employ that is an illegal alien subject to immediate deportation. We expect that those companies with illegal or undocumented people in their employ will take the necessary steps or else will find themselves subject to Federal Prosecution sooner rather than later. If one cannot find work in the US, then their only rational course of action will be to go back from whence they came. Hopefully it will be the latter, then in the years to come when the population of illegal's is winnowed down to a more manageable level, then and only then, will we be able to approach the situation in a rational manner. I have directed the Defense Department to authorize ten of our Drone Aircraft to assist the Border Patrol in observing the activities along our southern borders and have already directed our National Guard to assist the Border Patrol in their efforts. Units will be rotated on a ninety day TDY, or temporary duty basis, with a squad of armed Guardsman being attached to each Border Patrol man and under his supervisors as their commanding officer. They are there to assist for this purpose only and in each case the Border Patrol will make any necessary formal arrests. This will be supervised by the Justice Department. Each unit will be video equipped."

"Next, those Sanctuary Municipalities that willingly flaunt existing Federal Statutes in this manner, starting as of last month will discover that Federal matching funds, they so eagerly embrace, will be unavailable until they show complete compliance with all existing Federal laws and statutes. It is oddly interesting that the very people who scream out the loudest, that we are a 'Nation of Laws', are often the very ones who will play the scofflaw, regarding a law they may disagree with. All one has to do is awaken from ones slumber for a little while and watch the cable news programs.

"In closing allow me to offer a 'Modest Proposal' in the form of an analogy, to illustrate the State of the Union as it exists today. Imagine a ship of state, far from shore on a perilous ocean. This ship has experienced many captains and crew over the years and has gone through several changes in ownership, during the passage of time. The profit margin has always been of supreme importance, given the attitudes of each duration of ownership.

Far past original design limits, normal maintenance of the craft has been deferred year after year. The mechanical equipment has been kept operational with little more than a kiss and a promise with a leaky hull and the bilge pumps going day and night. Should the pumps go out the ship will sink. Should the engine breathe its last the ship will be dead in the water.

The crews pray for land while the Captain prays for a dry dock, where the ship can be made whole once again"!

"This is the state of affairs our society faces at this very moment. Not as I see it, but as it exists today. Others may choose to obfuscate, but I will not. This is a time for America, to stop its petty squabbling and come together for a common purpose and for the common good. In many respects it was far easier during the Second World War, since America had two very visible enemies bent on our destruction and we came together against a quite visible and common enemy. Today we have a largely invisible enemy bent on our destruction, in the form of extremist organizations and social upheavals from without, but even more insidious lays the enemy from within"!

Magnusson stopped for a moment taking a drink of water from the glass on the podium, before saying, "I thank you for your time and patience, now I will take your questions"!

The audience was quiet for a full ten seconds, for never before in anyone's memory had a Chief Executive, spoken with such passion and candor, telling everyone exactly what they didn't want to hear. Then a hand slowly raised and the President recognized the reporter, who stood and said, "Johan Stronefeld with Reuter's news agency. Mr. President. Recently it's been reported the mountain passes between Pakistan and Afghanistan have all been bombed, by the American Forces. Can you shed any light on this"!

"Of course Mr. Stronefeld. As many of you know, the border between both countries is long and mountainous, with a number of mountain passes that cross over between both countries. This is an escape route for the militant extremists and also a supply route between countries. Now if Pakistan was of a mind then we could have a hammer and anvil approach to sandwich the extremists, but since they've been reluctant to commit their military resources in fear of their mortal enemy India, so they say and do not want us traipsing over their sovereign soil in pursuit of the militant fighters, we were looking for yet another way. The satellites photos have indicated more than two dozen visible pathways that people travel between the countries, some of which were perilous pathways. The militant's use them not only for supplying there forces in Afghanistan but to have access and egress between countries. All I did was point this out and wonder why we have allowed this avenue of approach to exist? And to my surprise no one in the military could tell me? Then I discovered that the CIA had pointed this out several years ago yet it gained few adherents. Then I asked what would happen if we bombed all but one of the passes, making them impassable for the time being and setting a trap on the only other pass available for traversing? Pakistan couldn't rationally complain since we would accomplish this on the Afghanistan side. Of course they later did, but their rationale held no water internationally.

So the NATO Commanders got together and in the space of two days every pass between the Mountains except the Khyber Pass road and one other was bombed, thus making them virtually impassable and I'm given to understand we got two large units of extremists in the process. A week later, in the remaining pass satellites showed that yet another caravan was traversing the pass. The Unit Commanders on the ground had full authority do what they thought best. In short order requiring no other authorization, they bombed the pass, thus as reports indicated subsequent later explosions indicated, they were apparently transporting a significant quantity of ordinance into Afghanistan"!

"All in all a pretty good day for the good guys"! All the credit going to the NATO forces who showed that if politicians simply get out of the way, possibly we can bring this whole affair to a close sooner rather than later"!

Hands went up from the crowd as the President selected yet another reporter. "Thank you Mr. President. Margot Myers, the Associated Press. Reports have surfaced of the Pentagon relaxing their long existing, 'Rules of Engagement', regarding foreign conflicts. Will you enlighten us as to why"?

"I'd be delighted! While I've never been in the military, along with many of you, I can easily put myself in the place of a 'Grunt', on patrol in a foreign land, weapon at the ready, seeking out the bad guys. They wear no uniform, the hide behind women and children and suddenly come at you from every possible direction, then quickly fading back into the population. Should the military man fire in an inappropriate manner and hit a non- combatant, then he risks courts martial, by a very eager Judge Advocate General judiciary and thus Federal confinement. Thus even should he survive his tour of duty unscathed, he risks a very uncertain future at the very hands of those whose duty it is to protect him. One slip, even should he save lives, he risks retribution at the hands of his own people. He is in a no win situation"!

"Ever since the beginning of recorded history, there has never been a military arm so sensitive to the sufferings of those caught in the middle of a war, than our United States Military. Yet we ask our military to enter into a dangerous place, risking their lives, with literally one hand tied behind their backs. Our military even goes the extra distance to pay immediate reparations, or shall we say a bribe, upon a superficial field investigation virtually on the spot, to those who reportedly have inadvertently lost family members due to a firefight. In several instances, it was discovered at a later date, that those reported killed, were actually involved in the assault upon our military, yet they got reparations. Clearly they lied to the investigators. We have since negated that policy for the duration of the conflict"!

"What has occurred has been a relaxation, not elimination, but a relaxation, of the rules of engagement and an elimination of immediate reparations on the battlefield. Hesitation in the midst of a wily and skilled enemy will get one unnecessarily killed every time and that cannot continue. We have the best trained, best equipped and best led military in the world. When we send our volunteer force, up country amongst the hostiles, we send them to do one thing"!

"I see that Oliver Hastings has raised his hand. Please Mr. Hastings; feel free to ask anything that comes to mind"!

The assembled audience started to murmur, as well as the entire White House Staff, as they stood gathered around the various television sets. Van Harvanian said to both Goodwin and O'Bannon standing close by, in the tension filled office, "Now we see the shit hit the fan"!

"Thank You Mr. President", said Hastings with a ready question surprised that he'd been called at all, but with his chin turned up in his standard imperious manner, "Mr. President, there are those who say that,"!

Immediately Magnussen interrupted him by asking, "Are we going to engage with that old journalistic ruse, by beginning with the standard, "There are those who say", which usually follows or is accompanied by, "Some say"? "I've always wondered exactly who are those people are who say or ask? Whether they are real, or contrived? We mere mortals will never know, for the Press has a legal pass, according to the courts, against revealing a confidential source, if indeed that source ever existed, or was simply a contrivance, a ploy. But again we will never know, will we Mr. Hastings"?

Hastings was clearly taken aback for a moment, for never in his career had he been so aggressively attacked by an adversary in pursuit of advantage. As he quickly gathered his thoughts and made ready to speak, he was again interrupted by the President who said, "For the past year, you have assailed the Office of the President, the executive branch of government as well as me and what is the memory of my family in particular in the most libelous and scurrilous manner, without a shred of proof relying on your gutter wit and innuendo entirely. I've been too busy as of late to give you the attention that you deserve, but recently it has come to light that you are responsible for leaking the battle plans of our military forces overseas to the enemy. The FBI has been involved in a silent six month long investigation resulting in the arrest of your military contact, obtaining your name as the traitor that has been responsible for the security breach. So in front of the entire nation, I want to know what have you to say in your defense"?

Hastings face became flushed with fear as he tried in vain to find the words to defend himself, but like a common thief suddenly caught with the goods in hand, he could only stammer, as Magnusson finally said, "As I thought"!

"We have several members of the Justice Department as well as the FBI with us this evening. Gentlemen, there is Oliver Hastings at your service if you will"!

Throughout every room in the White House, was heard a simultaneous cheer as well as the trio of Harvanian, Goodwin and O'bannon who jumped for joy as Harvanian, suddenly stopped them, putting his hand to his ear saying, "If we listen very carefully, we will hear the sound of a bear trap slamming shut"!

Three agents of the FBI summoned a suddenly enraged Oliver Hastings, to come to them. His refusal to budge from his position amidst his volatile prostrations compelled the agents to come to him and forcibly place him in hand cuffs in the middle of all the reporters and forcibly remove him from the room screaming epithets as he was led away, prompting Magnusson to comment, "Me thinks he protested too much"!

After the commotion started to die down Magnusson continued, "Ladies and Gentlemen of the media, I must for what just occurred and it is to be considered in no way an assault against the members of the media.

However a point had to be made and it simply is, say anything you want, print anything you want, but I recommend that you have rock solid proof of your assertions. After all, isn't that what is taught in College Journalism classes these days"?

Just then another hand shot up, the President acknowledging him. "Mr.

President, Morton Collier, CBS news. Rumors are surfacing about yet another attempt of the Republican Party to pass a Campaign Bill in Congress, along with an attempt to initiate a congressional Term Limits amendment to the Constitution. Would you share your thoughts with the nation"?

"I'd be happy to Mr. Collier"! Magnusson took yet another sip of water while he gathered his thoughts, then looked up saying, "A very long time ago, sometime in the nineteenth century, a man named Lord Acton, a member of the British peerage at the time said and I'm going from memory here said, "Power tends to corrupt, while absolute power corrupts absolutely"! I think the man was onto something a long time ago. Now as I understand it, the framers of the constitution had no crystal balls, allowing them to see far into the future. They only had the examples of the behavioral patterns of the day to reckon with when they crafted the pathways of governance for the day and on balance I'd say they did a darn good job. Their original intent was that the smartest and wisest men of their day, run for political office, resolve problems, then after a certain appropriate period of time, relinquish their positions and return to society at large. Clearly that didn't last very long. For eventually men took a liking to congressional power and perks. For our seniority system provides a great deal of privilege and influence, thus equating to power, once an individual has achieved seniority status in the form of Committee Chairmanship. We have people, usually men, who serve their entire adult lives, far into their latter years, thus making a career in supposedly serving the people and the common good, when in fact they feather their own nests at the expense of the American Taxpayer and along the way feather the nest of friends they met along the way"!

"Lord Acton was quite accurate when he made that statement observing the morays of his day and guess what? Human behavior hasn't changed a scintilla, from his day until the present moment. Now post Second World War, Congress was quite right in limiting the power of the Presidency to just two terms and then he must step aside and join the rest of us. But they forgot just one little thing. They conveniently omitted to limit their own terms during the course of "Serving the People". All over America, State and local governments passed laws limiting the terms of Mayors, Governors, municipal councils and County Officials, yet our

Federal Legislature is somehow exempt, thus blind to human nature. They like the hustle and bustle of life on Capitol Hill, with all their power and perks and will fight the good fight before they give them up. The few arguments one may hear in defense of their reluctance to relinquish power doesn't even pass the laugh test. This must change sooner or later, for the common good.

The very same argument is applied to Campaign Finance Reform.

Many attempts to reform this egregious conglomeration of Overwhelming Amounts of Money, flooding into the Campaign coffers of those wanting reelection are designed to not only influence a pointy of view, but to further corrupt the object of lobbyists intentions. Somehow Quid Pro Quo deal making is insufficient, money must secretly change hands, with skillful acumen, wending its way through the various loop holes intentionally crafted by skillful lawyers. Thus begs the question, "Why do some people become Lawyers and Politicians"? And the answer is, "To craft laws that allow certain people to gain advantage"! That is the simple truth. Now there are a number of legislators on both sides of the aisle that are in complete agreement with this point of view, especially in light of the current perilous circumstances our economy and country finds itself in. They may disagree on any number of things, but in this they agree. Many members of congress will not give a constituent the time of day, unless he presents a certified check for their reelection campaign, for after all, they are very busy people and I might add, important. They are in perpetual motion putting the arm on constituents and others for cash to further their retention, thus being far too busy to actually read many of the bills their voting on"!

"Thus my "Modest Proposal". Any group, entity or private individual cannot, may not and shall not, contribute a greater amount than "One thousand US dollars per annum, or render any service or convenience, of an equivalent amount, to any sitting member of either branch of congress, or candidate for congressional office"! Now right away one can just hear the howls from those opposed to this. The vast legions of political advisors of every shape and kind will have to find other work. Their numbers will be winnowed down to a chosen few.

The words we hear from our legislators will more likely be of their own mind rather than talking points crafted by one of their handlers. The media may be unhappy about this, because every election cycle, the costly barrage of campaign ads will be less available. But crafty as our politicians are they will find far less costly ways of adjusting to get their respective messages to the people at large. They will claim falsely that this is an abridgement of free speech, while in fact in will be a more efficient and factual manner of free speech. In fact I expect these initiatives to die in their respective committee's for the present, at least until the fall elections. I intend to utilize the bully pulpit of the Presidency to advance this point of view to the people at every appropriate opportunity. Power tends to corrupt and absolute power corrupts absolutely"!

"Now the congress is already upset with me as all of you are aware, for my stance regarding waste in government. It's everywhere like a pestilent virus, sucking the lifeblood from our society. They're already angry with my stance regarding vetoes of any bills presented that contain any amendments not directly germane to the bill at hand. Think for a moment of how angry they will be, when the candy is removed from the child, in the form of a "Line Item Veto! Most successful corporations, especially those publicly traded have to submit an annual budget. A plan for profitability and in every instance the Head Honcho of that organization has the authority to line out any expenditure he thinks is unwarranted and yet in the governance of our country, our Chief Executive is held hostage, to the minority. And we wonder why our country is sideways and sliding into the abyss."? At this point Magnusson sought out the television cameras concluding.

"Now I'm certain that I've provided the members of the media, the body politic and the public at large, more than sufficient material to chew on in the weeks and months ahead. What I'd like to see is America to awaken from their slumber, read the papers, and digest the news of the day like our grandparents once did. Amidst the hectic schedules that many of you may have in getting through your lives, educate yourselves as to the problems that confront us all. Listen very carefully as to what is said, who is saying it, then make up your own mind as to who is telling the truth and who has their hand in your pocket. The decisions rest ultimately in your hands, via your vote every election day. So I leave you all, with this simple thought, "We have met the enemy and he, is us"!

"Thank you and May God bless America". At that Magnusson turned and walked down the hallway and disappeared through an open door.

The White House in normally a staid and respected edifice not known for raucous behavior, ever since the days of Andrew Jackson. This was why Lars Magnusson was overwhelmed when he went amongst the hired help after his Press Conference. Tears of joy burst forth from both genders along with everyone crushing around the President, insisting on shaking the man's hand and in the case of the women, giving him a well-earned hug. Goodwin sent several people into the kitchen area, summoning them forth to return with the entire staff, laden with bottles of bubbly and the glasses to go with it. Magnusson had expected some after action activity, nothing approaching this swarm of affection.

The glasses filled to the brim, everyone turned to the intrepid trio for some words of toasting; first in the pecking order was Melanie O'Bannon, who simply lifted her glass on high saying, "Mr. President, tonight you certainly kicked butt"! A cheer burst forth as everyone drank. Next was Vannevar Harvanian, who thought a second before saying, "Mr. President, I just don't know add to that, except, ah.... ." You certainly... Kicked butt"! Once again a raucous cheer followed by a round of drinking, with finally Orval Goodwin being pushed forward to say a few words. "Really can't top the previous two toasts, except I'm certain I speak for everyone here by saying, we're really glad that you're at the helm of our ship of state and no one else and in the days ahead, we all see what's coming down the pike and it's not pretty. Mr. President, we all have your back"! Once again a loud cheer as everyone finished off their glasses.

As the noise finally died down in expectation of Magnusson making a brief statement, everyone could see that his eyes started to mist up as he started out, "Damn sinus's, going to have to take a pill tonight. But I thank each and every one of you for your continuing efforts both great and small, for each of you are important elements in the machine of progress in the coming days ahead. Thank you one and all"! Once again an even louder cheer burst forth, before everyone disbursed, going their separate ways, with full hearts of hope and cheer.

The quartet went back to the Oval office and turned on the bank of television sets to observe the after the speech shows on the networks, with Harvanian serving as bartender and bringing everyone his favorite drink.

"Seems the Justice Department will be working late this evening", said Harvanian with a sly wink!

"Van, just how on earth did you pull this one off", asked Melanie?

"A friend at the Justice Department let certain things be known on the QT, so I simply asked him to adjust his time table of interdiction for maximum effect after checking with the boss here! Took the man five whole seconds before he gave me the head nod and the rest is history"!

"Well lets all hush up, drink our drinks and quietly revel in success at least for the moment, and watch what all the talking heads have to say", offered Melanie!

Magnusson peered out of the Oval office window into the night watching many of the staff working their way to their cars. Suddenly he longed for his family at his side. It would've been grand to have them close at hand. Taking a deep breath he decided to join the others to view his report card. Sure he'd made his points crystal clear and scored on each and every point of possible conjecture, but the perception of others was a political reality as everyone knew. People were either for you of against you and he wanted to shake things up amongst the populace, thus flushing the birds from the brush and that he did.

In the weeks ahead, Magnusson's press conference was headline news, pushing most other events of the day to the secondary pages, or below the fold. His image appeared on most all of the magazines of the day as a handsome man, placed alone by circumstance, a Don Quixote to some tilting at the windmills of ill fortune, struggling to hold back the tides of fate, with but his thumb.

Magnusson started a policy of making time each week for at least two hour long interviews with National and International Journalists, with each one being placed on guard, by his aggressive and articulate stance with the Nations journalists in a public forum. Each came away with an added level of respect for the man, regardless of their political bias, for the man was concise, and well up on the issues at hand, able to effectively articulate his point of view, without reference to prepared talking points from those "troll like handlers", as one columnist phrased it.

Of course those from the far left of the political spectrum, rose up virtually in unison, crying to the heavens that, "Magnusson, was a traitor to the Democratic Party and thus to America", for his actions regarding in "Righting the Ship of State". The Unions rose up almost en masse, with a series of strikes designed to bring chaos to both the Government and key manufacturing facilities, requiring the President and various State Governors to call out the National Guard to restore order. America at large never before seemed more vulnerable, to the world at large, than from the fractured and partisan activities, from the body politic within.

This prompted several Senators and Congressmen to convene secretly to see if there was a way to enter into impeachment proceedings, for the President was going too far in calling for a harnessing of their Congressional prerogatives. However the idea got nowhere, for there was a paucity of brave souls, who would join their cause, for a variety of reasons. Chief of which was that congressmen didn't achieve longevity in office by being overtly foolhardy. They were far from having a sufficient number of votes, regardless of how angry they were with the President and his staff.

There would have to be another way.

While this roiling of legislative discontent was loud boisterous and continual, the media started to run fifteen and thirty second, privately funded, non-partisan commercials appealing to the public to become more involved in the issues of the day, with the constant overlay of the cartoon Pogo Possum saying, "We have met the enemy and he is us"!

It was in the middle of the hottest and driest summers in most parts of the country that anyone could remember and these commercial offerings would run intermittently, all the way till the night of the elections in early November.

14

For the past several years, Salaam was busy disbursing Islamist revolutionaries to various Mosque assemblies throughout the nation. They were trained in colloquial English and Spanish and were appearance wise able to pass for someone of mixed Indian Spanish heritage from south of the border. They were brought to Salaam by well-known and well paid agents in Mexico, whose families had been successfully engaged in smuggling for generations. They arrived in two's and three's and Salaam's job was to be their Shepard once they arrived in the states then see to it they arrived safely in the care of any number of Imam's nationally. What became of them afterward was not his affair.

For the last several years he'd been a keen observer of general meteorological weather trends in the US, stressing on seasonal forecasts, keeping weather charts and making voluminous notes, when he decided that this very summer was about as good as conditions for his purpose, were ever going to get. The month of August in the States was historically the hottest time of the year, thus in Salaam's mind, it was time that Hell visited the infidel. Over the years, he'd built a network of key contacts all over America, in Muslim communities, visiting and revisiting these communities periodically as a self-appointed Ambassador of good will. Sometimes addressing the faithful at their Friday prayers, never once preaching violence and hatred of the infidels as others often did, rather making it a point to preach quite the opposite, sometimes being held in contempt by the more radical elements in the area.

The Christian teachings had a saying that was based on the writings in the bible and that was paraphrased, "There are those that talk the talk, while others say little and walk the walk"! Salaam was not a man who thumped his chest and was certainly not prone to boasting. He believed firmly that his actions spoke loudest, nothing more. He was content to stay well in the shadows, patiently waiting for the precise moment of weakness and lack of resolve from his mortal enemy and then, may Allah guide his hand and strike at the very heart of the infidels at such a time, from every direction to inflict massive damage that defied description and even more important, terror in the hearts of the apostates.

The nation's weather predictions indicated that August, just weeks away, was going to be the hottest on record.

He went to his Rolodex and started dialing the phone. The connection would be made. Salaam would greet the recipient and thus be acknowledged. Then Salaam would whisper the word that had been previously implanted subconsciously in the recipients mind. The recipient would then reply, "I understand my brother", as previously instructed, then hang up without another word. He, in turn would then go to his list of ten other soldiers and start placing a call to each, making certain that he was talking to the right individual, repeating the ritual, signaling the subconscious to do the bidding of Allah and proceed with the business at hand, then without another word, hang up. None of the men was exactly conscious of precisely why they were doing what they were about to do, but one thing remained clear. Their actions were about to strike a dagger deep into the heart of their infidel hosts in America. Each man had no knowledge of any other engaging in similar actions, for each was certain he'd received a message directly from God and must obey the will of Allah.

Since each man was a true believer and had a deep seated predisposition to inflict violence, the normal societal checks and balances to inflict harm faded away immediately, for in each man's mind, he was a 'Soldier of God'. It was three in the afternoon, Pacific Coast time, when Hakeem received his initial call from Salaam. He'd already seen his patients for the day in his podiatry practice and set about calling the others. By a little after four in the afternoon he was finished. He called his wife and told her that several emergencies had arisen at the hospital and not to wait up for supper and that he'd return late at night when his tasks were completed and not to worry. He'd already forgotten about the others he'd contacted and in his mind his actions were of the message he'd received from Allah and nothing more. When his task was completed, he, as well as all the others, would immediately forget what they had done. It was a segment in time gone forever. Being wiped clean by an unseen hand.

In Los Angeles, as in many of the other locations, each initial contact provided ten likeminded others over time for Salaam to imprint his directions from Allah. The day for action would be Friday and each was certain to have gone to his Mosque for Friday prayers. Those in the Eastern Time zones were contacted first by Salaam, as he worked his way westward and their subconscious was mindful to remind them to feel nothing one way or the other regarding the coming event and to go about one's normal schedule, when completed their performance at Allah's bidding.

Hakeem went to one of his favorite Restaurants and ordered a lavish meal which he lingered over for almost three and a half hours, for Friday afternoon rush hour traffic in Los Angeles, along with this seemingly endless heat wave this city and most of the nation was experiencing, was not appealing in the least. But once the sun started to dip below the hill tops, it signaled it was time to summon the waiter, pay his bill, leaving a good tip and depart.

Ten minutes later he arrived at the Storage Warehouse of buildings where individuals paid a monthly rental to store everything from soup to nuts. His small facility was in the rear of the video recorded complex, at the far range of the swiveling video cameras that kept a constant eye on events at all times. His storage space was no bigger than a large closet with a metal door, and inside was ten one gallon plastic petroleum cans, filled with gasoline along with ten timers and igniters. He opened the trunk of his car and placed each one of the implements in the trunk carefully, mindful of the camera some hundred yards away. Once in place, he attached the igniters as he'd been taught long ago. The timers could be attached and set with in the space of seconds, when he'd reached each of his chosen locations. Each location would be in a heavily wooded area, designed to be difficult for fire fighters to gain access to. Thus it went and by ten in the evening he'd reached his first location. Removed the gallon gas can from the trunk walked to the pre-selected location, set the timer, then calmly left for the next location. By the time he placed his last gas container and left, the first he'd placed ignited. By the time he was half way home, he could hear the sounds of fire engines, sirens wailing away into the night. And thus it went all over the greater Los Angeles area. Eleven operatives setting ten fire's each.

As he quietly slipped between the sheets, next to his softly snoring wife, Hakeem's last conscious thought before falling into a deep slumber was, 'And they think the earthquakes were bad'.

And so it went all over America, from the deep forests of Maine, all along the Appalachian Trail, to the forests of Georgia, to the deep piney woods of East Texas, the woods of the Michigan peninsula, Minnesota, Ohio, the entire west coast from Seattle to San Diego. If one was up astride a stationary satellite, one could see one by one, a light developing where it never normally would appear, near an adjoining metropolitan area eventually sending up clouds of smoke into the atmosphere. By the following morning, none of those involved had any memory of the events of the previous evening, yet watching with keen interest the national newscasts. Those involved came from the ranks of every level of endeavor, from Doctors, Lawyers, Professors, Accountants, Restaurateur's, Tailors, Plumbers, Truck drivers, Cab drivers and others and the only thing each had in common was that they prayed multiple times a day with a religious zeal. Those with a nominally calm demeanor remained so, while those more agitated remained exactly the same.

Of slightly more than a hundred operatives, seven were apprehended by the local authorities during their egress after they had set their last gas can. Most had run afoul of some traffic violation during their escape, during which they were pulled over by the authorities and during the process of writing out a ticket, heard an explosion near by seeing the fire and thus securing the individual and placing him in the patrol car as a precaution. In three cases, the subject made to escape in his car only to be engaged in a high speed chase in which his car crashed and he was apprehended and hospitalized. In one case in the suburbs of Minneapolis, a search of the car trunk revealed a single full gas can igniter and timer. Apparently this individual was on his way towards his last stop for the evening prior to his being apprehended. The local field office of the FBI was immediately notified late the following morning, but with everything going on all at once, it was ten AM, before an agent was assigned to his case and noon before he was able to be interviewed. By then the man in custody, a lawyer had one of the partners of his law firm to represent him.

By noon of the following day, the entire nation was placed on full Military alert by the President. Every military base, in the nation and abroad was placed on full alert and all leaves were cancelled. Military and citizens alike were conscripted into fire squads to help extinguish the thousand plus conflagrations that had risen up during the night while people slept. Many had just barely escaped from their slumber, with only the clothes on their backs, while thousands of others less fortunate perished in the flames, throughout the land. It would be several months before anything resembling a complete body count was completed.

The State Department was pressed into immediate service, contacting the appropriate countries that had aerial fire suppression aircraft that could lend a helping hand. Of the International Community, those that had the aircraft lent a helping hand, those that didn't help out as best they could in other areas both great and small. Every branch of the military was deep in the process of engaging the myriad of fires that raged day and night. Those not engaged were sent to assist every law enforcement entity throughout the land in controlling the raging mobs that were bent upon looting.

After the third day of intense struggle, with casualties mounting in the law enforcement community as well as their military auxiliaries, President Magnusson authorized the Secretary of Defense, to issue 'Shoot to Kill' orders to each military commander on the ground in his area of responsibility, as he saw fit. For days the inner cities were a battleground as many of those engaged in the rioting and looting, engaged the military in running gun battles in the inner cities all over the land. In the process, the streets were littered with the bodies of both the guilty as well as the innocents as the rioters and looters took shelter, held innocent hostages, settled long festering feuds, between families and individuals without regard to right or wrong. Manson's 'Helter Skelter' was at last in place.

The fifth day of the national conflagration, with rioting in the streets of every major city in the nation and part of the military fully engaged with the fire, other elements were busy assisting the various local authorities in riot suppression, various members of both houses of Congress rose up in righteous indignation, claiming the President exceeded his authority in declaring the nation on full military lockdown, for he'd violated "Posse Comitatus". The following day, the President convened a joint session of both houses of Congress, fully televised before the nation, arguing the point and defending his actions before the nation and the sitting Congressional bodies.

Magnusson berated those recalcitrant members of congress, for dithering inaction, demanding they set aside, "Posse Comitatus", on an "Ad Hoc", basis, 'For This Purpose Only', while the nation at large was at risk. Several members of congress rose to attack the President for his seemingly dictatorial directives. With Magnusson dressing them down, in response, in front of all America saying, "While the nation goes up in flames and our citizens are being shot and robbed in the streets, you would have me convene a tribunal of so called experts to consult their navels? This is what you think leadership is? Then he bored in on each and every congressman who challenged him by name, looking directly into the cameras and talking directly to the American people, verbally browbeating those who would stand idly by while 'Rome burned'. He demanded and immediately received, a joint congressional vote of almost unanimous approval to, allow the Military to perform whatever duties the Commander in Chief deemed vital to the situation at hand, thus setting aside "Posse Comitatus", for the duration of the emergency only.

Of course, the Television commentators had a field day, with some commentators railing about what a Benevolent Dictator, this 'non-elected' President of the people had become, while others staunchly defended the President for being a man of action and the man of the moment and other radical elements resurrecting calls for his impeachment.

Lars Magnusson being the man of the moment in these days of constant duress taking leave of the Oval Office along a few of his Cabinet members and staff, touring the besieged country, preceded by the Secret Service and a detail of Navy SEAL personnel all armed to the teeth and ready for any untoward interruption on the President's agenda of being amongst the people in their time of need. A special news pool of hastily conscripted news men and video types were attached to

Air Force One, as his entourage made its way across the land. Where Federal officials were hesitant in responding to the emergency at hand, Magnusson immediately replaced them with their subordinates, giving the new official his marching orders, in full view of the country.

When one reporter asked him about his seemingly Draconian actions, "Magnusson looked full into the camera, the entire country seeing that he was in need of a shower and a change of clothes as he said, "When I see a Federal Official dithering as not knowing what to do and standing around with one finger up his ass and the other in the air swapping off every thirty seconds, I know he needs to be somewhere else right away"!

The embedded News Media followed in his wake, bedraggled every bit as much as the President and his staff, yet there was a series of stories and dramas here, played out on a moment by moment basis. Love him or revile him, Lars Magnusson was a man of action, moving at warp speed to respond to a nation under siege. Gradually the nation responded, jerked from their slumber as neighborhoods all across the land formed watch groups in conjunction with the local authorities on the ground and the military ever present.

Never in the history of this great nation, could anyone recall the Chief Executive being seemingly everywhere at once, often in dangerous places and coalescing disparate element to unite for the common good. As the first week of the nonstop high winds fanned the nationwide conflagration came to a close, the National Meteorological Service was hard at work everywhere, scanning their data, looking for weather fronts that may contain the possibility of rain. Yet few seemed promising, with people everywhere praying for rain and especially those along the Gulf Coast praying for of all things a Hurricane.

While the Vice President assumed a Command post at the White House, the President worked out of the executive aircraft, Air Force One, issuing directives from whatever Air Force Base it was temporarily housed.

Never in their lives had the Executive pool reporters worked so hard, following the President in his wake, catching cat naps whenever they could, noting the endurance and drive of the Nation's leader. Going deep into the second non-stop week of the National Emergency and with events everywhere, showing no signs of abatement, a number of the reporters were about to throw in the towel, yet were held in place by their respective editors, reminding them that this was a story of a life time and that their departure would find them on their own and without a job. When reminded of the possibility of a reporters family being in danger, some of the assignment editors reminded the recalcitrant journalists, "If the President can do this with all he's been though, then so can you", before abruptly hanging up!

Interesting about how celestial serendipity can play a role in human events. Over the course of weeks, with riots raging in the streets in many of the major cities, a dozen of the Muslim true believers that started the fires had been caught up in the rioting and their lives extinguished, at the hand of others, while trying to seek safety. With the truth of their role in the events dying with them.

In many parts of the Muslim world, there were celebrations in the streets almost nonstop, equaling or surpassing that following the tragedy of the twin towers during 9/11. When certain information came to light in the media of possible culpability of disparate Muslim elements being a possible cause of the latest national tragedy, many of the radical right started to connect the dots, assuming that all of the Nations Muslim population was at fault and thus complicit, releasing a wave of retribution at many of the Mosque's in America and thus once again many of the innocents had to suffer for the actions of the few.

The future looked bleak for many of middle-eastern descent in America. Mosques began to be firebombed. Anyone that appeared on the streets in garb resembling Muslim clothing was either attacked of spat upon in public places. Those women that went for their weekly shopping in the store's, discovered that upon their return to their vehicles in the parking lot, all four tires had been slashed. Therefore entering the fourth week of the National Emergency, many of the same roving gangs shifted their anger to any one they caught on the streets that appeared Muslim. It made no difference if it was a man or women, a mother and child. To appear on the streets during this time meant taking one's life in ones hands. Business's that were owned by Muslims or that catered to Muslims were attacked during the night often being burned to the ground. All the while the nation struggled to gain control of the wild fires that were consuming the Nation's wealth and sanity.

Fatima Malanoush was returned to her family under military guard from the hospital emergency room, to convalesce after suffering a severe beating in the parking lot of her neighborhood grocery store. Her groceries stolen and her car torched, she suffered a mild concussion along with a myriad of bruises and contusions. The hospital ward was genuinelyfull, well past over capacity and could take no more, as was the case of every other hospital in Chicago and she was one of the lucky ones. Had she gone shopping dressed like any other person and wearing sunglasses, she probably would have returned unscathed, but her husband, Ahmad, a highly devout Sunni Muslim, insisted that she wear her native country Chador, when out and about and as a good and obedient Muslim woman could only but comply.

The previous day his dry cleaning business was set afire, in the middle of the day by a gang of men, who quickly drove up to his business in two cars. Four men emerged, with Molotov cocktails in hand, while the drivers kept the cars running ran into his business, lighting the firebombs, throwing them deep into the bowels of his establishment. As Ahmed tried to stop them he was knocked senseless to the floor as the men made their getaway. The initial explosions, killed five of his employees as Ahmed groggily struggled to regain his feet, while two of his counter clerks forced him out of the front door just in time before yet another larger explosion was triggered by the other firebombs effecting the business's on either side of him. As he lay in the parking lot, once again felled by the second explosion, the thought quickly ran through his mind before he lost consciousness, "How could this happen in America"?

Yet the following day, his pride, compelled somewhat a similar fate onto his wife, as she went about her daily duties.

Now at home, their larder with but perhaps a few days of groceries available, and with their young children afraid of appearing on the streets, they as a family discussed their immediate future.

"We can't go to the Mosque father, for their all being bombed", said Nathalie their oldest daughter! "Well, we can't stay here either", said

Hajid the eldest son adding, "Too many of our neighbors know who we are and it's only a matter of time for this place to go up in flames"!

Never mind that they were all from Lebanon. The five children, for the most part, were as assimilated as can be in the American experience, along with their mother. Only the father was of the old school, not radical in his thinking, but not completely accepting of the Western folk ways. The few friends he had were of the Mosque and all others he tolerated.

Unbeknownst to her parents, Nathalie's best friend was Anna Weisbrodt, the eldest daughter of Mordechai Weisbrodt, the City of Cicero's, Controller for many years, the keeper of the towns finances. Anna and Nathalie had been secretly best friends even since the first grade, their homes on the same city block separated by four other houses. Not even her mother did she tell of her friendship with the Jewish family that lived up the street and to reveal this to her father was completely out of the question. It was then that Nathalie excused herself from the gathering, saying that she had to go upstairs to the bathroom. She promptly called Anna on her cell phone as the only person she knew that she could reach out to. Twenty minutes later she came back downstairs as her older brother quipped, "Everything come out alright Nat"?

As the family dithered as what to do, they heard a knock on the kitchen door in the rear of the house. Nathalie ran to the door and a minute later returned with her guests announcing, "Mom, Dad, I want to introduce you to our neighbors down the street, Anna and her mother, Hannah Weisbrodt"!"Weisbrodt", asked Nathalie's father? "That's a Jewish name isn't it"?

"Why yes it is Mr. Malanoush. We are a Jewish family and when we heard about your recent situation we came to see if we could be of any help, to your family. Your daughter and my Anna have been class mates at school since they were little children. Fatimah was about to speak, when her husband interrupted her saying, "We don't need any", then Fatimah stepped in front of him, warmly smiling and said, "It's been a long day for my husband and I apologize for his rudeness, please come into our home"!

All the time of their marriage, Fatimah had proven to be a good Muslim wife, never once questioning anything her husband did or said.

Even when he was on the wrong side of an issue, or had over reacted to what was said or the events at hand she either held to silence or visibly deferred to her husband, except this once as Ahmad was dumbfounded when their Jewish neighbors entered into their kitchen.

"I heard about what happened to your business Mr. Malanoush and what happened to you Mrs. Malanoush and I was concerned. By the reports on television it looks like the street gangs are about to return and this time seek out Muslim families to kill. Anna has known your daughter for quite some time now and speaks highly of her and although we've never formally been introduced, we feel that yours is a good family. So I called my husband at work and we talked and he agreed to offer you shelter in our home, for the duration of the unrest. In fact from what he's given to understand, being at City Hall, he recommends that you join us"!

At that point the Ahmed and Fatimah, started to squabble in the native language, his point being that it would be a disgrace for a Muslim to ever take comfort from a Jew and her rejoinder was that he leave the old country prejudices alone. Here was a neighbor, the only neighbor that had volunteered to help the family at their moment of need. Then Fatimah turned to Hannah saying, "Again, please forgive the manners of my husband. Sometimes he still thinks he lives in the old neighborhood in Beirut and not in America. My family accepts your generosity and will be happy to join you at your convenience"!

Just then, the sound of distant volleys of gunfire was heard, some blocks away as every one became startled. "Please hurry and gather a few belongings for it sounds like the National Guard are engaged with the rioters, some distance away. Our home is just five houses away down the back ally"!

Fatimah, ignoring her husband, gathered her children and thanked Hannah, and then all ran upstairs to gather what clothes they could quickly, joined by Anna.

When they were out of sight, Ahmad turned to Hannah and asked, "Why are you doing this, for us"?

"Someone has to do it. Your Mosques are all burned to the ground and you can expect no help from anyone in your community. My husband is on his way home from work and should arrive shortly. If you wish you are welcome to ask him the very same question, for he is the Hazan, or Cantor of our Temple Beth Israel and a learned man. He will welcome you and your family Mr. Malanoush with open arms"!

Within the space of five minutes, they heard the pounding of footsteps coming down the stairs as everyone had a bag packed with only the bare essentials as they entered the kitchen, with Nathalie asking, "Father aren't you coming"?

"I'm thinking about it", he growled!

"Don't think too long, you old fool", said Fatimah as she hustled the children out the back door and into the ally.

The entire neighborhood was built back in the early nineteen twenties, shortly after the Great War, with two story brick homes crowded next to each other, one after the other.

Given that more and more people drove motorcars and needed garages, the rows of homes were all provided with a garage placed at the rear of each property, facing a wide alley that ran the entire length of the city residential block. So with those who drove motor vehicles to work and back, the rear kitchen door was their main point of entry and exit, while those that traveled by the trolley, usually came into the house by the front door.

The Weisbrodt's eldest son Daniel, stood vigil at the wooden gated door that led to the alley as his family and that of the Malanoush followed Hannah down the alley towards their house. As Nathalie passed Daniel their eyes met and Nathalie missed a step almost falling down as Daniel quickly grabbed her helping her to her feet saying, "Can't have you falling down now can we"? As both eyes again met, lingering just a bit at the sight of the other, Nathalie heard her mother whisper, "Hurry", as she hurried down the alley followed by Daniel bringing up the rear. For the rest of their time together, Nathalie and Daniel would occasionally steal glances at each other. She was almost thirteen and just on the verge of discovering her womanhood, while he was a robust teenager just shy of his sixteenth year.

In the days to come, both mothers would begin to notice this lingering attention to their children's unusual attention to detail to each other and begin to be concerned. A good Jewish boy and a good Muslim girl becoming interested with each other. No good could come of it. None at all.

Ahmed just stood there in the kitchen wondering why God had dealt them such a bad hand. He was a devout Muslim, praying the proscribed five times daily, at dawn, at noon, at mid-afternoon, at sunset and at night fall.

He's raised his family according to the Sharia and attended Friday Prayers without fail. His business firebombed and his wife assaulted with street gangs traveling the streets looking for Muslim families to wipe out, simply because they were different. This he'd thought he'd left far behind, when he and Fatimah immigrated to America, to start a business and have a family.

Surely in America this could never happen. But here he was in America, with a bombed out business, an injured wife and of all people, a Jewish family, neighbors down the street, that he would never normally give the time of day to, coming to the rescue of his family. His pride and everything he'd known to be true told him to stay put and stay with the house. But deep in his bones he knew that Fatimah was right. Her judgment over the years had been faultless. She was the brains and the common sense and he was simply the one who manned the battlements. It was Fatimah who selected the right location for the business and in the early days ran the counter while he was in the rear turning out the clothed for their dry cleaning business. Even while pregnant with their first two children she worked until the very last day. Eventually retiring by the third child to become a full time mother, but by then the business had grown to where additional help could be hired.

She'd select the home they lived in and even when he'd gotten into an argument with the real estate broker at the closing, turned things around to where the home purchase closed at even a better rate than he'd wanted. And yet his Middle Eastern Muslim pride, screamed at him to stay put, even though in his bones he knew the rioters would somehow find a way into their home and destroy all that he'd worked for.

From time to time, upon attending the Friday prayers at the Mosque, he would hear the fire and brimstone exalted by firebrands of how it was the duty of all true believers to be the 'Soldiers of Allah' and fight the infidels and bring them all to heel and kneel in obedience, to Allah the most merciful. Yet no one was trained to become a soldier of god, for here in America, they'd all become merchants. Thus a merchant he was, regardless of the temporary zeal he and others proudly displayed as they emerged from Friday prayers. By the time he'd arrived at his business, he was once again a merchant and nothing more.

Thus above all, everything he'd been taught from his earliest memory was that Jews were the supreme apostate. Yet here it was, a Jewish family just a few doors down the street, that was coming to shelter he and his family from certain death and destruction. His business was insured, his property was insured, he even had life insurance, but what if he wasn't around for his family when the grandchildren came? How could his presence in this house save his property? Surely he would be overwhelmed and killed.

Slowly and grudgingly he went upstairs and stared to pack just the essentials. As he looked for the important family papers, he discovered they'd gone missing. Suddenly he'd realized it was Fatimah. It was Fatimah who had the good sense to take the important documents with her, so the family could continue, regardless of whether or not he'd come to his senses.

He locked the doors as he left the house, even securing the rear wooden gate, to the back ally. Then he wondered, was it four houses down the alley on the right or was it five houses, as he made his way down the alley. At the fourth house he tried the rear gate door. It was firmly secured and wouldn't open. He tried the fifth gate and it opened. As he peered around the wooden door he saw that the kitchen door was open and caught a brief glimpse of Mrs. Weisbrodt in the kitchen window, then that of his Fatimah joining her and knew he was in the right place. He firmly secured the wooden gate and went up to the kitchen door and knocked.

Hannah Weisbrodt opened the door saying, "Welcome to our home Mr. Malanoush", as Ahmad slowly entered the kitchen. He'd never before had been in a Jewish home and was very nervous about the entire process. Just then the kitchen was invaded by all of the children, of both families who seemed to be getting along very well together, in the living room watching the Cable TV Newscasts. Tears started to well up in his daughter's eyes as well as that of his wife. Seeing this, even the matron of the house Hannah mumbled, "Scheist" as her eyes started to well up. For only the women knew just what it took for a Muslim to accept charity from a Jew. As the children led him through the house, leaving the women to prepare the evening meal, he discovered that this home was exactly similar to his with the exception that the basement had some time ago been made habitable, with hide a bed sofa, television, a bar, and extra bathroom with shower, alongside the laundry facilities.

Nathalie cheerfully standing alongside Anna said "You and Mom will bunk in down here all by your lonesome in private, while I'll bunk in with Anna upstairs and the boys will all bunk in together"!

Resigned to his fate Ahmad put down his suitcase and accepted Nathalie's embrace as she said, "I love you dad"! Just then a large commotion could be heard upstairs, as Anna said, "That must be father. Please let's all go upstairs, so you can meet my father"!

As Ahmed reached the top of the basement stairwell, he was introduced to Anna's father, who reached out a hand and said, "Hello, I'm Mordechai Weisbrodt. My friends call me Morty and I can see that you've met the family. Welcome to our home Mr. Malanouch". Ahmad gingerly shook his host's hands as Morty asked "Want anything to drink before dinner? I have a fully stocked bar from which to choose"! As soon as he made the offer Mordechai, knew that he'd blundered as a host by saying, "I'm very sorry I forgot about your religion. Hannah", he yelled, "Have we any refreshments for Mr. Malanouch, like iced tea"? Just then Ahmad decided to put caution to the winds and said, "Since you're the host and I'm a guest in your house, I'll have whatever you're having, Morty"!

"Never mind Hannah save the iced tea for dinner", he yelled!

"Well, let me see. What would be appropriate", he wondered as he looked over his liquor supply? "I see that you have a bottle of Southern Comfort", said Ahmed. "Many years ago when I was young, I tried some of that mixed with ice and found it pleasing"!

"The man wants some Southern Comfort on ice and that he will receive", said Morty as he reached for the bottle pouring an overly generous portion into a glass and filling the rest with ice, then reaching for his favorite Old Overholts Rye Whiskey and splashing the glass with ice saying, "A wee bit of Old Overshoes at the end of the day to keep the feet dry," and then turned to Ahmad saying cheerfully, "Up through the lips and over the gums. Look out stomach, here it comes", lifting his glass and tossing down half the glass.

"Les go into the parlor, join the kids and watch the news, while the women tend to the evening meal. Best we stay out of their way"!

As they watched the evening news regarding the vast wild fires that ravaged the nation and the running battles with rioters that raged throughout many of America's cities, they were amazed that the riots had spread across the borders into Toronto and Montreal Canada and as far west as Vancouver. Yet another news report from across the Atlantic, revealed that in several British Cities, similar riots were well in progress. While yet even more were occurring in cities all over the European Continent with significant Muslim populations.

Some were preemptively started by the more radical elements of the Caucasian population while others were initiated by Muslim radicals.

Regardless of who was the initiator, it seemed that each element of the population had had quite enough of the other and once again, blind hatred amongst the masses replaced common sense and decency. All fell silent as the reports came over the airways, one right after the other, as Morty silently thought of an old Texas cowboy he'd met years ago, who'd said, 'This is just Gods way of thinning' out the herd'! There was just no other rational explanation for what was happening.

Then came the local news reports, as they switched the channel, which was full of reports of what was happening in greater Chicago. A full dawn to dusk curfew was set in place throughout the entire area, as well as other cities, as National Guard troops were assigned to units of the Chicago Police Department on round the clock patrols of the city. The Police, the Fire Departments as well as the Guard troops were over extended and the nerves of the City were stretched well past the breaking point as the looters that came from the poorest sections of the city were involved in running gun battles with the authorities.

As it turned out, many of the dietary restrictions observed by the Muslim religion mirrored that of the Jewish faith as Hannah and Fatimah prepared the evening meal. As they called the families together for the evening meal, Mordechai sat at one end of the table and Ahmed was invited to occupy the other end of the table. The prayers prior to the meal were shared between both Patriarchs of the families prior to the meal. During the course of the meal in which small talk was occurring, a muffled sound of a distant explosion came to their ears startling everyone momentarily, but after the meal was concluded and dessert and coffee was served, Ahmed suddenly asked Mordechai, "Why have you helped us and been so kind to my family"? "Boy Ahmed, you get right too it don't you. Well you asked the question and deserve a proper answer"! Usually it is at this point, where the children usually decide to be somewhere else, but the children stayed glued to their seats eager to find out why.

"When I was young I used to hear stories about what happened to my people in Europe during the Nazi occupation. Eventually as I grew older I read many books written about what went on back in those days. Most Jews were headed for concentration camps and those with skills were relegated to slave labor factories and literally worked to death, producing weapons for the Nazi war machine. I was particularly taken with stories, like the 'Diary of Anne Frank', which recounted events about Christian families, taking in those few lucky Jewish families into their homes and hiding them from the Nazi occupiers. This was done at great risk for, should they be ever discovered, the Jewish families would be immediately shipped off to the concentration camps and their eventual death and the host families in Denmark, Holland or Belgium would be either shot on the spot or sent to the concentration camps themselves, to meet the same fate as the Jews and their property confiscated by the Nazi's. Which prompts the simple question why would someone do such a risky thing? Well, the answer is simple really, 'Because it's the right thing to do'! Back in those days few were inclined to do the right thing"!

"Then I recall wondering, if I were in a position to do the right thing, whatever that was, would I ever be up to the task? Then life took over, I got a College Degree, fell in love got married to a wonderful woman and had a family. Thoughts of my ever being in a position to do the right thing at the right moment took a back seat until today when Hannah called! It was as if she'd read my mind, for we'd never ever discussed that particular thing.

Her call to my office jogged my memory and of course I had to agree. Once again I was reinforced in my conviction that I had married the best woman possible for me, for she's is my soul and conscious. Every Saturday I perform as the Hazan, or Cantor in my synagogue and as such should lead a life worthy of such a position, sort of in the secular world as 'paying it forward', doing the right thing at the right time, because it needs to be done, without any expectation of return"!

"But there is even a greater example of why this family and I are reaching out to someone in need. I remember of a time when I was in school that I read the life history of Mahatma Gandhi and some years later there was a major movie made about his life. Here was a South African man of Hindi descent who leaves a thriving law practice to take his family to India, the land of his people and advocate for Indian Independence from the British. The man went through a great deal over the years, never once advocating for violence, but by simple peaceful non-violent protest over the actions of India's British masters. But this story skips to the end of the Second World War and with India on the verge of being granted self- dependence, by Great Britain; suddenly the country is tearing itself apart, with Muslims clashing with the native Hindi's. In every great city throughout India and what is now Pakistan, Bangladesh and Afghanistan riots are everywhere. Where the Hindis are in the majority, they attack the minority Muslims and where the Muslims are in the majority they attack the Hindi minority with the purpose of each driving the other out of their lands by whatever means possible. Old scores are settled, vengeance is the order of the day and this goes on for weeks on end"!

"Now over the course of time, Gandhi was about the only one that most all parties respected and usually one of his tactics to get his way was that he would go on a very well Publicized fast, consuming nothing by mouth until he got what he wanted. Now with the entire country tearing itself apart and no one trusting each other, the Hindu's hated the Muslims and the Muslim minorities in the Indian cities and countryside returned the favor. The death toll climbed as bloated bodies lay in the streets for days and weeks.

Everyone was afraid to come out of their homes to retrieve the dead. And there lay Gandhi on a roof top bed because it was too hot inside, with no air-conditioning to be had, excepting in the homes of the wealthy, days away from his death from fasting. He simply refused to eat until everyone stopped fighting with each other everywhere. Now here's where the story gets very interesting"!

"So weak from fasting as he lays up on this rooftop bed unable to rise up, barely able to open his eyes, surrounded by his weeping family and the important politicians of the day. Jena, the Muslim and Nehru all begging him to eat and each of their protestations falling on deaf ears, with Gandhi whispering, "When all is quiet everywhere, then I will eat"! Suddenly a dirty wild eyed man thrusts himself through the crowd and right away everyone thinks he's an assassin and grabs hold of the man who's yelling at Gandhi to "Eat for God's sake eat", or words to that effect. Now what is said next I'm going from memory, but I think he made some reference that it would be a sin against god for Gandhi to commit suicide and that India needed his wisdom, in these perilous times and that Gandhi himself was in danger of going to hell if he continued. Then the man says, "I'm going to hell for the sins I've committed, but you should not", or words to that effect. Now this gets Gandhi's attention and Gandhi weakly asked the man "What he'd done to make him think he's going to hell"? The man is highly agitated and then says, "When gangs of Muslims invaded our streets they caught my wife and children in front of my house and when I tried to save them they held me fast and killed them in front of my eyes and I could do nothing, then they beat me senseless, and left me for dead. When I came to, there they we're, my family laying in the street, dead"!

"I gathered them up as soon as I was able, dug the graves then buried them. Then I joined the Hindis as we invaded the Muslim neighborhoods again and again and did the very same things to the Muslim families that were done to mine. I thought revenge would bring satisfaction and relief, but eventually it made things worse. Ten times over did I do these things, but it didn't bring my family back and the guilt I feel because of my sins makes things worse"!

Mordechai paused for a moment before continuing, "Then Gandhi weakly opened his eyes and this is the part I can never forget, he says to the tearful, remorseful, dirty man, "I think I have a way out of your going to hell for you. Go into a Muslim neighborhood; seek out a young child whose parents have been slain. A child much like your own and raise the child as you would your own. Except raise the child as proper Muslim"!

Mordechai let that final statement hang in the air a moment before saying, "No religion has a corner on wisdom. Gandhi was not particularly a very religious man, but he was a moral man and wise and wisdom these days is in short supply"!

At that very moment yet another distant sound of gunfire occurred as the sun ways going down, causing Morty to slap his forehead and say, "Scheist, why didn't I think of this before? How many cell phones do we have among us"?

Between the two families they brought forth five cell phones upon the dining room table. Morty then grabbed his wife's phone and went into the kitchen, returning a few minutes later saying to Ahmed, "Have your family make a list of every Muslim family they know and their phone numbers.

Nothing we can do tonight because of the dusk to dawn curfew, but my Rabbi has just agreed to open up the Temple to shelter any Muslim family that can make it to any Jewish Temple come morning. He's calling every Rabbi in the city and the surrounding area. David, get a phone book and make a list of every Temple in the area, phone number and street address. Now when my Rabbi calls back he will give me a list of everyone he's contacted who's agreed to open the doors to Muslims. When I get those address's, every one of the Malanouche family get on the phone to every Muslim they know and explain to each that the Jewish temples will be open for sanctuary for one and all from the roving bands of rioters. They mostly come out at night so travel by day should be safe. Oh and one other thing when they go out, try and look as American as possible and leave the native garb at home at least until this whole mess is over. Oh, one more thing, tell each one they contact to call several of their friends and family and do the same as many times as they can. If all goes well we should be able to shelter a great many families, until the sun goes back down tomorrow night and the harpies come out to play"!

"Now if nobody minds I'll go upstairs to the bathroom and perform my bodily functions"!

By eight AM the following morning, every synagogue in the greater Chicago area was open for the business of sanctuary with the Jewish members greeting the Moslems that arrived in a slow but steady stream into their midst. At one time or another, some Jew would slowly shake his or her head and say, "Go figure already"!

No gratitude was sought or expected, for it was the right thing to do.

Perhaps in the days to come, this act of charity would be remembered, but to expect it was out of the question. What was expected was for the act to stand alone as a beacon for others to follow. Nothing more.

After the second week of non-stop traveling around the country following the President in Air Force One, the pool of reporters and cameramen were on the verge of open revolt to their editors. As best they could, fresh clothing and personal items were hurriedly shipped to them often delayed, due to the rapid nature of the Presidents movements. And as is usually the case often they were lost.

Of course, the President could always catch a nap in Air Force One and fresh clothes and food was in a state of constant replenishment from the stocks of the various military installations where he landed.

The news organizations finally relented sending in a different set of reporters and camera personnel, to accompany the President for no longer than two weeks, then yet another crew of journalists would replace them. Of course, being a part of the Presidents traveling entourage meant that the journalistic crew had the very same access to the necessary aspects of the military installations that the President and his staff had. They even had access to every installations "BOQ's", (Bachelor Officers Quarters), for access to a bed as they wished, while others chose to stay close as possible to the President, who quartered many evenings on Air Force One, staying in touch with the White House and key members of Congress via video conference calls as the situations on the ground warranted.

But time and events wait for no man and upon several occasions, Air Force One had to make sudden departures to another part of the country, leaving behind those quartered in the various "BOQ's", behind and stranded. From that point onward every member of the Presidential media entourage, decided that it was prudent to stay as close to the President and especially Air Force One as possible.

Entering into the fourth week of the National Emergency, the third shift of media reporters and crew assigned to the President arrived, replacing the worn and haggard second crew that was returning to their home bases. As one CBS reporter met her replacement on the Air Force Base tarmac, the incoming reporter said in greeting, "Hello Molly, you sure look like crap girl" "Mike don't even start with your crapola! I've been going nonstop for the last two weeks and am in serious need of hard liquor, tall glasses and a long bath"!

"Word is that you guys have been hitting up the Presidential bar tab on the POTUS craft to a fair thee well, so maybe that would negate the need for that stiff drink"!

"In lieu of the combat pay we're not getting, the booze will have to suffice. But thankfully every installation that we've landed at has been very gracious and seen to it that the Presidential bar was always fully restocked and I must say that we were all well fed in the mess halls whenever we could get there. We just stayed close to POTUS wherever he went. But the military dining halls are something else. I never knew what 'Shit on a Shingle' was until last night"!

"Molly, its creamed beef on toast. Typical grunt food"!

"Yeah Mike, I discovered that the hard way at two in the morning as we caught the last shift of Midnight Chow for the on duty flight line crews. We suddenly dropped in just as the cooks were starting to clean up and they had to rustle up some assembly line scrambled eggs and what was left of the "SOS"!

"So how'd ya like military chow"?

"It would take some getting used to for me, but since none of us had eaten since the previous morning, I hate to admit this, but it tasted sort of good. Get hungry enough and a girl will eat almost anything"!

"When you get back to the upper West side of Manhattan, perhaps you could toss a bit of a soiree' for the swells you hang out with and serve "SOS" and show them what a real babe you are"! "That'll be the day, Mike"!

"So what about the President getting involved in a full blown riot this morning, in Beverly Hills"!

"Filed that report at five o'clock, this morning and it was horrible.

There were no helicopters available for every single one was assigned to fighting the fires that raged around the city, so we had to get from one place to another by military convoy. So someone made the smart decision to drive through the heart of the Watt's section of LA, the very same that was torched years ago during the riots. We're all driving at a breakneck pace, when up ahead as we cross this intersection, we run right into a gunfight between the rioters and the Oriental shop keepers. This stops the entire convoy and the Secret Service, the SEAL team members and the regular troops fall out as were all being shot at by the rioters. President Magnusson dove out of his Hummer and was hustled by the SS to shelter, but while they were running, an agent caught a hail of bullets intended for Magnusson. One which the Kevlar vest didn't catch wounded the agent. So Magnusson drags the agent to shelter grabs the man's side arm and starting firing at the rioters that are firing at him"!

"So Molly did he hit any of them"?

"Hard to say since I spent most of my time trying to be as small as I could, but we have much it on tape, Mike"!

"Did our camera man get the shot Molly"?

"As far as I can tell, he got part of the footage, for he caught a bullet during the melee, but the Fox News guy got most everything and will share his footage with all the news organizations"!

"So what happened later"?

"From what I could gather, the Korean and Chinese businessmen were right at the point of being overrun by the rioters when out convoy stumbled across them and it appears we were just in the nick of time and saved their hides as well as their businesses for the present"!

"How long was the fire fight Molly"?

"I'm gonna say around the better part of an hour. Thankfully our military had greater firepower and were better shots, but I've gotta say that the rioters had a lot of automatic weapons"!

"So back to Magnusson for a moment. The man is under fire by the rioters so what does he do next"?

"The son of a bitch takes charge. He gathers some of the soldiers and picked up one of the M-16's and charges across the street, amidst a hail of bullets, with seven soldiers following in his wake, one of which gets hit just a few feet from safety. He orders the soldiers into firing positions to set up a cross fire and here's the kicker. The soldier that got hit held his ground, and covered their flank and as the rioters tried to circle around his position, the wounded soldier held them off killing six of the rioters. The President's group along with the others cut the rioters down fairly quickly after that and in about fifteen minutes later the firing stopped"!

"Jesus H. Christ Molly what a story this will make on the evening news"!

"Not so fast Mike. If you think about it for a second, how would it look if the President was seen by the world, gunning down citizens in the streets, during a riot? The extremists would have a field day, sparking even more riots. No, I think a little self-censorship is called for, like the President so often says, 'For the common Good'! Anyway, that decision is above our pay grades and I'm pretty certain the Suits will squash or at least heavily edit what appears to the public. If not, someone in Government will pay our people a hard visit"!

"But Molly that's Government Censorship"!

"Mike, think a minute. This is a national emergency we are in, all the way up to our necks. Just because we have the right of free speech, doesn't mean that we should reveal every little thing we deem newsworthy blindly. Think about it! As for me, I can wait awhile, and see it someday on the History Channel"!

"Well, I don't know about that Molly, for it goes against everything," at that point Mike was interrupted.

"Stop that Mike right now. I'm sorry now that I ever said anything about that to you. Should any of this ever get out amongst those blogger friends of yours, I'll know right away their source and rat you out in a heartbeat and you will be a mortal enemy of mine till my dying day. I will make it my life's work to dog your every step over this. Do I make myself clear? This man Magnusson is a hero by any meaning of the word and has earned my everlasting respect. I will not stand idly by should anyone do a single thing to damage his reputation. Do I make myself clear Mike"?

"You have my promise Molly. My lips are sealed", said Mike meekly! "They damn well better be Mike. Oh just so you know, the President got nicked twice in the firefight with the rioters. Flesh wounds, he was later treated and released by his private doctor and the military medics. He'll have some additional scars on his body to tell War stories about should he ever decide to write his memoirs"! As Molly Pringle walked away from her replacement, she cursed herself for being so candid with Mike Prichardt, one of the rising stars at CBS news. She quickly chalked it up to battle fatigue. What she had the good sense not to reveal was the body count during the incident at Watts, which ran just under a hundred, before she stopped counting. How many met the grim reaper, before the motorcades arrival, or because of it, was unknown. Somehow, some way, somebody would use it to make political gain of some sort. Yet she was a partial witness to the event, having the good sense to hunker down and leave the fighting to those well trained for such events. She hated firearms and usually had little use for those who were adept in the skillful use of such implements, yet were it not for those people she doubted that she would be looking into her compact mirror at this very moment, seeing someone who had witnessed death up close and personal. No doubt, with the exception of the three casualties suffered by her military escorts, those citizens that perished would be missed by few, if any and the world would be better off by their passing. Born into a world, with everything going against them witnessing the opulence of the few at the expense of the many their fate being predetermined by some unseen hand. Yet hadn't it always been this way, since the beginning of time? The Alpha's of the world will always hold advantage over the Delta's. Hadn't that itinerant carpenter from Nazareth said as much to Pontius Pilate, just hours before he met his fate, when he said, "The Poor will always be with us"?

She just hated getting all intellectual, because it made her head hurt.

Too much thinking and soul searching made her remember many of her sins of the past and yet here she was, a famous media reporter, thrust in a dangerous place and come out the other side unscathed, except for more memories. One of which was the memory of a man who was like no other she'd ever heard of. A man who had suffered a loss as few others had. A man of action and wisdom. A doer, not a poseur. That man was her President. She had observed him almost every moment for the last two weeks, taking charge knowing precisely what to do and when to do it, at a non-stop staccato pace, with recent memories of a man with no military training, taking immediate charge of a perilous situation and emerging victorious, then charging off when the situation was well in hand, to face other dangers and impossible situations. Thinking not of himself but of others at all times.

When she got back to New York, she was determined to call in one of her chits, from the editorial page of the New York Times and write a self- edited opinion piece for this guy Magnusson. She was a witness to greatness and someone had to spread the news. As she looked into her mirror, she had to agree with Mike, that she had seen better days and indeed she had been "Rid hard and put up wet"! But a tall glass, full of hard liquor, while soaking in a bath tub would solve that problem.

15

As Molly Pringle lay soaking in her bathtub, surrounded with the soft light of candles, she listened to Miles Davis playing the muted sounds of "Killer Joe" on the tape deck in her adjoining bedroom. She reached into the small bowl which contained the slices of cucumber suspended in ice water and put a slice over each of her eyes, then deftly reached for the nine inch tall thin glass, containing ice surrounded by thirty year old Scotch Whiskey. As she lay there relaxing, her mind raced as to her schedule the following day. In about an hour from now she would write the Op Ed article for the New York Times, to be printed 'as is', and hand deliver it to the editor. Over the years she'd bedded the bastard enough times to ensure that her scribbling received a priority status. Then tomorrow she would have lunch with her assignment editor at CBS and discuss the plans for an hour long news special in prime time to recount her travels with the President.

With the entire news divisions rating in the tank, they had no other alternative but to finally go with her. All the others that she was passed over for, had crashed and burned ratings wise and finally one of the 'Suits' in the Executive Suites had a moment of epiphany, deciding that Molly Pringle's time had finally arrived.

Back when the world was young, she'd received her undergraduate degree in Journalism from Rice University in Houston. Even did her time as a cheerleader for the Owls endlessly mediocre football teams, and received her Master's degree in that discipline two years later.

Her resume and style demanded that she join the local CBS affiliate as a fledging beat reporter while she was pursuing her Masters diploma.

Through rainstorms, floods and the dark of night, Molly Pringle had charged ahead of the others, usually getting there first, scooping the other reporters. Her raw, no nonsense style, was a hit with the local viewing public and at the first opportunity she jumped ship and joined a

CBS affiliate in Austin, specializing in Austin's affairs in the Municipal as well as at the State level of government, when in session. What brought her to the attention of the CBS big wigs at the Network in New York, was her series of stories regarding the scandal at the Governor's Mansion years ago when simultaneously the sitting Governor, the disgraced Head of the Pardons and Parole System and a Ft. Worth Commercial Real Estate Developer simultaneously disappeared, never to be found. As she worked the story, she discovered any number of layers of political mire, like a bad cabbage all leading to the illegal and unjust incarceration of a University of Texas football star, "The Uberballer".

The man with no name, was subsequently released, after a long stay from the State Prison unit at Huntsville along with several others and eventually became an international bounty hunter. In pursuit of the story, the name "Jaeger" kept coming up as a possibility, but the man made it a point to keep well out of the lime light, so after a while, especially after she was asked to become part of the CBS network in New York, she just decided to let it go.

Her good looks, long legs, slight Texas drawl and take no prisoners style of reporting made an immediate impression in the Big Apple. She eventually evolved into the 'Princess of Ambush Reporting', coming out of nowhere to confront the wealthy and influential and shed light on their activities. Of course, in the course of time this was bound to make enemies, of those at the highest levels of governance and business, but to the rank and file of the average man and woman, enjoying the more salacious aspects of the rich and famous, she became a celebrity. Invited to most of the important events and parties, she chose her bed partners wisely and with a purpose, never spending the entire night, but leaving a lasting impression with everyone she blessed with her bodily fluids. On camera, she was the model of dignity, grace and panache', but off camera she had her moments. When challenged, she could be as profane as anyone and in a multiple of languages. She was characterized by those who knew her well as one who could, "Strip the hide off a Rhino, with simply her mouth", that comment being able to be taken in a multiple of ways.

The following day went far better than she had any reason to expect.

Her Op Ed piece was eagerly accepted by the New York Times editor, who wanted to know when she'd be available in the future. She cheerily asked him to take a ticket and she'd get back with him at her earliest opportunity.

The long working luncheon with her producers at CBS regarding her upcoming hour long news report in Prime Time, regarding the Presidents activities during the emergency, went well turning into a daylong procedure and well into night. It was finally going to happen and as a result, before long perhaps a shot at an Anchor position somewhere.

When she returned to her Manhattan apartment, she went over her mail and one envelope stuck out from the rest. It was in an envelope that looked like many other 'invitation to an event' envelopes, yet of the finest paper containing cotton fiber, with a return address that said money and lots of it. As she opened the envelope, she discovered that it indeed was an invitation to select few. A soiree', at the home of the Countess Fabiola Hargraves.

She put the invitation down on the coffee table in front of the television, turned on the TV to one of the local news channels, went to her bar and made a drink, lit a cigarette and returned to her couch, picking up the invitation and changing the channels till she caught up with a channel that was reporting on the Presidents current activities. She watched the story till the end then as a commercial appeared, turned her attention to the invitation.

'Shit fire and save matches', she proclaimed inwardly. An invitation to a party hosted by one of Nuevo York's prima society Mavens was indeed a feather in her cap. She recalled being introduced to the woman a few years back, during the intermission of a concert at the New York Metropolitan Opera House. The bitch looked down her long perfectly sculptured nose, held a limp hand forward and said simply, "Charmed", moving quickly on to yet another clutch of the Four Hundred, eager to be in the presence of faux royalty.

Up from the ranks of the Euro fashion runways, she quickly rose. Her first husband, a world famous tennis star. The marriage lasted slightly over a year, ending with the untimely death of the man during a tennis match. It was match point, the next serve most likely to determine the winner. At the very point of his opponents serve, someone yelled an indignity from the stands at Fabiola's husband. As the hundred and fifty mile an hour serve rocketed off the opposing players racket, her husband turned his head in the direction of the heckler, the serve bouncing off the ground and slamming right into the players inattentive temple killing him instantly. Of course, since the husband was of some obscure Euro royalty, her brief union with him conferred upon her a title that she'd never relinquished.

Over the years she'd worked her way through three other well deserving and wealthy husbands, all of which, passed to their great reward in her bed 'with their boots on', as the ever popular saying goes. Leaving her with a significant portion of their wealth as a wee bit of Lagniappe', for services rendered above and beyond the call of duty. During her 'In between times' between husbands, she was known as a woman who took her discrete pleasures from both sides of the batter's box, as gossip would have it. So once again with her fourth husband just six months into the ground, she was again free to become the "Hostess with the Mostest", as the society pages reckoned things. She had always been visibly active with most of New York's charities, maxing out her annual tax deductions in the process, but now she was back to her private entertaining at her posh Manhattan, mid-level roof top apartment. Her four thousand square foot digs were reported to always bring in the best and most entertaining of guests, impeccably catered and with a small musical group playing in the main entertainment area and yet another playing outside, twentieth floor marbled patio.

An evening with the Countess, was guaranteed to be a memorable experience, where the latest gossip was exchanged and the selected elite, commingled with the equally selected up and coming 'Hoi Polloi' of the art world.

Thus an invitation to one of her events was not to be taken lightly. But for Molly Pringle to be recognized and invited by "The Countess" was a sign that she'd at last on the verge of arrival.

She made it a point the following day to return the RSVP signifying her acceptance of the invitation and although the next few days would be rather busy in preparation of her taping of her Prime Time special, she would find time to make the appropriate preparations.

As she prepared for bed, she took stock of her completely unadorned appearance in the full length mirror, coming to the conclusion that some five pounds, or so needed to be somewhere else in the next two days. A strict diet, time in the gym, followed by time in the steam room and drinking endless bottles of water, to help flush out the crud in her system ought to get her back in fightin' shape. If the fighters could do it to make weight then so could she. But all in all she wasn't doing so badly for an old broad on the short side of fifty.

In the words of her buildings door man, "She still had it goin' on".

Friday evening she would turn heads. For the next several days she toyed with the idea of inviting someone to escort her to the Countess's digs. But as she surveyed what was available at work, she decided to attend the event stag. Perhaps someone interesting would be there during the course of the evening.

The party was to commence at nine PM and her program was to begin at ten, Eastern Time. She made it a point to have the cab deliver her to the Countess's building at nine thirty, reckoning that the early arrivals were always the so called 'little people'. By the time she made her way up to the twentieth floor, it would be a quarter to ten, sufficiently tardy, to not seem awkward yet appropriate, since word had reached her ears that her telecast was to be the centerpiece of the event. In the world of high society, this could cut either way depending on the biases of those in attendance. Since the thrust of her reporting was in praise of the Presidents, relentless efforts, it would seem reasonable, that a Lion's Den of controversy would await her, after the program.

She promised herself to be nice at all costs, but one of her many faults was that she rarely ever backed off from a good old fashioned verbal tussle, never quite able to turn the other cheek and when sufficiently provoked, always gave far better than she received.

The cab ride uptown went well and as she entered the building, she encountered some people she'd met awhile back and some celebrities of note, who accompanied her up in the elevator. As they all reached the twentieth floor foyer, they followed another preceding group through the door and were greeted by the Countess's latest companion, an embarrassingly grand looking male model, clearly the woman's latest, boy toy of the moment.

A never ending monument of the trophies that wealthy Cougars flaunt at will. Having no wrap to stash, since it was a warm summer evening, Molly followed the crowd to the bar, passing by the proffered fluted glasses of tepid Champaign by the wandering hired help. After she hit the bar and placed her order for Jim Beam, two fingers, (being the designated forefinger and the pinkie giving no doubt that three inches of whiskey was the order of the day) straight up, she turned and surveyed the attendees. The dress that adorned her was a sleek black affair, cut sufficiently low in the front and to slightly below her waist line in the back, held up by a Herculean effort of those two little black spaghetti straps, that held the laws of gravity in abeyance, as long as they weren't put to the supreme test. Anyone with eyes took notice, that other than the shoes that clad her feet and the small handbag she carried, the dress was all they're was. No jewelry ever adorned Molly Pringle, for some women simply didn't need it.

Then through the crowd came her host, the Countess Fabiola, looking as flawless as ever. Although they were of approximately the same age, it was clear the Countess held a slight advantage in the visual realm, thanks to the latest in medical technology her face was tight and flawless, her body equally sleek and supple able to bring an erection from those six feet under while traipsing through a grave yard. Her makeup applied with the skill of a hired artisan, who no doubt studied at the feet of a Renaissance artist, while attired in an equally revealing gown adorned with what appeared to be diamonds.

As she approached, she held her arms out exclaiming, "Ah, the centerpiece of our little soirée', Molly Pringle, journaliste' extraordinaire'. I'm so happy that you could come", as she gave the appropriate embrazio and kiss of each cheek that always left a space in between.

As she put her arm around Molly, she turned and escorted Molly to an overly large settee in front of the massive wall mounted LCD television set, saying to one and all, "Gather round everybody for Molly Pringle's introduction to the world at large is about to begin"!

Taking her seat next to her hostess, Molly began to feel uneasy, for there she sat as a counterpoint to the usual course of feminine acquisition of great wealth. There they sat the Countess and the Molly. Perhaps it was the way Fabiola announced her name, with that apparent verbal smirk that signified one of an agrarian origin. Molly had never been in love with the name, especially since her college days in Texas, often considering changing it to something more upscale. But as her career progressed, she discovered that her accomplishments and her appearance overshadowed the name of a commoner, to such a degree that her given name was almost an afterthought.

The photographers all swirled around the duo, flashes of light intermittently signaling to strike a pose, while several of Manhattan's premier gossip columnists, of both genders peered around their photog's to catch the moment. No doubt with the latest in micro recorders lurking somewhere secreted on their body's eager to catch every word.

The countdown to the program started, as the wait staff faded away into the bowels of the residence as not to bother the guests, ready to return to quickly refill glasses during the two minute commercial breaks. With just under a hundred guests in attendance they would have to work fast.

After the intro and the lead in to the special, the craggy face of Les Crane, the networks premier journalistic icon appeared, peering over his signature rectangular reading glasses as he bid welcome to Molly. It was the standard scripted question and answer interview, interspersed with edited clips of video footage of Molly's fortnight in the Presidents wake as he attacked the problems of the Nations nightmare. All eyes switched back and forth between the program and the duo of Molly and the Countess Fabiola, sitting together on the settee. When the first commercial break appeared, as pre rehearsed the staff was out in a flash working the crowd with freshly opened bottles of chilled Champaign in each hand deftly filling proffered within the two minute break, then disappearing once again. It was during the break, as the glasses were hurriedly being refilled, that Molly began to hear the faint disapproving murmurs of some of the guests as draconian actions more befitting a benevolent dictator.

As the second commercial break came to an end, the murmurs again resurfaced during the brief interlude, as the stage whispers began to escalate in volume, with some stalwarts suggesting his complicity in the riots and the troubles that assailed the inner cities. Of course the footage of Magnusson's all too public image of the Chief Executive terminating the services of a Federal official, in full view of the traveling video cameras that would be seen all over the nation was distressing to the feelings of the Upper Crust Mavens of the Upper West Side of Manhattan. Yet this was simply a continuance of what Lars Magnusson's modus operandi, in previous encounters with bureaucratic incompetence. Everyone knew his style and knew what to expect when the man was in the area, yet long held habits are often hard to shed.

Yet it was quite obvious that a public dismissal of an official was a career ender and guaranteed to leave in one's wake an enemy. If a poll was taken of everyone in the room of precisely what it meant for an appointed federal official to be held accountable actually meant, from that tally one was bound to get a hundred different answers.

Entering into the second half of the hour long program, the Countess Fabiola's guests started to become restive, as the story of the encounter with the rioters in the Watts section of Los Angles unfolded, with Molly providing a verbal overlay to the video of the fire fight, to provide context.

The viewers were shocked as the vignette' unfolded, whereas never in the history of the Country had any President been actively involved in a shootout with his fellow citizenry. The video showed the Presidents military Humvee, coming under fire by the rioters and the President bailing out of his vehicle, led by one of his people, while under fire. It even revealed his taking of his wounded guards weapon and firing back at some unseen assailant, but thankfully no visual of him hitting anyone, or his taking charge of a squad of soldier escorts to provide a crossfire position against his assailants was made public, having been thankfully been edited out as previously agreed with the Network Executives.

One would think that many of those assembled would have been grateful the President survived such a dangerous encounter. While some appeared to be so, others took the counter view, still dogmatically insistent that Lars Magnusson was a traitor to their chosen political agenda and not a bit shy, as to where their sympathies lay.

As the program reached it final five minutes, the moderator, Les Crane, asked Molly just what she thought of the President now that she had seen him in action. Molly thought a brief moment, then slowly looked straight into the camera rather than at Crane saying, "Everyone who knows me and who has followed me in the media, is aware of my points of view. As a journalist, I'm supposed to perform a function of unbiased reporting, dealing on in facts that are verifiable. What has been reported this evening has been a realistic view of a man, thrust into a situation like no other of our Presidents in recorded history. As any fool can plainly see, the man leads from the front, plunging into harm's way, inadvertently taking charge, when others clearly have not, in a timely manner. Of course it's upsetting to an individual's career of governmental service, when it is terminated in such a public way. But in a time of national emergency, when an appointed bureaucrat fails to perform and literally lives are at stake, how is the violator of the public trust to be held accountable? Fortunately for them we don't live in a third world dictatorship or else the firing squads would be busy almost non-stop"! The moment Molly made that distinction over the airwaves, the entire room gasped in astonishment. Then her comments continued, "In the space of two weeks, my first hand exposure to the President, has been a gradual epiphany for me and turned me around, from a Presidential critic, to a supporter of the man, in our time of need, as a proper steward of our ship of state. The latest reporting of the casualties from the Wild Fires and the Rioting in many of our Cities has surpassed the twelve thousand mark. The man literally lives out of Air Force One catching cat naps when he can while many of us sleep soundly. There will be no rest or vacation for the man, until the very last fire is extinguished.

Until the next crises occurs. At the very least we can say an occasional prayer for the man's health and safety. And one final thing, May God Bless America"!

The camera than focused back upon the moderator Les Crane, who closed, "From the studios of the Columbia Broadcast System in New York, Good Night America. This is Les Crane"!

As the program concluded, the small trios in the main room as well as the outside patio started playing once again, as Molly rose up asking her host, "My kidneys are in need of relief, could you direct me to your nearest facility"?

Fabiola stood up and said follow me dear and walked her over to her private bathroom in her bedroom, half closing the door behind her as Molly swiftly hobbled to the facility to relieve herself hearing through the half open door, "I'm genuinely glad to have finally met you after all this time and hope that we can become fast friends in the future, but I must warn you that socially, you may just have relegated yourself to Manhattans version of the Leper Colony"!

Just then she heard the toilet flush, followed by the brief sound of hands being washed, then the door swung wide as Molly reappeared smiling and said, "Won't be the first time and certainly won't be the last Countess"!

"Please call me Fabiola, my dear"! Then taking her by the arm said, "Let us descend back into the teeth of the Lion's den and confront evil together shall we"!

Many eyes were drawn to the duo as they made their way back into the main room as both went to the bar, with Molly getting a new drink. As the bartender asked his evenings employer what she was having, Fabiola said, "Whatever she's having", to seal the bond between them both.

"You heard the lady pal, two fingers of Jim Beam", making the horizontal sign of a true Texas Longhorn, "but ya just might want to kiss it with some ice"! As the Countess took her drink, she asked, "Shall we toast anything? How about your emergence as a Cause Celebre' my dear"?

"Sound's good to me Fabiola, but you might want to sip what's in your glass, for it simply will not do for you to, perish at your own party"!

Plunging back into the crowd, it was easy to see just who had joined the ranks of Molly adherents and who stayed aloof, by watching who approached and who stood in clusters talking amongst themselves, casting the occasional glance at Molly and the evening's host. As they passed the buffet table Molly grabbed a stick of celery plunging it into a small crystal bowl of imported Alaskan salmon dip saying, I need a smoke, can we go outside? The music on the patio is wonderful"! Settling upon a spot overlooking the city lights, Molly reached into her purse and removed a pack of cigarettes as the Countess asked, "May I have one Molly"? Molly lit both of their cigarettes, as Fabiola asked, "What brand is this Molly, it tastes wonderful"?

"No brand, for I roll my own. Sometimes it's a pain in the butt, but I get just as good a smoke as a so called premium brand for a lot less money"!

"You'll have to show me how it's done sometime", said Fabiola! "Honey, with your money that should be the last of your concerns"! "Never the less, it's something I want to learn, for one never knows, does one?

"You have a point there, Fabiola"!

"Before we rejoin the party, there's something I want to warn you about"!

"And that is"?

"Just a few minutes after you arrived, I noticed the uninvited arrival of Mavis Knickerbocker. You know who she is don't you"?

"That old bitch. Who doesn't? What's she doing here"?

"Spying, reporting, snooping. In Manhattan, she goes where she wants, clubs, restaurants, plays, events, both public and private. Her nose is everywhere. I've sent out invitations from a carefully prepared guest list and she wasn't on it. Of course if asked, one has to chalk it up to a clerical error, by ones incompetent staff. The old bitty has been around forever and simply refuses to die from natural causes. Everyone reads her gossip column in the Times, disguised as a 'Journal of Current Events'. If by some chance she likes you, it's like becoming a made man in the Mafia, if not one becomes a social pariah"!

"Then why doesn't anyone tell her off and stand up to her, in public Fabiola"?

"The reasons my dear are both simple and complicated at the same time. But the simple solution is that we're all sheep and social cowards.

Those of us fortunate enough to ascend the heights of social acceptance, wish to stay there as long as possible. No different than when we were children in school. We wish to be popular, as so few people are. We strive to be interesting and inevitable, to see and be seen as relevant to the social swirl. If one composes a soiree', to be successful, then one must invite those of importance. Since we cannot be everywhere at once, we have to have a guide and Mavis Knickerbocker, through her column provides this service. If she smiles we are considered Haut Couture'. Should she frown, the Leper colony awaits! Thus as long as she lives, we are all in this event horizon with the danger of being swallowed into the abyss of the social black hole"! Eventually she will join her ancestors in the bowels of the far away depths, only to be replaced by another desperado

"A hell of a way to live your life if yaw ask me"!

"That it is, but it does have its moments, just so you know, the woman is an avowed Communist and will not view your reportage favorably"!

"Thanks for the heads up Fabiola. Let's get inside and rejoin the party"!

As they entered the apartment amidst the gaggle of those who wanted to meet both of the women, they saw Mavis Knickerbocker surrounded by a clutch of social climbers paying homage to societies self-appointed Grande' Dame. A positive mention of them in her column was worth ones weight in gold, publicity wise and everybody in the area knew it. Every instinct that Molly had indicated that Mavis Knickerbocker was keeping a keen eye on her from her perch across the room, looking like an old female Jabba the Hut. She wondered if at any point in her life, had she appeared appealing sufficiently enough to appeal to any gender in either a prurient or puellant manner. Deciding the argument of moot value, she turned her attention to those who were congratulating her on her performance on national television earlier. As the clock raced towards the midnight hour, the Countess took Molly by the arm and introduced her to the cream of New York society, all of whom were polite, some of which agreed with her assessment and some of those who didn't without putting too fine a point of things, all the while assiduously avoiding the Mavis Knickerbocker, who by this time had made it a point to not refuse a non-stop replenishment of her Champaign glass by the hired help.

Eventually a feral looking man approached the Countess looking at his watch and asking her, "Madam Knickerbocker is wondering if you could steer Ms. Pringle her way so she could have a chat. It's close to midnight and she will have to get to bed soon"!

"Working on her second Jim Beam in ice, a relaxed Countess repressed a giggle wondering out loud about the rapid approach of the 'Witching' hour and asked Molly, "Well Molly, are you up to this"?

"Well lemmeseeheah, I've got about six ounces of Kentucky Sour Mash Whiskey in my innards and I can catch a cab ride back to my digs. Why the hell not", she said with a toss of her head. "Lead the way Pal"!

As they approached in silence, both Molly and the Countess briefly glanced at each other, each putting on the eminent front with a grand smile as Molly was introduced by Fabiola, "Mavis, so good of you to attend, may I introduce the centerpiece of our little get together Molly Pringle"! Neither of the women made any attempt to shake hands or embrace. The gossip columnist sitting in her chair surrounded by her acolytes and Molly standing there ever regal and sure.

"Molly Pringle", said Mavis slowly. "That's your given name eh? Ever think about changing it to something less agrarian"?

Still holding on to her smile, yet with her eyes narrowing in on the enemy, Molly answered, "Yes, for an ever so brief moment, then I sobered up and thought of my wonderful parents"!

"I caught your little performance in behalf of that part time President we have to endure, which begs the question, since the death of his family a while back who's been providing him his male relief, if you know what I mean"?

"Mavis is your given name? Surely one would think it should be Monica, given your proclivities and why on earth would you ask a question like that"? Those assembled could sense the static electricity in the room.

The queen of the Big Apples gossip, finally matching wits with someone approaching her equal. Everyone held their breath awaiting the next response. As if on que, both musical groups stopped playing, so everyone could hear the verbal point and counterpoint.

Ignoring Molly's question as Molly had done to her, Mavis bored in saying, "Clearly the man hasn't been laid in a very long time and since he's not a bad looking man, I was wondering if during your time in his presence, you decided to do something about it", then she paused, "for the common good", using the Presidents favorite catch phrase!

Deftly ignoring her last comment Molly countered with, "Somehow you have elevated yourself as the premier gossip columnist in the greater New York area, using the Times under the cover as the "Journal of Current Events". As anyone can see you are someone of considerable talent and accomplishment in this churlish regard. Regardless of what ever anyone might say, it is clear that you of all people did not achieve the heights of your profession by sleeping your way to the top"!

Just then a palpable moan escaped from those assembled, followed by escaping several shouts from the kitchen staff, even at some distance away from the verbal carnage that was developing in the next room kept an eager ear to events through open doors. This had all the earmarks the standard Friday night 'Chop' battles, between teens on the streets, except for the location which was about as uptown as it gets.

"Just one moment Missy", said Mavis before Molly loudly interpreted her by walking over to the music trio and asking for the microphone, "Is this on"? The piano player quickly nodded his head. Molly now taking charge addressed the group, which now comprised all of those in from the patio and the kitchen staff and said, "The time has come, the Walrus said, to talk of many things. But rather than that, I say it's time to read Mavis Knickerbocker, or whatever her real name is, her rights, for the common good"!

Then Molly turned to her sitting target that couldn't bring herself to face the long overdue onslaught and said, "Mavis Knickerbocker, you have the right to remain silent. You have the right to remain incredibly ignorant and stupid. You have the right to retain a mouthpiece, for you need one badly. If you cannot afford a mouthpiece", at that moment she paused for effect casting a disdainful glance at her adversary before continuing, "I was about to say the State would provide you with a mouthpiece, but since the word is out that you are an incredibly cheap and venal individual, I've decided that you of all people can afford another set of chops"! Yet another moan from the guests and yet another shout from the kitchen staff sprang forth before Molly continued, "And I give fair warning that anything you say from this point forward, especially since we have a slew of video cameras in attendance, may and most likely will be used against you in the court of public opinion"!

"In addition, since the court of public opinion will clearly find you guilty, of bad manners, bad breath and a countenance most foul, thus the court will now pronounce sentence:

"You are to go to Hell. Directly to Hell. You shall not pass Go. You shall not collect two hundred dollars"!

"That said ladies and gentlemen, I see the witching hour is upon us, the hour is late and I bid you all a good evening"!

As she tossed the microphone back to the piano player, nervous applause started to break out from the edges of the crowd and the assembled staff, who immediately went back to their tasks. As Molly made her way through the guests, in triumph guided by the Countess, to the elevator, she was congratulated by others, clearly out of sight of Mavis Knickerbocker, all eager to touch her and read the following day's edition of the New York Times, especially the gossip columns that were certain to recount the evening's verbal carnage. As Molly rode the elevator down to street level alone with but the Countess, they looked at each other for a moment before the Countess spoke, "Molly you gave a bravura performance. Never before have I witnessed anyone more deserving, receive such a well-designed and complete tongue lashing. Now we shall put you in a cab. Next week we must get together for lunch. But from now on I shall have to be the one to watch your back"!

Then the elevator door opened at ground level as Fabiola and the doorman hailed a cab and watched it as it disappeared on its trip back down town into the night. By Ten AM, the following morning, Molly finally woke up with a slight hangover moaning as she gingerly got out of bed to make her morning coffee, padding into the kitchen dressed in an overly large, well-worn man's t-shirt left behind by some long forgotten guest. As the hot water dripped into the carafe, the phone rang and on the third ring she picked up the receiver saying a terse, "What"!

"Molly is that you? It's Chad Ramsay your producer! "I've been trying to call you for the last two hours and left three messages. Look on your recorder"!

Jesus Christ, Chad, its Saturday isn't it. I just woke up! Are you calling about the Program last night? Wait a minute while I get my first cup of coffee and a pill. I've got a bit of a hangover. Just a minute", she said sleepily putting the receiver down, several minutes later she picked up the receiver saying, "OK I'm back. I've a hand full of aspirins in me along with some coffee, now what's up? I did mention that its Saturday didn't I"?

"So ya called to tell me about the program last night? So what were the overnights"?

"Everyone raved about the Program last night, especially Crane, who says you got a lot of spunk and charisma on the tube and the ratings were extremely well, blowing away anyone in our time slot. But listen up girl.

That is not why I called. Look on your recorder and tell me how many calls you got"!

"Jus a second Chad, I'll look, when she came back she said, "There's fifteen calls on the recorder Chad. What in the world is going on"?

"So you haven't read this morning's Times or any other paper have you Molly"?

"Chad, I just woke up and I'm trying to escape a hangover and you're not helping with these questions. My head hurts"!

"The party last night at Countess Fabiola's digs? You remember that"? "How could I forget"?

"The word is that you got into a verbal scuffle with Mavis Knickerbocker. Is that about right"?

"Yeah, I gave her a piece of my mind. So I'll bet she's pissed and probably looking to sue over some indignity. So turn it over to the legal department. There was three different camera men there getting it all on tape. Fabiola will have the list of invitees. So tell me why I'm so popular all of a sudden to yank my chain"?

"The lady wants to know, so I gotta tell her", said Chad to himself, before saying, "Ya really don't know do ya"?

"Chad, will you quit screwing with me and tell me what's going on"? "Mavis Knickerbocker is dead"!

"What"?

"The old broad, the wicked witch of the upper west side croaked from a heart attack, shortly after you left around midnight last night"!

"Well the old girl was alive when I left her"!

"Doesn't matter, last night after you left, she started to gurgle, as the witnesses told it and keeled over from her seat and hit the floor. Seems like everybody just stood around and watched, with nobody calling 911, until the Countess reappeared from taking you downstairs and it was she who called 911. Ten minutes later the medics arrived but it was too late. She was officially croaked. They tried resuscitation on the spot and all the way to The emergency room, but no dice. The cops arrived, the graveyard shift and took statements from everybody there. Apparently the Countess didn't get to bed until 7AM after everyone left. The headlines in the Times are just hitting the streets and uh, well you just have to read em. Oh and the videos have already gone viral on the internet and no doubt by next week you will splashed all over the Tabloids as the girl who can kill with words alone. We haven't heard yet from the White House, Kremlin, or the Vatican but given that it's a full bloody moon, I wouldn't be surprised, So a couple of boys from the legal department are taking the train in from Long Island and wondered if you would be so kind to grace us with your presence in about an hour, for a little legal CYA just in case? Oh and don't return any other of your calls on the recorder if you please, make a list of who called and let the legal boys sort it out, will ya babe"? "I'm jumping into the shower soon as I ring off, but someone is going to buy me lunch or dinner and I'm talking to him. See ya in an hour"!

Of the three videographers at the Countess's party, two turned out to be savvy businessmen, saving their camera footage, for the Gossip TV Programs and the National Enquirer, while the lone cameraman that released his footage to You Tube in the hope of getting a scoop, the following Saturday morning came up short, financially when he could find no buyers for his efforts. The latter of which was viewed in the CBS News conference room early Saturday afternoon, by a room full of executives and two members of the legal team.

The entire footage was replayed, three times for everyone to see if there was any possibility for a lawsuit to be brought against either Molly

Pringle and or the network either jointly or severally. Several segments of the footage were slowed and preened over carefully like a mother eagle tending to her freshly hatched newborns.

"Anyone see anything, a single thing that can possibly signify that Molly and or us are culpable? Anybody", asked the President of the news division?

Alvis Kooperman, the senior staff lawyer spoke up saying, "First amendment stuff all the way through. Molly never laid a glove on Mavis Knickerbocker. It clearly was the old girl that tossed down the verbal gauntlet and quite frankly I'm impressed on how well our girl from Texas skewered the old girl, linguistically. Where did you matriculate Molly"?

"Well sir, ah done did my learnin' in reading', writin' and my numbers in a County School District an ah guess that Rice University took pity on poor lil ole me and let me hang round long enough to get my Master's Degree", she replied, in her finest affected Texan country drawl!

As everyone tried to stifle a giggle, the President of the News Division said sternly, "We're not here as an exercise in frivolity people. Now Molly, we're all here to get out ahead of this and in no way wish to ascribe a possibility of guilt, on your part"!

"And cover the networks ass in the process, right", injected Molly quickly!

"Just doing our due diligence my dear"!

"Good then we're all on the same page!

The conference room door opened and one of the secretaries came rushing in, handing a hand written message to Kooperman, who after quickly scanning it stood up saying, "Our friends downtown have come through. The Manhattan coroner has just completed his autopsy of Madam Knickerbocker and it seems that she has had a long standing heart condition and was on medication for some time for her malady. The official pronouncement will read death by natural causes. So it appears that any possibility of a criminal indictment

Is out of the question. Although there is a remote possibility of a civil action, I recommend we stand foursquare behind our star reporter in every aspect. As to why, after repeated viewing of the incident, there is nothing there in any fashion that indicates culpability. Further, in the coming days, especially after her good work on the Presidential Report, the networks ratings can only rise and this incident can only provide invaluable publicity.

The national rags will have some fun with it for about a week, and then some other scandal will rise to the level of the front page. As for you Molly, you may be involved in some challenging situations in the coming weeks.

Hold your water and it'll all subside"!

"Your agreement of standing by me legally in this can be fully executed in writing by the close of business Monday, can it not", asked Molly?

Kellerman cast a glance down at the end of the conference table, seeing the appropriate head nod slightly saying, "I'll draft the document first thing Monday morning for your approval"! "Good", exclaimed Molly, "Now which one of you cowboys is going to feed me"?

The Air France flight had just landed from Alexandria Egypt, to Kennedy Airport, with a refueling stop in Paris, as Jaeger peered out of his first class passenger seat, preparing to deplane. It had taken an entire month to corner "Abdullah, the butcher", one of the leaders of the "Muslim Brotherhood". With the assistance from his old friend, Nestor Magellan, he was introduced to several influential people in the Egyptian Government, who wanted to see the trouble maker gone. Since it was in their best interests to have a third party do all of the nasty work, all they had to do was pick up the phone, bark some orders and the way was made smooth.

Along the way, he picked up three expatriate Legionnaires, in Rome languishing in their retirement and always in need of some extra money to sustain their retirement. Half in advance and half upon delivery and of course all expenses covered was the usual deal. The last half of their fee was always deferred because it was understood, that should they fail, it was highly likely they would be dead. After all, jails and prisons abroad were usually a death sentence anyway. So when engaged, the "All or Nothing" attitude was the norm.

The target, "Abdullah the butcher" was a radical Muslim sheik that traveled freely all over the middle east. He was known as a collector. One who facilitated the funding for the various activities of the radical Islamic fundamentalists. In his earlier days, he successfully took part in the kidnappings and executions of a seemingly endless string of apostates to Islam. Of course his kidnappings were considered an art form, where as they always went off well and the funds paid were never recovered. The termination of his tactical activities came to a close when, after a string of kidnappings and after the ransoms were delivered, rather than the subject of the abduction being returned whole, he was usually returned in various parts, by post and always there were parts missing.

Of course, the Egyptian authorities had a general idea of the man's whereabouts and according to the US State Department, Abdullah probably could have been apprehended at any time, but for reasons of fear of reprisal or simply internal corruption, the man was permitted to travel unobstructed in Egypt and throughout the African Continent, where a significant Moslem majority was in power.

What brought things to a head, was when the American Ambassador to Tunisia was kidnapped in broad daylight and his body guards slain in the street. No attempt of ransom was made by the abductors. Two weeks later, in the dead of night, his mutilated body was dumped, in parts, in front of the American Embassy, as a message to the infidels.

For weeks the question of 'How to respond' was kicked around at the highest levels of government. CIA, State Department and the FBI and since America was involved in the Wild Fire emergency, a decision was made to seek auxiliary assistance.

J. Tecumseh Bollinger, Brigadier General USMC Ret., was sitting at lunch in an upscale DC restaurant, the guest of several old friends he served with during his time seconded with the State Department. He now spent most of his time in retirement, being a sort of Professor Emeritus at the FBI training facility at Quantico, Virginia.

Bollinger, never one to observe the political necessity's said simply between bites of his salad, The Tunisian Ambassador gets himself kidnapped and while the Nation is burning to a crisp, no one seems to want to make a decision. The Delta and SEAL teams sit on their butts and the suits at CIA and FBI dither. You need someone out of the loop to sustain plausible deniability should things go wrong. In short, a fall guy to capture this Abdullah guy alive if possible and bring him back to the Justice Department for a show trial, so America can make a political statement to the rest of the world. That about right fella's"? The two hosts briefly glanced at each other. Then Jerry De Forest said, "That's about right General. You know how things are around here"!

"Yeah Jerry I know. I know a lotta folks, but there's but one that comes to mind if it calls for getting the job done and 'Jaeger' is his name"!

"Jaeger? Never heard of him", said Dan Morris!

"When's the last time you did any field work Dan", asked Bollinger, who promptly answered his own question saying, "Never mind I think I already know that answer to that question"!

"I know of his work first hand, when my last assignment was to command an action in Africa, just prior to my first retirement and then one other, some years later around the time of my second retirement. He's not exactly front page material and he wants things that way"!

"But what's he done General", asked Morris?

"You can get hold of this Bail bondsman in Houston named Rafferty, then some guy who used to work for him as a chaser, named just "Hondo" and finally this female lawyer in Houston. Elizabeth Beauvior. Between them, if they're of a mind, maybe they can put you in touch with him, if one asks very politely. Piss any one of them off, and any one of them is likely to tell you to go piss up a rope. Of the three, the one to be very nice to is the lady lawyer. Try any Federal moral suasion on her and suddenly there will emerge a whole lot of people that will have their way with you and you will not like it. If anyone can get hold of Jaeger it's them. But the rumor is that his services don't come cheap. You may want to ask someone in the US Marshall's Department as they've tossed him some work from time to time, and I hear they've got some good things to say about him, or so I've been told. Now you both can turn off those recording devices, so we can enjoy out lunch"!

"What's the man's first name General", asked Morris?

"Marine Corps. records list him as 'Jaeger', no first name, no middle initial. It's on his birth certificate, just Jaeger and in Kraut speak is translates into Hunter! Now turn off the recorders fellas"!

The meeting with the State Department representatives went well, while at Buffy's offices in Houston. She had become a senior partner at her Uncles law firm, due to the retirement of Boyd Parmalee, who still held an office there being a partner emeritus. After hearing the men out, she negotiated the terms of service within ten minutes and within another fifteen had a contract for services rendered, fully executed. Just two main points of the contract were of concern, principally that should anything go awry the US government will do whatever is necessary to procure the release of the contractor, at the direction of one Elizabeth Beauvior, Attorney at Law, secondarily the fee which was set at the existing price of Five Million American dollars, to be paid half in advance to Attorney Beauvior along with a working capital amount of two hundred and fifty thousand dollars. In the event the subject was returned to US soil dead, the fee would then diminish to One Million American dollars. The subject was to be turned over to the US Marshall Service, anywhere on sovereign US soil which encompassed any Embassy, aircraft, or ocean going vessel. Any violation of this agreement by the Government, would grant the entire agreement null and void and the world press would be made aware of this agreement.

The further terms of the agreement were nonnegotiable. It took some forty eight hours for the government to respond, but after receiving the hand delivered copy of the fully executed agreement, by the Secretary of State, (an unheard of event never before in the country's history) along with the funds transfer into one of the firms accounts, Jaeger was set loose.

A quarter of a million dollars working capital can go a very long way in the middle east, when placed in the right hands. The right bureaucrat, ever in need of a better life, revealed a weakness in Abdullah's security envelope. When the right body guard was away from the rest, earning a long weekend of solitude with his favorite 'houri', he was immediately snatched by Jaegers Legionnaire's just after his 'moment of truth' with the young lady. Of course her throat had to be cut and they stayed till she bled out. She wouldn't be missed by anyone, since Cairo was a city of some sixteen million people.

Her former boyfriend was bound gagged, drugged, and then taken to a place far out in the desert where no one could hear him scream. With a member of the local Cairo constabulary along for his well-compensated ride along with Jaeger and his retirement community of Legionnaires, they flipped a coin as to see just who could make the poor soul reveal the whereabouts of his master and the timetable of his movements.

It took some nine hours of skillful manipulation by the interrogators, using nothing but their hands and other low tech implements readily available. Each one of them had a three hour run at it, steadily eroding the resolve of the object of their intentions in an excruciatingly painful way.

Then the Egyptian policemen took over, boring into the victim, his crooked teeth and his ever constant smile, taking the man ever closer to his breaking point. The accumulation of relentless activity over time, with the advancing and receding waves of pain, altered the subject's brain chemistry to a point where his will finally belonged to his interrogators completely.

Finally the prisoner began to talk freely. Through broken teeth and the muted pain of two broken legs, sufficiently mollified by some rather fine home grown heroin, the Egyptian official gleaned the truth of Abdullah's Travel plans for the entire weekend, translating into English the testimony of one who was about to join his ancestors. The Legionnaires took careful note, as Jaeger watched impassively marveling at the skill of this Egyptian.

He thought, 'No wonder the CIA turned over their captives to the Egyptians for rendition. After all, they had several thousand years to perfect their craft'.

When he was finished, the Egyptian stood up from his seat, turning to his ad hoc colleagues and smiled, saying not a word, for the chagrin on the faces of the Legionnaires was sufficient.

"Team effort gentlemen. A great team effort" said Jaeger, thinking the Frenchies would've probably broken the man anyway, but he was glad the Egyptian was along for the ride and his translation abilities along were beyond measure.

At a nod of Jaegers head, the captive was put out of his misery with a single bullet and taken outside of the structure and buried in a shallow sand grave. In time the shifting sands would reveal the corpse, but everyone would be long gone.

Abdullah the butcher always traveled at night and he was to be in Alexandria the following day for a meeting with the other members of the Islamic Brotherhood, to finalize plans for an upcoming assault on the Paris and London Metro's as well as a suicide bombing of the Chunnel trains under the English Channel. His body guard had revealed of such a plan before he succumbed to the Egyptian. No details mind you just the generalizations.

Knowing where Abdullah was and where he was headed was

invaluable and their Egyptian associate was of invaluable help along the way. Jaeger had marveled at what was made by the political meanderings of those supposedly in the know, of the inconsistencies of what was called torture, by the western world. Clearly their knowledge of the subject was incomplete at best. For in the hands of a skillful interrogator almost every man had his limit of endurance, the trick of it was to discover his exact point of vulnerability. The greater the personal will, the greater the task. Of course, in the rare case of someone with a death wish, or someone with a deep seated post hypnotic placement, then the limits of physical pain became apparent.

The next few hours would either re-enforce or reconfirm the argument one way or the other. Quickly the group went back to Cairo, so the Egyptian could get them together with an underground arms smuggler, to outfit them all with the necessary firepower for the pending confrontation. In short order, five WWII all metal Sten Guns with screw on sound suppressors was selected along with, four clips for each weapon with metal penetration ammunition for each weapon distributed equally for each member. The weapons were immediately tested in the large warehouse and found in good working order. Old they may be but highly serviceable and just the thing for close up work. The available Kevlar vests were all of a small size, suitable for women, therefore of no use. Thus all the men had to take great care, for everyone had to move fast in the coming hours and a serious wound meant that someone would be left behind to fend for themselves, in case things went awry. That was the understood risk that everyone knew to be true.

When Jaeger was satisfied with his purchase, he withdrew ten thousand dollars to pay to the arms dealer.

The rest of the day was spent finding a suitable coffin, contracting a hearse to drive them to Alexandria and finding the suitable medical supplies to accompany Abdullah to his trip to America.

Once again The Egyptian was invaluable in securing a bona fide death certificate and the necessary paperwork to release from local custody the coffin and its contents. Just before sundown at around eight in the evening, everyone was in position around the home in Cairo's suburbs, waiting for the emergence of 'Abdullah the Butcher' and his entourage. Three vehicles drove up, in front of the walled house and as the massive wooden gate opened, three men emerged, scanning the area for any sign of things awry. Seeing that all was in order, they signaled the others. As Abdullah was the last man to come out, Jaeger sprang from cover in front of the lead vehicle, firing a short burst at the tires, puncturing them immediately then firing through the wind screen to disable the driver, then firing at anyone who presented himself as did the others. Each careful to try and not hit Abdullah. By the end of each man's second clip of ammunition twelve seconds had elapsed as the Legionnaires closed in firing their sound suppressed weapons at the surprised minders, grasping for their weapons and finding a hail of well-placed bullets instead.

At a signal from the Egyptian an ancient Cadillac Hearse appeared around the corner of one of the buildings, gradually stopping across from the bullet riddled trio of vehicles. As he tried to crawl under one of the vehicles, Abdullah was hit across the head by one of the Legionnaires, rendering him unconscious as Jaeger and the Egyptian lifted him bodily up and crammed him into the waiting hearse. As it pulled away, another car pulled up from behind and retrieved the three Legionnaires, making their way north towards Alexandria.

Approximately thirty seconds had elapsed from the time that Jaeger had opened fire, to the departure of the second vehicle containing the retired Legionnaires. So much about any talk of old geezers not being able to pull their weight. If things continued to go well, quite apart from the money each of them would garner, in the coming days they could hold their head high come each Bastille Day for the rest of their lives. That no one caught a single bullet was almost a miracle. In a few hours, they would have to pull over and dispose of their weapons, prior to the hearse's appearance at Alexandria's airport. The slow Thorazine drip had been administered intravenously in one of the main ankle arteries in Abdullah and the multi bottle oxygen supply would only engage when the altitude exceeded twelve thousand feet. Of course Abdullah would sleep all the way across the Atlantic, in his sealed coffin. Just prior to their departure, Jaeger presented each of the Legionnaires with their second envelope for the final portion of the agreed upon fee along with their tickets back to Rome, except the fee was double that in which was agreed. The same went to the Egyptian as well as the hearse driver and the other driver.

Hey after all it was OPM and it went towards furthering international unity. When his flight landed at Rome, he bid a fond adieu to the old Legionnaires, made certain the sealed casket was placed in the baggage compartment of his flight back to New York, then sent a quick email to his contact in the US Marshall's Service informing of the arrival of the sealed casket.

Thus he and the Marshall's never met as he walked through Kennedy Airport to the baggage retrieval area, he saw a slew of men entering the baggage area, with US Marshall emblazoned across the back of their wind breakers, disappearing behind metal doors. As he retrieved his small suit travel bag and slung it over his shoulder, he glanced inside the swinging metal doors the Marshall's had entered to have a brief glimpse of them opening up a funeral casket. Jaeger smiled and decided to take a cab into Manhattan and spend a day or two in the Big Apple. After all he had the remainder of his working capital, some nine thousand dollars and the local economy needed a helping hand.

He checked into a hotel not far from Times Square and spent the rest of the Friday seeing the sights, even to a point of taking a tour bus and replenishing his wardrobe. He'd been to the Big Apple several times before, but they were just in and out affairs, barely putting his feet on Manhattan's terra firma. This time he would take a few days, to engage all of his senses. At days end he decided to call his contact at the US Marshall's service after he'd seen the news report regarding his delivery earlier in the day.

"Damn Jaeger, the guy was almost dead after we picked him up. Had to get him over to the nearest emergency room, to get him all thawed out"!

"Well Don, what did ya expect, with him traveling all the way over in a casket", said Jaeger!

"They said he was shot through with Thorazine"!

"I had it measured to a very slow drip, enough to immobilize, but not enough to fry him"!

"Ya got him stashed in a safe house"?

"Yeah. He's not going anywhere. He'll be offered up first thing Monday morning by the grunts at the Justice Department"!

"So the point being is the product is delivered in good shape and the contract fulfilled", said Jaeger"!

"Yeah, it is my man"!

"Then you'll instruct the Justice Department to email my contact in Houston immediately and have a hand delivered letter of confirmation to the same party first thing Monday

"Will do Jaeger. First thing Monday morning and in case no one else ever says this, Thanks and stay frosty"!

"Will do Don, take care"!

That evening Jaeger, while having dinner at a sports bar, saw a televised report regarding the Nation Wide wild fires, that were entering into the sixth week of duration, with finally the governmental forces, federal, state and local, arrayed in the front line finally getting a handle on the fires, with some long overdue assistance from mother nature. Thunder storms in Oregon Washington State and Northern California, made quick work of the conflagration, as well as various parts of the upper New England state crossing the border into Canada. The following day's satellite photos would reveal vast blackened areas, deforested as a result of the fires. Eventually, Mother Nature would replace the forestry, in her own way on her own schedule.

He was about to pay his bill when a CBS news special came on, Hosted by Les Crane, featuring Molly Pringle reporting on her two weeks with the President. Jaeger vaguely remembered the woman years ago, during his dark time, as in court every single day sitting right behind him, trying to gain access to him for an interview, only to repeatedly be rebuffed by Buffy his lawyer. He recalled a particularly spirited exchange between the two, when Buffy threatened to have the sitting Judge ban Molly from the court room. He recalled thinking that it stood little chance of happening, since the Judge had seemed to rule against Buffy on nearly every single objection she brought forward. Still, Buffy prevailed, running a bluff that silenced the reporter for the rest of the trial.

As the news report ran its course, he compared what he was seeing on the television to his memory of the woman long ago. They both had come far in the ensuing years and were pushing their midcentury point, but it appeared the years had been far kinder to Molly than they had to Jaeger.

She still looked good. Must be the war paint the TV studios apply before a telecast. As the report rolled on, he saw the President Magnusson in action on the streets of Los Angeles and thought about the last time they met on a cold football field in Minnesota. The man had come far and had been put through his own particular ringer, yet look at him, Jaeger thought. The right man, in the right job, at the right time and something he'd read long ago, about tough times never lasting, while tough people do.

The program over, he paid his bill and returned to his hotel room. The Jet lag was finally catching up with him and the hotel bed was calling.

Saturday Morning and the Nine AM call from the desk woke Jaeger and by ten, he was showered, shaved and dressed in the new slacks and sport coat he'd bought the previous day. He grabbed a brief breakfast and decided to hit the clothing stores once again and by three in the afternoon his stomach called halt as he passed a restaurant calling with the famous smells of corn beef.

Searching for a booth where his back was to a wall he quickly slid in, just as a family was leaving and placed an order for a New York Style Corn Beef deli sandwich. Good habits were always worth retention as he scanned those seated, already enjoying the heart attack food.

Half way through his meal, he noticed a woman peering around her partner, glancing directly at him. Since she only showed half of her face and that only briefly he ignored her, until the fourth time he viewed her glancing in his direction. Then he saw her say something to her male partner, rise and walk his way. There was something familiar about her that he just couldn't place as she approached. Perhaps it was the way she was dressed. Polo pull over, hair pulled back in a ponytail, slacks, heels and the way she walked.

The long stride of a Dallas type model that reeked of Texas. Her stride spoke with the full confidence of a woman who had been there, done that and had the marks to prove it. As she came to a stop in front of his table, she bent down and said, "Pardon me but haven't we met somewhere before"? There it was, you could take the woman out of Texas, but that hint of verbal four Alarm chili, never quite left as he said, "Heck I don't know. Remove the shades and we'll see"! As Molly removed her sunglasses, Jaeger gave her his full attention for a moment, and then returned to his meal saying, "Molly Pringle, ace news reporter. Caught your show last night on the tube. Great report. But why would a famous Texican woman like you take an interest in me", said Jaeger returning to his massive corn beef sandwich, never taking his eyes off of her for an instant.

"May I join you for a bit", asked Molly? Jaeger nodded his head for her to take a seat, his mouth full of corn beef, as he heard her say, "You have that Texican look yourself, but where on earth did we meet"?

Having swallowed his food Jaeger said, "We haven't formally", as he swallowed his beer!

"So we have, uh, encountered each other sometime ago but you're implying we've never been formally introduced"! Jaeger continued her line of thinking adding, "I'm surprised and flattered that I'm still in your memory banks"!

"This is driving me crazy, because I know we've crossed paths before, but I'm coming up with zeros as to just who you are"?

Jaeger then pulled up a newspaper with Molly's picture on the front page, above the fold with the headlines, "Words can Kill", referring to the full length article of her encounter with Mavis Knickerbocker and said, "If your that good with words, then I'd better be especially nice Ms. Pringle and say, you sat behind me in a Texas courtroom a long time ago"!

Then he saw her jaw drop, then she quickly recovered saying, "Jaeger, the UT Uberballer. I just knew it"!

"Yeah, but that was a long time ago. "From hero to zero, in the space of a few weeks", was the phrase you coined I believe"! It took a great deal for Molly Pringle to be speechless, for if anything she was imbued with a world class wit and as had been previously demonstrated could verbally slice and dice with anyone, yet here she was sitting with someone who was a legendary presence as far as she was concerned. Finally she came to her senses and said, "I'm terribly sorry for what I wrote at the time. Most of us bought the circumstantial story of your family's death, being led in the direction the prosecution wanted. After all after the season you had, your military background, and especially your last game in the Cotton Bowl", her voice trailed off to nothing.

Jaeger glanced at the front page; Molly's picture emblazoned across the front page in her full length black dress, and then said, "You certainly do something for a little black evening dress! Hanging out with a Countess and the social elite. You've done well Ms. Pringle"!

"Please call me Molly", she asked?

"Then Molly it is. Now we are formally introduced", replied Jaeger as he hefted the massive Corn Beef sandwich, taking another bite. As he chewed his sandwich, this attractive woman that sat across from him, just stared at him without saying a word.

"Cat got your tongue", asked Jaeger after he swallowed the corn beef? "Yeah probably. It's just that some time back after your trial, when I was all aggression and some short of common sense, I always had the thought of seeing you again some way, somehow. But after you were sentenced to life in prison, upon the insistence of the jury, I quickly forgot about that and went about my life, forcing you out of my mind. But here I am, sitting across from you far away from Texas and wondering about the fate of Serendipity. What're the odds of our finally meeting years later? Right here, right now"?

"Probably so enormous, the Cray Computer would blow a gasket trying to compute", mused Jaeger absently.

"So tell me, what have you been doing with yourself after all this time"?

"Got out of Prison and went straight"!

"I remember hearing that you became a 'Chaser' for a Bail Bonding company in Houston for a while and while you were in prison, completed your degree and even got a graduate degree at Sam Houston State"!

"All true Molly"!

"But how did you get out of prison? And why did the Governor grant you and two others a sudden pardon"?

"Not clear on all the facts there, but you'd have to talk to Elizabeth Beauvior my lawyer"!

"Ah yes, her. If I recall she threatened to have the Judge throw me out of court"!

"She just might have mellowed, over the years, then again maybe not. One thing is certain. I'd hate to get between the two of you, if y'all ever decided to have a catfight"!

"So tell me. What brought you to New York"!

"A little business and a little pleasure"!

"I can see you were shopping Jaeger"!

"Mighty perceptive of you"!

"You're not going to open up to me are you Jaeger"! At that point, Jaeger leaned over on the table, steepled his hands together and said, "Molly Pringle, you're a world famous reporter, headline news and a prime time celebrity. Anything I might tell you could be used against me in the court of public opinion. Can it not"?

"What if I gave you my solid oath, never to reveal a thing, you've said"?

"Molly, you're a reporter. It's in your blood, your genetic makeup, your education. How can you not"?

Just then she looked at Jaeger saying, "My kidneys are protesting. I've gotta go tinkle. I'm leaving my purse right here in your care, please be here when I get back and order me whatever you're drinking", then she got up and disappeared hurriedly to the rear of the restaurant.

When she returned five minutes later, in front of her was a fresh bottle of beer and her purse hadn't moved an inch in her absence, as she sat down saying, "Stay around over the weekend and allow me to show you around the Big Apple. My treat"!

"Molly, are you picking me up"?

"I certainly hope so Jaegermeister, I certainly hope so", she said flashing a huge smile.

"Then hold that thought while I get rid of all that used beer, order us both another and I'll be right back, directly", he said rising out of the booth.

Several minutes later he returned, taking his place in the booth staring at two additional beers and said, "What have I done to be so blessed by your presence"?

"Or cursed", she added slyly. "It's just that, I've been through a lot lately, what with the President and all, plus last night at Countess Fabiola's party and the aftermath, at noon with all the CBS lawyers and the Network suit's covering their blessed asses. When I saw you sitting here alone, something pulled me towards you. Now that I've gotten to know you a little better, I sense there's something good and true that runs deep in you. Maybe I'm all wrong, but I've always trusted in my intuition and it's served me well so far. So I'd really like to get to know you better. I believe in serendipity and fate. Something brought us together, whatever it is"!

"Jesus, I hate it when that happens Molly"!

"What's that"?

"You've just discovered my main weakness and it just might do me in"!

"And that is"?

"Beautiful Texican women who are smart, aggressive and highly articulate"! A gradual smile came over Molly's face as she searched for words eventually saying, "Big fellah, whatever happens you can be certain of one thing, we'll keep things light, I'll respect your boundaries, and what passes between us is nobody's business but ours"!

"Oh before I forget, should you ever need a top notch lawyer, ya just might wanna give Elizabeth Beauvior a ring in Houston. She runs her own law firm and they don't call her the "Princess of Darkness" for nothing down around those parts. Now tell me about your two weeks with the President, for I'm all ears. She then scooted around the booth closing the three feet that separated them and spent the next two hours filling in all the details of her adventures with Lars Magnusson that never made air time.

When she concluded she said, "You really oughtta meet the man"! "I have, but not formally. A long time on a football field in Minnesota."! Suddenly Molly's eyes opened wide as she exclaimed, "Yes, it was you", she gushed!

"I've always regretted that hit, it ended his football career"!

"Please don't feel that way. One door closed while another one opened.

Instead, he completed his degree, went to law school, entered politics and he ended up as probably the best President we'll ever have"!

"It also took away the family he clearly adored, wife and children. Got them blown to bits. Not enough bury and damn near put him in the ground"!

"Did you ever stop and think what you both have in common", asked Molly? "The passing of your family and the passing of his"? They both remained silent while the sounds of the restaurant swirled about them. "Yes I have"!

"Then just as we've come together, the fates will bring the both of you together. In their own way and time"!

There comes a time between men and women, not all that often, when a single word or phrase, can overcome obstacles and defenses, drawing two people together without a further word, as Molly then broke the silence saying, lets go back to your place, drop off your clothes, then join me at my place, so I can reprise that black dress, then we shall hob nob the night away and do a little social work among the rich and famous.

An hour later, Jaeger found himself riding up in an elevator with a revamped woman wearing the very same black dress as the previous evening, up to join the Countess Fabiola Hargraves and her Metro companion for a chauffeur driven night in the city that never sleeps.

During the evening's festivities, Fabiola drew Molly aside and said, "Where in the world have you been keeping this man Molly? He looks delightfully dangerous, not at all what I've been accustomed to"!

"You might say that lately I've been living right and I stuck in my thumb, pulled out a plumb and climbed the tree of life. And you're absolutely correct when you say that he's a very dangerous man"!

At three in the morning the Countess's limo dropped them both off at Molly's digs and once the front door closed to her place, they came together with such a force of passion, where Molly was tearing at Jaegers clothes, after simply dropping the straps of her little black dress, allowing gravity to do the rest. Barely making into her bedroom, it had been far too long for either of them while they explored every nook and cranny of the other bringing each other to the crests of passion, then diving back into the swells of each other, commingling their bodily fluids, until there was no more, allowing their joint release to drive them deep into the arms of Morpheus, two bodies united by a single lifeline, gradually withering back to its normal state as the duo fell into a well-earned deep slumber in each other's arms.

Late the following morning Molly lifted one eye open, the shut it again savoring the long overdue odor of a man on her sheets. Her mind going over the memory of a wonderful day with a man. A real man, of considerable accomplishment. As she stretched and rolled over to embrace her supreme conquest she discovered that he wasn't there. In a modest panic she jumped up from the bed and went into the bathroom hoping that he'd be there. But the bathroom was empty. Then she went into the living room, bare as the day she was born hoping that he'd be there sipping on a cup of coffee. But there on the glass coffee table, next to a half-finished cup of coffee, was a note. She picked up the half-finished cup of cold coffee, taking a sip, noting that he drank his coffee with cream and sugar, then picked up the hand written note, which read; "Coffees made in your kitchen. Sorry that I had to leave. Almost didn't. Heart said to stay, while the head said move on and cherish the memory. But you'd be the death of me and I have a ways to go before the pilgrimage is completed. But there's one other thing. Something else is in the way. Sorry, can't be helped"!

Memories, locked away in a private place "J"

Molly slowly put the note down, took up the coffee cup and savored the cold coffee slowly and wanting to find it all a dream, slowly put her hand down between her legs, feeling the moist remains of the previous evening, and remembering the words and feelings exchanged, in that all too swift time together, reclaimed reality.

He was gone. Reality returned. The world would keep on turning. All too soon, her innards would take a turn south, the skin would lose its elasticity, and she was at the pinnacle of her career, with no one to share it with. Still, it wasn't a dream. It was a glorious memory of expectations, dangled, then jerked away by some unseen hand. She cradled the coffee cup in both hands and started to cry.

Jaeger looked out of the aircrafts window, noting the time was shortly after noon as the Continental flight out of Newark climbed to cruising altitude on its way back to Houston. He'd no doubt that he'd be seeing Molly Pringles face on the evening television again and again, wondering if he'd done the right thing by leaving her. He momentarily closed his eyes and still felt her softness, her image in and out of that little black dress would haunt him for a while, as well as her incessant physical hunger for sexual release, over and over, until the combat was concluded. She would indeed be missed, but something else was in the way.

17

The Presidents aircraft flew into Andrews AFB at 0100 hrs. in the morning. Lars Magnusson was on the verge of exhaustion as he wearily climbed into the armored Humvee and fell into the small entourage of military vehicles that sped him back to the White House. The first thing in the morning, he would meet with his personal physician and the visitors from the West Coast for a complete physical and to see how well his implants were working. For almost twenty years, several people in America had been the test dummies for the highly secret, nanobot implantations, to provide a non-stop internal healing mechanism for the human body. The program was privately funded, with no more than a precious few highly capable individuals working on it since its inception.

The system was flawless in its working ability, the submicroscopic nanobot's constantly roving through the body, providing rapid healing capabilities in the case of injuries and the range of viral and cancerous intrusions the average human would endure in a normal life span. In a few cases it had proven to be a life saver, especially where Lars Magnusson was concerned. Still, in all the years of empirical study, the doctors and scientists, never fully grasped the true limits of the nanobot's capabilities in the human body. During the early day's workups, on rats and animal test subjects, they severed limbs, to see if the little bots could self-seal the arteries to stem the loss of blood. Those studies provided mixed results with some of the larger animals perishing while other smaller creatures survived.

What was of chief concern was not of the efficacy of the nanobot's, nor their implanted dime sized computer that served as the mother ship for the sub microscopic critters, but in endeavoring to lower the costs of manufacture, while still maintaining the quality of service. Thus far this had remained elusive, for the time being, but the decision was made to provide the little bots to selected people of merit to maintain their effective productivity.

By noon the President was pronounced fit by all concerned and the visiting doctors were sequestered upstairs until after dark when they were spirited to Andrews AFB and boarded the private Gulf Stream jet back to the west coast.

During his absence from the White House, the assistant press secretary was the only senior official to accompany the President, while everyone else stayed in place in Washington. The Vice President worked out of the Oval Office during Magnusson's absence and was in daily contact with the President, as well as Orval Goodwin, the Chief of Staff and Van Harvanian, the Press Secretary. As sure as cream always rises to the top, so does inefficiency and incompetence reveal itself during times of stress and serious emergency, with a stream of senior agency replacements suddenly stepping in to assume quickly vacated posts. For the logistics of the emergency had to flow unimpeded, to where they were needed most.

Excuses were not tolerated and reasons not given, for results were the only thing that mattered.

While the Nation's military was busy overseas and during the conflagrations, the Southern Border States began to see an escalated influx of armed penetrations by Drug and Human smuggling operations, by the various Cartels in Northern Mexico. The rationale being the assumption that while most of the military were busy fighting fires elsewhere, the southern door to the nation would be wide open for business. Thus for the first week of the fires and street rioting in the Nation's big cities, this thinking started to pay big dividends for the smugglers as the southern border was stripped to the bone of personnel. Yet after reports of heavily armed escorts of human and narcotic shipments, clashing with disastrous results, with various out gunned local law enforcement entities andmanpower requirements running thin, Magnusson in a conference call with the White House and the Joint Chiefs of Staff, interrupted the conversation, by asking, "What about the various non-essential military clerks that can shoulder a rifle and the various militia groups around the nation. The Constitution provides for a well-regulated militia, so here's an opportunity to bring them into play. If the nation was being over-run by military invaders they would be pressed into service anyway. So most of them are armed to the teeth.

Here's an opportunity for them to serve their country. Quietly but quickly contact those we feel are responsible, provide what munitions from the local armories, put them in uniforms, equip and feed them as needed, offer a small stipend if necessary for the duration, then attach them to serve under the appropriate Military or Border Patrol operatives, given the operational rules of engagement that currently exist. I'll bet we are overwhelmed with the response. Forget about vetting them, just have your people use their best judgment as to whether they're serviceable or not, for time is our enemy. I expect to hear about these militia volunteers being deployed along the southern border, no later than forty eight hours from the time we get off the phone"!

"Orval Goodwin will provide you with the appropriate Presidential directive and the Vice President will execute it within the hour gentlemen. Now are we all on board gentlemen"?

The room met with a resounding "Yes Sir".

"Then make it so people", the line going dead for the President had hung up abruptly. Within the time constraints of forty eight hours, the first contingents of civilian militia coupled with other members of the military able to demonstrate their ability to handle effectively firearms, started to arrive along their new duty stations on the southern borders. They were under the strict military control of the US Military and the Border Patrol, having been previously sworn in and provided written copies of the existing rules of engagement, then assigned their duty stations. Within twenty four hours, the first arrivals encountered their first contact with the southern drug smugglers and upon being fired upon, suffering casualties, drove the drug smugglers off capturing several four wheel drive vehicles that crossed the Rio Grande River during the dry summer months, laden with a haul of Amphetamines.

When the dead were inspected, it was discovered that armed elements of the Mexican Army were providing a vanguard for the smugglers, provoking an international incident. The Mexican Consulate was immediately called on the carpet by the Vice President and showed concrete evidence of the intrusion of Sovereign American soil by members of their military armed with weapons and ordinance paid for by the American Government. Their response was less than satisfying as further reports came rushing in of additional incursions escorted by elements of the Mexican Military overrunning in some cases, American Border operatives. As the casualties began to mount, the Vice President called Secretary of Homeland Security and gave a direct order to initiate direct military action, with extreme prejudice, on any elements on American soil especially if they were provided with armed escorts, in or out of a military uniform. This was roughly interpreted by the boots on the ground as a "Shoot on sight" directive. In all cases the border was to be observed and no pursuit of any one across the border to occur, unless otherwise notified.

A few old helicopters were pressed into service, along with a half dozen armed Predator drone aircraft. During the initial week of the operations on the border one of the armed drone aircraft patrolled the Big Bend area of the Rio Grande River spotting a convoy of five vehicles crossing the river, at a fording point just after midnight, utilizing its night vision capabilities at some six thousand feet. Waiting until the last vehicle in line was well across the river, the order was given to fire as the Predator released its payload.

Some ten miles away and closing in rapidly was a rapid reaction group of two vintage Huey choppers, filled with militia members accompanied by active duty military and two members of the Border Patrol, all coordinated by a mobile radar unit of the US Army.

The Army helicopter pilots saw the multiple explosions in the distance as they descended and in five minutes landed in the path of and behind the string of blown up vehicles, five miles north of the Rio Grande River. By sunrise a team of forensic inspectors was flown in from Dyess AFB in Abilene Texas, by Osprey VTOL aircraft to inspect the wreckage. Six four wheel drive vehicles, with the lead vehicle and the last in line clearly showing Mexican Military markings along with the dead bodies of armed members of the Mexican Military in combat attire

Two days later, in Southern Arizona some twenty miles east of

Lukeville, yet another convoy of Quadra track vehicles, entered American territory, being tracked overhead by another Predator drone aircraft.

Traveling at night during the new moon when the reflected light was the least, still wasn't sufficient to hide the convoy's activities in Arizona from the drone aircraft overhead. The order was given to the operator to release the two Hell Fire missiles on the convoy below, the first slamming into the lead vehicle and the second hitting the second to the last vehicle, one right after the other, split seconds apart.

Within the time frame of fifteen minutes, two Army and one of the Border Patrol helicopters landed in front and in the rear of the vehicle wreckage site, disgorging fifteen armed military militia and Border Patrol members who immediately secured the area. As they approached the wreckage site, several of the surviving Mexican Military and Cartel members opened fire on the advancing American Military. A half hour fire fight took place, in which time additional military help came to the fight.

When it was all over, the intruders were down to two survivors, one being a Cartel smuggler and the other a Mexican Army Sergeant on active duty assigned to a Northern Border Unit.

As the Predator drone aircraft circled overhead, a Mexican Military jet aircraft was sighted on the mobile radar station, gaining altitude as it closed on the Predator drone aircraft. The drone was directed to fly back to Luke AFB, outside of Phoenix, with the Mexican jet closing fast. As the drone flew over the small community of Gu Vo, it exploded in mid-air as a missile from the Mexican Jet slammed into it. As the jet made to turn back to Mexico, it met its end as it was met with a missile from an USAF F-16 closing in on him. The pilot had achieved his very first kill in combat as it was all video-taped by the onboard camera, and loitered for a brief time radioing in the crash site co-ordinates to a small hoard of Army operatives closing in on the crash site. The Mexican pilot had ejected and lay prostrate with a broken back when the Army units closed in, taking him prisoner.

By order of the returned President, the Mexican Counsel General was summoned to the White House, two days later and confronted with direct evidence of Mexican Government complicity in the drug and human trafficking business. That evening, every news broadcast ran stories, of the successive incursions. The evidence was clear and unassailable. Mexican army vehicles and soldiers and Mexican fighter aircraft had attacked American military equipment and personnel and the wreckages and operatives were clearly found on Sovereign American soil. The President went on nationwide television and one again recounted all that had recently occurred on the southern border, and suggested in the strongest terms, the Mexican President visit the White House, to iron things out before they got any worse.

Three days later, the Mexican President came to the White House with his entourage of high military and cabinet officials. The meeting between Chief Executives was clearly laid out. There was no more room for misunderstanding between parties. Mexico would take whatever steps necessary on their side of the border, to prevent any more incursions, by anyone, either civilian or military. The message was delivered loud and clear, with both governments having interpreters on hand and a tape recorded message of the meeting to be played on all Mexican media out lets through the land as well as America, in unedited form.

Further, no more international remittances would be permitted between America and any nation south of Rio Grande River, which included all of Central America. Finally, the Country of Mexico should consider any and all military aid to be held in abeyance, until further notice and make preparations for a return for an influx of its citizens.

As the Mexican Ambassador left the White House, with the Secretary of State he asked, "Can your President do these things"?

"Senor, no doubt some will bring suit in our courts against such action. Our government will vigorously fight any lawsuits in that regard for at the very least, the remainder of the President's term of office. The way things look right now, he's a lock in for re-election should he choose a second term of office, with an approval rate in the eighty percentile. You're President and your government should consider yourselves fortunate, considering recent events, for many members of our government were for a return visit of the War of 1847 and if you'll recall things didn't turn out very well for you then did it. You can thank Lars Magnusson for pulling in the reins of our Military leaders and cabinet officers. For years your country has permitted your problems to be deposited on our doorstep. All the President and our government are doing is returning the favor. I heartily suggest that you tend to your problems and we will tend to ours"!

The illegal's in America, were thus given a choice, of a one hundred twenty day moratorium, to leave the country now, settle your affairs as you see fit and take whatever assets with you, outside of the borders of the United States. After this period anyone apprehended and found without the appropriate documentation will be immediately deported, and any and all assets seized by the State they were domiciled in.

Goodwin and Harvanian viewed the Mexican Governmental officials depart, then returned to their offices as Harvanian said, "The crap is really going to hit the fan now Orval"!

"Van, we've been neck deep in the crap ever since day one. This is just another form coming from another direction. You've got the distinct pleasure of letting the White House reporters in on events in about an hour. Are you up to it"?

"Hell, I better be! Has the President given the Attorney General a heads up regarding the slew of lawsuits certain to result from his directives"?

"He was on the horn with the Attorney General, Homeland Security and the FBI Director, since dawn and everyone knows what's to be done. ICE will start resuming the workplace investigations and the AG is reshuffling his department to put in place enough attorneys to tie things up for a while.

No doubt some Congressional investigations will be instituted, but a guerilla action will be mounted to allow the President's actions to have effect. Day after tomorrow he'll be back on Air Force One heading for the funerals of those killed"!

"Ya know it might not be a bad idea to invite Molly Pringle of CBS back along for the ride with him. She gave him a great review on her program a little while ago and she's a card carrying liberal. She could've released the footage of his charging the rioters but saw to it that the key portions of concerned video footage was edited out. She's tough but fair and I think she's starting to have a thing for the President"!

"Might be a good move Van. I'll run the idea up his flag pole this afternoon"!

In the weeks since Jaege returned, he'd been meeting with Architects and builders working out a set of plans for the resurrection of the Ranch and farming community that had been in McLennan County for generations.

The initial twenty sections of ranching and farming communities, ceased to exist shortly after the murder of Jaegers immediate family and his incarceration in Huntsville prison for that act.

The family estate had been illegally dissolved and much of the land had been sold to other parties, being commercially and residentially developed. Over time, Jaeger had re-securedseveral sections of land out of the original twenty, surveyed by his forbearer Heinrich Jaeger long ago. Chief of which was the graveyard containing the graves of all of the generations of the family of Jaeger, along with the gravestones of the two Wolves Chani and Akila and those that followed after. It took some doing but with the help of Buffy his lawyer in Houston, he purchased the copse of ancient trees that surrounded the grave area and the home of the family that abutted the area.

Pay someone twice the appraised value of a property and offer to pay to move them into an adjacent property and people realizing a wind fall profit will usually comply.

It took a while, but Jaeger now had the funds required to resurrect the MHM ranch. At a certain point in the future he would fade from view and become a retired rancher. He'd need a big house, a barn; some hired hands, implements and some livestock start out with.

He remembered the stories his family would recount of how Henry Jaeger and Mendoza had started out across the Rio Bravo River, now known as the Rio Grande, after the Mexican American War, with twenty Longhorn cattle, a small remuda of horses and two wolves, settling near the Waco settlement and carving out a small ranching and farming empire. This was his goal to restore as much as possible, of what had been lost over the years.

He hadn't had anything to do with farming or ranching since his seventeenth year, when he departed for the Marines. Jaeger wondered if he could ever remember the things his father taught him so long ago. He could almost hear his father's voice bellowing down from above disapprovingly that he'd become far too citified and would never be a true cowhand much less a rancher that was worth anything. But if there was a heaven above, his dad must be aware, that to effect this resurrection that some unseen force was driving him to accomplish, many men had to die at the hands of the hunter. Now the money was there to make it happen. Jaeger was pushing his fiftieth year and he didn't have a lifetime ahead of him like his forbearer had. He had no family nor any children he was aware of, so why was he wanting to restart the MHM brand, he often asked himself? He just had to trust that driving force, trusting that things would be revealed in due course.

Yet at the heart of it all, was the memory of the two wolves, Chani and Akila. Two orphaned wolves from Southern Ohio, that became every bit a part of Henry Jaeger, when he was young as if they were of his blood.

Somehow, to make things complete he had todiscover two foundling and abandoned wolves, naming them Chani and Akila, bring them to the grave sites of his forbearers and seek their recognition and acceptance. He'd trusted in divine providence before and would have to continue down that path.

Monday mornings are at best a chore for most working people. You have to haul your lazy butt out of bed, perform your daily ritual of getting ready for work, fight the traffic in a metro area, hoping the crazy drivers chose this day to sleep in, then either attack a boring or difficult workplace for yet another week. 'At least Lars Magnusson was shielded from daily traffic jams', he thought as he worked his way through a hurried breakfast at 0600 hours in the morning. He was joined in the White House kitchen by Orval Goodwin, who sat on a stool, in front of the stainless steel work area, next to him. His cup of coffee was immediately placed in front of the Chief of Staff and his daily dose of oat meal was soon to follow as he said angrily, "Have you read the piece the Times printed on the front page"?

"The one following the headlines, "Magnusson, the Political Apostate", asked the President scanning the sports page"?

"Yeah that one", fumed Goodwin! "This time they've gone too far in their egregious slander"!

"Let me see what our options are Orval! Ah, I have it, we can send out a raiding party of Militia, escorted by the Justice Department, have a kangaroo court convened, as the entire editorial staff and publishers are perp walked in front of Rockefeller Square, tried then immediately hung on the spot", Magnusson said as he turned the sports page. "While I might start to feel great at that sight, I don't think it would go over too well on Main Street USA. Then we'd have nothing but headlines. So, let's not, say we did, and let America have its say. Until then I'll still have my place as "Chief Arrow Catcher"!

"The media south of the border is having a hissy fit with you, Mr.

President, for speaking so harshly to their Governmental officials the other day and of course all of the leftist regimes are having their say as well", fumed Goodwin!

Then Van Harvanian appeared, in the bowels of the White House kitchen saying, "Senator Scarsdale is demanding a meeting with you today to discuss your recent, pronouncements with the Mexican Government", as he grabbed an offered cup of coffee by one of the cooks!

"The very same Morton Scarsdale, who is the brother in law of the Time's publisher? The Senior Senator of New Jersey", asked Goodwin sarcastically?

"The very one", said Harvanian!

"So the man expects me to push him to the front of the line and ignore all of the pending obligations that have been piling up during my absence", asked Magnusson?

"The man is considered to be the 'Senatorial Lion', Mr. President," said Harvanian looking none too pleased, because a session with Scarsdale would serve to be a verbal blood-letting session for those involved, and prompting yet another long session with the White House correspondents. "My initial inclinations are to let the man go pound sand", said Magnusson wearily. "I'm not going to disappoint those who have been kept waiting for their Executive Moment"! "Wait a minute" said Goodwin. "Of course you just have to go through with your preset schedule so do it, but accede to Scarsdale's demand, but make it towards the end of the day. Van, have Melanie ring back Senator Scarsdale's people and tell him the President will be able to squeeze him in around three in the afternoon"!

"But he's booked up until after five in the afternoon and you know these things run, like a Greek wedding, always running behind schedule", said Harvanian!"Precisely", replied Goodwin. "Keep the Son of a Bitch waiting; only keep him waiting in Melanie's office! She'll know just how to handle Scarsdale, as he fusses and fumes about being kept waiting. She'll plant the hook because the man is a fool for a shifty skirt, always has been. Now starting around four in the afternoon, the President makes a very brief and hurried appearance in front of Scarsdale and is full of apologies, saying that things just couldn't be helped and that he really wants to get together with the good Senator and that he'll be with him directly. Now of course Melanie will have already contacted, the Republican House Majority Leader, Roland Stonecypher and will have gotten a commitment from him to join you for a consultation at about five thirty. He arrives on time and is escorted into the Oval Office through another door. When he's seated, then we announce that you are ready to receive him with apologies, a few hours late and as he enters he sees Stonecypher already seated. Now the man is a classical Alpha type who sports a high blood pressure history and who doesn't listen to his doctors, who just can't stand waiting"!

"Now if he decides to croak in Melanie's office, aid will be rendered as soon as possible and if not and he gains an audience with you and the House Majority leader, you can sit back and let Stonecypher carry your water for you, since I happen to know that he deeply respects what action you've taken since you've assumed the Presidency. He's said not one derogatory thing about you since you've taken office. Of course he's not going to cheer you on politically, but of the range of issues, the both of you are in lockstep, in a sub rosa sense. With any luck, our good Senator will be fit to be tied, he'll scream and rant and it'll be all caught on the Oval Offices video system, and with any further luck, then the man will keel over", concluded Goodwin with a smile and a flourish!

"Van, are you sure you haven't been a bad influence on Orval", asked Magnusson with a wry smile? "Gentlemen, sounds like a plan so set it up, but sometime tomorrow, make certain that Melanie is rewarded with an overly large bouquet of flowers and box of Belgian chocolates, since she's not normally entitled to receive combat pay"!

By ten in the morning, Melanie had contacted Senator Scarsdale's office, firming up the Three PM meeting time with the President, and just minutes later contacted the Republican House majority leader Stonecypher, turning the call over to the Chief of Staff Goodwin to finalize the five thirty time slot. She was made aware of what was to transpire and dreaded having to spend several hours with Morton Scarsdale looming large in the vicinity of her work place. Further, she would have to make certain that she had no reason to leave her desk during his extended visit, for the man was known not to be above rooting around in private papers. She'd started the day off feeling very feminine and thought the day was going to go well, yet by mid-morning a feeling of foreboding ran through her mind as she made certain the Oval offices secret video and audio recorders were certain to be in operational condition, especially the feature that allowed her section to be under scrutiny.

Most had thought the Oval office feature of secret recording devices were a thing of the past Nixon era, yet some years ago at the insistence of the Secret Service Presidential detail, a secret state of the art Audio Video system was quietly installed, with powerful directional microphones, that could pick up a shielded whisper from across the room. Of course the President's desk had a simple, switch installed that could disengage or engage the system whenever he felt it appropriate. By noon, all systems were tested and placed operational.

Senator Scarsdale had a un nerving habit of always arriving at meetings no less than fifteen and sometimes a half an hour late. It was a time tested purposeful ploy to enhance his importance. He saw to it that everyone waited for him and not the other way around. To achieve the station of Senator, took a supreme ego and to rise through the ranks, took the energy of a master politician, a puppet master of the little people and Senator Scarsdale relished it his role. All day long Lars Magnusson was hurried along meeting with the variety of social groups that required Presidential attention, Boy Scouts, Girl Scouts, Veteran Associations, all being hastily assembled for their long overdue meet and greet with the President.

Everyone understood the man had been busy as of late and were grateful even for the abbreviated time allotted. As one event in one part of the White House concluded, the President was rushed to yet another continually, eventually being glad he'd not consumed a large breakfast, for there was just no time for a potty break.

Morton Scarsdale arrived with a small entourage of two other Senators at precisely three twenty in the afternoon, as he hurriedly rushed to Melanie's Desk saying, "Good Afternoon Ms. O'Bannon, I'm here to see the President"!

"Well Senator it's a good thing that you were running late, for I'm afraid the President is in the very same situation, so if you'll have a seat, I'll notify the Chief of Staff that you're here. But I was told this was to be a private meeting between just you and the President"!

"Things change missy", blurted out the Senator highly irritated that he was not shown directly into the Oval office. I'll just go inside and await his arrival"!

"I'm sorry Senator no one is permitted to enter the Oval Office without the express approval of the President, as per the Secret Service"!

"When did that all start? That's ridiculous, we're going straight in", replied an angry Scarsdale as he made to open the door.

When it wouldn't open he turned at Melanie and said, "The door won't open", in a surprised manner. Seconds later a Secret Service agent rounded the corner asking, "Is there a problem here"?

"I'm being kept from my meeting with the President. I'm Senator Morton Scarsdale and", the Secret Service agent interrupted the Senator saying calmly, "Senator I know just who you are and if you'll be kind enough to take a seat, the President has been on a dead run since sunup and he'll be glad to attend to you shortly I'm sure. Besides, Ms. O'Bannon is the keeper of access to the Presidential office, as per the Presidents directive. So if you'll be kind enough to take a seat", then Scarsdale abruptly interrupted the agent asking, "What about them", referring to the two other Senators. As Scarsdale made to speak, he was interrupted, by the agent

"Senator, we were told that just you would be attending to the President and we were told to provide but a single seating device. We were not directed to provide three. So it looks like the gentlemen will just have to stand, unless you wish to relinquish your seat Senator"! Then he turned to Melanie and said, "If you need me for anything Mel, just hit the button", crisply turning and left. Nothing makes time pass more slowly than someone in a hurry, who is to be kept waiting. Especially keen is the pain of waiting, when one is prepared for combat, either physical or verbal and the maintenance of the razors edge gradually erodes with the passage of time.

Such was the case for Morton Scarsdale, the most influential man in US legislative history.

He picks up the phone and things happen, except he'd now kept waiting.

At the stroke of four thirty in the afternoon, the President hurried past the trio and Melanie with Van Harvanian hard upon his heels. As he past the Senator and two others he hurriedly blustered, "Goddammit, I'm sorry gentlemen. They've got me so booked up and Backed up I can't even take a dump. As he charged into the Oval office, Magnusson yelled, "Mel, where in the hell is that folder I need"?

"Upper left hand desk drawer Mr. President", she yelled back as the President replied, "Got it Mel, thanks" and charged back out the way he came, with the Secret Service minder closing the Oval office door in his wake.

As Magnusson passed Mel's desk he gave a brief wink, for they both knew his appearance was a simple canard and the file, was nothing more than a file folder, thus firing for effect to maintain the illusion of a man under great stress, as Magnusson hurriedly said to his guests as he rounded the corner, "Back as soon as I can"!

"The son of a bitch is really smoking", mused Scarsdale aloud to the others, causing Melanie to respond, "Short of some coffee and a cruller at 0600, the President as you can see has been in a track meet gentlemen, going from one event after another. I doubt if he's has anything to eat since then, much less time for anything else. So he's bound to be a bit cranky until he gets something in his stomach, so if he's eating a sandwich while he's talking to you, please excuse his manners"!

Turning back to her work, she noted Scarsdale, give a knowing glance at his two associates, and then silently concluded the staged event had served its designed purpose. Scarsdale and associates would now be happy to await the President a little while longer, sensing weakness.

Shortly after Five PM, Roland Stonecypher arrived and was ushered into the Oval office by way of the Chief of Staff's adjoining office, then was served a freshly brewed cup of coffee by the steward who quickly departed.

As Magnusson rushed back to the Oval office just short of Five Thirty, he was again full of apologies to the Senator and his colleagues as he bid them to enter, nodding at Melanie to press the button as an audible buzz signaled the Oval office was opened for business.

As the President entered the Oval office he took visible notice that Roland Stonecypher was already seated and waiting and said, "Oh crap, I'm sorry gentlemen, must've been a scheduling mix up of some sort. But while we're all here I'm certain we have plenty to discuss", as he made for his desk and the glass of freshly brewed iced tea and a sandwich awaited him.

"What the hell is he doing here", asked Senator Scarsdale, visibly agitated that his mortal enemy, the Republican House Majority Stonecypher was in the same room. "I was given to understand this was to be a private meeting"!

Never in the history of both houses of Congress, had two men hated and had visceral contempt for one another, than Scarsdale and Stonecypher.

Each going out of their way whenever possible, to scuttle any legislative initiative that bore the others signature. Not since the days of Andrew Jackson and Senator John C. Calhoun, had two men held each other in such low regard that if it were legally possible to publicly hang the other, they would.

"As it's been stated Senator Scarsdale, clearly a scheduling foul up, however noting the presence of the Chairmen's of the House Ways and Means Committee and House Judicial Committee here, clearly you wished it not to be a private meeting Senator, unless you have a different meaning of what is private from the rest of us. Look gentlemen, it's been a long day all around, certainly for me, so tell the porter what you're drinking and lets all try to be civil", asked the President as he sat upon the front of his desk and took a bite of his sandwich. As the porter left after serving the drinks, Orval Goodwin entered and silently took a chair on the periphery of the meeting. "So Morton what's got you so clearly vexed, to such a point that you just had to have a face to face"?

"Your entire position on the undocumented aliens in our midst and the recent closing off of all remittances by them south of the border, then the recent addition of militia members to supposedly assist our military, not to mention the addition of the Military on the entire southern border, being a violation of "Posse Comitatus", and finally the way you acted to the representatives of the Mexican Government was and is abominable and I and others in congress protest in the strongest manner. President Dobbins, god rest his soul, would never have done this"!

"Well Senator, since you claim to have certain intimate knowledge of his thinking patterns, you just might be correct. But the man is resting in heaven now with his family and sitting here in front of you is someone quite different"!

Roland Stonecypher sat there listening to the Senator rant and placed a brief glance at Goodwin sitting just within his peripheral vision who failed to return his glance and knew in an instant that his presence in front of his arch enemy was simple Machiavellian ploy to gain the upper hand on the good Senator. So he smiled inwardly and decided to enjoy the moment and play along, waiting for an appropriate opening to buttress the President and perhaps skewer that bastard"!

"You must immediately rescind your recent directives that you initiated without the approval or consent of Congress"!

"Didn't you forget to say something like, "Or Else", Senator"?

"I intend to reconvene the Senate and settle this egregious issue once and for all. Further my colleagues in the House Committees intend to block all of the funding for the conflicts in the Middle East, for the foreseeable future, thus no money to fund the war and the boys have to come home"!

"Seems to me Senator, that either you're hard of hearing or have a mental block of some kind", mused Stonecypher calmly! "In the media you keep stressing that we will penalize the illegals and make them pay any alleged back taxes and as of yet financial penalty of sorts then get in back of the line and learn English et cetera, et cetera. Now the President here has already addressed the issue of where in Sam Hill are they going to get all the money to accomplish that very thing, since many of them live low on the hog and send a large portion of their cash back down south to their people, by way of remittances. Now by blocking any foreign remittances to be sent south, they just might have enough 'Dinero' to become a citizen, short of that, Nada Senor"!

"Since Labor Day recess, for both houses of Congress starts after the close of business tomorrow and everyone is eager to get out of town and start campaigning, those that are up for reelection in November Senator, ask yourself, how likely am I going to be able to herd all of the cats back into the Senate and in the House of Representatives, you have no chance at all. Am I not correct Roland"?

"Stonecypher nodded his head casually as he took another sip from his coffee cup, his eyes never leaving that of Scarsdale's, as he said, "Now Morton, I can see that you're all sixes and sevens over this and since you have this blood pressure problem of yours why don't you try and calm down and take a deep breath. The Presidents executive orders all well within his authority as the Chief Executive and I suspect that he'll be somewhat busy while all of us are back home celebrating the holiday"!

"Gentlemen, any attempt to block funding of our military deployed overseas, will meet with failure as you well know. All it'll do is get you send many of you into an early retirement in a couple of months, come reelection", said Magnusson.

"And you know this how", asked Senator Scarsdale, trying desperately to regain the advantage!

"The very fact that this subject has been brought up by you and your acolytes here, might be made known to every rank and file American over the holidays. All three of you are up for reelection in a few months and the word is that each of you is in a tight race. Should word of this somehow leak out of this office and into the media, I would think that whatever slim advantage you had in the polls, would vanish in a heartbeat. Of course I could be wrong gentlemen, as everyone knows and says that I'm a lousy politician", said the President"!

"It'll be our word against yours", replied Scarsdale!

"Senator, you just keep on thinking that", said Magnusson!

"Are you trying to say this has all been recorded", asked Scarsdale in horror? Magnusson shrugged his shoulders and took another bite out of his sandwich, as Orval Goodwin stood up and walked up to behind one of the couches and said, "There are the three of you sitting on one side of the room all proud Democrats. There is the President sitting on his desk, trying to finish a well-earned sandwich, a lifelong, card carrying Democrat, there's yours truly here, a lifelong Democrat and finally Representative Stonecypher here as everyone knows is a proud Republican and House Majority Leader. An Honorable man who's political philosophy as everyone knows runs often counter to that of the President. Gentlemen, here are the six players in this little vignette. Should this conversation goes public, who are the voters going to believe"?

There was a brief silence in the Oval office, as the truth of it was neatly presented to all, without revealing the presence of the recording devices reintroduced to the Oval office several presidents ago. Should it be necessary, they were always a CYA device to chronicle events as they actually happened, the Presidents hole card.

Then Goodwin asked, "Senator Scarsdale. Are you all right? You're looking quite flushed"!

Scarsdale struggled to rise saying, "You can all go straight to hell" and stormed out of the office, followed by his two colleagues, without a further word!

As they departed, in rushed Van Harvanian, followed by Melanie O'Bannon who eagerly wanted the lowdown on what was said. The executive porter then entered from another direction as Roland Stonecypher, looked at Goodwin and said, "Next time you invite me to a political hanging, just give me a little heads up, OK Orval"? As Goodwin sheepishly nodded his head, Stonecypher said, "Mr. President, I believe you understand the concept of Quid Pro Quo?

Magnusson nodded his head saying, "As long as we can afford it Roland. As long as we can afford it"!

Then Harvanian looked at the Steward saying, "I take it that it's after normal working hours"? The Steward nodded his head saying, "Yessir, I believe it is"!

"Then would I be remiss in asking whether or not it's time for tall glasses and hard liquor, so our beloved Henry can clock out and go home to his family"?

"Henry, if you'd be so kind to get a round of drinks for everyone", asked President Magnusson, then go join your family with our blessing. Within several minutes the executive Steward returned with drinks then took his leave.

"Gentlemen, I know I sit here in the enemies camp celebrating the hoped for demise of a Mortal enemy and I must say thanks for the invitation. To see that look on his face was beyond measure. Let us at least say a prayer the good Senator gets through the evening without further complications"! At that everyone lifted their glass to join the toast.

"May I make a further suggestion Gentlemen and Lady"?

The President nodded in assent, as Stonecypher continued, "I'm given to understand that a CBS reporter, one Molly Pringle, a rising star at that network delivered an excellent bit of reporting in your behalf. Seems to me the woman was an objective journalist who played things straight down the middle. So taking advantage of her recent popularity and yours, it just might be appropriate if Mr. Harvanian here invited her for an exclusive sit down with you Mr. President, for another thorough briefing to the nation of your efforts, the whys and wherefores"!

As Magnusson briefly glanced around at the others, seeing heads nod in agreement, he said Van; can you and Mel here make it happen"?

Mel then chimed in, "Mr. President, does the sun always rise in the east"? As everyone laughed, the Oval office bank of televisions was turned on to the local DC area evening news reports just in time to see emblazoned across the screen an urgent bulletin reporting that Senator Morton Scarsdale was being rushed to one of the local emergency rooms after suffering a massive heart attack after meeting with the President.

Roland Stonecypher, then rose to his feet, tossed back the remainder of his drink and said, "With any luck, looks like your party just might be down one vote in the Senate come the November elections. I'm heading towards the hospital and will call you if I hear anything significant"!

18

Bypassing a host of other more famous Television journalists, Van Harvanian, contacted the producers of CBS, to come to the White House, for a series of documentaries, regarding the history of the White House, and the various forms of the government, Executive, Legislative and Judicial, from the perspective of the Executive branch of government. In the coming months, similar documentary's would be produced covering the very same ground, of the three equal but separate branches of government, but from the point of view of the Legislative and the Judicial branches.

Historically, there was a great deal of important material in which to report and there was just no way to winnow it all down into an hour, or even a two hour viewing schedule. So the decision was made to develop a series of six programs, divided into one hour sessions during evening prime time viewing. Thus when all was said and done, eighteen hours of prime time reporting would occur. Sufficient to last an entire viewing season.

Of course this was madness, many in the executive ranks concluded and they would normally be correct in their assessment. The average evening viewer wasn't interested in serious history for the most part, they wanted to be entertained. The old bread and circuses concept that proved that in spite of technology, the common man hadn't changed much for the last few thousand years. They had short attention spans then as well as now.

"So we'll entertain them as well as inform them historically", said Marc Conrad, Vice President of Network Programming. Normally Network Programming suits, (decision makers) didn't get involved in the affairs of the News Division, except when it involved making way into the normal offerings of Prime Time telecasting. At first glance he was dead set against the concept and wanted it to be developed then sold to one of the cable networks. A rather good idea, but not for CBS Prime Time.

As he stood up with full knowledge that his veto alone meant the project could either be shelved entirely or peddled to one of the cable channels, he said, "Sometimes, you can have it both ways, not often, but sometimes"! He stood silent for a moment allowing for that statement to sink in, before continuing. "True, the great unwashed must have their Circus Maximus and their life and death matches in living color and I propose that we give them the bitter, with the better. The choice for the reporter and narrator of Molly Pringle is an inspiration. Next the people, who always gravitate to the salacious, can have it, for as I understand it, both the Executive and the Legislative branches of government are neck deep in the arts of mendacity, even the staid judicial branch has had its moments. Hell, the History Channel has made their bread and butter out of this for years. Thus so will we. It will all depend on how artfully we inculcate the relevant history of each branch of government, with the salacious and eventual prurient. The mendacity of Presidents, members of the congress, and the Judiciary can be easily revealed as a roadmap of our nation's political development, in such a way to be historically accurate as well as being sufficient to becoming of great interest to the average viewer"!

Since most folks in Network television operate under the herd mind set, heads began to nod in agreement all around the executive conference table. The head honcho had made an executive decision and everyone could get on board. If it flopped ratings wise, it would be his neck on the chopping block and none else.

For the next few months, Molly Pringle and her team would be traveling back and forth between New York and Washington DC., on the Acela train, putting together interviews from a historical perspective with key governmental officials. America would soon discover how their government functioned, in such a way that would infuriate some, while enlightening others. The bitter and the better of how the sausage has always been made, since the early days of the Republic. Soon America would discover how fragile in some quarters, government was and the truth of a former President's commentary that in Washington, if one wanted a true friend, then a dog should be a constant companion.

Thirty days later, the initial production team went down to Washington for a brief meeting between themselves, the President and his immediate staff and discussing their concept and the boundaries, if any that were to be observed. Magnusson had no immediate objections regarding the subjects disclosed other than to ask they leave him a copy of the format so he could run it by a historian he knew for accuracy especially where the more salacious aspects of prior Presidents was concerned.

"Ms. Pringle, I'm looking forward to working with you on this project and I want you to interface directly with my Secretary Melanie O'Bannon as regarding anything you'll require and of course scheduling"!

"Thank you Mr. President we're also eager to get started", said Molly as she and her staff shook hand with the President and departed for their next appointment after lunch to see Roland Stonecypher, to gain his for the Legislative branch of government. The following day they would have a brief meeting with the Chief Justice of the Supreme Court, to discuss content and scheduling.

Later on in the day, as Melanie was in the Oval office rounding out the details of the news team's next arrival, as well as blocking out some time for Magnusson to meet with his favorite Presidential historian, Melanie said, "You better keep an eye on that Molly Pringle Mr. President"!

"Oh yeah. How so"?

"She's got a bit of a thing for you"!

"And you know this how Mel", asked Magnusson as he kept signing documents slated for the Secretary of Defense?

"Women's intuition, Mr. President. The way she conducts herself in your presence, body lingo and the fact that she's a Texas woman!

"So it's the old takes one to know one thing, eh Mel"?

"Yup"!

"Well, I think either you had better stop drinking in the middle of the day, or take a side job as the Truth Sayer"!

"I'm just saying Sir; keep your guard up when in her presence"!

"Mel, if she was ever going to skewer me, she had plenty of opportunity when she was tagging after me, when I was out on the West Coast. But her news program self-edited some fairy hairy moments that we'd rather not be made public, for the foreseeable future. I promise to keep my guard up, but over all I think she'll be just fine"!

"Thanks for listening sir", said Mel!

"Tell you what, when she's in town next, you'll be interacting with her and her crew a great deal. Have lunch or dinner a few times with her and expense it to my account. Get to know her on my nickel, then tell me if she wears a white hat or otherwise"!

"Any place in town"?

"Within reason Mel. Within reason"!

Since schedules had to be coordinated between parties, it turned out that the CBS crew, started out with the Supreme Court first, spending the better part of three days fitting in interview time between court scheduling and meetings between justices. A week later, they were back for a longer series of interviews with Roland Stonecypher. Once again sandwiched in between his busy schedule, as the Republican Majority Leader of the House of Representatives. Finally she was traveling back to Washington DC, for the final segment of interviews with the President.

Each time she came to Washington, Molly and Melanie made it a point to get together for lunch and as luck would have it became fast friends, engaging in salacious gossip and general banter keeping things light.

By the time Molly and her crew were busy working on the Legislative Branch of government, she invited Mel to come to New York and go along with her to attend one of the famous parties hosted by the Countess Fabiola Hargraves.

"What's the event to be celebrated by the Countess", asked Melanie? "Her Manhattan digs have been redecorated, thus the reason for the party is to celebrate her taste in drapes, I suppose. I haven't known the woman all that long, but for some reason she's appeared to take a shine to me and she does toss one hell of a party"!

"Yeah Molly, it made all the papers a little while back. No press agent on the planet could've staged such an appearance, So tell me about the Countess. Need to know the lowdown on my hostess"!

"All I know about her can be found in the papers. Every gossip columnist has covered her for the last twenty odd years like a wet blanket. The paparazzi are everywhere she goes and she never says "No" to a photo op. She's had four husbands and has done very well for herself financially. She's about our age, yet whoever her cosmetic surgeon is, he serves her well. Don't expect her to ever remarry, since she has no need to, if you catch my drift. They say one is known by the company one keeps? Well it's safe to say, Fabiola is the Cougar Supremo of the Big Apple. I just wish she'd be a bit more cognizant of her personal security. One thing though.

She's a wonderful sense of self-deprecation and will be the first to say that, "She's as pure as the driven slush", so all one can do is, smile and go with the flow. But I wonder about that girl.

"Do as I say not as I do", mused Mel!

"Exactly that", smiled Molly!

"Does she know who I am"?

"She said for me to bring a guest. Gave her your name and that was it. Don't think her guest list follows the political section of the Times much and you do keep a low profile Mel, so I wouldn't worry about your arriving amidst a sea of notoriety. Do you some good to see how the so called literati spends their time, at least once in your life and if someone connects the dots, so what. Usually the Presidential secretary is someone of a dowdy nature, wouldn't they be surprised to find a card carrying babe shields the President"!

"So what are you wearing Molly"!

"Since my recent finances have yet to catch up with my sudden good fortune career wise, it'll have to be the very same little black dress, I wore at the last party. I've been told that although simple, it apparently worked"! "I think I've something that would match that. Haven't worn it in a while, but it'll have to do"!

"Good. Then it's settled. We'll both take the Acela train to New York, Friday night. I've aspare bedroom that's yours at my place and Saturday evening well show up at the Countess's party, both looking fabulous. Two tall Texas females invade enemy territory and show them what real women look like"!

"Just so I can get a train back to DC on Sunday afternoon. The President is up by five in the morning and in the saddle by six, if you catch my drift"!

They rode the Acela train up to New York making more small talk on the way as they got to know each other better, discovering they both had roots in Houston. Molly a Rice University graduate and Mel a graduate of the University of Houston. The inexplicable concept of serendipity once again making itself known. When they arrived at Molly's apartment, they unpacked and made comparisons of the dress's that would adorn them the following evening, discovering that it appeared that both dresses were designed by the same couturier and similar in appearance, with the exception of Mel's dress being a flaming Red in and Molly's being the ever elegant Black.

"Tomorrow, since you've never been to Nueva York before, we'll see the sights, but it'll have to be salads all the way, if we're ever going to do those dresses of ours good service"!

"As they both rode up to Fabiola's party the following evening in the elevator, each took notice of each other by the reflection in the gleaming brass elevator doors, saying the word "Bookends", together and laughing at the coincidence. Their dual entrance was guaranteed to turn heads all evening long and a woman, any woman could never get enough of that kind of attention. As the doors opened they followed another group of invitees into Fabiola's, to see the ever present Andre greeting the guests as he said, exclaimed loudly "Molly, so good of you to come", hugging and bussing her on both cheeks saying, "And who is this lovely woman you've brought to attend us"?

"Melanie O'Bannon, this is Andre, the Countess's ever present concubine"! Andre gave Mel the same greeting saying to them both, "The last time here it was a full moon and you quite nicely dispatched the wicked witch of the west. Und 'Viola', here it is a full moon once again Molly, who'll meet their maker this time"!

"Cool your jets Andre, not here to be the floorshow. Just here to grab a few drinks, pay homage to Fabiola's taste and get in a schmooze with the Hoi Polloi"!

"Work your way amongst the guests, when you hear a shrill voice, look around and you'll see our host, or by the way the both of you look, she'll find you by following the direction of all the men's leers", he said with a toss of his head, immediately turning his attention to another group of arrivals.

As the two women worked their way through the room, marveling at the obvious expense of the decorations Molly said, "That woman can really spend some money. I was here a few months ago and what's here now looks nothing like what used to be here. All this got done in the space of a few months"!

"What's the story on this Andre guy", asked Melanie?

"Her main squeeze, you mean. There are others from time to time, but the word is he doesn't seem to care, for there are no strings there. In case he looks familiar, he's one of New York's finest male models. Everything from billboards to magazines and a few television commercials. The supreme Metro Sexual. All hat and no cattle. The Countess has him on her arm for, several reasons. First look at him, he's gorgeous, he's well mannered, and according to the gossip, he can lick his eyebrows", she said with a knowing nod of her head. But according to Fabiola, he's the only man who could ever make her squirt during sex. "Leaves an embarrassing wet spot on the sheets so large", at that her voice trailed off. "Now you're wondering how large aren't you"? Mel nodded her head, bidding for Molly to continue her statement. "So large it forces them on the floor"! "Don't know if I'd ever want to live like that no matter how much money I had", said Melanie.

"Damnable Lone Star values. Well neither could I Mel, but it certainly is a hoot, to be in their midst a time or two", said Molly with a smirk.

After they made their way to the bar and each had a drink in their hand, they clicked glasses and Mel said, "Well girl, the eyes of Texas are upon us"! Just then they were startled by a shriek, turning around seeing the Countess cutting her way through the guests and heading straight for them. "Brace yourself", mumbled Molly as he heard, "Molly dear, and who is this vision of loveliness at your side"? Then before Molly could answer, Fabiola stepped back looking at the duo and said, "My god, you're both wearing the same dress"!

"Actually Fabiola, that's not exactly accurate. She's in red", blurted out

Molly. Then turning to Mel said, "Melanie O'Bannon, may I introduce you to the Countess Fabiola Hargraves, our hostess for the evening"! Both women went thru the ritual of the greeting hug and dual buss on both cheeks, as Mel said, "My friends call me Mel"!

"A bit masculine, but Mel it will be"! Then she stared at Melanie for a moment and said, "Molly, why is this woman's face so familiar to me"?

"Gee Fabiola, I don't know. She's just a hard working girl in Washington that works for the government"!

"That's it", exclaimed Fabiola! "I know where I've seen that face before. She's the Presidents private secretary. See Molly I often read other things rather than the society rags. You've done well, by inviting such a lovely representative of our government to my humble home"!

"Why Countess thank you very much", said Mel in reply.

"My friends call me Fabiola and I truly wish you to be every bit of a friend as Molly is"!

"Then Fabiola it is"!

"Viola. Now follow me, so I can show you both what I've done with this wretched place", as she took them both arm in arm and escorted them through her entire living quarters. Opulence, yet tasteful opulence was the only way to describe this woman everyday existence, as the trio worked their way through the place. As they passed through her lavish bedroom she quipped, "And this is my work area, along with a little recreation", she added with a sly wink.

Then working their way back to the main room, they went by the bar to replenish their drinks, listening to the musical sounds of the jazz ensemble, she'd hired for the evening. Then the trio worked their way around the room, being introduced to the Manhattan literati. All eyes were on the three women, as Fabiola said to Mel in front of Molly, "Darling by tomorrow, every gossip columnist and their paparazzi attendants will combing their archives to discover just who you are. Eventually they will discover your bona fides on their own, and your pictures will be front and center. I hope you don't mind the publicity"!

"As long as I'm on my best behavior, what can go wrong", said Mel, noting the glance that passed between her host and Molly, who jointly replied, "Plenty", then laughed.

"You will notice that it seems like all eyes are on us. Normally I might be a little jealous, being in the company of two equally attractive women, such as the both of you", exclaimed

The Countess continuing, "But somehow, at this very moment, your presence, completes the evening, being flanked by two such lovely, ah, . Bookends"! At that very moment Mel and Molly glanced at each other and broke out laughing, explaining that they had said the very same thing on the ride up the elevator, prompting the Countess to join in the laughter. "By the way before I forget, Andre was telling me several weeks ago the very evening after my last party that you attended, of running into you and your beau, the very next evening at some night club. He said that he'd said hello to you and this man. He described the man as large, good looking in a roughhewn dangerous manner, fit and a rather good dancer. He also said that you appeared to be completely enamored with this man, by the looks of it. So I almost expected to bring him along this evening rather than Mel, but I'm very glad you chose to come Mel", she said turning her attention back to Molly. Andre said his name, but somehow I've forgotten it"!

From a laugh to a frown he face went in just a very few seconds, Molly answered, "Oh he must mean Jaeger. That didn't work out as I'd hoped"!

Melanie suddenly stiffened, for she'd not heard that name mentioned in quite a few years, and then quickly recovering her composure asked, "What was his first name, his full name Molly"?

"No first name, no middle name, just Jaeger", she replied wistfully, noting the sudden change of expression on Mel's face. Then asked, "Mel, what's wrong? Is it something I said"?

"I think I need another drink", said Mel. Time for a tall glass and hard liquor"!

Feeling that somehow Fabiola had inadvertently stirred up a hornets nest with her newfound friends, she said, "Ladies, follow me to the bar"! As they approached the bar she summoned one of the bartenders saying, "Give them exactly what they want"!

Mel looked at the bartender saying, "Fill a Tom Collins glass full of ice, then pour 'Jack Black' in between the cracks"! "Same here" said

Molly". "And me as well", said Fabiola", continuing, "There's another musical trio out on the patio, bring my drink and I'll go ahead and shoo away some people so we can be alone"!

A minute later, onto the patio came Mel and Molly passing a few angry people that had relinquished their place for their hostess. Twenty stories above street level one could barely hear the echoes of the street traffic down below in Uptown Manhattan, just the lilting music of the jazz trio, recreating Dave Brubeck's, 'Blue Rondo Ala Turk'. As the women settled into their chairs, Molly asked sincerely, "Mel what did I say that upset you so much"?

"It could only be one person in the entire world. Jaeger!

"You knew Jaeger too," asked Molly incredulously?

"Now I know just how Rick felt in the movie Casablanca, when he saw Elsa"!

"I repeat Mel, you knew Jaeger"?

Melanie nodded her head slowly, saying "Yes, a long time ago! I think about him every once in a while, but then come to my senses and drown myself in work till things settle down. Haven't thought about him in quite some time, until this very moment"!

"Who is this mystery man that goes by just one name", asked Fabiola? Molly started, "Well it looks like someone has got to connect the dots, so I might as well start. Clearly the man broke Mel's heart as well as mine. First time I laid eyes on the man up close, was in a court room in Waco Texas. He was on trial for murdering his family. Of course he didn't do it and was neatly framed by the local court. His lawyer was a girl just out of law school, working as a public defender and this was her first case. I was working for a local television station in Houston and was sent up to Waco to cover the trial. I sat two rows behind Jaeger and in my eagerness to get a story locked horns with one Elizabeth Beauvior, his lawyer. Now Jaeger came from money, scads of land, livestock, farming and a host of other business's, that went back almost a hundred and fifty years, to the days right after the Mexican American War. Now one he's in the local jail and there's a story to tell there, the rest of his family gets the local judge to freeze all access to his family accounts, because no will had been found anywhere. Now at the very same time Jaegers family is murdered, so is the family lawyer dies under questionable circumstances the local county authorities fail to investigate. Well, Jaeger is found guilty and goes to prison for just under nine years. The trial over I get on with my career in television.

There's more to this story that I've uncovered, a lot more, so I'm giving y'all the short version"!

"This Beauvior lawyer never forgets Jaeger and joins her Uncles law firm and becomes a terror in Houston never losing a case and eventually obtains Jaeger's full pardon, from the State of Texas in less than a month's time. Now when the state grants parole or a pardon, things moves at a glacial pace and for this to occur in less than a month is unheard of. During his time in Prison a number of attempts to murder him occur and he escapes serious injury each and every time. Now what's curious about Jaegers pardon is this lady lawyer, gets two of his best friends in prison, sprung at the very same time that he does. An Australian con man and weapons smuggler named Roy Seltzer and a former bank robber named Duke Vultee"!

Both Mel and Fabiola are completely engrossed in Molly's narrative as the pack of imported Dunhill cigarettes Fabiola ordered arrived as Molly said, "Dammit and I was trying to quit smoking as the pack was passed around and Fabiola mused, "This story reads like a best seller novel replete with treachery and intrigue"!

"So I thought also but there's more", said Molly! "His lawyer having sprung him and the two others puts them both to work managing three Gentlemen's Clubs in Houston. These are supposedly high class places, full of the finest women in the area and the lady lawyer is the owner. Several additional attempts are made on not only the lawyer Beauvoir's life but on Jaeger as well. Subsequent investigation reveals that killer groups from the Northern Mexican drug Cartels were hired to perform the hits, but in each and every attempt, all of the assailants were killed before they could be questioned by the authorities. But I think Jaeger all along knew exactly who they were and was biding his time. As a result they came to him. Now while all of this was happening, an investigation of his original conviction was starting to bubble up in the State Capitol in Austin. A death bed confession by the Judge that originally issued the arrest warrant while he was in College, at the University of Texas, revealed that he was paid off to issue the warrant by a Texas Ranger who later became Governor of Texas and the long serving Sheriff of the county where the Jaeger Ranch was located and a Ft. Worth Real Estate developer. Now in the aftermath of all that's going on, the trio are indicted by Grand Jury"!

"Now here's where things get murky. Jaeger comes from wealth, but nowhere is there a record of his father having a last will and testament. His father, mother and both sisters are murdered. A record of a Will is filed at the county courthouse, but no copy can be found. A search of the family records and surviving documents reveals no will. Now at about The very same time of Jaeger's family's death, their long time family attorney, in the Waco area, dies under circumstances that are suspect, yet no one makes an attempt to investigate. I mentioned that before, didn't I. Now one would expect a long time family attorney to have a fully executed copy of the last will and testament of his best client. He has other documents of Jaeger's father as well as copies of legal documents of his other clients, but no Jaeger will is discovered. So Jaegers more distant relatives file a motion with the county court to have the entire estate placed in probate court and his father thus declared as dying "In testate" or without a will. As I'm following this I'm selling a very dead rat. I try and get my station to report my discoveries, but they put the clamps on me. So all I can do is file a daily report and get on with my career, I sold out. Oh what about the prosecutor in his original case? Well a few years after Jaegers conviction, he dies from apparently natural causes. Now years later after Jaeger is out of prison and just about the time the sitting governor, a former Texas Ranger, the Sheriff of McLennan County and former head of the State Bureau of Pardons and Paroles and the Ft. Worth Real Estate Developer are about to have themselves brought up on a criminal indictment, germane to Jaegers original conviction, all three of them disappear. They fall off the face of the earth. They are last seen at a Gentlemen's Club on the Dallas Ft. Worth Turnpike, owned by the Developer by a waitress that served them together in one of the clubs, VIP rooms. The authorities attempt an investigation, but no leads come forth. Not a single one. They even call in Jaeger and give him a grilling, but he apparently was in in the verifiable presence of his attorney, Buffy Beauvior for the better part of a week. Far away from the Dallas Ft. Worth area at the same time. So that particular case is languishing in the Cold Case file somewhere in Austin. Was Jaeger involved in any respect? I really don't know, but somewhere deep down I hope he was and I suspect he was"!

"Now here is where I come in", said Molly turning toward the Countess. "Remember about a month ago, during your last party, approximately one renovation ago"?

"How could anyone ever forget? A tour de force performance. The old fat witch Knickerbocker, hoisted upon her own petard with nothing more than words. The only thing I regret was her vomitus on my rug the moment she croaked"!

"Well, late the next Saturday morning I was summoned downtown to network headquarters for a meeting between the top executives and the lawyers. We spent several hours reviewing every aspect of what happened, with the suits concluding that no one there was culpable for the woman's demise, brought on by a little known heart condition of long standing. I made my producer take me to lunch so I could destroy one of those famous Manhattan Corn Beef sandwiches. I'm almost finished when who walks in the restaurant but Jaeger. It had been some years, but during the trial I was able to memorize his every movement. We'd both gotten older, but despite the age and some visible scars I didn't remember, he still looked good. So I took a deep breath got up and approached Jaeger, sitting in a booth with his back to the wall seeing everything that came before his eyes. A trademark of real professionals, I've discovered that makes sense"!

As Molly revealed the mystery of Jaeger's life, the little things she revealed, started the process of dot connection.

"I introduced myself rather clumsily, trying to turn on the appropriate amount of gushing charm, which wasn't too difficult when I think about it, because the man does have a certain presence, but eventually he was gracious and invited me to join him. We spent the rest of the afternoon engaged in small talk. Like I recalled the time when he was playing football and I attended a football game in the Old Rice Stadium in Houston. Texas was playing Rice, my alma mater and it wasn't a pretty sight. Texas ran roughshod over Rice, or should I say Jaeger, the "Uberballer", almost single handily destroyed my team. Then I hated the man,

But years later, sitting right there in front of him, things got very turned around very quickly. He was polite, charming and engaging, yet knowing what I knew and suspected about the man, he was walking death, depending on the circumstances. Time flew by, and I remember asking him what he did for a living these days and he replied that he was an investor"! "The very same thing he told me", Mel said in a rush! All three women passed knowing glances with each other, as Molly continued. "Well, it was Saturday night, two grown people in Manhattan and I suggested that we do the town together. He agreed, we took a cab back to my place so I could change and then I introduced him to Big Apple night life. That's when we bumped into Andre and said Hello. Of course the evening ended well. I had sugar plumbs dancing before my very eyes. The following morning when I awoke, he was gone, and had made coffee, leaving a hand written note. I hate thinking about it, because as much as I try to limit expectations about anything, some things ya just have to hope for. I remember that he'd drunk half of the coffee in the cup so I picked up the cup he'd touched and gradually finished it, reading and rereading the note he'd left. One thing though, the last thing he mentioned, was that "Something else was in the way", haven't figured that out yet and probably never will"!

"Sounds like you really fell for the man and hard", said the Countess looking as melancholy as everyone else"!

"We only had one memorable evening together Fabiola, and had little time to really bond together. Yeah I flipped for the guy and I hope I never see him again, even though he promised nothing and fulfilled all the dreams I ever had for a memorable evening with the man. If I work hard enough I can forget him in time and get on with things. Had we stayed together longer, that just might have proved impossible. One thing though, the very last sentence of his note disturbs me, as if that something that was in the way was the memory of someone else"! As soon as the words left her lips, both women turned and looked at Mel, as if a moment of sudden revelation hit them both. A prior involvement that could never be, perhaps?

As Mel looked at them both, she could see Andre, over the Countess's shoulder standing silent guard at the door to the patio, holding inquiring guests at bay wondering where the evening's hostess had gotten to. Loyal Andre, for reasons unknown protecting his patroness's from intruders, directing them elsewhere.

"I suppose this is where I connect the dots further", said Mel matter of factly. "Years ago after the death of my husband in an auto collision, I was in a bad place. Fighting his family for custody of my son, his family was a train wreck but had money, and legal fees were wiping out my insurance settlement. I was living in an apartment in the Northwest of Houston and working full time as a secretary. I joined the local health club and worked out five days a week and there I met the man we call Jaeger. Large well built and with some scar tissue he never talked about. I couldn't afford a personal trainer and after he casually pointed out that I was doing things all wrong, we introduced ourselves to each other and he became my personal trainer. It started out very slow at first, we'd work out together, and I followed his advice and got more out of each session at the gym. But time was an issue and I had a small son to consider, so my time had to take a back seat to my obligations. One day when I thought things couldn't get any worse in the battle of my son's custody; we cut our work out short and went for coffee, where I explained everything to him. A few weeks later, my former in laws drop their lawsuit without any reason and I was in heaven. I mentioned this to Jaeger and he just smiled. But the way he smiled told me that somehow he'd gotten involved. I never pursued the issue, but gradually we got to know each other. Eventually a certain comfort level existed. I knew absolutely nothing of the man except of the here and now. I do remember asking him what he did for a living, just like you did Molly and was surprised when he replied that he was an 'investor'. He didn't look like any investor I ever saw. Investors usually have no shoulders and are immaculately attired, while this man had shoulders and could pass for a bouncer in any night club in town. I do recall one of his workout friends called Randy. The man was so massive he could blot out the sun."

"After some months, as he was often away from time to time, he suggested that we all go to a movie, including my son. Any relationship I might've had depended on him, and of course they fell in with each other right away. He taught him so much. At the age of eight, my son became a crack shot, for at least several times a month they would go do guy things at the firing range together, eventually involving me and despite my then aversion to firearms, learned to handle them thanks to Jaeger, who would joke and call us his, "Little Pistolero's".

"He was always a gentleman, well-spoken and moderate in his actions, except when he was with my son. They would always go down by the pool and have these long talks. I would always ask my son what they talked about and he would reply, "Aw Mom just guy stuff ya know".

"One evening I recall, he spotted some people tailing his car when we were out one evening for dinner, with my son along"!

"The car was following us, we entered the restaurant, we ordered, while we waited for the food, he excused himself, to go to the restroom. When he returned he seemed a little short of breath and I recall him saying that we could now enjoy our meal without any concern. In those days he drove a renovated white Ford muscle car that was very fast, I remember our leaving the restaurant and pulling out onto the freeway after dark and the same car began to chase us.

We drove down the freeway and then they started to shoot at us. He suddenly pulled off the freeway and when the car tried to follow, the wheels came off of the car and the trailing car crashed into the another, with both crashing into a building on the access road in flames. At that very moment, I fell for the man completely and without any reservations. He resurrected my position as prime parent in some way, he was pals with my son, he was an excellent driver and he saved my life. Nothing more to be said, that night was the pivotal moment in my life, we made love together repeatedly. I simply could not get enough of the man. Of course he'd be away for business from time to time always returning and bring presents for me and my son from some far off place. Then one day he simply never returned. No notes. He wasn't seen at Ballys anymore and no one knew where he was"!

"Some months later, I received a call from a lawyer in town named

Parmalee, concerning an inheritance or so he said. It was a sizeable amount, designed in such a way to set up a trust fund for my son's college education and for my continued subsistence. Of course my son never needed that money for he ended up getting an appointment to the US Naval Academy at Annapolis. One more year and he'll graduate and his intention is to become a Marine Officer, so one day if he ever runs into Jaeger that Jaeger will have to salute him. I ended up in politics working on President Dobbin's campaign staff. And the rest is history I Now work for President Magnusson another magnificent man. A long time ago I wouldn't give up looking for Jaeger, so I hired some local private investigators to see if they could find out what ever happened to the man. A week or so went by and in each case the bulk of my upfront money was returned, by each investigator, retired detectives from the City of Houston Police Department. Seems that each of them had an accident and they were both extremely closed mouthed about what happened. So I gave up and went on with my life. So that is it ladies, there's nothing more"!

There was several moments of silence between the women, as the sounds of soft jazz filtered across the sky patio, the piano player, lightly tripping across the ascending and descending chords, followed by the timpani of the drums and the back beat of the Bull Fiddle, when the Countess and Molly both glanced at each other with the Countess saying "Dahling we now know just who the missing link is, don't we Molly"?

"Mel, that very last sentence in the Dear John note he sent me was about you! You, Melanie O'Bannon, the Head Honcho's secretary, were the very thing that stood in the way of Jaeger ever completely giving himself to anyone. Neither I nor anyone else ever stood a chance. You were the one who filled his heart at least for a time and place. Thank you, now I don't feel so bad"!

"Ladies, it is I that thank you both for this revelation. I shall never watch another soap opera ever again. For whatever reason, those Sopwith Camel writers cannot hold a candle to what you and Mel have recently revealed. Oh this is an evening to remember and it shall stay buried deep within. Yet someday Molly you should write a book about the entire thing, of course leaving out any mention of our dear Mel"!

"Yeah, that's an idea, but there are still gaping holes in the story line that only Jaeger himself and his Houston lawyer Elizabeth Beauvior can shed light on, but I doubt that either one of them will ever talk to me about it. Sort of makes one wonder what ever happened to the Governor, the Sheriff and the Real Estate Developer, since they were all in the scheme to imprison Jaeger, then on the very moment of their legal 'Come to Jesus' moment, they all disappear all at once"!

"Then Fabiola stood up and glanced at Andre saying, "Andre, you can announce the reemergence of the three goddesses back into the bowels of the party"! Then she turned back to Mel and Molly saying with a flourish, "Ladies the public awaits shall we"?

19

As Salaam sat watching the evening newscast, reporting on the latest apprehensions of suspects of the Nations six week struggle with the wild fires, that consumed vast stretches of forest land as well as urban growth and properties, he could only but smile. The entire event exceeded his wildest expectations. The nation was scarred for generations to come. The property and casualty insurance companies would be especially hard hit and if not sufficiently capitalized, go under from the vast influx of claims. No doubt, the state and federal governments would intercede with tax payer funding to facilitate the claims in many cases.

Then there were the casualties. The dead and injured. The death toll alone exceeded ten thousand, directly attributable to the wild fires, with the injured doubling that figure. Greater Los Angeles alone was especially hard hit, with the outlaying populations in the hillsides completely devoid of any growth. The few homes that survived the fires were ripe for rock slides as there was no growth on the hill sides to hold the earth together come the first heavy rains.

But completely unexpected was the rise in those in the inner cities across America. Almost as if someone had taken the lid off the jar called 'Hell' and let loose the demons amongst the land. Not one major American city escaped the anger of the damned. Most every Mosque in the land suffered some physical damage as well as those who came for their daily prayers. When news reports of suspected Muslim terrorists were made public, it served as a perfect excuse for individuals to join together for a little payback. At some point the target shifted from the Muslims to the various neighborhoods in general. Soon everyone was a target. It even touched the President, when he was touring Los Angeles, completely an unexpected gift as far as Salaam was concerned, yet the President survived.

No doubt the Federal authorities would interrogate those few that were caught, but that would lead to no end. Borrowing a page out of the French resistance against the Nazi's during WWII, Salaam had set up cells of followers in the major cities. None of these cells knew of the existence of the other cells, much less those involved. Both the leaders of the cells were placed under deep hypnosis, as well as the followers. After the event, upon their return, each man would become overwhelmed by the need for sleep and once he reached the stage of REM unconsciousness, his mind would be rebooted and any memory of his recent deeds be completely eliminated, as if someone deleted certain information on a computer's hard drive. Even in the unlikely event the authorities should be able to retrieve the subjects memory of the events at hand, only their local leader, the one on hand who set everything in motion, was the only one who's identity could be revealed By the names of the few captured revealed to the public, the best the authorities could hope for was to round up a few cells. If every local Imam had followed Salaam's directions down to the letter, none of the participants in each locale would know of the identity of any other in his cell.

Now that very best part of this marvelous catastrophe, was that those who were selected to be the local cell commanders, were very visible members of the Muslims of America, the largest extended congregation of black Muslims in the nation. At the very best, any and all avenues of investigation would lead directly back to those people and not Salaam or any of his acolytes. Absolutely no comebacks, none at all. What ever happened to them would misdirect the efforts of the authorities. After all, they wanted publicity? They wanted to rant and bluster? Now the stage was all theirs, allowing Salaams activities to fly under the radar of the authorities. For several years now, Salaam was filtering into the states through Texas, one or two Muslims, that would be delivered across one of several fording spots across the Rio Grande river during the summer dry season. Of course they would be wearing only the clothes on their backs and carrying several rucksacks full of the finest Columbian Cocaine or Peruvian Heroin. The quality was the highest, thus when processed down to safer limits for consumption, the profits were enormous. In exchange for what was in their rucksacks, they would be provided with new identities and papers and transported to a new location in either the

US or Southern Canada. Since they were all conversant in the English language and had jobs awaiting them and twenty thousand dollars in cash.

Each one was special, similar yet different from Miguel Montero when he emigrated, and each went through a special processing as they passed through St. Louis. Each was blindfolded and brought before Salaam, who put each into a state of hypnosis, interrogating them until he was certain of their genuineness, then placed them in a state of deep hypnosis, quite similar to that of the others, who had served their purpose for the moment.

The current people were placed in deep cover, to lead normal lives, blending in with the culture of their locale as best as possible. Doing whatever jobs they had and biding time. There would be some significant use at a later date. But for now their chief function was to lie still in the tall grass until summoned.

All transactions of the 'products' were done via private postings. An innocuous message sent by US mail to a known customer. A package of well worn 'Benjamin' currency and an order sent back to a private postal box, (each time a different location) then by return private posting a well- sealed packet of the desired 'product' guaranteed as agreed. Thus the trained 'mules' would proceed into America carrying product, be processed by Salaam and disbursed to a given locale to await necessity. A self-funding entity, to await deep in the bowels of their host country. Of course, an integral part of Salaams processing was to discover any behavioral anomalies, wipe them from their mind and replace them with a new set of habits that would allow them to function normally, until summoned.

The only exception from this was the earliest arrival, Mike Montero. He had served his original purpose and performed beyond expectations. In the near future, he would be called upon to perform other functions as required. Those who mattered in Cairo and Tripoli were pleased. Salaam wondered whether or not those in Cairo had adopted his methods and adapted them to other countries, especially in Europe. But he quickly forced that from his mind, for human hubris, the over reach of one's capabilities always led to eventual failure. Salaam had his job, he knew just what he was about, everything was working as planned and as far as the future was concerned, he would leave his fate directly in the hands of Allah, the beneficent and merciful.

The President spent the morning with his National Security Council concerning the conflicts in the middle east. He was in an angry mood because the best source of new about what was occurring in the Iraqi and Afghani theaters were beating the Presidents handlers to his ears.

"Gentlemen, there can be two possible explanations for this", said Magnusson angrily. "First it's going through far too many hands along the info pipeline and getting edited. This office doesn't want things edited.

Time is of the essence, first last and always. "It's either the incompetence of edition, or something more sinister. Someone is covering up something"!

"In both countries, reports keep coming in regarding local subcontractors, not being paid in a timely manner. In some cases it's because of shoddy work, while in others it's because of the general contractors, simply getting out of the country with literally bags of cash and disappearing. As of now everyone who gets on an aircraft, no matter their rank or status, gets their luggage searched for contraband or cash. Border crossings notwithstanding. Anyone caught carrying cash out of either country is to be apprehended, no matter who they are"!

"The way we fund our non-governmental contractors is ridiculous. I want tangible ideas on my desk by noon tomorrow on how to tighten things up there, or else there will be some vacancies around this table by the close of business tomorrow night. My current thinking is the military has far too much to do, yet too much dependence upon our auxiliary contractors is in existence. Where's the oversight? I will know by noon tomorrow, gentlemen".

"Next, is apparently my viewpoint on the relaxation of the rules of engagement is not being shared by the rank and file commanders in the field. The troopers on the ground are a bit restive to say the least. Yet I'm grateful for their discipline and sense of purpose, or else a number of those reluctant commanders would not be with us. Gentlemen, do I make myself clear? Stopping well short of outright theft, rape, or murder, our soldiers will be aggressive and become the dogs of war we all know there trained for. Hesitation gets our boys killed. Supply vehicles need to find several routes of access and egress so they are not sitting ducks for roadside IED's. If someone appears like an enemy, then consider them as such. We're in a goddamn war over there, not a court of law. Quite frankly gentlemen, all of you are trained in the arts of war, yet around this table all I'm seeing is politicians. I'm not seeing the leaders of men in battle. I should not be the one telling you these things it should be the other way around. We all talk about victory when not one of you is doing anything rational about achieving that end"!

"How many of you have read Machiavelli's, "The Prince"? A show of hands please? Ah as I thought, not one of you has found the time.

Interesting. In the book he talks about either being loved or feared. It would I'm certain accrue to all of your benefits in reading that book. I think every bookstore has multiple copies somewhere. Focus if you will on the fear factor. In WWII, we defeated two mortal enemies in a great struggle, and in the end those enemies learned to fear us, for we had a very sharp sword in one hand and an olive branch in the other. After it was all over it was the fear they had for us that caused each of them to capitulate, was replaced by respect after they saw our sword, being replaced by the olive branch. Since then, no enemy of ours has feared us since and why? Because we were reluctant to engage our swords. Gentlemen, first the sword then the olive branch. I might remind you that since then Germany and Japan have rebuilt their societies and have been staunch allies. The book is easy to find and is in paperback and a quick read. By tomorrow morning I expect two things, for each of you to have read 'The Prince' and for our clear verbal directives to quickly find its way to the battle commanders in theater, by noon tomorrow our time. We will not bargain with the enemy for the enemy will break any agreement as soon as is practicable, read the Koran and you will quickly see why. Now if anyone at this table has even the slightest problem with what has been directed please speak now"!

"As I see that not one hand has risen I will take it that all are in at least tacit agreement"? At that Magnusson scanned everyone present, then rose up saying, "Good Gentlemen, so now we can all get back to work and I trust we will all know something about Machiavelli sooner rather than later"! As the President strode out of the conference room he joined Orval Goodwin who had just arrived asking, "How did things go with the Big Brass"? "I laid it all out for them, in no uncertain terms. Kill the enemy, period. They have until noon tomorrow to get the message through to the field commanders in theater. Either they will or I just might get a visit from the Delta boys. We need an exit strategy and aggression is the strategy. No more pussy footing around. It's costing our lives and cash money we just can't afford. Any good news Orval"?

"The bitter with the better Mr. President, which do you want first"? "The better Orval, the better"!

"Doesn't look like Senator Scarsdale is going to make it. Everyone knew he has a heart condition and what we've recently discovered is the he was on meds for both his heart condition, but in addition, he was a manic depressive and was on a medical regimen for both afflictions"? "Why am I not surprised Orval"?

"The docs could find no evidence that he had his meds in his system in the aftermath of his heart attack, which as you know, developed into a severe stroke the following day. He's been in intensive care ever since and is on a respirator and seems to be fading fast. A discussion has been going on all morning as whether or not to give his last rights"!

"That serious, eh"? Goodwin nodded his head as they walked.

"Just the Lords way of thinning out the herd! What's the other good news"?

"The sanctuary cities have finally gotten together in a law suit against your action of holding up federal funds, because of their complete lack of enforcement of our illegal immigration statutes"!

"Oh let's see, they ignore federal statutes, because they want to court the Latino vote and then when the consequences come due for their action they cry foul even though they're scofflaws pure and simple. What's next"? "The ACLU is filing a class action suit against the Government regarding your Executive Order cutting off all wire transaction remittances to anyone south of the border, claiming that you exceeded your mandated executive authority"!

"Sounds like we need to get together with the Solicitor General soon as possible"!

"I've blocked out your entire afternoon, for the both of you to discuss strategy Mr. President", said Goodwin as they passed Melanie's desk.

"What's the news on the Montag/Duquesne, Mag Lev mass transport elevated train projects"?

"The Miami, New York projects as you know have all gotten off the ground Mr. President", said Goodwin, "With Two of the four initiation points with over a hundred miles of elevated track in place and the ancillary equipment following close behind. The other two IP's are just getting under way and are behind, because of the roadblocks from the environmental groups that want studies performed and the Unions that want in on the projects. However the task force that was created to interface with various state and municipal concerns is slogging its way through everything. Now the Los Angeles, San Francisco, Seattle project is pretty much in the very same condition, but the West Coast Federal Task Force, is tangling with the various legislative units. The LA, Vegas Mag Lev line is two months ahead of schedule; of course, it was started during the prior administration and has mostly unpopulated desert to cross. Desert Jack Rabbits fortunately have zero constituency in the legislative bodies. Seems that a bipartisan coalition of legislators have really cleared the way, in this regard"!

"Just make it be known that the White House prominently gives them recognition in the media at every turn regardless of their party affiliation or their cooperation and service rendered to the nation, Orval. As far as those who are standing in the way with their cry out for committee studies, sic Harvanian on them"!

"Already on it Mr. President. After all, if you want to stop a piece of legislation, then appoint a commission to study the issue and we just can't let that happen. Although you will have to meet with a coalition of environmentalists the day after tomorrow, that are standing in the way of our wind and solar initiatives, along both coasts, the Gulf and the Great Lakes as well as the Rocky Mountain region"!

"Any idea what they want Orval"?

"Depends upon which ones you talk to. Some are concerned that the Wind Towers will disrupt migration patterns of birds; others are concerned about visual pollution, while others along the coastlines have concerns about fishing. Ask a hundred of them about their concerns and you'll end up with seventy five different concerns. Like herding cats"!

"Service to all is service to none Orval", mused Magnusson as he rummaged across his desk for a memo he was seeking.

"Harvanian is on it. By the way, he has to duck out for tomorrow afternoon after his news conference and visit his sick relative in New York, for the evening, but he'll be back the following morning. His assistant is up on all the issues in case things crater during his absence"!

"Thanks Orval. On your way out please send Mel in and tell her to bring her memo pad"!

Later on in the day, the Director of FBI, was summoned to the President's office. After the initial greeting the Magnusson said, "Thank you for coming Director! What progress has been made in the interrogations of the Muslim terrorists"? "Sad to say very little Mr. President"! "And why is that Director"?

"Well as you may know, early on the ACLU has provided each of them with counsel and we are obliged to have them president during every interrogation session. Although they are all conversant in English, we have an interpreter, out of sight, listening in on all conversations, just in the event they say something in their native language"!

"Why isn't the interpreter visible, in order to give visual impressions regarding the questioning of the prisoner, Director"?

"Mr. President we are obliged to go by the book and the existing protocol does not require this"!

"Excuse me for a moment. I want the Chief of Staff to sit in on this meeting if you don't mind"?

"Of course not Mr. President"!

Magnusson picked up the phone and summoned Orval Good-win into his office. As he entered Magnusson said, "Of course you know Orval"!

Both men acknowledged each other as Goodwin took a seat.

"Certain elements of the media are crucifying both you and I for taking so long to get any actionable information of any kind from the terrorists, Director and the public wants to know why"!

"If I may Mr. President, 'Alleged Terrorists' at least until their proven guilty in a court of law"! Magnusson then looked at Goodwin and asked, "Orval, you know a great deal about the history of the Oval Office, so can you tell me of any time you can recall, that any Chief Executive has been corrected by a subordinate, especially when the subordinate is being called on the carpet for lack of results"!

Glancing briefly at the Director, then back at the President, Goodwin replied, "No Mr. President I can't"!"Just as I thought. Director, you've just confirmed my growing suspicions"!

"And they are Mr. President"?

"That my confidence in you has been on the down slope for quite some time and Director at this very moment you are on the bubble"!

"We all serve at the pleasure of the President", said the director, seeing the calm demeanor of the President growing fainter with each passing moment.

"Historical and Hollywood clap trap Director. Talking points. I despise talking points coming out of the mouth of anyone in government service.

Yes loyalty to a sitting President is nice, but loyalty to the nation that employs you is the greater loyalty. Loyalty to the people, the extant laws that govern us are but a means to an end any that is end is relative peace and harmony. We are at war Director, in case you haven't noticed. So now tell me what you are going to do to obtain information from the terrorists"?

"Mr. President, the current laws of the land, limits what we can do"! "As I thought", replied Magnussen! "Orval, if you'll be so kind to do the honors"?

Goodwin reached over to the President's desk and opened the leather folder, presenting it to the Director along with a pen.

"What's this Mr. President"?

"It's the letter of resignation that you are going to sign, before you leave this office. I tried find a way for you continue in your current position, but you just sold me out of that idea and thank you for that. By the way on your way back to your office to clean out your desk, inform the Assistant Director, that I'll be expecting his letter of resignation on my desk no later than 1700 hrs. By 1800 hours you and the AD will be gone from your office. Any personal items will be trashed, after 1800 hours. As you depart a moving company will arrive, at your building to accommodate you.

Within the next fifteen minutes a news bulletin will appear on most of the media channels announcing both your and the AD's decision to resign.

Depending on what the both of you say to the media in the aftermath of your departure will determine the appropriate response from this office. The Recess appointment as your replacements will be in place by 0800 hrs. tomorrow. Sorry things had to come to this Oscar, but you called it on yourself. Now sign the goddamn letter and get out of my sight"!

After he'd left, with a copy of the resignation letter in hand, Goodwin said, "You know the Attorney General and his number two will also have to go to accomplish what needs to be done, for they've been giving the Director political cover for a long time"!

"The replacements in the wings"?

"Yes, Mr. President, they are just two management levels down from their boss. Discussed the possibilities with them last week. Ran your concerns past them and their answers are exactly what you will want to hear. These are guys that will find a way to get the terrorists to spill the beans and give us the straight skinny, even if it means inviting the boys over from Langley. By early next week, after all of this key personnel change business is out of The way for the most part, the prisoners will be whisked away from the current place of incarceration and just a chosen few will be in on things"!

"Should it ever come to this and it probably will, The official position will be that the prisoners in question have been taken to a secret medical facility for an in depth physical examination, which is sort of the truth, Mr. President. In reality, they've been looking a little peaked lately. Not near enough sunlight, so a little physical rehab is in order in a sunny climate, somewhere in the Caribbean area". While Congress is on vacation as of yesterday, we will have two whole weeks, to get things in place"!

"What about the ACLU attorneys for the prisoners, Orval"? "Checked the interrogation schedule and it was announced that no questioning sessions are normally scheduled for the next ten calendar days. Sometime late tomorrow morning, after the New Director takes office, a secret habeas corpus directive will be issued by a friendly Federal Judge, who has already announced his retirement by year's end, to release the prisoners to the US Military, for a destination to an Air Base in Alaska, where an experienced team of interrogators will await their new charges. All military transfers will occur in the dead of night"!

From two different locations, teams of Federal Agents departed with their four prisoners. From various locations in America teams of experienced interrogators departed for that Air Base in Alaska. Four different Quonset buildings were hurriedly made ready for the arrivals of the visitors, with a team of experienced Air Police and US Marshall's in charge of joint security. Welcoming them all was Brigadier General Mark Sherman, the Base Commander, saying, "Welcome everyone, we could spend time making nice with one another but I understand that time is a luxury we don't have. Assembled here we have, representatives from the CIA, the FBI, the NSA, and some medical specialists from Cal Tech. What needs to be done first I'm told, is to discover effective avenues of approach in which to obtain the maximum of information within a ten day window of opportunity, with a maximum of two weeks, while our congressional leaders are going on their reelection campaigns. With due respect for our FBI brethren, several months have gone by while their interrogators had the shackles on their activities. As of now, I've a directive from the head honcho himself, the shackles are off, with the minor exception of visible bodily injury, inclusive of bruises or penetrations that leave a visible indication of possible foul play. Short of that you ladies and gentlemen have carte' blanche with these guys. Just remember they have to be returned to their lawyers unscathed. That said, Colonel Moore is at your service with anything the US Air Force can provide to be of assistance"!

The General promptly departed and as he passed the Colonel he said,

"Remember Carl, this is every bit a Black Ops, Security Class Alpha. See what you have to but quickly forget and at all times, CYA. What you don't know can't hurt you"!

"General, this whole thing is a career ender if news of this gets into the wrong ears"!

"So let's just make certain that it doesn't"! For the next several hours over a midnight meal of Smoked Salmon and scrambled eggs brought over from the Officers Mess, the various well experienced interrogators, poured over the previous interrogation records of the subjects, looking for the obvious weakness' in personalities, but given the fact that Miranda Rights for prisoners were in the way, along with the constant presence of legal counsel limiting what could be answered to, the records were virtually useless. Four hours later and seemingly endless discussion between parties about the very best method of approach, compelled Dr. Mara Romanofsky to raise her hand and ask a question.

"Gentlemen, I'm Mara Romanovsky from the Rand Corporation. My specialty, at the Think Tank has been Bio Weapons and my Doctorate is from MIT is in the field of Bio Weapons Technology. However back in college my first love was in the field of Human Narco Analysis as it applied to peering deep into the human mind. We clearly are starting from scratch with the subjects at hand and time is of the essence. No doubt, given the time, and without the existing constraints, no doubt many of the well- practiced techniques so many of you are adept at will work. So I'd like to offer a modest proposal. Narco Analysis. Polygraphs won't yield the desired results because one would require a willing subject and anyway there are several well-known ways to defeat that technique. Voice stress analysis is a way to observe human veracity along with someone adept at reading the micro expressions of the human face along with the subconscious body language clues the subject's exhibit over the course of repeated interrogations. However all of that requires sufficient time to employ and observe. Hypnosis is also out, because one would need a willing subject. The science is therefore incomplete, for there are a sign cant number of people in the world who are resistant to hypnosis at the deepest level of somnambulism. Then there is always post hypnotic suggestion that would place an almost impenetrable firewall, unless the appropriate key was discovered. What I propose is a way to penetrate that firewall, via Narco Analysis"!

"Doctor Romanovsky is it? I'm Dan Jackson from the Behavioral Analysis section of the FBI, in Quantico Virginia. I've two questions for you. First of which is the fifth amendment, prohibition as to violating ones right of self-incrimination and back in law school I recall several old cases of apparently settled law that prohibit use of any substance that would compel a prisoner to self-incriminate himself. Then the second question relates to the efficacy of Narco Analysis as a truth serum. Scopolamine, Amino Barbital, Sodium Pentathol as well as several others have indeed proved very useful in opening up the lips of resistant patients to reveal their inner secrets to psychoanalysis, but prove only a way to get people to start talking, often leaving truth and wandering off into the land of further psychosis. So even should we go down this risky road legally, what guarantee would we have that what we learn is the actual truth"!

"An excellent question Agent Jackson and I'll even tell you one other thing wrong with the Chemicals you've listed. They require an injection site and depending upon the subject, sometimes exhibit undesired physical after effects. Plus sometimes the subject may recall the subliminal questioning at some later date"!

Most of those in the room nodded their heads, some even having used narcotics in the past in interrogating a subject to diminish the will. "But Gentlemen, what if there was a chemical substance, that could be orally administered in any liquid either hot or cold, leaving no taste, or color, or odor, or physical after effects or any recollection of interrogation or questioning of any kind, simply a gap in time, since the subject would simply drift off for a nap"! At that moment, Dr. Mara Romanovsky paused to let that sink in for everyone.

"There is a drug that could do all that", asked Agent Jackson, prompting Dr. Romanovsky to continue saying, "Back in the mid-eighties the Bio Weapons Division Twelve of the Soviet Army developed such a drug. It was extensively tested for its efficacy for many years on animals and humans alike in Siberia. The reason for the development was for the private use of the military exclusively. Eventually the old KGB got hold of it and now their successor uses it to vet everyone, spies, theirs ours, common criminals, governmental officials suspected of malfeasance and of course in their mental institutions. It works very well; they just don't talk about it. We have our DNA proof; the Russians have SP-117.

"Sound much like that date rape drug doctor", came a voice from the far end of the table. "Similar, except it does not affect the sexual sensory aspects of the subliminal. While the so called date rape drug works as desired to remove inhibitions, it has aftereffects in many people and in some cases hypnotic therapy can restore memory of the event. Once SP-117 is administered and the desired information obtained, it acts exactly like a computer hard drive that has been repeatedly written over with all previous data deleted. Oh, one thing more, any post hypnotic firewall that may have been put in place on the subject prior to his current examination will be obliterated and when the subject awakens not only will he have no memory of his interrogation, but the subject(s) of the interrogation will also be eliminated from the subjects memory forever. The only thing that shall remain is a hole in time that can easily be explained by the subjects drifting off into a nap"!

"Now gentlemen, it seems to me, the only impediment that remains is the Fifth Amendment. I would be happy to administer the drug to the subjects, then sit back and observe, while the rest of you went to work.

While you decide, I'll go outside in the snow and have a cigarette"!

Before she could reach the door, several people called for her to come back. After an hour of consultation it was decided that Dr. Mara Romanovsky would administer the drug, SP-117 into the subject's drink of choice during the next scheduled meal. The first interrogation should serve as a pattern and test case for the experts at hand. Everything was videotaped from beginning to end, with the others watching the video screens with keen interest.

The meal was served to the prisoner, who sniffed around a bit, but his hunger drove him to finally take the first bite, in what he thought was complete solitude. From time to time he drank from the large mug containing lemonade, going back to his meal, each time. When he finished his meal after having consumed his lemonade, everyone looked at each other and nodded knowingly. Then a stopwatch was activated and within twenty minutes, the prisoners head began to nod off. Finally after several minutes more, Dr. Romanovsky said, "Gentlemen, you may begin"!

Then she went outside into the cold arctic evening, to light that long overdue cigarette. After several minutes, she was joined by Special Agent Dan Jackson who asked, "May I join you Doctor? I seem to have forgotten my cigarettes"!

As she offered the Agent one of her own she said, "I heard you were a non-smoker, Agent Jackson"! "Please call me Dan. Normally I avoid the evil weed and even abstain for months at a time. But eventually I always drift back into the fold, especially when the stakes are high like the present. Things could be worse, for I might be addicted to snuff, or chewing tobacco, or Cuban cigars. I suppose when I eventually retire, I'll gradually drift into pipe tobacco"!

"But that's not why you joined me here is it Dan", said Mara, looking at the far off dimly lit skyline. "You wanted to get a handle on how I know so much about old Soviet style narco analysis interrogative techniques and get a feel on whether or not this woman with a Russian name can be trustworthy or is a sleeper agent"!

"That obvious eh"?

"My people came over to America from Vladivostok, in the Russian far east in the latter part of the nineteenth century. My forbearers helped build the Trans-Siberian railway, since one of my grandparents was a construction engineer. I'm told that many died during That period of Czarist rule. My father escaped the worst of it, since he was a designer and engineer and was needed. When connection was made in the east, he was settled in Vladivostok, the terminus of the railway. He eventually married a woman from St. Petersburg. An Arranged marriage I've been told, between families. She traveled three months to meet him and within a week of their arrival, they were married by the local Russian Orthodox Bishop, who just happened to be drunk at the time and barely got through the wedding, passing out upon the altar, as they were making their way out of church"!

"Have another cigarette Dan", said Mara offering him her pack and as they each lit up she said, "In case you're wondering why I choose to hold a cigarette in the continental manner, between the thumb and the forefinger, it is because I choose to, not as a force of habit as we in the west choose to between the fore and the middle digits", she mused with an arched eyebrow.

"Still a few steps ahead of me", said an embarrassed Jackson wondering just how she picked up on his well-practiced glance.

"No doubt you will check into my background upon your return to Quantico and discover that I was married long ago during my undergraduate days, wondering why I still retain the family cognomen? The reason was simple. I was a victim of infatuation not love. When I finally discovered that the man was a fool, I left him immediately. The relationship lasted six long months, ending in divorce. Perhaps I should've waited, for he came from a wealthy Southern California family and three months after out divorce, he was killed on the Pacific Coast highway in a high speed police chase, trying to elude the California Highway Patrol. Had I prescient abilities and a bit of patience, I might have enjoyed a significant inheritance and saved a great deal in legal fees in obtaining the divorce. I resumed my family name and it's been that way since"!

"As for my heritage, my great, great grandfather ran afoul of a corrupt Czarist government in the Far East and in the dead of night rounded up his family and left all of their possessions behind in Vladivostok boarding a tramp steamer for Hong Kong. Six months later they landed in San Francisco, with little more than the clothes on their back. Yet he was indeed fortunate in being a top notch construction engineer, with European training he found work quickly working for the Union Pacific and was employed there for the rest of his life, or at least that's how legend has it", she added with a sly wink! As for any knowledge I've obtained regarding our current project, please remember who employs me and given that what I do is also a hobby of mine, I do not regard this as work but an avocation"!

"Are you saving me a lot of needless time and effort, Mara"?

"Perhaps so, but I doubt it. Just observe what I do here and now then make up your own mind of my fourth generation American credentials"!

"That is what I will do Doctor", said Agent Jackson!

"Good, now that my lungs are clear, shall we rejoin our associates and enjoy the crumbling of mortal wills in behalf of America"?

The first prisoner took approximately forty five minutes, before the information regarding his prime contact began to come forth. Name, contact information and delving deep into his heretofore locked subconscious, revealed that he was a subject of deep hypnosis administered by someone named Salaam. His immediate local handler was identified and as to the others involved, he had no certain knowledge. At that point Dr. Romanofsky asked the interrogators to ask the subject to speculate just which members of his Mosque Were predisposed to engage in such an event. Five minutes later, the subject started to offer possibilities and categorize them according to probabilities. By the end of the second hour, the interrogators wrapped things up and emerged with the others, smiling and saying "One little Indian down and three to go"!

Seeing Dr. Romanovsly waiting with the others, One of the CIA interrogators asked, "I hate to admit this, but the old saying my wife hammers me with all the time, "Leave it to a woman", genuinely applies here folks. Now I hope you have more of this SP-117 on hand so we can complete our job Doctor and oh by the way will you write us all a prescription for the stuff"!

"After tomorrow mornings meal, the three remaining subjects will be interrogated and we will be directed by Dr. Romanovsky. With any luck, we'll have all we need by afternoon and then escort our charges back to the lower forty eight and start the long search. Let's all get some shut eye everyone, for we're up at 0500 hrs. breakfast at the officer's mess. At 0600 and we go to work after the subjects have their morning vittles at 0700", said Agent Jackson"!

By lunch time the following day, each subject had opened up to such a degree, giving information of names of suspected terrorists involved in the summertime conflagration that swept the nation, that Agent Jackson admitted the FBI hadn't sufficient manpower to pursue effectively, saying "Need to know basis gentlemen"! "Our agency is going to be overwhelmed with information in the effective pursuit of these terrorists. When you get back to your superiors have them request an eyes only meeting with the White House"!

"Doctor Romanovsky, I'm certain that I speak for everyone here, that we wouldn't have this kind of success without your skills on site.

Should you receive a call from Washington asking for your help; will you entertain the possibility of helping your nation in its time of need"?

"Agent Jackson, my presence here, away from the beaches at Malibu should answer that question don't you think"?

The officer's mess was open once again to the visitors as the base security readied the prisoners again for another trip. This time to their original destination, to the southern tip of Cuba where, they could work on their tan. Interestingly enough, the prisoners had no recollection of the detour they'd taken, much less of what they revealed.

Three days later, the Directors of the FBI, CIA, NSA and all the military intelligence arms met after hours at the White House for a collective meeting of the minds in how to effectively collect the swarm of terrorists that lay in the county's midst. Sitting at the table was Dr. Mara Romanovsky, quietly listening, as she sat next to the newly appointed Attorney General of the United States.

The meeting was conducted by the newly appointed, during congressional recess, Director of the FBI, as he briefed the President and his immediate staff of what had recently transpired.

"Thanks to the splendid efforts and skill of Dr. Romanovsky, we've not only cut the time of interrogation down to almost zero, while we think will obtain the optimum of quality information as to the location of the suspects, Mr. President"!

"Director, I've already received a pre brief of what went on and am I correct that it's been suspected that each of the suspects involved was placed under hypnosis, much akin to the Manchurian Candidate scenario, yet after the event have no recollection as to what they'd been involved in"!

"Yes Mr. President that is what we all currently agree on. Now I think I know where you're going with this. If they have no recollection of what they'd been involved in, what would be the rush in rounding them all up at once"? Magnusson nodded his head.

"It's' already been demonstrated that we've been able to break through the firewall their original controller set up, by our new technique, thanks to Dr. Romanovsky. Now the best psychiatric minds we consulted, on a need to know basis, agree on the simple fact that the human mind is a highly complex thing and one little thing unforeseen may, mind you, one little aspect of news reporting, may be sufficient to have just one of them suffer a recollection event and then alert one or more individuals he may suspect that was also involved. Since we wish to apprehend as many of these people possible, and put them through the very same process of their predecessors, we must move swiftly and surely"!

"I understand Director, that one individual has been singled out by all of those already put through the process, as you put it, as the prime initiator.

Someone they all refer to as Salaam. My recent reading of the Koran and Middle Eastern history tells me that the name Salaam is the Muslim term of greeting meaning 'Peace'. Am I correct"?

"Yes Mr. President. All four coincided in that information. They all came at it at different times during the process and from different directions, which we conclude must be genuine, rather than preprogrammed"!

"I see that if we employ, those in the Behavioral Analysis Section at both Quantico and Langley along with some people of similar behavioral interrogation skills from the NSA and the intelligence sections of our military, we just might have the manpower to affect this"!

"Yes sir we just might pull this one off", interjected the Director of the CIA", provided that we employ the services of Dr. Romanovsky. Her employers have willingly placed her at our service, for as long as she's needed"!

"This SBG-117 substance the old KGB employed and that we effected on the prisoners, I'm told crosses the path of the Fifth Amendment is that not the case, and if so poses a potential legal challenge, does it not? So operating from the podium of Murphy's Law, which is ever present, what would happen if someone let it slip in a moment of weakness that person X is being, or is about to be interrogated by the Federal Government and somehow some lawyer, let's assume the worst case, the lawyer is from the ACLU and he's with his new client every moment of the time during interrogation as has been the case in the past. What's to be done"?

"May I answer that question Mr. President"?

"Please do, Dr. Romanovsky"! Standing fully erect she began, "In such an event the subject of interrogation is accompanied by counsel, we simply offer them both refreshment such as coffee or tea. In twenty minutes, both will be in a deep slumber for the next six hours or so and we go about our business with the interrogation. Should the subject awaken before the lawyer, we spirit him away making the excuse that he took ill. Should the lawyer awaken first we'll have sufficient time to spirit the subject away with the same reason and have a medic of sorts available to tend to the lawyer who fell asleep from apparent fatigue. Either way, no memory of the event will be in the mind of either party. Simply a period of time they cannot account for. If skillfully done this contrivance usually is sufficient.

Now if the lawyer will accept no open container of refreshment then we go on with the questioning for an abbreviated period of time, and then send the subject back to his cell. The lawyer will have to return home. The subject will be fed his next meal and in the tray will be liquid refreshment and once consumed the questioning begins anyway"!

"Thus Check and Mate, is what I'm hearing"?

"Precisely Mr. President", replied Dr. Romanovsky!

"I assume gentlemen that Dr. Romanovsky has been appropriately vetted and that no one at this table has even the slightest problem working for and or with this women on an interim basis. If anyone has the slightest reservations about her abilities or where her loyalties lay lets here it now"! As the President looked around the table, his glance was met by silent agreement of nodding heads.

"Thank you lady and gentlemen. This office will execute an executive order this evening and each of you will have an individual arrive at the Chief of Staff's office to receive and transport the hand delivered directive back to you. By 0800 hours tomorrow the COS will have a list of those who will arrive as messengers, am I agreed"!

As everyone arose, Magnusson said "Gentlemen, good hunting"! As he walked out Magnusson called over his secretary saying, "Dr. Romanovsky is going to need transport and a place to hang her hat each day for her stay here in Washington Mel"!

"I have a perfectly good bedroom that can be used at my place and I'll tell the head of the secret service to have an unmarked car and driver at her beck and call every day that he's needed. Don't worry I'll get her through the system in no time.

Mara Romanovsky placed a call to her brother who usually worked late most evening conducting experiments at Cal-Tech University while acting as Chairman of the Chemistry Department, for the University.

"Your dime shoot", was how Dimitry always answered the phone irreverently while his sister always replied, "Shoot who, you Cossack"?

"Aha, my adoring sister, who's off doing secret work for god knows who. How are you Drushka"?

"Just calling you to ask you to collect the mail for a few months at my place and I'll call you later and tell you where to send it"!

"Ah, the work of my brilliant sister goes on. Consider it done. What else can I do for you"?

"Before I left, I took some of the very special ingredients you cooked up for me a few years ago and I'll need more much more"!

"So you finally had need for my brilliant synthesis for your Narco Analysis. So how well did it function my dear"?

"That's the main reason for my call Dimitry. It worked as we both expected it would and we will require a great deal more! So how many doses have we left and how much can you synthesize in the next week"?

"If memory serves, I'll have about four dozen on hand in vials in the refrigerator and if I allow myself only four hours sleep each night along with my normal schedule for the University and limit my sparse social live to absolute zero, I can probably furnish around five dozen more vials of your precious substance within the coming week. But only if you'll tell me what you're up to"! "Remember your very favorite movie brother. The one where Jake and Elwood go on their Crusade for the Penguin. Well, I'm in the Nation's Capital and I'll be here for a while and the Nation needs your talents. That's all I can say at the present, so can I count on you brother"? "Little Drushka, you've always been able to count on me. Send the federal messenger west for the first batch in the morning. It'll be ready. But little sister it'll cost you"!

"What will it cost me Dimitry"?

"Dinner at the finest most expensive restaurant Los Angeles, sister"?

"Done, little brother and perhaps it'll even get better than that God willing. Thank you and good night I'll call you in the morning"!

As Dimitry Romanovsky hung up the phone, he suddenly exclaimed, "The Blues Brothers and I'm on a mission for God"!

Starting in the cities where the list of suspects were quietly apprehended by the various task forces, Mara Romanovsky was in attendance for each interrogation. As anticipated many of the initial interrogations were successful in revealing other involved in the investigation, which started to spill over into other cities affected by the recent conflagrations.

Where, other interrogations were not successful, the participants were quietly deposited a block from their residence of record, in the early morning hours, shielded from any witness's, to awaken with the dawn with no recollection of where they had been or what had occurred. Simply a twelve hour or so, hole in their life they could not explain.

In the instances where the interrogations yielded hard evidence of other involvement in the conspiracy, then selected investigators were sent to glean hard evidence, albeit after the fact, to corroborate their suspicions thus establishing probable cause. Of course this may have proven to be a problem in the event they were ever brought to trial.

Of course, what was occurring at a rapid rate was out of the normal bounds of American Juris Prudence, everyone involved was certain that none of these cases could ever be brought to trial, for a host of laws had been contravened, thus each case would be thrown out of any Federal Court in the land.

Some thought that with the wiping clean of the memory of what each individual had done; simply releasing them like the others would be sufficient, for they would recall nothing. Others argued with conviction, that their individual normal propensities would still be in effect, thus leaving a potential cancer still alive and well in their midst.

So while the investigation was moving along at a rapid pace, almost a hundred individuals were placed in temporarily isolated high security federal facilities throughout the land, while a meeting of minds convened in the Oval office. Brought out of retirement was an old war horse of long service to the nation, who sat quietly while others argued as what to do?

Clearly the Administration's secret investigation had painted them all in both a legal, but political corner.

"General Bollinger, we haven't heard from you yet, said the General Maxwell Ottenger, Chairman of the Joint Chiefs of Staff, of the US Military. "Have you any useful ideas you can come up with"?

Bollinger put down his coffee and thought a second before voicing a comment. "General Ottenger, President Magnusson, I thank you for including me in this. Now I'm not a lawyer, simply an old retired Marine. An old war horse, at last at peace with the world, comfortable in his pasture. However a few things are crystal clear to us all. Those in custody, what is it currently, some ninety five people, many of which are naturalized citizens, along with many who are not, even under the best of circumstances, are guaranteed to clog up our federal judicial system for years to come, yet the circumstances of their apprehension are at the very best questionable if not illegal. Therein lay the irritant. What to do with the prisoners? The accused! Now we all know they are guilty for many of us have seen and heard the videotapes. Were we in a declared war with a sovereign country, fighting an enemy clad in Uniforms according to the Geneva agreements of long ago, then perhaps we could make a case for our speedy action. But we are in an undeclared conflict with an enemy that hides in plain sight and I suggest this will be the case for years to come"!

"Our freedoms and laws that govern us do not make sufficient provision for the current situation and of course there is no way our founding fathers could have foreseen the current reality. All of us in this room realize the current course of action is for this purpose only, yet here we are setting precedent for future actions. Something must be done, on the fly and soon, for time is not our friend. Now if it were up to me, with no constraints, I'd immediately have them all executed by firing squads. Thankfully it's not up to me. Plus an argument could be made that it would be murder, straight up. Yet they cannot stay, they cannot be tried and incarcerated and they should not be murdered, so thus my modest proposal. Now before I begin, I understand that a number of missing person's reports are staring to occur in various localities. Should this trend continue a dangerous set of circumstances is certain to develop that could place everyone in this room in legal and political danger, therefore in my mind things distill into two very simple alternatives"!

"First of which, the existing prisoners are all cut loose, like the ones determined not to have any involvement, in the dead of night, near their own neighborhoods, while other investigations are developing hard evidence, that can be brought before a judge, who will issue a warrant for their arrest issuing from probable cause. Then they are officially apprehended, interrogated as much as is possible and tried in a court of law.

Of course, in instances where no hard evidence can be obtained, these people can be disposed of in yet another way. The other alternative"!

"There exist an island, northwest of the Bering Straits. An apparently barren island devoid of what we would call normal vegetation. The island is, as I am given to understand, uninhabited and rather small, being some fifteen square miles in landmass. Part of its mass is miles of peat bogs, which if dried can be used for fuel. Of course it lay's well above the Arctic Circle and enjoys perhaps two months out of any given year, of anything resembling a normal climate. It is on the bare fringe of what Russia claims as its sovereign territory and any aircraft that approaches it from a ceiling of not exceeding three hundred feet in altitude can both enter and exit their airspace without detection. In addition, I know where some five hundred old eastern bloc parachutes and arctic clothing can be quickly obtained, for the purpose of inserting these people, via a Lo Lo static line insertion, low altitude, low opening landing of those selected. Of course the prisoners will be kept under their current sedation schedule and if well administered will wake up shortly after their landing, finding themselves on a deserted island.

Of course, shortly before their scheduled to jump, each of them will be armed with an old Soviet issue knife for purely survival purposes. Of course none of the individuals will have received any arctic survival training much less any training in parachuting. This should be of no concern to anyone, in this room. We will be giving them a better chance than they gave our citizens who perished from their actions"!

"General Bollinger, asked the newly appointed Attorney General,

"You suggest we parachute them on an deserted arctic island, what happens if Russian radar detects approaching aircraft"!

"Interesting question! Let's say you're a Russian radar technician in the arctic and all you see is flocks of birds passing across your radar screen all day and night long. Further let's say you've developed a love for Vodka, to numb yourself from the boredom of Arctic service. Further, is a known fact that the very best of Russia's vastly underpaid military does not Perform Arctic service, for it is but one step above a Gulag and the island in question is on the very fringe of the nearest Russian radar stations scanning area"!

"But General Bollinger", asked General Ottenger, "What about the survival possibilities of the prisoners? Some may not survive the Lo Lo insertion and those that do will be ill equipped to survive the Arctic winter"?

"Once again General, why should that be any concern of ours? We would be giving an opportunity for survival. A slim one, I'll admit, but an opportunity none the less. We save the cost of prosecutions and incarceration. They are deposited far from any land mass; they will each have a knife and arctic clothing for survival and a source of fuel if their clever enough and just one more thing, the island is full of seals and walrus's. Some will not survive, while some may, it should not be of any concern to any of us. Just one thing more gentlemen. Depending of what religious theory one relies on, what is Hell like? We all think it is deep in the neither regions, where thanks to Dante's writings of the Middle Ages, we've been given to believe. While others make reference to Hell, being a very cold place where one is kept in a constant state of stasis, fighting for survival. Yet it is clear, whatever one believes, Hell is a place where God cares not! When one has earned his place in that very place, hope does not spring eternal but is a distant memory, fading rapidly from ones memory"!

"Gentlemen, I've given what council I could and I've placed alternatives before you. Whatever is chosen must be done without delay"!

The General had given them all much to think about as he excused himself to step outside for a cigarette for a few minutes. Upon his return he saw General Ottenger on one of the offices phones issuing orders.

Had it been the Attorney General he'd have known what the decision would have been.

Magnusson and the Attorney General approached him as the Attorney General said, "I hope your correct in your assessment General, for my office is up to the gunwales in prosecutions and investigations. If this works, good. If it doesn't.... . his voice trailing off"!

"Sir, remember Ben Franklin who said something like, "We must all hang together, lest we all hang separately".

After he departed, Magnusson said, "General Bollinger, I'd like to have you stay after the others depart and share dinner with me. Would you do me that further service"?

"Mr. President, I'd be happy to join you for dinner"!

During the rest of the afternoon, General Bollinger allowed himself to be shown around the entire White House, by Melanie O'Bannon. As they walked he said, "Never ever have taken the White House tour Mrs.

O'Bannon and I thank you for showing me all of the artifacts and spending your valuable time with this old war horse"!

"Thank you General so very much and I relish the break in the action. By your reputation I feel quite honored to be in your presence. By the way we never hear of a Mrs. Bollinger"!

"And with good reason, for she passed on some years back during child birth. The child also didn't make it"!

"So in all the years since you've never chosen to remarry"?

"Didn't seem to be much point in it all. I loved Mary with all my heart. Chat briefly with her every day, so what woman would or could ever put up with such behavior. Besides my work usually kept me away from her for days and weeks at a time on a fairly regular basis. Mary adjusted to it or so it appeared. The woman never complained once about my absences, nor had a jealous bone in her body, she was about as well grounded a woman as it gets. We'd looked forward to that child it was to be our first. But it wasn't to be. My good friends at the time were all five by five and took turns staying with me through the dark days afterwards. Oddly enough it took three Liters of Tequila consumed over a three day period of time, or so they all told me, to drive most of the demons away."!

"A three day bender", asked an astonished Melanie?

"Yes indeed. But my men were at my side at all times. Then I took a long shower, for I had a unit to run and a life to live. Mary is in a very good place and we'll join up soon enough and be together. But what about you Mel"?

"Oh me", she said with a downward glance. Married my college soul mate, or so I thought. Big time man on campus and All American football player. Even got drafted by the old Houston Oilers. We had the entire world and life ahead of us, or so I thought, until early one morning, a Houston Police officer knocked on my door and told me that my husband had been killed in an auto accident. Later at the coroner's office, I discovered that he had company in his car. A partially clad stripper. She lay right next to him on the autopsy table.

It was headline news in the papers the following day. The only thing that kept my sanity was that I had a little boy from our marriage that I had to raise. He's starting his junior year at Annapolis and he's doing well.

Wants to become a Marine officer and a career Marine at that"! "Sea Marine, Aviator or Mud Marine" asked the General? "Don't think he's quite decided yet General"?

"Well if he's anything like his mother and I'm certain he is bring him around some fine day and we can discuss Annapolis, tell war stories and perform a quality control function on my imported Tequila. But one thing I'm curious about. Here you are, still a very beautiful woman and like me you haven't remarried. Seems like we were traveling two different roads only to end up in the same place as for me, I'm well past my line of marketability to the fair sex and anyway I'm far too set in my ways. But in the passing years, hasn't there been anyone that struck your fancy"?

"In the aftermath of my husband's death, all I could think about was my son and eventually later my former in laws who were hell bent for taking my son away from me. Then there was the fact that for a very long time, emotionally, I just couldn't trust another man. But eventually as time passed I did meet someone", he voice trailing off to nothing!

"I hope you're not going to keep me in suspense young lady", said the General.

"It's just that even to this day I wonder what went wrong with us? We met at a local gym, Ballys it was and gradually became workout partners. He was also an ex-Marine, had more than his share of scars. He was a big man, fit and well built. A former collegiate football player I think but he never talked about it. Certainly not the Metrosexual good looks one sees these days, but handsome in his own right. Very wellmannered and he and my son were as thick as thieves. He'd take him out to the firing range from time to time and eventually my son developed into a crack shot with the pistol and the rifle. He and my son would have long talks by themselves down in the patio, strictly guy stuff. I don't know how he did it but one day my former in laws dropped their law suit against me for custody of my child. On a date we had, he saved my life from some people who were chasing us on the freeway. By that time I'd fallen in love with him. Some days he would just stare into the distance. He never spoke of his family or what he did for a living. But he would sometime be away for days at a time without a word, but always bringing back a present for both me and my son"!

"Then one day he never returned. Weeks and months went by, when finally I was Contacted by a local attorney who apparently represented him, and this 'Jaeger' left me and my son a fair amount of money to apply to my sons education. Haven't seen the man since. I still think of him from time to time and wonder how he's doing"!

"Did I hear you say the name 'Jaeger', young lady? What was his first name?

"That's the odd part about it all. He had no first name, or middle name.

I know he's still alive somewhere because someone I know made his acquaintance by chance, not long ago, in New York"! Then Mel took notice of that look on the Generals face as he stared away at the buildings across the street. "General is there something you're not telling me about Jaeger"? "You know of the man, don't you General"!

"Interesting how fate can often bring people together", said Bollinger still staring at the buildings in the distance. "Yes one can say I know of the man for our paths have crossed a few times in the past. I know quite a bit about the man and as I look at my watch, it seems that you will have to return me to our President for our dinner engagement. Don't quite know how long that'll last, but afterwards I'll be happy to meet up with you anywhere you like to help fill in the blanks"!

"I'd like that General", said Mel. "Please call me anytime this evening, when you and the President have concluded your meal. Don't worry about the time. I won't be asleep"!

The evening meal between The President and General Bollinger went well and as they enjoyed their after dinner drinks, Magnusson asked, "General I only know you by reputation and no one comes more highly recommended than you as someone that can get things done and think outside the box. This afternoon your alternatives provided put the nail right on the head with your assessment of the situation and the appropriate remedy. Clearly you're not one of those armchair Generals who are adept at politics and push paper around. So one of the reasons were having this get together is that I need a man like you to look at a problem and connect the dots"!

"Thanks, Mr. President, but I'm retired and there must be someone else in the government that can push the right buttons"!

"If there was then I'd be talking to that man. But there isn't! General Ottenger and Director Bolling of the CIA have both indicated that you are the man"!

"Mind if I light one up Mr. President", asked Bollinger? "Suit yourself General", replied Magnusson.

"What do we do if we ever catch up with this Salaam character? We can't try him for any good lawyer will probe into the government's case and discover eventually what we've all been a party to"!

"But you've acted in the common good Mr. President"!

"Nice talking point and line in a speech, but in court it will not hold water"!

"Then you find the son of a bitch and kill him. Cut up the body and dump the pieces into a fifty gallon barrel full of acid. In twelve hours or so everything disappears. But if the rumors are true you've even bigger problems"!

"And they are General"?

"Last week the papers were full of reports, that the two Secret Service agents, that were in charge of perimeter security during yours and President Dobbins Inauguration Parade were found dead. They both died by poison during approximately the same evening. They were both examined by the very best minds in the country. Polygraphs, voice stress analysis etcetera, prior to their death and came up clean. Yet all signs pointed to them both as the ones who somehow permitted the terrorists to infiltrate the perimeter.

They were removed and assigned desk jobs. Then time passes and they are killed. Now the question is how reliable is the Secret Service personnel on the Executive Detail and are there anymore"!

"So what's to be done General"?

"I'd think the answer is simple. When Dr. Romanovsky has finished with her assignment of administering SP-117, you ask her nicely for one last favor. I hear she's tearing em up"!

"Now how on earth did you find out about that"?

"Saw it in a dream, Mr. President. Saw it in a dream", mused Bollinger with a sly wink.

"What about this Salaam fella"!

"With any luck, the Behavioral Analysis boys at Quantico will run him to ground then you call in someone to take him out, then make him disappear completely. While I'm no lawyer, even I can see the trail of information that will lead you to this man, if we are fortunate, is tainted. So the only alternative is to somehow find who this individual is, where he is, try and capture him, hand him over to Dr. Romanovsky for several hours, then make him disappear"!

"But General, who in the government could do such a thing"?

"A number of highly trained people in the military would and could perform such operation, but if discovered, would not only be a career ender, but subject them to a long term of inside the walls duty at Leavenworth. No, one has to go outside the government for such an operation. To answer your next question, there is someone I know of that is more than capable of getting the job done and keeping his mouth shut. In fact if memory serves, the both of you came in contact with each other, repeatedly, on a cold fall afternoon in Minnesota, some time ago"!

The President looked at Bollinger for a moment, the last sentence somehow not registering immediately, and then slowly said, "Jaeger, the Uberballer"!

Bollinger slowly nodded his head, then reached for his pen and started writing as he said, "I could tell you quite a bit about the man, from what I know, but all I'll tell you is that when he was a Marine, I was his last commander on a mission he didn't have to go on. The mission was highly successful, under the most harrowing of circumstances. He saved American lives and received no recognition in return. Of course, this was about a year, before you had the pleasure of meeting the man. Much has happened to him over the years and our paths have crossed a few times. The names I have just written down are some people who know about the man close up and personal. He's not usually one who seeks publicity of any kind you can understand"!

Magnusson took the sheet of paper and after glancing at it, quickly looked up in astonishment exclaiming, "Mel knew Jaeger"?

"Something I just recently discovered this very day prior to our dinner. After you and I have concluded, I'm to call her so she and I can have a little chat over that very thing"!

"Seems like I've some catching up to do this evening", said Magnusson picking up his phone and punching in some numbers. As he waited for the phone to pick up, he said to Bollinger, "Can you run by here late in the morning General? I've got a lot to do this evening and have a meeting with the Defense Secretary early tomorrow morning, after which I'd like it if we could put our heads together. The phone finally answered, as the President heard, "O'Bannon"!

"Mel"? "Yes sir", she answered immediately recognizing the voice! "Just wanted you to know the General is on his way over to your place and I'm writing out the address"! An astonished Melanie could only answer, "Yes sir, I'll be here"!

The early morning meeting with the Defense Secretary encompassed an off the record progress report with the Department of the Defense regarding the conflicts in the Middle East and a variety of other developments.

"Mr. Secretary, I'd like you and the Secretary of State to get together with the local ambassadors via a video conference call and tell them to convey my displeasure with the lack of progress being made by them in insisting in accountability regarding the foreign aid received and them to remind their counterparts about the 'Golden Rule' philosophy. 'They accept our foreign aid, and then we make the rules', philosophy! Every dollar is to be accounted for if they want the aid to continue, or else I'll persuade Congress to cut off their funding"!

"Finally gentlemen, I was watching a TV report from a Texas Station regarding the activities of their Texas State National Guard. Not only has the State Air Guard acted in an egregious manner towards their female members, but it seems to me the Air Guard is overwhelmingly top heavy in Senior Officer Personnel. I suspect this is going on to greater and lesser degrees throughout the land. So I'm directing you Mister Secretary to have every element of our reserve components gone through with a fine tooth comb by the appropriate inspector generals, reporting directly through you and to me. The Inspector Generals can start by visiting major news organizations in each state no later than the day after tomorrow. I'm certain the fifth estate will be more than happy to show them the way. In no event will the heads of the various National Guard and Reserve units will be notified. If their running a clean operation they shouldn't mind the scrutiny, if not they will howl. I'm given to understand that 'I G' information already exists growing cobwebs. In thirty days from today, I expect that you will be before me with answers to my questions. Now Mr. Secretary, I expect that every Inspector General will receive Carte' Blanche' cooperation in this endeavor. I'm certain that what will be discovered is that a lot of make work projects at the Senior Officer Level of the reserves is in existence via the 'Old Boy' connections. This will come to a swift end. I trust I am completely understood gentlemen, am I not"?

As everyone filed out of the Executive Conference room, ever present on the Secretary's mind was the orders from the Chief Executive, "The Boss". Above all else that he had to contend with were the seemingly impossible task of building a fire under the ambassadors on the ground to get the so called allies to accelerate their activities against the extremist terrorists by whatever means necessary. On top of this was the deadline imposed by the President in shaping up the various Guard units around the country. He as well as his predecessors was aware if their failings, for years being a country club for secondary officers not quite fit enough to be a part of the regular military. Time long past due to clean house of the driftwood.

More sleepless nights lay ahead for him and a cadre of others, yet it was past due.

20

As the stretch Humvee Limo pulled up to the rear entrance of the new Texas Stadium, Pierre Duquesne and Vannevar Harvanian emerged from within. "We'll be the Montags guests in his executive box suite, on the fifty yard line, with a full view of everything. Well take the long way up so you can appreciate what the Dallas Cowboys owner and his partners put into this edifice, to football"!

"But tonight Pierre, we attend a Rock Concert", mused Harvanian as they made their way up through the porticos and into the bowels of the vast state of the art Arena. Everywhere they looked it appeared that money had seemed of no object, when it came to construction of a first class venue, for the display of brute force.

"And someday if society so clamors, this grand arena could display gladiatorial combats"!

"I don't ever think we'll see that in our lifetime, Pierre"!

"The Romans did it for hundreds of years in the Flavian Ampetheater, what we call the Coliseum and while it didn't bring down their crime rate, they had no prison population to contend with and everyone who won the state run lottery got free entertainment. Plus it created an entire industry of sorts in gladiatorial schools where Lanistas bought slaves and convicted prisoners, taught them skills and brought them together for the entertainment of the citizens", said Duquesne as they made their way up to their reserved box for the evening's entertainment.

"So tell me Pierre, what have we in store for the evening"! "Several things on several levels my friend. First we shall be entertained by what just might be the best rock band in the entire world, according to my son and after hearing them and following their progress, I believe him. Six months ago the returned from their grand tour of Europe. From London to Moscow, from Stockholm to Cairo, yes even Cairo my friend, they've played to nothing less than sold out crowds, in sports arenas alone, for those are the only venues that were large enough to encompass the audiences. In every one of those cities, they had to eventually provide public address loudspeakers in abundance on the outside of the arenas, so those without tickets could enjoy the music as well as those inside, lest there be riots. Of course their album sales are off the charts. One wonders which cames first, the popularity of their music, begat their tours, which were all sold out, which begat more album sales and the wonderful thing is they have not one original song they've written. Everything is well out of copyright. What they do is take an old classic, be it Rhythm and Blues, Rock, Jazz, Classical, Mambo, Samba, a Tango rhythm, Electronica, Trance and put their own brand on everything to greater and lesser degrees from lyrics, to the music itself. The genius of their business model is that everything has already been done before and all they do is restyle it and out comes a money maker. Now usually when one makes an album, there is only one or two songs intended to be "A" material. What they've done is select old classic's already "A" worthy and upgrade them to current day tastes and "Viola"; they've gotten an album that sells in abundance."

"Sounds like you're envious of their business model Pierre"?

"Goddamn right I am! Wish I had just a major piece of their action"!

"Implying that you're a partner"?

"How do you think you're sitting right here, right now", said Duquesne with a sly wink!

"How did they come up with their name, 'The Moog', pal"?

"Trivia question 6B. Legend has it that one night in a recording studio when they were in the process of coalescing into a group, they worked their way through a keg of beer and came up with the name. Now of course it all sound ridiculous, but another legend of the origin of the old rock group "The Who", is similarly ridiculous. As teenager's long ago, they had a name that no one could remember and when they approached their first agent he asked them what the name of their band was. When they told him he asked, "The Who", as if he hadn't heard them and the cognomen stuck, "The Who"?

"Now the members of this group are almost a United Nations, Two are Americans, a Swede, an Irishman, a Brazilian, a German, a Mexican et cetera. Two Drummers, a bass, rhythm and lead guitar, a keyboardist, a horn section and woodwinds, plus some troll, out of sight that manipulates a control station, that blends visual graphics and dancers. Then a small army of technicians and construction types, that see to the construction and tear down of their sets, everywhere they go"!

"Must cost a fortune to produce each show"!

"At the very least, but an impresario friend put some numbers together on their two concerts, in Madrid last year and came up with an approximation of five million Euro's post tax net on net profits from each concert. Their ongoing costs of production are tremendous, but the income generated by ticket sales is far greater. Of course that is only one income stream, the other being the album sales, which benefit from their concert tours"!

"That's mind boggling Pierre. Sounds like they're a money machine"! "Van, it's far better than stealing, it's legal and fun thus far. You'll see when the event starts up"!

"But what about their America's tour"?

"Toronto, Detroit, Chicago, Minneapolis, Seattle, LA, of course here in Dallas kicks everything off, then Miami, New Orleans, then four concerts alone in Mexico City, two in Rio, two in Buenos Aires, then if their still all talking to each other and healthy, back to New York, to rest up for a year.

Then they plan to attack the Far East, the following year"! "Any concern about security south of the border"?

"Always a concern, especially there, but we've greased enough palms, in a number of ways already so that shouldn't be a great concern"!

"Which implies, I take it, that money is just one of a host of mediums of exchange"?

"Ah, ever the quick one to catch on, you are Van. In addition to the best tickets liberally divided amongst the politicians, Bronko Lubetska and his merry operatives, will be delivered good information as to whom to focus on abroad, as we are doing this evening. For our purposes, almost two dozen of the offspring of key politicians, union bosses, judges and the like have been furnished free tickets to attend. These people of influence have already been targeted to be additional roadblocks to both, the Presidents ambitions and policies as well as our own business interests. Lubetska has a number of his operatives that will identify those invited that will be at the ground level in the swirling melee of literally thousands. We have learned in Europe that many very interesting things happen at ground level, where the light level will be minimal and liquor and the effects of drugs prevail. His people will work in teams of two and they've honed their craft well. Each observer will wear special non-prescription glasses, connected with a cell phone with a fully charged battery. All one has to do is look at an event occurring close at hand. If the light level is insufficient, a small flash light appears for a brief period of time. Inhibitions are tossed to the winds due to the music, the swirling crowd and one's stupidity. It's worked in the past as you know in small Euro clubs where the rich and randy go to cut loose, only to discover later that their activities have brought disgrace and dishonor to their families. In Madrid, we discovered two Parliamentary Ministers, brought low, by the activities of both their teenage children as well as their wives at a Moog event. Of course, the ministers resigned their positions in due course, victims of public pressure. They were an impediment to progress"!

"By any means necessary", mumbled Harvanian, as a waiter brought their drinks and a plate of flaming fondue!

"Now, now my friend, don't look so glum", said Duquesne, dipping his sourdough bread into the hot cheese. "Of course Democracy is not supposed to work this way. But where is the benevolent dictator when he's needed? And of course whenever he arises, wars occur, vast numbers of people die unnecessarily and in the end he's disposed of. Democracy is not working as intended right now, thus certain steps need to be taken, to procure progress. Steps that admittedly sacrifice a few for the greater good. That few were corrupt, at any rate and beyond forgiveness and redemption. Thus with a minimum of targeted focus, obstacles are removed"!

"Yes of course your right Pierre, it's just that there is always the slippery slope to consider. If used judicially and for a selected purpose only, then put aside, that's one thing, but if such tactics become the norm, then hubris welcomes the land of the shortcut. Posing the question that as long as our interests coincide, for the common good, this will be tolerated, if our interests diverge at any point in the scenario, then what happens"!

"Your point is well made my friend. At the present we've invited the Devil to our dance party and at some point we must be wise enough to sever that relationship. Trusting to the correctness of our purpose to limit our activities. Put another way limit our greed. Tyler and I have studied the scenario very well. A chess game, with an innumerable degree of possibilities. Your President is a fine man, operating in a valiant manner against all odds and serving the country well. Yet what happens if something untoward occurs? That instance goes against our purpose and that of the country. Thus it is in our best instance that Lars Magnusson is safe and successful in all of his endeavors, for they exactly coincide with ours and the country as a whole and will do so for the foreseeable future. It is precisely because he is a man that requires our assistance, for this purpose only, which of course must remain on a Sub Rosa basis"!

"Of course we have other business interests abroad, so measures must be taken unfortunately that insure certainty. We are comfortable with our relationship Van because we know we are dealing with honorable people and that if either of us should decide to break the bond between us for whatever the reason, it would lead to our mutual destruction. The President will remove certain impediments to our progress and when possible we will assist him in that endeavor. He's an able ball carrier and we trust him because he's earned it"!

"Of course your right Duquesne, I'm just pointing out the obvious"! "Good. Now we shall enjoy the evening. Good entertainment, good food and good company and by dawn you shall be back in Washington with torrid memories"! Then he reached for a hand held television channel changer saying, "With the single push of a button, I'll engage the bank of TV monitors, a dozen in all and thanks to modern day science, I can engage all of the monitors that are connected each one to a two person team of operatives working the vast confines of ground level, attired like the natives except they are sober and on the hunt"!

As Duquesne pushed each numbered button, a monitor came alive.

Harvanian looked around for the waiter and fining him gone, heard Duquesne say, "He has now turned into a guard for the rest of the evening. He's being paid well so he'll be a reliable guard for our door, rather than a waiter for the rest of the evening. We are on our own as to the refreshments we receive. Should the unforeseen arise, I can shut off all of the monitors with the push of a button. Each team's visuals will be transmitted to a separate recorder, to be burned into a DVD diskette. As long as a team is transmitting it is being recorded on a separate diskette. The concert is approximately two and one half hours long and their video phones batteries are good for over three hours of transmittal"!

Finally the last of the monitors came on revealing the swirling mé-lange of humanity on the playing field eager for the appearance of "The Moog"!

"Now Van, all we can do now is sit back and observe. Whenever a target is sighted the operator down on the field will push a button signaling a monitor that a target has been identified and is under observation, for our enjoyment and recording"!

"I'm out of my element here Pierre, but I just have to ask, what happens if something unforeseen occurs, to any member of your team. I'm thinking Murphy's Law here"!

"That is why our operatives work in teams. Then we cause a minor diversion. The members of the group on stage are old hands at concerts and know they can get a bit rowdy. The only thing that would get them to stop playing and compel them to leave the stage for safety is the sound of continuous gunfire. Each of them has served their journeyman duty as back up players for other groups"!

"Well hells fire Duquesne, you seem to have covered all the bases"! "For the moment my friend, for the moment, which is why we get paid the big bucks"! Then a long, intermittent klaxon came over the public address system, along with a blinking of the Stadiums lights, signaling the show was about to begin, prompting Duquesne to say, "Show Time, in the big D"! As the stadium crowd grew silent, the lights grew dim, casting long shadows everywhere, with only the emergency lighting in the exits providing sufficient lighting.

The massive circular stage located exactly on the fifty yard mark, began to slowly move in a clock wise manner revealing twin graduated steps on either side, designed to scoop up the performers as they approached in a counter clockwise direction, all the while a visible psychedelic montage grew on the giant screens above the stage. Spot lights slowly illuminated main stage, flanked by two other smaller stages reserved for the dancers bathed in the hushed earth toned lights. The dancer's task being to serve as a visual counterpoint away from the main stage and their movements exactly choreographed to match the various rhythms of the music.

Suddenly a loud series of staccato clicks came over the loudspeakers. Each syncopated click was measured to occur two to a second, as the first of the two drummers began their long march to the rotating stage from a darkened area behind the end zone. Each of the drummers was wired for sound as they made their approach. As the first drummer made his way to the stage, a lone spotlight illuminated his path through the silent morass of humanity who eagerly made way on the field. As the first drummer approached the slowly rotating stage, he timed his approach precisely to the approach of the rotating stairway, catching the first step without missing a beat and each step elevating him to the top in precise syncopation to the click of his drumsticks. He approached his drum set taking his seat, hisclicking drumsticks never giving way until his down beat on the base drum, signaling the other drummer to approach, clicking his drumsticks in a similar manner, taking over that Task from his predecessor, who by now changed the focus of his beat to his drum rims, serving as a precise counterpoint to the second. As the second drummer made his way towards the stage, every eighth beat of his drumsticks, was met by a single beat from the first drummers base drum. Eight clicks followed by a resounding Boom, signaled the dancers to approach their respective stages, one by one, bathed in a single spotlight as they made their respective ways through the silent crowd on the field.

As the second drummer took his position on stage his second bass drum beat joining the first signaled the bass guitar player to make his approach.

As the third performer joined the other two, he picked up his gaudy axe and started his staccato riff, signaling the rhythm guitar player to commence his approach through the crowd, who by this time, started to feel the excitement building of an seminal event in their lives. The rhythm guitar in place, playing a counter veiling melody to the bass, signaled the lead guitar to approach and upon his elevation to the stage, the soaring electric wails of his lead, summoned the first of the horn section to approach. Eventually the horn section in place as well as the woodwinds, led by the throbbing beat of the Baritone Saxophone, signaled the approach of the final segment of the group, the keyboard artist, who eventually sat between his electric piano and organ, joining in with the rest for the final measure of the intro, prior to diving right into their signature piece, a seven minute long version of an old Booker T and the MG's piece, "The Song with No Name"!

The driving tempo of the music, soared into the heavens, and then dove into the depths, emerging, swirling and soaring once again as the stadiums light show overhead, coupled with the gyrations of the dancers, compelled all eyes to drift back and forth from the performers to the massive video screen and back lest they miss something significant. All the while those at ground level swirling about in the shadows, provided little interest to those in the seats, as they allowed the music to lead them from ecstasy to ecstasy, in a host of ways.

Yet working their ways through the swirling morass of the very young were the teams of voyeurs, some having identified their targets early on as the entered the stadium, while others were still in search of a target. As the terminus of the first song approached, six of the dozen targets were identified by their shadower's, with the others still in search. By the end of the fourth song all of the monitors in Duquesne's private box had the small red light blinking on their screens, signaling that all targets were in view and being recorded.

As Harvanian sat in awe, staring at the stage and the video screens back and forth, Duquesne said, "What a show, eh"?

"I can now see why this group is a moneymaker. Never seen or heard anything like it"!

"We might as well enjoy the music, for I don't expect anything significant to appear on the screens for at least another half hour. Should anything noteworthy occur, each team will signal us via their cell phone and a second red light will appear on the monitor"!

"Doesn't the band take a break or have an intermission, for a piss call or anything"?

"No they don't Van. To take a break would be to interrupt the mood they create. What they strive for is elevation of the musical sprit. Of course, after each performance all are exhausted and seen to by a group of keepers.

They are all in rather good shape and if you will notice, the type of songs alternate from the wild and woolly, to the slow and spiritual in order for them to endure two nonstop hours"!

Minutes later one of the monitors, displayed a second red light on the periphery signalingthat tangible activity was about to occur and sure enough, one of the subjects of their attention was on her knees, unzipping her escorts pants and visibly working on the man's member, as one of the watchers simply stared on, intent on capturing the moment for posterity.

"And that is the daughter of Murray Weinstraub, Senior Vice President of the Teamsters Union International. The very man that's causing our efforts in the Mag Lev train construction, delay after delay. But not for long after this night", said Duquesne!

Then another screen's second red light, revealed two young women, deep into the crowd, oblivious to any observance, deeply involved in a passionate embrace, with one of the young women, sinking to her knees, her head disappearing under the others all too brief hemline, while the object of her intentions, face rose up in ecstasy, revealing her identity, to the keen spectacled observer close at hand. Be it the drugs, liquor, or the hypnotic driving sounds of the music, one by one, the observers captured the mostly unobserved activities of youth for posterity. All too soon there they would be. No longer the innocent product of a misspent upbringing, but their excesses laid bare for the entire world to see.

One by one, every target of Pierre Duquesne, willingly displayed a hitherto unknown side of themselves, the final display being the most important. The young wife of the Senior Senator from New Mexico. Half his age, yet secretly on the prowl constantly for younger suitors, was in full attendance on the field of play. Despite the sunglasses worn in the dark recesses of the secondary stage, the dancers working their magic above her, the Senators wife, in a moment of reckless abandon, hiked up her hemline and sat on the open lap of a willing young male, gyrating up and down to the rhythm of the dancers overhead, several of which who upon seeing her started to mimic her ministrations. In the midst of her display, one of the teeming passersby inadvertently bumped into the duo, knocking the sunglasses from the Senators wife's head revealing her identity, all of which was immediately captured electronically.

Just then one of the roving stadium plainclothes security staff, placed his hands upon one of Duquesne's operatives yelling above the din, "Hey, what's going on here", as his eyes drifted down to the gyrating Senators wife, squatting on the ground, intent on completing her very necessary mission.

Immediately the other member of the team pulled out a can of naphtha lighter fluid and began squirting the flammable liquid all over the back of the security officer's clothes and in a few seconds with the other hand removed a cheap lighter and lit the back of the security agent, before fading back into the crowd. As the flames rose up the back of the hapless officer, the other agent kept squirting the naphtha down his legs and back up while taking cover behind someone else. In the space of eight seconds the officer lit up like an Aggie bon fire, running through the crowd, screaming and crashing into others, while the Senators wife was in the process of completing her sacred mission.

"That is why our people work in teams Van. Now as to the last of our objects of scrutiny, Senator Mondragon's wife will soon be famous, if the son of a bitch doesn't kill her first. Either way, just one more impediment to our Presidents programs will soon be eliminated. Within days her image will mysteriously appear on the internet and every media station in New Mexico. Either he'll divorce her and toss her out of their house, like his last wife, or he'll shoot her, which knowing him is not out of the realm of possibilities"!

"Seems our work is done Van, so why don't we relax and enjoy the final closing song of the show, while I call in our security to collect the diskettes and enjoy the rest of the Program"! On the late night flight back to the east coast in Duquesne's private jet, Duquesne revealed that seven additional targets were viewed and recorded by the crew on the ground, making this foray far better than they had hoped. He needed not recall the forthcoming chain of events, for it simply would be a repeat of the format previously established. Harvanian would be certain to monitor the main stream media in its entirety as best he could, to keep track, sudden retirements, resignations out of the blue, suicides, divorce announcements and the like of politically important personages, in a seemingly random fashion. This Lubetska character, appeared to be a master of subversive threat. Once he had incriminating video of a target, that person was already burnt toast. From here on out one of Lubetska's lieutenants would be conducting the events, following "The Moog", from venue to venue through the entirety of their tour. While Duquesne rejoined his senior partner Tyler Montag, in doing what they both did best, make money.

While they made small talk on the flight back, Harvanians mind compared what had been done to a number of people in the recent past, all connected to powerful people who stood in the way of the Presidents plans for America. More, resignations, firings, forced retirements, suicides, heart attacks and in a few cases perhaps a murder or two, were on tap in the near future.

Then his thoughts shifted to the Middle and South American venues of the tour. There was no doubt in Harvanians mind that Montag and Duquesne were operating on a much larger scale than anyone could imagine. What Harvanian, Goodwin and the President were aware of was only the tip of a very large iceberg. No doubt the duo were successful in Europe, ferreting out troublesome politicians who posed a threat to their business interests, finding then exploiting their weakness', in such a way to destroy them politically and professionally. The justification was that they were irretrievably corrupt anyway and untrustworthy. Going over in his mind, those in Europe who succumbed, Harvanian would be hard pressed to argue against what they were accomplishing. Since they refused to pay a bribe of any sort to any impediment, they would simply bide their time and destroy that individual from long distance, using the individuals hubris against him. The unfortunate aspect was that many of the innocent would have their lives altered in one way or the other. Then came the fact that many of the alleged innocent weren't so very innocent after all.

No doubt a treasure trove of possibilities would surface for there were a host of American cities yet ahead of "The Moog's" tour, much less the

South American tour which would no doubt provide a treasure trove of possibilities. In every country south of the border, corruption and bribes were part of the ongoing business curriculum for any enterprise. A few Dictators here and there, a Democratic Oligarchy or two or three, then a vast variety of political agendas, to overcome. Harvanian wondered if Montag and Company would succumb to their policy of not paying bribes of any kind, or relent whenever the situation warranted. After due reflection he decided that thus far, what they were doing was working very well for them so why change. After all, as they say in Texas, 'What works is good.

What doesn't work ain't good"!

21

J aeger awoke with a start, bathed in sweat. Although Houston was having another Indian summer, with the overnight low temperature in the high seventies, his air conditioning was working just fine. Still, why the sweat? He plodded into the kitchen and got about the business of making a pot of coffee. He glanced at the clock on the wall and seeing that it was just after 4AM, concluded that he's gotten about six hours of sleep. He lit a cigarette as he was waiting for the coffee to drip, thinking about why he'd awakened. Then elements of the dream came filtering back into his consciousness. He stared out of the glass patio door and reached under the kitchen table for the .44 snub nosed revolver he kept housed under the table by a secured clip and placed it on the table without any conscious effort. As he glanced at the revolver, he reasoned that it was habit, built up over the years.

For the first time in a very long while he began to experience real fear. But, of what? The cigarette, having burned down to the filter was crushed into the ashtray as the small 'ding' of the coffeemaker rang.

He sat down again after putting cream and sugar in his early morning coffee and stared at the revolver and fired up another cigarette. He closed his eyes as the dream gradually began to reappear in his conscious mind. Of course everybody dreams from time to time he reasoned and that dream state usually manifests itself during the REM portion of the sleep cycle. Usually, when ever Jaeger dreamt he woke up with scant memory of what he'd dreamt, if any at all. But this time it was all there in living color. He opened his eyes, staring at his revolver, but it and everything else in the dim light of the kitchen only served as a back drop, for the cavalcade of faces that paraded before him. This had not happened since his time in Huntsville Prison, where he had every reason to experience fear of the unknown on a daily basis. He recalled Roy Seltzers favorite saying, plucked from the musings of his favorite comedian George Carlin,

"Paranoia, is simply the flip side of complete awareness"! Only those who had experienced the all too real fear of the unknown on a daily basis, day after day and oft times down to the very minute, grew to really appreciate the caustic humor of those words.

What saved his sanity in those dark days, what drove him to survive without a scintilla of tangible hope, was that 'Unfinished Business' lay ahead, that only he could accomplish. But precisely what that business was eluded him, as he viewed the silent faces that paraded before him in his mind's eye. His parents, his sisters, his forbearers, namely the legendary Heinrich (Henry) Jaeger and his wife Melanie, all of his immediate relatives that existed from then till now, then the faces of two wolves, the offspring of Chani and Akila, made themselves known by their silent howling.

Then the faces of all those who met death at his hand, filtered into view replacing the others, all those while serving in the military drifted into view, then vanished quickly, replaced by yet another, some he recognized, some he didn't. Then in a timely fashion, those who met their death on the gridiron came into view, one by one, ending with Dexter Mankiller. Then those he crossed paths with in prison, chiefly the giant 'Elsasser', going to his death, out in the Ellis Units main yard, during a prison riot, while holding two of his assailants by the neck, elevated from the ground below, in a death grip while they repeatedly plunged their prison shanks deep into his torso, looking right at Jaeger as he yelled to the heavens before keeling over to the earth.

Then drifting into view, were the faces of the unholy trio, that took part in the death of His family and his incarceration, sinking slowly downward bound and gagged on the three long poles, they were impaled upon, pleading with their eyes for mercy, while the buzzards waited patiently for them to breathe their last. The teams of killers that came for Jaeger an his friends during the period after his release from prison, quickly ran by, then a host of others that followed, all replayed in his mind, followed by Ortega, as he drifted into his death spiral, his entire side of him blown away at close range by a shotgun blast from Jaeger, as he tried to focus on Jaegers eyes, knowing that all was lost. Then as if it were an intermission, everything faded from view for a moment, followed by a reappearance of his forbearer great grandmother Melanie, and then fading from view, the image of Melanie O'Bannon appeared. He immediately felt ashamed for leaving her the way he did. Perhaps the only woman he'd ever loved. His all too brief time with her, cut short by what rationale he couldn't fathom. As he gazed into her phantom face, he longed to see her once again, to hear the sound of her voice. He recalled one precious moment as she prattled on about political affairs of state while he simply stared at her in abject wonder she suddenly stopped and asked Jaeger what he was staring at? "Just enjoying the view", he replied. That comment took several seconds for the true meaning to sink in, before her frown slowly turned into that wonderful smile. At that very moment they both knew that they were meant for each other.

His regret had always haunted him, but eventually he forced her from his mind through sheer force of will, at least he'd provided for her and her son sufficiently. He wondered what had happened to her and hoped that she'd remarried, for a woman of such fine qualities, should have a good husband to share a life with.

Then the face of Lars Magnusson came into view. The last time they met was on a cold football field in Minnesota. The very best player he'd ever encountered. Played a clean game, yet his as hard as anyone Jaeger had ever met. Again he felt regret, for the aftermath of their collision on the field of play. Except for that single event, the man no doubt would've had a distinguished career in the NFL ahead of him, full of fame and fortune.

Instead, his dreams no doubt dashed, he had to undergo months of physical therapy to even recover the ability to walk again. Any possibility of contact sports again a pipe dream. The man was now President of these United States, while Jaeger the very one who came out on top from their last encounter, a pardoned felon. Had he never encountered Magnusson, perhaps his family might still be alive. His children grown to maturity and he and his wife drifting into old age and greeting their eventual departure from this mortal coil, as a friend offering eternal rest, rather than being blown to bits, by craven terrorists. He then saw a look of defiance, followed by sheer terror, on Magnusson's face, followed by further defiance, followed by faces he could barely recognize and finally the crying face of Melanie O'Bannon, somewhat older now but still appealing. Then he awoke from his dream bathed in sweat.

He wondered what Mel was doing in the same dream with the President, as he lit yet another cigarette and took a sip of his now tepid coffee? Jaeger had somehow felt he owed something to the President, but what? Somehow he sensed a further danger befalling the President, but what? What in the hell did the dream mean? The dreamscape, now lifted from his subconscious, the dim light of the kitchen came back into full view. It was all just a bad dream he reckoned, or was it? Then right in front of him appeared the visualization of Melanie, sitting across from him smiling, looking wonderful as he once knew her. As he simply stared, enjoying the view, he recalled something he'd once read by a French author, who's name escaped him for the moment, "There comes a time when a woman must be beautiful to be loved, then there comes a time, when she must be loved, to become beautiful"? Something caused his head to turn and there on the kitchen counter was his old harmonica. He rose from the table and retrieved his harmonica, taking it from the case and sat back down in front of his table. He'd not played the harmonica in a while and only played it during moments of deep concern. Linus had his blanket, Jaeger had his harmonica as he began to play the three notes over and over, the cigarette went out and the coffee grew cold.

Wrapping up his early morning meeting with the President, preparing him for his itinerary Orval Goodwin mentioned, "Then there's the situation with Senator Mondragon"!

"What's the status Orval"!

"The bad news is that ever since he's murdered his randy wife. He's been rendered 'Hor's de Combat and is being under a suicide watch in New Mexico's State Mental Facility. Three days after the Moog concert in Dallas, he and his 'Cougar', toss an invitation only party with big wig money people at his house in Santa Fe. He's got a string of commercials playing on his big TV for the well-heeled guests, to add to his re-election kitty, when someone had interjected the You Tube video just starting to make the rounds of his wife banging some poor soul in the shadows of the Moog Concert in Dallas. The wife faints and the Senator disappears for a few moments, reappearing with a semi auto shotgun full of double ought shot shells. She's now been revived and tended to by the guy she was humping in the video. The good Senator, quick as you please, pumps a few rounds into his wife, then a few more into her lover sitting right next to her before anyone can intercede. Everything is on video as are all of his campaign events, so everything is open and shut"!

"Christ Orval", exclaimed the President! "The man is in a tight reelection race, three weeks away and he blows away his wife"?

"Now more bad news, your party is now down two votes in the Senate to the opposition, because his Republican opponent is a lock to get elected"!

"The State of New Mexico will now determine the Senators fate Orval"!

"The good news is that when the Republican wins, he'll be a staunch advocate for most of your policies, but that follows with more bad news of your party grumbling that somehow you relish Senator Mondragon's fall from grace"!

"The man marries a woman half his age and he's in his seventies", mused Magnusson. "He should've known what he was getting into when he got in bed with her"!

"Lust is blind Mr. President! She was a high priced model that traded upon her looks even well into her thirties. It was said that Mondragon worshipped her and treated her body like a temple, while everyone with eyes knew that she treated her 'Sanctus Sanctorum' like an amusement park"!

"I'm hearing things about those militia men that we rushed to the border to plug the holes with the border patrol, Orval"!

"Suggest we walk that one back, for some of them have had to be restrained by the military and have been quietly sent back from where they came with our thanks for their service"!

"So what was the problem? Too quick a trigger finger"?

"That plus, they simply weren't as disciplined as we'd liked. Held up well enough during the few shootouts that were engaged with the smugglers, but were and still are a concern"!

"So I take it our manpower concerns across the border are stabilized and that traffic of all kinds has diminished"?

"A confluence of several events Mr. President. The economy, crack downs on workplace enforcement, the sweltering summer, with three hundred dying in the desert by trying to come over and the military presence on the southern border is bringing the poll numbers down some.

Plus those that are here, are unable to wire back their remittances back home. Many are afraid to even approach those outlets for fear of apprehension"!

"Why don't we quietly release the existing militia from their border duty with their country's gratitude. How's the ninety day temporary rotation working out for the various guard units"?

"Quite well sir! Border patrol duty isn't exactly rocket science. A working field unit of squad size is assigned to each border patrol agent as backup. They assist in apprehensions, but the agent is the one who makes the determination officially as to the actual arrest. Every ninety days their rotated back home and replaced by others, thus minimally disrupting their lives. Plus reports are filtering in where they are all celebrated upon their return and as the now old grizzled border veterans they now all are have a host of war stories to tell that normally wouldn't be in their social quiver. For a few months they all had to rough it, living in tents and sleeping bags, but each in turn, will receive an official service badge, in the months to come"!

"Anything else Orval"?

"Last on tap, is the news that Harvanian's number two will be leaving us a week after the coming mid-term elections, when she's slated to give birth to her first child. She's pushing forty and this'll be her first, so she's going to spend at least a year with her first child which is understandable"!

"So I assume Van is on top of things in getting her replacement"? "He's in conversation with someone, this very moment. Someone that will indeed have an impact. Someone who is at the pinnacle of her professional career currently, whom you've met and who is certain to protect this administrations flanks as well as anyone", said Goodwin!

"Well, are you going to keep me in suspense? Out with it man, without the buildup"!

"What do you think about Molly Pringle, from CBS, taking a leave of absence and joining the White House as Harvanian's assistant press secretary"?

"Molly Pringle, eh? Have her vetted completely. If nothing comes up we may have to explain and Van is high on her abilities, then I've no problem with her coming on board! She seems to be nimble, articulate, well versed in government and not a member of the egalitarian elite. CBS should be happy that we have selected one of their own to place on loan to our administration. Have the White House legal department work out any kinks she might have on her contract with the network"!

Jaeger was out shopping one Saturday a week before the federal midterm elections. The last stop on his itinerary was at the Academy Sporting Goods Store, to stock up on shot gun shells. While he was inside, with his camo baseball hat and black wraparound sunglasses on, something caught his eye on the periphery. Adjusting his head slightly he caught sight of someone he remembered encountering awhile back. Something he couldn't explain told him that should they ever cross paths again, this was someone worth keeping an eye on. The man was patiently waiting in the checkout line, with Jaeger out of his line of vision, while Jaeger struggled with remembering just who that person was and where they had met? Jaeger glanced several times at the individual partially hidden behind a rack of sweat pants, studying his every movement, wondering all the while why he was so familiar. From time to time he'd forget a name but he never forgot a face once imprinted. It was just that paradox that confronted him currently.

As the man eventually came to the cashier, paid for his purchases and walked out of the store, Jaeger followed him at a distance, keeping his vehicle in sight in the event he'd have to shadow him. The feeling was gradually coming to mind that he was simply a stupid voyeur grasping at phantoms, when the object of his attention dropped his purchases at his pickup truck and made his way to a restaurant across the parking lot.

Rather than pursue the man, Jaeger made his way back to his car, retrieving a GPS monitoring sending unit with lithium, long lasting battery pack that would magnetically attach to the metal undercarriage of any vehicle. In less than a minute, he worked his way back to the parking space, where the person's pickup truck was parked and slid beneath the undercarriage. In a few quick moments, he selected a spot that would escape all but the most intense scrutiny, placing the heavily magnetized sending unit to top portion of a cross beam and turned the unit on, sliding quickly out from under and working his way between the cars to a spot where he could observe the subject approach.

As he came to his place, he saw that he'd done just in the nick of time, because his quarry was on his way back to his truck carrying some bags of takeout food. The truck backed out of its parking spot and drove off.

Jaeger was considering pursuit at a distance, but then reconsidered, when it finally hit his mind just who the person was. Over a year or so ago at the shooting range, the Latin looking individual, and an expert shot with both the pistol and the rifle. It was the pickup truck he drove that brought his mind into focus, yet the name eluded him. No matter, the GPS sending unit was of intermittent transmittal power. When the vehicle was in motion, the motion detector would engage the unit, then turn on and off intermittently in order to conserve battery usage. When the unit stopped the unit would register the GPS location and then turn itself off, unless it was engaged by Jaegers calling unit. At that point, it would briefly broadcast its location, and then turn itself off, until summoned once again, either by the vehicles motion or by Jaeger. Its broadcast band was at an ultrahigh wave band level in order not to interfere with any radio reception by the subject vehicle.

His work done, Jaeger went back into the store to continue his shopping. The Unit he'd attached cost him a pretty penny and when he returned home, he'd activate the unit and for the next week he'd reactivate the unit from time to time to track the individuals travel habits. He'd be pretty certain in about a week or so, if he was on to something or not. If not he'd simply retrieve the unit and go about his business, no harm no foul.

As he drove back to his residence, the name suddenly came to his mind. 'Mike, or Miguel Montero', was the name of the pistolero. Now we would see what we would see. Upon his return, he activated the GPS monitor attached to this Montero's truck and made a note of the location coordinates then turned the monitor off.

Early the following Monday morning, just before sunrise he turned on the GPS monitor and made a note of the location coordinates, then disengaged it again. Comparing the early morning figures with that of the Saturday coordinates and finding them exactly the same told Jaeger, this was his residence. He turned on the television and went through his early morning routine. At nine AM, he again took a GPS reading and noted the different coordinates. Clearly this must be his work place. He then picked up the phone and called an old associate, for he was about to call in some favors.

"Rafferty here" came the gruff old voice on the other end. "Whadda ya need"?

"I need a phone number ya old fart", barked Jaeger!

"Now who the"? "Only one piece of Texican turd in the whole world would talk to me like that! Jaeger…. Long time no see pardner. Ya still livin' in town"?

"Yes Rafferty and I need you to search your memory, its important"! "Heard ya gone International and have ratcheted up your game. That true"?

"True enough, I reckon but I still need ya to search your memory and give me a name and number of someone we worked with a while back.

Could be of vital importance"!

"Then talk to me friend. What ya need"?

"Remember my lawyer Buffy Beauvior? Well she had a retired cop on retainer that had his hooks deep into the local and county computer records"?

"Ya must be talking about Randall White. Yeah, he's still in business with his own PI firm. Does the bulk of his business with Buffy's law firm, but takes on private clients also. Why don't you call Buffy for his number"?

"Perhaps for other things, but not for what I need at this very moment. You on good terms with White and think he'll remember me"?

"Yeah, White and me do business from time to time and from time to time, your name gets brought up whenever the cold beer bottles come in hand and war stories need to be retold"!

"Can ya get White to call me? I need to engage his services and his access to law enforcement data records"!

"Give me your number and I'll call him soon as we hang up"! Jaeger then gave Rafferty one of his cell numbers, and then asked, "Hondo still work with you"?

"Yeah he does, gave him a piece of the business, so I can't get rid of him"!

"How are you doing personally"?

"Good of you to ask. Other than high blood pressure and a touch of gout and just plain old age I'm doin' right well thank you. Ya ought come down town and pay us a visit. I know Hondo wouldn't mind seein' ya again and if'n you're real nice, we might just sashay on over to the Silver Dollar and say hello to Rae"!

"Thought he was in the printing business, Rafferty"?

"Oh he still is, but since his old lady is partial to the other side of the street and the grub at the Solver Dollar Café, they had a chance to buy the place for pennies on the dollar a few years back just when it was on the verge of going belly up. Since it's just down the street on Montrose Boulevard it made sense. The place is always full, the grub is great and the staff and customers be the very same floorshow as before"!

"Like listening to a room full of escaping steam", mused Jaeger!

"The very same. Now let me off the phone so I can call White, for ya"!

"Thanks Rafferty and we'll get together soon"!

Thirty minutes later, Jaegers cell phone rang and it was Randall White, who began with "Heard you went International on us Jaeger. So how ya been"?

"Every day above ground is a good day, is it not Randall"?

"That it is, that it is. So what can I do for you"?

"Need to engage your services, to build a dossier on someone, who might want to lay low"!

"Yup, you gone international sure enough with that 'dossier' stuff. So you want to start a 'file', on an investigative subject, What do we have for openers"?

"We have a possible name, Mike, or Miguel Montero; we have a pickup truck and a Texas license plate number. If my memory serves he works for a Mechanical Engineering Company. Finally I have two GPS coordinates; one that I think is his residence and the other possibly his workplace"! "Got it Jaeger. So can you fill me in on what this is all about"?

"Just a hunch mind you, but about a year ago, I ran across this guy out at the Hot Wells firing range. He was a crack shot, with the rifle and the hand gun. We started World War Three for a morning and got to talking back and forth casually. The guy was an uncommonly good pistolero. Much more than what one would normally see at the firing range. Didn't think much of it at the time but since it was just after the time of our local bombing of the buildings in town, made a mental note that if ever our paths crossed, I'd give this guy the once over. Well last Saturday I caught sight of the guy again and planted a GPS device on his truck, thus the coordinates"!

"You think this guy had something to do with the bombings, Jaeger"? "Don't really know. It's admittedly the wildest of hunches and there is probably nothing to it. But the Feds have zip leads and are still thinking that it was a well-trained group of sappers that are long gone. The local FBI agent in charge, this Corinne McKay, has floated a theory that runs counter, that someone local is responsible and is hiding in plain sight. So call it what you will, an idiotic hunch, there's this thing that just will not go away, regarding this guy and I need you to get on your puter and tell me if I'm full of crap or not. So I'm willing to buy some of your time to find out"!

"You want me to get right on it Jaeger"?

"Sooner the better I reckon. If you'll give me your address, I'll be down after lunch with my checkbook to pay your retainer and give you my billing address"!

"Well get on it right away friend. By the way do you want me to get Buffy involved in this"?

"Not just yet Randall. If there is nothing there, just give me the bill for your time and we all forget about it, but if there is something to it, who better than Elizabeth Beauvior to bring this all out in the open"?

"See you after lunch Jaeger", said White and the line went dead. With time on his hands till his meeting with Randall White, Jaeger drove down to the Silver Dollar Café, to see if he could run into Rae, during the lunch hour and sure enough there he was, with his tattoo laden larger than life partner in business as well as life. They all embraced and reminisced over old times and as Jaeger could see, from eleven in the morning, through two in the afternoon, the place was packed to the rafters, with the artsy crowd hankering for the finest in stick to your ribs heart attack food, like your momma used to make. For dessert five different types of apple pie and six versions of cherry pie was on the menu. If that didn't float your boat then take your business elsewhere, the dessert portion of the menu proclaimed.

During an abbreviated lunch of one slice of apple and another of cherry pie and coffee, Jaeger asked Rae quietly if he'd heard from Duke Santee over the years"!

Rae quickly glanced around, then replied cautiously, "He's been very quiet ever since, the big to do in the Galleria a few years back if you'll recall. See him drift in from time to time for the food and the floor show, if ya catch my drift and then for months at a time nothing"!

"Just curious as to if he's still with us that's all. Might have something of interest for him. I'll know later this afternoon. Think he's still around the neighborhood"?

"The mans like you in many respects Jaeger. He really doesn't have to work for a living any more. He keeps a low to the ground profile and just doesn't want to be found. "He's here, he's there, he's everywhere. He only talks to those he really knows and trusts. Although he's Asked about you from time to time and I tell him the very same thing about you, being that you're both two birds of a feather"! "Well, gotta go pay a quick visit to Rafferty, said Jaeger as he pulled out a 'Jackson' from his wallet and laid it on the table. "Tell the waitress to have that mole on her arm looked at as soon as she can", he said as he started to rise. Then he asked, "She is a she, isn't she"?

"As far as we know, she pisses sitting down, said Rae with a smile!

Fifteen minutes later Jaeger pulled the big Ford into a selfserve parking lot two blocks from Rafferty's Bail Bonding, one block from the Harris County Court House, walked the city block and entered into the ancient two story structure. It wouldn't have been there, a potential victim of downtown renewal, had it not been for the building having been declared a "National Historical Monument", by the federal government some thirty plus years ago, thanks to the political manipulations by Rafferty some thirty five years ago, in by a long departed local Member of the US House of Representatives. As long as the building stands and is not considered a fire hazard by the local government. Rafferty's position as the Premier Bail Bondsman in Houston, by gawd Texas, was assured.

As Jaeger entered, he could hear Rafferty yelling over the phone, no doubt at some hapless court bailiff who once again screwed up some paperwork germane to a prisoner. As Rafferty slammed the phone on the hook, he turned in his ancient swivel chair and saw Jaeger standing there before him not a few feet away. "Damn fucking bailiffs, trying to screw with my surety. Didn't we just talk on the phone just this morning Jaeger"? "Your memory's still keen as ever old man", said Jaeger as he sat down next to Rafferty's ancient oaken roll top desk.

"You ever hook up with Randall White like ya said"?

"We talked right after you called him, in fact when I get through with my visit with you I'm heading for his office. Just came by to say thanks and sorry that I haven't stayed in touch"!

"So can ya tell me what you're into"?

"Rather not for the present. White's in the process of setting things up to determine probabilities. If things pan out then I might be giving you and Hondo a call, if not I'd like it to all die a silent death. For now it's simply at the long shot hunch stage"!

"Hunch or not, If you'll recall the arguments we both had over your long shot hunches"?

Jaeger smiled as he said, "We certainly did go round and round, over my hunches"!

"What used to piss me off was that over all of the fucking bets we had over who bought supper over your goddamn hunches, I never once collected on a dinner. Always I paid, and you always brought in your man or woman as the case may be. So I'm a believer in your hunches, never once having to forfeit a surety to the courts over your hunches"!

"We'll see how this develops and in respect, I'll fill you in either way it goes"! As Jaeger rose from the chair he said, "Gotta go visit White next so I'll look in on you later. Tell Hondo I said Hi", as he turned and walked out the door.

"Good to see you again Jaeger. Here take a seat and I'll show you what I've gotten thus far and thank you Janet, for showing Mr. Jaeger in", said Randall White as he took a seat behind his desk and opened the newly created file.

"First there is a Michael Montero and here is a copy of the man's Texas Driver's License. Is this the man we're talking about"? Jaeger looked at the photo copy of the TDL duplicate and nodded his head saying, "That's The man in question", handing the sheet back. "Before you leave I'll have Janet make a copy of everything we've uncovered so far and I'll email you anything we develop in the future, if you'll give her your email address.

Next I tossed both of your GPS coordinates in the county computer records system and you were right. The first one was a residence built some years ago by a Mike Montero way north of Houston out in the northern part of Harris County, just shy of BF Egypt. If county records are accurate and that's a big if, the man's land straddles the Harris and Montgomery county lines by some twenty feet. The guys way back deep in the trees, like someone who doesn't want nosey neighbors"!

As White turned over the next sheet of paper, he said, "The next set of GPS coordinates indicated a three story office building, that is home to Harris County's largest mechanical contractor and apparently that is his work location. So we know that he works for a Mechanical Contractor in some capacity. Then thanks to my nephew who is a genius computer wonk, we can secretly access the company's computer files. Took him all of a half hour to sneak through the company's fire wall to access their personnel files and here is Mike Montero's personnel file with the company from the very first day he went to work there. You will note that he's a Master's Degree in Mechanical Engineering Design from Texas Tech University. So I had my nephew access Texas Tech's data base and get a print out of every class he took both in his undergraduate and graduate studies. Took him an hour to penetrate their firewall, but he got er done. Every grade and every professor from his time there and it indicates that he was awarded in fact, a Master's Degree in Mechanical Engineering, specializing in design and construction of HVAC systems in High Rise office buildings. Now we go back to his personnel records and discover that Mike Montero designed and was key in the construction phase of a number of first generation high rise office structures in the downtown central business district. Apparently he was so good, that after construction the owners and managers awarded his company the ongoing maintenance contracts for the very structures he designed and built. Over time he developed a portfolio of high rise structures, both in the CBD and in the suburbs and two Hotels near the Galleria area of town. This guy is a hard worker and a very successful man for he holds the current title of VP, Operations Downtown"!

"Now on a hunch, I compare the addresses of the properties he had a hand designing, building and maintaining, with those that initially exploded and I find them identical. So Jaeger a rational man can only conclude that either this man is very unlucky and that this is all a severe coincidence, or that somehow he had some involvement with their destruction"!

For an entire minute the importance of White's discovery was stunning for both men, before Jaeger said, "I was hoping that I was wrong. That there was nothing to this"!

White then interjected. "There is something here my man. If it looks like a duck, well I won't belabor the rest! Now back to the Texas Tech connection. We can't access their database for class pictures of their students, simply because they currently have a computer glitch regarding their data base to show class photos of their students, one would usually find in their annual year books. So what if this Montero came into the country illegally with a set of skills learned elsewhere? Now his student information indicates that he emigrated legally from Mexico and obtained his citizenship prior to his enrollment. But what if that is all bogus? The University will only check someone out so far and usually it's a lick and a promise vetting. Someone needs to go to the University and see if there is any photo on record of this student in the student annual of any mention of his attending. If none exists, then we can readily make the assumption that someone well placed at that institution at that time, placed a bogus record of his attendance and matriculation at that institution in the data base. For unless there was probable suspicion of foul play and most business's simply have little reason to delve so deep, it just will not get done"! "So it looks like a little trip to the Student Library in upcountry, is in order wouldn't you say and if no mention in the year book or no picture can be found, it looks like this guy is a duck"!

"While your gone up to Texas Tech, I'll hustle up my nephew to get that facial recognition access program into the DPS Driver's license data base, up and running. If my suspicions are accurate then this guy will have one or more Texas Drivers Licenses in different names. Not exactly legal to penetrate the TDL data base without a court order, but you're not going to tell anybody will you"?

Jaeger then pulled out his checkbook and a memo pad. He wrote his billing address on the memo pad, then started to write out the retainer check out to White saying, "How's about a five thousand retainer for your services and here's my billing address for the rest. Keep on pulling the thread while I drive up to Lubbock tonight and nose around Texas Tech's student library.

Should be back day after tomorrow, one way or the other. Then we can compare notes. My current thinking is that if there's something tangible to this, then we get Buffy's firm involved to work out the legalities involved and interact with the local FBI Agent in Charge. Either way give Rafferty a heads up, so he can round up some off the books help if need be"!

"See ya in a few days Jaeger" said White as Jaeger rose to leave.

By four in the afternoon Jaeger was on his way out of town heading in a northwesterly direction towards Lubbock Texas, with is radar detector fully alert as the ancient Ford Galaxie's big supercharged engine roared to life on the open road. Traversing the state during the dark of night Jaeger had the presence of mind to bring along selected cassette tapes of his favorite music to help pass the time. West Coast Jazz might seem out of character to most as he charged through the dark night of the central Texas state roadways, but Jaeger had never developed a taste for most Country Western music and he knew the closer to Lubbock he got, that was about all he was ever going to hear on the FM Radio.

The headlights cut a path into the dark night as the moon was in its quarter phase, shedding little light on the earth. As he left one town for the endless stretches of open road, he switched to his thousand candle power road lights, that peered ahead a quarter mile, into the gloom as the critter suppressor broadcast far into the distance that a large object was coming and it was best to be somewhere else for the moment. As the sun peeked over the horizon in his rearview mirror, Jaeger stopped at a Kettle Restaurant for breakfast, gas and perhaps a morning paper. For he guessed the Student Library wouldn't be open until after nine in the morning and he had the need for coffee and grub at the moment.

The stroke of nine in the morning brought Jaeger to Texas Tech's campus library. After consulting with one of the librarians, Jaeger was provided with issues of the student yearbooks, for the years that Mike Montero was to have attended the University. He went right to work scouring each issue for any picture of Mike Montero, then finding none reexamined each of the books for any mention of Montero. Student transcripts indicated the man attended and even graduated from that institution, yet nowhere else was it indicated that he ever was there.

Jaeger then took all of the books to the main desk and asked to see the head librarian. As he was shown to the office and introduced to the librarian in charge, he presented his conundrum to her and then arrayed each of the University's annuals for her perusal saying,

"I have in my possession this man's student transcript from the time he entered the university until his eventual departure upon graduation, yet no mention of any kind occurs, of his time here, no pictures, no names, nothing. Which makes those I represent wonder if his degree, that hangs in his office is genuine"?

"But that is not possible", said the head librarian!

"Then explain how the transcript exists, naming him and his social security number and nothing else, no past student registry for any of the years verifying his being in attendance"!

She promptly got the campus registrar on the speaker phone and explained the situation. In a few minutes the registrar came back on line and was very apologetic, saying that she just couldn't understand how this could happen.

"Clearly someone has compromised your campus computer facility.

Sounds like it may be an inside job. Either way I shall have to alert my organizations HR Department and you may be hearing from our corporate counsel via registered letter within the week. If you'd be so kind to provide me with your name and contact information, then I can be on my way"!

As he left the library for the long drive back across the state, he dialed Randall Whites number on his cell phone. "White here", came the gruff response from a man who was clearly busy, late in the morning.

"Is Jaeger, Randall and what we talked about has taken form. No record of Mike Montero exists, other than his transcript that indicates that he ever attended Texas Tech University. Personally examined every year book for the time he attended the University, talked to the Head Librarian then talked to the Campus Registrar. Not one shred of evidence indicates that Montero ever set foot on the campus"! He then gave White the name and address of the Campus Admissions director saying, "You might want to give Buffy a heads up regarding all of this, in case she wants to get the local FBI involved, or float a preemptive heads up letter to the institution. At any rate, I'm heading back right after lunch and I'll call you tomorrow"!

The drive back to Houston was largely uneventful yet as he glanced at Montero's file laying on the seat next to him he decided that if he got back in time, he now had the man's residential address in the country side and if the was still day light available, he just might take a casual drive by the man's place for a brief recon visit, before heading home. As he was cruising southward on US 290 passing through Hempstead, he decided to visit Montero's place the next day, whereas rush hour traffic was building and the rapid decline of the sunlight signaled that it was time for headlamps. Plenty of time tomorrow. He'd call White check and see if anything else developed, then recon Montero's place in detail.

The following morning Jaeger set out for Montero's property. It promised to be a long day in the piney thick woods of northern Harris County. Dressed in Camo, heavy boots, a canteen full of energy drink, several energy bars, a county plat of the property's boundaries in a waterproofed sheath, his old Bowie Knife and a compass to guide the way, he set off, just after the morning rush hour. On the way, he rang up Randall White and told him what he was doing, then he folded the cell phone up and put it in his buttoned trouser leg pocket. By nine thirty he was on the road heading north as he passed the small township of Magnolia. So small that one could drive right through it and be unaware that you were there.

He turned off the main two lane paved road, following the county map directions and onto a smaller two lane gravel road, which promised to go on some four miles back into the woods, if the county records were correct.

Driving slowly he looked to his left as he drove, looking for a fence or a small gravel drive way or perhaps a rural route mail box. As he drove on slowly he saw a small round concrete culvert covered with crushed gravel that sat in place in the drainage ditch that flanked both sides of the road and a wooden gate some ten yards in from the roadway. He slowed the Ford Bronco to a crawl as he glanced at the county map and decided this must be the place, even though there was no sign of address. He thought, 'What would a man who wanted his privacy want with a street address sign?

Further, what would he ever need a visible mail box for? Just rent either a post office box at the nearest postal station, or preferably a private postal drop, since they were all over the place. The latter was what Jaeger did and thus so would Montero.

Two hundred yards up the road was a spot to his left, an old concrete culvert straddling the drainage ditch covered with the remnants of old gravel with small patches of hardy grass peeking up through where he could cross, just past Montero's property line. The great part of this location was the foliage flanking the old path being so thick so that it immediately snapped back to its old position, allowing Jaeger to drive the Bronco some twenty yards deep into the brush. He shut off the ignition and walked back through the brush to the gravel roadway. As he viewed his entrance he could not see any obvious signs that a vehicle had passed through the brush. Again back at the Bronco, he removed what was needed for his reconnoiter and headed to his left with the compass in one hand and the county property plat in the other. It was slow going, what with his clearing thick brush way from him from time to time and his constant checking for any trip wires close to the ground. Twenty minutes on he came to a barb wire fence than ran from selected tree, to selected tree, in a south westerly direction. As he checked the county plat, with his compass, the fence line compared favorably with the surveying direction of the county real estate plat. The barbed wire fence was overgrown all along most of its length with growth which was allowed to take its natural course. No doubt from time to time some unfortunate critter might run afoul of the hidden fence line, but what would the owner of the property care? It was humans he wanted to keep out and after all it was his property.

The indications were that Montero was astride of ten acres and as Jaeger tried to peer through the thick foliage he could not see any structure, so he decided to follow the wire line the length of the property. Any man that would go to the trouble to keep such a low profile must have a purpose other than simple shyness. An hour later as he skirted the property line, Jaeger saw something on the ground straight ahead. Not six inches above the ground was a small mound of compacted dirt that crossed a path way beaten by the critters. As he carefully dug into the mound, he saw a single strand of metal wire. He then followed an unseen line the wire must have taken, slowly and carefully and, there attached to a tree, were four claymore mines, attached to each side of the tree, about waist high. They were well camouflaged and only the utmost scrutiny was able to peer through the vines that had over grown the booby trap. He carefully disengaged each of the mines. Then made a mental note of their location and moved on. As the noon hour came upon him he reached the rear of the property having disabled three more Claymore mines locations en route. At the rear of the property the property sloped down towards a small creek bed as Jaeger measured each step with the greatest of caution. Something drew his attention to his left and so skillful was the opening hidden by the dense overgrowth, he almost passed by a six foot tall concrete culvert hidden by a wooden framed chicken wire round gate, securedby a simple padlock behind the growth. Jaeger carefully peered into the interior and turned on his flashlight, there it was an escape tunnel that if one pressed on would no doubt carry one back to Montero's house. Jaeger decided to leave it alone for the present and continue his recon chore. As he reemerged from the culvert and made certain that he left no visible signs of his passing. He climbed to the top of the culvert and there not a hundred yards or so was Montero's house, he made a note on the plat and moved on. By three in the afternoon he had skirted the entire perimeter of Montero's property having dismantled six additional Claymore mines, in the process and saw the gravel road some twenty yards ahead. He then decided to turn around and retrace his steps, still careful to move with caution, leaving no visible signs of his presence and on the lookout for any other booby traps he might have missed along the way. Every single thing was important as he made his way back the way he came. He wondered how often Montero had inspected his perimeter? He wondered why Montero hadn't planted some 'Bouncing Bettys' along the perimeter and concluded that somehow, wandering critters might inadvertently have touched one or more of them off and an unwarranted explosion at any time and the possibility of a forest fire might bring unwarranted attention to him. Everything about this guy said, "Leave me Alone". As he made his way, he searched his memory for the morning they both spent together at the firing range. How he spoke, how he moved, the great care and respect he had for his weapons. While not Jaegers size, he had to assume the man was good with a knife and skilled in the arts of hand to hand self-defense and he carried himself on his toes and appeared to be fit enough to stand great pain if necessary. There was clearly more to this guy than met the eye at first glance. He had the eyes of a killer, who would take a life in an instant without an instant of remorse. That very fact, plus his uncommon skill with firearms was what stuck in Jaegers mind from the time they spent together. This guy would have the patience to lay in wait, for hours, even days, without moving. Finally around five in the afternoon Jaeger approached his Bronco. He had noted on the county plat, the locations of each of the Claymore Mines, now disabled and had discovered no other booby traps along the perimeter. In a week or so he would visit again and retrace his steps, visiting the mines to see if they had been re engaged. If so it meant that Montero was alerted to the presence of possible intruders and might be ready to run to ground. What Jaeger just could not have was an assault team, run afoul of the Claymores at the worst possible time. Claymores were a nasty piece of work designed to flay a creature, human or not, into unrecognizable strips of protoplasm.

As he carefully drove back onto the gravel road, the brush he'd come through had sprung back into place covering any evidence that it had been penetrated. As he came to the intersection of the gravel road with the paved two lane road, Jaeger turned right and headed back into Houston. Evening rush hour traffic was just starting build as he approached the Tomball intersection wondering if they had passed each other somewhere along the way. One coming while the other going. Jaeger picked up his cell phone and rang up Randall White and told him he was on his way back in and would meet up with him early the next morning for a confab.

22

The last eighteen months, since the local destruction of Houston's downtown buildings, for Mike Montero were about as active as he could imagine. All of the reconstruction of the High Rise office structures meant a refocus of his HVAC General Contracting Company's activity into new construction. Eighteen hour days were the norm in order to bring his company to the front of the line with the various bidding process's involved. His bosses were busy schmoozing with City and County Officials as well as the various Insurance and Commercial Property Developers, selling their proven abilities as those who could repeatedly bring home a project on budget and on time, while Mike and the various architects worked out the engineering problems involved. Far into the night he often worked, rarely visiting his home in the northern part of the county, spending his nights at his secondary apartment inside the city limits in order to cut his commuting time to work and back. But every weekend, mostly on Sundays, he was able to make the long drive out to Magnolia and enjoy the country.

Now that there were nine projects coming out of the ground, in varying phases of development, he was better able to visit his primary residence in the country. He felt guilty not being able to engage in the daily ritual of timely prayer, so central to his Muslim faith, but he reasoned that Allah would forgive him for this interruption as long as his prayers were faithfully performed early in the morning and at night prior to his retiring for bed.

A recent visit to the firing range indicated that his shooting skills had diminished somewhat, so it was necessary that he visit the nearest firing range on a twice a month basis to keep his skill sets up to his high standards. He eventually made time to visit every so often, a parcel of property in Liberty County close to the Gulf where he had sufficient room to test his long range shooting skills. He'd discovered this location sometime back when invited to a duck hunting party by some of his vendors. For miles around, the only thing that occupied this particular land close to the Gulfs waters were small critters, ducks and the occasional gator. Thus he could shoot up a storm without concern from human intrusion as long as it wasn't duck hunting season.

He followed the daily newspaper every day, especially during the aftermath of the local bombing, for a variety of reasons, especially concerning any reported progress in the investigations. One reason for his concern was buried report on page two regarding the local Agent in Charge of the FBI, Corinne McKay, expressing a theory that perhaps the bombing was conducted by far less people than originally thought. Perhaps even by a lone actor. Admittedly there was no actual proof of this, simply a theory.

Still Montero thought it prudent that he get to know this Corinne McKay as much as possible, as soon as his daily schedule permitted. Gradually information began drifting in from a variety of sympathetic yet sub rosa sources and eventually he knew her office location, her transportation, her various phone numbers and her home address. Eventually verifying all of this information personally. He concocted an initial and a backup plan for her destruction.

The wonderful thing about the FBI as far as Montero was concerned, was the fact the organization as firm policy rarely, if ever, operated on hunches or speculation. Provable facts were what drove this organization, from a strictly legal standpoint. Concern over the possibility of private lawsuits and negative publicity against the agency and the various possible abridgements of individual freedoms, constrained their agents from acting in a rogue manner. This was both a strength and a weakness, for the organization as a whole.

The very various policies designed to protect citizen's freedoms, constraining the activities of its agents, with rigidity of purpose, also limited their flexibility of action. Since no reporting indicated that Agent McKay's suspicions were gaining any traction with her superiors in Washington, didn't necessarily mean that nothing wasn't being done on some level. His investigation into Agent McKay's background was as in depth as his limited resources could develop, allowing only superficial knowledge of the person. He had no possibility of gaining access to the FBI data base, to examine her personnel dossier, which would have revealed volumes about her. Yet what could be gleaned was that, she had achieved the status of management of others and the rumor was that she was strictly a "By the Book" manager of resources. One didn't get promoted to a position of responsibility, by a hide bound, "By the Book" organization by running against the grain. He knew that, by logical inference, from his time at his very own organization.

Still, the fact that she had mentioned at all, another possibility regarding the source of the local bombings, indicated that, she was capable of "Outside the Box" thinking and rationale.

He agonized about the possibility of her destruction, raising the possibility of the fact that her theory was a distinct possibility, or whether or not to let sleeping dogs lay, eventually concluding that a year had passed since that statement had been made known. With time comes a tendency of memory failure and he concluded that perhaps her time for departure was close at hand. Now the question was precisely how?

By midmorning, Jaeger had drifted into Randall White's office just as he was hanging up the phone. "Good", said White. "I see you have your coffee in hand, so take a seat there's much to discuss. Just got off the phone with Special Agent McKay of the local FBI office. Prior to that I faxed her all of the material we've developed about our man, this Montero or whatever his name is, plus the fact that I had someone out by his place yesterday on a recon mission, without mentioning your name. You can do that if and when. What I didn't know when I hung up with you was whether or not my nephews program to penetrate the Texas Drivers License's data base, with his facial recognition program was going to work or not. Well, it worked", exclaimed White with a huge smile. Mike Montero has three different TDL identities and here are your copies", he said shoving over three photocopied pages to Jaeger.

"Agent McKay has everything we have Jaeger, yet she needs more. You know how the FBI is, by the book. We have her complete attention however since what's been uncovered thus far buttresses her suspicions of a local lone actor in the downtown and uptown bombings. Yet not enough evidence is sufficient to develop a case for probable cause for her to get a search warrant from a Federal Judge"!

"What about the state and local judiciary? Isn't this more of a State and local matter since no evidence has been developed that indicates a crossing of state lines"?

"Normally, Jaeger you'd be right except long ago if you'll recall, the Governor called the FBI and formally requested that they get involved. Especially since the theory still prevails that a variety of foreign elements are involved. So like it or not we got to go with the FBI. Plus I suspect that Agent McKay had been stepped on hard by some higher up in even voicing her opinion that ran counter to the norm without any evidence, just by the way she was talking. She's a career agent and is not going to jeopardize her career by getting into a pissing contest with a higher up which would result in a less than desirable, annual efficiency report. Remember? You had them back when you were in the Corps"!"So you're telling me that you need more proof that this guy is our prime suspect"!

"I'm convinced, but Corinne McKay is the point gal in all of this and pictures, fingerprints etcetera, will be needed to get in front of a Federal Judge. You know the drill. But we have McKay thinking as of the present"!

"I'd think she'd be predisposed along those lines anyway", mused Jaeger! "So it looks like I have to go back in. I know the perimeter, but haven't been inside the fence line. No idea whether or not he's got the place televised on CCTV, then need a master locksmith and some techie to gain access to the tunnel. I haven't picked a lock in years"! Jaeger then picked up his cell phone and made two calls. The first was to Rae the printer, to put out the word that Duke Vultee was needed muy pronto and the second call was to Rafferty, to see if Hondo was available, for a little up and back?

"He just got back last night from bringing in a runner. Should be asleep right now but I'll ring him up soon as I get clear of you and see if he'll bite"!

Soon as Jaeger hung up he asked White, "You talk to Buffy yet"? White responded, "Gave her a brief call first thing before I called the

Feds. She's in court till midafternoon. She'll call me back as soon as she's free. What'll you be doing the rest of the day"?

"Gotta plan how I'm going to get into that place tomorrow. Guessing I'm going to have to get in by the tunnel. Can't believe that a guy like that wouldn't have his property inside the wire televised. Didn't see any evidence of CCTV outside of the wire, but to tell ya the truth I was more concerned of stuff on the ground rather than up in the trees, which would be where the camera's would be located"!

"If ya did run afoul of cameras outside the wire, no doubt he'd be alerted by now and ready to didi out of there", said White!

"I'm going out there right now and go back over the perimeter once again to check for CCTV cams. Should be there in an hour or so, traffic permitting. Your nephew, is a computer wonk right"?

"That's right, also a video and audio wonk"!

"How would he like a little adventure in his life tomorrow? Sure could use his expertise"!

"I'll ask him real nice, but just don't get him killed or injured. Need him too much. And as for me, my days of shoot outs are long over ever since we had that run in in Montrose years ago, at Odessa Robillard's house"!

"I'll keep that in mind", said Jaeger rising as he made for the door. He raced back to his place got dressed in his camos and switched to his Ford Bronco and drove north back to Magnolia. As he reentered the same spot north of the Montero property, he got out of the Bronco and started to retrace his path along the property perimeter. Working with the plastic covered property plat, he slowly concentrated this time in logical spots where a CCTV camera would be located in the trees. Since he'd seen no telltale wires on the trees before, he'd assumed that any camera must be battery operated, with a motion sensor and rotational hardware like that would be very expensive and must be checked periodically and no doubt would be set off by any animal movement, coming within range. If the guy really was working alone, this might prove an onerous chore, yet it seemed this guy was capable of great detail. He almost got to the rear of the property, when he felt the cell phone go off"!

It was Hondo saying, "Long time no see sport. How ya hangin'"?

As Jaeger switched hands and stopped, he said, "Hangin' tight and right now am deep in Bum Fuck Egypt, in the middle of a recon job, sweatin' up a storm. I'm going to give you the number of a PI named Randall White, ex- cop who has his own shop. He'll fill you in on the details if ya call him Pronto. You still good at pickin' locks"?

"Only guy I know better than me is Vultee, but he's dropped from sight"?

"Got a call out for him as of this morning. But need you to join me tomorrow early possibly for a little in and out evidence gathering. It all depends upon what I find in the next few hours. Ya up for it"?

"Do I need to bring heat"?

"Don't know yet. Let you know later"!

"I'll call White right away and get up to speed. Call me when you get clear"! Jaeger folded his cell phone and put it back in his pocket as he cautiously moved forward. As he approached the rear of the property near the tunnel he surmised if any place to put a camera this was the place, he stopped and took careful stock. Peering deeply into the trees. He moved a few meters forward, picked up a small piece of rotted wood every so often and tossed it ahead of him looking for camera movement in the trees, before doing the same thing again and again until he was satisfied that there were no cameras at the rear of the property. He looked at his watch and saw that it was well past one thirty in the afternoon.

He had another side of the property to examine, so he best get to it.

By Three PM, he reached the part of the property that was near the gravel roadway in front of the property and having discovered no cameras lurking in the trees turned back, reexamining each Claymore Mine as he passed to be certain they had not been made operable. In a half hour he'd reached the rear of the perimeter again and stepped inside past the hanging shrubbery that covered the entrance. He examined the padlock that secured the wired enclosure and finding that it was a relatively simple but large padlock, made note of the brand and style then pulled his flashlight and peered into the darkness of the tunnel. Unable to see more than twenty yards ahead into the gloom, he almost turned, until he saw single tire tracks leading to the tunnel entrance. He followed the tracks out of the enclosure, embarrassed that he'd not caught that earlier and followed them down a brief hill past a partially dry creek bed that worked its way around the rear of the property. Then he saw a series of ruts in the dirt that could only be made by a trail bike. The light went off in his head. Of course, this way his escape route, in the event that his place was discovered. He followed the track along for a half mile before he discovered that it ran into the rear of an adjacent gravel road, before making note of it and heading back.

Upon reaching the tunnel he decided to climb around the tunnel and look out onto the property through the thick brush. Some hundred yards away he saw the house and another structure that looked like a very large garage. Perhaps it doubled as a work place?

Tomorrow Jaeger would find out, he reasoned as he made yet another series of notes and carefully withdrew. As he made his way back to his Bronco, checking the Claymores along the way, he knew the exterior of the property was clean. He also knew that the tunnel was an escape hatch that was rarely used. What he didn't know was if the tunnel was televised with motion sensors, or that if the interior and exterior of the home was monitored in some fashion. When he got back to the Bronco, he called Randall White to give him the results of what he'd discovered and his concerns. "Hang on a minute sport and let me round up my nephew to join in our little confab" said White. A minute later he came back on the line and talked with White who by now had his nephew on the line via the speaker phone. After he again outlined the problems and his concerns, Jaeger asked, "What do ya think sport"? "Geeze Mr. Jaeger, never been a burglar before, but I'm up for it. Don't ya worry. I've some hardware that can tell us well in advance if we're being monitored, visually or otherwise. I also have some night vision equipment I can bring along that can get us through the darkest tunnel. I also have some hardware that can detect motion detection sensors well in advance and temporarily disable them. If the guy has a computer, give me an hour and I can get past his firewall and security device and download everything he's got on diskette. I can bring along a ground metal detector in case he's got the place mined. Finally I can bring along something that can detect laser barriers just in case. So when do ya want to meet up"?

"Call me at this number, young man around nine tonight and

have available everything you've mentioned and get ready your country clothes. Nothing flashy, keep it plain Jane. Now give me back to your Uncle Randall"!

"Is this kid easily excitable, Randall"?

"Not if ya tell him early on how the cow ate the cabbage. Make it clear, up front eye to eye, "I say you do", and everything will be fine"!

"How old is this kid"?

"Lemmesee, he should make his nineteenth year sometime next month, if the creek don't rise too much. He dropped out of his senior year in high school because of boredom. He's got a registered IQ of one seventy six. Just make certain he comes back in one piece, or else I'll never hear the end of it from my sister. He still lives with her, cuts the lawn and does chores"!

On his way back into town, Duke Vultee finally surfaced and after the initial, "Long time no see", discussed what might be needed and where to meet up the following morning. Of course the classic question came up, "Think we need to bring heat, sport"?

"Might not hurt, just as long as we assume the worst case"1

"Then he called up Hondo and told him that Vultee had surfaced and was coming along for the ride the following morning and where to meet up and when the following morning! At the stroke of Nine PM, Randall Whites nephew called and asked where and when to meet up the following morning?

"Should I bring heat Mr. Jaeger", asked the eager nephew? Jaeger, mindful of what Randall White had told him about his nephew, laid it on the line, "Son we need you for your brain. There will be, including myself, two others along that will be your guardian angels, readily capable of being pistolero's. Your uncle needs you back in one piece, Que Sabe? So you'll be with me at all times, unless I say otherwise. At all times, I say, you do just what is asked, and nothing more unless directed otherwise, by either myself or whoever I might hand you off to. Are we agreed"?

"Yessir, Mr. Jaeger", replied the nephew calmly!

"Good son. Now get some sleep, were going to be busy tomorrow and I'm glad you're coming along"!

At six thirty the following morning Jaeger was at the Kettle Restaurant, having secured a booth and ordering coffee. In five minute intervals in walked Whites eager nephew, Hondo and Duke Vultee as they all got quickly reacquainted and the plan of attack gone over.

Jaeger made everyone aware of White's nephew's expertise as the eager young man told them of what he'd brought along to pave the way. At a little past Eight in the morning with the bulk of the early morning traffic heading towards Houston, everyone helped unload the hardware from Whites Nephew's trunk into the rear of Jaegers Bronco and headed north Towards Magnolia. A half hour later the Bronco pulled into the spot off of the gravel road and unloaded the equipment from the Bronco, each taking a piece of equipment as Jaeger made it very clear, "Gentlemen, I've been here twice in the last few days and am fairly certain that I've disabled everything that can hurt us, but were dealing with a very smart man here and a killer none the less, so until I say otherwise, step where I step and pay keen attention to everything. Once we gain access into the tunnel and the unseen we'll be guided by this young man here", referring to Whites nephew, "And then we step where he steps until we gain access to the interior of the house, then we play things by ear very carefully. We're on an evidence gathering trip here and nothing else"!

All seriously nodded their heads as they followed Jaeger through the forest each carefully stepping in the steps of the one who preceded him. A half hour later, the quartet reached the rear of the property and the overgrowth shielding the tunnel. As they approached the round frame that held up the chicken wire that shielded the tunnel entry, Hondo fell to the task of opening up the padlock. He brought out a round ring of old skeleton keys and after looking at the lock selected one and inserted it into the lock and turned the key. The lock sprang open as Jaeger said to Whites nephew, "Son, work your magic and lead the way. Upon his request two flashlights illuminated the dim interior if the tunnel as the nephew took a step inside then removed an aerosol from his backpack and carefully sprayed the path ahead searching for an indication of a laser detection beam. Finding none he handed the aerosol off to Vultee and engaged the motion detection devise he'd brought along. Seeing that nothing registered, the group advanced cautiously, every ten yards, spraying the path ahead, and then finding nothing pointing the motion detection device ahead. Eventually they came to a point where the tunnel ended and a wooden stairway loomed in their path. At the base of the stairwell just to the side sat two trail bikes on their kickstands.

As the nephew carefully examined the wooden stairwell for pressure detectors and wires, Jaeger made the executive decision; to simply remove the ignition wires from the sparkplugs, in such a way that they looked like they were connected, but with the slightest motion would fall from their precarious perch thus making the bike unable to start.

Once the nephew pronounced the stairwell safe to climb, he examined the overhead wooden door to the interior of the house for any sign of an intrusion alarm device and signaled Jaeger to climb the stairs and proceed then into the house. As Jaeger got to the top step, he was stopped as the nephew, pulled out some cotton shoe covers and asked each man to cover the soles of their shoes when inside, so tracks would not be left on the floor and further that they would not create any static electricity as they walked.

Into the interior of the house, the nephew again produced for all sets of police lab rubber gloves to wear in order not to leave prints anywhere in the interior and two sets of police finger print removal tape and media to attach the tape. In addition he brought out a number of plastic bags of varying sizes in case something had to be isolated while carried away. As the team carefully made their way through the house, following Whites nephew and his hardware, they discovered the man's computer workplace.

Then Jaeger told Vultee and Hondo to go over to the garage and work area, while he and the nephew stayed in the house. Each team had a small video camera and digital camera in which to take pictures. Between Vultee and Hondo there was no locking device that could keep them out, but just in case, he sent the nephew along with them to ensure that no other detection devices lay in their pathway or in the garage interior. While they were gone, Jaeger and the nephew searched the interior of the house videotaping every inch of the interior while searching for a possible weapons cache. He discovered several hand guns strategically placed around the place in exactly the manner Jaeger had placed his hand guns around his place. Six semiautomatic weapons in total. His respect for the man growing with each discovery. As he came to each weapon, he had the presence of mind to unload half of each clip, just in case of a future encounter. To completely unload each weapon would be easily detected by the lack of weight, but if a fifteen round clip had only six or seven rounds in it a nasty surprise would result. Of course, each weapon had a round already in the chamber ready to fire if need be.

A half an hour later, the nephew and Jaeger came back down the wooden stairs. Thenephew eagerly made his way to his first love, the subjects computer and sat in front of it, removing categorized diskettes from his back pack and an assortment of multigigabyte flash drives, saying, "Give me a half hour and I'll milk this cow clean down to the bone"!

As Montero's computer downloaded the last byte of information, Hondo and Vultee, entered the house and went over to Jaeger who was by the computer.

"The garage and work area were clearly an area where explosives could be concocted. There's remnants of chemicals and a lab that can be used to that effect. Everything is videoed and pic's taken on the digi camera.

Carefully went over the entire place and found no place he could store weapons, so they must be in a storage area somewhere. If we had the time to take this place apart, but we don't. You wanted an in and out and ya got what ya asked for. We left the place as we found it and the place is buttoned up"!

Just then White's nephew said, "There, everything this puter has is now ours"! Looking up at Jaeger, he asked, "Time to boogie"?

"Time to boogie son", replied Jaeger with a nod. They all made their way carefully back down the hidden stairwell and back through the escape tunnel. As Hondo seemed to lag behind searching the left hand side of the walls for something, Jaeger turned and said, "What's the holdup Hondo?

"Almost forgot to mention the garage area has a trapdoor similar to the one in the house. I found it while Vultee was busy taking pictures. Sorta forgot to mention it in the hurry and all. But my guess is that it comes out somewhere along this side and maybe we overlooked it as we came in", he said as he shined the flashlight along the concrete side of the wall, Five yards later, there it was, well hidden and mudded over. But a small metal concave door well fitted to the slope of the wall, opening into the main tunnel.

"There's a single GI type metal bed on the far end of the garage in a separate room. Underneath the bed lays a small trapdoor, with a simple wooden ladder. Easy to miss unless yam know what you're looking for. The tunnel is probably small but no doubt. Here is where it comes out"!

As they made their way out of the tunnel, Jaeger and Hondo grew more respectful of Mike Montero. They closed the wire door behind them and secured the padlock just as they found it, careful not to leave any telltale footprints as they left.

As they drove back towards town Jaeger stopped at the same restaurant they all met up at and bought lunch, handing each of them an envelope, with the hand written message, "For services rendered", with Vultee shoving his envelope back with a sneer saying, "Don't need it Sport"!

While they waited for their orders to arrive, Jaeger placed a call in for Randall White. "White here", came the gruff response! "We're all done and I'm bringing your nephew back in one piece. Not so much as a scratch on him. Glad we brought him along, got videos and pictures and your nephew downloaded everything in the guy's computer. The man certainly has some place there and we should be back in your office after lunch. If Agent McKay wants proof that something is going on, I suggest that she be at your office when we arrive"!

"I'll call her right away"!

"How come y'all know each other", asked White's nephew? As they all looked at each other, Vultee spoke, "Haven't seen Jaeger since that big storm hit the Galleria, a bunch of years ago and I haven't laid eyes on Hondo since, what was it Hondo, ah yes, the shootout in River Oaks even longer ago"!

"So what have you been doing all these years Duke", asked Hondo? "Took Jaegers advice, made a career change and became a professional investor. Remember that Ft. Worth Real Estate Developer, all wired in with the Governor as the press speculated. Well sir, I bought his club at auction, for pennies on the dollar and thanks to Jaegers lawyer, who got the both of us started in the Gentlemen's Club business years ago, parlayed that into a string of clubs in Texas, Oklahoma and Louisiana. Renamed the club in Ft.

Worth, the "Itty Bitty Titty Club". Of course there are no dancers in the club with Itty Bitty Titty's, but the name caught on and that's all that matters"!

"So how come you jumped back into the danger zone Duke", asked Hondo"!

"Well sir, I'm getting' up in years and life's been treatin' me very well. In the process of livin' the good life, ya tend to get soft. Might wanna call this a last hurrah. Some good memories to last awhile, that gets your heart rate up. Besides it probably for a good cause and then there's the fact that Jaeger and me go way back. Anything he needs, he's got it and its reciprocal"!

"But you don't even know where each other lives", said the nephew. "I mean where do you send each other Christmas and Birthday cards"?

"Son they got something way better than friendship", said Hondo looking at Jaeger who nodded. They both been to the shithouse and came out the other side without the stink"!

"Include yourself in that statement Hondo", said Jaeger as Vultee nodded in agreement, adding, "We don't need any fucking Christmas or Birthday cards to remind us of the past. It's seared into our brains, boy! In anyone's life, you're lucky if just one person you know can be truly depended on no matter what. Including Rae and Rafferty, we each have four others that can be depended on, no matter what. None of us have anything to prove to each other. It's all past history. When this meal is over, we'll all go our separate ways. We may never meet up again. We might never speak to each other again. But if the need arises, we'll all get together somehow, to do what's needed, no questions asked"!

"Wow", exclaimed the nephew, before diving back into the Chicken Fried Steak.

At One Thirty Jaeger and the nephew came back to Whites office just behind Special Agent McKay and two other of her associates. After they all introduced each other, Randall White started the narrative germane to the series of events that led up to today's action,

Saying, "Agent McKay, you wanted proof? We believe we have the proof you need to compel your superiors to redirect your investigation"! "Before my associates get fired up with the legalism's involved, the proof you apparently have will simply not pass the smell test with any judge I'm aware of at the Federal Level. Randall, you of all people, being a former officer of the law, should know that evidence illegally obtained without a court order is just not admissible should it go to trial. I haven't got a chance in hell of getting my superiors to even look at this"!

Then one of her associates said, "There was burglary committed here and", just then Jaeger, who remained silent through all of this, interrupted, "Don't even think about finishing that sentence. This entire event will never even get that far. This guy will go down in flames, before he'll let the cuffs get put on him. He's like no one any of you have ever come up against.

He's clever, very intelligent, patient and resourceful, single handedly blowing up a host of buildings after having patiently setting things up for years. If you see what we have in the videos and the digital pictures, even a blind man can see that he's got a virtual fortress up north deep in the woods.

Just take the time to look at the video's we've obtained. Then say 'No' at the expense of your precious careers"!

As Whites nephew ran the two videos in silence, one of the agents with McKay asked, 'Who are the people that accompanied you to the subject's property"?

"Heckle and Jeckle", answered Jaeger. "Please just watch the damn video"!

An hour later, after the video's had run their course, Jaeger again took up the narrative saying, "Just ask yourselves these questions, What kind of man would surround the perimeter of his property with illegally obtained Claymore Mines designed to kill humans? What kind of man would have multiple identities? What kind of a man would have clearly false transcripts from a Texas University? What kind of man would lead two different lives? What kind of man would have the means and the remnants of chemicals to craft multiple explosive compounds to bring down buildings? We've all seen the reports in the media of where structural experts reported that the buildings substructures were attacked precisely at their maximum point of vulnerability. Clearly this guy has the education, training and skill level to bring down those structures. In addition I met this guy inadvertently about a year and a half ago and I can tell you he's a crack shot at the range with both the rifle and the hand gun. He uses HK, nine millimeter's with fifteen round clips. He has a number of them placed around his home strategically located"! Then he carefully emptied his pockets without touching the contents onto the table saying, "I took the liberty to empty half of each clip in the event the place had to be breached. Instead of fifteen rounds, each clip only contains six, plus one up the pipe. There ought to be his prints on the shells, feel free to take them with you, but be careful. You will notice that half of the rounds are hollow points that have been skillfully converted to an explosive round, via a drop of fulminate of mercury, while every other round is a Penetrator, designed to penetrate Kevlar vests. In addition we've obtained several sets of prints your welcome to take with you. I don't think you'll find any prints in your files in West Virginia, but I could be wrong.

You might want to give Interpol a try but I somehow think this guy's prints may be elsewhere"!

"Agent McKay, we know what constraints are placed upon you in the course of your sworn duty, but after a year and a half, without a single lead to the source of the bombing, don't you think it's time to look in a different direction. None of us are asking for an Atta Boy, we just want your time to be productive and besides, you know in your bones this is the right path to take. Time has arrived for a little out of the box thinking, don't you think"?

"How much time will it take, for you to make copies of those videos and digital shots, so we can take the originals, for complete examination along with the prints Randall,", asked Corinne McKay?

"About the time it takes to dwell over a cup of coffee", said White his face breaking out in a smile. "I'll get my nephew right on it and bring back a round of coffee for us all, while we wait"! After White left the room, Jaeger reached into his pocket and removed a pack of cigarettes and lit one up taking a deep drag, much to the distaste of the agent that previously mentioned his act of burglary, who asked disdainfully, "Must you light that up"?

"First cigarette of the day Agent and I think I've earned it. The room is well ventilated. If your constitution is in such faulty condition then perhaps you should consider a career change"!

White then came back in with the coffee, for everyone, quickly departing without a word as the Agent who spoke to him said, "Now I remember the name! 'Jaeger". You're the guy who killed that Miami player in the Cotton Bowl, years ago! What was his name? It was on the very last play of the game"!

"The guys' name was Mankiller and you failed to mention what he did to our players, especially the Quarterbacks"!

"I seem to recall, Mr. Jaeger that you were responsible for several other Miami players demise in that game"!

"The gridiron van be a very dangerous place if one is not careful", replied Jaeger as he tasted his coffee.

"Come down off your high horse Harvey", said the other agent, who until now had remained silent. "Mr. Jaeger and I met a long time ago in Rice Stadium. You probably don't remember me, but I remember you. The third game of the season. Texas had lost its first two games and since we never had much luck against the Longhorns, the Rice Owls had illusions of grandeur, of winning our second game of the season. But you stopped that cold. Seems you sat on the sidelines the first two games they lost, being a walk on player and all. But you ran through me all afternoon. In the fourth quarter, you put me out of my misery by putting my lights out. That's never happened before or since. I was on a full jock and academic ride at Rice University and to have a 'walk on' eat your lunch? Well I never heard the end of it from the coach, until the season progressed and we all saw what havoc you wrought on the football field. So Harvey, thank your lucky stars that Mr. Jaeger here is in an expansive mood, for if he wanted, he could eat your flesh and drink your blood. Just have to say that the hit you gave me was a clean hit. Hardest I ever received which quickly redirected my thinking toward the career path I'm currently on. We've never been introduced, but my name is Rex Wallace", said the agent reaching his hand out in friendship!

"Glad to finally meet you Agent Wallace" said Jaeger reaching out his hand, then asking, "Of the two of you, which one of you has seniority"!

"Agent Wallace has seniority and better annual ER reports", said Corrine McKay chuckling at all of the male testosterone that filled the office.

Then Randall White reappeared in his office with the originals of the videos and the digital prints, along with his nephew, for the agents as they rose to leave. The agents then gave out their cards to everyone as Corinne McKay said, should anything further develop, please let us know. Until then how may we get in touch with you Mr. Jaeger?

"Through Randall White if you will. You can also reach me through either Rafferty's Bail Bonding or Elizabeth R. Beauvior, Attorney at Law in that order should the need arise"!

After theyleft Jaeger and White sat down and looked at each other, after having refreshed their coffee cups.

"You and your crew have done a man's work again today", said White. "So how did my nephew do again"? "He did exactly what he was told and did it well. You have a very smart young man by your side Randall. Just set out the terms in advance, lead from the front and this guy will follow.

Everybody was impressed. Hopefully the local FBI will take it from here and we can get on to other things"! "Jaeger, if this guy is everything you say, he's a real scary character"!

"Have you ever known me to embellish Randall"?

"Nope, can't say that I have"!

"Just hope this guy is acting alone and doesn't have a lot of help close at hand", mused Jaeger as he lit up another smoke!

"Think anything will come of the fingerprints"?

"Not really. A guy that smart and that dedicated to his work will be relentless and will not go quietly into the night. He'd have to be a common felon to have his prints on file with Interpol. The entire organization is little more than a clerical clearing house for the international law enforcement community. This guy has never been in any jail or prison and my guess, is that this guy has never formally been with any military organization therefore his prints might never be on file anywhere. The Feds will be chasing shadows if they depend on prints to run this guy down. Make work for the clerks. But at least we know where he sleeps, or at least one of the places he can lay low. Should the Feds ever get close, he'll go out with a bang and take as many of them with his as possible. It'll be Alamo time"!

"How do you know that Jaeger"?

"Because that's exactly what I'd do"!

"Think they'll catch him"?

"No! And I know what you're thinking Randall. You have some friends in the Constables office and the Sheriff's Department, along with some friends in the Montgomery County Sheriff's Department. You set up a task force to drive by his residence occasionally, in a place where almost no traffic passes each day and that won't alert him that eyes are on him? Then you might set up road blocks to apprehend him either early in the morning while drives to work or late at night when he comes home, you know what he drives, his license plate and what he looks like. You think a shootout won't happen? Then you might try and apprehend him at his work place, but do we know if he's armed or not? The possibility of hostages? Let's say you do apprehend the fella. Do you think that kinda guy is going to wilt under normal questioning procedures? He's gonna be savvy enough to want a lawyer straight up. The first thing the gonif is going to ask is where the probable cause is and Agent McKay is right. It all was obtained via illegal procedures. The guy goes free and fades from view. No, Randall, let the FBI handle it from here. Even that might not be enough. The very laws and procedures that protect the innocent from overbearing police are grossly ineffective in protecting citizens from really well trained professional terrorists"!

23

As Corinne McKay and her two associates rode back into town, to the FBI office she was going over in her mind just what she was going to do. Rex Wallace was driving while she sat in the front passenger seat. She had to attend a meeting to go over the existing investigations her office was involved with as soon as she returned. Yet the possibilities of finally breaking this stalemate were far too important to just shelve. She, of course, would have to write a full report to her superior, sending it off by encrypted email. She had little confidence that if she told him everything that he would approve of pursuing this lead, yet she had to try. It would be Seven PM before she could ever get started as she asked Agent Wallace, "Rex, what's your case schedule look like, progress wise", knowing full well that all of her agents were at the maximum case load already.

"So you want to know if someone can be spared to do a little surveillance on a location, knowing full well how short-handed we are manpower wise"!

"I'm thinking about locating this Montero's alternate addresses and verifying his work location. Shouldn't take more than single day manpower wise. Then we can have a better view of the guys fall back positions. Ultra low profile all the way"!

"I'll check the agent's progress on their other cases when I get back and let you know after the meeting. Harvey, what about you"?

In the back seat the agent silent all the way back in towards downtown said, "If you can't get someone else, I suppose I can visit his fall back locations this weekend and drive my personal car into the office late Monday morning and stake out his workplace, to see if he shows up in his pickup truck. Let me know after the meeting"!

By Ten PM, Corinne McKay finished the report to her superior regarding the new local bombing suspect Montero, with all of the collated attachments. After the email was sent, she paused, reconsidering her next move which most certainly was a career killer if this didn't pan out just right. She had been a, 'by the book', agent all of her career and just one act of insubordination was sufficient to send her, or anyone else, to the boon docks forever and yet she had little confidence in her superior, that he would approve her recommendations. So she looked up the email address of someone she had met long ago that was serving in the White House. Someone she knew had the ear of the President and knew how to finesse an issue when necessary. 'Ah, there it was', she thought. Vannevar Harvanian, the White House press secretary. After she put his email address on the blind copy, she wrote him a brief two paragraph, "Eyes Only" memo regarding the importance in this new lead and the manner in which the evidence had been obtained. He would know exactly how to circumvent official procedures in case nothing else happened.

The long drive back to her town house in the Houston suburb of Sugarland was pleasant. The seasons were changing away from the oppressive humidity and heat of the long South Texas weather, no longer the widows up requirement when driving her car cruised along the Southwest Freeway with the windows down while listening to a slow Brazilian Samba CD. Everyone in the office was detailed out for the weekend on their assignments where necessary and if all went well, perhaps her cell phone wouldn't ring even once. But she wasn't going to count on it. Every chance he got, Mike Montero verified the back and forth travel patterns of Special Agent McKay. Usually she went to work via Houston's Southwest Freeway and traveled back to her town home the same way. The reports verified what he suspected, that being the Special Agent in Charge of the Houston office, her function was more administrative, Rather than investigative and like most boss's her hours were more regular like anyone else, therefore predictable in her travel habits. He knew that usually she passed right under a walkway bridge that traversed the Freeway within a half hour time frame every working day of the week. He knew the car she drove and the license plate number and he knew exactly what she looked like from many angles.

He selected the day of Monday, during early morning rush hour traffic, when the speed of traffic seemed to be at a virtual crawl for reasons unknown at that very location. Given that there was a choice of a large Pin Oak tree on either side of the pedestrian bridge that traversed the freeway, he climbed each tree to discover an appropriate firing angle and limb platform from which to fire. He finally made note of the sound decibel level at that location along with any ancillary sounds that seemed to be the normal course of morning rush hour traffic, finally selecting the tree on the northern side of the freeway, in which he could target the incoming traffic firing into the driver's side of the vehicle's windscreen. On his way home from work he would stop by the storage warehouse and remove the big bore Soviet Dragunov Semiautomatic Rifle and a clip full of armor piercing shells. He considered for a brief moment whether or not to bring along the screw on sound suppressor, deciding to bring it along in any case.

He'd heard a rumor that FBI supervisors had bullet resistant windscreens in their vehicles and bullet resistance was an entirely different thing from bullet proof. His big bore armor piercing round would make short work of the windscreen and any Kevlar vest the driver might wear and probably end up lodged in the left rear tire given the firing angle he'd chosen.

He'd fallen in love with the Dragunov weapon because he'd helped redesign the weapon with the help of an El Paso gunsmith, who suddenly became gravely ill right after he delivered the weapon to Montero, having a severe brain hemorrhage. The weapon broke down into various elements, thus was easily transportable.

For the final two weeks prior to his shoot, he made it a point to spend three nights a week in his backup location near town, so he could be up before dawn and reconnoiter the location, climbing the selected tree and clearing away a few selected branches, that might hinder his visibility. All was in readiness by the time he reached his home in the deep woods.

As the Saturday morning dawn light came through his bedroom window, he awoke with a start. He went downstairs and got the early morning coffee going and then while he waited, decided to go over to his garage and see if anything was amiss. He slowly walked through the garage and carefully looked for anything out of place. On the work tables, on the floor, everywhere. He went over to his small room in the corner that housed the never slept in metal bed that covered his escape hatch and peered underneath, seeing that somehow the accumulation of dust had somehow been disturbed. He looked at the dust a very long time, wondering, then went back into the main house and got his coffee. Then he went over the house completely looking for signs of entry and telltale signs of disturbance, indicating another presence. He then went to his main trapdoor to the tunnel and examined it, lifting the covering of the large rug that covered it. Since he personally kept the hardwood floors dusted weekly there was never a time when dust might accumulate. He raised the trapdoor and peered onto the wooden stairs and as he shown the flashlight down there it was, minute indications of what looked like multiple footsteps leading down the ladder. The evidence was indeed faint, yet since the house had been built years ago, the few involved had succumbed to an early death in a variety of ways. No it wasn't anyone he knew, he considered as he made his way down the stairs and into the tunnel following the light from his flashlight all the way down to the end by the chicken wire door. The hanging vines and brush didn't seem to be disturbed and he saw no further signs of footprints. He then turned around and made his way back to the house, sitting at his computer desk as he booted up his computer to read the online newspaper and scan an email.

While he perused his email finding nothing of interest, he decided to get dressed and examine both the inner and outer perimeter of his property to see if anything was amiss. Starting with the front entrance gate to his gravel driveway he slowly walked around the inside wire perimeter of his property especially looking for any signs of disturbance in the foliage that covered the wire especially the lowest strand which had attached to it a separate electronic security wire, that if significantly disturbed or cut, alerted the security alarm on his computer. Yet no sign of a perimeter alarm was evident when he turned on his computer. By midmorning he had made the circuit of his property and finding nothing decided to open the main driveway gate and examine the outer perimeter. He turned right and started in a southerly direction and slowly made the rounds. He was fifteen minutes into it when he approached the first location where he had secured a grouping of well hidden Claymore

Mines on a tree. He knelt down to examine the barely discernible mound that covered the pressure trigger and finding it undisturbed, decided to examine the Claymores themselves. He'd meant to do it anyway, for it long was past due for their monthly scrutiny. If he found nothing wrong, he decided to call things off and spend the rest of the day relaxing.

As he moved the covering foliage away from the mines, his eyes grew large as the lead wires just hung there unconnected. There was no way that this could happen unless someone had done this. He calmly reconnected the wires and went on the next Claymore and finding it in similar condition reengaged the mines. By noon he had made operational each one of the Claymores as he walked back up the gravel driveway. As he sat in his kitchen drinking a fresh cup of coffee a certain feeling came over him. The feeling wasn't fear, more of a deep concern of his discovery. Someone else was clearly in this house and most likely his garage. Whoever that someone was, was clearly skillful in covering his tracks, but not quite good enough.

He would spend tonight at this place, then tomorrow night in town, prior to Monday morning. He would drive the Mini Cooper rather than the pickup truck into town, but before he left he would leave a little surprise for someone at the main gate just in case he was visited at a later time.

The early morning alarm woke Mike at 4AM. He got up and made several cups of coffee to brew while he took his early morning shower. He'd brought a suit along, for after the hit, for it just wouldn't do to arrive in the office, in mufti. He'd change in a service station restroom. The previous evening he obtained several license plates from several cars in town switching them from one to another and keeping the last set of plates, to put on the Mini Cooper. He'd change back to his original plates afterwards.

He arrived at the location at the stroke of 5AM, looked around and seeing no one climbed the selected tree with his over large gym bag. He selected his hide rather well, for no one could see him unless they were directly under the tree and had a reason to look directly up. What were the chances of that happening? But just in case, he brought along a silenced .25 caliber Beretta automatic loaded with hollow points. Should he need to fire the Weapon, the sound would be little more than the sound of a bb gun. He carefully assembled the big Dragunov rifle and loaded the clip half full. If all went well all he would need is a single round. He'd calculated that traffic would be moving at around twenty five miles an hour. The drop angle of his shot would be 38 degrees downward deflection and the distance involved no greater than between a hundred and a hundred fifty yards. The Dragunov along with a thirty power scope would be more than sufficient to make it a single shot. Of course there would be collateral damage with other vehicles in the aftermath, but that was of no concern to him. She usually took the far left hand lane into work which made the angle of the shot significantly easier.

Prior to 6AM, inbound traffic moved along the freeway briskly, but the closer to 6:30 in started to slow down as more vehicles of all sorts crowded on to the roadway to get to their destinations. Montero's mind was clear and his pulse calm; for this was simply one more exercise of the thing he did the best. One more to join the rest of the infidel apostates that dared to get in the way of his work. The penetration he'd discovered could only have been done by the FBI, he reasoned. Soon he'd bring their work to a complete halt as far as he was concerned, by cutting the head off the snake. He gradually began to smile, the smile of someone completely certain of the outcome.

Seven AM came and went as the traffic had now slowed to an intermittent crawl, traveling between ten and twenty miles per hour he estimated, sometimes speeding up to even thirty miles per hour then slowing down again, thanks to erratic drivers responses. He quickly glanced to the east as the sun began to clear the horizon. It would be shining directly into the eyes of the drivers, he noticed, as driver's side sun visors began to drop down and sunglasses began to be put on heads.

Then there it was at the stroke of a quarter past seven in the morning. In the far left lane as he predicted, was the government sedan about a quarter mile away, heading towards Houston's Central Business District. The noise level that came from the freeway was literally music to his ears as the government vehicle entered the kill zone. Apparently in the outbound lane of the freeway was the largely unruffled sound of a big bore V8 engine racing out of town, just as Montero gradually began his gradual pull of the two stage trigger, calmly concentrating on the target as the V8 roared past, underneath. Suddenly the big gun bucked and an instant later he saw the round hit home.

Corinne, had a calming weekend for a change, for the phone rang not even once, a sign from heaven she reasoned that this just might be a very good week for her. Yes the traffic was a bitch especially on Monday mornings, and the daily grind at the office just might prove to be a welcome relief. The following week she would have to commence every ones annual efficiency revues, something she always dreaded. But that was the way things ran in government service. Yet the bothersome heat of the summer was gone and she had the mild winters of Houston right ahead. Her only concern was the two extensive emails she'd sent to Washington concerning this Montero character. If Jaegers assessment was on the mark, this man was going to be difficult to run to ground.

Suddenly out of the corner of her eye, she saw an ever so brief wink of light to her left at about ten o'clock high, and then the windshield starred, while she felt a force hit her like none she ever felt.

Montero's round hit the target windscreen and was ever so slightly deflected downward by the steering wheel, penetrating Corinne's sternum, again slightly enough to sever part of her spinal column, coming out her back and through the body of the vehicle, coming to rest in the right rear tire blowing it completely.

Although she had the presence of mind to know that she must have been shot, she tried to make her arms and legs work and discovering that she had no control, saw her vehicle gradually drift over into the lane of traffic to her right hitting the car that was next to her, which caromed off into a tanker truck. Since Corinne was in the process of acceleration when she was shot her foot was stuck on the gas pedal as her car sped up, still drifting to her right into the other lanes. Her last thoughts were as she tried to take a breath before she crashed into a panel truck and her lungs wouldn't work.

Montero didn't have to wait around to view his kill shot. In ten seconds flat, he had the big gun disassembled and into the oversized gym bag and was climbing down the tree. He heard the sounds of all of the cars crashing into each other in the freeway down below as he calmly walked up the side street to his car several blocks away. He briefly turned after he'd put on his sunglasses to see one housewife in bedclothes and curlers two doors away from where the tree was walk outside and wander towards the pedestrian overpass, but her attention way on the freeway and never did she glance at Montero who by now was turning the corner.

Ten minutes later a mile away, he pulled into a Shell Station filled up with gas paying cash, got the restroom key from the attendant and made his changeover in the Stations Men's room, leaving the key in the sink upon his departure and making certain that no finger prints had been left on anything grabbing the door knob with a paper towel as he left. He decided that he'd eat a hearty breakfast before he went to work at the nearest House of Pancakes. Traffic out bound was of course sparse as he passed those poor souls inbound trudging along in the stop and go morass of a typical Monday morning.

As he gave his order to the waitress, he noticed the News Bulletin come on the large wall mounted television in the dining room, during the early morning local news interval. Seems the collateral damage from his shot was far greater than he'd realized with no less than eleven vehicles affected by his single shot. Eventually the local authorities would get to the bottom of this event and realize this was not your run of the mill traffic wreck.

As he drove into his buildings parking lot, he went to the rear parking lot where the executive covered parking canopies were. Slowly driving into the lot, he noticed a dark blue sedan parked in the red fire zone curbside of the building. In the sedan was a seemingly uninterested individual just sitting there watching, in the general direction of his assigned space.

Montero quickly decided to bypass his own covered space and parked in an unoccupied space somewhat away from his spot. He emerged from his Mini Cooper, with his briefcase and his wraparound sunglasses on and started towards the building's entrance, keeping an eye on the governmental vehicle for any signs of movement as he entered the building.

As he entered his offices main reception area, he greeted the receptionist and picked up his messages, walking quickly to his office on the third and top floor of the building. Only three messages to return and none of them of vital importance. He looked out of the window towards the red fire zone in the rear parking lot and still saw the car parked in the area. He quickly went to his briefcase and removed his small Beretta automatic and screwed on thesmall silencer and placed it inside his waistband in the rear covered by the suit coat he was wearing. As he left the office he grabbed an old issue of a newspaper, passing the front desk said to the receptionist, "Hold any calls for a bit, for I have to see a man about a horse", implying that he was to be in the men's room for an extended stay!

He walked towards the men's room, entered looked to see it anyone else was inside, finding none left and proceeded down to the floor level by the inside fire stairs. At the bottom of the stairwell, he removed the automatic, flicked the safety into the fire position and placed the weapon inside the folded newspaper, exiting the building from the front entrance. During the midmorning most vehicular and foot traffic usually was at a bare minimum.

Harvey was just about to cash in his chips and go to the office. For he saw nothing resembling a pickup truck enter the rear executive parking area, much less park in this Montero guys assigned parking spot. His weekend efforts did produce a result of interest. Of the three locations registered with the Texas DPS, on his three different driver's licenses, two were abandoned residences, while the third was an existing apartment complex. He would tell Corinne McKay when he got into the office. He looked at his watch and decided to give the stakeout all of another five minutes more before he packed things up and headed for the office.

As Montero came around the side of his building, he noticed that all of the blinds were drawn to shield the office workers from the midmorning sun and that no one was around near the building. He casually walked around the rear of the car, as he noticed the lone occupant in the driver's seat look down. The driver's side window was rolled down as Montero approached. He bent down and said, "Excuse me but"!

As Harvey turned his head to acknowledge the comment, he saw a man in a business suit, speaking to him. The man's face seemed familiar, as his right hand quickly came up revealing a folded newspaper. It seemed odd to Harvey the newspaper was pointed in a slanted downward angle until the newspaper erupted, with a single hollow point bullet tearing through his eye, till it came to rest embedded in the passenger seat.

Montero had enough sense to fan open the folded newspaper just as he fired the gun, thus avoiding any possibility of any blood spray back, on any part of him. The driver of the vehicle simply slumped over the seat without a single sound.

Harvey's last fleeting thought before the lights went completely out, was a single name, "Montero", then he heard a sound like the report of a bb gun, and felt the pressure of another round slam into the underside of his jaw, as it entered his head.

The coupe' de grace administered, Montero quickly put the weapon inside his rear waistband, covering it up with his jacket and walked towards the building as he passed the trash receptacle he tossed the folded paper into the spring loaded flap into the bin and went back into the building taking the fire stairs up to the third flood and reentered the men's room, this time to examine himself for any telltale signs of blood back splatter. Finding not a single drop, anywhere front, side or rear, he decided that, the horse had finally arrived, so he best take a stall and tend to the animal.

Five minutes later he reentered the office and as he passed the receptionist she asked with a saucy smile, "How's the horse"? "Out of the barn and down the street", said Montero with a wink as he moved to his office. He returned his calls spending time on the phone working out engineering problems with his subordinates on the job site and with a few subcontractors. At noon Montero left the office for lunch telling the receptionist that he was going around to the job sites and put a "hands on", inspection to resolve problems. As he emerged out the back door with his briefcase, he glanced in the direction of the federal sedan still parked over in the corner of the rear parking lot in the red fire zone, with its driver side window still open. As he sat in his car for several minutes, he saw a number of people emerge from the building intent on going to lunch, several of which came within close proximity of the sedan, not one of which gave the sedan a second glance. He drove off into the fray of lunch time traffic. All during the rest of the day people came and went into the building, thus at the end of the day, everyone went home and there lay Harvey, the former FBI agent, slumped over onto the passenger's seat, his single eye wide open staring blindly and seeing no more.

It wasn't until one in the morning, when a lone private security guard drove by making his rounds of the three story building, operating his front mounted security light, when it came upon a single parked car standing in the red fire security zone, with the driver's side window down. He stopped his patrol car and got out with the lights full on the vehicle. As he approached on foot, he noticed the car looked like those as part of the federal car pool and as he approached from the rear, the sight of federal plates on the vehicle confirmed it. As he approached the driver's side he shined his flashlight into the interior and saw the dead body of the agent staring into nothingness with his single eye wide open. He was about to say something, when it became abundantly clear the body in the seat was incapable of response.

He went back to his patrol vehicle and reported in to dispatch all that he saw. The first to arrive fifteen minutes later was his field supervisor, who upon confirming what was there, called back into dispatch to confirm, saying, "Ya better get the Sheriff's department to have some investigators on the scene and while you're at it, call the local FBI dispatch and have them send some honcho's out soon as possible, for it's a Federal pool vehicle and this just might fall right into their juris diction.

Rex Wallace was just about to head home, for he'd been up all day long. It was almost two in the morning when he got off the phone with the last conversation with his superiors in Washington. As of early this morning with the sudden death of Corinne McKay, he was now Acting Special Agent in Charge of the local branch office of the FBI. A team of specialists were being formed up to fly to Houston ASAP, and was to arrive at Ellington AFB no later than 0600 hrs. this morning. He was to be there to pick them up and afford them complete access to everything for a full field investigation of what was clearly a murder of a Senior Agent.

Upon notification by the locals of the death of one of his agents by the local Sheriff's Department Investigators, he was just too busy to wonder what had happened to Agent Harvey Johnson. But when the Senior Patrol officer of the Harris County Sheriff's Department read his name out, Wallace quickly rounded up the two remaining agents writing reports in advance of the Washington team's arrival, to head north. Speeding along in two different vehicles with lights flashing, the two vehicles made it to the buildings location in twenty minutes flat.

After the brief introductions and in conjunction with the local forensic unit that was already going over the crime scene, Rex Wallace identified the slain agent as one of his people and asked the local forensic technician, "Any idea as to time of death"?

"Hard to say Agent Wallace, but my SWAG would be sometime late yesterday morning. Of course, the next stop will have to be the Harris County Morgue, for your Agent for a full on autopsy. Since you've a full field investigation going on concerning your predecessor, we will extend you every courtesy. It's a Harris County matter initially, but since both people slain are federal agents, I'm certain my people will be OK in letting you people take full charge in this matter. Oh, before I forget, here is one of the bullets that put your agents eye out", as he handed the small evidence baggie to Wallace. "Twenty five caliber automatic bullet, hollow point, hand crafted by the looks of it"!"There's probably a second round somewhere in the front seat area, but you can have your forensic people go over this in your garage where there's more light. Tell you one thing though; whoever did the hit was a pro. Your agent never saw it coming, one in the eye, and the second after he keeled over, the second shell is probably lodged in the interior of the passenger door. The shooter pulled the trigger on the driver's side and by the apparent lack of blood splatter on the driver's side; he used something to shield his body and shooting hand with"!

Wallace could not help but mention a single name slowly, "Montero". This was the last stop that Harvey was investigating before he came to the office. It was where Montero worked each day. He grabbed Harvey's briefcase sitting undisturbed on the front passenger's seat. As he picked the briefcase up he noticed a bullet hole in the side of the conveyance. Upon opening it up he notified the local forensic tech to approach saying, I think this is the second bullet we're looking for as he removed the spent misshapen round with his rubber gloved fingers and placed it in the small plastic bag. He squatted on the curbside and went through

Harvey's notes, discovering that of Mike Montero's three known TDL addresses, two were vacant residential structures and the third was an apartment complex. He noted the time as the County ambulance drove up and several wreckers were in the parking lot if needed to tow the agent's vehicle back to the garage downtown. It was a little past four in the morning and they'd done all they could do for the present moment and Rex Wallace was tired, but somehow he'd have to find the strength to continue. He hadn't had a chance to eat all day and his mind and body were shutting down from lack of food and sleep. He searched his mind for something else to do while everyone was here, but when nothing else came to mind, he directed the agents body to be taken to the Harris County Morgue and the sedan towed to the Federal Garage in town, for everyone to plunge into first thing in the morning.

He had visitors from Washington to pick up at Ellington AFB at 0600 hrs. and before this day was out it would be all balls to the wall and zero sleep for everyone involved. When he arrived back in the main office at 0430hrs. He was surprised to see everyone there ready to be directed. Most had gone home, eaten, showered, then returned waiting to be put to use.

While Agent Harvey Johnson was generally considered to be a pain in the ass, he was after all part of the family, while Corinne McKay was well respected and considered a very competent leader and would be missed dearly. No one had to be told, to be available, for this was on their time not the governments. Wallace fortified himself with some freshly made black coffee and directed his troops to contact the various local SWAT units to be on hand as much as possible to put together a two different tactical assault teams one to head north and the other to engage in a secondary location in the city. Then the legal team was to contact a friendly judge for the necessary warrants. Looking at his watch Rex Wallace told two others to follow him towards Ellington to pick up the visitors, as they all raced south on Interstate 45 to greet the dawn.

The executive Gulf Stream Jet touched down at Ellington AFB at precisely 0600hrs. asoriginally planned and after making their way down the runway and taxiway stopped at the indicated spot in front of one of the hangers, where three black Federal SUV's were at the ready waiting to transport them back to local headquarters in town.

After the brief introductions back in the office everyone was assigned different duties along with selected members of the local constabulary, both city and county. All assets available were placed at their disposal. By 0800 hours a federal and local judge were advised of the selected evidence at hand in order to gain approval of the two pronged assault, When One of the local judges noted that part of Montero's property lay astride the Harris and Montgomery county lines of jurisdiction. A minor sticking point to be sure, but three hours' time was spent rounding up a Montgomery County Judge, in order to gain the final judicial assent for a warrant.

Grumbling all around was the attitude of those ready to roll. Hurry up and wait until all of the legal loose ends had been secured was the feeling of all. Yet they all knew that no going by the book gave defense lawyers all the legal means to throw uncounted man hours of investigative work and effort down the legal drain, worst case. They all assumed this was going to be like any other felonious apprehension. It was not the case.

Montero was busy all night long and far into the morning, in preparation for his departure. He set up many traps in his workplace garage as well as the house, as well as the interior of the fence line in several locations. Finally since someone had gone to such serious trouble to gain entrance to his escape tunnel. He decided to place a booby trap there as well, right under the stairwell. A single pressure plate that was not there before, that would trigger a multiple of explosive devices to destroy the concrete tunnel as well as the entire home and all it contained.

The combination of C-4 and Semtex explosives that triggered gasoline cans full of petrol were sufficient to send them all to hell in Montero's mind. As he drove past his main gate, he stopped his Mini Cooper and went back to the cattle guards that came just before the main gate as one exited the place. He placed two simple contact land mines just under a wooden beam he installed some years ago when the place was built. It barely fit between the two wooden support beams and his Mini Cooper could probably drive back and forth over it without setting them off. But a large SUV such as the Feds drove weighing much more was sufficient to provide enough weight to depress the beams toward each other and "BOOM". They would all be very careful in their assault he knew was coming and he'd assumed correctly since the place had been carefully reconnoitered that they had identified all that could be done to intruders. They would be wrong.

As he drove off down the crushed gravel road towards town, Mike Montero wondered whether or not he was over reacting. The next twenty four hours would be the judge he reasoned. When he reached the main road towards Decker Prairie and Tomball he turned right and headed south, driving at speed. As he approached Decker Prairie the road turned into a two lane highway running both north and south, separated by a wide esplanade that varied in its width from fifty yards to a hundred yards. As he was traveling south he noticed a convoy of black SUV's traveling very fast heading in the opposite direction. Montero then knew his instincts were right and the Federals were heading north to apprehend him. But they would be too late and in for a nasty surprise.

Jaeger sat glued to the television set most of the previous day. He just knew this was the work of Montero, but how had he been tipped off. He went over in his mind over and over, his insertion activities at Montero's place in the woods. Clearly two possibilities came to mind, either there was a mole in the local FBI office, or somehow he'd missed something. He didn't want believe the former, and the latter was the only possibility, but what? With Corinne dead he wondered whether or not she'd gotten off a report to her superiors before she'd died. She certainly seemed on board with the probabilities, with only the question of the legalities of evidence acquisition a roadblock to immediate attention. He considered calling up Rex Wallace to find out but decided that Agent Wallace would be having all he could say grace over at the present. He went to bed that evening wondering whether or not to insert himself into the equation, eventually deciding this was a Federal affair and to let them handle it. The following morning he saw on the morning local news cast that a Federal Agent had been murdered the previous day while on a stake out and they gave the address on the Beltway 8 toll road that fronted the building. Jaeger's ears perked up as he heard the address, the building where Mike Montero worked. He called the local TV Station to verify what he'd heard, whereas usually first reports of an event usually proved inaccurate at least in part. After holding on the line for some twenty minutes, a reporter came on the phone and verified the building location where the murder took place, saying they'd just arrived as the local police and the FBI were leaving the scene and followed them back into town. There was no mention of the second event in the Houston Chronicle's early morning edition and he doubted the evening edition would shed any further light on the subject.

The Feds had a firm policy of no leaks to the media, other than what they chose to reveal.

He lingered over his morning coffee, watching the local newscasts, he wondered if the locals had connected all of the dots. The murder of the second agent told Jaeger that they were checking things out. He decided to visit the building in question and give the murder scene the once over, if for nothing else as something to do.

As he arrived at the building he quickly parked his Ford near the site where the second agent was killed. Something he'd heard in the earlier newscast disturbed him and he couldn't quite put his finger on it. He saw the crime scene was cordoned off with the yellow tape and as a civilian with no legitimate standing, watched the local sheriff's investigators go over the scene again and again searching for what, no one was saying. Then as he was reading the newspaper report something struck him as odd and he called over one of the deputies and started up a conversation. Posing as just a good old boy with nothing better to do than kibitz a crime scene, Jaeger asked why there was no report of blood splatter and if anyone working in yonder building was involved, as someone who avidly watched the crime shows on television?

The deputy said that the current theory was that some kind of shield was placed between the shooter and the victim. But then the question was posed what kind of shield and the deputy posited the answer as a newspaper as his mind began to work. Jaeger casually asked what might have happened to that newspaper, given that the killing probably happened in broad daylight. Both agreed that either the shooter took the paper with him as he left, or if he worked in the building he'd have to dispose of it prior to entering the building. The Deputy's eyes grew large as he said, just a moment and went over to one of the investigators and they huddled deep in conversation then walked over to the building and searched thebushes close up to the building, working their way towards the rear entrance. By this time Jaeger had walked back to his car and sat there as the deputy and the investigator stood by the trash container scratching their heads. Then the investigator turned towards the trash container, removing the round covering and looked inside. He then removed the entire plastic bag containing the contents and after a bit of rummaging slowly removed a still folded newspaper, calling over several others to see what was found.

By this time Jaeger had started the big Ford, but it in gear and slowly dove off, back towards the beltway.

"Got the idea from some guy I was talking to", said the Sheriff's deputy turning around to see if Jaeger was still there. But he was gone.

"No matter", said the investigator, holding the blood splattered newspaper by his rubber gloved fingertips. "I'm seeing a partial finger print in the dried blood. The shooter must have been in a hurry so he ditched the paper in the trash receptacle". "Pick up the rest of the trash and well take it over to the Sheriff's office, so he can turn it over to the Feds, after our boys get done with it"! As Montero drove towards Houston, he toyed with the idea of closing out all of his bank accounts locally, then he thought better of it because, he'd put nothing of a personal nature on either his work or home computer. No account numbers, bank locations, passwords, nada nothing.

Then he drove in the direction of his back up apartment on the other side of town, south of the I-10 Interstate, if all went well, he'd hole up there for a few days. And decide what to do later.

As he turned into the small esplanade divided street running past his apartment he slowed down seeing a small army of Federal vehicles, there as he slowly drove past, bunched up with a few other cars coming back from the lunch time interval. Local constabulary were directing traffic as he glanced to his left seeing a number of SWAT personnel taking cover. As he drove away from his former hide out he then decided that this was the time to clear out his bank accounts and go completely to ground. In a Metropolitan area of over four million people he had the skills and resources, to hide in plain sight, for at least a month or so. By the close of the day's business, he closed out every single one of his accounts, converting all except one to cash and the lone holdout had to issue a cashier's check because they had an insufficient amount of cash on hand to cover the request. He'd open an account somewhere else the following day in one of his alias's names, since he'd emptied all of his safety deposit boxes with his varying personal information.

The following day he'd trade in his Mini Cooper, for yet another suitable vehicle and muddy up the water a bit for his pursuers. During the interim, he would change his appearance just enough, to get by and have to buy some new clothes. Tonight he'd check into some nondescript motel and get a good night's sleep. After all, he'd earned it!

As the fire trucks and county ambulances raced north on US State Route 249 towards the farthest reaches of Harris County, two news helicopters circled overhead, broadcasting the latest news bulletin of an FBI assault on a suspected local terrorist compound, gone terribly wrong.

Rex Wallace sat there nursing a ruptured eardrum from the initial blast deep in the access tunnel to Medrano's home and he was one of the few lucky ones. The initial SWAT responders, mindful of the original booby traps gave them a wide berth as they circumvented the exterior of the property. They had approached the property in absolutesilence from both the northern and the southern perimeters of the subjects propertymeeting at the tunnels rear entrance and penetrated the simple padlock that secured access to the tunnel, but as they climbed the wooden stairway entrance to the interior of the home, they triggered the recently installed pressure plate that set off the Semtex and C-4 explosives that set off a chain reaction of explosions obliterating the house and the garage workplace. The only thing that saved Agent Wallace was that he was held back by one of the Washington arrivals to quickly go over further tactics for securing the entire property.

The initial explosions set off the strategically placed gas containers that set off secondary explosions to the property. As other personnel made their way along both exterior paths of the property, in their haste as a cause of the explosions, they apparently ignored the directives of the Claymore Mine positions, setting off three of them as they Ran ahead to the rear of the property, of the ten casualties from these explosions, five of them expired on the spot, with only barely recognizable remnants of their shredded bodies available on the ground. A rapid decision to breach the front gate to the property was approved by one on the new Washinton arrivals. The padlock was cut and one of the Federal SUV's drove straight through with six fully armed operatives. The vehicle traveled just eight yards inside the front gate till it crossed the cattle guard, the weight of the accelerating vehicle sufficient to trigger both land mines. The resultant explosion was more than sufficient to lift the vehicle straight up into the air, exploding the gas tank, flipping it over on its top trapping everyone inside.

The conflagration was far too intense to approach as many tried and fell back. Within minutes, all inside were consumed by the fire, yet another surprise was in store for those brave enough to approach, something Montero had not considered. The heat from the explosion started to ignite the ammunition carried by the agents, firing off intermittently in all directions, severely wounding five more operatives.

As Wallace struggled to his feet, he climbed the hill on top of the tunnel entrance to see what had happened. In the distance was the main house completely obliterated as well as the garage work area. Even a fool could see they had walked right into a trap and on the top of his list were two names, Randall White and Jaeger. It was slowly building in his mind that he'd been given bad information. But why?

He started to go overland and climb the covered fence towards the house, when the Washington honcho cautioned him to climb back down and back track along the perimeter towards the gravel road. As they walked, they passed two of the locations with dead and injured from the Claymore Mine explosions. And summoned medical techs to the location by their radios. Within a half hour they were at the gravel road and Wallace dropped to one knee from a combination of lack of sleep, food and the small concussion he'd suffered from the blast effects. He was one of the lucky ones. He'd eventually be back to duty within twenty four hours after medication, food and rest, suffering only a ruptured eardrum as battle damage. As for many of the others, especially the initial penetrators. They were all gone. Of the initial assault group of fifty three people comprised of Federal, City and County law enforcement personnel, fifteen were outright dead with another eighteen casualties from the serious to the walking wounded. Of the original visitors from Washington two were the walking wounded while two others located in the gravel road command center remained unscathed. Yet two of the local FBI suffered casualties demanding hospitalization. The other assault went off like clockwork. Within the space of fifteen minutes, a warrant was served, to the apartment management, the access gates opened, the assault teams took positions and the apartment was entered. No one was present and the residence was treated like a crime scene, with Federal and local law enforcement personnel doing their duty searching the small apartment for clues while others examined the management office for anything germane to the subject. The name on the lease was other than Mike Montero.

His picture was shown to management but no one could recall what he looked like. The property was sold twice within the last five years and the original managers were elsewhere. All rental checks arrived on time and in the mail. The following day when the local FBI went to the bank the checks were drawn on they discovered the account had been closed the previous day. Montero had only used that specific account to pay the rental on his hide out.

The following day the local office had paid a visit to Montero's workplace, only to discover that he'd not shown up to the office since the day before, late in the morning and then off to some construction sites. No one had seen him since. A call was placed to the office of Randall White, by the now partially recovered Rex Wallace, the acting local Agent in Charge. The call was recorded as from this point on all conversations would be recorded one way or the other, especially since a full on effort from Washington was ordered by the Director himself. Another team flew down from Washington into Ellington Field to stay for the duration. Houston was now on the front page once again in every media venue in the nation, for all the wrong reasons.

While all this was going on, Jaeger and Randall White were in constant communication as was Buffy Beauvior having been brought back into the mix. After his call to White, Jaeger placed a call to Agent

Wallace from his cell phone while he was on the freeway in towards town to Buffy's law office.

"Wallace here", he answered, from his one good ear.

"I hear you want to talk with me and White", said Jaeger.

"Yes we would", said Wallace trying to sound calm. "Why don't you come in to our office where we can chat"?

"Why don't you return your phone calls in a timely manner"!

"What do you mean Jaeger"!

"Soon as I heard on the morning news that Agent McKay got hit. I called your office and left a message for you to call me. I figured that you would try an assault on Montero's place up north and I was going to offer to go with you and show you the way, since I'd been there before, remember"?

"I never received your call"!

"Stands to reason since you guys have been a bit busy for the last few days. How are you by the way"?

"Busted ear drum in one ear, and some other scrapes and bruises, other than that fully functioning"!

"Randall White is fit to be tied over this and your call shook him up a bit", is the reason for my call Rex. I wish I'd been able connect with you before you guys went charging in, up north. The media says that your other event went off like clockwork, didn't it"?

"Yes it did Jaeger"!

"I'll tell you this, either my crew or myself inadvertently left some kind of clue to our insertion several days ago, or someone in your organization is a rat, plain and simple. I disconnected all of the Claymores when I was there and even gave you all of their locations, yet somehow they all got reconnected. Clearly you bypassed them all or else we wouldn't be talking would we. So I'm willing to meet with you and anyone from Washington that might be around at a certain location in town as soon as you can get there, provided that you leave Randall White out of this. He's stuck his neck out on this an in no way is culpable, or should even be considered a person of interest, nor should I. As a sign of good faith, I'll even tell you in advance, if you don't already know, where you can find a bloody newspaper that might have Medrano's prints on it and where it was discovered"!

"Where is it Jaeger, the bloody newspaper"?

"A sign of good faith"?

"Yes, a sign of good faith"!

"Check with the County Sheriff's Department, their forensic people. They found it yesterday in a trash can in the rear of Montero's building. My sign of good faith. Now in a few minutes, I'll be in the law offices of Elizabeth R. Beauvior. I'm sure she'll have the conference room available. It'll be me and her, versus the small army of people you'll bring along. Round up a polygraph examiner to bring with you if you like. If necessary I'll answer only questions germane to the events at hand and none else"!

He then gave Wallace, Beauvoir's office phone number and address and disconnected.

An hour later Rex Wallace was standing at the firm's reception area with five other suited agents announcing their presence for a meeting with Elizabeth Beauvior and her client known simply as Jaeger. They were shown into the plush conference room with the overly long teakwood conference table as the trio of Beauvior, Jaeger and old Boyd Parmalee, the former managing partner of the firm, now in retirement possessing 'Emeritus' status as one of the originating partners. He was just in for the morning tending to some personal business, in a small office that was provided.

Soon as Buffy received Jaegers call to arms, she gave Boyd a heads up, for he always liked Jaeger and wanted to do what he could to keep him out of any difficulty. As the FBI agents congregated at one end of the conference table, Special Agent Brian Hoffmeister, took special note of the photographic mural that graced the entire wall behind Ms. Beauvoir who took up her position as head of the firm. It was a photo rendering in stark black and white, of the surface of the moon taken by the LEM long ago in low apogee as it traversed the surface, indicating the pockmarked moon surface in stark contrast with the far distant stars in the background. Hoffmeister immediately took the subliminal meaning of the entire wall rendering, from wall to wall and from floor to ceiling to mean that he was playing in this woman's ball park and that she had the gold and made the rules. Further, what did she ever want? The Moon and the Stars!!

As soon as the initial introductions were accomplished, everyone took a seat except Buffy who stood at the apex of the table, flanked by Jaeger on one side and the coatless Boyd Parmalee, sitting there with his sleeves rolled up in silence, his role as observer.

"Gentlemen, we agreed to this little sit down given a few basic rules, first of which is this only concern's your interest in my client Jaeger. That agreed, I'm wondering where the polygraph examiner is"?

"We won't need that kind of technician at this time", said Brian Hoffmeister, taking charge from the Federal Investigative point of view"!

"That's too bad Agent Hoffmeister, for that bit of Lagniappe is now officially off the table, never to return. Next, we assume that this is strictly a fact finding meeting only and that in no way is my client assumed to be culpable in any way, shape or form and after what has been divulged will not be considered a "Person of Interest" or any derivative of the word, nor anyone he may or may not have engaged in the obtaining of the evidence that has been provided to your organization. Finally the last item is that we insist that all recording devices be turned off and place in the center of the conference table and that all coat jackets be removed and given to our Security Guard to hang in the coat closet. Of course you may still have your firearms on your person as is your right. Failure to comply with any of these reasonable requirements will bring this meeting to a grinding halt! So boys, what'll it be"?

Hoffmeister, being the senior man at the table slowly removed his coat and removed his recorder from its pocket and clicked it in the off position, closely followed by Agent Wallace and the others, handing their coats to the Security Guard who took them to the cloak room and hung them up returning to the room and leaving the cloak room door opened.

One of the other Agents said, "Our jackets are off, what about yours"? "You silly little puerile creature. You apparently know nothing of women's fashion, for it you did; you'd know that underneath this jacket lays a simple bra that stands between me and partial revelation. Now if I peak your prurient interests to such a degree that you insist upon observance of my udders tell me now and to be fair I'll have to comply"!

Agent Hoffmeister said, "That will not be necessary Ms. Beauvior. We will agree to your terms as this being a fact finding visit only and will limit the scope of our inquiry along the limits agreed to"!

"Good Agent Hoffmeister, and to reciprocate good faith, I will now disengage the conference rooms recording device". Then she simply removed what appeared to be a simple black expensive looking ball point pen from its position in the coral display in front of her. What Boyd Parmalee knew sitting at her side quietly was that when the pen was removed from its resting place, it indeed turned off the initial recording device, but then automatically turned on the video and audio master recorder that was good for the next four hours if need be, with directional mikes aimed at each well placed chair in the room, sensitive enough to record the slightest whisper. Parmalee measured the movements of each of the agents in the room, cognizant of every motion without seeming so and giving away nothing in return visually. His special gift. Old man he may be, but that was why those who knew him well, referred to him as "The Truth Seer"!

"If we may Mr. Jaeger, since you and Agent Wallace have made previous acquaintance and since he's closer to the facts at hand as we know them, please allow Agent Wallace to carry the ball from here and hopefully I'll be able to interject a question of clarification to the equation from time to time agreed and Ms. Beauvior I do hope you'll permit us all to take notes as needed"!

"Gentlemen that's why in front of every seat lays a legal pad for your convenience. I assume y'all have pens at the ready so please Agent Wallace begin"!

"Mister Jaeger, will you please chronicle as best you can, in time line form, your involvement, no strike that, your first and subsequent encounters with the subject known as Mike Medrano, as you've related to myself and Agents McKay and Johnson in the offices of Randall White, if that's all right with you Ms. Beauvior"?

Buffy nodded her head in agreement bidding Jaeger to continue, as he did, in time linereciting chapter and verse, how he first encountered the subject Montero at the gun range, then over a year later by accident at a retail establishment and then his discussions with Randall White, and what they had discovered, then his first foray out to the subjects property and his discovery of the active Claymore Mines on the perimeter of the property and his deactivation of the mines, then following day with some help from people not germane to the heart of the investigation, the second insertion in detail and what was discovered, that the FBI never had an opportunity to see.

He then related his reaction the following Monday when agent McKay was slain and the following day when he heard about the murder of the agent surveilling Medranos office. He related what he'd seen in the parking lot of the office building the next day adding, "If you check with the County Sheriff's Department, you might find they have a bloody newspaper that Medrano used to shield the blast from his weapon. All I did was connect the dots from the news reports and make certain suggestions to the Sheriff's Deputy, on site. They recovered the newspaper from the trash receptacle at the rear of the building"!

"Yes I just found out about that this morning and the partial prints matched the prints furnished by Jaeger upon our first interview in Randall White's office. In addition the blood splatter on the paper was the same type as Agent Johnsons along with a charring of the paper that most likely was the result of a weapon being fired"!

"If I might guess, what do you say about the caliber of the weapon? Most likely small bore, and hollow point don't you think", asked Jaeger?

"If I may Mr. Jaeger", asked Agent Hoffmeister, "Your serendipitous encounters with the subject and the correct speculation regarding the manner in which our agent was dispatched, seems odd to these ears. Can't quite get my arms around that. Please help us understand precisely how you come to know these things"!

"Agent Hoffmeister, your coming dangerously close to violating our agreement", said Buffy testily!

Jaeger said, "That's OK Elizabeth, let me help the agent understand what he's got hold of if I may"!

"This is your agenda sport; I'm just trying to be the good referee"!

"Agent Hoffmeister, if I might ask, what is your religious affiliation"?

"What's that got to do with anything"?

"Just trying to help you get your arms around what got a hold of everyone in this city, so please answer the question"!

"I was baptized Roman Catholic"!

"When was the last time you attended Mass"?

"A number of months ago, probably last Easter"!

"Good. Now you remember the Apostles Creed, the thing everyone recites about half way through every Mass"?

"Why yes I do. Why do you ask"?

Then Jaeger said, "Sorta goes like, I believe in one God, the Father, the Almighty, maker of heaven and earth, of all that is seen and unseen"! "Now that might explain how random fate, inexplicable chance, brought this Medrano and me together. Can't explain it, so won't even try. Why do some survive combat while others don't? Why did a fine woman like Corinne McKay get killed when lesser people in this world still keep going? I can't answer that question and not one you know can. So hopefully that will answer your first question or not. Now as to your other question, I'm fairly certain you haven't a clue as to what you're up against. This Montero guy is a real pro. He's given up a residence out in the piney woods where his privacy has been violated; his backup plan has been interrupted. Now he didn't have to kill agent McKay, but somehow he got the notion that he might be on her list and he reasoned he better act first, knowing full well a shit storm might result. This guy has instincts that are off the charts. Has a nose for survival he does. He got his engineering training somewhere and it wasn't at Texas Tech University. The man never set foot on the campus.

Armed with that degree and knowledge of Mechanical Engineering he caught on with some firm locally and worked his way up the ladder. This guy is a true believer. My memory of him is that he looks and breathes of Mexican descent, but so do a lot of Middle Eastern types. Something about him reminds me of someone who has spent time in the Balkans. Maybe he was raised there, I don't know, just something about his mannerisms. If so he'll probably be Muslim born with a name that ends with a "C", but is pronounced as if it was "ich". Clearly he's a master munitions maker, I saw that in his shop and y'all experienced it firsthand. I can tell you first hand he's a dead shot with a hand gun in either hand, and with a long gun he's probably on a par with anyone in the military, capable of a thousand yard shot, most likely. He's somehow got the instincts for survival of a wolf, sensing the unseen and constantly making adjustments. He's no doubt closed out all his accounts locally and is on a cash and carry basis, for the foreseeable future. He's gone to ground and has gotten rid of whatever he was driving and has new wheels by now. He'll have access to whatever funds he needs and has changed his appearance just enough to be unrecognizable on the street. He's very fastidious in his habits and has self- control that's off the charts. This guy will lay doggo in the tall grass for as long as it takes to eliminate whatever is bothering him and will be relentless, because he's a true believer and is in complete control. He'll use eastern block ordinance at all times, because that's what he's comfortable with and it tosses you guys for a loop. He'll just keep coming. He's not going anywhere. He's been one or two steps ahead of all of us all along.

This guy will never put himself in a position where he'll spend a single day in any jail or prison. He will never see a courtroom and the sooner y'all get your arms around that, the better. Oh and just one last thing, he enjoys killing, just like the lyrics in the old Johnny Cash song, "He shot a man in Reno, just to watch him die"! That gentleman is what you're dealing with. Time to start thinking just like him, is my suggestion"!

"That's quite a description of what were up against Mr. Jaeger", said Agent Hoffmeister slowly. But how can you assess this man's potential and his propensities so readily"?

"Because I spent a morning with the man, taking his full measure and what I've told you about his capabilities is precisely what I would do if I were in his shoes"!

The room became deathly quiet, eventually interrupted by Boyd Parmalee who offered, "There is a man who's retired, who knows Mr.

Jaeger as well as any one. I'm told he's a legend at Quantico, which is where you gentlemen presumably call your operational home. He's a retired Marine General and his name is Bollinger. Jaeger once served under the General and the General as well as some others, if their still alive, at Langley and perhaps the State Department may still vouch for the veracity and bona fides of this man! Ring up General Bollinger, is my suggestion gentlemen"!

The name of Bollinger carried great weight with all those who passed through Quantico for the last twenty odd years. Agent Hoffmeister rose from his chair as a signal to the others, thanking Jaeger, Buffy and Parmalee for their forbearance, gathering their things and left without a word. As the elevator door closed, Buffy said, "With any luck we'll have seen the last of those Bozo's"!

"Luck may not be with us in one fashion or the other Buffy, regarding your Bozos" said Parmalee continuing, "They've got a whirlwind on their plate and are in need of assistance they cannot know how to accept given their corporate culture. Haven't seen the General in quite a while. Hope he's still with us and if so they'll get in contact with him for certain. If so expect the Bozo's to come knocking at your door, with an olive branch wanting to make nice. Now son, I'll leave you two for some private time together.

Have to get back to my office and my rat killing"! As he went through the door, he stopped, turned and said, "Good to see you again my boy. Don't be such a stranger. Hell, your almost like family around here"!

As the conference room door closed, Buffy took a seat and bid Jaeger to do the same saying, "It's been years since any of us has seen or heard from you pal. Then this morning, it's all hands on deck. What gives"?

"Came close to getting my tit in a wringer and you were the only one who came to mind. But it hasn't been that I've exactly been a stranger. Been running through my acquisitions of the old estate back in Waco through Boyd. Since he's retired, he will not send me a bill for his time, so I run the buy money through him and he sends me the papers to execute. He keeps mumbling, "Pro Bono my boy, Pro Bono", over and over. I suppose it keeps his heart beating and serves a greater purpose. Anyway, I'm grateful. He knows that when his time comes, I'll be holding down the anchor spot on his casket"!

"Heard rumors from Rafferty years ago that you went International"! "Yeah, something like that. Pays far better than chasing runners for Rafferty. Don't work quite as often, but when you do its intense"!

"So how's the family estate coming? Boyd's awful closed mouth when it comes to your affairs for some reason"!

"He seems to have acquired, much of the original land that was appropriated that wasn't developed of the old estate. Best let sleeping dogs lay for the rest. He turned me onto this architect that did some work for you on your Uncles River Oaks home. I approved the plans, wrote him a check, set up an escrow account where he could approve payment for the General Contractor and construction started six months ago, to resurrect the estate. house, barns, corrals and eventually livestock"!

"You have enough cash to see it through, Jaeger"?

"Yeah, there should be enough money in the till to complete the project. After all, this is what I've been working for all these years"!

"I can see that now. After we drifted apart, I was bitter for a while, but I eventually came to realize that we were moving in two different orbits. Once that was made clear I understood"!

"Heard that you remarried for a while, and then ran the guy off. Hope ya treated him better than ya did your first. What was his name, Archie or something"?

"Made the classic female mistake. Hooked up with this fine looking, corporate elite Metro sexual, after his first wife had run him off for infidelity. Helped get him elected Mayor even. We had a three year run at it, until I put Randall White on his six for a while. The man was a disaster as Mayor and still couldn't keep it in his pants as far as others were concerned. But ya just gotta give the man top marks for sheer Chutzpah. Divorced him in his last year of his first and only term. Odessa had a field day. Made all the papers. Headlines material, Page One. He even wanted me, of all people to run his reelection campaign after all he'd done. Well, the Bird said "No"! Of course he lost the election and I heard that shortly thereafter he'd had his "Come to Jesus" moment and got saved by some Holy Roller preacher.

Then rumor had it that his first wife took him back and the last anyone heard, he was selling open range ranch land in Colorado and Wyoming"!

Jaeger tried to stifle a chuckle but was losing that battle. As Buffy looked at him and said, "Yeah it's all ironic enough. Smart woman like me, falling for the same kinda man twice in one life time"!

"Learn anything", asked Jaeger drifting towards the serious? "Plenty, before and since, which is why I was so attracted to you in particular. We had plenty in common yet were in many ways an attraction of opposites. Besides I owed you. Later I invested in you and the dividends reaped were enormous. Plenty memories to last a lifetime. Besides, I'm now a card carrying member of Houston's Junior League and the neighbors in River Oaks have clasped me to their bosom. So for me life is as good as it gets. But what about you"?

"Hell Buffy, I don't know? When we drifted apart, I was still chasing runners for Rafferty for a while, then somehow I threw in with this guy Ortega, for about six very hairy months or so, somehow I emerged from that with some cash and then somehow got involved internationally. Seems like I've been being nudged in some kinda general direction in my life, for a purpose. Now with the resurrection of the ranch becoming more and more a reality, I can see just why certain things fell into place"!

"But what about your personal life? Has there ever been anyone you've really gotten nuts over"? Jaeger turned in his swivel chair and looked out the window out on the city, then said, "Yeah, there was this one woman long ago"!

"Well, what happened? I showed you mine, so now you gotta show me yours"!

Clearly uncomfortable with revealing his private life, Jaeger never the less, relented for in reality he was no public figure, he'd spent time with Buffy long ago and he owed her a great deal as he started, "Girls name was Melanie. Met her at the gym working out. She was married to an NFL lineman who died in an auto wreck on the Loop 610 interchange. She was having trouble with her former in laws in a custody dispute over her son. I exerted some moral suasion and persuaded them to give it up, which they did and we had a great time together. Then this Ortega got in the way and I decided there was no way I could possibly expose her to this guy. So I had to leave her in a lurch so to speak. Six months later, things with Ortega ran their course, I came out on the other end in good shape financially and got you involved, if you'll recall setting up a College fund for her son and shoving some cash her way to provide a cushion. You put Boyd on it and he did just fine. Lost contact with her. She was as fine a woman as there is and if it wasn't for this thing that was driving me so hard, I might have asked her to settle down with me"!

"Oh yeah, now I remember. She was the one at the Enron party. Just can't see you in a rose covered cottage Jaeger. You're too restless. You slave to the rhythm of danger. Which is why you know so much about this Montero or whatever his name is. You live long enough you just might settle down to live a long life. But it might be a lot better if you had the right woman making your bed each night. Especially since you're on the cusp of achieving your goal of righteous restoration. Might want to think about that"!

"Might be right Buffy, but that chapter has closed in my life. There was this one woman that had a grip on my heart and I pissed it away. I broke her heart I imagine and in the process broke my own. How can this be forgivable? How can this be explicable when I don't completely understand it myself"?

Buffy thought a moment, Clearly here was a man conflicted by his mission in life and his lost love for another. Time together lost in the process. She owed him wisdom and right at this moment. But where in her life was the personal wisdom to come from when her past choices had proven to be without personal merit? Suddenly she said, "In the meeting with the Feds, you recited the first verse of the "Apostles Creed" and you put your finger right on the spot when you said, "And all that is seen and unseen"! Seems to me that your whole life has been on a first name basis with the concept of Serendipity. You and I came together long ago and I screwed up your trial. Couldn't get that out of my mind and it took me years to make things as right as I could and eventually we came together again and I greatly value that experience. You encounter this Montero and then sometime later encounter him again as an act of coincidence. Fate! I suspect if you examine your life you'll find a continuum of accidents, reencounters, serendipity! Now how does one rationalize that? How does one explain the unseen, the irrationality of events? I suspect that you will, quite by accident run into this Montero and when you do I'm fearful of the outcome. But if you get through it somehow, life just might finally reward you with a long overdue pleasant surprise! Don't know what, when or where, but if anyone has earned it you have, so stay frosty pal. You have a ranch up north to get up and running. Oh yeah before I forget, your architect is as good as it gets. He'll ride herd on the contractors and make certain you get value for every dollar spent. After all he did really well on Uncle Leo's place as well as others and he'll do the same for you. Just stay alive long enough to enjoy it all"!

She then rose up and gave Jaeger a long overdue embrace, briefly bringing back fond memories of their time together saying, "Now scram cowboy. I gotta be in court this afternoon for a summation to a jury, just make certain this is not the last time you enter this office, ya hear"?

24

The following morning, another team of FBI operatives arrived at Ellington AFB and was taken to the local FBI headquarters, which was by now turned into a Command and Control Center. A task force was created with the single object in mind in apprehending the person known as Mike Montero. This group was comprised exclusively by behavioral investigative specialists. After a brief introduction to the various other investigative groups that comprised the newly created task force, the new people on the block were taken to the Mechanical Engineering Company that employed the subject. Still involved in pouring over every scintilla of documents Mike Montero might or might not have been involved with, they joined another FBI team that had round the clock occupancy of the premises, examining everything.

For the rest of the day and far into the night, the behavioral specialists interviewed every single person in the company, inclusive of Corporate Officers, in order to build the profile on the subject. Field personnel that had contact with Montero were brought in to add their input as to the subjects mannerisms, traits, tendencies, apparent likes, dislikes any detail regarding the individual. Nothing was too small to pique their interest.

The apartment management where Montero maintained a secondary backup unit was brought in to be re-interviewed, yet was unable to shed any additional light on the subject. Meanwhile a quiet all points alert was put out to every law enforcement entity in the City and surrounding Metro Counties, with the full knowledge that as soon as the media became aware, Montero's picture of what he may have looked like were most likely to become posted everywhere, with the "BOLO" acronym of "Be On The Lookout"! Every manner of egress from the area was under as much scrutiny as possible by the authorities, but everyone knew that a clever, well-funded individual could find a way out of this mouse trap.

The best way to achieve this was to lay low, become invisible and blend in to the surroundings.

From the various interviews, once collated to form an operative profile on the subject, determined that Mike Montero seemed to be many things to many different people. Even though Rex Wallace was the interim head of the local office, everyone knew that Brian Hoffmeister, down from Washington was the Senior Agent in Charge of the Task Force, during this emergency action. Should things go well eventually, he would be the one standing in front of the media, thanking all of those who gave invaluable assistance. On the other hand should things not go well, it would his ass and career on the line. The man liked his ass as well as anyone.

"So your saying Agent Bergdorf, this man is a Chameleon if I'm understanding you correctly"?

"Amongst a host of other things, that's exactly what I'm saying. Your search teams discovered nothing of value from the wreckage and debris of his primary residence, and nothing from his secondary residence. In his office, nothing of a personal nature, not even one single finger print.

Amongst those in his office and out in the field that came into constant or intermittent contact with the man, the only constant was his abilities to detail and his affability. He had no known enemies, no close friends, only acquaintances. Some could readily remember his face, while others did not and had to be coached before vaguely remembering. When out in the field he usually wore sunglasses, prescription he usually said, in the office he wore glasses, prescription he said, intermittently. Even the owner of the company, the very man who hired and promoted him, worked hand and glove with him, could not agree with others regarding habits and mannerisms. Clearly one of theconstants are the man didn't matriculate at Texas Tech, at all to obtain his abilities displayed in the field of Mechanical Engineering. He obtained that expertise, somewhere else. That information was gathered and known early on by someone outside of our agency.

"I believe that man's name is Jaeger. Why is it that we don't know his first name and where is he"?

"I can answer that Agent Bergdorf if I may", said Rex Wallace! "Please enlighten us, Agent, uh, Wallace"!

"Because that's how he came into the world. That's what's on the man's birth certificate. That's what is on his Marine documents, and his enrollment documents at the University of Texas and on his pardon documents from the Texas Department of Pardons and Parole. NFN, NMI, Jaeger"!

"Oh yes now I recall, from our briefing from General Bollinger! I see only notes from the interview with Mr. Jaeger. Why is it that no audio or video recording of that interview took place. From the few notes taken, my guess is this man has some insight into the workings of this Montero that are currently eluding the rest of us because of the paucity of factual data"! "The answer to your first question, Agent Bergdorf is that we we're not permitted to record out interview by his attorney and secondarily his operating expertise are outside the policies of the FBI"!

"Agent Hoffmeister, everyone knows you're the one in charge of this investigation and we're only here to assist in any way possible under your guidance and direction. Also we know that we're coming up croppers with any clues by our own initiative. In addition, it's commonly known the Bureau wouldn't enjoy its reputation over the years, without help and cooperation from a variety of sources, outside our mandate and policies. It seems to me this Jaeger fella has some unique insight into the depths of this Montero, the rest of us do not. General Bollinger spoke well of him briefly in passing and I for one have learned to rely on that old man's common sense over time. So I'd like to ask your permission to enlist this Jaegers help by whatever legal method possible, even down to the possibility of saying Please, if necessary"!

I'll approve your request Agent Bergdorf, with one exception. Should anything go awry, anything at all, resulting from the insertion of this man into this investigation, you will be the one to catch all of the arrows.

Agreed"?

Bergdorf nodded his head asking, "Who here can get in contact with this Jaeger individual"?

Wallace simultaneously raised his hand while the other was speed dialing the law offices of Elizabeth Beauvior. Within minutes he had her on the phone, explaining the Bureau's further need of interviewing her client and possibly enlisting his assistance as part of the ongoing task force, in front of all those assembled. He put Agent Bergdorf on the cell phone to explain the Bureau's need.

Apparently Bergdorf sealed the deal as an hour later, Buffy called Wallace back saying. "He'll be in my office inside of an hour, Agent Wallace and if y'all are real nice we just might allow you to record the session."!

Promptly an hour later Agents Wallace and Bergdorf were escorted into the law firm's conference room and Preston Bergdorf was introduced to Jaeger and his lawyer. This time the quartet was the only ones in the room and sat close to each other, Buffy at the head of the conference table and Bergdorf sitting to her right while Jaeger and Wallace to her left. Bergdorf graced up at the wall to floor moon and star scope, arching an eyebrow and saying, "I can see that I'd best be on good behavior my good woman"!

"Any gentleman should and would be but humor me as to why Agent Bergdorf?

Nodding his head toward the moonscape he said, "Because all that you are about are the Moon and the Stars, everything else are details"!

Wallace and Jaeger gave each other a brief glance as Buffy replied, "Saw that right away did ya now. Well most don't and few ever connect the dots. Seems that I'll have to be extra careful in your presence and have the presence of mind to keep my legs together. Now that were all friendly like, lay out exactly what you need from Jaeger and how he can help you and what if freedoms of action he might have, should he choose to become involved, purely as an act of good citizenship, mind you"!

"First, my interests are in Mr. Jaeger's unique abilities of observance. Given the few scrawled notes permitted in his earlier interview with Agent Wallace present as also in an even earlier interview prior to the assault in Randall White's office, given by Agent Wallace's notes and verbal offerings, I'm interested in your client's assessments of this Montero.

Clearly the man is a very unique individual. Usually when we go after an individual either he is mentally or emotionally unbalanced in some way, thus eventually allowing us to make an apprehension of the individual by the errors he makes. The subject we seek is clearly of a superior mind and abilities. He'll have no capability of fear, only concern for an outcome. He's highly detailed to the extreme, his spotless work record and subsequent events exhibit this. He automatically shows, without any recognizance or conscious effort, different parts of himself to different people and somehow categorizes and remembers which face he's shown to whom. Have never encountered someone like this in my career. There are other things but to be brief, your client's assessment that this man will never see the inside of a Federal Court Room, I tend to agree with, much to the dismay of others who come at things from a different perspective"!

Now this is a long way around from saying, "I'd like to go over what you've related once again, with Agent Wallace present for the obvious reasons and record his statement and impressions from all of us in this room if we may with your approval. This is for the purpose of study only and will not be used in any other way. You have both our word assurance and that of the head of the local task force Agent Hoffmeister"!

Just then Wallace briefly glanced at the expensive pen set sitting in front of Buffy and remembered that her recording device was in an "Off" position, wondering if push came to shove, how much stroke in the Bureau, Agent Bergdorf really had"?

"Finally, should I see a value in having Mr. Jaeger join our task force, he is to work with me and I am to be responsible in every way imaginable for everything he does. Now I'm perfectly willing to use the prefix of "Please", in this exchange"!

Jaeger and Buffy exchanged glances and at his brief nod, she turned to Agent Bergdorf and said "Preston is it? The floor is yours. Bring out your recorder and ask away"!

Two hours and two pots of coffee later, Jaeger brought them all to the present moment. Buffy just sat in amazement as Jaeger recanted every jot and dot his involvement and she watched Agent Wallace as he coaxed his responses of affirmation from his occasionally at first then after a while she noticed Agent Bergdorf look to him occasionally for affirmation.

When Jaeger had wound down to the present moment, Bergdorf turned off the recorder. He'd made voluminous notes on the legal pad placed in front of him and looked at the other mini cassette tape in front of him saying, "It's even worse than I thought. This man appears from out of nowhere, seeming of his own resources, although I doubt that and patiently inserts himself into our society for the purpose of sowing terror amongst us and that he did. Clearly by the accident of chance, you and he encountered each other and then again later on. By your initiative and a long hunch which our organization abhors, you alone made the initial connection and apparently a successful initial recon, then later an insertion to gain evidence which you turned over to our organization promptly. Agent McKay, unbeknownst to everyone but myself stayed late the Friday before her death and wrote a long report to our office pointing out, in detail, your role and she suspected that of several others in the insertion. That is of no interest to me the assistance you had Mr. Jaeger. I only discovered her report by accident as I was preparing to leave my office and join the team to Houston. I dare say it is sitting still in my superiors in box in Washington. Clearly we need you on our team if we have any chance of apprehending this individual, but as of the present I'm not quite certain how to employ your talents. However, I'd like to go on record of asking you to formally assist us, if you will"!

"Is there a 'Please', inserted somewhere along the way", asked Buffy?

"Please consider it said and asked"?

"When and where do you want me to start", asked Jaeger?

"How about right now", asked Wallace? Jaeger nodded his head in agreement.

Buffy then interjected toward Agent Bergdorf, "Preston, you silver tongued son of a bitch, you just cried Havoc and let loose the dogs of war. Now when all of this is over and if you're still with us, you can call on me some evening so I can show you the finest Texian food there is"!

"But I'll have to be alive and successful in our endeavors won't I"?

"Just listen to Jaeger there, listen closely and you'll be alright"!

On their way into the main office up town, Agent Bergdorf said to Wallace, "Mind if I ride with Jaeger and we'll follow you, since this town is your turf"!

"That's OK Rex", said Jaeger continuing, "While I drive, we can talk shop, so the man can take further measure of me"!

Ten minutes later they arrived at the Main office and Wallace saw to it that Jaegers car was assigned temporary access status. True to their word, Jaeger indeed quickly compared notes as they drove, each taking the full measure of the other and quickly concluding that each one brought certain unique talents to the table. The question remained, would they be a perfect fit. As they all rode up in the elevator, Jaeger said, "You guys are the investigators. You are good at connecting the dots. What I think I can offer is a different perspective; see what's not exactly visible. What I'm good at is the hunt. The tip of the spear initiative. The initial grab and bag stuff where possible"!

"My conclusion exactly", said Bergdorf as the elevator door opened to a swirl of activity.

After the initial round of introductions, Agent Hoffmeister announced a meeting of the unit heads in their conference room. To discuss a progress report he had to write later in the evening. Jaeger sat between Bergdorf and Wallace as the meeting commenced, commanded by Agent Hoffmeister.

As the meeting began to wind down an hour later, Hoffmeister looked at Jaeger and said, "Since everybody has had an opportunity to see our latest Ad Hoc visitor who's agreed to assist us, I'd like Mr. Jaeger to stand and offer a few comments as to the direction this operation is going seeing that he's been jotting down a few notes. Mr. Jaeger, the floor is yours. Enlighten us, please"!

Jaeger slowly stood and looked at each of the agents around the table and said, "I wonder where this guy is, if he's still in town. He's a true believer in something. He's not your ordinary criminal. He's exceedingly good at practically everything he does. He has almost a sixth sense for survival, he's got the cash and he's resourceful. Someone else in the country is a provider, where they are is currently unknown. My sense is that somehow he's involved in the same bunch that was responsible for the rash of forest fires that recently consumed us. Masterful stuff if you're a terrorist. Really low tech that did more damage than the 9/11 attacks. If he's still in town and my gut says that he is, he's lying low. He's changed his appearance, he's either living in another apartment or a low rent motel somewhere. Since the discovery of a parked car in the parking lot of his backup apartment, in the name of one of his aliases, he's probably gotten rid of his other vehicle at some used car lot and is driving something else"!

"So in case no one has thought of it, we might try having your in house artists, providing a series of different looks on the known pictures we have for him courtesy of the local DMV. Simple changes of appearances, glasses, a moustache a goatee, etcetera. Then fax them to every apartment complex in the area, the management office and every single hotel and motel in the greater Houston area. Then we do the same to every law enforcement agency in the state, the nearby states and the nation. Then we put the arm on every law enforcement agency in the area for additional manpower, for plainclothes personnel. We want them scruffy looking the scruffier the better. They'll bitch and moan about other cases in their respective hoppers, but if ya say 'Please', I'll bet they'll come around. We don't want to go to the media just yet. We want to put the squeeze on this guy, hammer and anvil stuff. He's in his comfort zone and doesn't spook. Now we can assume that Mike or Miguel Montero is not his real identity. I assume that Interpol has been alerted, but this guy probably has never been finger printed or been incarcerated or in any formal military so there probably isn't any record of his prints anywhere"!

"That said, if y'all will be nice enough to provide me with a BOLO picks and print file, I'll be willing to play a long shot and contact someone I know well and have worked with who has his fingers in practically everything in Europe. The man flies under the radar, but is legit and he knows many people who know other people, all of which are marginally trustworthy. But there is a certain honor amongst thieves and money is only one of many mediums of exchange. I'll get him on the phone, soon as this meeting is over and get his overseas fax number and fax him what you release and let him nose around. If what I suspect is true and it's only a hunch, this guy is of European origin, is a true believer Muslim and as for the rest, we'll just have to see. If we can come up with his real name, long since buried and put it to a picture, then just maybe we can get him out of his comfort zone and get him to make a mistake. That's usually when you guys shine, when mistakes are made by others"!

Minutes later Jaeger contacted Nestor Magellan still at his office working late, far into the early morning on a contracted bid. After the usual greetings and affirmations, Jaeger told Magellan what he was involved with and asked for his help. "But of course Mon Ami, fax me what you have and I'll make some discrete inquiries. I should be here until dawn a few hours away finishing my bid offering. When everyone arrives at the office, I'll turn everything over to my secretary and go home for some sleep, unless I receive your fax, then I'll have to remain awake for a little longer. I'll confirm your fax as soon as it's received. When I have something I'll call you first then fax what I have minutes later. Bon Soir my friend"!

An hour later, Jaeger faxed the inquiry and what prints and a picture of the subject to Magellan. He knew that a record of Magellan's fax number would remain in the FBI's possession but it couldn't be helped. He hoped things never would lead to them ever needing Magellan. He decided to give Magellan a heads up after all of this was over.

Jaegers message to the agents did not fall upon deaf ears, with quiet solicitations going out to other law enforcement entities in the area for additional plain clothes personnel to join the task force. Most of the clerical staff was busy sending out faxes and emails for the next several days to all rental unit complexes and every known Hotel and Motel in the area and state and even the surrounding states. Every car dealership new or used was alerted as well as banks and credit unions and every policeman was placed with the task of providing a pictorial of the subject and contact information to every gas station in the area. If the guy was in town something was bound to surface.

Montero was starting to feel the walls close in living at a No Tell Motel for the last seven days, in Houston's suburbs. Risking dive through forays at fast food restaurants and eating his meals in his cramped quarters. All he did all day long was watch the television and read the newspapers for any hint of information as to what the authorities were up to. Use of his credit cards was out of the question. Too easy for the Feds to track his movements. He had opened up an account the previous week in order to park a cashier's check written by one of the smaller banks that hadn't sufficient cash on hand to satisfy his withdrawal request. But for the last week he'd been steadily been drawing down those funds, with only ten thousand left in the account. He needed a house. Preferably a furnished house, preferably a patio type home with an enclosed yard, where he could relax and regroup a while, away from prying eyes.

He scanned the real estate section of the daily papers; from the few pay phones still available and finally settled upon one add that caught his eye.

He made an appointment with the owner. An older woman who inherited the home from the death of her husband. It was perfect, a furnished patio home that once the carport garage door was closed, completely shielded him from prying eyes. He charmed the woman completely signing the lease on the dotted line and paying with cash, to close the deal. Since it came complete with cable television he had no need add any other services, since all of the utilities costs were built into the rental. By nightfall, he abandoned his motel room, leaving behind just enough luggage and toiletries to give evidence that he was still there. After all, he paid in advance and had almost a week left of his former occupancy, before any flags went up.

The following day he decided to make one final visit of his private postal box to see if anything arrived from Salaam. To his surprise, there was a single letter in the box. As he pulled the letter out of the box, he examined the envelope. In the upper left hand part of the envelope was the single asterisk where usually the return address was placed. A sign certain that it was from Salaam. He closed the box and left the facility without a word.

Two hours later, two agents from the local task force, visited the very same Private Postal Box and print shop where Montero had for years received mail from Salaam. They showed their badges and federal authorization to gain immediate access to any box used by Montero. They talked to a reluctant owner of the facility who after seeing their credentials and hearing the name of the subject of their inquiry, quickly put things together, along with the daily newscasts of the area wide dragnet for the terrorist saying, "Oh Mr. Montero? Why I think I saw him only an hour, or so, ago visiting his box. Yes, I remember. Two days ago I received a letter for him and placed it in his box, whereupon he immediately showed them the box in question. Within the hour a forensic team was at the private postal facility and interviewed a very scared owner who verified that Montero was the one who was one of his very first customer's years ago.

They went back through years of his records, comparing samples of his hand writing with that of others gotten from his other banks and the engineering company that employed him.

Jaegers hunch was proven correct; the man indeed was still in the area. But where and for what purpose if any? Once again Montero was just a step ahead of the authorities. Upon their departure, Agent Hoffmeister visibly impressed the proprietor to call them immediately should Montero return.

"But he only comes by every once in a while, never a regular visitor", said the proprietor!

"Tell no one that we we're here, not any member of your family or friends, nor anyone from the news media. Do so and you will risk the full prosecution from the Federal Government for obstruction of justice. When found guilty and you will, you'll go to prison for a very long time".

He abruptly left and directed one of the local agents to leave his card.

The proprietor, who was Pakistani origin years ago and had been in America for over twenty years, started a business, raised a family and himself became a citizen just five years ago, quickly sat down and began to shake. He had never wanted to become part of this Jihad business, he heard many times at the Mosque during Friday prayers. He was not of the warrior class or had any inclinations to that end. He was simply a merchant as his family had been for as long as anyone could remember. He had made friends in this new country. His three children were all in local colleges, working their way through. Although he and his wife spoke English with an accent, both were conversant in the language and had adopted most of the morays and folkways of American life. Of course his children were completely indoctrinated to American life to such a degree, they tolerated their sessions at Friday prayers at the Mosque, complaining they wanted to have nothing to do with the old Moustache Pete's and Bearded Freaks that pounded their chests at the infidels that surrounded them in America.

Although his children had a working knowledge of the language of their parents origin, Urdu, they refused to converse with their parents or anyone at the Mosque in that language, pleading innocent ignorance. This apparent ignorance served unexpected dividends as others spoke in their presence of a variety of matters, some concerning their parents, since everyone knew the children were completely assimilated in the land of the infidels. As time went on, the children's attendance at Friday prayers became less and less, finally dropping off to zero by the time they were of college age. Their spiritual leanings were not co-opted by any other form of worship, simply put in stasis for the foreseeable future, much to their parent's dismay. But since the times they lived in were strange and those they lived with had seemed to accept them all without a hint of reservation and most important since the children had been mostly obedient and good students, never causing a hint of trouble, the parents decided to live and let live, never to be overly parental or concerned, until today. This evening he would have reason to confide to his wife and resume the daily prayer ritual he'd permitted to atrophy over Searching for a silver lining in all of this morass, Montero found solace in the fact that now he could find time to pray at the appointed times every day as the prophet had instructed. He had much to be thankful for. For somehow he'd escaped the jaws of the infidel and was able to strike a blow for the cause of Jihad. Of course he'd had little in common with those, who promoted strict adherence to Sharia Law as literally was the cornerstone of the world wide Jihad everyone was talking about. He viewed that concept just as it was an adaptation by the Prophet, of the existing morays and folkways that has existed for thousands of years, prior to the existence of that illiterate goat herder long ago, who received his visions, in the mountains while tending to his goats. Islam simply adopted the habits that existed, as they marched their merry way towards conquest of nearby lands. They did one good thing in the mind of Montero, limiting the number of wives a man could have to four. After all, how many wives did King David possess, or his son King Solomon have?

Montero had little time for women, much less allow someone so inferior to share his bed and his secrets, except for the basest of his instincts to be periodically expunged. No, he'd endured the propaganda and the stupidity and back biting of those who promoted Jihad, as a way to gain revenge for what the Serbian thugs had done to his family long ago in Bosnia Herzegovina. He'd traveled a long journey to that end and in his mind the journey was not completed by a long shot. Although his hatred for the infidel had known no limits, this pilgrimage he'd traveled, had taught him many things other than the skills he'd acquired, mostly patience, endurance, humility and control of one's self. With any luck, he'd find a way out of this wretched country and make his way back to Bosnia, to hunt down and kill the Serbian vermin that destroyed those he loved long ago in the name of Ethnic Cleansing.

His daily prayers to Allah the merciful were directed now exclusively to that end. Any impediment towards that end would meet with Allah's wrath and Montero would be the instrument of that destruction.

His prayers concluded, he went to the kitchen counter and picked up the letter from Salaam, opening it. The news after the contents decoding, was what he wanted. He was to make his way to St. Louis and to another private postal facility where a completely new set of documents and money was waiting. Then he was to make his way to Tampa Florida where he would meet an Imam for tickets on a Travel Cruise to Kingston Jamaica. There he could meet a trustworthy Rastafarian, where for a price, could book him on a flight to Rome. From there it would be simple to hire a car and travel back to Sarajevo where additional work awaited.

His heart sang in rejoicing. For this phase of his own private Jihad would be over and now he could strike terror deep into the heart of the Serbs. They would learn to fear the night, before he was through.

But he thought, since Allah was clearly with him as he'd been all along, perhaps there was one final thing he could accomplish before he shook the dust from this wretched land. But what? He would take several days in silent repose and consider the matter. When concluded, he could depart in the dead of night of steady driving and be out of Texas in a matter of hours, crossing the state line into Arkansas by midnight and into Missouri by dawn the next day and into St. Louis by noon, then some eighteen hours of driving before he arrived at Tampa, his future assured. Of course the local Imam in Tampa would have to disappear, but that was of no consequence.

But what final thing could he do, before departing Houston? He would pray on the matter repeatedly. For he had faith that Allah would visit him in his dreams. He always had done so before. Gradually he started to have his dreams once again after a brief interlude, but they were unorganized and their message obfuscated from clarity. He began taking long naps in the afternoon, just as old people often do. He reasoned that whatever Allah had in store for him would take strength and endurance, so the afternoon interludes went directly to that effect. After about a week of eating in so much he noticed the local TV and Radio stations ran news reports of Mike Montero and his alleged activities less and less. With time would arrive a waning of interest of the infidel's short attention spans. Time was their enemy not his. After all he's changed his appearance enough over the last ten days to befuddle the average man. Cut his long hair short, had enough growth of his neatly trimmed goatee and had bought some several pair of cheap low optic glasses, with varying rim styled from the local Dollar store.

He yearned for savory Chinese Food, rather than the endless cheap Convenience store offerings he'd endured over the period. The Chinese Buffet was only a mile away and he would venture forth at Five PM during the rush hour traffic. Tail end of the police shift change he reasoned and rush hour traffic would be sufficient to shroud him from observant eyes.

Everyone so much in a hurry to get home after a hard day. True to his reasoning, he encountered no patrol cars en route to his much anticipated evening meal.

He'd not eaten the entire day in anticipation if the culinary delights that awaited, subsisting on the original pot of coffee brewed at six AM. After going through the buffet he sat down and removed the wooden chop sticks from their paper container. When he first started eating at Chinese Restaurants, he shied away from attempting utilization of Chop Sticks, eventually trying them out with less than desirable results, but after a month of weekly attempts he gradually developed the skills necessary to get the morsels into his mouth rather than his lap. The Won Ton soup was another matter. Even the Oriental apostate's used a spoon. The trick was to lessen the trip from the plate to one's mouth. He wondered briefly how the high born Geisha and the Samurai of old mastered the trick of plucking from a bowl of rice with two simple sticks and feeding another from across a table.

No doubt endless practice he reasoned. His current level of adeptness was sufficient, he concluded.

The food was indeed wonderful by any culinary measure, that he made a second trip to the buffet table. A leisurely hour later, as he was finishing, he wondered whether or not should The Universal Caliphate become a reality, would Oriental food in all of its forms be acceptable to Islamic laws of cleanliness, a later derivation from the Jewish Kosher laws. There would be this everlasting problem with pork, shell fish and all of its derivations.

He had developed this weekly craving for sweet and sour pork, knowing full well it conflicted with Islamic doctrine. He'd mentioned it in his daily prayer from time to time, as often as he mentioned his periodic visits to Men's Clubs to recruit some willing whore for an evening of complete exchange of bodily fluids at the going rate of exchange. A man did have his occasional biologic needs that had to be satiated and he was certain that with all he'd accomplished in the name of Allah the merciful, exceptions into the kingdom of heaven would be granted with little fuss or bother.

Then of course, there was the obligatory fortune cookie at the end of every meal. Hiseducation level and discipline forsook any adherence to the concept of fortune cookies, for he knew they were simply random sayings generated by a computerized library of composures. As far as the lucky numbers were concerned, again randomly generated by a computer and printed on the reverse side of every fortune message.

As he cracked open the fortune cookie, he wondered what his faux future would read. But the thin, half inch by three inch strip of paper was blank as was the other side of paper. He'd never seen that before. Never even heard of that before. He absently put the blank strip of paper in his pocket, rummaged in his pocket for a tip, then went to the cashier, paid his bill and left, thinking not a thing about it.

On his way back to his rented patio home, he drove past a random half dozen County Sheriff and Constable vehicles on patrol now the evening rush hour traffic was thinning out. One of which was clearly behind him as he drove and eventually beside him as the both stopped for a light. The officer never gave him even the first glance as the light turned green and the officer quickly accelerated, turning on his lights and siren apparently being called to some life of death event down the road somewhere.

Mike felt as if the hand of god was again shielding him from the vision of those who were seeking him. His previous 'faith' in Allah had been true and constant over the years, gradually evolving into the certain 'confidence', that Allah was smiling and that all he'd done was in the name of Allah the merciful. His protection from his enemies, his stunting of their senses, was all part of the continuing plan. His cause was righteous, his faith unshakable, his pathway cleared of every obstacle.

A few days later he would revisit the two storage warehouses, north of his current location. The first one held his cache of weapons and munitions and the second, right in the next space contained his prize possession above all things. An early seventies hand made Ford Pantera, two seater sports car.

He'd had the presence of mind to cut through the connecting metal walls that separated the two spaces, installing a single door between them.

Stripped of all creature comforts save two seats, an FM radio and a police scanner, the car was built for two things, speed and maneuverability. The only time he drove it was at night along the back roads of the county and the freeway. The only mechanic he trusted to lay hands on the vehicle being a simple Korean man who knew little English, who tuned the normally aspirated big Ford engine twice a year to such a degree it's full race cam engine, had little or no vibration during idle speed. Having proved itself several times during the endurance races at Sebring and Lemans over the years, he was confident that no vehicle possessed by the Highway Patrol could ever hope to match his speed or maneuverability on any of the local roadways. This was to be his grand getaway car, to St. Louis and beyond.

He'd had installed two additional twelve gallon petrol tanks engine, crafted to the vehicles sparsely spaced undercarriage, sufficient to carry him a very long way between fuel stops. It was too bad the vehicle would have to be abandoned after his departure from Tampa. He loved that vehicle, but he loved something else far greater.

The days of waiting after reaching out to Nestor Magellan were nerve wracking to every member of the FBI task force. They knew the man was still in town for the time being at least. It was easy to figure the man had changed his appearance, but to what? As news reports became less frequent, with no hurriedly flashy bulletins revealing breaking news, it seemed like most of the initial enthusiasm gradually diminished. Now everything seemed in slow motion. Nothing to report. Nothing to inform.

At the end of a week of futile searches and nonstop investigations, the local's law enforcement entities began to gradually scale back their manpower contributions to the task force. After all, a host of investigations had been stopped in mid-stream and had to be resumed. Both Jaeger and Agent Preston Bergdorf were in agreement that the Terrorist Montero may well still be in town lying low for the moment, but had scant indication other than a week old sighting of a visit to a postal box. As Jaeger and Bergdorf were looking out of the window at the City, discussing the case, Agent Hoffmeister came over to them asking if any new information surfaced regarding their efforts. Discovering that all current avenues of investigation were bearing no fruit, he mildly admonished them for not putting in enough effort. As soon as the words left his mouth, he apologized, for he knew as well as anyone, the needle in a very large haystack situation they were involved with.

Normally this agency relied on the mistakes of those they pursued, or in informant information to apprehend their quarry. Yet their quarry was not about to yield to error, being the clever and industrious soul he was, nor was any actionable information surfacing.

"We've just got to be patient a while longer", was Bergdorf's rejoinder. "I just know the man's still in the area. I can feel it in my bones. A little more time and patience is called for. We're hunting a very clever bunny"!

"I've got a report to write to Washington and I've nothing to tell them", said Hoffmeister testily. "And as to your feelings quotient, feelings are for cows and women"!

As he walked over towards another group of agents to vent upon,

Jaegers cell phone rang and on the other end was Nestor Magellan calling from the Continent. "Mon Ami", he began, "Do you have a pen and paper handy"?

Scrambling to reach a desk he commandeered a paper and a pen saying, "Nestor, what do you have for us"? He put the phone on speaker with agents Bergdorf and Hoffmeister joining in to listen quietly.

"Write this name down, BESLANBUJOVIC, pronounced Beslan Bujovich, the 'ch' is important in the pronunciation of the cognomen, for it indicates a Muslim origin, somewhere in the past history of the family. I am faxing to you what little I've discovered about your quarry. Yet I'll briefly tell you the high points. He matriculated at a Serbian University in Belgrade, specializing in Mechanical Engineering, obtaining a Master's degree in that discipline in just under four years with the highest marks. At that time he barely made it out of Belgrade alive, just ahead of some purists that were determined to rid all of the former Yugoslavia of ethnic infidels, namely suspected of Muslim origin or sympathies. Apparently something horrible happened to his entire family, shortly after he arrived back in Sarajevo, his point of origin. Shortly thereafter he joined the Bosnian partisans in the street fighting to capture the Capital of Bosnia/ Herzegovina. Then he somehow evolved into a firearms and munitions expert, and a master sniper, credited with some several hundred confirmed kills, many of which were of Serbian snipers in an urban setting. There's a bit more but I'll let you read the faxed report and make your own determination. I trust that is helpful Mon Ami"?

"My friend, you've described this guy right down to the ground. I thank you for this effort and after all this is done I'll fly over and take you to dinner anywhere you choose"!

"One thing more, Mon Ami" said Magellan. "Take great care with this man his instincts are reported to that of a wolf on the hunt"!

"Thanks for the heads up. We've gathered that already, but a reminder is always important. See ya"! Everyone ran to the fax machine and Hoffmeister called all of the unit heads into an immediate meetings and announced a break in the investigation. Apparently there was a twenty year or so old grainy photo of their quarry along with a three page dossier of the man Beslan Bujovic, AKA, Mike Montero. Copies of the dossier were hurriedly printed and distributed to everyone.

Hoffmeister read dossier to those assembled as they followed along with their own copies, finishing up with, "People, we now have a better idea what this guy is all about and what he's capable of, any questions or comments"?

Jaeger then raised his hand to speak. "Yes, Mr. Jaeger, you have a question or comment"? Rising, Jaeger began, "The man I got this information from, I'd trust with my life, as he would with me. If this man says the sun will rise in the west tomorrow, bet he knows something. I've met this man who we now know as "Bujovic" and I just have to tell ya, he's a pro of the first order. Guys like this will not spook easily but everyone has a weakness. He's been ahead of us every step of the way and he's gotta be laughing right now. So given his mind set is that he's dealing with a bunch of whatnot's, let's surprise him. We need to flush the quail from its nest and get it up in the air"!

"What are you suggesting Mr. Jaeger", asked Hoffmeister?

"We have the media all over us, for a lack of progress, so let's do a little selective media release, with an well edited release of his real name and his pictures then, as well as now, and post an hour long BOLO on every radio and TV station in the surrounding area, for two days. Freeway signs, Toll Road flashers, etcetera. If this guy has a little good bye present to leave before he makes tracks out of this area, it should spook him enough to abandon those plans and depart. Now when he finally leaves, expect the optimal time to be during afternoon rush hour traffic where he could hide in plain sight"!

"How do you come by an afternoon exit", asked Hoffmeister?

"Because that's exactly what I'd do if I were him"!

"The man has a point Brian", said Agent Bergdorf!

"Exactly! People we'll now break up and Agent DeSoto, call your media contacts and get them over here pronto. Agent Tharp, make the calls around to your folks in the local law enforcement community. We're going to need more man power"!

Montero arrived back at his quarters after the local evening televised news cast, his belly full from the Chinese Buffet, took a shower and went to bed early, forgoing his evening entertainment. He was eager to embrace sleep, where he was certain the final problems would be ironed out in his dream state by Allah, the most beneficent and merciful. He engaged in his evening prayers with an ardor he'd not experienced in quite a while. Tears came to his face as he exhorted Allah for the solution to his plans. Allah the most merciful, had always shown him the true path before and would once again he was sure, Allah, the most powerful, saw clearly deep into the heart of his most loyal disciples and warriors, who never evaded their duty in advancing the Jihad against the Kuffaar. As it was in the beginning, the present and in the future Allah would reign supreme over all mankind.

As his head hit the pillow for the rest he would need the coming day, sleep gradually overtook him. As he gradually drifted off, he recalled a verse he'd read from some book of Islamic prose that may have attributed to the meanderings of the prophet in his latter

Year's when a group of young acolyte's sat adoringly at the prophet's feet while attending him amongst his sheep up in the hills, by the camp fire. When asked what the future held in store for the followers of the prophet, Mahomet was to have thought a moment before saying, "None can portend the future. Not even the angels in heaven. Only Allah, the beneficent and most merciful who sees all can say. But he tells us this that 'Each man's fate is writ large in the sands, at his moment of birth'. Thus trust in the will of Allah, for he will reveal all to the most faithful"!

As Beslan nestled in the comfortable bed, the nightly local news reports from all local channels, revealed the original identity of the one sought by the Federal Government. Devoting an entire half hour of the broadcast in an area wide alert regarding one Beslan Bujovic and all of his known pictures and alias's. It was shown during the evening and the ten PM newscasts without commercial interruption, as a government service. The message was that he was still believed to be in the area, armed and extremely dangerous. The Federal Government pulling out all of the stops and offering a million dollar reward for any information leading to the apprehension and conviction of the subject. The following morning it was once again shown, this time with the normal commercial breaks, yet now was briefly inserted at the top of every hour for sixty seconds.

Every radio station in the area followed suit some devoting their entire schedule of both AM and FM broadcasting schedules to the subject.

Of course the predictable flood of crank calls and misinformation overwhelmed every media station, Police, Sheriff and Constable Precinct in the multi county metro area as well, as the local FBI office. Sandwiched in between all of those calls was a little old lady who had slowly recognized the subject's face, by one of the renderings that was published. Since the man she leased her patio home to, a little over a week ago wore wraparound sunglasses and a the beginnings of a small goatee and paid cash in advance, somehow the least likely of all photos and facial renderings by police artists finally bore fruit. The more she thought about it and besieged by every TV and Radio station she looked at every telecast, hour after hour before the certainty of it all became clear. She had leased one of her properties to this killer and she began to fear for her life. She dressed and called up the Sheriff's Department, then the City of Houston, then the local Constables office, but at every turn the lines were busy. She finally looked up the local FBI, number but their lines were busy too.

Tired from all that effort, she just sat there watching the television. She tried to go to sleep, but sleep would not arrive. So there she sat for an entire day and far into the evening, wondering just what to do. Finally she went to sleep shortly after midnight, but woke up after only three hours unable to sleep. She then decided there was only one thing to do and drive into town to FBI headquarters. She found a parking space nearby around six AM and joined the line of people waiting for the office to officially open. After two hours of waiting in line, she suddenly felt faint realizing she'd failed to eat breakfast and take her medication. Try as she might, she suddenly fainted. Waking up in the emergency ward of a nearby hospital. After she'd been stabilized, she grabbed one of the doctors and pleaded with him to contact the locale FBI office and get through somehow, for it was an emergency and told the doctor why.

He eventually got through to one of the Agents, who drove over to interview the patient in depth. By noon the old lady had recovered sufficiently to be coherent as the local Federal Agent conducted his interview, eventually getting Agent Bergdorf on the line to direct the interview via speaker phone on his cell line. He instructed the agent at the hospital to remain in place by the lady's side until re-contacted. All through that night Montero tossed and turned, never quite waking up, yet never drifting into that deep REM sleep that was required to achieve the ideal dream state. Something blocked that somnambulistic deep level, something unknown. Unconsciously Montero at some level, tried to reach out to the Prophet, in his sleep and he saw him in the far distance as a shadow in the background. Of course he'd never looked upon the Prophet in his dreams, for that would be blasphemy and one never heard the Prophet as one would hear another mortal and of course Allah was in Heaven on High. One simply felt the message of the Prophet in ones dreams. Only the mentally afflicted actually heard the "Voices", and they were of the 'Jinnah', the unclean spirits of the underworld.

Montero in his state of unconsciousness, reached out to the Prophet as he never had to before asking for his guidance in his furthering of Jihad, but heard nothing in return. Finally he saw the dim shadowy figure turn his back and felt the message filter into his being, 'My son, each man's fate is writ large, in the sands of time at his moment of birth'. Then the shadowy figure slowly dissipated from view.

Montero tossed and turned in his bed as never before, wanting to wake up but remaining asleep. Finally at six thirty in the morning he fell out of bed and groggily got to his feet and padded into the kitchen to make his early morning coffee. He then turned on the Television set while the coffee was brewing and went into the bathroom to take his early morning shower. While he was taking the hot shower trying to shake the rigors of sleep from his mind, the newscast came on that revealed, his true identity for everyone to see. But the news cast was only for five minutes and by the time he emerged from the shower, the newscast had finished, until the top of the hour arrived.

He dressed and went to the coffee maker and savored the morning's first cup of coffee and watched the news for any sign of the hunt the Federal and Local authorities had for him. As he watched the early morning National newscast, with little interest, he worried about the previous night's dream message. He thought about it and eventually the occurrence made itself clear, especially the part where that which was in the shadows turned his back and mentioned the verse equating each man's fate with the drifting sands. His mind was in a deep quandary as to what that meant. Never before had the Prophet left such an ambiguous message.

He turned down the volume and decided to drop to his knees and engage in his morning prayers. Somehow his beseeching of the Prophet would bring things back into better focus, they always had before. He muted the volume and commenced his ritual. When he was concluded he got up and sat on the couch and turned on the volume, to receive his local morning newscast. He was greeted by the photo of himself long ago and a stream of likenesses and the mention of his name "Beslan Bujovic" and the rapid run through of his bio and accomplishments. His mind reeled as the newscast droned on, revealing him to the world.

When the news cast was over, he turned down the volume, got to his knees and yelled out to the ceiling, "Why"? Then something told him to reach into his pockets and find that sliver of paper that was inside the fortune cookie he'd consumed the night before. As his hand emerged slowly from his pocket it contained the crumpled thin strip of paper. He opened the paper, there it was. Nothing printed on either side. It wasn't a bad dream, because there is no message for someone that has no future. Then the message in his dream became clear.

The Prophet wasn't going to waste time on someone, Allah had deemed expendable. Of course he'd turned his back, leaving the import of his message crystal clear, the shifting sands writ large each man's fate at the moment of birth, but that fate could take many directions, just as the sands could drift first this way and then another. The sands of the hourglass were running their course. Time was running out at long last. Soon his burdens would be lifted, but not before he left one final glorious surprise.

For the very first time since his teenage years back in Yugoslavia, he felt fear. Not necessarily fear of his fellow man but fear of failure.

Somewhere in the background was someone who would stand in the way and that someone must be obliterated at all costs. He would know that man when he saw him.

He turned off the television and made ready to depart. Old habits die hard as he mindlessly went through the house, wiping all signs of fingerprints from view. He spent an entire hour cleaning and going over any where he might have touched the last several days.

Then he threw his few dirty clothes in the washing machine and eventually the drier. While waiting for the machines to do their work, he made another cup of coffee and turned the television set back on as a way to kill time prior to his departure. He would leave this place as soon as possible and go to the storage facility. He looked at his gym back full of garnered funds and the other back with which he'd put his few clothes, currently being washed and all else would be left in place. He went over in his mind what he would retrieve once he arrived at the storage facility, mostly several firearms and assorted munitions like grenades. Of course he would have to change vehicles, and take the Ford Pantera to a filling station down the street for a complete fuel fill up. Then he planned to wait until late afternoon drive time before emerging from the area heading north to St. Louis for the papers that lead back to his old life. He almost couldn't wait until he had the Pantera out on the roads at night. Of course he'd stay off the Interstates and travel the secondary roads. He made it a point to leave all of the electronic devices behind except for the Police Scanner in his Pantera.

Now he eagerly changed the channels to see if any nationwide BOLO was in effect and finding none was relieved as he continued to watch the television for any further word.

The downtown FBI headquarters were now in a state of high alert as a SWAT team was being hastily being assembled at lunch time. One of his agents was hurriedly assembling the paperwork to present to a Federal Judge for an arrest warrant, while the others were quietly being assembled to the drive north.

As the others drove off towards the subject's location, Jaeger decided to follow in his own vehicle, as strictly an observer. This was the Federals show now and all he could do was watch. His laundry finally finished, Beslan Bujovic quickly folded his clothes and crammed them in his bag saying over and over, my name is now Beslan Bujovic over and over. He'd not used that name for quite a while and at first it felt rather strange, almost an out of body experience, but with each repetition, he finally grew back into the name of his youth. He loaded everything he was going to take into his used car and went back into the house. At first he was going to turn off the television, but thought better of it, turning up the volume as if someone was still there. He locked the door, went to his car, started it and punched the button of the automatic garage door opener, backed his car out of the driveway, hit the door up button and as the garage door slowly closed sealing off the property, he slowlydrove off down the street. At the very moment Beslan drove off, the task force vehicles drove out of their buildings parking garage, hurrying out to the suburbs and the subject's residence. They would miss him by a scant half hour. Once again he was a step ahead of them. The storage facility was a five mile drive from the location, as Beslan leisurely drove down the street. A mile before he arrived, he noticed a Service Station where he would take his Ford Pantera for a complete fill up of Petrol. He stopped at a fast food restaurant and went through the drive through and brought his lunch with him to the storage facility. There, after opening up the overhead door that housed his Pantera, he sat down inside the vehicle and took his time enjoying the food. It might be quite a while before he had another chance to refill his stomach.

The Task Force surrounded the house, awaiting any indication from those downtown, that an arrest warrant was approved. Everyone was watching their wristwatches as time crawled by slowly. As they knew, few judges at any level of juris prudence allowed themselves to be hurried in making a decision, no matter how many times one reminded them of that old legal aphorism, "Time is of the essence". An hour after the Task Force arrived and was in place, the word finally arrived. The warrant was approved and was on the way. Some of the Task Force grumbled to allow the assault to proceed, before children started to arrive home from school, but Agent Hoffmeister, ever a stickler for procedure, gave strict orders that not one single thing was to be initiated without his approval. Thus all were to remain in place until the warrant arrived in person.

Jaeger stood in place, behind a tree a half block down the heavily tree shrouded street with Agent Bergdorf. After all, Jaeger was simply an observer and was allowed the courtesy to tag along, more for the purpose of identifying the subject after apprehension. His weapon was in his car down the street and around the corner. Thus everyone waited the arrival of the paperwork.

Finally the agent arrived from down town with the fully executed Arrest Warrant, delivering it to Agent Hoffmeister, who quickly read the warrant, line by line before releasing the Task Force to scale the brick walls that surrounded the residence. As the agents surrounded the structure, one of them could hear the television program from inside the home and all assumed that someone must be inside, regardless of the fact that no vehicle was occupying the carport. Two agents were flanking the side sliding glass patio entrance, where the inside blinds we're clearly drawn, while two others were at the front door. No one could see inside for all of the blinds were drawn. At a given signal, the wooden front door was breached and a flash bang grenade was tossed inside, quickly followed by the two agents from the front while the others stood their ground outside every window. Quickly five other agents flooded the residence clearing each room in turn and as the sliding glass door was opened, to let out the smoke, one of the agents came running with a fire extinguisher to put out the small fire that was started by the flash bang device.

The residence secured, Bergdorf and Jaeger ran to the house as everyone else milled around. Clearly someone was recently occupying the residence and everyone knew in their bones the subject if their manhunt was the one. Everyone looked at Brian Hoffmeister in silence, for he was the one who was in charge of the task force and the bird had flown the coop once again, ahead of his pursuers. Forensic technicians were called in to give the place a top to bottom examination.

Jaeger was overheard saying to Preston Bergdorf, the behaviorist, "A complete waste of time Preston. Our boy's a pro and the place'll be clean.

He's somewhere on the road most likely"! "Goddammit Mr. Jaeger, you're here as a courtesy, I'll remind you and as of now that courtesy is rescinded. Your presence is no longer welcome", Agent Hoffmeister fumed, approaching Jaeger up close and personal.

"You need to start brushing your teeth more often Hoffmeister, your breath smells so bad it'd knock a buzzard off a shit wagon. Now I'm gonna give you till the count of three, to Get your mug out of my face, unless you want to go back to Washington in little pieces", growled Jaeger.

Two agents got between the parties and forced Hoffmeister to retreat, while Jaeger turned around and made for the door passing Agent Preston Bergdorf saying as he shook hands, "Nice working with you Preston, but its time I went to the house. Besides my car is almost out of gas and needs a fill up. Good luck in catching that fella"!

As Jaeger made his way back to his car, he noticed a block away the Sheriff's Department had cordoned off the entire area, just in time to prevent the horde of school children from reaching their respective houses. As he passed a crowd of young children complaining to the Sheriff's Deputy he gathered them around saying, "Now kids, listen to the officer here. The FBI is trying to run down a very dangerous man. Just be a little patient and I'm sure the officer here will try to let y'all get home as soon as he can"!

"So what happened inside", asked the Sheriff's Deputy?

"We missed him and I'm going to the house. Their doing their due diligence but the danger has passed. You might want to get someone on the horn to verify that, so these kids can get home"!

As Jaeger got to his car, he noticed several of the area media's, on the scene trucks approaching. They'd be pissed they missed the non-event but that was just too bad. The last thing this or any neighborhood would need is a full bore, shoot out. Whoever ran this Bujovic to the ground could expect every bit of that and then some.

As Jaeger started the big Ford, he noted his fuel gauge and saw the dial hugging the empty line. There was a Race Track service station several miles down the street and he'd fill up there.

It was a typical South Texas Indian summer day, warm and humid.

Mother Nature's last shot at giving Houston one last taste of summer before the short winter set in sometime after the first of the year. Tomorrow was Election Day and everyone was going to vote, while this Bujovic fella was enroute to somewhere else. He would have liked to have been there when the guy was rounded up and have the satisfaction to look into his eyes and have him know that Jaeger was the one who brought him down. But the more he thought about it, the less likely this guy was going to be caught by anyone, must lest be captured alive.

As he drove into the Race Track station he parked by a pump, took out his credit card and went through the procedure at the pump. Out of the corner of his eye he noticed a flashy looking exotic yellow Ford Pantera sitting at the far pump. 'Talk about your standard American built sports cars', he thought, 'Other than a Shelby Cobra, the Pantera Ford was probably the least practical car one could own. Not exactly the kind of vehicle one drove to the Wal-Mart and back for ones vittles'.

As he pushed the 93 Octane button on the pumps selector, he noticed a man approach the Pantera from the inside of the service station. As he had his head down and his sunglasses on he put the nozzle into the tank and started to pump the gas. The service station had four lanes of pumps, with Jaeger and his Ford at one end and the Pantera at the far end of the lane of pumps. Something told Jaeger to keep his eyes on the Pantera and the man who approached with wraparound sunglasses. As the man addressed his pump, he brought down his sunglasses briefly to see the pump selection of octane grades, then making his selection readjusted his glasses as he started to fill his tank.

Jaeger couldn't believe his eyes. There not thirty yards away was this Beslan Bujovic, plain as day. His attention was towards filling the tank of his Pantera as his back was turned Towards Jaeger. Jaeger briefly toyed with the idea of approaching him straight up while his back was turned, but thought better of it. Yes his back was towards Jaeger but all he had to do was turn around and he might be armed. Good bet that he was armed, while Jaegers weapon was in the back seat, a vintage single action Colt .45 fully loaded, but secured in a pistol bag. Then there was the issue of a possible gunfight at a service station and the collateral damage. No, Jaeger would complete his fill up and try and follow the guy. He still had his cell phone, with him. Perhaps in route he could call up the posse' and try and corner him someplace, before things to too much out of hand.

The very last thing he wanted to do was get into a "Bullet" style chase, for while his big old Ford Galaxie was reengineered from the ground up at great expense and fast and maneuverable as a car that size could be, it was no match for a Ford Pantera on any back road. Sure it was Autobahn worthy top end, but if this guy was a skilled driver Jaeger would be hard pressed to keep up with him. Besides, he'd seen the movie many times and he knew exactly how Detective Bullet's car ended up. Food for the junk yard. He'd avoid that at almost any cost, yet he just couldn't let this guy get away. If it cost him his car so be it.

Jaegers tank filled, he replaced the nozzle back on the pump and got into his car and sat still. Bujovic while looking around periodically had not looked behind him, so perhaps he knew nothing of Jaeger being onto him. Time to be patient, time to be alert, his eyes on Bujovics every move, he reached into his back seat and brought his weapons pouch onto the front seat. Had he any inkling he'd be in this predicament he'd have brought along something more appropriate, like his Ruger .357 revolver with a half dozen speed loaders. But dumb as that here was the old Colt and he would have to make do.

Bujovic completed his fill up got in his car and slowly drove off, without once turning his head in Jaegers direction as Jaeger brought the engine of the big Ford to life, he placed it in gear and drove off, careful to keep the yellow Pantera in sight even though it was almost a quarter mile ahead. Soon the rush hour traffic would start to build and that would be impossible. He got on the cell phone and pressed the speed dial trying to get through to the local FBI office, but the lines were all tied up. Jaeger then placed the big Colt in his waste band and tried the speed dial again, but with the same results. Driving north on the esplanaded street he was careful to stay in the right hand lane, while the Pantera was in the left hand lane, keeping the same approximate distance between them. In the process he had to slow down and run a red light weaving his way between cross traffic amidst honking vehicles, but there the Pantera was now an eighth of a mile ahead, signaling a left hand turn waiting for passing traffic as Jaeger drove right past him, still pressing the speed dial button, while keeping pace with the other cars. Sure would've been nice for a local cop to be passing by as he'd run that last light. Where were the cops when ya really needed them?

Keeping the Pantera still in sight through his rear view mirror, he noted that it was a storage rental facility Bujovic was entering and soon as he could, Jaeger made an immediate Uturn around the esplanade and raced back to the entrance of the Self-Storage facility as the yellow Pantera disappeared into the interior of the cluster of buildings and the gate came down.

He quickly stopped the Ford at the gate, put the gear in neutral and applied the emergency brake and ran inside the office. The attendant was on the phone with someone as Jaeger yelled, "Hang up the phone right now"!

The attendant not about to comply with the demands of a total stranger started to reach in his desk as Jaeger jumped over the counter knocking the man to the floor and, the gun in His hand flying to the other end of the office. He grabbed the phone and dialed 911, and finding that busy hung up. As the man groggily tried to rise, Jaeger ran to where the small revolver had come to rest and opened the receiver and dropped the shells on the floor then returned to the man dragging him to his seat. He held the man's head in both hands saying, "Pay attention now and there might be a reward coming your way"!"The man that just came through your gate is the terrorist the FBI has been looking for as well as all the cops. I've been trying to call the FBI office but the lines are busy. There's a whole shit load of Feds not five miles away that assaulted a house but they missed him.

Now you're gonna open the gate right now and call 911, tell them there's a robbery in progress and that a patrol man is under fire. I'm going onto your property, to try and put a hold on the guy till the cops arrive. Now open the fucking gate"!

The clerk still groggy from the collision reached out for the button that raised the gate as Jaeger ran to his car calling out behind him, "Remember call 911". While he was in the office, he caught sight of a map of layout of the buildings, which ran parallel to the length of the ten acre property. He jumped into his car and sped through the gate as it swung upwards, barely clearing the Fords roof. Coming to his first group of buildings he could see the entire length of the property there was no vehicle parked, so he turned left and slowly moved forward as his car stopped at every intersection, where he could see down the long rows of metal buildings. At the second intersection he saw a large panel truck with several people unloading furniture into a storage unit, moving on he slowly passed several alleyways, pausing briefly at each intersection and seeing no vehicles parked moved on. At the fifth intersection as he moved forward, he glanced to his right and saw a glimpse of a bright yellow sports car about a hundred yards down the long alleyway. He moved past the intersection and put the Ford in neutral, engaging the parking brake and left the engine running. He quickly grabbed several handfuls of shells cramming them into his pocket and the vintage Colt revolver and got out of the car. As he peered around the corner he saw the Pantera Ford sitting in front of an open storage unit with the door up, about a hundred yards down the long alleyway. He was about to move forward when he saw Bujovic emerge with two large bags of something and place them into the lone passenger side of the car, turning away from Jaegers direction and disappear back into the facility. Jaeger noticed forty yards down the alleyway an insert in the building's exterior that housed air conditioning compressors and quickly ran to than spot, coming to a quick halt and pressing himself between the humming compressors and the side of the metal building. Bujovic emerged once again, this time with a small wooden box, similar to what munitions might be placed in and placed it inside the passenger side of the vehicle. As he emerged from the vehicle, he rose fully erect and raised both arms skyward as if to stretch, when Jaeger stepped out from the building insert and yelled, "Freeze Bujovic! Don't move a muscle! Keep your hands up and turn very slowly to your left"! As Jaeger stood there with his big Colt zeroed in on his quarry, the pistol at full cock in a two handed firing grip, Bujovic slowly turned to see what confronted him. As he came to rest, Bulovic peered over the top of his wraparound sunglasses to get a better look at his antagonist. Jaeger slightly moved his aim towards Bujovics left, towards the buildings entrance, figuring that if he was to make a move it would be towards the building's interior. He had a hair trigger on the Colt, yet he knew that at forty yards he'd have to lead him some bit.

"Why do you look familiar to me", yelled Bujovic?

"We met a while back"!

"I usually have a good recollection for faces and your face is not registering"!

"We spent a morning at the firing range, about a year or so ago"!

"Ah yes, now I remember! That was in another life and as I recall I out shot you. Is that what you're here about"!

"Call it what you want Bujovic, I'm looking at a mass murderer"!

"You keep calling me Bujovic as if you know me. Are you the one that has turned my life upside down"?

"Seems so pal"!

"So what do we do now, my friend"?

"We wait for John Law to arrive"!

"By the way they've been acting lately it seems that they'll be late once again, don't you agree"?

"Could be but we'll wait however long it takes"!

"I'm sorry but I've an important appointment", he said swiftly moving to his left just as Jaeger fired the Colt. Even with the lead on his aim, Jaeger was a hair too slow, the bullet grazing Bujovics right shoulder sufficient to tear a long strip of fabric and skin from his shoulder causing pain but not enough to immobilize him. He quickly grabbed a grenade from the box just inside the door, tearing out the safety pin and flipping it around the corner in Jaegers direction. The entire movement took two seconds and Jaeger quickly ducked back into the buildings recession as the grenade came his way, followed quickly by another, then another and another in rapid succession. The grenades exploded ten yards ahead of Jaeger, with the shrapnel, tearing jagged holes in the thin aluminum buildings outer fabric and ricocheting in all directions, some of which found their random way towards Jaeger, leaving him with a number of superficial wounds.

Bujovic grabbed several more grenades and quickly emerged from his shelter, lobbing them one at a time towards his antagonist as he ran to his car, jumping inside and firing up the engine, throwing the gearshift in gear and burning rubber as the Pantera's engine propelled the vehicle down the alleyway in a weaving manner.

Hearing the Pantera's engine come to life, Jaeger stuck his head around the corner, ducking quickly back as yet another grenade landed just five yards away, exploding and sending more shrapnel coming his way. The Pantera Ford now tearing down the alleyway, Jaeger again jumped out from behind the building and seeing the fleeing yellow Pantera careening down between the buildings, took two carefully aimed shots at the car, then turned and ran back to his own car, throwing it in gear and lurching forward, taking the first right turn and paralleling his way towards the rear of the property. While, he was repeating the phrase, "Oh shit", over and over, he was quickly trying to think if there was a back exit on the premises. While driving very fast he was mindful of the fact that perhaps at some point he might be driving right into an ambush like some stupid rookie, yet as he emerged from between the buildings, he saw the yellow Pantera at the rear gate held up by the agonizingly slow upward motion of the metal gate.

Jaeger had a hundred yards of gravel to cross, deciding that if he ever caught this guy at the gate, he'd ram the Pantera and keep his pedal to the metal, sacrificing his precious relic, but as the gate rose, just sufficiently to clear the low slung Pantera, it rocketed forward onto one of the back streets, making a skidding hard left, tires screaming in a Smoky protest as they gained traction and threw the vehicle forward, through the back streets of suburban Houston, through the maze of newly constructed apartment projects. Jaegers Ford barely came under the still rising gate as he drifted the big car sideways to the left, tires screaming in protest of the chase that was under way.

Five minutes after the first grenade explode, the first of several County Patrol cars arrived at the storage facility. It took the befuddled clerk some time before the entrance gate rose and he haltingly told them what had happened. As a few of the county vehicles made their way into the bowels of the vast storage facility, they came across the site of the explosions and while one of the vehicles stayed behind at that location, the others followed the tire marks to the rear of the property, radioing the Senior patrolman in the office to direct the clerk to open the rear gate so they could pursue. "Goddammit, that's what I've been tryin' to say all along. This big guy that roughed me up, me said sumpthin' about a terrorist and an FBI assault not five miles away. I did what he said, but it wasn't until I heard the explosions that I figured that maybe there was somethin', to what he was yellin' "! Just then a report from a southbound County Patrol car on the Northwest Freeway said there were explosions in the northbound lane and that he was taking a U-turn under the freeway to be in pursuit of a White Ford Sedan pursuing a yellow sports car of an undetermined model at high speed. Minutes later another patrol car stuck on the on ramp access lane echoed that report of the ongoing chase, radioing the lead yellow car was throwing what may be hand grenades on the roadway while weaving in an out of traffic at high speed.

As Bujovic sped out of town he knew he was in a superior vehicle, but it did have its limitations, while Autobahn ready, he had to get off of the Interstate very quickly and onto the back roads, where the road quality would diminish very quickly. He would stand a better chance on the county back roads. On the Interstate there were always radios and road blocks to consider, along with the dreaded overhead helicopters. As he drove through the building traffic seeing the big White Ford in the distance in his rear view mirror, he occasionally reached over into the passenger's seat and removed a grenade, extracting the pin with his teeth and tossing it flipping it behind him as he swiftly changed lanes between vehicles, ever mindful of the forward inertia of his vehicle. The first reports of his chase were now coming through on the police scanner, as he saw a familiar exit to a cross county road that would provide him further opportunities to zig, zag his way into the piney woods of east Texas away from the roadblocks certain to be placed on the main thoroughfares and away from the prying eyes of the overhead choppers. His fuel tank was full of petrol, he had several candy bars in his rucksack, money, weapons, munitions, skill and most important a vehicle that was faster than the wind. His heart sang at the adventure of it all. In future years he would tell and retell the story of how this true believer out witted the infidel repeatedly. In his wake he'd left a trail of destruction with more to come. His little goodbye plan now shelved, for a far greater adventure. He was now convinced that 'The Prophet', turning his back on him in his dream, was nothing more than a test of his eternal fidelity and then when he was on safe ground, 'The Prophet' would return and sing his praise.

He glanced at his rearview mirror, catching a brief glimpse of that big white Ford, barely discernible in the distance changing lanes, then Bujovic weaved in between two Semi Trucks and took the off ramp to the cross county road that headed east, leaving the two Tractor Trailer rigs, to weave into each other causing one of them to jack knife at speed and the other to skid uncontrollably to a cross lane halt stopping all of the vehicles behind Except the big white Ford that worked its way to the far right hand lane, keeping in sight the fleeing yellow Pantera as it flew down the exit ramp and onto the access road. Soon Jaeger's car ran down the very same exit ramp catching a brief glimpse of the yellow car ahead cutting through a gas station to avoid the traffic at the intersection. As he hit the access road, he caught a brief glimpse of flashing lights in the far distance of the access road. As he weaved his way through the gas station he hoped the patrolman was a better than average driver or else he'd end up in one of South Texas's plethora of drainage ditches that flanked the roadways almost everywhere. Come to think of it, he might end up with that very same fate if he wasn't careful. He just couldn't allow that to happen, not since he'd come this far and put in so much effort to bring this guy to heel. It had somehow become very personal all along and deep in his bone marrow he knew, his quarry would never see the insides of a courtroom. It was an option that neither one would allow.

As he emerged from the gaggle of the service station, he saw some one point in an easterly direction as if that where the muy rapido car was heading. Skidding onto the roadway he could see no sign of the car ahead, but for the dust cloud left behind from a very fast car speeding along a dusty Texas blacktop road, Jaeger floored the accelerator, kicking in the full power of twin superchargers, ramming compressed air into twin Holly carburetors that fed a 427 Ford engine that was operating full out. As Jaeger power shifted up through the gears, the ancient vehicle pressed him back in his seat with a vengeance, he never thought possible. Not glancing at his speedometer, since he was going too fast, he prayed that no one would cross the six lane road. He would never be able to react in time, to stop and be fodder for the drainage ditches. Yet after about two miles of straight and level road, following just a trail of dust ahead, he caught a glimpse of yellow in the far distance. He had a little more travel in the depth of his accelerator, yet in fourth and final gear, with the tach reading over 7000 RPM's, and a .270 high speed driving rear axle, he was going faster than rational thought allowed. Yet he appeared to be slowly gaining. Just then he sensed the Pantera down shifting ahead of him and at the last moment a wink of the brake lights as the Pantera turned left and headed north out of Harris County. Jaeger anticipating he'd better break ahead of schedule, went through his down shift scenario, heel and toeing the big Ford into the best short drift he'd ever performed and midway through the corner skid, punched the accelerator driving the beast onto solid blacktop escaping the drainage ditch by inches, once again raced into the secluded overhang of trees shielding anyone overhead from witnessing the life or death duel occurring below. Seeing that he was making far less headway from his pursuer than he anticipated as they raced through the gently winding blacktop roadway through the heavily wooded forest, Bujovic quickly reached over for one his last grenades in the box on the passenger's seat and crammed it between his legs. Quickly downshifting for a side road he knew was coming up, he slowed sufficiently to make a gradual but rapid turn to the east, midway through the turn he grabbed the grenade, pulled the pin with his teeth and tossed it backwards onto the roadway, quickly accelerating.

The grenade took one bounce on the blacktop and given the laws of forward inertia, landed in one of the drainage ditches.

As Jaeger tried to make the right hand turn heading east, he punched the accelerator midway through the turn and felt an ear popping explosion close by. But since the grenade was deep into the drainage ditch, it had little effect on the big Ford that raced past, other than make a very nice fox hole for the critters come winter.

Jaeger quickly took heart as he raced past the blast, reckoning it with his days long ago when he played on the gridiron against those who would do anything to win, no matter what.

Somehow he was gaining on the Pantera, on the back roads, something that shouldn't be. His adversary was clearly a supposedly a skilled driver in a roadworthy vehicle. He sensed something bad was ahead and slowed down just a bit, when the yellow Pantera shot ahead. He quickly down shifted and hit the accelerator and his Ford followed suit. Jaeger gritted his teeth and became one with his vehicle, matching the Pantera at every turn, miraculously gaining ground, through the twists and turns of the back roads. Eventually he came up on Bujovics rear bumper, and as

Bujovic was down shifting his lighter car on the gravelly blacktop of the east Texas back roads, Jaeger's Ford nudged his Pantera's rear bumper just enough to cause the Pantera's tires to lose adhesion to the road, sending it spinning into a drainage ditch as the Ford slid past almost following it in the same way yet recovering just enough to slide to as stop some thirty yards ahead. Jaeger turned off the ignition and looked in his rearview mirror, removing his Colt revolver from his waist band and reloaded the three shells expended from his shoot out at the storage facility and slowly got out of the car.

The Pantera was almost nose deep in the drainage ditch as Jaeger approached, its engine steaming from its exertions and the crash. He placed the big Colt in his waist band. wondering how anyone could've survived that crash. His old Ford had performed wonderfully and he had driven the best he'd ever had in his life. Clearly he had some sort of celestial help along the way, he wondered. He peered into the passenger side of the car and saw the dim outline of Bujovic in the rapidly diminishing light of the forest. He looked done for all slumped over in the drivers' seat, still in his racing seat restraints, bleeding from the forehead. He went around to the driver's side, squatting down and reached over to disconnect the drivers restraints and as he did that and started to reach down to lift Bujovic up, his eyes opened and his right hand suddenly appeared holding a black automatic pistol that stared Jaeger right in the face.

Jaegers face suddenly went pale and his heartbeat raced to keep equilibrium. All of this work and effort, down the drain because of a rookie mistake. Without having to be told Jaeger slowly backed up as Bujovic glared at him at first and then started to smile, as he saw the look of fear in Jaegers eyes. As he slowly and clearly painfully made his way out of the wreckage of his precious car, his eyes never once leaving that of Jaegers, he made he made his way out of the ditch gradually, clearly in great pain.

"You're through Beslan. It's all over" said Jaeger!

"I'm holding the gun on you and you're the one that's telling me, that I'm through"?

"That's right, look at you? You can barely stand erect, your left collar bone must be broken by the way your left arm just hangs there and you've just gotta be in great pain. Even if you get past me, you'll not get far. Hand over the gun and I'll call in an ambulance"!

"I'm holding the gun on you and you're telling me to hand over my gun", asked Bujovic shakily?

"This is the way it's going to be", said Beslan slowly clearly struggling to overcome his pain!"I'm an honorable man no matter what I've done in the name of 'The Prophet', and you will hand over the weapon stuffed in your waist band, then unload everything in my car and transfer it to yours.

I'll be taking your car and will leave you alive to make your way back to where ever you came from. If you're wise, you'll give up your quest for me and live to a ripe old age, giving thanks for my benevolence. I'll have your weapon Now"!

As Jaeger slowly brought his right hand down to the waistband of his trousers, Bujovic clearly weary but still dangerous said, "Stop! You will hand the weapon to me slowly and butt first, do you understand"?

Jaeger nodded his head and his right hand continued its slow journey towards its destiny. Once that Colt was out of his hands his prospects for survival grew dim and that could never happen. He slowly pulled the Colt out from his waist band with his right hand, turning it over in his hand with the left still in the air, his eyes never leaving that of Bujovics. Grasping it slowly by the barrel in an upright position and the barrel facing him, he slowly offered it forward towards Bujovic and as Bujovic reached forward to grasp the weapon, Jaeger flipped the weapon over the barrel now facing Bujovic, his thumb pulling back the hammer at the speed of an eye blink as the big Colt fired right into Bujovics chest knocking him backwards as he pulled his trigger, the barrel being deflected and firing at Jaegers right shoulder tearing off a bit of fabric and skin almost in the very same spot that Jaeger had fired at Bujovic back at the storage warehouse.

As Bujovic fell backwards, Jaegers left hand came down came down and quickly fanned the Colts hammer, firing two more rounds quickly into the man's chest, quicker than an eye blink, causing his hand to release his 9MM Makarov as he lay against the bank of the drainage ditch. Jaeger, ignoring the pain of his wound quickly retrieved the weapon from Bujovic, and then stood over him for a bit watching the man, seeing if he had any more tricks in the offing. He then squatted down beside him and looked straight into his eyes saying, "In case you're wondering why, as you present yourself to 'The Prophet' in a few minutes, you can tell him the reason you finally failed was that you ran into a hard case. An ex-Marine, from a family of Texas Rangers going back generations. The son of a US Marine, who's family never failed to teach their sons, the secret of the Road Agent Spin. You may be a sly bunny, but so am I. I'm not going to worry about seeing you in the next life, for you're never gonna get your hands on those ninety nine virgins, or smooth faced boys they've been telling you about where you're going. It's all been propaganda sport"!

Then Jaeger rose up wondering about whether or not to administer the Coups' de Gras as he slowly brought the barrel up to Bujovics face and cocked the hammer.

Bujovics final thought before the sprit left his body, was of the Chinese Fortune Cookie and the empty message it offered and then his body breathed its last, the audible death rattle signaling the heavens that the herd had been thinned by one more soul, to do with it what you will.

The death rattle signaled Jaeger the final bullet was unnecessary. He could see it in his eyes. The man was Kaput. No longer a concern to anyone. He went up to the road, went to his car and reached into his glove box, for a cigarette and seeing the harmonica removed it. He hadn't played the harmonica in a while. He lit the cigarette and went to the trunk of his Ford, removing two road flares. He went back to where the roads intersected, lighting one of the flares and dropping it on the blacktop, then went to the wrecked car and lit the other flare and dropped on the road.

Then on an impulse, he went back to the crumpled Pantera and in the rapidly dimming light rummaged through the interior, finding a rather full gym bag. Removing it from the car he slid the zipper open revealing a full bag of twenty and fifty dollar bills. His fee, for his time and trouble. He took one of the stacks of twenties handling it by the edges and sprinkled it over the car interior, then went back to his car, lit another cigarette and for the next several minutes, played those three notes over and over on his harmonica. A fitting funeral dirge to send Bujovic on his way. Then he lit up another smoke and went back to his glove compartment and turned on his cell phone and called Rex Wallace's number at the FBI. Wallace answered the phone as Jaeger asked, "Where are you Wallace"? "Jaeger?"

Just about ready to ask you the same thing. We're all at the storage warehouse where you had your shoot out with Bujovic. Seems the lines were busy and we eventually got the message and rushed right here. The place is a treasure trove of weapons and munitions and by the way where are you"!

"Tell ya the truth, I'm not quite sure. Somewhere in southern Montgomery County on a back road somewhere in the vicinity of Bum Fuck Egypt. Bujovic is dead and his yellow car is wrecked. If you've choppers overhead, tell them to look for two road flares to mark the spot for the County Mounties. When y'all arrive you'll fine Bujovic dead in a drainage ditch with three rounds from my old Colt in his chest. I'm tired right now and am going to the house and get a good night's sleep. Think I'm getting too old for all this stuff. In case Hoffmeister gets on his high horse, tell him I'll be by your office in the morning for a debriefing with my lawyer. Bujovic's weapon is at his feet. Of course he'll want me to bring in my vintage Colt revolver for forensic testing and I'll do it as long as the weapon never leaves my sight. You'll see an empty box on the front seat where his grenades used to be"!

"Hoffmeister, will want you to hang around, for the rest of us at the site", said Wallace weakly.

"Rex, I'm tired, thirsty, hongry and the skeeter's are making their presence known. I've done all the hard work and I don't feature getting another dose of malaria and if Hoffmeister don't like it, then fuck him and the horse he rode in on. See la late tomorrow morning"! Jaeger then turned off his cell phone. He'd rather have told Hoffmeister straight up his closing comment rather than Wallace, who seemed like an able agent. But if he'd hung around any longer in the condition he was in, it was a certainty that he and Hoffmeister would lock horns.

He slowly walked over to his car, marveling at how the old girl held it together. He'd resurrected it from a junk yard years ago spending a great deal of money completely rebuilding the old girl, that resembled its old self in its appearance, but not in its innards which were of the current state of automotive engineering. As he walked around the vehicle he saw no apparent harm save a long scratch on his left front bumper. A battle scar from the recent PIT maneuver that brought things to a close.

As he came around to the driver's side he took a large step backwards from his car, smiled and said, "Thanks Babe! You sure are a sexy beast"! In the depths of the forest all was quiet as he turned the ignition key and the massive Ford engine came to life. Time to go to the house. Sometime in the next several days, he'd detail her from stem to stern and lovingly apply a wax job to her exterior. She served him well, now time for Quid Pro Quo.

25

"You're like a bad penny always turning up when my schedule is overflowing", said Buffy as she listened to Jaeger. As he related what happened that afternoon, she turned on the late night newscast that featured the remnants of the extended chase and the string of wrecked cars and trucks on Harris County's Freeways.

"So you braved grenades and whatnot in order to run this fella down", asked Buffy?

"Hey, no telling' when the cavalry was going to arrive! What's a guy do? Let him get away?

"No! You did righteous work this afternoon, said Buffy continuing. It'll be their hide bound procedure that'll insist on capturing him and when you tell them he had a gun on you and you still put three rounds in him, they'll not believe you and this Hoffmeister will insist on bringing you up on charges of probable murder"!

"I've got an answer for that. Just need you to run legal interference for me for a while, then after I get my relic back I can answer that question right at Hoffmeister"!

"Late morning you say? Around eleven? OK. I have to be in court at nine, but I'll ask for a continuance, the following day. Best I can do sport. You have me for the day only, starting late morning"!

The following morning Jaeger showed up at FBI headquarters and walked into the conference room where Buffy was there already with Agents Wallace, Hoffmeister and Bergdorf. He brought his vintage Colt revolver with him, unloaded, with a half dozen rounds in its leather carrying case, inside a gym bag.

Jaeger was feeling a bit aggressive this morning and wasn't about to give an inch to Hoffmeister saying, "Good Morning Buffy, Agent Wallace, Agent Bergdorf. Now let's get one thing straight. I'm here as a courtesy and nothing else. Have my Colt Hog Leg here and some rounds that can be tested by your firearms folks, so y'all's loose ends can be all tied up. Y'all can debrief me while my weapon is being tested. Hell, you can even tape the conversation as long as my counsel can do the same. The weapon is well over a hundred years old and is an heirloom and will never leave my sight. Now Hoffmeister if that isn't to your liking, I'm gone. What's it gonna be"?

Hoffmeister stood up and said, "Let's go down to the armory"!

As they walked down to the basement of the building to the firing range and the weapons testing facility, Bergdorf conducted the inquiry, on a moment by moment time line, from the moment Jaeger was directed out of the rental house, through to his encounters with the subject Bujovic, the chase and the apprehension.

While the technician accepted Jaegers vintage firearm, he prepared the weapon for testing, Jaegers eyes never leaving him for a moment, continuing his answers of each question. After the test was concluded, the technician returned, handing Jaegers vintage heirloom to him and saying to everyone else, "This is the weapon that terminated the life of the subject.

The rifling, lines up perfectly"!

"I'm still not satisfied Mr. Jaeger", said Agent Hoffmeister finally asserting himself. From what I see, all the evidence shows that you murdered the man in cold blood, from a fit of rage, rather than detain him for our legal apprehension. You say you've been wounded as a result of your encounter. Where's the proof? Further, if the man had his weapon on you as you say he did, and your weapon was in your waist band of your trousers, there is no way on god's green earth that you could have reversed things. No jury could buy such a story"!

"Boy Hoffmeister you just never give up making an ass of yourself do ya", said Jaeger sneering with utter contempt. He then reached into the gym bag and removed the shirt he'd worn the previous day, pointing out the torn patch on the right shoulder. He then removed his shirt revealing the bandage and removed it showing a wound consistent with the tear in his shirt, adding, "The shirt hasn't been laundered and has my sweat and blood still on it. Have your people check it out. Now Agent Hoffmeister do you have your service weapon on your person"?

Hoffmeister nodded, taking his weapon out of his waste holster.

"Please unload the clip and the chamber and hand the rounds to Agent Wallace and I'll unload my piece. You find it quite unbelievable that someone could reverse things, when a weapon is being held on him right", said Jaeger as he checked his weapon and finding the cylinder void of any rounds, placed his Colt in the front of his waist band.

"Now hold your weapon on me and tell me to give it up slowly"! Hoffmeister complied as he weapon was fully cocked and pointing at Jaegers midsection from just five feet away. As Jaeger slowly removed his Colt from his waist band, he turned it over with one hand and offered it to Hoffmeister butt handle first ever so slowly. As Hoffmeister reached his arm out to grab the weapon, Jaeger swiftly twirled the well balanced Colt upright cocking the hammer and in a flash jerked the trigger, then his left hand swiftly fanned the hammer twice on Agent Hoffmeister before he could react. Hoffmeister still hadn't pulled his trigger, as Jaeger twisted around swiftly, knocking Hoffmeisters weapon from his grip.

"The last move was for show pal. In truth at least Bujovic got off a shot where you'd be dead. Now your dead sorta, thanks to the "Road Agent Spin". Don't they teach you guys anything at Quantico? Better stay at a desk son, because you just ain't ready for prime time. Oh you can keep the shirt as a souvenir and a reminder, never to draw down on me ever again"!

As Jaeger collected his belongings, putting on his shirt as he walked to the elevator with Buffy, she looked at him saying, "Ya just made a lifetime enemy and ya had to show off didn't ya"!

"The son of a bitch can get in line Buffy"!

"The line must be a short one, because your enemy's don't ever seem to last very long"!

As the elevator arrived at ground level Buffy said, "OK sport give me a hug and a kiss, I have to get back to the office and I'll send you a bill for my time next month"!

Just a mild joke between two old friends, the bills never arrived, because they were never sent. After the fall elections and both houses of Congress returned to Washington, Lars Magnusson invited the Majority and Minority leaders both houses of Congress to join both he and Vice

President Mulvahill in the Oval office for a long overdue meeting of the minds.

As they were ushered into his office, he and the Vice President greeted them as if they were long lost friends, with initial cordiality and grace. One only wondered how long that would last. Rather than sit behind his desk, the President bid them to each take a seat around the large ornate coffee table saying, "Gentlemen, so good of you to come. Seem's that both houses of congress will have a host of new members, to be sworn in over the next few days. But let's get right down to several things I have in mind"!

"I'm concerned about the all-time low polling numbers that your branch of government has been experiencing as of late. Both political parties have experienced recent adjustments in this area. A host of office holders with seniority have been voted out of office. Committee chairmanships will be exchanging hands. I hope we are in agreement the people have spoken, for better or worse and are desirous of positive change. After extensive review of the polling data and the election results that everyone knows, we know this one thing. The average citizen holds both houses of congress in low regard. Almost forty five percent of incumbent office holders in both houses of congress and of both political parties will have been replaced come the first of the year. Over half of the most senior members of both houses and of both parties will not be with us in a few months. I congratulate you gentlemen for making the cut, but one has to ask, how long can this egregious division go on? In the last year, in both houses of congress, twelve members, half of which were committee chairmen were lost in one way or the other to political scandal. Please gentlemen, let that sink in for a moment. The average citizen of this country has but few expectations of our legislators, our lawmakers, the 'Levites' of our great country. They simply desire and expect legislators of wisdom and character. Please let that also sink in. Wisdom and personal character. Anything else is gravy"!

"Now that average citizen asks himself why, when the country is having such a difficult time politically, economically and spiritually, why are not our congressional leaders sharing in our difficulty? Perhaps part of the problem is of my own making, for I've always been one who thought leadership came from those who led from the front. Early on in my administration, I took a rather severe haircut in my rate of remuneration. I did this on my own, with few expectations. We were then as well as now in a severe deficit position and I didn't necessarily need the money. Within a few days every single one of the White House staff starting with Vice President Mulvahill, decided to do the same. The couldn't afford it and that became readily apparent for this is an expensive town we reside in, so I met with all of the department heads and we scaled the program back to a more reasonable level. After a few days I mentioned this to my cabinet members, privately and suggested they offer a similar program to every senior member of their departments on a purely voluntary basis, discretely. Foolish me, for I should have realized that no secret can last long in this town.

Within days, a rumor is being spread all over creation that I ordered cuts in salary for all Federal workers. This gentlemen, is a lie! And some of you in this room have eagerly gone along with it behind the scene"!

"Some members of congress, in both houses and of both political parties, have chosen to offer the same choice, on a sliding scale basis to their staff. Not near enough of them to make a difference, but amazingly enough each and every one of them got reelected in their respective districts by a land slide, on purely a voluntary basis. This was unexpected, but the facts speak for themselves. 'Vox Populai', the people have spoken! Now what has gone on in the past, is history and the purpose of this meeting is to see if there isn't some common ground we can agree on from this point onward"!

"To begin with, I gathered together while everybody was busy campaigning, a group of brilliant Governmental Affairs students from the area Universities, mindful the group had to be comprised of half liberal and half conservative students. We met in the dark of night and the task I set forth for them was to research the congressional archives in detail and that they did all fifty of them, in secret, and come up with archaic laws that go all the way back we've discovered to the Mexican American War, that still are in effect. Yet in this day and age are of no intrinsic value or importance"!

At that Magnusson, nodded at Orval Goodwin and Melanie

O'Bannon to pass out the collated laws to the Congressional Leaders saying, "Gentlemen this is what the students, have unearthed, that are still with us"! "It seems to me that Congress could earn back some much needed good will from the American people, by rapidly reviewing these laws, all of which are horribly out of date and have been ferreted out by students of both political persuasions at some great personal expense to their personal time and interestingly enough we all are in perfect accord with one thing. None of us is desirous of personal mention should you gentlemen decide to immediately act in behalf of the nation in this regard. The credit will be all yours to enjoy assuming that all of you act with due and swift diligence"!

"One final thing, the students asked me to impart on all of you and this is their idea. We've recently gone through the twice a year adjustment from Standard to Daylight Savings time and each and every one thought this was a supreme pain in the butt. Perhaps appropriate when we were a primarily agrarian society but these days of absolutely no use. Oh, there's a five year old polling of the citizenry that was buried in the archives, never seeing the light of day, reflecting the public view for your review"!

"Gentlemen, the reason why we've gone to this effort is that with the newly elected congress about to soon begin its work, those remaining as well as those soon to be elsewhere, can contribute to the regaining of your congressional, 'Mojo', their words not mine. The feeling amongst the students and I agree, is if you can't come together on these simple things, what hope is there for the most complex of initiatives that consume us. In short, they want both houses of Congress to try and develop some new working habits. "Time is of the essence", said one of the students and all agreed. So what do you say gentlemen"?

The congressional leaders all looked at each other and nodded their heads, as Magnusson said, "Good"! "I will immediately sign what your findings will be as a standalone bill, with no attachments as you gentlemen well know," said Magnusson as he stood up. They all smiled and shook hands as they stood and filed out of the Oval office, each laden with a small stack of documents their respective staffs would be soon be pouring over.

"This should keep them out of the bars for at least a little while", mused Melanie!

"I wouldn't count on that Mel", offered Goodwin sarcastically, "But at least it was an offer of executive good will that will be difficult to criticize.

"What's the prognosis on Harvanian, Orval"?

"Your standard Government Issue heart attack. Long hours, no exercise and too rich a diet. He'll recover in a few weeks but we'll have to keep a lid on him, in the event of his return. In the meantime, Molly Pringle will be thrown to the wolves and take over the press conference. She's been at Bethesda Hospital with Van all night and is up on everything. She ought to hit the ground running"!

"God help the reported that screws with her. Can I get an Amen on that"? Magnussonreadily complied.

As Melanie gathered up the remnants of the meeting Goodwin said, 'Did you hear the latest scuttlebutt amongst the Federal Agents in Houston on the running down of the terrorist Bujovic? None of the media has gotten wind of it yet, but it seems that our boys weren't the ones that killed that guy at all. It was a civilian bounty hunter of sorts. He only has one name and it's simply Jaeger, which means "Hunter" in Kraut speak"!

Magnusson looked up from his desk, just as Melanie turned and said, "What did you say"?

"What do you mean what did I say", asked Goodwin in reply?

"The name Orval. That name", asked Melanie?

"You mean the name Jaeger, Mel"? She quickly nodded her head.

"He apparently was the mystery man working with the local field office that uncovered the guy who had the Chutzpah, to hide in plain sight. All of our modern technology and training failed to lift up that single rock. Plus he was the guy that chased him down and killed him, then disappeared, only to reappear the following day at the local field office with his lawyer.

Apparently she's some kind of legal legend in Houston named Elizabeth Beauvior. Seems she's never lost a case. Anyway he allowed himself to be debriefed, en camera, in her presence. Seems the task force leader, an agent named Hoffmeister, wanted to put the cuffs on him for some reason but apparently Jaeger talked him out of it. Seems that the former Agent in Charge that was murdered was working with Jaeger, McKay was her name faxed a report to Quantico and to our office, the Friday night before she was murdered, but as usual the thing somehow got buried"!

"What kind of car was he driving", asked Melanie?

"Let me think, I think it was a 1963 Ford Galaxiie. The guy was driving that ran this Bojovic to ground. Why do you ask Mel? Do you know this guy"?

"There can only be one man who goes by that single name that drives that kind of car. Yes, I know him"! She then sat down in the nearest seat saying, "And so does Molly"?

"This world we live in seems to be getting smaller and smaller", said Magnusson sitting on his desk as wide eyed as Mel.

"Don't tell me that you know this guy also", said Mel!

"If it's the same guy I'm thinking about, he's the one who altered my career path years ago on a football field in Minnesota. What is he doing these days Orval"?

"Things are kind of sketchy, but it seems that he's some kind of International Bounty Hunter. There's this retired Marine General named Bollinger that advises the guys at Quantico that can probably give you the real skinny on him"!

"Yes, I met the man. Very impressive", said Magnusson!

"Want me to invite him to lunch, Mr. President"!

"Yes very much so. Command performance stuff, but don't put too fine a point on it Orval. But Mel, how come you know this man"?

"That, Mr. President was long ago and personal, having nothing to do with government"!

"You mentioned Molly as one who knows this man", said Magnusson! "Ask her if you wish, but I'd think she very bluntly give you a reply not much different than mine"!

"Seems this man gets around a lot", sad Magnusson exasperated by the lack of information. "Orval, go ahead and ask General Bollinger to a private luncheon or dinner, then ask the local Agent in Charge in Houston if he can get hold of this Jaeger and offer him the same invitation to the White House. Somehow I need to reconnect with this man. Oh and his local lawyer, what's her name"?

"Beauvior. Elizabeth Beauvior, Mr. President"!

"Please find a way for her to make a visit, but separately if you will"!

As Goodwin left the Oval office for his own, Magnusson noticed his secretary still sitting in the chair staring out the window, with a blank stare on her face reminiscent of the thousand yard stare he often found himself engaged in during his private moments, thinking of the past and how each man's life placed heavy burdens upon each of us. The office was quiet as he said, "By your silence, it appears this man is a memory for you that I'll respect and we need talk of it no more"! His words brought a flood of tears to her eyes as she bowed her head and wept openly, the emotions of time long past coming back with a vengeance. Magnusson had never seen her like this. The Oval office Alpha Lioness, that protected the besieged President with such grace and charm, while providing what shielding she could, from the scallywags in this town. Abrasive with those that didn't matter, while lubricant with those who did, she as well as many others made things work in a world of chaos.

He walked over and sat down opposite her, waiting until she had regained her composure, and then said, "I recognize that look Mel. I've had it more times than I care to say. Clearly this guy has touched you deeply in some fashion. Should you ever need an ear to just listen, sing out. If not, I'll understand"!

Mel then stood, wiped away the tears saying, "I'll keep that in mind Mr. President and thank you. Now it's time we both got back to work" and left the room gracefully.

Jaeger arose with the crack of dawn, went to the kitchen and made the morning coffee and turned on the TV while the coffee was brewing. The cable morning news programs were full of the post-election gossip, of the political strategists twisting and spinning their own views of election results. He wondered how construction was going on his ranch up in Waco, concluding that before the week was out it was worth a visit. He padded to the shower, checking his shoulder wound. The skin had all but completely puckered over the long, almost half inch wide wound he'd received from Bujovic, a week ago. A series of butterfly bandages kept the edges of the skin together, while the hoard of little nanobots inserted years ago were doing their job as advertised, accelerating the healing. It would leave a scar, but that would join the many others that laced his body.

While he was in the shower he mulled over the phone call he'd received from Buffy last night. Seems the President's office in the form of his Chief of Staff, wanted to invite him to the White House for a special ceremony, as a point of thanking him for his recent service. After negotiating the terms of his visit in Jaegers behalf, Buffy called Jaeger and explained his planned itinerary, ever mindful of his desire for existing without publicity. Jaeger approved and was told that Agent Rex Wallace would contact him the following day. On cue Wallace called him promptly at 0800 in the morning and suggested the both make a day of it and drive up to Bujovics old residence to look over the place at their leisure. Jaeger agreed and told him where he'd meet him in about an hour for breakfast.

"So they want to give me a medal do they, mused Jaeger while they waited for their calorie laden breakfast at the Kettle Restaurant! "Seems to me they've forgotten a few folks, like Randall White and his nephew.

Especially his nephew. The kids got a lotta snap. Never got past high school's senior year I'm told, but he's a genius with computers and will do just what he's told if led properly. Seems to me Quantico could use someone like that and a Presidential Medal on his resume would go far, don't ya think. Then there's a guy I used to work with named Hondo. He works for Rafferty in town as a Chaser. You people or the Marshall's Service could put good use for his skills on a consultancy basis"!

"Anyone else come to mind," asked Wallace taking notes on a napkin? "Yeah, one other, but I'd have to think about it awhile and see if he wants the recognition"!

"Do you trust him Jaeger"?

"Yeah, I'd trust him with my life, but his credentials are a tad bit iffy, if ya catch my drift. Don't know where he is, but I know someone that can get in contact with him. I'll run it up the old flag pole and see if he salutes"!

While they ate breakfast Jaeger inquired what happened to Agent Hoffmeister.

"Oh, he's been relegated to desk duty somewhere deep in the bowels of FBI Headquarters in Washington. Seems the higher ups went over all of the after action reports and found the man wanting in several areas. I don't think we'll be seeing him leading any task force units anymore for the rest of his career. He's in a purely staff level capacity"!

"What this about the President calling in General Bollinger for a consultation"1

"A prelude to getting together with you. Apparently he gave the President the complete low down on you, before, during and after your incarceration in Huntsville. That apparently put the wheels in motion to get in touch with you personally. Besides, the President said that you two were never formally introduced, from years ago and that he wants to reconnect, but this time with a handshake"!

As the bill was presented by the waitress, Wallace grabbed the bill saying, "This is on the taxpayer from now on. Your money is no good here, for the foreseeable future"!

Driving out to the site of confrontation in his Bureau vehicle, Wallace continued by saying, "Both this place and the backup apartment of Bujovics, have had every inch of the property swept by the techies, for any other nasty surprises. Don't want a repeat of what went before. Thus far your need for secrecy and the Bureau's need for positive publicity go hand in hand, regarding Bujovics demise"!

As they drove through the gate and around a large crater created by an explosion, Wallace continued, "If you agree, tickets and lodging arrangements will be sent to your attorney in your name. I'm to accompany you to Washington on the same plane. Seems we'll both be flying Coach Class, what with the White House's current penchant on Federal economy. Different seats will be booked. We'll both be at the same Hotel but on different floors. You'll be picked up by the Chief of Staff's assistant and I by the local office. We are to arrive separately. No decision yet has been reached as to the time of day we meet with the President. Have you a preference"?

"None that I can think of. The man is pretty busy these days. Just as long as we don't encounter any reporters or camera men"!

"Every precaution will be taken, but I'm certain you have a hat and wrap around shades knowing the drill as you do"! They both laughed as the got out of the car and both went on a tour, of the ruins, Jaeger filling out some of the few missing links that never made it on the various after action reports. Finally entering the escape tunnel, Jaeger pointed out the auxiliary tunnel never explored saying, "We were on a clock when we initially came in. Strictly in and out stuff, taking care not to leave any signs the place had been compromised. We discovered the beginnings of the garages escape tunnel but never explored it completely just going slowly on our exit to determine where it came out. You might want to have your people get into it and see if there are any surprises left", said Jaeger!

As they walked back to the car, after inspecting the entire perimeter and interior of the property, Jaeger finally made up his mind asking, "They going to give you a medal too, Rex"?

"It would be news to me if they did. No this trip is strictly for you and I'm just along for the ride and maybe a slight bit of Lagniappe"!

"Seems that if the President himself had his folks go to all of the trouble of inviting the both of us to the White House, it would be impolite to accept don't ya think"?

"I'd tend to agree", answered Wallace.

"Well then better set it up, with Buffy, at the Presidents convenience".

Wallace broke into a smile as they got into the government car.

"Are they out of their fucking minds", said Duke Vultee over the phone to Jaeger? "We're convicted felons"!

"Were convicted felons", replied Jaeger. "I've received a full pardon from the Governor in writing, if you'll recall and you've served the remainder of your parole and have the paperwork to prove it. All the White House is going to do is send you a Medal honoring your service to the country. You don't have to come to Washington. They can send it to Rae and then he can get to you when ever"!

"Buffy put her blessing on this"!

"Yes she did"!

"OK, then have her set it up with Rae and you watch your keester fella. You just might get to be some kinda celebrity up there"!

"That'll be the day. By the way how're you doing"?

"Doin' Ok I suppose, but life's getting boring. The clubs are all making money, got my hands on all the trim a man can handle, but there's this big fat bank, just outside of"! Jaeger cut him off by saying, "Enough of this talk about a bank Duke. You don't need the aggro at your age"

"Yeah, I suppose you're right, I was just sayin', that was all. Have em mail whatever they want to Rae. In a month or so I'll check in with him and maybe catch a lunch with him at the Silver Dollar"!

26

The late afternoon Continental flight to Washington went off without a hitch. Jaeger parked his old Ford Bronco in long term parking and took the shuttle bus to the terminal. He caught sight of Wallace at the gateway prior to entering the aircraft. Neither of them acknowledging the other. They passed each other in the coach section, again oblivious to each other and stowed their single bags in the overhead bins and settled in, with Jaeger sitting at the rear of the aircraft. Both hailed a separate cab upon arrival and took it to their hotel, with Jaeger arriving right after Wallace checked in.

He settled in for the evening, ordering room service to be sent, for he was to be ready for a phone call by the White House at 0730 Hours, signaling him that an official car was to be sent for him. Thus an early evening was in the offing.

The following morning at 0730 sharp, his room phone rang. It was the desk saying that his transportation was ready down at the front desk. Within five minutes he met the individual that escorted him to the waiting government sedan. As he entered the rear seat, he was greeted by an old familiar face.

"General Bollinger. What are you doing here", asked Jaeger?

"The President asked me to be the one to greet you and escort you to the White House and son I just couldn't say no to the President"!

"Damn sir, it's certainly good to see you. Can you tell me what I've gotten myself into"?

"Yes I can and will, but before I shed any light on your itinerary for this day, a bit of advice. Just relax if possible? Today is to be your day of days for you've traveled a long road and while you'll not be getting any overt recognition, for services rendered, you'll be well regarded by those who matter. Have you had your breakfast yet"?

"No sir, I rarely eat breakfast anyway"!

"Well son your then eat hearty at lunch. Seems what was going to be just a brief visit in the Oval office has morphed into some other things, the President wants your opinion on. Oh, there will be time for old friends to reminisce and a brief awards session. But given your talents and things that have recently come up, the man needs your unique perspective. Both Agent Wallace and I will be with you all day long. Good to see that you've worn your snap brim hat and shades. It'll keep any prying eyes from recognition. Oh and Wallace will be right behind us. The FBI Headquarters sent a car for him. It appears that he's been no less than a one man press agent to the management, without the press of course. Seems that after the ceremonies in the Oval office, some folks I know of want you to conduct a class in 'How to turn the tables on an aggressor'. I think they're talking about the road agent spin move you introduced to Agent Hoffmeister"!

Jaeger was only half listening to the General as he gazed out the window prompting Bollinger to ask, "Are you OK son"?

"Oh, I don't know General. It's just that I've never been comfortable with people making a fuss about me. Even by my mother, God rest her soul, when I was a little boy, standing knee high. Never got any medals in the Corps. for what I did and just don't see why now"!

"That's understandable, given the background you came from. Your father was a hard taskmaster, who came from generations of hard taskmasters. Yet look what it produced? A hard boned, mostly self-sufficient human being, who's always done the right thing at the right time. Had you not so doggedly stayed on the tail of this terrorist and let him get away after all that he'd done, you wouldn't have been able to live with yourself"!

"Those you sent to their great reward deserved it and the world is a better place for it. Most folks in this world labor in relative obscurity all their lives. In the brief time that is before you, you will be quietly recognized by people who matter, for the outstanding service's you've rendered to a host of people and just perhaps all of the crap you've gone through, the injustices, just might be made right once more"!

The car slowed to make its turn at the check point entering the White

House grounds, Jaeger said, "Perhaps you're right General. Time to turn another page in the book"!

"The General then said, "Somehow I'm thinking that somewhere up top on some cloud, your family is looking down at this moment with a sense of pride"!

As the car made the slow turn approaching the entrance portico, General Bollinger opened the rear door, smiled and said, "Smile son, it's show time", as Wallace joined the group.

On the second floor looking down was Melanie watching Jaeger emerging from the sedan. There was a sharp involuntary intake of breath at the very sight of the man she'd not seen for years. Wearing wraparound sunglasses and a snap brimmed hat, sports coat and slacks, he looked every bit of the nondescript man she'd known long ago. She wondered if his appearance had changed any over the years. What would his reaction be when he caught sight of her? What would her reaction be? She could only control herself not her surroundings as she promised herself to be gracious, charming, welcoming and above all business like. Although she's already written her private number on a slip of paper and would find a discrete way of placing it in his hand. If he never called her, then that chapter in her life would quietly close, but if he did, then what? She quickly went down stairs and took up her position by her desk, to greet the man with everyone else.

Jaeger followed Bollinger into the White House and was introduced by the General to Orval Goodwin, the Presidents Chief of Staff. Who quickly guided them to the Oval office. As they went down the corridor, Molly Pringle emerged from one of the offices with a leather bound folder, winked at Jaeger saying, "Congratulations Sport", following them as they went.

The last person he'd ever thought he'd see again was Molly. Suddenly he felt as nervous as a whore in church. As they turned the corner, approaching the Oval office, Goodwin said, "And this is the real power behind the President, his personal secretary", as he said those words, Melanie turned around, a vision of loveliness, reaching for Jaegers hand in greeting with both of hers saying, "So good to see you again Mr. Jaeger and congratulations", as she pressed home the vital slip of paper, that just might determine what came next in her life, or not. She saw by the look of complete surprise in his eyes that he was not expecting to see her, yet the transfer of that slip of paper went off without a hitch, with his palming of the missive and slipping it deftly into his pants pocket.

Following in the wake was Molly Pringle who witnessed the transfer, giving Melanie a sly wink whispering, "Nicely done girl", and signaling her with her head to follow them inside the Oval Office for the brief ceremony. "Mr. President", said Goodwin, "I'd like to introduce you formally to Jaeger"! As Magnusson came around the desk he walked up to Jaeger grasping his hand and said, "We've met"! The two men just stood there grasping each other's hand in greeting far longer than one would expect, staring at each other, smiling head to head saying not another word for what seemed like an eternity, when Magnusson said, "That's quite a grip you have there Mr. Jaeger", both men slowly disengaging from the other, each determined not to show a hint of evidence of the pain they received from the other. "You're not so bad yourself Mr. President", said Jaeger his mind starting to become overloaded with the confluence of events. The President he expected to see, but then Molly Pringle, an off handed one night stand from awhile back, but what really hit him to the core was the sight of Mel. His precious Mel, from long ago. She was still as lovely as ever. The memory of her touch over riding the pain he felt from the Presidents hand shake. The slip of paper burning white hot, in his pants pocket.

As the two men shook hands with each other, performing the ritual of male bonding that only men of action enjoyed, Molly stood there with Mel, anxiously clasping each other's hand with until the men unclasped, discretely flexing their fingers to bring back the circulation.

Standing there in the background was Bollinger, taking each and every nuance in between parties. In the last few minutes, it seemed like all of the stars were in alignment for a singular purpose that perhaps only wise old General could grasp.

Then Molly stepped forward and handed the folder containing the awards to Goodwin who in turn handed it to the President, commencing the ceremony. As Molly rejoined her, the White House photographer stepped forward to illustrate the event as was the custom.

Again the two women clasped hands, each deep in their own thoughts of the occasion, with Magnusson droning on with the award recognition, Molly proud to be serving such a fine President and Mel, proud that she at least touched the life, if ever so briefly, of such a man as Jaeger. Midway through the ceremony Mel started to fight back tears of regret. As Molly turned to her, she slipped a small paper tissue into her hand mouthing silently, "Yeah, I know, sinus"!

The presentation concluded, the pictures taken, everyone in the room broke out into applause, each in turn congratulating Jaeger, except for Mel.

She wanted to go up to him and shake his hand, even embrace him. But there was just so much self-restraint she could muster as she turned around and silently slipped from the room. She quickly checked her phone for any messages and finding none made her way to the nearest bathroom. There she would get rid of the sinus problem even if it took a half an hour.

Jaeger turned around and caught sight of Melanie leaving the room, then turned back to the President who was smiling from ear to ear. Still shaken from the sight of Mel, he put forth the eminent front and smiled for all those assembled as Rex Wallace clasped his hand and asked, "Well Jaeger, how does it feel to be awarded the top civilian award, The Presidential Medal of Freedom"!

"I don't quite know yet. Perhaps in a few days it'll all sink in, but right this moment I've no answer"!

"Well said Jaeger", said Magnusson putting his arm around Jaeger! "Now if everyone except Jaeger, Agent Wallace and General Bollinger would please leave us, we've a few things to discuss"! After they left Magnusson bid them all to join him around the coffee table, eschewing the formality of sitting behind the desk. He started out by saying, "I want to apologize for that hand shake Jaeger. Perhaps still some of the residual of that red ass I felt for you after that hit in Minnesota long ago. I went over the tapes of that encounter many times and even though it was a clean hit and you got hurt too, you recovered and I didn't. It changed a few things for me. Made me have to redirect my life and really think about things, putting them in proper perspective. Rehab took quite a while and much effort.

Thanks to General Bollinger and Agent Wallace bringing me up to speed chapter and verse, it seems this award you've just received is but a pittance of what you should receive"!

"Thank you Mr. President but"! Just then Magnusson gently interrupted him by saying, "Please, just amongst us I'm Lars. Please continue"! "I was just going to say, that I too have been following what you've been involved with for the last few years and it seems to me that you've got about all you can say grace over"!

The expression on Magnusson's face changed from that of complete seriousness, to that of relief as he said, "I was hoping you would say that. Congress is giving me fits and there's a small movement that wants me out of here by any means necessary. I can handle the political end of things, but I need someone working below the radar to solve some problems"!

"I'd think that would involve two things. That somewhere in the secret service are one or more people who were involved with President Dobbin's assassination on Inauguration Day and then somewhere out there is someone, who's involved with all those forest fires"!

"Have you spoken to Jaeger about this General"?

"Not a word Mr. President. He just figures things out on his own it seems"!

"Just as Wallace had said then. The man has the instincts of a timber wolf", mused Magnusson continuing, "The itinerary for today if you're agreeable is to get you over to Quantico and show some the instructors the finer points of the Road Agent Spin. Seems you've impressed Agent Wallace here with your firearms acumen. The rest of my day will be involved with various group involvements that require the Presidential touch not unlike what you've recently endured. But I'd like to spend much of the day with you tomorrow, along with Wallace and the General and a few others and get some fresh thinking planted on a few items of interest if that's agreeable to you"!

"My time is yours for as long as you need me", replied Jaeger!

"Oh yes, before I forget, We've sent by special courier, the Presidential medals you've requested for the others that helped you run this Bujovic fella to ground, but it seems there's one more"?

"Yessir there is", offered Rex Wallace. The man's name is Duke Vultee and I have the contact information of someone who will get the award to him.

"Duke Vultee? That's a rather gaudy name for someone", mused Magnusson!

"Yessir", answered Wallace. "The man's a former acquaintance of Jaeger from his past. A convicted bank robber who's served his time and enjoys his privacy. Jaeger vouches for him completely as does the General"!

"Then before you leave get with the Chief of Staff and give him the information. The man should have the appropriate recognition, even if it's, en camera"!

Magnusson then rose from his chair, offered his hand to Jaeger saying, "A friendly grip between friends this time eh? I'll have to use this hand later on"!

The trio then left the office passing Melanie's desk as Jaeger glanced at the desk with a mixture of elation coupled with disappointment at not seeing her. As they walked down the hall Melanie rounded the corner just in time, to see them walk out of sight.

"I could have him, brought to you in hand cuffs, but you already know which Hotel he's staying at. The man's going to be in the area for the next several days", said Magnusson watching Melanie approach he desk.

"He has my number. The ball's in his court. If he calls me that's one thing, if he doesn't, that's another. If you love somebody you have to set them free. If they come back to you it was meant to be. If not", her voice trailing off into nothing.

"Now Mr. President you've got an entire day of glad handing ahead of you. So get to work"!

As he went back into his office, he had to get the last word saying over his shoulder, "Somehow when your tour of service is completed here, I think the folks at Langley could make use of your talents Mel"!

On the way helicopter trip over to Quantico, Jaeger sat silent gazing out the window, while Wallace and the General engaged in amiable conversation, the sound of the engines muted by the sound proofing. Jaeger opened the folio containing his medal and the ornate document that signified that he was at long last an American of some significant accomplishment. All well and good of its own accord, but something was missing. Then he thought of the slip of paper in his pocket and taking it out read it, "Time we talked, then a phone number, then Mel"!

He knew why he left her, or so he thought over the years. Each time the memory of her and the time they spent together surfaced, he'd embrace the memory then force it back down deep in the recesses of his mind. Each time he weighed the time he'd lost, the memories they'd never experience, against the sheer adventure, the excitement of the chase and the eventual satisfaction that derived from capturing or killing those who needed badly to be excised from humanity. As time passed, the momentary exultation began to diminish and the memory of Mel gained ground. Was he getting too old, or soft? Probably!

Were there others just as capable, if not more so, somewhere in the pipeline of humanity to do the work that needed to be done? He certainly hoped so. He had far enough memories to last several lifetimes.

He'd done well financially. Certainly restoring much of what was the Jaeger family estate that had survived the many generations since the founding of the fledgling nation and eventually the State of Texas. So perhaps at long last it was time to lay things down and join the rest of humanity and become normal, or whatever that was. He needed someone to take off the rough edges. He vowed that before the day was concluded, he would take the first step and call Mel and see if divine forgiveness was an option.

Just in time for lunch, Jaeger and his small entourage were introduced to all of the firearms instructors in the area of Washington. Every agency was represented by someone amounting to an audience of thirty men, each in their own right outstanding marksmen, with all firearms.

After lunch, they all gathered as Jaeger addressed the group en masse saying, "I'm certain that many of you in this gathering are better marksmen than I am, under normal circumstances. However some of you will realize that a face to face gunfight at close quarters just ain't a normal thing.

Somebody could get killed, just as long as it isn't you"!

The gathering to a man gave a sporadic chuckle, where some had indeed come face to face with death emerging out the other side, while others had yet to experience a trip to the ferryman.

"No doubt word of my recent encounter with this Bujovic fella has reached your ears. So in advance I just have to admit I was very lucky"! He then took them all through a step by step rendition of his encounter concluding, "The man was badly injured from the crash whereas I was not, just tired from the chase, so no doubt his reaction time was a tad off. My advantage, his disadvantage. Now what I'm about to demonstrate takes an endless amount of time to practice, whereas it becomes an automatic response. Tell y'all the truth? In all of my encounters, Bujovic was one of a few times I had an occasion to do the spin. My daddy was and ex-Marine and a former Texas Ranger. Most every one of my forbearers served with the Rangers and each generation passed that skill on to the next. Don't have any War stories to tell about the spin except to say, from the time I was old enough to be standing to my daddy's knee, he bought be a set of kiddie cap pistols and holster and set me down and went through each step of the three different procedures I'm about to demonstrate. All will be provided in the video recording that's being taken"!

"Endless practice it took. I remembered crying at first because I kept dropping the pistols all the time, but my daddy was patient and kept on with me slowly repeating over and over just how to do it. Eventually one day I didn't drop the cap pistol, never thinking there would come a day when I had to use it.

"Now the weapons that have been provided are arrayed on the display table. Now I have some bad news for everyone. Seems many of you love the automatics, for their sheer capacity of rounds, never mind that some will be prone to jamming at the worst possible time. The counter to that is to keep the weapon clean at all times, but what if you can't? Next every single automatic is not balanced, with most of the weight being in the grip of the weapon that houses the clip, full of rounds. Next, is the trigger position of the automatic. Way too far forward in the trigger housing group. It'll snag your finger every time you try the spin. Only the old Colt 1911 automatic has the trigger far back enough in the trigger housing group to be viable, yet it still is too far out of balance. My guess with enough practice and concentration one might be able to execute the spin successfully, but I wouldn't want to bet my life on it"!

"Now here is a Ruger replica of the old Colt Single action .45. "The trigger is far back in the rear of the trigger housing group; it will not impede or snag your finger when in action. It is both single and double action and I find the balance acceptable. Yet the design is that of an ancient weapon as modern weapons go. Now as we move to the short barreled single and double action revolvers that many, including myself prefer, I bring to your attention the placement of the trigger once again. Far too far forward in the trigger housing group thus snagging your finger when you try and do the spin. As we in Texas say, 'That dawg won't hunt', but a skilled gunsmith could cure that along with the trigger and hammer pull that's far too heavy, to be of any use, to any skilled pistolero"!

"Thus if my presentation is to be put to any practical use, a partial reconsideration of the choice of hand guns for agents in the field is necessary. Utilization of revolvers, reengineering of the trigger position and the pull of the trigger and the hammer and then endless practice with both hands will bring you up to speed. You hopefully will never in your lives an occasion to do the spin, but some of you might want to train your students in defensive tactics effectively, or simply want to show off to wives or girlfriends. But seeing that this room is occupied by serious men and women please belay the last comment"!

"And now let's get to it. Let me preface this by saying short of several pistolero's, who earn a living by firearms demonstrations, and there can't be but a handful in the nation, skilled in the art. The Road Agent Spin is purely an American thing. Been all over the world and not once have encountered anyone who knew what the spin was or even heard of it. Now assuming your antagonist has the drop on you and your weapon is in your holster, please observe the three possibilities you have of have of reversing the tables on the rascal. I'll be using the Ruger replica .45, unloaded of course", as he checked the weapon for rounds, finding none, commenced with his demonstration. Going very slowly step by step, he broke each movement down to its lowest common denominator for the video camera, repeating again and again for the purpose of future editing. When he concluded his demonstration he added an additional element. "When you have a subject under the gun, of course you tell the subject to clearly remove the weapon by his fingertips and slowly place it on the ground, then step to the side and lay in a prone position. Of course you kick away the weapon from his reach. But what is not taught anywhere that I've seen is a very simple thing. Face down on the pavement and arms and legs spread wide, prior to cuffing, but what about the position of his hands? "Palms Down" on the ground, gives the subject the leverage to move, where 'Palms Up' with the thumbs facing inward towards his feet, minimizes the subjects leverage towards rapid movement. It's worked for me for a very long time and in Texas we say, "What works is good. What doesn't ain't"!

"Gentlemen, I thank you for your patience and kind attention", said Jaeger as he concluding his demonstration as everyone rose in applause. Within moments everyone surrounded him flooding him with questions.

Wallace watched in awe, as he said to Bollinger laughingly, "See General what you've wrought"! "Rex, the man was well wrought by the time I ran into him. He's lived more in one lifetime than most of us can ever even conceive. With any luck he'll soon slide out from living memory and live to a ripe old age. But I think there's a few more things ahead of him, before that happens. Let's say a prayer for the guy, for I think there's more to come. By the way are you going to sit in on the meeting with the boys at Langley with us tomorrow"?

"No sir, have to get back to Houston tonight on the red eye. Please make my apologies to the President tomorrow, for a few things have arisen regarding other cases in progress that need my attention. I'm going to be picked up tonight at my hotel by HQ and have a ride to Dulles Airport"!

By 1730 hours in the afternoon the trio was in the chopper on its way back to the White House, as Jaeger reached into his pocket and removed the slip of paper, while Bollinger and Wallace were engaged in conversation.

He placed a call to the number given on the paper by Melanie and after the fourth ring encountered her voicemail. He left a message that he called and wanted to see her at her convenience.

Fifteen minutes later, he felt the buzz of his cell phone and saw that it was a text message from Mel that read: "2000 hrs. at The Palm. Any Cabbie in town will get you there. A reservation will be placed in your name. Be there"! Mel…Jaeger was buoyed by her response. Probably she was at her residence he concluded and he wondered just what would be in store for him when they met. He steeled himself for the worst. Of course a woman in her position would not allow herself to exhibit an ugly display of emotion. His time with her long ago taught him that even under the most onerous of circumstances', she always conducted herself with grace and dignity. Habits that most people chose to ignore of either gender.

Which gave him precious little time to shower shave and change shirts.

He'd not planned for staying more than a night or two in Washington. At seven forty five in the evening his cab pulled up to 'The Palm'. As he entered and encountered the Maître' D Restaurant, he gave his name and was shown to a booth. She hadn't forgotten his old habit of keeping everything in front of him. Perhaps a good sign.

As the designated waiter approached, Jaeger bid him to lean over whereupon his slipped him a fifty, saying, "Bring me a Beefeaters and tonic, dash of lime and when my guest arrives bring her a Wolfschmidt's and tonic with a dash of lime"!

Normally, Melanie was a punctual individual. That built in clock of self-discipline demanded it of herself. She'd taken great care to quickly shower and choose her attire carefully opting for a French Tweed outfit, and a simple camisole underneath. Selecting her Scent, she opted for Ambush.

Not too much as to be noticeable past five feet away. The cab had arrived at her town house on time as it whisked her away towards her rendezvous. She glanced nervously at her watch, seeing that she was going to be late. As the cab got stuck in traffic, she wondered if Jaeger had received her text message? If so, would he be there or not. Or perhaps he was unavoidably detained. She checked her blackberry for any response and finding none let it be. He was just as punctual as she was. He would be there.

As the cab pulled up to the curb, the door was opened by the uniformed doorman as she emerged. He went before her and opened the front door to The Palm. She was greeted and directed to the table. As she approached she caught sight of him, smiling at her. She deftly slid into the booth next to him, putting her purse carefully between them. Here in this very public place, was perhaps a rekindling of two sprits, perhaps.

As she came to rest she said, "Sorry I'm late, the traffic you know". Just then the waiter arrived and placed her drink in front of her saying, "Madam, Wolfschmidt's, tonic, with a dash of lime I believe", then withdrew. In this world there is nothing like a fond memory of ones' preferences to break the ice, as Melanie picked up the glass, sampled its contents saying as she glanced at Jaeger, "You remembered"!

Jaeger then picked up his glass as she said, "Beefeaters and tonic, splash of lime" and sipped of his drink, nodding her head. To which he replied, "You remembered too"!

"Always sit in a booth whenever possible, keeping everything in front of you. Always have your pepper spray in hand along with your car keys.

Always be aware of your surroundings at all times. Trust your instincts. See what others won't, or cannot. Should I go on", Melanie asked as she took a rather unlady like draught of her drink, emptying most of the glass and signaling the waiter to bring two more of the same.

"Just want you to know that I'm no longer angry with you. I rounded that corner long ago. Although I'd be less than a woman if I didn't admit that I want, no, need an explanation of your disappearance long ago. Please take your time. Whenever you're good and ready. But before you say anything, I just want to say that I'm very proud of you and the way you responded to the President this morning"!

"The guy has quite a grip"!

"That I wouldn't know", she said finishing her drink as the waiter brought the second round.

"So how is your son doing? He must be of college age by now"!

"He's in his junior year at the Naval Academy at Annapolis. Just barely squeezed into the top ten in his class academically and is the leading scorer as an attack man on the Academy's La Crosse team. The word is that come this spring he'll be an All-America candidate for certain. In addition he's received the academy's highest marks ever on the shooting range, equaling the instructor's best shots. They've told me that from the start, they had little to teach him in long range shooting. In escape and invasion techniques he constantly bests his instructors and will be invited to join them this coming summer break to help teach others. The instructors swear he must have some Indian blood in him, so I suppose the time we spent together and the influence you had on Rory went far towards furthering his education"!

Mel picked up her drink; this time sipping demurely, the edges of the event now rounded smooth then concluded, "Rory's doing just fine"!

This was the moment for the pregnant pause, as each took another drink wondering what to say next. The wide chasm of the passing years seems insurmountable almost when Melanie finally said, "I'd ask how you are, but clearly you're on top of the world. However", she then hit the conversational wall, clearly at a further loss of words, saying, "Help me out here. I'm out of words"!

"I had no idea that you were working for the President, so this morning when I saw you standing there, I went into brain freeze. Everything after that went in slow motion"!

"Well sport, you certainly did well enough with the executive hand shake", added Mel with a slight smirk.

"That was the autopilot working. Throughout everything all I could think about was you and my bailing out on you and your son"!

"Look Jaeger, other than purely selfish reasons, I have no rational reason to be angry with you. This gentleman, the lawyer Parmalee, did your bidding in providing me well enough to continue and the fact that you set up a College fund for Rory, which by the way his appointment to the Academy made a moot point, said to me more than words could possibly say"!

"You deserve a why, so here's the short version. From the moment we first met, I was completely nuts about you. From the moment I woke up, all through the day, until the time I finally fell asleep. You were my

Alpha and my Omega. Even occupying my dreams at night. In addition, I quickly drew attached to your son Rory. But there were things about me that I just couldn't share or expose the both of you to"!

"I recently learned about your unfortunate incarceration and the death of your family, thanks to Molly Pringle. We've become fast friends and in case you're wondering, that 'Thang', doesn't matter, so please continue"!

Jaeger took a deep breath, lit a cigarette, took a drink, then looked up from the table and continued, "After I was freed from Prison I did a number of things trying to get the direction of my life straightened out finally coming to work for this guy named Rafferty who had the biggest bail bonding firm in Texas as a Chaser, aka a bounty hunter. Did this for a while, then I met you and it seemed to change everything. I couldn't see me with you and your son being that I was a Chaser. Yet I couldn't find the words to let you go. You became an integral part of me"!

Looking at the table cloth he continued, "Then I inadvertently fell in with this guy named Ortega, the biggest drug smuggler and distributor in Texas. Shortly thereafter I was involved in some things I just couldn't let go of and I couldn't risk the chance that he'd ever find out about you and Rory. And he would've eventually found out, for he had his fingers into just about everything in Houston but was skillful enough to avoid publicity. He was a killer of everybody he came in contact with. So I had a Hobson's choice on my plate".

"Couldn't expose you to this and wouldn't let this guy get away with things. So I made the choice"!

"So what ever happened to this guy Ortega, there was nothing in the papers about him"!

"He disappeared"!

"He disappeared? How?"

"Let's just say that there is nothing left of him. What remains is with the fishes"!

"What about his associates"?

"Much the same thing, except for this one guy and we've become friends. He has a legit business in Paris"!

Melanie, leaned back a bit, then leaned forward, just enough to allow the full force of her scent waft past Jaegers nostrils saying, "There is certainly far more to you than meets the eye sport. Now that I have the short version in pocket, please summon the waiter for another round of drinks and the menu. I'm hungry so feed me"!

As Jaeger summoned the waiter for another round and the menu, he gazed into Mel's opalescent eyes and weakly said, "It's been too long. Far too long"!

As the waiter brought the menu along with the drinks, Mel studying the menu let slip, "Yet the evening is still young sport", with a wry smile on her face.

Jaeger suddenly became awake. There he lay next to Melanie, in her bed. Remembering they'd raced through their meal, hailed a cab and went back to her town house in virtual silence. It had started to rain a little as they went up the steps and he stood guard watching the streets as she fumbled for her key. Once inside, they eagerly fell into a long overdue embrace, probing the depths of each other with a passion beyond comprehension. She then half guided and pushed him up the stairs shedding garments along the way, breathlessly falling into her bed, writhing like two reptiles with a hunger for each other. For the next several hours it was like unarmed combatants with the demons of Eros, silently guiding the duo towards that old pathway towards mutual release. In the aftermath they both silently reacquainted each other with the past, relishing the present as well as the past, as their fingertips explored, followed by their lips and gentle caresses. All was possible and nothing was out of bounds. Eventually finding the energy and overwhelming desire of urgent necessity to reengage with such ferocity that was certain to bring ultimate rigid release, with neither one wanting to uncouple. That is how they feel asleep.

He silently got up and went to her bathroom, rubbing his arm that had fallen asleep back to life and quickly got back into bed, next to this goddess, who briefly stirred. He glanced briefly at the clock radio which read 0330 hrs. in the morning, then put his head next to hers as she turned, one eye opening saying groggily, "Don't even think about leaving me ever again"!

"Not even to dip the dew from my Wilson"!

Without a further word, she placed his hand between her moist thighs and placed her hand on his flaccid member saying, "You better get used to this pal. What time is it"?

"0332 in the morning"!

"Good, stay put and I'll be back shortly", then she got up and in all her glory went out of the room and shortly came back saying, "Your shirt is in the washing machine and your slacks are on the chair"!

As she approached the bed, Jaeger said, "Stop. I want to see you as you are"!

"But it's chilly out here. Stupid man I'm jumping in bed next to you where it's warm"! As she nestled next to him resuming her previous grasp in his bodily part she said, "At five the alarm will wake us. You can call whoever you have to let them know that you have a ride to the White House. Your meeting with Magnusson and the others won't be until nine. I'll be your driver. I trust you know how to operate an iron for your shirt and trousers"?

"Yes I do"!

"Good. The coffee will come on automatically at five. So be quiet and let me snuggle"! For several minutes they were quiet in each other's arms before Jaeger whispered, "Mel"?

"What"?

"Thank you"!

"You're welcome"! Then a few minutes later Mel whispered, "Jaeger"?

"What"?

"I take it that we're branded"? Jaeger then held her head gently between his hands and whispered, "For as long as I live"! They came together with a gentle and slow kiss neither wanting to take their eyes off of the other, drifting off into that halfway world of gentle slumber.

At 0900 hours, Magnusson strode into the Oval office, as everyone rose to their feet saying, "Good Morning Mr. President"!

"Good, I see that everyone is here. Gentlemen please be seated", said Magnusson as he took his seat behind his desk. "Jaeger, I presume you've met Gordon Hathaway who's come over from Langley and you already know Preston Bergdorf from Quantico and of course General Bollinger. Orval I presume the all of the recording devises are turned off"?

"Yes Mr. President"!

"We have two particular problems that require Mr. Jaeger's unique skill sets. One internal, the other external. Let's allow Mr. Hathaway to explain the external first.

"Thank you Mr. President", said Hathaway continuing. "Months ago our country experienced a wave of very clever cyber-attacks on not only the Defense Departments computers, but that of a number of our banking houses. The Cyber boys traced the penetrations back through our satellite system and in time were able to send back to the overseas servers, many of which were operated by the Chinese and North Korean governments, a series of virus's that penetrated their firewalls and literally turned the computers on themselves melting their internals. Faced with useless servers the bad guys could only guess who their assailants were, with no proof. Of course they remained silent on the matter. Their computers and servers literally imploded, setting them back on their heels. Well, gentlemen they're back, but coming at us in a variety of ways now from different directions.

What we have are multiple firewalls, all circulating at a varied rate, that our people cannot penetrate. Think about the old Nazi cipher system of the last World War. Their cipher system operated on a rotational basis, with ciphers changed periodically. Their current system of firewall rotation is purely random, with no way of prediction. Our best minds have given it the old college try and came up with nothing. Now we have a pretty good idea where there servers are currently located and have zeroed the personnel involved down to a few of the Russian Mafia operatives, all of which are former KGB. Very nasty and brutal fellows. We could kidnap them and put them through the rendition but that would take a while. Too long. The local government is not aware of this as far as we can determine. To make matters worse, we've finally traced a number of their servers, to the suburbs of Paris. Seems the Russian Mafia had joined up with Moroccan Muslims, to give it another go, this time avoiding the satellite system and operating via the overseas land lines. Relatively low tech but very effective. They've not penetrated anything yet but are apparently making significant headway. Of course we could send in some of the Delta boys in but they don't know their way around and should things not go well, an international incident would occur. What is needed is a simple plan to blow up the buildings in question and everything and everyone in it, solving the problem. Seems that rumor has it that you've done some work along those lines Mr. Jaeger"!

"You've a good handle on the buildings involved and where they're at and the pics of the people involved"?

"I've a complete file in my briefcase"?

Jaeger then took out his cell phone, punched in some numbers and said, "Excuse me gentlemen while I make a call, to an old friend who might be of help"! A minute later Jaeger said, "Nestor, Como se Va"! Ten minutes later he disconnected his call and said. "The man I Just talked to is Nestor Magellan. He has an electronic security company in the suburbs of Paris.

Nestor is ex Foreign Legionnaire and we've known each other for years. For a reasonable fee, he will assemble a group of very capable and reliable people locally that can help. Everything required will be there. Everything local. Complete memory loss of the event guaranteed, thus no blow back either way. His phone lines are as secure as any and his word is beyond reproach. We can either fax by secure lines the file to him for study or it can be hand carried by me. One more thing, he has friends in the French Security Service, very good friends"!

Hathaway thought for a moment saying, "Funding for this can be made available with discretion. Yet despite his capabilities I'd feel a lot better if the data file was delivered personally"!

"As you wish", said Jaeger!

"Mr. President", said Hathaway, "Your verbal is all that's required"! "Jaeger, are you up for this", asked Magnusson? He nodded his head in agreement. "Then make it so gentlemen. Gordon you'll see to it that Jaeger is taken care of and will have whatever he needs without delay"!

"Of course Mr. President"!

"Good now hang around while we attack this other local problem relating back to the rash of fires last summer. Preston you're on"!

"Thank you sir! The upshot of our secret investigation of those few we luckily rounded up last summer revealed a very good suspicion that one man, in the Muslim community was central to performing a

Manchurian Candidate scenario upon a host of Muslims in this country, predisposed to violence. We've apprehended several of them, probed their minds and think we've figured out the plan all centering on one lone mastermind who is still out there. As to the others, they are well north of the Arctic Circle no longer a threat. Yet there are the others out there, with no conscious memory of what they've done. The bad news is they could most likely be activated at any time in the near future, by one lone individual. Coupled with that is the still lingering fact that no one has a handle of who was responsible for allowing access to the inauguration site to the terrorists. We narrowed it down to two or three Secret Service Agents, responsible for perimeter access by civilians. Yet polygraphy, voice stress analysis, and injections of truth serum all gave them a clean bill of health. Not one shred of proof, thus they were put back in service, yet in a less important capacity. I believe those in question are involved currently in counterfeit currency apprehensions. Now I'm reluctant to mention this, but in depth investigation to their heritage, reveals a definite relationship to a middle- eastern heritage several generations ago. Certainly nothing that could be presented as evidence in a court of law anywhere in the western world.

Now before anyone says anything we know that is pretty slim and we're grasping at straws. Those involved have no known religious affiliations one way or the other. Yet everything points to them"!

"Jaeger, your thoughts" asked Magnusson. "Preston, what's their annual reviews look like"?

"Everything seems operating in the norm. Nothing detrimental, nothing spectacular. Not management material. More followers rather than leaders. They know the policies and procedures, they're all single and have been in service for a decade or more and most importantly they all operate within prospective guidelines"!

"What about their weapons and munitions capabilities Preston"?

"All grade slightly above average. Capable but not superior"!

"So not one single thing about these guys stands out correct"?

"Yes Jaeger, not one single thing"! Suddenly Bergdorf's eyes grew wide as if he'd reached an epiphany. "Of course", he slowly said, thinking on the run!

"Well out with it man, what are you thinking", asked Magnusson?

"Hide in plain sight. That was it all along! What Jaeger was leading us to was right before our very eyes. Very simple really. If one is to plant a sub rosa operative deep in the ranks, one must have the patience of the biblical Job. A great deal of effort and expenditures must be brought forth, which means a governmental task by someone. Most likely the Russians or the Chinese. Not one thing can go wrong. Mental and emotional conditioning must be engaged in from a very young age. So deep seeded as to be almost at the genetic level. One single word, so obscure as to not be engaged by accident, is required to engage the subconscious, to act a certain way. What we believe the Muslims did, yet far deeper seated. Their actions or lack thereof came from one source, while the arsonists in America got their marching orders from another"!

"All extremely speculative and nothing that'll stand in any court of law", mused Jaeger casually"!

"Correct", said Bergdorf!

"Any handle on the one who triggered the arsonists"!

"We have a name, Salaam and that's all currently. We're trying to canvass all of the Mosques throughout the US, one by one, but adequate manpower is a problem. Like looking for a needle in a haystack with a tweezers"!

"Yeah, it'll take a while especially since the word 'Salaam' in Arabic means Hello and Goodbye", said Jaeger!

"Gentlemen allow me to make a modest proposal", said Jaeger as they all nodded their heads. "Hypothetically, we have received information of the existence of a plant on the outskirts of Paris, capable of printing the Super Bills in American currency. We all know they're out there and the bain of our Treasury Department. Current suspects are the North Koreans and the Iranians. But now they're on the Continent and along with cranking out perfect American currency, they're turning out perfect Euros. Thus a secret task force is to be formed and the agents in question are to join that task force. They will arrive in Paris and be greeted, briefed and equipped by myself and the locals. I'll be a State Department Attaché, with the appropriate credentials, which will shortly thereafter disappear. Our operation on the sites will proceed as planned, yet the suspected agents in question will become unfortunate casualties and disappear completely. Thus two problems solved at the price of one"!

"But how can you guarantee the complete disappearance of those in question without negative blowback", asked Hathaway?

"Two words. Mexican Stew"!

Silently sitting at the fringes sat General Bollinger trying to suppress a smile, but it caught the attention of the President who asked for his opinion.

"Of course Mr. President. Mexican Stew, haven't heard that term in years. But it comes in two flavors that I'm aware of. A dismembered body placed in a large container of hydrochloric acid. Within forty eight hours tops there's nothing but shards of bones which are then poured in the sewers and the entire location quite liberally hosed off. No forensic evidence remains. The second flavor was the favorite of the old French Special Action Group that operated for a while under General DeGaulle when he ran France. The deceased would be taken to a certain Boulangerie on the Rive Gauche, or left bank of the River Seine, that specialized not only in the finest baked goods, but the finest Boeuf Potage, or beef soup in all of Paris. Everyone raved about the soup, likened to the mythical Soup Nazi skit on Seinfeld. The subject completely disappeared, rendered completely on site down to his skin and bones which would find their way into the depths of the English Channel before noon the following day. The patrons of the eatery raved over the soup with long queues of people waiting for their fare. The owner of course had no problem because it cut down on his food costs. The governmental officials involved had no problem because an individual problem ceased to exist. But the poor patrons of the eatery began to have a problem when the government disbanded and retired members of the Special Action Group, sending many of them off to old age pensions, or their graves. Horse meat had to be substituted, sending the food costs up just a bit and modest complaints from the customers that the recipe had been altered"!

"No one the wiser General", asked Magnusson?

"Of course, this is all speculation and legend Mr. President", said the General wryly!

"Jaeger, please then put your plan into action as discussed, and Mr.

Hathaway, jump in the middle of this to make it happen. Of course no one was here and we never had this meeting agreed"!

"You'll be spending the rest of the day at Langley Jaeger", said Magnusson as everybody started to file out of the Oval office, "However late in the day you might want to check in with your official ride, if you catch my drift", said Magnusson nodding his head in Melanie's direction.

"You don't miss much do you", said Jaeger with a grin!

"Don't worry about the time. She's not on any time clock. Whenever you're though call her"!

Jaeger then followed the others out of the office, giving Mel a brief smiling nod as he passed. After they were out of sight, Magnusson emerged and asked, "How's my schedule keeping Mel"?

"You are ten minutes ahead of schedule, Mr. President"!

"Oh yes before I forget, sometime before the day ends someone will call you for a ride. It's Friday and that individual will be in need of transportation for the rest of the day, if you catch my drift. You even might have to provide transport for the entire weekend. If so, suggest the individual check out of the federally funded lodging and into more appropriate surroundings. Capeesh"?

27

Melanie stared out of the rain swept window in a state of complete melancholy. A normally happy and content woman with a son she could be proud of and a career that was pretty much at its peak. She reviewed the times in her life that threw her for loop. Her husband dying in a high speed car crash with a dancer in the passenger seat and his missing male member in her mouth. Followed by the attempted lawsuit by her former in-laws to gain complete custody of her son. Then Jaeger's sudden and complete disappearance and now this. Three weeks since their wonderful reunion and she'd heard not a word. She recalled what her mother had said about life in general being that good always followed bad and vice versa. After her husband's death she eventually met Jaeger and fell completely in love with the man, yet knowing very little about him other than he was thoughtful, polite and great with her son. In the middle of things, suddenly her former in laws mysteriously dropped their custody suit. Then his sudden disappearance for over six months, followed by a session with a downtown lawyer and the legal papers she had to sign from a mysterious benefactor, setting up an annuity for her and a sizeable college fund for her son.

Seems her mom knew something about life. Bad follows good, followed by bad and endless series of crests and shallows. Still her son Rory was doing well at Annapolis and was bound for service in the Marine Corps., upon graduation. He was more like Jaeger in almost every way, yet not a scintilla of the man's gene pool did he possess.

The almost week of their reunion was a magical time for her. She tried to hide the almost schoolgirl glee she felt every time they touched. Being chased out of the office on a Friday afternoon by the President and having to drive over to Langley to pick up Jaeger, then to his Hotel to check out then back to her townhouse to spend that magical time together. He wanted to take her dining and dancing, yet she firmly put her foot down by insisting they spend their time together alone and in her bed as much as possible. She briefly relented the following day by allowing him to acquire some traveling clothes, and then back to her place, to eat, talk together and make love as much as possible. She made it a point to drain him of his bodily nectar every chance she could and during the aftermath examined his scars, prying out highly edited stories of how they came into being.

The following week, she'd drive him to Langley meeting with god only knows who, then pick him up after work and brave the rush hour traffic back to her place where they would prepare the evening meal together, then spend the rest of the evening talking, touching and making love every night. Other than the lovemaking, the very best part of their time together was that they had almost everything in common. He would start a sentence, she would finish it and vice versa, just as before.

On the evening before she had to put him on his flight to Paris, they were making dinner together and while she was dicing onions, she caught him staring at her. She stopped her cutting and asked "What"?

He replied, "Oh not much, just enjoying the view"! An entire book of love poems could not have come close to touching her heart as much as those few, off the cuff words.

The following morning when she dropped him off at Dulles International for his flight, he said, "I'm going to be very busy over there so don't expect me to give you any progress reports. The next time you can expect to hear from me, is when I call you to pick me up. Ya follow"?

"You got it sport", she replied. "Just one thing. Come back to me. You hear"! He gave her a kiss, nodded his head then got out of her car disappearing into the growing crowd of traveler's on their way to everywhere. Then back to work at the White House. Putting on the brave face and doing her job. Other than several luncheons with General Bollinger, slowly peeling away the layers of the onion that was Jaeger, from the man, she had lunch several times with Molly Pringle, who eventually filled in all the missing pieces of the story of Jaegers incarceration and his family's death so many years ago. After all she did have a front row seat for the entire trial.

Yet there was something afoot in the White House. Something that had not as of yet surfaced. One evening she had Molly over for dinner and in the aftermath the subject of the President surfaced. Mel wondered how much longer he was to mourn for the loss of his family.

"Molly he needs a good woman at his side once again", said Mel as she poured out another glass of wine. "He has two fine women watching his six at all times", replied Molly feeling quite relaxed. "You and me"!

"Of course Molly but that's not what I was talking about. He needs a woman in which he can confide"!

"Again Mel, he has two of the finest fillies in town that he can talk to"! "Again Molly you're not getting the message. He needs someone he can love, who will share his bed and keep his confidences. Someone he can talk to. I've seen him before staring out the window at times with that melancholy look of sadness. Like pictures of Lincoln during the Civil War"!

"Yeah, fat lotta god that did him. He was married to this short matronly woman who constantly had the vapors. He would've been far better off being single at the time"!

"I agree, but be that as it may, someone needs to introduce the President to someone suitable"!

"I take it that you're suggesting a Dolly Levy or something like an online dating service? Tell me you're joking"?

"Hell I don't know Molly I'm just thinking out loud"!

"Well now, I've an idea. We can always hook him up with the good Countess Fabiola Hargraves. She's suitable, sort of and has a shit load of money. Hell she'd be able to refinance his reelection campaign in a heartbeat and not miss a farthing"!

"Fabiola Hargraves", exclaimed Mel. I think not! The press would have a field day. Now you're the one who's joking"!

"Of course I am. But I wouldn't worry about that. With any luck, that bridge will be crossed eventually. Nature hates a vacuum"!

"Bridge crossed", wondered Mel out loud. Her mind racing with the possibilities. Then she looked Molly straight in the eye and said, "Molly you know something you're not telling"!

"Oh Christ. Me and my big mouth. Another round please if you will"!

While Mel poured the wine in both of their glasses, Molly started. "The man ran off all of his speech writers, if you'll recall and ever since he's been cranking them out himself sometimes with Harvanian's help and other times with Goodwin's. He had this speech about two weeks ago the day after you cut loose Jaeger to go to Paris. Well I had to go help him craft his speech for the next day and we worked till about ten in the evening. He had the staff bring in dinner and we worked straight through munching and working. Then Hell I don't know, we kissed. Nothing intended on either of our parts I don't think. We just kissed. Then we kissed some more and then a long lingering kiss. From that point on I was toast. The man owned me body and soul. Of course the speech was completed and he had it down cold. The work was finished. I think it started when I locked horns with a few of the Press Corps during the news conference and later when I locked horns publicly with Senator Kleptocrat"!

"Did you coin that phrase", asked Mel?

"It just came to me, I think. The son of a bitch is the biggest ear marker thief in Congress and doesn't give a fig who knows it. Anyway, I think you and Jaeger might have had something to do with it, for as any fool could see, for a whole week you were on cloud nine, so perhaps that might've been the catalyst. Who knows? But I remember asking, him if he was ready for this? He paused and mumbled something like, He had permission! You can figure out that one anyway you choose. Then head said for me to wait a few minutes and follow him upstairs. He left I waited a suitable interval then went upstairs. How could I not? He's clearly available. He's a very attractive man and after all, he's the President. Believe me I didn't want a repeat of the event several years ago when President 'Randy was nailing everyone he could. That kind of publicity no one needs. Still there was a joint chemistry there that is not going away"!

"So you succumbed to his lustful advances", said Mel with a slow wink!

"I like to think we both jointly succumbed, reluctantly, but with abandon and good cheer"?

"So inquiring minds just have to know, how was it"? "Nothing short of wonderful, girl"!

"Anybody see you in the Presidents quarters"?

"Don't think so and even if they did, you know the staff, their all in his corner foursquare"!

"So what about any repeat performances"?

"Every other night for the last few weeks. Pisses me off though. I have to leave at three in the morning and neither of us is getting much sleep.

Which is why some other accommodations will have to be made eventually. If you noticed he's now taking mid afternoon naps for a half hour each day and with my work load I can't. Still, I'm absolutely smitten with the man.

Just have to offer it up to the higher power and see what develops. Now I know just how you feel towards Jaeger and girl I just want to say that my sincerest wish is that he makes an honest woman of you, so the both of you can grow old and cranky together"!

"Back at ya sister", said Mel starting to tear up.

"Damn it, now you got me going", said Molly starting to cry herself.

Out of gossip between them Mel filled Molly's goblet once again saying, "You're in no condition to drive anywhere tonight and neither am I, so you have the guest bed room all to yourself. Feel free to sleep until noon and if his majesty calls, I'll tell him you're pooped and that it's all his fault"!

"Meanwhile, let's turn on the TV and catch the news.

Flipping through the cable channels the settled on the BBC Europe just as a Reuters report came through regarding a massive explosion and fire rampaging through a series of warehouses in the far northern suburbs of Paris.

"Isn't that where Jaeger was headed two weeks ago"? "Yes but that probably had nothing to do with him", said Melanie weakly, wondering if it were true and if Jaeger was safe.

The following day, the girls spent the morning together and by noon Molly departed for her place, to spend the week end catching up on the personal essentials of her life, while Melanie devoted herself to doing the same. By nine in the evening her work completed, she'd just settled down with a glass of wine and opened a book she'd been reading. The TV was on low volume and was of no distraction. She'd gone no more than two pages, when the phone rang. She picked up the phone saying, "Mel here, speak"!

On the other end she heard, "I wonder if that free cab service is still available"?

"Jaeger"?

"No darlin', its Jose Jimenez! Of course it's me"!

"Are you alright"?

"Let me look around for a moment. Yep, seems everything is in place"!

"When are you coming back"?

"Get something to write on and I'll tell ya"!

"I'm boarding the Chunnel Train in a few minutes heading to London. I'll be taking the first flight out of Heathrow". He then told her the flight number, departure and arrival time at Dulles International as she hurriedly wrote it down! Just be in your car at the arrival queue at the airport and I'll find you. Before she could ask any more questions, he said, "They're announcing the train boarding right now, so just put a staple in it and I'll see ya soon"!

"Be safe", said Melanie as the line went dead. She hung up the phone and looked up at the ceiling thanking that higher authority, simply giving thanks. Wanting to call someone, or scream out loud, she did neither and closed her eyes asking yet another favor of the unseen, to bring her man back safely, to the comfort of her home.

Of course time never passes so slowly as when one is awaiting the anticipated return of a loved one. Seems Einstein overlooked that in his equations long ago. Every other hour she phoned the airlines to verify the flight arrival time, if for nothing else, to have something to do. Her body told her she ought to eat something, yet her mind rebelled at anything more than the obligatory cup of coffee. Normally a regular attendee of church services, she asked the eternals forgiveness just this once, for her absence. As time drew near for her to depart for the airport she threw on some slacks and a blouse, ran a comb through her hair, checked her appearance in the mirror and left.

The Federal tag on her windshield, served her well as she waited in her car at the arrival area. The airport police staff kept moving cars along and gave her a wide berth, as she stood by the fender of her car. The flight was supposed to have landed a half hour ago and still no Jaeger. She checked her cell phone for messages and finding none put it back in her jacket pocket. Just as she looked up, there he was, trudging through the exit door looking all around, then finally catching sight of her, gave her a head nod and walked her way smiling. The car trunk open he tossed his bag inside and slammed the trunk lid, as she slid into his arms, putting one hand around his head and pulling it towards her for a passionate kiss. As they finally pulled apart she laughingly asked, "Is that a banana in your pocket cowboy, or are ya just glad to see me"? Before he could answer she pulled his head towards her for round two. Just then a police whistle sounded and they turned around to see the airport traffic cop approaching. "Hey you two, get a room and move it outta here"! Jaeger nodded his head and said, "Drive woman"!

As she drove away on the exit ramp Jaeger said, "Just keep your eyes on the road. Be too bad if an accident occurred at this juncture. Besides, I like the view of your profile. Makes the Mona Lisa look bovine in comparison. "What do you want for dinner sport? I'm in a cooking mood", asked Mel?

"How about you for an entrée', then for dessert let me see? How about you"!

"What about your choice for the after dinner drink", she asked, her face starting to grow flush. "Same answer", he said pausing. "You want me to drive"?

As soon as the door closed in her town house, they hurriedly climbed the stairs to her bedroom and closed the door as Jaeger dropped his bag.

Three hours later as they lay in bed she said, "You know I haven't eaten all day in anticipation of your arrival"!

"Damn it, why didn't you say something earlier", asked Jaeger in mock anger?

"Because your dinner came first", smiling at her feeble attempt at a pun.

"I take it the kitchen is ready for my attention"?

They both tossed on some clothes, he a pair of pants and Mel a wrinkled Naval Academy oversized T-shirt that barely came to midthigh and went down stairs and she watched him direct her to the counter while he prepared them dinner.

"So sport, what's on the agenda for tomorrow"?

"A few days with this Hathaway guy and the General at Langley for a debriefing, then wait for a phone call from my contact in Paris about something else that's on the burner. Then I just have to zip back to Texas, attack my mail, pay some bills, check on a project I've got going in Waco, then back here with your permission of course so I can examine at length the space between your shoulder blades"!

After dinner as they sat next to each other on her couch, she asked him about the project in Waco?

"Something I've been working on for years. It's been a secret, a project of resurrectionof my birthright. Been working on it for so long and wondering why"! Then he looked at her seriously and said, "Now, at last I know why and it has everything to do with you"!

"Me you say"?

"Have you any accrued vacation time coming"?

"Of course"!

"Take off a few days. A very long weekend"?

"Depends what on the President's agenda"!

"Then when all this stuff is done, we can jump on a plane head for Houston, and then drive up to Waco, so you can see for yourself and tell me what you think"!

The following Morning Jaeger met with Gordon Hathaway, General Bollinger and Preston Bergdorf, at CIA Head Quarters in Langley Virginia. Secluded in one of the conference rooms, Hathaway commenced the meeting which was an after action review of the recent effort abroad.

Working from the original file he gave to Jaeger he asked him, "Is this the original file you took to Paris"?

"Yes it is"!

"Were any copies of this file made, either in its entirety or in part"? "Several copies were made in part as we commenced to develop the plan"?

"For what purpose"?

"As Nestor Magellan, my host and contact, and I developed the plan several things began to come together in his mind. As you must know, Paris, as well as the rest of France has a significant Muslim population. Of the people he brought in to assist the operation, several were old timers.

Retired members of the disbanded Special Action Group of the French Bureau of Internal Security along with two other current operatives that provided important access to things. It's accurate to say all of these people were, in a word, Islamaphobic. Be that as it may, it served our purposes sufficiently to affect the desired outcome. Several names and pictures we provided were loaned to them to run through their data base, which a day later came up with several others not directly involved with the operation at hand, yet might have some bearing on other problems here at home, that I'll get into later"!

"The following day, the Secret Service people that were suspected arrived and Magellan and I picked them up at the airport"! His governmental operative was in the lead on this one, with Magellan playing the role as driver. The State Department credentials furnished to me convinced them that I was purely along for the ride as an observer. In all, eleven operatives were involved, including myself, Magellan, the three Secret Service people, the two genuine French cops, and the three retired SAG operatives"!

"We put the eyes on the several buildings involved. Once we were certain that we had the right place and the right people involved, two days were spent, secretly loading up the places with explosives. The Secret Service people in question were under the complete impression this was to be an apprehension of an International Counterfeiting ring as the original plan called for and not a demolition so great care had to be taken to compartmentalize things, as one can imagine"! "So what happened next" asked Bollinger?

"Our observance told us during the course of several weeks, of their daily routine and apparently their several locations of the servers being in close proximity of each other in the Parisian suburbs, told us of the optimum time of their activity. Seems they were all night owls and did their best work at three in the morning local time. Thus we determined that 0330 AM was the optimal time. Within a ten second span of time everything went BOOM. With all identified parties inside and hard at work supposedly"!

"What happened to the Secret Service Agents", asked Bergdorf? "They were in the rear trunks of three different cars with plastic bags over their heads, Hor's de Combat"!

"Who and how Jaeger", asked Hathaway?

"Three of the retired Special Action Group people took care of that, with silenced .25 cal automatics, just prior to kickoff. They were quickly determined to be dead. These guys have had much practice in this so we weren't about to question their abilities. The plastic bags were placed over their heads to minimize any blood residue. They were loaded into the trunks of the three vehicles and on the road away from the locations three minutes before the explosions. Thirty seconds before the explosions the rest of us were on the road in different directions"!

"So we can't be absolutely certain that all were inside the structures when the explosions occurred", asked Hathaway?

"Not 100% certain but in the high ninety percentile, that almost three weeks of direct observation gave us regarding their nightly work routines. The Euro media reported no apparent survivors, with everyone burned to a crisp or crushed beyond recognition. Common sense dictated prudent action namely that we all de de out of there at a reasonable speed.

"Once again Mr. Jaeger, if you will", asked Hathaway, "The three American Secret Service Agents, in what manner were they disposed of"!

"Their skin, cranium and bones, lay some fifty miles out in the English Channel, as a modest gift to Neptune, so I'm told. They clothes and identifications are currently somewhere in a land fill, having been removed and scattered in a host of trash dumpsters the following day".

"But the remains man, the remains. What happened to the remains", asked Hathaway, while Bergdorf and Bollinger sat back trying to stifle a grin? "As Agent Bergdorf previously referred some weeks ago, Two of the retired SAG operatives operated successful restaurants on the left bank of the River Seine and they are famous for their 'Boeuf Pottage', and

Bouillabaisse. I would not recommend a trip to Paris any time soon for gastronomic curiosity. So as for the three individuals in question, it's no longer an issue I suggest. But they did come in handy while they were there"!

Hathaway looked sheepishly at Bergdorf and the General saying, "Your comment regarding disposal slipped my mind Agent Bergdorf, but as of now it remains firmly implanted. Have all the funds to the operatives been disposed of"?

"Half upon initial engagement and half upon completion. Standard Operational Format. Done and done again. Nobodies complaining, especially the restaurant owners"!

"What about this other thing this Magellan came across, regarding American activities"!

"Nestor, when I departed the other day, didn't have it nailed down yet, but one of the pictures shown to him of the suspected computer hackers, hit some kind of raw nerve in his head. Several days later, he said a single name. A man known as "Le Bossu", which means "The Hunchback". He's trying to nail down a picture of the guy, but scant chance of that happening. Apparently he's an Albanian from birth that found his way to France when he was young. Magellan says he came in contact with him briefly fifteen years ago. The man appearance is literally grotesque, being a hunchback, standing no taller than five foot six in height. Given his appearance he only operates at night and from the shadows. He has extensive contacts in the middleeast which makes sense, since he was born Muslim and is said to practice the religion daily, yet completely in private. Given his appearance one can understand his reluctance to attend Friday Prayers at any Mosque"!

"Now here's the interesting part. He knew this Bujovic very well back in the day, during the siege of Sarajevo by the Serbians. He has connections of some sort with the Islamic, or Muslim Brotherhood in Cairo. Spiritual and business connections. He had something to do with Bujovic coming to America and further rumor has it that another remains, here that he's the American conduit and mastermind. He's working on that very thing for us currently. So should we express any interest, especially since the other name he mentioned was the name Salaam"?

"Further, his business interests are everywhere, from drug and gun running, counterfeit products of all sorts, Turkish whore houses, you name it and he's got a piece of it. Now part of what he's involve with is the Euro and middle-eastern porn business. He's got this string of girls he runs in and out of where ever he's at, for he has a multiple of residences along the Adriatic Sea area. He's a penchant for German women especially one who's a bottle redhead who's stage name, is 'Leloo' in the porno film business.

They get together, she is blind folded, for the obvious reasons of his grotesque appearance, they perform, and he gets satisfied. Then she gets paid and whisked back to where ever she came from and gentlemen, that is his Achilles heel. Now if "Le Bossu" can be got hold of and rendered, he just might reveal where the headquarters of the Muslim Brotherhood is in Cairo. If what has happened recently in Paris can be duplicated in Cairo, this just might knock them down a bunc. h. The international funding for Jihad may emanate in Riyadh and Tehran but the spiritual heart of Jihad is in Cairo somewhere. Should what just occurred in Paris, be able to be duplicated in Cairo and possibly elsewhere, its certain to knock them back significantly. Now, if unofficially some go ahead might be given to a plan that is in the works, the Israeli Mossad just might be interested in providing assistance. The whole point being that these people are bullies at heart and bullies always cave to overt pressureIn a straight up life or death scrape, few if any will stand their ground and fight it out to the end"!

"Mr. Hathaway, I'm certain you'll agree with me on the following points", said the General continuing. "First, no decision regarding this can be made at this level. Next, we ask Mr. Jaeger to stay around for just a few days and enlighten those of a decision making capacity, finally involving the President as before. Finally we look around and determine the most optimum assets and their availability. Once this is all lined out then we can proceed, to the next step of preemption

The rest of the day was in endless meeting with a few key department heads, in the development of a hypothetical plan. The key element being precise information on the ground. More and more the name of Nestor Magellan arose as a key contact point. Rather than task their other assets around the world, many of which were currently involved in other activities, the logic of employing another became a growing reality, for political as well as reasons of provable ability and existing contacts. The presence of commonality of purpose and the all-important dollar was the tie that brought serious people together.

Things were starting to draw together very quickly, with Jaeger having to get back to Houston for at least a day, gather and sort his mail. Pay some bills then fly back to Washington within a twenty four hour window. While in town and amidst all the rush, he checked both his primary and secondary residence for any signs of intrusion and finding none, reset his security devices before his departure. By this juncture, Jaeger had paved the way for a relationship between the CIA's Gordon Hathaway, the FBI's prime behavioral investigator Preston Bergdorf and Nestor Magellan. Once certain procedures and protocols were established, data began to flow at a measured rate between the two entities on this Ad Hoc basis, for interaction.

When Mel picked him up at the airport upon his return, she noted that he was carrying two larger pieces of old olive drab military luggage, rather than the large overnighter he usually carried.

"Planning for an extended stay sport", asked Mel?

"Muy permisso, Chulita", said Jaeger with a smile, adding it's just starting to cool off in South Texas if you'll recall while snows just around the corner here in Yankee land.

The following morning Jaeger once again joined everybody at Langley. Before he departed for Texas there was some discussion of including several other agencies including the military for their inputs. When asked for their opinion, everyone gave theirs as whether or not engage others in the operation. When it came around to Jaeger he said, "As most of you know, for a number of years I made a living being a bail enforcement agent in Harris County Texas. Now being a chaser running down mostly common criminals, who might be long on clever but short on smarts, taught me many lessons. Gradually I upped my game and started to be a Chaser of a more unique and clever sort of criminal. Either way, they always came back, one way or the other. One of the basic lessons I learned was to fall in with those on the local ground whenever possible, who can bring unique talents to the table. One tests them or vets them for reliability. Super stars and too many Alpha types knock down your Chances for success. Give me reliability over pure ability any day. Now we have a contact on the continent that is reliable. I've known the man for a long time. He delivers. Been on a few operations with the man and never seen him make a bad move or decision even once. He speaks multiple languages fluently and has a working knowledge of many more. His involvement in this is as a favor to me. He is a man of personal honor, dealing in a world of criminals and bad actors.

Those who work for him are like minded and paid rather well, thus the probability that he'll be compromised in any way is minimal. Now one of many of our commonalities is the belief of traveling light and fast. He has access to people on the ground that are reliable and serious people. They know and trust him. A trust that has been hard won over time. The recent operation in Paris is a textbook example of what he's capable of. The job got done, with no comebacks. Listen very carefully to him. Provide only what he might ask for and nothing else"!

"Now phase one of the operation concerning "Le Bossu", the hunchback his apprehension. He's made some initial moves in that direction. We'll know something better in a few days or whenever he calls. Once "Le Bossu" is contained, he can be examined, that's when our people can join in with his to extract what is needed. Depending on what is extracted by our joint efforts will determine what is possible in Cairo, where two key members of the Egyptian Police are willing, for a remittance for their efforts, to put an end to the Moslem Brotherhood. A real thorn in the side of the Egyptian body politic. Now if we really get lucky then perhaps Le Bossu or even someone in Cairo can shed some light on this Salaam individual operating in the US"!

"The more people on our end that know of this, other than the President, is a guarantee of the summoning of Murphy's Law. Gentlemen I'll have no part of that and neither will Magellan. Please don't take that as a demand but nothing more than a simple fact. Keep things small, light, fast and invisible and good things have a better chance of happening"!

Just then the phone rang and on the other end was Magellan. Forty eight hours later Jaeger sat in the back seat of a gray BMW 745i as they shadowed a big black Mercedes Benz sedan carrying 'Le Bossu' to his rendezvous with his favorite redhead plaything, 'Le Loo'. Things had gone exceedingly well for the troll as of late with his latest munitions shipment to the rebels in Ghana, being paid for in blood diamonds from Sierra Leone.

Money being only one, of many mediums of exchange. He'd selected a sizable bauble of several rough carats to give to Le Loo this evening after her exertions as a little something extra. Of course it would have to be cut and processed by a jeweler he knew in Zagreb, for her final examination, but that was a minor affair certain to bring her heart towards him for at least a little while. After all, did not an act of kindness reward Quasimodo after he saved the lovely gypsy woman Esmeralda? Every time he looked in a mirror, he saw what others did. A grotesque individual with a heart of darkness. He knew from life's experiences, that happiness was fleeting even in the best of times and there was never a single day of his life that could be called the best of times.

So be it. Life had dealt him a bad hand in one respect while rewarding him in other ways.

As Magellan and Jaeger weaved their way through the winding mountain roads of the southern Bosnian landscape, almost a mile back with their light out, they could barely make out the headlights, of the black Mercedes sedan as it rounded the bend in the road. Suddenly, over the handset of the side band phone was the sound of a crash and the word, "Bingo", which signaled Magellan's driver to accelerate carefully. In a little more than a minute later, they arrived at the crash site and everyone piled out of the BMW, with guns drawn.

The intermittent patches of fog were helpful as the Mercedes rounded the bend in the road and could not help but run right into the big Lorry that had suddenly driven on to the road. The immaculate timing was due to one of Magellan's crew sitting on the hillside in the dark preceding the bend in the road and signaling the Lorry driver, by his cell phone to, "Go now"! The sedan had bounced off the Lorry and turned over quickly saved only from careening down the mountainside by a single guard rail some fifty yards down the road. The Lorry had been stolen some twenty four hours earlier in Belgrade and was promptly wiped clean of any prints, as the others fell upon the car finding the driver dead and the body guard in the front seat just coming around. A single muffled shot to the head prevented any unpleasantness. Le Bossu sat in the back seat worse for wear, his seat belt unbuckled at the time of the crash.

"Is he alive", asked Magellan from one of his operatives?

"A bad bump on his head, but he'll live. His breathing is slightly laboured but he'll survive"!

Then Jaeger reached into the pocket of his jacket and produced a syringe which he quickly injected a quarter of its contents into the crumpled body. They bound and secured his arms and legs, wrapping him in a tarp, then lifted him up and deposited him into the trunk of the BMW. Another sedan dove up behind them. It was the sedan of those trailing the BMW.

One of the men in the sedan went to the still idling Lorry and got behind the steering wheel putting it in gear and pressed the accelerator as it lurched forward driving it a short way down the road, jumping free at the very last instant onto the road as the Lorry plunged down the slope, smashing into trees along the way, ending up in the valley below.

A minute later the two sedans continued on down the mountain side to their rendezvous with a yacht docked in the Marina below, for a trip out into the Adriatic. They passed a small hotel, on the edge of a village where on the very top floor, was a small suite of rooms where "Le Loo", lay in preparation for a rendezvous that was never going to happen.

As the two cars drove through the fog of the sleepy fishing village deep in the neck of one of the Adriatic Sea's many inlets, they stopped at the fishing Marina, quickly and silently unloading the unconscious Le Bossu into a small life boat. Their task completed, Magellan gave each of the men an envelope and his thanks, watching them as they drove off into the fog shrouded early morning.

He then joined Jaeger and their passenger in the boat as the boat's owner, simple fishermen, started the small outboard engine, disappearing into the fog, on its way to meet the yacht some five miles down the inlet. A half hour later the motor boat pulled alongside the yacht as several men from the vessel helped bring the cargo aboard and down into the yachts interior. Magellan produced another envelope giving it without a word to the fisherman.

As the little boat motored back to the small fishing Marina, the grizzled fisherman opened the envelope, briefly scanning its contents, before putting it back into his coat. Inside the envelope were a year's earnings as a fisherman in a good year. Not bad pay for less than an hour's work.

As the two Delta operatives unwrapped the hapless Le Bossu from his tarp, they deposited him on one of the couches in the boats main salon. Jaeger directed them to remove the bonds that secured him.

He made the introduction between Preston Bergdorf and Magellan as Bergdorf asked, "Who owns this boat, if I might ask"?

"A very old acquaintance, Agent Bergdorf", said Magellan continuing. A wealthy Russian businessman, whose interests coincide with ours, for the time being", he offered with a fingertip tapping the side of his nose"!

Turning towards Jaeger Bergdorf asked, "How much of your jungle juice did you pump into this guy"?

"Less than a half cc. My guess is that he'll be out for at least six hours, before he comes to. Then I suppose you'll want him to stabilize for a while before you commence"!

"One of the Delta's that accompanied me is a medical Corpsman; he'll be responsible for seeing to it that he is in good shape medically during the interrogation. I'll conduct the interrogation. The boats captain is to pilot the craft to the middle of the Adriatic then slowly up towards Venice, where the boat is normally docked. Should take a few days sailing time. If the SP-117 works as well as I'm given to believe, we'll have everything this guy has to give in twelve hours. Since my grasp of linguistics extends only towards the Kings English, I'd appreciate your assistance Mr. Magellan at any time along the way"!

"That you shall have Agent Bergdorf. I see that the entire event will be videotaped, given the equipment set up in the salon"!

"Just part of the procedure. An aide to memory. But tell me what's to be done with this Le Bossu guy afterward"?

"Oh that", said Jaeger. "He'll be processed. Nestor this is your department"!

"But of course. Please Agent Bergdorf follow me to the boats stern"! As they all, including the Delta operatives emerged from the salon to the stern portion of the boat in the early morning fog, they turned off the lights from the shrouded interior of the salon and Magellan briefly turned on his shrouded flashlight that briefly illuminated a tarpaulin covered mass.

"Under this tarp is a specially prepared fifty gallon oil drum", said Magellan continuing. "Welded to the drum are four chains and attached to those chains are a hundred and fifty kilos of lead weights. Next to the oil drum is of eight kilos of hydrochloric acid. Welded into the drum is a snorkel like device. When the cow is milked for all it's worth, he will be placed inside the drum. A single bullet will be fired into his head, finishing him off. The acid will be carefully be poured over him and the lid will be secured to the drum and sealed. Then he will be hoisted over the side and we sail away. The drum will sink to the bottom of the sea. As the body rapidly decomposes, the snorkel devise will permit the gasses to escape without letting the water to enter the container. Within seventy two hours tops, a gelatinous mass will be all that is left. All evidence that Le Bossu ever existed will be no more"!

"You people have this business down cold", said Bergdorf!

"It is the recipe for preparing Mexican Stew, as my friend Jaeger has often coined it" said Magellan! In the darkness, both of the Delta operatives looked at each other with a recently acquired knowledge worth knowing.

Later in the morning Le Bossu recovered, was resecured and his clothed cut from his grotesquely formed body. A small portable EKG machine was brought along to monitor his heart beat and the electrodes attached. He was injected by the corpsman with the KGB truth serum, placed on the floor over the tarpaulin that initially covered his entrance and the questioning commenced, as the yachts captain held the course steadily in a northwesterly direction towards his home port in Venice. By night fall Le Bossu had revealed a wealth of information, of times, places, locations and names of individuals involved in a variety of events far exceeding expectations.

Magellan's expertise in linguistics was vital, as Le Bossu, unconsciously switched back and forth from his native Albanian dialect to Greek, then to Serbian, to French, to guttural German and every once in a while bad English, with a running narrative that lasted from beginning to the end. Twelve solid hours of video taped information that was gone over and over. At ten in the evening, their task finished the Captain of the craft informed them of surface radar revealing no craft within twenty miles of their location. A compliant Le Bossu was carefully placed in the oil drum, the Coupe' de Grace administered, the acid carefully poured and the drum sealed, with all the men taking part in hoisting Le Bossu over the boats stern as it made its way towards Venice. Magellan quickly turned on his flashlight to see if everything was all right. Then quickly turned it off turning and declaring, "Gentlemen, the hunchback is no more"!

As the boat sailed through the night, everything in the salon was put right as the galley produced a fine dinner for all. Every one was pleased as things went off without a single hitch. They discussed at length the possibilities that lay before them, agreeing that a two pronged effort was in order. A quick assault on the Islamic or Moslem Brotherhood in Cairo was in order, given that a political meeting between certain elements was scheduled by the Grand Muktar in Cairo within the next thirty days. It was agreed that Magellan was to inquire of his contact within the Egyptian National Police.

"Just as a point of inquiry, why should they be trusted", asked Bergdorf?

"Quite simple really", said Magellan continuing. "They are Coptic Christians, who long ago secretly converted from Islam. They attend Friday prayers at their Mosque, but only continue that charade as a point of survival. Even their wives are unaware of their conversion. Of course each one only has one wife. Things are simpler that way. Should anyone ever get wind of their conversion, their careers would be finished and their lives as well as that of their immediate families wouldn't be worth a farthing. They would be considered all, apostates. Their families at the very least would turn against them, for they were raised Muslim and of their own free will seem to have turned their backs on the Prophet. Now of course they will have to be well compensated for their risk, but as to their zeal to get the yolk of extremist, non-tolerance off their backs, make no mistake of their intensity. Both Jaeger and I have placed our lives in their hands before and emerged whole"!

"Your thoughts Jaeger" asked Bergdorf?

"Been to Cairo once before. What interested me more is this Salaam fella. The Hunchback mentioned he'd been specially groomed. Imported from the bowels of the Great Satan, America, as he put it long ago.

Completely trained and examined by their elders. Sent to them by the American Imams, whoever they were. Returned to the Great Satan, to serve Jihad. To erode, to destroy, to provide service to all believers from deep within. Then he mentioned something about the long road of this Bujovic fella, through Cairo, into Mexico for a while, then on to America. He knew nothing about his Mexican contacts, so we'll have to leave that alone. It might never be known. What'll be known lays in Cairo, but that's going to have to be a quick in and out operation should it come to pass. He mentioned something about the city of St. Louis, saying that it was a transit point. A transit point for what? Money, papers, drugs? My interests lay in the middle of America. Magellan can and should head up the Cairo operation"!

"Can you provide us with a cost factor of the Cairo operation Nestor", asked Bergdorf?

"Should be a few days but I'll be in contact".

"Good", said Bergdorf. "Now perhaps we can enjoy what's left of out cruise"!

The two Delta operatives had remained silent thus far, drinking it all in, when one of them asked Agent Bergdorf, "Excuse me sir. We've been sittin' on our duffs too long and feel we can contribute while we're over here. I've a working knowledge of Arabic and George is a Paramedic and munitions expert as well as myself. We look the part and with the right people can blend right in"!

Bergdorf looked at Magellan and Jaeger saying, "They're on loan from the Defense Department, not under my preview, for the duration of the operation. If the operation hasn't concluded and they're presence is still required, I suppose I could pass along a request for their continued involvement"!

Magellan glanced quickly at Jaeger, then at the two Delta operatives, then said to Bergdorf, "If the gentlemen wouldn't mind a long drive back to Paris, with Jaeger and I please make the request of whoever you have to for their continued involvement"!

28

As Jaeger removed his seat belt once the flight back to Dulles Airport achieved its cruising altitude, he opened his small case and removed the small package given him by Magellan upon his departure. He removed the note from its envelope and opened it. It read; "Our friend no longer has any need of such baubles. Rumor has it that you may be in the market. Any good diamond cutter should be able to bring out its finest qualities"! Jaeger promptly opened up the small box to find a rather large rough looking stone. He quickly concluded this was probably one of the so called 'Blood Diamonds', he'd heard about. A result no doubt of activity conducted by the Hunchback. Lifted from him by Magellan, prior to his examination.

Since Magellan was a happily married man, or so he proclaimed and had no other involvements, he'd no other course than to take the man at his word and thank him after a jeweler had appraised it. Then his thoughts drifted to Melanie and he knew exactly how to put this rock to good use. The only thing that disturbed him was how on earth Magellan thought that he was in a position to put it to good use?

As Jaeger and General Bollinger lagged behind the rest as they made their way towards one of the White House conference rooms the General said, "Since you've taken up with Mrs. O'Bannon recently and I understand it's a long overdue acquaintance, you might want to consider taking a day and driving over to Annapolis and spend a few hours with a certain young man"!

As they walked on in silence a bit further, he recalled seeing pictures of Mel's son all over her town house. He was a fine looking specimen, resplendent in his Naval Academy uniform.

The General added, "When he graduates, he's going to commit to the Marine Corps. Ground Assault units."!

"The Mud Marines, eh General"?

"Exactly. I've talked with him. Visited some of his instructors and they all give him high marks in field craft. Somewhere along the line, someone taught him to be a shooter. Top marks at the firing range with the long gun and the hand gun. Don't have any idea where he might have picked that up do you"?

"Have a lot on my plate right now General as you know. If all this mess works out as planned, I'll be hanging things up. Then I'll drift on down to Annapolis and make myself known"!

As they entered the room the General said, "Good enough"! They both took a seat at the end of the conference table, next to Agent Bergdorf, of the FBI and Gordon Hathaway of the CIA. It was a selective meeting of those immediately concerned with the two phases of the operation. The Defense Secretary sat next to the Chairman of the Joint Chiefs of Staff, flanked by a single trusted assistant each.

The Presidents Chief of Staff Orval Goodwin entered the room, followed by the President as all rose in unison.

"Gentlemen please be seated and thank you for coming at such short notice. I don't need to remind you that no notes or recording are to result from this meeting. Everything is strictly verbal", said the President as all nodded their heads.

"Thanks to Agent Bergdorf of the FBI, on assignment to us for this purpose only, the Balkan operation in the Adriatic yielded us a boatload of actionable information, for external and internal operations. First let's discuss the external. Agent Bergdorf tell us that within three weeks and we have a date certain, a meeting of most all of the political terrorist factions in the Middle East, will secretly gather in Cairo for a unity meeting. Most of the big honchos will be there. Mr. Hathaway, why does the CIA have any interest in this? Let's allow that all goes well. How will their deaths cripple them severely and couldn't a few F-117's, or YF 22's drop a few well- placed bombs, strictly on a quick in and out mission"?

"Thank you Mr. President", said Hathaway rising. "The information gleaned from Le Bossu was finally vetted by our contacts with Israeli Military Intelligence and The Mossad. I might add that only the aspects of the Cairo Meeting were made known to them with all else redacted. They knew something was up, but it took our information to finally connect the dots for them. They were thinking along the same lines as we were, but now that we all have the most complete picture of all the anticipated players, they are willing to take a back seat for this operation and provide us with valuable on site assistance. In addition thanks to Mr. Jaeger's overseas contact, which has proven vital to the success of the Balkan operation, there exist reliable contacts in the Egyptian Government that will also assist our efforts in that regard"!

"Now the question may be asked, why would anyone in the Egyptian Government want to assist in an operation in Cairo, a city of some twenty million people? So gentlemen, lets step back in time a bit. Years ago Anwar Sadat made nice with the Israeli government and the Moslem Brotherhood, with operatives deep in the Egyptian Military has him taken out. Mubarak almost got the horns too but survived. He's run the country as successfully ever since. Some say that he's a benevolent dictator and they might be right. But Egypt during his turn at the wheel has achieved a level of prosperity from his long efforts. He's growing old and is in the process of grooming his son to take over some day. Now the Moslem or Islamic Brotherhood wants to bring Egypt into the universal world Caliphate. Thus is a mortal enemy to the current Egyptian way of life. The view all secular governments as apostates and any reading of the Koran indicates that all apostates must be killed. This technically includes the government of Turkey. So you can see their dilemma. Do we embrace our current progressive way of living, or do we embrace chapter and verse the Koran"? "It's our view that those key people inside Egypt will give us assistance, because it's in their best interests to do so. They and the Israeli's will provide logistic, munitions, infil and exfil assistance, transportation and temporary quarters for the operation"!

"Now to the question as to why are these people meeting anyway? For ages they've all operated on their own, like a multi headed hydra. Few of them like each other, much less can get along. They each trumpet their success's as much as possible and rarely if ever cooperate with each other. Israel likes it that way, for if they ever were capable of unity, Israel would be in for a very nasty and long slog. Thus apparently the Islamic terrorists have finally had their, pardon the expression, Come to Jesus moment and want to find some other common ground, putting aside all of the enmity that exists between Sunni and Shiite factions"!

"Now we could bomb them through the air with our stealth fighters and probably get in and out without a problem, then again maybe not. Always a first time for everything. Even if successful, the only two parties with that kind of capability would be either Israel or the US. Even the most casual observer could put those dots together and our President and the State Department doesn't need that kind of problem"!

"Now Mr. Jaeger over there next to General Bollinger, a while ago went into Cairo and brought back a felon to the US Marshall's service, using the efforts of the very two Egyptian operatives that are in assistance today, with of course, the help of his European contact. Now gentlemen, there are key elements in each of the entities that have agreed to meet in Cairo, that want nothing to do with the others. They distrust anyone that is not one of them. Sort of tribal loyalty that keeps a unity of purpose at arm's length. They are in conflict with their own leaders. I'd like that very fact to sink in for a moment"!

"This is their Achilles heel for us to employ to our purposes. Their lack of unity. We go in, we skillfully prepare the ground, we lay doggo in the tall grass, they arrive, and we wait until the last of them arrive. We set the timer, and then depart blending into the Megalopolis that is Cairo, in many different directions and then Boom. We do to them what's been done to us.

Chaos ensues and amidst the chaos the good guys escape. Now who's to blame? No one knows! Who are the suspects? Where's the proof"?

Then General Ottenger spoke up as the Chairman of the Joint Chief of Staff saying, "Mr. Hathaway, the plan as it exists seems to have covered most all of the contingencies, yet as every military man knows battle plans often go out the window at the commencement of conflict. Move and countermoves being expected"!

"An excellent point General, but this is not an expected battle between two gargantuan armies that expect confrontation at any moment. We know that a meeting is going to occur and why. We know where it will be. We know its top secret and the only reason we know this, is because they expect certain members of the Cairo Police loyal to their purposes, to provide security. Of course our guys have discovered that one of the policemen involved has a certain sexual problem he wished he didn't have. Namely homosexuality. Should it ever become known his true preferences, he'd be dead before sunrise. Thus a guarantee of silence in the aftermath.

Plus they don't know that we know, thus the advantage"! "But what about the explosives used, Mr. Hathaway"? "I'd like Mr. Jaeger to speak to that General. Mr. Jaeger"?

Jaeger sat up when addressed saying, "General, The Eastern block guys, back in the day tended to use Semtex explosives whenever and wherever, whereas we tend to use C-4. Both do very well in obliterating a target, but with different chemical formulations explosive experts can detect. The name of the game is misdirection. Our middle-eastern friends learning their craft long ago from the Soviets tend to use the Semtex formulation almost exclusively. Now this guy that blew up the buildings in Houston, made everyone crazy using C-4, Semtex, and another formulation according to newspaper reports. My contact in Europe that will be running the operation if approved, will be using Semtex. Our fingerprints will in no way be on this operation. In fact one other recent event that just occurred yesterday might prove useful. The Israelis have a terrific plan to easily spring several mental patients from a local facility, indoctrinate them and place them in the proximity of the site in the aftermath claiming responsibility for the bombing. It's not in place yet, and might not be if impractical, but if so it'll go a long way in misdirecting culpability"!

"By the way General, two of the Delta operatives in the Balkan operation are still in Europe and available to join our European contact with your verbal approval, for the Cairo operation."!

General Ottenger gave a brief nod of his head. Signaling President Magnusson to ask, "Do we have any objections at this table for the operation to commence", as he looked around and seeing none said, "Make it happen gentlemen"!

"One thing more Mr. President", said Hathaway, "I and Agent Bergdorf will be acting jointly in this operation and Agent Bergdorf will be heading up the US part of a different operation to run this guy Salaam to the ground. Plus you have received a copy of the expense pro forma estimates for the Cairo operation"?

"Yes I have and will turn that over to the Defense Secretary for secret funding", said Magnusson.

"Get with me after the meeting and will find some nook or cranny that has the funds, Mr. Hathaway"!

"Good, now that we have that out of the way and operational, I'd like Mr. Jaeger. General Bollinger and Agent Bergdorf to stay and discuss this Salaam fellow"!

After the room had cleared the President asked, "What have we learned Agent Bergdorf and how do you suggest we proceed"?

"Mr. President. Several sessions of questioning of the owner of the Private Postal franchise yielded little in information. This Bujovic fellow acting under the cover name of Mike Montero, had the postal box in that name for over fifteen years as far as the records of the postal franchise revealed. He apparently received little mail over that period. So we requested that he willingly submit to hypnosis. He willingly agreed and under hypnosis his scant memory of events revealed that perhaps he vaguely recalled that St. Louis was the point of origin for most all of his mail. Given the vast bulk of mail delivered over a span of time, it's impossible to trace the mail point of origin given the logistic constraints. So all we have for the present is possibly St. Louis as where this Salaam might be. We've alerted the local FBI office and have requested federal electronic monitoring of all Mosques in the greater St. Louis area. However the local federal judge in the area, has the request still under consideration"!

"How long has this consideration issue been in place", asked Magnusson?

"Tomorrow will mark the forty fifth day"!

"What's the local Agent in Charge doing about this"!

"He's going by the book Mr. President"!

"What's the Attorney General doing about this"?

"The AG is cognizant of the lifetime appointments of Federal Magistrates and will not do anything to influence a Federal Judge"!

"Even during an event involving national security"?

"Sir, that argument was placed before him, with him countering with the separation of powers concept that he feels strongly about. In short, he refused to get involved"!

"Hide bound, by the book son of a bitch", fumed Magnusson. "The man is cruising for an early retirement"!

"If I may offer a comment Mr. President", said General Bollinger!

"Please do"!

"Any action regarding the early retirement of the current AG or the Agent in Charge of the St. Louis FBI office will do nothing but raise red flags all over the place politically, human nature being what it is"!

Whatever their future is in your administration would be better served politically after the fact as they serve at the Presidents behest. A lack of confidence in their abilities would be sufficient cause for their resignation"!

"So your modest proposal is what General"?

"The Secretary of Defense and I have known each other for years. The man is a staunch patriot. Moreover, he's been known as a highly creative figure, especially where the securityof our nation is concerned. I can ring him up this afternoon and we can meet soon thereafter, if I may bring your name deftly into the conversation, when appropriate. I can outline the St.

Louis problem and the bottleneck that prevails. He'd been at the DOD long enough to know who and what he can rely on especially regarding circumstances of national security. It may be necessary to go outside of the Government and procure the services of a proven cadre of ex-military. In fact we have and are currently doing this already, witness our efforts abroad and the presence of Mr. Jaeger. Now he may have a few ideas himself of reliable people that can be employed for this purpose. Be that as it may, perhaps it's time to explore the facilities of the Old Boy network. Preferably this Salaam will be apprehended, examined at length and reveal the rest of those involved in any way with the nationwide conflagration last summer, best case. Worst case this Salaam is killed without revealing the others. At any case none of those involved can ever see the inside of a courtroom. We now know how to make them disappear"!

Magnusson then leaned back in his chair and stared at the ceiling thinking, before coming upright saying, "General, can you come back on the Federal payroll and help out Agent Bergdorf for the time being and that includes you also Jaeger. You'll each have White House credentials to use as you see fit, answering only to me. Goodwin will see to it"!

Bollinger nodded his head as well as Jaeger. "Good, now I can get back to the simple world of politics. Gentlemen stay in touch", said Magnusson rising.

As they walked out of the conference room towards Orval Goodwin's office Jaeger said, "Good to be working again for you General. Never thought I'd see that day"!

"Tomorrow, I want you to tag along with me to the Defense Secretary's office. Prepare to be available the entire day. There's much to discuss and coordinate. We'll be pretty busy from here on out. You might want to pay a visit to Mel's son down at Annapolis to reconnect. I'm certain a DOD motor pool vehicle can be had for the asking afterward"!

"I'll discuss this with Mel this evening and let you know tomorrow General"!

The following morning Bollinger arrived at Melanie's town home at 0600 hours just as Jaeger was coming down the steps. As he entered the Generals sedan, he buckled up. "We'll have breakfast with the Secretary at seven and after that we just have to be flexible. Goodwin called him and has paved the way"!

"Discussed that thing we talked about with Mel. She called her son Rory at Annapolis and he'll be done with his classes by 1400 hours today. I briefly talked with him and he seemed in good spirits. So we have a rendezvous spot all set up at a coffee house off campus. We traded phone numbers in case anything comes up"!

An hour later they were shown into the private dining area for the secretary as the introductions were made. As they sat down to eat the Secretary said, "Saw you in that Cotton Bowl game years ago. A magnificent game you played. Inspirational"!

"Thank you Mr. Secretary", said Jaeger tending to his waffles.

"Was on the fifty yard line. Never thought you'd make it to the end zone, but somehow you did. Was a damn shame what happened to you later. But seems those involved just vanished forever. Must've been divine providence", he said raising an eyebrow. Even saw the after action report on your running down that terrorist in Houston. Great work son. Now you get to work with the General once again don't ya"!

"Good to know you do your homework Mr. Secretary", said Jaeger.

"Now General, what can I do for the President"? For the next half hour Bollinger outlined the problem and the suggested remedy in St. Louis to the Secretary.

"Needs to fire the AG and the St. Louis SAC, ASAP"! "Already been discussed Mr. Secretary, after the fact!

"Well well. Another off the books operation. Two at the same time", he said wiping his mouth with his napkin. "Time to make a few phone calls and see what I can do to put you two in action"!

By 0830 hours the General hung up saying, here's the people you see, written in this napkin. They're expecting you. They know the drill and know who can fly low and who can't. They won't ask questions, they'll simply facilitate. Tell them what you need and it'll happen off the books. Wonderful thing about the Pentagon. One stop shopping under one very big roof"!

As they all rose in unison, as Bollinger and Jaeger thanked the Secretary for his time. The rest of the morning was spent visiting three different department heads, all ex-military, who operated verbally over secure phone lines. By 1300 hours, everything was in motion, manpower and equipment, all to meet in a Motel in the suburbs of St. Louis, in three days, as Jaeger left the General for the motor pool, having a government car for his afternoon transportation to Annapolis.

By 1400 hours he found the coffee shop right off campus, where he was to meet Melanie's son. He ordered a large coffee got a seat next to the last window in line, with everything in front of him and a wall behind him and waited scanning the streets. Three cigarettes later he saw a tall rangy individual making his way down the street in civilian clothes, wearing a Naval Academy windbreaker, sporting a regulation haircut and striding in a military manner. The young man entered the coffee shop and headed straight towards the counter placing his order with so much as turning around. After his coffee arrived, he turned and scanned the premises, seeing a large man deep in the corner with his hand lifted in recognition. As he approached he saw the friendly face of a man somewhat older than he remembered offering him a window seat across from him. The man said as he reached out his hand, "Hello Rory. Thanks for coming"!

Rory shook his hand. Remembering his overly large hands enveloping his completely when he was much younger saying in return, "It's been awhile Mr. Jaeger"!

"You're a grown man now so you can drop the Mister"!

"So you and mom are together again"?

"Hopefully this time for good"!

"What brought you to this neck of the woods"?

"Doing some work for her Boss and we met strictly by chance in his office"!

"You're working for the President"?

"Strictly need to know business son. I'm taking a chance in telling you, but by all accounts you know how to keep your mouth shut. Can't tell you any details and even your mom doesn't know what I'm involved with, so don't ask. You'll eventually find out after the dust clears"!

"So tell me why you and mom split up if you can"!

"I owe you that at least, so here's the short version. I became involved with some very bad people. Don't ask why, for to this day I can't explain it even to myself. As I was drawn deeper into his operation, I realized that if he ever discovered who my private life involved, he eventually would use them as leverage against me. That's how he worked. He would have eventually discovered you and your mom's existence and I just couldn't risk that happening.

That is why I severed the relationship as I did. In my defense I left her financially secure in the process"!

"It crushed her for weeks, but eventually she got over it"!

"Crushed me too and I thought about it for weeks and longer, but in my mind it was the only way. What doesn't kill us makes us stronger, someone once said"!

"Funny that you would mention that quote. We're studying the writings of Friedrich Wilhelm Nietzsche at the Academy. An interesting character.

He wrote that comment in the book I've just completed, 'Twilight of the Idols'. Soon after he was committed to a mental institution. Seems he went completely around the bend. Some speculate that he contacted syphilis while serving and a medical assistant in the Franco Prussian War of 1870. But the fact remains that even in his warped mental state; he was capable of a few profound statements. He checked out a few years later"!

"Well, shut my mouth. Seems your mother chose her son well", said Jaeger continuing. "I'm impressed. Really. I recall reading one of his earlier works years ago. Think it was something regarding some Old Persian philosophy. Anyway it was at a time when all I had was time on my hands. But tell me about the Academy. General Bollinger tells me you're in the upper echelons of your class, a damn good marksman, and want service with the Mud Gyrenes after graduation"!

"You know General Bollinger", exclaimed Rory with surprise?

"Know him very well for a very long time. Served under him as my last action as a Marine prior to mustering out. He knows you mom too. A great man if there ever was one. Our paths seem to be crossing each other's time and again. I've always paid close attention to whatever he said. But tell me what's in store for you once you hit your stride as permanent party somewhere"?

"Well, as a Second Lieutenant, I'll know nothing of the ins and outs of the military and as you said, 'Listen to the General' and he recommends that I listen to the Sergeants, for they're the ones that really run things in the Corps. After eighteen months' time in grade, I should make First Lieutenant and then if I've earned my Commanders respect, have a go at the SEAL program"!

"Never did that, for the Corps. Had other assignments for me that kept me busy nonstop it seemed, but I can tell you this, those that survive the ordeal are real studs. Met a few along the way after my time in the Corps. And they all had that look. They were and are men who matter in this world. Met a few others along the way, Delta's, a few French Legionnaires, Spetznaz and the British SAS. All of considerable accomplishment. No if that's what's on your radar, then go for it. I can see that you've the juice, the grit"!

"So what's on your radar? You going to make an honest woman of my mother"?

"You get right down to it don't ya. Well let's turn that around. If she'll have me, after I get through working on these special projects, I'll hope she'll make an honest man out of me! The whole point of my being here is to get your thinking out in the open"!

"So if I'm hearing you right, you're asking for my permission to marry my mom"?

"That's the plan"!

"And you're not going to break her heart ever again"?

"There are three things that prevent your mom and me from unity. You, her and my death. I love her more than life itself and have always felt that way"! For a long minute Rory stared at his coffee, then looked up and said smiling, "Well then you just better stay alive if you two are gonna do the right thing after all this time and welcome to the family"!

"Thank you Rory. Takes a hell of a load off my mind! So tell me what weapon do you prefer when at the firing range"?

"Just like you taught me long ago, the old Colt revolver. Bought a Ruger replica, they let me keep locked up in the armory. Talked the gunsmith into tinkering with it. Shoots the long Colt .45 ammo and kicks like a mule. Had him tinker with the trigger and hammer pull a tad and it's both single and double action. Thinking about having pearl handle grips put on it just like General Patton"!

"You might want to check with General Bollinger about that. He's a bit of a military historian. When back in the day, a reporter asked him about his pearl handled revolvers, he politely corrected the man by saying, "Pearl handles on a revolver are for pimps. These are pure Ivory"! If you're gonna be a SEAL eventually, get used to doing nothing that will bring unwanted attention to yourself. When you're a famous General then you'll be part politician, then you can sport Ivory handles on your shooter. But check with the General"!

"When are we going to go to the range and start WWIII"?

"Soon as I get clear of my special projects and your mom makes me legal". Then I'll have a thing or two to show you that might come in handy one of these days. I hope you don't mind that I'm staying with your mom at her townhouse when I'm in town"!

"Not a problem. Just as long as you stay out of the spare bedroom she keeps for me", Rory said with a wry grin! As they both finished their coffee Rory said, "Time to saddle up and make tracks. I've got a lotta studying to do tonight. Have a term project coming due in a few days and I'm behind schedule"!

Walking up the street where Jaeger had parked his government sedan. Rory asked, "Driving government wheels these days. What ever happened to that old Ford you used to have"? "These wheels are on loan and have to give it back tomorrow. Just to get me down here and back. As for the old Ford, Still have it and its bigger and nastier than ever. Muy Rapido"!

Driving back to Washington, Jaeger felt better than he had in a very long time. He'd longed for the day when the 'Dark Ride' would be over. Just a few more very tricky hurdles to get over. He was quite pleased that Rory had accepted him. Now if the almighty would hold on for a little while longer, perhaps his seemingly endless voyage to the dark side of humanity would come to an end and everything before would become just a bad dream that had to be endured. However after seeing Rory and how well he'd grown, he knew the next generation of Ubermenchen would serve humanity well.

It started to rain as he drove up to Melanie's townhouse. He drove past the home and to the end of the street, turning right and finding a spot midway down the block parked the car on the street and made his way back to her place. He knew she would be there, thanks her call on his cell phone en route, during the evening hour traffic. He walked up to her in the kitchen, turning off the burners from what she was preparing and asked. "When was the last time I said I loved you"?

"Been a long time sport. Can't remember exactly when"?

"Which is more important to you words or deeds"?

"Both pal. Women are very greedy when it comes to certain things"!

"Then I'll just have to tell that I love, no, adore you. My very life is in your hands"!

"When is this going to happen"?

"Soon, very soon"!

"When the sun rises in the west"?

"Far sooner than that"!

"So until then I'll have to settle for mere deeds"?

"After dinner, for I'm hungry"! They came together for a long and passionate embrace, with lips caressing each other, hands raking each other over relentlessly, then coming apart with Mel saying, "Good thing you had the sense to turn off the burners on the range or else dinner would be crispy"!

29

Of the team of thirty operatives assembled in the greater St. Louis area, only five were from the ranks of active duty military. Two were supply and logistics experts fully adept in the skills of a military 'Dog Robber', or those able to purloin needed equipment, munitions and supplies from a variety of sources, with or without formal orders. The other three, were electronics experts capable of tapping into formal in line phone traffic, or scanning the electronic frequencies of cellular communication devices. All others were from the civilian ranks, former military who have taken vacations from their various jobs, for the duration of the operation.

They all met in an open field, in the northern county area as Jaeger said, "Gentlemen, thanks' for your time. I trust that you've all received your remunerations? Good. You've all been briefed on the operation at hand. The silent monitoring of every Mosque in the greater St. Louis area. This initially is a fact finding mission to uncover alien terrorists. We can expect no assistance from the FBI, the judiciary or any local civilian entity. Zero visible profile all the way. You all were selected because of your proven skill sets and the fact that all of you fit's a certain ethnic profile. Seven of you are in fact active policemen from your own localities, who have worked undercover in an urban setting. We are depending on you to quickly bring the others in each of your teams up to speed quickly in the arts of blending into your surroundings. The overall mission is observance and recording. The initial mission is to tap into each Mosque's or office, or homes phone system where aver possible. You are to initially assist each of our electronics experts in any way possible. Then we wait and monitor.

Every vehicle has police scanners and a high tech state of the art encrypted cellular system. So intercommunication between us should not be a problem. Everyone has a silenced weapon, just in case. You are divided into three teams, each attached to a monitoring position in one of the suburban Motel's. You will work as close to twelve on and twelve off schedules as is possible. Some of you I've worked with before and even though you've seen to have grown in size somewhat, if all goes well ones physical shape should not be an issue, but silence and invisibility is. If ever alertness and situational awareness was important, this is it. Should it be necessary to silence someone, do it as a last resort, remembering that if someone goes missing, that alone might be enough to send up an alarm prematurely. Should that happen get in touch with your team leader immediately so steps can be taken. When the hammer falls, we don't want to give them any advance notice. Remember this, every assignment is important, every single one. Any questions"?

By the weekend every land line phone on every Mosque in the area, had an active tap on it and information was slowly starting to flow. Every call to or from a given land line phone revealed another phone number. Electronics in each monitoring point revealed another phone number, either cellular or land line. Every call was recorded, stored and eventually collated.

Three weeks later Jaeger was on a conference call with General Bollinger and Agent Bergdorf giving them a progress update.

"Thanks for the three clerical types sent over for the project. Our intercepts are yielding a treasure trove of information. First of all no sign of this Salaam. He slipped out of town several days before we arrived. Where he is as of yet is unknown. What is known is the fact that for years all of those so called storefront Mosques in this area, including the few that have grown in size, are distribution points for Coke, Heroin, Crystal Meth and god knows what else. They've been operating a very disciplined organization for years. Product arrives from out of town and that which is not has been spoken for locally finds its way across the river to East St.

Louis, then up to Chicago. We have information that some people inside the St. Louis Police Department may be on the pad to look the other way. Most of the activity occurs during each Mosque's Friday prayer services, giving a whole new meaning to the Eagle flying on Fridays. Of course all of the conversational intercepts are in Ghetto code speak, so the undercover officers had to be pulled off their original assignments to translate"! "So who's running things, when this Salaam is elsewhere", asked Bergdorf?

"His Segundo is this great big fella who goes by 'The Blade'. Was recruited from Joliet prison in Illinois when he had his, 'Come to Mohammad', moment and was converted to Islam while in prison. A certified badass he is. Apparently many of their key players were converts while in Joliet. Turned their lives around, gave them a certain discipline they never had before. They stay low to the ground and when dealing with nonbelievers always use a go between. If things go south, the go between gets bail and disappears. They were talking about a deal gone wrong two weeks ago, when their cut out got busted. They bailed him out and by dawn the next day he was in pieces in the Mississippi, food for the carp. Case dismissed"!

"So every Mosque in the area is involved in some fashion", said Bollinger!

"Every Mosque in every way has some that are very busy", said Jaeger continuing. But something just came up a few hours ago on an intercept by this 'Blade' fella. Apparently in response to a question from one of his acolytes, he let slip in Ghetto jargon, that Salaam went east somewhere in pursuit in the service of Jihad. Now the boys that have been tailing him are very good. I've been with them on a few of their surveillances. My guess is that this 'Blade' has gotten sloppy over time and almost never checks his back when on the street makin' his moves. He knows something about Salaam's whereabouts. He usually travels a standard route every day and during the night. Sort of a working under boss. We can set up a snatch and grab off the street and a nice quiet place to examine him. But we're going to need a little pharmaceutical help if this is to go fast and easy"!

"Sounds like a call out west is in order, said Bergdorf! "General can you do the honors"?

"Soon as we ring off", said the General!

"What about the rest of the pack" asked Jaeger?

"Like we all knew, none of this would ever make it into a court of law, being the source of information being illegally obtained", said Bergdorf!

"We can't do a Cairo Operation repeat, for the press and the ACLU would be all over it in a heartbeat. Hate crimes and all that. Besides, there's the whole collateral damage thing to consider. Besides the Cairo affair has its own time table which we don't know", said Bollinger!

"What we could do after grabbing and sweating, 'The Blade', is put the arm on a smooth dozen of those we've identified, as transit points for the Swag they deal in. Given enough pharmaceuticals we could grab them, make them give up everything, pour the contents in the Mississippi and give the fish a great meal. Everything disappears"!

"How long would that take and would we get everybody", asked Bollinger?

"Probably the better part of a week if we were lucky. We've got three teams and all we know their routines. The biggest problem will be getting 'The Blade' and I've a plan for that. It would mean a loss of sleep for a lotta guys but I'm certain their up for it"!

Bergdorf and Bollinger agreed that pharmaceuticals would be in Jaegers hands within twenty four hours, with Bergdorf asking, "How certain are you that everything will go as planned Jaeger"?

"Two reasons. First the discipline they might have learned long ago has apparently eroded over time. Each team that has had them under surveillance has commented on that. I've seen it myself. Second thing is, I've done this before"!

"Do what you feel is necessary", said Bollinger, "and the product will be on its way by morning"!

The following morning, Jaeger brought together his three team leaders and outlined his primary and secondary assault plan. Each team leader had made his recommendations, as Jaeger said, "Good. We will have the product necessary by noon. The messenger will stay with us and administer the product on each one that's delivered. For tonight's target, the 'Blade', we will have five vehicles, four cars with two men each, running parallels and switches on our initial subject. The fifth vehicle will be an older panel Van that one of our agents will have borrowed from a used car lot, in the suburbs. Everyone will wear the Kevlar vests with the ceramic inserts, just in case. We're all connected by cell phone, and portable police scanners. We make the grab after the 'Blades' last stop for the night. He'll be going to his crib for a good night's sleep. There is where we make the intercept. Any questions"?

All night long Jaeger took part in the surveillance, yet on the fringes, monitoring the activity by his cell phone plugged into his cars cigarette lighter. The portable police scanner was on his front seat on low volume. At around one in the morning he broke off the tail and headed for the 'Blade's' crib. He drove around the block several times to make certain that everybody was asleep. It was a Thursday and with one more day of the week, the working class neighborhood should be asleep. As he made the final circuit of the neighborhood, he received a call. "The Blade is heading your way from the nightclub, but he's got company"!

"What kind of Company", asked Jaeger?

"He came out of this club with some trim on his arm. A bit skinny for my tastes, but it appears he needs someone to keep him warm tonight. What do we do with the woman"?

"We play it by ear, but my instincts are to bring her along. It all depends on how this plays out. Tonight just might be her lucky night. We'll just have to see. What about the Van"?

"It's on the way. Two men and a driver. Should be in place a block and a half up the street from your position with its lights out in just a few minutes. They'll have eyes on you. As for our boy he should be there in about twenty minutes. We've got eyes on him. Just a thought, but the size of this guy. He's huge. How are you ever gonna take him out"?

"Knuckle dusters! Might have one of the other cars close at hand in case one of us gets a hernia to help carry this guy"!

"Ten Four", said the voice on the other end. Jaeger found a parking spot on the street a half block away from the 'Blades' crib, got out of his car and seeing no activity on the street, slowly walked up the street, climbing the stairs of the stoop in front of the brick row house and faded into the shadows. He tightly gripped the brass knuckles in his jacket. Big man or not, surprise was his advantage and he'd yet seen any man survive a knuckle duster flush in the face.

The time passed slowly as he saw a Van circle the block up the street twice, before coming to rest two blocks up the street, flashing its lights once, before shutting off its engine. Everything was in place, with time passing at a snail's pace.

There it was', thought Jaeger. The black Chrysler traveling slowly down the block, looking for a parking space and finding one a half block away in front of a fire hydrant, the car came to rest and the driver emerged walking around to the other side and opened up the door, helping his partner for the evening out in a gentlemanly manner. Jaeger heard the chirp of the auto alarm as the 'Blade' pushed the button on his auto alarm. The duo slowly made their way up the street towards Jaeger as two people out on the town with a load on would, weaving their way drunkenly across the street and up the sidewalk.

As they reached the bottom of the stoop, the girl stopped a moment and then 'Blade' grabbed her lifting her up above his head as she gave forth a slight squeal and slowly brought her down as if to kiss her.

Jaeger took a silent step out from the shadows and leapt. Seeing his form coming from the shadows, the girl started to scream. Her action caused 'Blade' to move his head slightly. Jaeger was aiming his blow for that sacred region just behind the ear, guaranteed to put the lights immediately for any mortal human. But in a split second his blow simply stunned his target, as the hapless girl was knocked senseless by the sudden collision and flung toward the curb, her head coming to rest rudely against a hubcap.

Momentarily stunned but not helpless, Blade's instincts took over and his gleaming switch blade sprung into his hand and he swung at Jaeger missing him by a hair.

Those in the Van seeing the initial action by binoculars sprang into action, with the Van pulling out of its parking spot and driving down the street with its lights out.

His senses quickly returning and focused on his assailant, his blade making swift horizontal figure eights in front of him Blade said, "Damn boy you shore do hit hard, but now you're gonna die, as he quickly charged Jaeger, driving his blade into his chest and finding out it was going nowhere, after two quick and painful blows to his face, instinctively lifted the razor sharp double sided blade in an upward blindly slashing motion, cutting the front of Jaegers jacket and catching the side of his face, from the jaw line, past the eyebrow.

Staggered by Jaegers blows and unable to see, he felt his entire mouth explode as one final punch with the full force of his body, closed his eyes, his entire mouth a dental nightmare.

The Van slowly and silently pulled to the curb and two men stepped out, swiftly applying large plastic tie wraps to the Blades ankles and knees, then flipping him over and securing his wrists and elbows behind him. Then another car pulled up and the passenger leapt out and helped them manhandle the large body into the Van. Then a bloody Jaeger said, "Take the girl with you and give her a shot to keep her out as well as our guest. After you drop him off, stick a round in her head and find a dumpster for her. One of you get the guys car keys in his pocket then, get in his Black Chrysler down the street in front of the fire hydrant and make it disappear in a parking lot across town. Don't want the cops issuing him a ticket do we? Finally have someone ride with me to pinch this wound on my face closed. Within the space of thirty seconds of the van coming to a stop, it was loaded and started down the street, with one of the men trotting down the street and getting into black Chrysler, while another walked with Jaeger to his car down the street and around the corner. They stopped and opened the trunk of the Ford and removed the first aid kit, then Jaeger tossed his keys to the other member of the team and said, "You drive"!

Sitting in the passenger seat, Jaeger watched the Ford drive out of the neighborhood, while he sat there pinching the wound on his face closed. "Once we get some miles away from here find some place where there's sufficient light and park the car. You're gonna do a little work on my face, while you're at it turn up the volume on the police scanner so we can hear what's happening"!

"That's a wicked wound you have on your face. Might need a doctor to tend to it", said the driver!

"Out of the question. Find some nice quiet place with some light. We'll park the car and I'll guide you right through it and I'll be fine", growled Jaeger. The pain of his wound was now starting to make itself known once the adrenaline had worn off. Ten minutes later they pulled into a park on the banks of the Mississippi and drove until they found the right spot, under a tree, but with just enough light from a street lamp to see. Jaeger had toyed with the idea over the years, of replacing the bench seats in the front of the Ford, with bucket seats. Now he was glad he didn't, as he rolled down the passenger side window to let in the cold night air.

"Gonna be cold for a while, but that's what I want so the skin and the blood vessels will contract. Now open the aid kit and remove the bottle of alcohol. Now remove the cotton swabs and the cotton balls and put them on the dash. Good, now remove the butterfly bandages and find a tube of super glue and put it on the dash. Good, now while I'm pinching the wound closed, start cleaning way the blood with the alcohol drenched cotton balls and toss them on the floor. We'll clean that up later"!

When all of the wound was cleansed of blood Jaeger said, "Now prepare about six of the butterfly bandages and lay them on the dash board in a row"!

While the driver did what he was told, he marveled over Jaegers ability to manage pain somewhat stoically. Alcohol in an open wound was nothing to sneeze at, as he heard the occasional grunt as he worked.

Still holding the wound together Jaeger said, "You'll see a small cloth in the aid bag. Use it to wipe the area clean of any remaining blood"! When that was finished he said, "Now cut the tip off the Super Glue tube, very carefully and put a thin strip of the glue from the jaw line to just below my lower eyelid, while I still hold the would closed. Then take one of the cotton swabs and remove the cotton from one end and use that end to smooth the super glue evenly over the wound. When you get done with that, we wait five minutes for it to dry, then start applying the butterfly bandages from the jaw line to the lower eyelid sealing the wound closed"!

Ten minutes later the last butterfly bandage was applied as Jaeger said, "Now do the same thing for the upper brow. This should only take two butterfly bandages to secure the wound"!

When the procedure was completed Jaeger rummaged around in the bag and removed a small bottle, removing several pain pills and said, "I'm going over to the water fountain to wash these down. Clean up the bloody cotton, best you can and toss them in the trash can"!

As they drove across town to the storage warehouse where they rented several on the ground storage units Jaeger said, "Thanks. You did real good fixing me up the way you did. Now call the rendezvous point and tell them we're on the way"!

After the call was placed, the driver said, "That was something back there, what with the pain and all! How did ya know to do all that"?

"I read books. Call it underground first aid"!

"Gonna leave a big scar. How'd ya deal with the pain, what with no anesthetic"?

"No other choice. Had to hold still so you could do your work"!

"The pain must've been a son of a bitch"? "The pain pills should start to kick in, about fifteen minutes from now. Takes the edge off things. Now as for pain I'm not sure how I'd respond if someone was drilling into a perfectly good tooth with no anesthetic, while I'm all hog tied asking, 'Is it safe', over and over"!

As Jaeger was driven across town he began to wonder just how well those little nano bots, implanted long ago, would work deep in his innards. They'd been tested from time to time and his rate of healing from injuries suffered was remarkable. His annual physicals by the folks out west, all came back with a wellness quotient that was splendid for a man approaching middle age. But this would be the acid test. He'd been cut badly and took the appropriate steps to seal the wound. No doubt a vivid scar would remain. In two days he would examine the wound and change the bandages then he would see what medical science had wrought.

He listened to the police scanner on the way over and hearing nothing regarding the recent event smiled. Phase one completed.

Five minutes out the driver called ahead to those at the storage warehouse and told them of their arrival. They drove past the three rented cubicles and parked down the alleyway. The driver tossing his keys toward Jaeger and without another word got in another car and drove off while Jaeger entered the recently opened door, where their subject was in seclusion. He asked one of the men, "What about the girl"?

"Twenty minutes ago dropped off in a half full dumpster and covered her up. She was a whore and will not be missed by anyone for a while

I reckon"! As Jaeger approached the single folding picnic table covered with a white sheet with a large naked black man on the table. He noticed a bank of six car batteries, one of which was powering two bell shaped shop lamps that provided illumination and an electric space heater.

"What happened to his clothes"?

"His bowels let loose while in transit. Smelled something horrible. Had to cut the clothes off him. Everything's in a sealed plastic bag over in the corner. Shortly we'll dispose of it"!

Jaeger said, "Cover the guy's midsection with a towel. I don't want to keep looking at his schlong for the duration"!

"Kinda ends that myth that Spades have a bigger Wang than we do", commented one of the men, only to be met with the reply by another, "Winters coming. It's getting cold outside. Male shrinkage"!

"All right settle down", said Jaeger! As he walked over to where one of the team members who doubled as a Med Tech said, "That what he did to you Jaeger"?

"Yeah. By the way who picked up the blade from the street"? "I did. You want it", came a voice from the darkness!

"No keep it or toss it away. Just wanted to make sure it wasn't left behind"!

"What kind of condition's he in"!

"Just got him cleaned up we did. He'll still be out probably till early morning, from the Thorazine injected. Without an X-Ray machine it's hard to say, but since all his front and lower mandible teeth are gone or shattered my guess is that his upper mandible has a break in it for sure and probably his lower as well. You can infer that from the hematoma's displayed. Only thing I've ever seen do that much damage is a baseball bat or some knuckle dusters. I'm guessing the latter"!"You'd be guessing right. The question is will he be able to talk, or did I fuck things up for fair"!

"No, it's just that it'll take a little longer. There's the video recorder on a tripod, focused on his face exclusively. Attached to his head will be an audio headset plugged into the video recorder. We've the portable EKG machine attached to him to monitor his vitals all during the procedure"! "The tech that's coming from California with the joy juice is due to arrive at 0900 hours. She'll be picked up and taken straight here from the airport, for the procedure. She'll train me while she's here and then leave after were done with the Blade"!

"The motor boat for the disposal of the Blade afterwards"!

"Done and done. Up river in a boat dock all gassed up and ready. If all goes well, we can use the boat over and over during phase three of our operation"!

"Nothing to be done until approximately noon then", asked Jaeger?

"You might as well go back and get some shut eye. You look all done in"!

"We have any food around here? I might as well stay put. Keep the traffic in and out of this place to a minimum. Don't want to draw attention, to our operation"!

Once again time passed slowly as Jaeger as well as everyone else in the storage facility could do nothing but wait. The steady soft drone of the police scanner being their only contact with the outside world. He reviewed in his mind eye the events of the early morning hours, concluding that all had gone as well as could be expected, with the exception of that little hiccup that he'd display for the rest of his life, everyone had performed admirably. Too bad no formal recognition for their work would ever come. But that was par for the course as far as he was concerned.

His thoughts drifted to Mel and her son as he slowly ate the sandwich gotten from the picnic cooler. He was glad he went back to Houston and gave the big blood diamond to the jeweler to craft a set of earrings and a ring for Mel. Now all he had to do was stay in one piece in order to give them to her. Her son Rory was a magnificent young man. So much like him in many ways yet clearly his own man with ambitions and intellect. It was because of this that he began to silently pray. He had not celebrated Mass in quite a long time and if he was permitted, he promised himself to correct that very thing. He asked the eternal for forgiveness of his sins and those he was to commit in the near future. The slate must be wiped clean of all his tasks before he was through, for was there not a greater good at stake?

He looked at his watch seeing that it read 0930 hours and felt the throbbing in his face start up. The pain pills were wearing off so he reached into his jacket pocket and retrieved the bottle removing two more pills, washing them down with a canned drink.

At 1100 hours the medic's cell phone rang. He hung up quickly saying, "Our visitor will be here in five minutes"!

Shortly thereafter they all heard a car stop, a door open and close and a knock at the door. Jaeger opened the door, as a woman stepped inside saying, "Hello Mr. Jaeger I'm surprised to see you here. Are you running things"?

"Hello Dr. Grabowski. Haven't seen you in a while"!

"What on earth happened to your face"?

"A slight mishap earlier this morning. But with luck the little gremlins are doing their work. Let me introduce you around, so we can get this over with"!

"That's fine but I want to have a look at that face and give you a complete once over after all this is finished. You missed your last appointment with us, if you'll recall"!

After the introductions, she set to work with the team's medic, examining The Blade in detail. "What was the subject subdued with", she asked?

"Thorazine", came the reply"!

"Nasty stuff that. What was the dosage"? She was told the precise dosage by the med tech, to which she answered, to which she replied, "That shouldn't fry his brain too badly. I see that he's under restraints, immobile and partially lucid, the effects of his prior sedation all but worn off"! The she peered over the subject saying, "Can you hear me"?

The Blade groggily hissed between broken and missing teeth, "I'm cold. Where da fuck I at, he mumbled"?

Dr. Grabowski looking at her patient for the time being said, "He's sufficiently lucid for us to continue. Shall we begin"?

After she prepared her syringe, she leaned over her patient and said, "Now just relax. Soon you will feel all the warmth you'll ever need or want.

I'm going to inject you with a wonderful substance and you'll gradually feel warmth and an overabundance of wellbeing"!

"Jus as long as I kin fuck your lights out when, we be done wid dis", said The Blade, his voice trailing off into nothing as the effects of the injection of Kickapoo Joy Juice, as the SP-117 became known as, gradually took effect.

Ten minutes later, she asked her subject some simple test questions to gauge the depth of his compliance. Thus passing the test she said, "We can remove his restraints, he is now ours completely. Please turn on the recording equipment and be ready to take notes. Mr. Jaeger, he's all yours"! As Jaeger commenced his interrogation, Dr. Grabowski drew aside the Med Tech asking, "What's to be the disposition of the subject when the questioning is completed"? The tech, reluctant to answer stammered, the she interjected, "Come now young man I'm completely vetted regarding this operation and shall we say the sensitivities involved. Is it to be Mexican Stew, dismemberment or what"?

"We have a large body bag, we were going to poke holes in then dump him in the Mississippi and let the holes fill with water dragging the corpse to the bottom of the river, miles downstream from the city"!

"No, No, No, that will not do. All wrong, all wrong! The man is too large and far too unwieldy to dump over the side of your standard boat. Is there one among you that knows the area well? It's Friday and we will search for a medical supply house. Well make the rounds and bring back what you'll need. You'll have to dismember the subject, leaving the torso intact, but first drain all the bodily fluids from the body, inclusive of his blood, which will end up in a five gallon gas can, easily cleanable and reusable. The blood drain will cause the subject to drift into an eternal sleep and the heart beat will stop. Thus the body drained from most of its fluids will be far less messy to dismember and easier to transport. As I'm given to understand there may be more individuals that need to disappear, so you will have to know the correct way in which to effect this procedure, so there is no possibility of negative comebacks"!

By late in the afternoon Dr. Grabowski had returned after her shopping trip, with the trunk of the car laden with the necessaries. The three team leaders arrived in her absence to be on hand for her seminar regarding the proper way of disposal.

As the clock struck seven in the evening Jaeger had concluded his interrogation. By seven thirty the subject had expired. By eight thirty the subject had been dismembered and his less massive torso slid into the body bag and zipped closed, with his extremities each placed in a separate heavy duty plastic bag and sealed. By ten in the evening the cargo was loaded onto a simple motorboat, that motored south past the City and by midnight the three men punctured the bags containing what was formerly the Blade and slipped them quietly over the gunwales into the river, one by one every quarter mile or so. The outside temperature hovered just over forty five degrees and the boat made the slow turn and headed northward. Its task for the day done.

Anita Grabowski settled comfortably into her first class seat as the mid- morning flight back to Los Angeles gained altitude. She looked out the small window as the jet flew past gray cloud echelons that looked white far below. With luck she would be back in time for her Saturday afternoon class back at Cal Tech. Yet another dinner she owed her brother for his work.

She closed her eyes and allowed her mind to drift back to the previous evening. After her seminar on remains disposal to the ex-military operatives, she went back to the Motel where Jaeger was staying. The team leaders followed close behind. After checking into her room, they all followed as Jaeger gave a running commentary to them all regarding what he'd gleaned from the interrogation. As he spoke she examined his facial wounds, interrupting him periodically with questions as to his on the spot first aid effort, in front of the others.

The bandages off, she discovered to her amazement, the little nano bots were indeed hard at work, for the wound had closed rather nicely and the puckering of the skin surfaces with each other gave evidence the wound had closed, normally a process of ten or more days.

"You say you used Super Glue to unite the wound surfaces"? "Read about it somewhere that some hospitals are using a form of Super Glue instead of sutures to close wounds. So I thought I'd include a tube or two in my first aid kit. It worked didn't it? Gave time for the little gremlins underneath to do their work"! The last comment having no meaning to the others of Dr. Grabowski's work with the help of others long ago.

"Since Super Glue creates a great deal of heat as it cures, didn't it hurt", asked the Doctor?

"Sure it hurt but the pain was the least of my problems then"! "It's healing nicely", said the Doctor, "But you're going to have a lifelong scar, reminiscent of the Heidelberg dueling scars in the latter part of the nineteenth century. Thank god the blade missed your eye, but your left eyebrow will have that sinister appearance for the rest of your life"! "Hollywood's never been seeking me out in the past and I see no reason for them to start now", he said in response!

"I'm going to clean and reapply the bandages, just as before, but since the wound is healing nicely you can dispense with them sometime tomorrow evening"!

Then his attention turned back to the team leaders, telling them what was gleaned and that a Presidential threat was in the offing by this Salaam.

They were to continue the work here against the drug dealers, apprehending them, interrogating them, then disposing of them in the proscribed manner. Once the last were disposed of, a file would be assembled and in it names, especially those of legal community, times, places of illegal drug interactions in the Midwest area. Copies of which were to go to the White House, the Department of Justice, The FBI and finally to every media outlet they could think of simultaneously.

As they all left his room he placed a call to a woman. Clearly someone he cared about by the sound and tonality of his voice. The conversation was short, but he directed her to contact the Chief of Staff that very night and tell the President to have no public meetings till he got there. He hung up shortly thereafter. Accompanying him would be a complete set of video tapes of the interrogation. Strictly for the Presidents eyes only.

"Working for the President are you", asked the Doctor? "Seems that way"!

"Well you'd better get a good night's sleep if you're going to be on the road all day tomorrow. Give the President my best wishes", said the Doctor, "For each of you has in you what I've placed in you"!

30

Jaegers eyes suddenly opened. The pain in his face would allow sleep no longer, the medication had worn off. He looked at the luminous dials of his watch in the dark which read a little past 0300 hours. 'Time to rise', he concluded. He padded into the bathroom and delved into his bag fishing out two tiny pills, swallowing them with a fist full of water from the faucet. He quickly showered and shaved, packed everything, wiping the place clean of any prints and left. After paying the sleepy night manager for his room in cash, he quickly found an open service station, gassing up the old Ford, getting their largest cup of freshly brewed coffee and drove off into the chill early morning fog. He selected the I-64 Bridge across the Mississippi River as the straightest route to Washington. Stay awake, drive hard and see everything. His police scanner and his CB radio were his connection with the world outside, as well as the radar detector. As soon as he crossed the river he turned on his old CB radio and said, "Breaker one nine, you have the one Cincinnati Kid, needin' to head east, 'muy rapidemente'. Need to find room in someone's rocking chair. Come back"!

Seconds later the CB radio crackled back, "Hey Kid, this is the Road Ranger headin' east on Sixty Four with some friends. So what's your twenty"?

"Just came over the bridge about a mile back. Come back"!

"So what's your hurry? Come back"!

"Ever seen the movie the Blues Brothers? Come back"!

The laughter crackled over the radio as the sender said, "Ya mean the one where the Penguin put them on a mission for God? Come back"!

"That's the one. Come back"!

"So you're on a mission for God? Come back"!

"Almost. Come back"!

"You make a gas stop sport? Come back"!

"The tank is full of high test motion lotion filled up just west of the bridge. Come back"!

"You awake? Comeback"!

"A little over an hour ago, clean and mean. Comeback"!

"What you drivin'? Comeback"!

"A white sixty three 427 Ford Galaxie, fully restored. Two Holly AFB's on top, high lift cam with dual supercharger's if needed drivin' a two seventy rear axle. Comeback"?

"Well then how can you be denied? I'm headin' a convoy, should be a couple miles ahead of you, just crossed this long ridge and are on the down side. Look for five trailer rigs all lit up, like whore houses. As you approach, hit your high beams twice and we'll know it's you a comin' up on our six. Some room'll be made for you between the two and three rigs.

Keep your ears on all the way. Come back"! "On my way and thanks"!

As Jaeger approached, he saw the convoy in front of him. He flashed his high beams twice and in recognition the truckers flashed theirs once in return, the rearmost three rigs slowed a bit and made room for Jaeger. The wind noise immediately diminished and Jaeger noticed a four hundred RPM drop in his tachometer.

"Ya all tucked in sport? Come back"!

"Ten Four, Road Ranger"!

"Good. Now everybody travel up to two five and check in"!

One by one everyone turned to channel twenty five and checked in with the convoy leader, "Good. Now my speedo is reading at seventy and on the count of three we're gonna pick things up a bit and level out around a hundred. The road ahead is empty for the time being and we'll slow down before we hit Louisville. By my count"!

At the count of three all of the truckers accelerated in unison. Not five yards separated each vehicle as the finally hit the designated speed. It was early morning and the sun was just starting to peek over the horizon. The cold morning air passed over each of the vehicles in the convoy as they settled down to the rhythm of speed.

"Hey Kid", came the radio, "Y'all comfy back there"!

"Like Mothers milk Ranger, Mothers Milk"!

"So where ya be from Kid? Cincinnati? Come back"?

"Some say I'm from parts unknown! Comeback"!

"Yeah, but what do you say? Come back"?

"Houston, by gawd Texas. The Baghdad on the Bayou. Comeback"!

"Sorta bad choice of monikers for a town, seeing they bombed the shit out of both a little while back. Come back"!

"Very bad Juju. But they're rebuilding and will be back bigger and badder than ever. Come back"!

"I was born and bred in Cut'n Shoot, just north of your twenty", said the Road Ranger, Come back"!

"So hello neighbor", replied Jaeger. "Comeback"!

"So let that be a lesson to y'all, that everthang in Texas is just up the road apiece. Now enough of this pitter patter. Next stop, Lexington by gawd Kentucky for a piss call"!

The radio went silent as the wind passing by the big Ford in relative silence. For this was the art of open road drafting which took concentration as the convoy headed into the sunrise at speed.

By nine in the morning they crossed the Wabash River into Indiana and shortly after noon crossed the Ohio River into Louisville Kentucky. The convoy had to slow down entering into major urban areas and Jaegers fuel tank was heading towards empty as he left them temporarily for a filling station on the Kentucky side of the river. But having to negotiate the hills of western Kentucky was bound to slow them down a bit, Jaeger quickly caught up with them just as they passed through Shelbyville. An hour later they had to part company for their scheduled stop in Lexington. Since he was traveling alone from here on out, the Road Ranger gave Jaeger a brief heads up as to where the speed traps lay in the path of his trip to the nation's capital.

Traveling at the posted speed, the Road Ranger said, "Adios Vaquero"! "Back at ya and thanks boys", as Jaeger, down shifted into third, pulled out of the line and quickly accelerated away from the rest, shifting into fourth gear, the power of the superchargers making itself known. His police scanner, radar detector and his CB radio were now his partners in travel, as he sped eastward, into the afternoon. By the time the sun became visible in his rearview mirror, he was pulling into Virginia for a brief gas stop. "Just up the road a spell, look fer the exit that says 'Washington'. It'll be a couple of exits past Fishers Hill an ya wanna go east on I-66", said the service station attendant who looked on with envy at the big Ford as Jaeger pulled out of the service station armed with a cup of hot coffee and a full tank of high test. An hour and a half of hard driving northward, up the back bone of the Appalachian Mountains brought him to the turning off spot to I- 66 and Washington. He decided to make one final fuel stop just outside of DC. Then he'd place a call to Mel and tell her of his arrival.

As he drove onward, something jogged his memory of a tale passed down from generation to generation regarding his early forbearer. The first Texican, Henry Jaeger. The immigrant that fought the Comanche, during the days of the Republic. His long quest for those that killed his family. The Shawnee renegade called Red Hair. He felt a strange presence around him that he couldn't understand. Must this be what Heinrich Jaeger must've felt as he trudged north from the Austin Colony in search of Red Hair? This Salaam was in the greater DC area, he felt it in his bones. He must not let this guy get away. Things could only end in one way. Gradually Jaeger felt a certain peace surround him. He hadn't taken a pain pill for his facial wound in over six hours, yet the pain hadn't returned. He felt his face as he drove onward and it felt fine. All that he needed was in the trunk of his car. He was far ahead of schedule when he pulled in for his last fuel stop in Arlington.

He placed a quick call to Mel to tell her he was OK and for her to call the President and have him call him on his cell phone for a meeting this very evening if possible.

It was a little past eight in the evening as a tired Jaeger was let through the White House security gate by Orval Goodwin. Mel was waiting in the entrance and guided an unshaven Jaeger, into the Oval office to meet with the President. Jaeger had removed the bandage from his facial wound at his last pit stop before entering DC and even that drew comments from those who knew his previous appearance.

"Nasty Cut you've got there. Shaving", joked the President!

"'One might say that", said Jaeger! "While I'm thinking about it Dr. Grabowski sends her best wishes"!

"You know Dr. Anita", asked Magnusson?

Jaeger nodded in reply saying, "She says we have a lot in common, but that can come later. What I have are the results from our interrogation of one of this Salaams Lieutenants. A guy named 'Blade'. Let's just watch the videos and then we can talk later. Just then Molly Pringle arrived with General Bollinger into the Oval office, joining the President and Mel along with a recovered Van Harvanian and Orval Goodwin who asked, "What are you drinking", to Jaeger?

"Anything that's a hundred proof, straight up"!

As the video started, it became clear that Jaeger was the interrogator and the camera was focused on the 'Blade' from the chest upward never moving an inch. In the foreground was a partial image of the back of the interrogators head. Most everyone in the room at the time had heard Jaeger speak so it was evident that he was the interrogator as the questioning droned on. For the first hour several late arrivals trickled into the Oval office, each and every one on the need to know list, thus aware of other operations currently ongoing. Since it was going to be a very long night, the kitchen staff was alerted to provide a continuous supply of hot, strong coffee.

All through the evening, Jaeger intermittently stopped the tape to provide an explanation and give proper context to what was seen, before continuing. At two thirty in the morning, the last tape concluded and the lights came on as the blackout drapes were drawn shut.

"So let's recap what we've seen", said Jaeger! "We have our subject, a former pimp and inmate of Joliet Prison, who along with a number of others are converted to Islam while in prison. Once out on the streets, they fall back into their previous ways and become apostates according to Islam.

Comes along this mysterious guy called 'Salaam' who doesn't allow pictures taken of him and gradually brings them back to the true path towards Allah and the teachings of the Prophet. Along the way they work hard to make Islam grow in a Midwestern city. Just one thing they need an income stream and fast, so they find an exception in the Koran that justifies any action taken against the infidel as Ok to engage in, regarding the path of Jihad, or conversion of the infidels in whatever manner available. Now what is more profitable than the illegal drug business? Nothing if it's conducted in a smart manner. Soon a cadre of highly disciplined believers surrounds Salaam and his efforts grow and prosper. As each neighborhood Mosque is brought into being another disciple is chosen to run it. Over time a string of small neighborhood Mosques are open dispensing the teachings of the prophet every Friday and serving as a distributing point on other days, to other groups in the Midwest, right under the noses of law enforcement in the area. Eventually our subject, aka 'The Blade', earns the trust of Salaam and is renamed 'Segundo Farad', becoming the head guy whenever Salaam is out of town"!

"Connecting the dots, we can assume that Salaam was the catalyst for garnering up the operatives responsible for the host of conflagrations we suffered all over the nation recently. He'd travel to a number of cities and preach in the Mosques, gather a number of predisposed people around him and plant post hypnotic suggestions. Upon a given signal at a later date they'd go into action and when their assignments were finished, all memory of what was done vanishes deep into their subconscious. Every indication available says that he was the one who facilitated the arrival of this Beslan Bujovic, aka. Mike Montero, who single handedly exploded a large section of Houston's commercial buildings awhile back. All signs pointed to the St. Louis area as the point of origin, for money, documents, and etcetera"!

"According to our subject we missed Salaam in St. Louis by a matter of just a few days, for he was headed east to pick up a team of shooters, for a little project in the DC area. The kill team is comprised of three people.

Three Africans who as small children cut their teeth in the Blood Diamond wars in West Africa back in the nineties. We don't have a picture of any of them except a verbal description of their appearance, but we do know what name they go by, Blood Alpha, The Killer and The Chameleon. Of the three, we find the Chameleon is of Mulatto heritage with very light brown skin that's been known to pass for white, with the rest of standard African appearance. The Chameleon speaks English with a Euro accent while the other two speak with a thick African accent.

Further, according to our subject, these bunnies have come far since their days in the killing fields of West Africa."!

"As a point of context, back in the late nineties when DeBeers finally put the clamp on the world wide purchase of Blood Diamonds from West Africa. The black market for them dried up but only for a short while. Then mysteriously Middle Eastern types, presumably Al Qaeda, persuaded certain moneyed interests to step in and fill the void, thus earning money for the World Wide Jihad. According to our subject, the three men somehow found their way to Tunisia, were converted to Islam, sent elsewhere to hone their weaponry skills and thus put to work doing what they did best. Kill whoever was pointed out as the infidel. Seems they've been quite busy with a string of well planned assassinations all over the Mediterranean area, thus puffing up their resume without putting one foot wrong. The current target is in the DC area. Someone of great importance in the Federal Government and most important we don't know where or when. The final thing we learned is that the team will have help from within the government"!

"Well sir', said the Defense Secretary, "It appears that most anyone of us could be a target. How certain are you that you've gleaned all that you could from this Blade character"?

"I had expert help in my interrogation. An individual the President and I know very well. You'll note, Mister Secretary, I cut short the last video, because I kept going over and over, just who the target was and the subject just didn't know"!

"So I presume the subject was the one who gave you that little present on your face"! Jaeger nodded his head in silence, as the Secretary then asked, "Where is the subject of your interrogation"?

Jaeger thought a second then said, "In another dimension, quite apart from this one"!

"Gentlemen, it appears that this calls for all hands on deck"! "Mister President and Secretary, if I may say something", asked General Bollinger sitting quietly all the while"!

"Please General, take the floor", said the President!

"Not quite all hands on deck Mr. Secretary, but a lot of them, all working en camera so to speak. Roll playing a minute and putting myself in their shoes, I have to ask, where is the biggest bang for my buck? The members of the Supreme Court? Any of the Cabinet members? The leadership of both houses of Congress? The Vice President? Although I'd advise everyone to stay away from restaurants and food prepared by others for the time being, poisoning is just not the terrorists Modus Operandi. The first World Trade Center bombing was less than successful, but years later came 9/11 and bingo success from their perspective. Any cabinet member or Supreme Court Judge, or Congressional leader goes down and the world still keeps turning. Say what you will of the terrorists, they're a determined lot. Whatever they go after they want headlines. A huge slash or bang and what piece of 'unfinished business' still remains for them"?

At that point all eyes went towards the President and silence hit the room like a hammer. "So while covering all the other bases I've mentioned, just in case, I see but two options before us. One is make the President a veritable hostage in the White House, covering him like a blanket, every minute of every day, and cowering in fear, while the assassins might for a while lay low in the tall grass, eventually giving up and going elsewhere, an unlikely event given their track record, or we could take a calculated risk, that would if done well would flush the bastards out of their rat hole, so they could be visibly eliminated"!

At that point Magnusson stood up to the horror of Melanie and more important Molly Pringle. "Makes sense to me General. You're going to need a stalking horse. A target for those guys to fixate on while others close in for the kill"!

"I'm sorry Mister President, said Bollinger!

"Don't be sorry General. It's a rare thing that someone hears wisdom in the political environment. A President must lead by personal example.

Can't have an image of me cowering going out to America, or more over the world at large. It can only end one of two ways. Either way I win. Either way America will come together. The sinking of the Lusitania, Pearl Harbor, 9/11 all brought us together for at least a little while. Just as long as all of the terrorists are disposed of one way or the other. But who in the Government can be trusted?

"Offhand Mister President, only one person comes to mind and he's standing in this room"! Eventually all eyes came upon Jaeger who stood an arm's length away from the President. This he hadn't bargained for as he glanced at Melanie, then at Molly standing right next to her. Her interest in the President more than simply casual, then briefly back at Mel again, then back at the President saying, "You asking" "I'm asking", Magnusson shot back!

"I'm going to need help. Need this FBI agent from Houston, Rex Wallace, then a guy named Hondo, works for Raffertys Bail Bonding in Houston. Then one other I'll get in touch with. Then I'll need to get together with Agent Bergdorf in Quantico. The entire White House staff has to secretly be re-vetted, concentrating on anyone involved with scheduling of appearances. This is inclusive of the Presidential detail of the secret service. Everything on the QT"!

"Let me get some sleep and I'll want to get together with some other folks. Now if the General will allow, I'll want him to direct my last action"!

As everyone filed out of the Oval office the city was still asleep. Jaeger followed Mel back to her condo, while Molly stayed behind with Magnusson after everyone left her tears no longer able to be constrained.

Magnusson sat down next to her and reached for her face, holding it gently in his hands saying, "Don't you see Molly? Either way America wins!

Can't have you being involved with a coward can we"?

"It's just that when I finally meet a man I can fall in love with, he now risks getting himself killed. Damn it Lars, it just isn't fair"!

"Life isn't fair Molly. Try looking at things another way. After my family was obliterated, I saw no reason to continue. I was oh so in love with my wife and children and my loss was so great I was determined to survive and join them later up top. I just knew that I'd never recapture that magic ever again in my life. Then eventually you came along. Changed everything. I began to have hope for a life after the Presidency. Have someone by my side to grow old and cranky with. Then this. Can't ignore it. Can't walk away from it can we"?

"Now dry those eyes and go back to your place, we all have a full day starting at nine AM. With luck we can spend tomorrow night together. Time for some of that Texas female grit to make itself known"!

Jaeger followed Mel back to her condo. As they entered her home, she finally broke into tears. He held her in his arms at the foot of the stairs and said, "We both need to get some shut eye, for I'm all in! Now I know what you're thinking, that something is going to happen to me. Something already has. You and I are not going to allow anything to get in the way of us ever again. You know in your heart I'm right. Besides, I owe the guy. I got him into this and I gotta get him out of this. When it's all over you can take some time off so we can drift on down to Texas. There's something I want you to see. Something I hope you'll like"!

As he gradually drifted off to sleep, Jaegers mind reeled wondering how in the world he was going to catch up with those guys. Perhaps Hondo or Vultee had the answer.

31

The President placed a call into Dax Sonntag to see how the progress was going on the construction of the Nation's first Mag Lev interstate transport system.

"Just called to get a progress report on how things were going, Dax"!

"Thus far things are going exceedingly well, Mister President. The idea of placing the tracks above grade and following the already existing train right of ways has removed almost all of the political barriers that would've existed otherwise. The Unions have gotten out of the way, allowing us to place work schedules on a seven day a week construction schedule. Of course work on agreed upon holidays are off scheduled. As you know each of our vendors and contractors utilize American made implements and products. There were only two exceptions where we had to go off shore and they were minor but important parts only found from a German manufacturer. We are currently in negotiations to license the American manufacture of these products by years end. Now within days we should be able to announce a test run of our initial phase of the project, from Miami to Jacksonville. We should be able to easily take a load of people up to Jacksonville from Miami in just under two hours"!

"Think there's any room for someone like me Dax on that first run"? "I'd prefer you ride on the second run if you don't mind Mister President. Just in case there are any bugs to be ironed out of the system. The invitation is all but printed just waiting from the go ahead from our engineers"!

"What about the West Coast Mag Lev project"?

"Same thing to report, although Pierre is heading up that effort. We should have the structures coming into Los Angeles from San Diego next week. Our project from LA into Los Vegas is a week behind schedule due to that wildcat strike, but that's been settled and everything is back to normal.

"Any right of way obstructions, due to your wind farms and your solar power projects, you and Pierre are in partnership with"?

"Out west, the Bureau of Land Management has mysteriously turned on a dime and has and currently is fast tracking our land lease and acquisition efforts. It's wonderful sometimes how a change in management can redirect an entity forward"

"How's the stock trading on all of your enterprises, germane to energy and transportation"?

"Have your people read the Journal and watch CNBC, or Fox Business Channel. The stocks are all on a steady rise. With the economy what it is we have no shortage of manpower or vendors to choose from. We are well funded and even the big banks are all lining up with extended credit lines, should they be necessary"!

"Glad to hear it Dax. Anything else we can do for you"?

"Yes run for re-election Mister President. Anyone else in your position would not have the foresight, and sheer will power that you've provided to help us nudge these projects towards completion. I'll tell you one more thing that Pierre, I and all the other partners are in complete agreement on. Your mention of the balls to the wall Manhattan Project, showed each of us what was possible in this great land of ours if we all pull and push in the same direction. Within five years with all our conservative projections indicate we can have Mag Lev interstate transport of people running north to south on both coasts and from the East coast to the West Coast in a northern, central and southern latitude position. Further, we should be able to supply thirty five percent of the electrical energy required by the nation"!

"That's an awfully optimistic projection Dax"!"There is a proviso to that projection. That is under the assumption that the nation has no hiccups of any kind, politically, economically or engages in any protracted foreign conflicts that can sap the economic and political energy from the body politic. Or anything else unforeseen. In five years, if left alone we can show the world what American knowhow can accomplish. Then the economic Juggernaut of America can really take off. In fact I'm glad you called this morning, for I've just gotten the news that our chemists have finally figured out a process to make Coal Gasification that is turning coal into petroleum products cost and energy effective. As you know we've had this partnership with the Air Force to make jet fuel from common coal. The problem was with the cost of production and particle emissions into the atmosphere. We have a projected two hundred year supply of coal, with the Continental US and we think we've turned the corner cost wise"!

"Didn't Germany run its military effort almost exclusively in this manner the final two years of the second World War"?

"You're correct Mister President, but they didn't care about the costs involved and political attitudes regarding atmospheric pollution were nonexistent back then"!

"That makes sense Dax"!

"Soon we'll engage with several of the Oil and Energy companies in a possible partnership. Of course all this is for your ears only Mister President, but you can surmise the rest"!

"Mums the word Dax. Just glad things are going well"!

Magnusson hung up the phone, happy that things he was pressing for were working out well. Now if he could only stay alive long enough to see everything into fruition.

"Mister President, do you have a moment", asked Orval Goodwin?

"Certainly Orval, please come in"!

"How did things work out with Dax Sonntag"?

"Extremely well. All of his and Duquesne's efforts are proceeding on schedule. Good news for a change"!

"Then you'll be ready for some bad news to balance things out"!

"Give it to me straight Orval"!

"White House General Counsel has just been served papers. Seems that one of the political organizations the House Majority Leader has been secretly backing has filed suit against you and this administration, in federal court for your actions on the southern border some months ago. Their contending a violation of Posse Comitatus, for your executive order directing National Guard troops to the southern border"!

"I was wondering what took him so long Orval"?

"His cloaked efforts to impeach you coming up with zero support, have directed him along another path"!

"He and his cronies are still angry about my stand on congressional pork acquisition, appropriation procedures and earmarks aren't they"!

"That amongst a host of other things"!

"The man has been in office far too long"!

"He's worked long and hard to gain his position and is not about to give it up, Sir"!

"He's a walking, talking example of term limits for congressional members if there ever was one. Any more bad news"?

"There is news to report. If you'll be so kind to accompany me outside you'll find the White House staff assembled for your review"!"My review"? "This won't take but a few minutes Mister President. If you will", said Goodwin walking towards the door"! As Magnusson rose to follow Goodwin towards the door, he wondered what in the world was going on.

His birthday was months away. Walking outside he saw the entire staff assembled, along with several photographers and news cameras.

There, at the single microphone, was Molly Pringle who said, "Thank you Mister President for joining us for this brief ceremony, in celebration of a former President, Harry S. Truman. We realize that you have a great deal on your plate and everyone has chipped in to get you a token of our esteem. Melanie, if you will"?

At that point Melanie emerged from the middle of the crowd, cradling a small puppy. With a collar and a leash. Handing it to Molly for presentation. Cradling the puppy Molly turned to the President saying, "The puppy as of yet hasn't any name Mister President. That will be your job. The area animal shelters were combed intently for the appropriate type, with the only criteria being that of cuddly. He obviously is a mixed breed puppy and the duties of daily maintenance have already been taken care of. Your only task is to enjoy his company and walk him daily on the White House grounds, as a daily reminder of one of your predecessors"!

With that she handed the Chestnut colored puppy to Magnusson, who stepped forward to receive the puppy, as it eagerly reached up to lick his face. Holding up the puppy to his face as it wiggled and licked as small puppies are want to do he said, "Harry Truman, eh"! The cameras were flashing like crazy. No doubt this small interlude was bound to make the evening news as he added, "I think the man said that in this town if one wants a friend, get a dog"!

Molly then joined in by adding, "Mr. President that is what was reported true enough, but everyone here as well as the rest of America, is the cake. The puppy is the icing"! At that everyone applauded as the cameras rolled, as Magnusson said, "Molly, Looks like your fine hand is behind this"!

"Not entirely true Mister President. The original idea was your secretary's. All I did was implement the selection and the details. Now I believe the little critter needs his first official walk"!

Magnusson put the puppy down and as the crowd made way; he followed it some distance as it instinctively put its nose to the ground and led the most powerful man in the world forward, sniffing out strange scents to get familiar with its new home. As the entire staff followed at a distance, the puppy eventually settled on a certain spot, squatted and relieved itself in a dual capacity. As the staff cheered and applauded, Magnusson turned and said, "Give it a little time folks. I'm sure he'll get the hang of lifting his leg"!

As the staff disbursed, all rapidly going back to their tasks, Magnusson followed the puppy around the grounds, followed at a discrete distance by his Secret Service Praetorians. Molly and Melanie stood together for a brief moment more as Molly said, "God almighty Mel. I never knew it was possible to love a man so much"!

As they turned and joined the others going back to work Melanie, of all people, knew exactly what she was feeling. Half way round the grounds, Magnusson sensing the puppy was getting tired, picked it up and cradled it in his arms lovingly, saying to members of his detail, "What do you guys think is its mixture", as he turned to go back to the executive mansion?

"Please don't walk in a straight line Mister President. Makes our job more difficult. A weave pattern would be better"!

"Sorry guys, what kind of mix breed do you think it is"?

"Has the long muzzle of a Border collie I think, with a little bit of long haired Afghan", replied one of the agents, his eyes constantly scanning the surroundings. "When you get back, please turn him over to the executive steward sir. He's the one who'll take care of the First Mutt"!

"The First Mutt", said Magnusson. I like how the words roll out of the mouth. Tell Ms. Pringle to announce it during her press conference this afternoon, but tell everyone else, that, "Thor", is what his real name will be"!

In Seattle Washington, Dakar received a phone call at work. Answering the phone, he said "Dak. So speak"! The reply came back "Salaam", whereupon Dakar replied back, "Assalamu Alaikum" and the voice over the phone came back, "Masha Allah"!

At the response, Dakar sat erect in his chair, his mind at full alert. The mind trigger had been pulled once again, but Dak had no previous memory of his prior service, so a repeat performance was not out of the question.

The instructions were precise. Allah had need for you're his services against the unbelievers. He was to go to his bank and clean out his safety deposit box during his lunch hour. Amongst the money and other things were a revolver and a box of ammunition he'd purchased long ago. He was to return to work and continue as he normally would. On his way home after work he would pull his car over to the side of the road and load the revolver. A simple enough task even though he'd never operated a firearm before, he saw a video tape long ago that taught him how to load and fire a simple revolver.

Upon arriving at his residence, he was to go through his normal routine of greeting his wife who was preparing the evening meal, the go to their bedroom and change his clothes as he normally would. He then was to remove the revolver from his briefcase and take a pillow to each of his children's bedrooms, where they were normally at their computers finishing up their homework for school the following day. After greeting them he was to press the pillow to the back of each of their heads and fire the revolver into the pillow and thus their heads with a single shot each. Of course the pillow would muffle the report of the gun. His last task was then to return to the kitchen, hiding the firearm behind him and go up behind his wife and fire a single shot into her head.

Then Dakar was to pack a single small bag with enough clothes to last a week. He'd been given an address in the greater DC area to travel to where he was to be given shelter and await further instructions. While he traveled eastward, at every place he had to stop for fuel, he was to purchase a five gallon plastic gas can and fill it up with fuel and place it in his trunk. He could feel free to use his credit cards as currency during his travels. He was to travel no more than 600 miles each day and seek shelter for the evening and obey all traffic laws during his pilgrimage.

As Dakar crossed the State line into Montana traveling east, he briefly thought of his wife and children. It had been an arranged marriage between two Sunni families in Jordan, right after his graduation from the University. With a job offer in the States and a family of long established Cousins and Uncles, the transit documents to the States were issued quickly. In time, the two gradually grew closer to each other as man and wife and those that knew them would actually swear they were a loving couple. They quickly assimilated to their surroundings, as both worked in their own jobs outside the home. Dakar would miss the family he'd fostered and the friends they'd made, but a higher calling was the gravity that was pulling him eastward.

'After all', he reasoned, 'They would join together once again on the other side, knowing in their hearts his cause was just'!

In ever big city all across America, men received the phone call that compelled them to action, with instructions of where to go and who to see.

Families were quietly murdered and left in place. It would be days and in some cases weeks before the decaying bodies would be discovered. By then it wouldn't matter. Every time the greeting, "Assalamu Alaikum" was given and the reply, "Masha Allah" heard, the desire to serve Allah in any and every way possible was cemented in deeper into each of the pilgrim's brains.

Ninety men were in transit from every corner of the country to the greater DC area. Each armed with a single pistol and a box of ammunition, along with containers of fuel in their trunks. Of course their locational necessities had to be provided for by their hosts, all of which had families of their own, but not for long. They had received the same phone call from their coordinator. The man known as Salaam.

In the month he'd been in the DC area, he'd made his connections.

After picking up the fire team of imported hitters, deep in the Chesapeake Bay at night from another transit cigarette boat, he'd secreted them away in another true believers home in Baltimore, the following day procuring them clothes that would help them blend in to the local surroundings.

Their lodging was at the expense of the former members of the family on their eternal vacation, sleeping quietly in the upstairs attic, wrapped tightly in heavy duty construction plastic wrap. Afterwards the entire house would be blown up and any evidence of their existence would be eliminated, or so the thinking went.

Jaeger received a phone call from Vultee several days later. 'What's up sport", asked Vultee?

"Problems in the nation's capital. Presidential problems. Got a call in for you and Hondo to help out"! "Yeah I heard a few minutes ago from Rae. Called Rafferty and talked to him asking for Hondo, but Hondo's out of the country tryin' to take up the slack you left behind and he's on a serious chase. Means a big payday if he can pull it off"!

"Well then let him be. What's your twenty and your availability Duke"?

"In the Dallas Metroplex and I don't have anything on my plate I can't walk away from"! Then Jaeger went into a shorthand version of what he was involved with ending with, "Sure could use that head of yours up here with me in Washington. You'd be on a Presidential team comprised of Government and Bureau people"!

"Me, in Washington? In the belly of the beast? Why son I'd feel about as comfortable there as a Whore in Church"!

"Duke, your clean ain't ya? Your up to date on your taxes aren't ya? No one is on your six are there"?

"Not that I can reckon Jaeger"!

"Then you can come up and help the cause". Before Vultee could reply Jaeger said, "Give me your number, so I can have a trusted soul make arrangements at DFW Airport to get you up here pronto. The woman is someone close to me and her name is Mel. She's the Presidents personal secretary and someone I'd trust with my life Duke"!

"Hell son, I'd trust you with my life and even you don't have my phone number"!

"Duke I'm calling on a private line. I could be calling on a line that could be monitored by the Feds and cell phone or not they could provide me with your number and location within minutes. But I'm not which is why I'm asking"! After Vultee reluctantly gave Jaeger his number he asked, "Need me to bring anything sport"? "Hell, no what with all the airport fuss. Just bring yourself and a week's worth of clothes. Any other outfitting will be handled locally. You should get a call back from Mel in about a half hour or so. Oh, one thing more. General Bollinger is heading up our team"!

"That old fart comes out of retirement for this. Why didn't you tell me this before? This crap must be really serious"!

"Just keep the phone handy and be ready to giddy up"!

Jaeger picked up Vultee at Dulles for the last flight of the evening and drove him to Hotel in Alexandria across the Potomac River from DC. As he drove Jaeger filled in the blanks for Vultee and when he was finished Vultee said, "We need to think like them. What would they do? What are their options? Is this a one way trip for them to the Promised Land, or do they have an exit plan"?

"So Hondo's out of pocket eh", asked Jaeger?

"Talked to Rafferty himself. Runnin' down an embezzler out on bond from Harris County. The Bond was two million and the guy gave up his passport. He was gone the next day and came up in Panama. Had Randall White run his credit cards on a hunch and sure enough he's leavin' a trail. He's got some offshore accounts in Panamanian banks so once he gets his hands on the cash God knows where he could be. He had papers to get out of the country all set up before he left. The amount embezzled was in excess of twelve million. With that kind of gelt, one could disappear for a very long time"!

"Yeah Duke, but he made his first mistake using his credit cards and he'll make another"!

"Anyway, I called Rafferty back after I talked to you and told him that if Hondo surfaces anytime soon to give your number a ring"!

"So you're still drivin' this old Ford are ya", asked Vultee?

"Oh she ain't so old. She can still make tracks "Muy Rapido". Under the body, the seats and the frame, everything is almost brand new. She's a keeper"!

The following day Jaeger picked up Vultee and they drove to the White House to get his credentials from Mel, then onto Quantico for a meeting with Agents Wallace and Bergdorf and General Bollinger. As they walked from the car Jaeger said, "I know your nervous being around the Feds, but stay frosty Duke. Bollinger you know and I've recently worked with this Bergdorf and Rex Wallace and their not cut from the same cloth as other Federal Agents. Besides I've alerted them to most, not all of your background and they know that you've served time, why and they didn't bat an eye. You're OK to gain entry into the White House and you'll be with one of us at all times"!

Once the introductions were made between the Agents, Bollinger, Jaeger and Vultee, all gathered around a small conference table, with General Bollinger calling them all together saying, "Thanks for your coming Agent Bergdorf. I know your handling two operations simultaneously and we'll try and be economical with your time. But first let's hear from Jaeger so he can bring us all up to date with what his team in St. Louis has discovered"!

For the next fifteen minutes, Jaeger brought everyone up to speed with the high points of his discoveries.

"That scar must've been a present from the 'Blade', "said Rex Wallace!

"His version of cosmetic surgery", said Jaeger!

"Where is he now", asked Bergdorf?

"Food for the fishes I imagine, Preston"!

"Probably for the best. Courts all clogged up as well as the prisons. The taxpayers need a break"! At that everyone gave a brief chuckle, which broke the ice for Vultee a bit. 'Perhaps Jaeger was right about these two feds', he thought.

As Jaeger concluded his briefing, Agents Wallace and Bergdorf looked at each other and Wallace nodded to Bergdorf to start things off.

"Gentlemen. For the week reports have been filtering in from every corner of the nation of a series of mass murders of family units across the nation. When the first reports started to filter in it was concluded that someone was murdering family's en mass. Then as reports started to filter in we thought that several mass murderers were involved simultaneously. The Behavioral Unit to which I'm a member quickly tossed that theory out when we saw that in each case, the head of each household had gone missing completely. Now interestingly enough something the media had as of yet failed to see, is that each and every household is of the Muslim faith.

With this morning's early reports we have thirty one Muslim families from every large metro area in the nation slain by either gun shot or knife wound. Now what makes this even more of a concern, is that every killing of a Muslim family and I must point out there were no survivors, is from an area that experienced the wild fires during the summer months"!

"I think we'll all agree, this news passes up the bounds of mere coincidence by a wide margin", added Rex Wallace!

"And in each and every case, the entire family was taken out except for the husband, who vanishes without a trace", asked Vultee?

"At first we thought about kidnapping as a motive", said Wallace continuing, "But given their wide expanse of work from white to blue collar, this didn't fit a logical pattern and especially since the same modus operandi was in place. Some households had aged relatives living with them. Wives, Children and the old folks all gone in the same manner and the bodies were discovered where they had originally fallen"!

Then Bollinger chimed in, "So days go by, men and or wives don't appear at their normal workplaces, children are absent from school. Calls are made to the respective homes, messages left that are not returned, people pay a visit to the house, which is all locked up. Perhaps one car is still there but the other is gone. Days go by, someone breaks in and discovers the bodies or the police are summoned"!

"In a few cases General the bodies were able to be seen by interested parties through the windows dead where they lay, and then the cops were called", said Bergdorf"!

"A one way trip to somewhere by Dad", said Jaeger. Just then the phone in the room buzzed and the call was for Bergdorf. When he hung up, he looked at everyone and said, "Four more cases have been reported.

One in Minneapolis, one in Boston, one in Denver and the final one in Detroit and all with similar MO's"!

"Just wingin' it Agent Bergdorf, but are any of the murders in the greater DC area", asked Vultee?

After hurriedly going down his list, Bergdorf lifted his head and said, "Not a single one. The closest one is in Philadelphia"!

"So what does that tell ya", asked Vultee? "That we are going to have a lot of visitors to the nation's capital, with perhaps many more to come", said Bollinger.

"Well they gotta stay somewhere", said Vultee!

"A long shot but all hotels and motels need to be canvassed within perhaps a fifty mile radius", said Wallace.

"Going to need a lotta help from local law enforcement and politically it'll be a bitch, for if all there looking for are recent check in's from those with Muslim names, you can see what a shit storm that'll cause", said Jaeger!

"If I was doin' this, I'd go for private residences", said Vultee. A lot less visible"!

"What about the current residents in those households? Same MO", asked Bollinger?

"Except the bodies would have to be disposed of to make room for the new visitors", said Bergdorf?

"Still a manpower concern. See no way out of including the locals in the hunt", said Wallace!

"Well, you Bergdorf and the Bureau have the juice to get the locals to help quietly so's not to spook the livestock", said Jaeger adding, "They want something here and what they want is the President. We know about the kill team they've assembled from St. Louis interrogations, but what are the others here for"?

"Remember what happened in Houston years ago", asked Vultee to Jaeger? Jaeger gave Vultee a quizzical look and then the light bulb went off in his brain. Vultee's small finger on his right hand gave an imperceptible twitch to Jaeger away from the sight of either of the agents, as a sign that it was OK.

"Yeah, misdirection play. I remember reading in the local paper about a series of bank robberies in town a number of years ago. Somebody timed a cold front blowing through town during early morning rush hour traffic.

They tossed a lotta funny money C note's from on top of a building in mid- town. Talk about a real mess, in the scramble for the money everyone ran into each other. Traffic was frozen for miles around, never getting sorted out until the following day. A host of banks on the west side of town were simultaneously held up. Choppers couldn't get in the air and the cops were busy elsewhere. That's what our visitors are for. They are here to create a diversion away from the real target. My guess is that once a place is selected for the President's address, since these guys are adept arsonists, they'll use the very same method once again"!

"Wallace and I will go back to FBI HQ and I'll help him get the ball rolling with the local law enforcement people in the canvassing of the local motels and hotels in a fifty mile radius, just in case. Then I'll get back to helping Hathaway with the operation overseas. The General will get your man Vultee equipped with a Kevlar and a firearm. Then I'd appreciate it if the both of you would join Agent Wallace in screening any and all missing person's reports in the surrounding area for unresponsive households. A task force will be in the making and perhaps a chat with the President and the head of his Secret Service detail should occur tomorrow", said Bergdorf!

Several days later when the canvassing of the areas hostelries came up with nothing useful other than a few drug deals agents wandered into by sheer luck, a decision was made to canvass the areas missing person's reports and even examine the unexcused area school absence reports. Little by little the combination of both sources of data drew the attention of the task force that was now commanded by General Bollinger and Agent Rex Wallace. Members of the task force were made up with those who readily blended into their various surroundings. The tip off to many of the residences, were the existence of unfamiliar vehicles parked on the various residential streets with out of state license plates. When these residential addresses were compared with those children who had unexplained school absences, the team knew they were on to something. When the politically incorrect question was asked as to the nationality and religion of each family and the answer came back in each instance, muddle eastern and Muslim, everyone was certain of the current contents of each residence.

Eventually ten residences were placed under round the clock surveillance, both visual and electronically.

Two days prior to the announcement of the forthcoming nationwide televised holiday Presidential address to the nation of Thanksgiving, at the foot of the Lincoln Monument a discussion was held as whether or not to monitor every roof top within a two thousand yard visual radius of the speaker's podium.

That idea was quickly discarded, by a senior commanded of an FBI SWAT team who said, "As I understand it we want to capture these guys just before the hit so they can be interrogated to give up others, correct"?

"Yes Agent that is the current plan", said Rex Wallace!

"That's fine Agent Wallace. So let's put motion sensors on every roof within two thousand feet visual references. We set up a monitoring facility day and night with a response team on ready stand by twenty four seven.

Ask yourselves how happy they'll be when they have to have a serious look see every time a bird lands on the roof? Now let's say connect a video hookup to be engaged with the motion sensor. Very doable. Right? But then ask yourself if a well-trained long range shooter would be dumb enough not to look for such a thing especially since the life of the President is at stake. If it were me, I'd look and I'd find the video camera, then I'd dee dee out of there mose skoshe'. By that time the response team would be under way and a shootout would occur. We may or may not be successful in capturing any of the three, much less all three at the same time. They may or may not be true believers and even if they don't care about their own skin, they wouldn't want to knowingly fail in the attempt"!

"The deck's open to the dealer Agent", said Wallace!

"What I think the agent is getting at is that we might not have thought this trap of ours through to completion. There are three ways' I can think of to gain access to mid and high rise building roofs. An air drop by chopper, scale up the outside of building and up the fire stair's and through a metal door. Now has anyone ever heard of a shooter so adept or crazy enough of doing an HALO jump onto a roof and have the skill of a long range shooter? I take it from your silence that's a no. Above the Capitol and the White House area is a no fly zone. A radar monitor would have to be asleep or complicit for a HALO jump to succeed. Now has anyone ever heard of a shooter with the skill or the balls to be a climber? I take it from your silence that's a no again. So the only viable way to a rooftop is via the fire stairs up through the building. Agreed"?

As Jaeger looked around he saw every head nod in agreement, so he continued, "We have an electronics expert here"? A man in the corner raised his hand. "Is it possible", Jaeger continued, "To rig up motion sensors, to coordinate with a sensor that would indicate an open roof metal fire door, independently of the buildings normal security system.

Remember the intruder would be good enough to defeat the existing buildings security system"!

The technician thought a few second's then said, "Yeah that would be possible, I could have the motion sensors placed on every rooftop with range of say a thousand yards or so, set the sensors to a slightly below medium setting so they wouldn't go off every time a bird landed, then place a small battery operated independent electronic door monitor that would, Broad cast a signal to an overhead monitor centrally located, say a few large balloons flying overhead from a set position. They could be propaganda balloons saying something like, 'Way to go Mr. President'. It could be set up to send an alert, when and only when the door is opened, then movement on the roof is detected. But I've a question here. Isn't it common knowledge pretty much that we have counter snipers on roof tops in position for such events"?

At that General Bollinger who had remained silent throughout it all said, "Yes son, but I'd hardly say it's common knowledge"!

"Then how come I know about it General? If I know about it so do the bad guys"!

"So your thoughts on the matter son", asked Bollinger?

"Isn't a good urban sniper taught to shoot from the shadows? Be able to see without being seen? Lot'sa buildings in the area. Most of them modern with sealed windows that do not open due to the buildings HVAC systems.

But I'd say there were a few still standing that had casement windows capable of opening just a little bit, not so much as to be noticed but a good shooter should be able to shoot through an opening not much wider than the width of his barrel. Isn't that correct"?

Of course the young man was completely correct and they all knew it as General Bollinger asked, "Where son did you gain your perspective on long range shooting"?

"Video games General, Video games"!

"Of course gentlemen we'll have to do both. Son I like your idea of large balloons overhead attached to a receiving and sending unit that works in conjunction with the rooftop motion sensors. But we'll have to hide its real intent. I'm thinking about one of those camera setups they have on professional football games where the camera goes back and forth on video shots. Can you set that something like that up with the live network feed"?

"Damn great idea General, of course I can"!

"Then you're in charge of setting that up. You'll work through me.

Anything you need it's yours, as of this moment. I'll get you together with the White House Press Secretary a Ms. Pringle this afternoon for the details, so you're with me for the rest of the day"!

"Of course the three highest rooftops in the visual radius will have counter snipers placed upon them so work out the details of your monitoring with Agent Wallace", continued the General!

Jaeger and Vultee will work with and assist in a dual role, initially with the Bureau SWAT commander in selecting interior and exterior building firing sites you think are most likely to be used by the intruders. When that's concluded then Jaeger and Vultee will get back with me so their expertise can be used in the hunt for the arriving terrorists. Gentlemen we have our tasks ahead of us so let's get to it"!

32

Officer Larry Davis of the West Virginia State Troopers had just come on duty for the evening shift patrolling the West Virginia side of Interstate 79 running East and West across the northern most sliver of the state, into Pennsylvania. He was on the eastern side of the Ohio River Bridge, monitoring traffic speed as east bound travelers entered the long tunnel through the mountain and the long uphill climb of the interstate over and through the mountains and the short twenty mile or so trip into Pennsylvania. It was getting dark and in his rear view mirror was an older Chevy Cavalier that was about to pass him without even as much as his parking lights illuminated. Within minutes it would be dark and feeling helpful he put the patrol car in gear and started after him. The vehicle was traveling at the posted speed in the right hand lane as he pulled up behind him. He briefly flashed his overhead lights and announced to the driver to pull over to the side of the road and the driver complied. As both cars came to a halt he noticed the out of state, Colorado plates at the rear of the vehicle.

Putting on his patrolman's hat he emerged from the patrol car and approached the car and asked the driver to turn off his engine. "Good evening sir. The reason I pulled you over was to let you know that it's against the law to drive at night without your lights on. While there's a little light still remaining, it's very dangerous to operate a motor vehicle without any lights on at dusk"! He then asked the driver for his standard driver's license and insurance papers and went back to his patrol car to run the license and make of the vehicle, through the system to see if any warrants were outstanding or if the vehicle was stolen. The systems computer was running slow this evening and he decided that if nothing came up he was going to give the driver a friendly verbal reminder to turn on his headlights and leave it at that"!

He was thinking that when the system finally responded he'd

apologize to the gentleman and send him on his way. Then just as the system finally responded, the Chevy Cavalier started up and started away through the tunnel and up the long hill. 'Something spooked the driver', he thought as he started to give pursuit and notify the dispatcher that he was giving chase to a runner. 'The man seemed calm and was sorry', as he explained why he'd been pulled over for such a minor violation. But since he was running and in an old Chevy up the long interstate hill, something was very wrong here. As both cars climbed the long hill Larry Davis dreaded what was possibly going to happen. A ten year veteran of the troopers, he never failed to wonder why drivers thought they could elude the police in a chase. Only in the movies did that ever happen. Should the guy crash, the paperwork and the scrutiny would seem endless and there was always some desk driver who was eager for advancement on the back of a trooper for the most miniscule of procedural infractions.

As both cars reached the top of the long hill they were both doing just under eighty miles an hour. Now a ticket for a moving violation was a certainty, as both vehicles gained speed down the long hill that came ahead of them. In about twelve miles they would be in Pennsylvania and what most folks didn't think about was that the chase never ended once a state line was crossed. Cross jurisdictional agreements were long a standard between states, especially during traffic violations. Those chased never got away and by the erratic way this guy was driving, high speed driving just wasn't his strong suit! Suddenly as they were approaching a bridge crossing one of the Chevy's front tires just flew off the rim and the car swerved violently back and forth across the road.

Something told the trooper to break off his chase and gradually hit the brakes and a split second later the Chevy Cavalier swerved one last time driving straight into the bridge abutment and exploded into an extraordinary fireball. Coming to a full stop some fifty yards away was not enough distance for the trooper's car as the edge of the fireball enveloped the patrol car briefly singing the paint. The trooper quickly scrambled to bail out of the passenger's side of the car rolling on the ground and running some distance away. As he looked both ways he could see patrol cars approaching from both directions. He walked towards the exploded Chevy but saw there was nothing he could do as the vehicle was ablaze wrapped around the bridge abutment.

The first patrol car on the scene came to a halt facing the flaming wreckage, as the patrolman said, "Ambulance and fire truck are about five minutes away and comin' fast"!

"Be nothing' for em to do when the get here, especially the ambulance. Look at that fire", said Trooper Davis in amazement!

"So how'd it go down", asked the second trooper on the scene? "Help me get these road flairs out on the road to slow down the oncoming traffic and I'll tell ya as we go", said Davis! Within the next five minutes several patrol cars were directing traffic around the accident scene as the Ambulance was the first to arrive, followed minutes later by a local community volunteer fire truck, as the firemen knocked down the surrounding brush fires before attacking the vehicular fire. As the shift supervisor came upon the scene, he questioned Officer Davis on the entire pursuit and the approximate cause.

"The guy seemed OK, a little nervous maybe. But since he was traveling a long way and hell Sarge I don't know what spooked the guy.

Unless it was the ten minute wait he had to endure while I ran the standard check on him. But he came back clean. He cranked things up just as I was getting out of the patrol car and off he went. I have it all on the patrol dash cam and the second officer on the scene has what came after on his cam"!

"We'll examine it later after we get back to the office, Davis. But what do you think accounted for the large explosion? Obviously the fuel tank ignited upon impact"!

"Sarge, we've all seen gas tanks explode and for a car of that size and age it'll probably have a twenty gallon tank. Plus gas tank ignitions these days are rare and even if it was recently filled, hell Sarge it beats me"!

"Back in the day, I seen napalm do that kind of damage, but there's something about that explosion Davis"!

"Lemme think Sarge", said Davis squinching his eyes shut reliving the crash in his mind's eye. "I saw his front drivers side tire separate from the rim, then he was swerving all over the road, was when I decided to hit the brakes. Then he swerved left straight into the bridge support. The explosion didn't happen upon impact, but maybe a half second later and then an eye blink after that another explosion. Wait a second; one other thing just came to me. After the initial contact when I was walking back to the patrol car to run his makes and wants on the computer, I noticed out of the corner of my eye a suit case sitting in the rear seat. Never gave it a thought at the time.

But when traveling isn't a car's trunk where the luggage usually goes"? "The second shift accident investigators are just minutes away and maybe they'll be smart enough to tell us what went down, but go help with the traffic for the time being and afterward we'll milk the dash cams of you and the other officer for the report we have to write before we go off shift.

Over a six day period, four similar situations were repeated across America. One vehicle ran off a small bridge in Oklahoma in the middle of the night traveling east from San Diego. The single driver was killed upon impact. The car didn't explode upon impact but the trunk was filled with five gallon plastic gas cans, some of which were compromised upon impact. The driver was also of Middle Eastern origin.

Another vehicle ran into an over the road tractor trailer rig, while making a lane change in the dead of night without using his blinkers or looking to see what was in the next lane, causing the Big Rig to run right over his vehicle, jack knife and crash in the middle of the interstate median, heading north from Florida.

Each incident taken on its own was not sufficient to warrant an alarm.

But wracking his brain in trying to make sense of the hoard of disconnected dots that confronted him Rex Wallace decided to play a hunch and put several agents on an interstate computer search to see what traffic tickets or accidents middle eastern types might have traveling either east, north or south towards the DC area.

The following day his hunch paid dividends and he discovered four accidents each unusual in their own right, but similar in which multiple containers of fuel were in the vehicles trunk. He then gathered the address of each drivers motor vehicle operator's license and personally contacted the appropriate agency to visit the house where it was suspected that multiple murders may have occurred, with the caveat to keep the news they might find away from the press, for the time being, for the purpose of national security.

Before the day was concluded, reports began to trickle in regarding the visits to the homes in question. In each and every case, everyone in the house was murdered and found where they lay. In two incidences, the local media discovered what had happened but not being aware of the larger picture ran the story as an isolated incident, going nowhere and an all-points bulletin was issued for a man that no longer was alive.

While Molly Pringle was announcing the Presidents occurrence and location of his pending holiday address, to the media White House reporters, Rex Wallace was in the Oval office with the assembled team of General Bollinger, Agent Bergdorf, Jaeger, Vultee, Orval Goodwin, The Defense Secretary (on a secure video feed from the Pentagon), and Vannevar Harvanian, (still recovering from his heart ailment).

As Wallace presented what his team had discovered, regarding the travelers heading towards the Washington area, he concluded with, "And gentlemen in each and every occasion they left behind them a family of dead relatives. Every single one of middle eastern origin"!

"Gentlemen, I'm certain that bit of information is the icing on the cake", said Bollinger!

"Cannon Fodder", said Vultee adding his two cents!

"Come again, Mister Vultee", asked the General as a point of clarification?

"They're all cannon fodder. Part of the great misdirection play.

Everyone's coming to the DC area with full gas containers in their trunk. Their all assigned a place to stay, which has been previously cleared out for the visitors. Now the visitors will be assigned places to go and start fires far enough away from the site of the Presidential address, to draw manpower and equipment from the point of attack. The timing has to be exquisite. If done well, there will be sufficient confusion for the escape of the shooters"! "You didn't mention what comes after Duke", said Jaeger!

"Thought I'd leave that up to you sport, since that's more your area of expertise"!

"Should the shooters be successful and effect their escape, there will be one or moregathering points, for them to go to either to be paid off of to lay low. At that point each of them will be snuffed. They'll never see it coming"!

"As if it weren't already complicated", said Wallace! Jaeger continued by saying, "I'll wager the paymaster is our boy from St, Louis, Salaam and the shooters will never see the next sunrise"!

"Your reasoning for this Jaeger", said the President!

"Mister President, my man Jaeger is exhibiting his SWAG credentials", offered Vultee, prompting a knowing smirk from Bollinger.

"Scientific Wild Ass Guess, based upon years of experience as a chaser of evil people. It takes one to know one"!

"I understand", said Magnusson completely out of his depth and he knew it! "Agent Bergdorf, how is the operation abroad coming along"?

"Mister President, I've done everything that can be done on my end. Jaegers friend abroad who is running the show on the ground locally has made his connection with the Mossad operative last week. The Defense Secretary has personally communicated, last night with the two Deltas' on the ground that are part of the operation. Everything they need has been provided. Now we wait and watch the news reports from abroad"!

"Good, now what do we do with the area media" asked Magnusson? "My area of expertise" said Harvanian. Tomorrow, Molly and I will be meeting with all of the heads of the area media. This afternoon she and I will meet to outline a course of action. The media thrives on news. This is their mother's milk. Even more important a compelling story line is necessary to sell newspapers and media time. Only the owners of the various media groups will be invited to attend a secret off premises meeting away from the White House. This story if crafted properly is of epic proportions and each aspect of the media will be guaranteed a significant aspect of the story, given that it has a multiplicity of angles, but only if it is permitted to play out to the very end. This way everybody will receive a slice of the pie, if they collectively hold their water till the bitter end. Now you're going to ask just what happens if just one aspect of the media reneges and spills the beans early on and the answer is their ass. Their very visible culpability of causing the possible death of a sitting President and very possible joint and several criminal prosecutions in a federal court. The legal costs to anyone would be astronomical who even thinks of ratting out. I'm confident that once Molly and I sell the program to the scribes, they'll get on board, because the story line is simply too good to screw up"!

"Van, my concern is that someone will be concerned that they'll get the short end of the stick. You know how those media types are", said the Defense Secretary over the video feed from the Pentagon! "That's where Molly and I come in. It's called salesmanship.

Obfuscation. Spinning what is currently known to advantage. Painting the carrot gold. We'll make em an offer they can't pass up. This is what I do for a living. This is why I'm here"!

The following day Molly and Harvanian met with the various heads of the media and hung out the virtual golden carrot for all to see. Both worked completely in synch with each other flawlessly. For Harvanian his legacy as a human being was at stake, for Molly, far more than life itself. Of course it was moral suasion on steroids, but that's how business is done sometimes.

To keep busy, Jaeger and Vultee toured the known assembly points at various times of the day and night in order to familiarize themselves with the lay of the land.

"Almost too bad we can't get the cop on the beat to join in", said Vultee!

"Too many cooks in the kitchen already", said Jaeger in response! "We have a few days until D day to set things up. Maybe we'll get lucky"!

"Did I tell ya about Tina Aquatain", said Vultee?

"Lemme guess. She's you're new main squeeze", replied Jaeger! "That woman is so fine, she give a blind man a case of premature ejaculation, at midnight, fully clothed. She's in her mid-thirties and has had a very successful career in porn. In great shape she is, but has pulled the train for so long that we got little in common except for the bedroom"!

"So when this all wraps up give her away to somebody in dire need and simplify your life, like say Hondo. He's a hardworking man with simple needs as long as she's ready to settle down", said Jaeger. "She have any tattoos? Hondo don't have any truck with a woman sportin' tats"!

"Just a little yellow rose on the inside of her right thigh"!

"A minor thing I'm sure he'll overlook, as long as that's the only one", said Jaeger!

"Has anyone thought of tracking the makes and models of the out of state cars just sitting in front of the various safe houses? I know Agent Wallace said in the meeting they tracked down the pilgrims that didn't make it to Washington, but what about the others", asked Vultee?

"Damn it. Slipped my mind too. Here, take my cell phone and call Wallace directly. Maybe he's already thought of it"!

After Vultee hung up, he handed the phone back to Jaeger and said, "Our man had a hitch in his throat and admitted the oversight. The area keepers will note the visiting vehicles first thing in the morning and make the necessary contacts, keeping things quiet"!

"Wallace has got a helluva lot on his plate these days", said Jaeger who suddenly handed Vultee his phone again saying, "Damn! Here, get Wallace back on the horn again and put the phone on speaker"!

"Wallace here"!

"Rex, its Jaeger. Another thing crossed our minds. Are there any vacant or empty homes in the areas that we have under surveillance"?

"Yes, a few of them have been identified and in those cases they are our observation and monitoring points"!

"Are any within close proximity of the homes under watch? I'm talking across the street, down the street a few doors, behind the residence, within say thirty yards or so from the surveilled site. Not directly adjacent but within tunneling distance. A man has to have a backup plan. In case his house is assaulted by intruders. History tells us, these guys are great tunnelers, look at Gaza strip. Tunnels everywhere. It would be a cryin shame if one of your observation points had a tunnel coming up in the basement of the house you were occupying. You might want to check that out and think like them if possible Rex"!

"Roger and thanks for the heads up Jagmeister", said Wallace!

He then pulled over into a service station for a fill up saying, "Are you up to pulling another all-nighter Duke"?

"If these duds can stand me a little while longer, I suppose I can. But if I don't get under a shower soon, I'll run the risk of smelling so bad; I'll knock a buzzard off a shit wagon"!

33

Yaakov Kitterman had been deep cover in Cairo for the Mossad for so long he was indistinguishable from any Arab in the world. A product of the loving union between an émigré Russian nuclear scientist that fled the old Soviet Union after his time in the GRU and a Cypriot Turkish Muslim mother. They met in Sidon on the Lebanese Levant, she a budding young and idealistic journalist and Yaakov's father a Russian Jew on the run from the KGB. Muslim women, especially those liberal beauties raised in a secular environment are not supposed to fall in love with any sort of Jew, ever and never. But from the very first moment Yaakov's mother and father laid eyes upon each other, their fates were sealed in stone. She knew the right people and accompanied him across the southern Lebanese frontier into Israel and the start of a life together. Forever forsaking her family and friends. It was the late sixties and Israel was in need of scientists and dumped right into their midst was an unexpected gift. A Russian Jew, of extraordinary intelligence, trained by the expense of the Soviet State to achieve a doctorate in nuclear physics. This was a golden time between the two as they waited in limbo in a small apartment in Tel Aviv for the clarification of their status. His mother was torn between leaving her work for a Beirut TV station as a producer and severing all ties with her family. Of course, Yaakov had no family, being a ward of the state and raised in an orphanage in Siberia. Had it not been for his spectacular intellect detectable at an early age, he would have spent his life laboring away in obscurity. He was culled out and sent to state run schools graduating from his baccalaureate studies at the age of fifteen. By his twenty second birthday he was awarded his Ph. D in Nuclear Physics.

His cognomen singled him out as Jewish as he was growing up and he was subjected to all of the Communistic Doctrine that was standard in any State run institution. As he grew up he had little knowledge of his ancestry or memories of a family unit. The single most thing that signaled his heritage was the fact that he was circumcised shortly after his birth, whereas none of the other boys were.

Several years with the intelligence gathering arm of the Soviet Military, known as the GRU specializing in evaluating data germane to nuclear intelligence gathered abroad, taught him many things, in the art and science of reverse engineering. During this period, he lived as frugally as possible acquiring the skill of playing poker along the way. Careful never to win too much, from others, lest he incur their wrath. While others got by in life utilizing their strength and cunning, Dimitri made it a point to be better than anyone else, in the utilization of the one thing he was best at. Thinking at Warp speed and making all the acquaintances he could while gathering no enemies. In an environment of highly intelligent people he always discovered other people's weaknesses and carefully exploited them at the tables, in subtle ways.

His unit stationed at the Crimean seaport of Odessa on the Black Sea, was especially proud of his prowess at the poker table and volunteered to stake him to a game between the three best players in the GRU and the three best players of the Black Sea Naval fleet. It was to be a marathon session. Table stakes and the last man standing being the winner.

Sometimes these sessions were concluded within a day or less but sometimes they went on for days at a time. Just to make things interesting, part of the table rules for the duration of the session was that every hour on the hour, each of the remaining players had to down a shot of hundred proof vodka, so the game might come to a speedier conclusion.

Eighteen hours later, Dimitri emerged the winner, raking in his winnings then as he rose up from the table, he turned took two steps and passed out in a drunken stupor, the victor. He was far too drunk to hear the cheers from his comrades and they meted out each man's shares of the winnings, placing six thousand Russian Rubles inside his pants deep into his crotch where it would be secure.

The following day his commander, (one of the winners) gave him several days leave with which to sober up. By nightfall Dimitri had boarded a Bulgarian freighter bound for Istanbul. By the time Dimitri had been declared missing by his Commander in Odessa, Dimitri had successfully debarked from the freighter and embarked on a Greek inter island tourist boat headed for Beirut Lebanon. He almost felt sorry for his Commander leaving in the way he did, but he had a life to live and a destiny to achieve. Something was drawing him towards Israel. What he would do when he arrived, he hadn't a clue.

After his fortnight long sojourn along the Aegean Sea and across the Eastern Mediterranean Sea, he landed at Beirut, cleverly navigating around the customs inspectors at the port ending up sitting one sunny morning at table, drinking pungent thick coffee and thinking about what came next.

Only there was this quite attractive woman, quite alone at the next table taking her morning breakfast and reading the local newspaper. Clearly she appeared to be on holiday relaxing and soaking up the sun by the seashore. Her spilling of her coffee on her sundress was a signal for Dimtri to be of help.

Their eyes met as he tried in vain to help her with her and ordered another cup of coffee. From that point on they were inseparable. They sat together all day long just talking and drinking coffee. When she suggested they go for a swim, Dimitri had to admit he had only the clothes on his back and little more, pointing to a small gym bag that contained his toiletries and a few other things, as the rest of his story gradually began to emerge as the sun worked its way towards the sea. As the sun went down they were still talking oblivious to the others that came and went around them during the day, ordering a sparse dinner, neither one of them very hungry and by nine at night, Fatima arose from her chair complaining that her ass hurt from sitting all day long and that she was going for a swim and Dimitri was quite welcome to join her.

"But I have no swimming attire Fatima"!

"Neither do I except for up in my room and that's too far to travel", she said as she made a grab for Dimitri's bag and said follow me so we can visit Poseidon. Its dark by the shore and no one will see us except each other.

They made love together in waist deep water, slowly and tenderly so as not to allow the moment to pass into oblivion. When they concluded he said, "Fatima, we know so little about each other and". She immediately put her finger gently upon his lips, as she adjusted her legs around him, his member still swollen in the aftermath, deep inside her as she said, "We've been talking almost nonstop for over twelve hours. I know your of Jewish heritage and your know that I'm a Cypriot Turkish woman raised as a Muslim. You have given me your heart and soul as I have you. From this moment on Dimitri my destiny is inseparable from yours. We will go to Israel if that is where your destiny leads you and we will be as husband and wife in whatever manner you chose. I will bear you as many children as possible and we will be together inseparable. Do you agree"? "How can I not agree, when Jehovah has provided me with a goddess"? They then uncoupled reluctantly and went to the beach where they put on their sandy clothes and Dimitri followed her to her room where they showered together and then spent the rest of the night repeating what Poseidon had provided. The following morning Fatima made two phone calls and they checked out, taking a taxi down towards the Israeli check point and their destiny.

It took several months of investigation, interrogation, polygraphs and finally truth serum before the Israeli Mossad was convinced they had the real thing a brilliant gift from God and not a Soviet double agent. All the while they made love each and every day in the sea side apartment that was theirs for the moment. Fatima had made the fateful decision to follow her star. It was her Kismet, her destiny. She never looked back or had one moment of regret.

Shortly thereafter they joined the small community of scientist deep in the Negev desert working for the fledgling Israeli nuclear industry.

Similarly vetted as her husband by the Mossad and the IDF, work was found for Fatima, in a different department utilizing her multiple linguistic as well as her writing and media abilities. They both studied the scriptures and within the year became not only Israeli citizens but Jewish in almost every way. As Dimitri's work grew in stature so did Fatima's amongst those who worked for her. As she grew up in a mostly secular Moslem household, she observed that other Muslim households in Cypress were less than tolerant of their family unit. Although she was not forbidden to have direct contact with the Greek Eastern Orthodox families, it was almost impossible to completely shield her from social interaction and she began to silently question various aspects of the faith she'd grown up with. Always a very good student she was awarded a scholarship to a University in Beirut, eventually obtaining a degree in Journalism and landing an entry level position at the local TV station.

Of course her family tried in vain to introduce her to what they deemed a proper young Moslem men and she grew to dread the encounters. While always demanding virtue and virginity from their future wives as was the custom for millennia, they never the less, tried their utmost to put their own special brand on their chosen life mates before the ceremonies were even started. When rebuffed as an improper advance, suddenly the object of their ardor becomes a whore, in their eyes…At least in Beirut, a more cosmopolitan and secular island in a sea of intolerance, there was freedom to be her own person. Then came Dimitri and that changed everything.

As part of their wedding vows, each vowed to place the other first in their lives, above every other commitment except that of the eternal Jehovah. Each vowed to always be a proper example to their children at all times, by the way they conducted themselves with each other, with utmost respect and above all, eternal love for each other. Fatima clearly understood the demands placed upon her husband, regarding the irregular hours that he kept in the course of his research and made each moment together as if there was no tomorrow. As a uniquely spiritual individual, with the rare ability to see that not readily seen by others, she rejoiced silently, several years later when she missed her first period, deciding not to release the news to Dimitri until she was certain.

During dinner, late one evening she presented him with an envelope of the size usually reserved for greeting cards and when he opened it, it had but a simple question; "If it's a boy, what shall be his name and if a girl what shall be her name"?

He simply smiled and said, "My love that I shall have to consider at some length, but should it be a girl, that shall be your responsibility, for you are the most sensible person I know"!

Several days before she was to deliver they were driven to a hospital in Tel Aviv, where they spent every moment together talking, planning. "Have you settled on a proper Hebrew name yet Dimitri"?

"How does the name Yaakov sound for the little boy"?

"Hebrew for Jacob", she mused? "Yes I like it. But there's something I've been thinking about, at some length, that I'd like to discuss with you"! "I'm all ears my love"!

"After little Yaakov arrives, its customary in the Jewish religion that he be circumcised is it not"?

"Yes it is, according to scriptural teachings and tradition", said Dimitri! "Why do you ask"?

"Because, I have seen the future my love and I'm about to ask you to do something counter to all of our teachings after his birth and I want you to agree, for Yaakov's sake and his future safety"!

"What is it my love"?

"Do not allow him to be circumcised"!

"Not circumcised? But why?"

"For it will save his life someday. I had a vision that I can't explain. Similar to the vision that I had in my lonely days, that my prince would arrive and that unlikely prince was you in the flesh"!

Dimitri then got up and went to the window, staring out to the sea. His entire adult live he dealt with logic and mathematics. The seen. For him faith was very difficult to come by for it was illogical. Faith was that unseen element that had no provable structure; you couldn't quantify it by any of the known and understood sensory devices. Couldn't see, touch, feel, taste, hear, or smell faith, just like one could not rationally prove the existence of the Creator, the Godhead, Jehovah, yet one knew in ones bones he existed, via the vehicle of Faith. He then turned and went to Fatima, sat down on the bed and said, "By some improbable, celestial accident or design we were bought together and since the very first day. I grew to trust and respect your opinions and judgment and a better lover and partner a man could never have. So why now should things be any different? Yaakov shall not be circumcised. He will grow to maturity with all his body parts intact. That is my word on the matter"! "Thank you my love", said Fatima!

The following day Yaakov Kitterman emerged into the land of the living, a gift from God. In the subsequent years that passed, time passed rapidly, what with each pursuing their work and raising their child. Then one day Fatima during the evening meal with a little five year old quietly eating his meal, Fatima, placed another envelope in front of her husband. Dimitri raised an eyebrow remembering the last envelope that had been placed before him, and put aside his utensils and opened it. The message read, "According to the recent ultrasound, little Yaakov will soon have a sister to love"!

Once again Dimitri looked at his beloved wife and said, "How come the Lord has chosen me of all improbables to be blessed with such a wonderful wife? Yaakov, looks like you're going to have a little sister", he said then getting up from his seat and going around the table to kiss his wife. "Have you decided upon a name for her"? "Not yet. Right now Rebecca is in first place, but I'm still considering. You know how difficult it is for some women to make up their minds"!

Months later as her time grew near, a lull in the activity of the plant in the Negev desert proved beneficial, for a month's pregnancy leave to be granted to the Kitterman's. Packing up for a month's stay, during her delivery in Tel Aviv, Dimitri obtained a month's lease on a small apartment just a block from the seashore and a short two mile bus ride to the hospital. They vacationed for a week sunning themselves watching little Yaakov cavort in the sea, something a boy raised in the desert had never been exposed to. To both Dimitri and his beloved Fatima, this was a golden time full of rediscoveries of the love that united them. Both felt truly blessed by God.

The day before Fatima was scheduled to deliver, little Yaakov was placed in a kindergarten class at one of the day care centers while Dimitri escorted his wife to the hospital. They would ride one of the busses the two miles to the hospital and get Fatima checked in the Dimitri would return later to retrieve little Yaakov and take him back to visit his mommy.

Patiently waiting at the bus stop for the short trip to the hospital, both felt sorry for leaving little Yaakov at the day care center, for he didn't want them to leave, crying as they left. It was nine in the morning and as soon as Fatima was checked in and examined he would return to the kindergarten and get little Yaakov and return to the hospital sometime in the middle of the afternoon. If all went well she would deliver the following morning and once again he'd retrieve little Yaakov from his minders and present the gift of his little sister.

It was going to be a warm and sunny spring day in Tel Aviv. A fine time for the beginning of a life. They both commented to each other as to the discomfort the two Muslim women waiting for the bus at the far end of the stop, must feel having to wear the fully covering attire their religion and tradition required as they made their way about town. Then they saw the bus arriving as it slowed to a stop in front of them. The bus appeared crowded as the two Muslim women rushed to board ahead of the Kitterman's. As Dimitri helped Fatima rise from her bench seat, he was the very last one to board the bus; with her overnight bag in his hand he helped her up the steps. There would be just enough room for him to squeeze into the lower portion of the steps, as he struggled to place the fare into the collector. As the bus started to move forward he bent down to tie his one shoe lace that had come undone, as the explosion tore through the entire bus, obliteration the back of the vehicle, its force moving forward through the front. A minute later he came to bleeding and unable to hear out of his left ear, with a ringing that wouldn't go away. Seconds later he yelled "Fatima"! He'd been blown through the half open front of the folding pneumatic doors on to the roadway, a simple untied shoe lace being the only thing that saved his life. He wiped the blood form his eyes looking for his beloved Fatima and discovered her blown through the front windshield in front of the bus, as the inertia of the still moving bus barely missed running over her as it came to rest all aflame into some parked cars on the opposite side of the street.

He limped to her side, as she lay in the street, knelt down and cradled her limp body in his arms yelling for help. He could hear the sirens approaching which indicated that help was close at hand. He felt for a pulse, at both the wrist and the neck yet in his diminished condition wasn't clearly able to get a clear feeling. As the sirens came closer from his right ear, the direction of the hospital, he started waving his one arm, to gain attention and yell out loud, "Help, we're still alive and badly hurt"!

Then he felt her move and her eyes open just a little, as he yelled some more to gain attention from the first ambulance that arrived on the scene. "My wife is pregnant and we're on our way to the hospital", yelled Dimitri as the first responders quickly descended on them. For they were one of the few bodies on the street, the others appeared dead and as for those still on the burning bus, one look told them that nothing could be done for anyone inside that inferno. The ambulance quickly scooped up the limp Fatima, her clothes now shredded and burnt. She was barely responding, drifting in and out of consciousness as all Dimitri could do as the ambulance careened around corners on its way to the emergency room, was stay out of the way as the technicians worked at a feverish pace two save two lives. As the ambulance skidded to a halt under the canopy the rear doors were flung open and hands reached into the ambulance and hoisted the foldable gurney to the ground and whisked her into the emergency room entrance. In the brief time he was with her in the ambulance, Dimitri kept hearing a mixture of Hebrew and English saying; we're losing her and saw an IV placed in one of her veins as she disappeared inside.

He limped after her as best he could but then passed out not twenty feet inside of the hospital.

Dimitri woke up a half hour later on a gurney himself, his wounds cleansed and bandaged with an IV in his own arm. As he tried to rise, one of the doctors went to him saying, "Just a second, please lay back down. You're not in any condition to rise yet"!

"But my wife, she's pregnant and we we're on our way to check in for her delivery", mumbled a weakened Dimitri!

"There's a team of doctors already working on her. They're doing everything possible, to save them both as we speak. You two were the lucky ones, for everyone else on the bus was incinerated, except for three other ones that were blown free, but they were dead before they hit the street"! "My son is at a day care center just up the street from the bus stop.

What'll I tell him"?

"Give me his name and I'll send some people to bring him here" said the doctor. A half hour later one of the doctors emerged from the operating room, bathed in sweat, tearing as his face mask in disgust as he approached Dimitri asking, "Are you Mister Kitterman"?

"Yes Doctor. Have you news of my wife"?

"Here come with me over here and we'll sit down. We've tried to save your daughter, but apparently when your wife was blown through the bus's windshield, she landed on her stomach bouncing several times before she came to rest, by the look of her wounds. The baby's skull suffered severe and irreversible damage we discovered during the post mortem exam. Your daughter died in her mother's womb. As for your wife, her entire right side struck the windshield and the blast effects did a great deal of damage to the left side of her body. Frankly I don't see how she's lasted this long. Her skull has suffered a great deal of serious damage due to the blast effects and we've been successful in abating some of the sub cranial bleeding, but her brain functions are seriously on the wane and she hasn't much time left. We have her under moderate sedation and I'm certain she's feeling no pain since she's asked to see you"!

Just then little Yaakov yelled at his father running to him and asked, "What about mommy and little Rebecca"?

The few doctors that joined them and the few nurses, then burst into tears besides their best efforts. They all had seen carnage up close and personal of every possible kind, yet even the most seasoned of them were crushed when a child came to a realization that one of his parents was gone.

Dimitri gathered his son to him hugged him a moment then drew him back saying, "Yaakov, now look at me. Little Rebecca has gone to be with God and the angels up in heaven. Your Mommy is soon to join her. Let us both go and say goodby to Mommy. Time to be brave"! He gathered up his son and followed the doctor into the operating room. Fatima had been drifting in and out of consciousness since the explosion. She had dim memories of her bloodied husband holding her in his arms crying out for someone to come help them. She vaguely recalled the sight of her husband sitting there in the racing ambulance, with blood running down his face.

Then the view of the long tunnel bathed in an eerie white glow. Just out of her reach was her daughter, somehow wrapped in white linen. Hanging suspended by Jehovah's grace waiting for her mother to join her. Rebecca was what she'd decided would be her name. She told little Yaakov some days earlier, but in the rush it just slipped her mind to tell Dimitri. Perhaps Yaakov would remember to tell him afterwards. It would be important.

She started to emerge from the tunnel as she opened her eyes, to see Dimitri holding little Yaakov. Both had tears in their eyes as Yaakov said "Mommy", as Dimitri placed him gently on the bed so he could grasp her hand. Seeing her husband she said weakly, "Sorry, I forgot to duck Dimitri"! Then she saw her precious son and said, "Now Yaakov, soon I'm going to join your sister with the Angels. You be a good boy and obey your father in all things for he's a very smart and a wise man. He's going to need you now more than ever. Do you understand"!

"Yes mommy", blubbered Yaakov bravely fighting back his tears as best as a little boy could! Then she turned to Dimitri and slowly said, her time running out, "My love, it's been a grand ride. I'll be waiting for you and Yaakov when it's your time. Don't be in any great hurry, I'll be there waiting. I've always loved you even before I knew you"! Then she slowly closed her eyes and took her final breath, her head slowly rolling to one side. The doctors and nurses all quietly left the room for the Kittermans final moments together. An hour later as Dimitri and Yaakov emerged for a final time; they were met by a stern looking Captain wearing the uniform of the IDF who said, "Mister Kitterman. I'm Captain Isaac Komitsky. My unit and I been assigned to accompany you and your family back home for your final services. We will handle everything. You wife and daughter will receive a proper burial"!

"Of course Captain and thank you", said Dimitri holding his son. As they emerged from the hospital, a squad of very tough looking and armed soldiers were there to greet them. Before the sun went down the Captain made certain of the attendant paperwork attending to the deaths of Fatima and Rebecca Kitterman, having them transported to a nearby mortuary and appropriately prepared for a funeral. Mother and child in a single stainless steel casket.

The following day the casket was flown deep into the Negev desert, by military helicopter to join the rest of the family for the funeral. Dimitri was hard at work personally digging the grave at his own insistence. Not a very robust man and unaccustomed to manual labor, he quickly grew painful blisters as he tried to break through the hard packed desert soil. Seeing his father painfully toil as the grave slowly made its way to the proper depth, his young son joined him in the cramped quarters of the grave site, doing what he could to help his father. They were both attended by those who worked with Dimitri at the facility, with offers to help them dig the grave seeing that Dimitri was having serious difficulty in the hard scrabble earth of the desert.

"Why are you doing this Dimitri? There are those who would gladly help, or better yet Take over this onerous task"? He stopped for a moment to readjust his bandages that shielded the blisters on his hands, looked up and said, "It's keeping my mind occupied and it's just something I have to do"!

"But why do you allow your son to suffer along with you in this manner", he was asked?

"He is his father's son and he will do what he must! What do you say Yaakov"?

"I am my father's son", he said working valiantly but making the progress expected of a five year old, not bothering to look up but keeping his scratching at the earth.

At dusk he had been digging all day and attended as he was by his coworkers at the plant, tending to his and Yaakov's hands, they made only four feet's depth of the standard six foot depth necessary for a proper burial.

Breaking only for water and scraps of food, lights were brought in to help the cause. Hour after hour father and son toiled finally at one in the morning they reached the desired six feet depth. Finally Dimitri asked for a carpenter's level. Both he and Yaakov were almost done in from their joint efforts of the day, yet neither would allow themselves to give into fatigue.

When one of the secretaries that worked closely with Fatima asked Yaakov to climb up and rest for a while, he wearily said, "When my father says to stop, then I'll stop. Besides Mommy and Rebecca are watching from heaven". At three in the morning amidst a crowd of onlookers, Dimitri proclaimed a perfectly dug burial site, the crowd cheered and pulled the exhausted pair out of the gravesite and hustled them back to their lodging at the facility. Feeding them, tending to their painful blisters, further cleaning them up and putting them both to bed.

The following morning the Prime Minister got wind of their ordeal and immediately ordered an aircraft to fly him to the secret facility, (canceling all of his appointments until further notice) in the desert, to pay his modest respects and attend the funeral.

A modest burial stone was placed at state expense at Fatima and Rebecca's burial site and the funeral proceeded, the Prime Minister made some brief remarks, and then came Dimitri who simply said. "I loved that woman more than live itself. Now that love is directed to our son in remembrance of her. A man long ago was purported to have said, "Each of our lives is writ large in the sands at our moment of birth"! So it was said, so it is done"!

The following week the entire country was abuzz, as the greatly edited story of the death of a woman and her unborn child circulated throughout the entire country's media, of course changing the identities and locations of the individuals involved. Adding a firmer resolve to each and every citizen for the example of the bravery of a woman and her son.

For a brief while, special care was taken with the remainder of the Kitterman family. Dimitri had proved to be a brilliant and exceptional part of the Nuclear family in the desert and like his father, little Yaakov had tested out superior in his earlier years. From the moment of his mother and sister's burial, no one had witnessed him shedding a tear. His genius, apart from his fathers, had taken the route of linguistics. He had a special gift recognized early on for middle-eastern semantics. Thus by his twelfth year was placed in a special state run program to accelerate his training in all aspects of middle-eastern culture. By Yaakov's fifteenth year he was completely versed in the Koran, the Talmud and the Christian Bible as well as a fluency in all of the Middle Eastern languages, with a working knowledge of its various dialects and sub-tongues. Quite apart from this was his constant training in the Israeli self-defensive art of Krav Maga, knife fighting and a complete emersion, in the handling of firearms. When he chose to he could pass for any Arab he chose to, often sneaking into East Jerusalem and Ramallah to wander around and simply listen and observe.

Every Jewish young man's arrival into manhood is celebrated by a Bar Mitzvah. A tradition so ancient few can recall its exact origin, except Yaakov chose to beg off from that tradition, feigning illness. After several attempts to reschedule the ceremony ended in failure people just let it pass. Yaakov had another rite of passage in mind. He bided his time and was patient.

Several days prior to his seventeenth birthday, the suicide bombings in Israel began to start up again with renewed vigor. No one had a good view of where the munitions were being manufactured in the West Bank territories. The current government in power in Tel Aviv was eager to negotiate with the Palestinian's yet heard no meaningful response from the other side as what passed for negotiations dragged on while the terrorists blew up restaurants, stores and public transportation, again employing women rather than men as often as not. Knowing Jerusalem and Ramallah like the back of his hand, Yaakov neatly eluded the checkpoints and spent the next three days aimlessly wandering the back alleyways of Ramallah. No one ever noticed the new face in their midst as Yaakov looked and listened hiding in plain sight. There was one person he was watching for, the man adept at crafting a bomb that could be secreted into a vest worn under the flowing garments. He even caught a glimpse of Yasser Arafat as he passed the well-guarded compound of the PLO. But there was someone else in his sights of greater importance. He'd seen grainy pictures of the master bomb maker and one evening there he was sitting with his retinue of protectors eating in a restaurant. One of the many talents Yaakov had acquired was the reading of lips, coupled with his fluency quickly told him he was close to his target. He saw the car they got into as they left the restaurant and reckoned they were going back to work from what his target said.

Yaakov had narrowed the search area for the bomb making plant to a five block radius of Ramallah, housed in three possible structures, so he walked back to the area reasoning that where the car was so would be the plant. The second site he chose had the very car parked in front, thus there he would find what he was seeking. Of course the site was guarded, but during the wee hours of the morning and under the weight of full bellies, guards will tend to be less vigilant in their duties. The first guard was foolish enough to allow Yaakov to draw near as he asked the guard in his finest drunken Arabic for a light for his cigarette. The guard was not completely foolish as he moved towards Yaakov to push him out of the back alleyway. With one swift, well-practiced move, Yaakov sunk his razor sharp flick knife deep into his throat, severing his spinal cord. The guard dropped silently to the ground. He was disarmed and his body well hidden in a nearby pile of rubbish. Now he had a Makarov 9mm automatic, with two clips to augment his flick knife and razor wire garrote. He opened the wooden door and made his way inside. From the intelligence that was known at the time, the munitions were crafted and assembled always at night under the cover of darkness and then reassembled and fitted if necessary, during the day into the various garments to be worn by the bombers, along with a brief videotaped ceremony for their family afterwards. As he carefully made his way up the stairs, mindful to gently place each step on the side of the stairwell rather than the center of the stairwell, certain to always force a creaky board to signal an approach, he heard several voices.

At the top of the stairs he hid behind several large boxes, as someone said in Arabic, "You better go down to check on Fawzi. He looked sleepy after what he gorged himself on"! A large man passed him and went down the stairs. As Yaakov heard the door open he quickly Followed after and heard the man grumble that Fawzi was nowhere to be found. As the man re-entered the wooden door, he was about to speak when he felt a sharp object plunge into the nape of his neck where the spinal cord enters the brain. Silently he dropped to the floor. The last thing he remembered was the feeling of two arms preventing him from crashing to the floor. Yaakov quickly moved the dead man into the shadows beneath the stairs and waited.

Several minutes more passed by when Yaakov heard a loud voice upstairs saying, "Go downstairs and see what is happening. It's taking him far too long to see what the matter is"! Once again a man thundered down the creaky wooden stairs, cursing with every step. Just as he opened the door, Yaakov once again plunged his flick knife deep into the back of his neck plunging deep into his brain, bringing the man silently to the floor, then to join his compatriot under the stairs, for the last trip into that other dimension.

Yaakov climbed silently up the stairs and made his way behind the very same large box, watching and listening for the sounds of any others. There he was, all alone. "The Butcher", as he was known to the IDF. Repatriated some years back during a political exchange, hoped to be a sign of good faith between the government at that time and the PLO that ran the West Bank territories. As soon as "The Butcher" was repatriated his release was celebrated and he was immediately put back to work crafting ordinance. A swarthy looking man in his middle years, he was clearly a master of his craft concentrating keenly on correctly wiring his latest project, regardless of the time. After he was finished, he put down his soldering iron and looked up grumbling and made for the stairs, to see what was going on down below.

As he passed Yaakov, the sharp garrote was quickly lassoed around his neck as Yaakov grasped the two wooden handles twisting them as his body twisted around to where his back joined the back of "The Butcher". Yaakov quickly bent over holding on to both handles lifting his target off his feet, grasping for his neck, unable to breathe much less utter a sound. The sharpness of the razor wire severed the arteries that brought the body's blood to its head, as the subjects heart pumped wildly to no avail, for the artery that served the brain spewed blood with every beat of his heart, while the other, just seeped blood. Yaakov counter slowly to twelve and seeing the blood on the floor, quickly stepped away as The Butcher fell to the floor, soon to be no more.

He quickly flipped the body into a prone position, its blood quickly spilling onto the wooden floor. There was still consciousness in the man's eyes as Yaakov kneeled down and said in guttural Arabic. "Remember when you are greeted by the Prophet and his master Allah, that you were killed by a teen age Jew, without firing a shot. Tell the Prophet there will be more many more"! Then he quickly stood up and stepped away as to avoid any more blood on him, watching the man's eyes stare into nothingness.

His seventeenth birthday was tomorrow and for him no greater gift was necessary. This was his long awaited Bar Mitzvah. He was now a man amongst men. But he had to be across the frontier before daylight in several hours. He also had to have unassailable proof of his accomplishment. His manhood. The head, hands and feet of The Butcher, were removed and left to drain their remaining fluids on the wooden floor as Yaakov, searched for a suitable container to transport his proof back to Israel proper and place in front of the IDF Commander. The day after tomorrow they were about to mount a search and destroy operation after The Butcher. Now it would be unnecessary. Finding a plastic bag large enough to accomplish his purpose, he gathered the proof and wrapped each artifact in oily Rags, then went around and found enough explosive and petrol to blow the entire block to kingdom come. Fortunately he'd discovered the joy of cigarettes just six months ago and he pulled one out of his pack and lit one up carefully placing it between the book of matches and gently placed them on top of the petrol laden rags that were placed on top of the table surrounded by every munition he gathered. He reckoned it would take some five minutes or so for the cigarette to ignite the book of matches and thus the petrol and thus the explosives. God willing he would be blocks away by that time seeing a very brief but nasty harkening of an early dawn for the faithful.

As he moved swiftly through the alleyways of Ramallah, he was cognizant of everything around him. All were asleep in the city and then the roar of the explosion illuminated the early morning sky. He didn't even bother to look back, for the Lord was his Shepard.

By 1300 hours the following afternoon, Yaakov wearily trudged into his Commanders office, asking to be admitted. He was greeted by, "Where in hell have you been. I'm filling out the paperwork to declare you missing.

You didn't appear for this morning's classes. And is that blood on your clothes young man and what have you in that bag"?

"Sir, may I speak, sir"?

"Speak away"!

"Please contact Commander Richter of the IDF and tell him that his mission to Ramallah tomorrow night will not be unnecessary, for the target their after, The Butcher, is no more"!

"What is that in that plastic shopping bag"?

"The last remains of The Butcher for verification, the rest of him went up in smoke early this morning"!

"You were responsible for that explosion Yaakov"?

"My birthday is tomorrow sir and I will be seventeen. What better gift can I receive, than a gift I provide to myself"!

"This is", the Commander sputtered, "Wait right here young man and have a seat", as the Commander went out of the office. Twenty minutes later he returned with Commander Richter who went immediately to the bag, looked inside, then turned to Yaakov saying, "It's The Butcher alright. I put him in prison nine years ago. How did you know to remove the head, feet and the hands"?

"Sir, may I speak, sir"?

"Speak freely and sit at ease young man"?

"In order to stop the incursion tomorrow, I had to have proof of my assertion that it was unnecessary. If the head and extremities of our enemies were sufficient proof for our ancestors, it should be sufficient for us in modern times"!

"A bit over the top, but I find it hard to argue the point. Not yet seventeen and you pull this off all on your own with no assistance. You were gone for several days and were about to be reported missing. What shall we do with you"?

"Asking my recommendation sir"?

"I could use a shower and a meal and ask to be excused from my classes for the remainder of the day and nothing more, sir"!

"How about a god damned birthday party tomorrow"! "Only if you insist sir"!

"Before you get out of here, I'm only going to say this once, don't ever pull a stunt like this again, or I will have your ass on a spit over a hot fire. Your party will be at seventeen hundred hours tomorrow and as of next week you will join the advanced class"! "Are we understood"?

"Yes sir", said Yaakov!

"Good. Now get out of here and the rest of the day is yours. I suggest you make the most of it"!

After Yaakov left, Richter as Senior Commander of the training unit said, "Put this Yatsel on an accelerated training schedule and do what is necessary regarding his attendance record. Are we understood? I'm going over to Command HQ to give them the good news"!

With that the legend of the "Ghost" was born! For the next fifteen years, Yaakov Kitterman saw service, in Tehran, Kabul, Istanbul, Yemen, Amman, Algiers, Tripoli and finally Cairo for the last three years prior to meeting Nestor Magellan. Yaakov Kittermanquietly, murdered, abducted, tortured, exploded and wreaked havoc throughout the Middle East and northern Africa.

His initial insertion, as part of the Israeli diplomatic mission in Ankara Turkey, proved a timely introduction into the world of espionage and the dark arts. He'd learned his craft from the best in the world, elevating his natural propensities and survival instincts to an entirely new level of competence. His chameleon like abilities, coupled with his quick witted abilities to talk himself out of any situation, in the native tongue and dialect of his surroundings, yielded a bountiful fruit. Gradually he began to infiltrate various Islamic political groups in Turkey, earning his spurs conducting a series of dangerous missions, in their behalf, often at the mortal expense of their sworn enemies. He made a number of seemingly loyal friends along the way that would swear on the lives of their loved ones and ancestors, that he was a true believer in the cause of Jihad. There was always enough work for Yaakov, for in the middleeast, every self- anointed Muslim organization had a mistrust of the others, almost down to the genetic level. Thus Yaakov, using his abilities to the fullest, was usually successful in his ability to turn this mutual mistrust of the various factions and groups inward towards each other, in such a way to deflect suspicion away from him and toward anyone he chose, for everyone had a weakness and he was a master ferret and agent provocateur.

As he would be moved, from group to group, with the highest of recommendations from his minders, he always went through a variety of tests to vet his background and gauge the level of his eternal commitment to Jihad. Somewhere along the process, it would be necessary to display his private parts. One Muslims always knew in their minds eye was the deep tradition of circumcision with the young males of the Hebrew faith. Thus the discovery of his male member being intact and not altered in any visible way from the moment of birth was proof sufficient to welcome him to the fold. This was usually followed by a call to prayers, in which Yaakov always was able to recite with perfect precision. During the quiet times between recantations, he silently invoked the prayers of King David during his dark days asking the eternal to "Cloud the eyes and senses of his enemies"! Then he looked even inward still, thanking his mother for prevailing upon his father to allow her sentient wisdom to be followed. For it was his trademark.

There were several missions where Yaakov was called upon to destroy a Jewish owned business or entity, fortunately he was able to effect a less than desirable outcome for his current masters, by casting responsibility on a key member of the attack who was lost in The event. Not one Jew ever perished by his hand. Over time he'd gradually become one of The Mossad's greatest assets, with only a chosen few knowing of his existence.

The various Muslim terrorist organizations passed him along recommendations from group to group, before one day he was blind folded and led to a secret place in Cairo where he was introduced to the Muslim brotherhood and examined at great length, by Islamic scholars, doctors and operational commanders, to further cement his bona fides. He would either pass scrutiny or end up in the Nile River, in pieces, food for the fishes.

After several days without food or water, enduring nonstop, relentless, round the clock scrutiny, he was finally fed, cleaned up and led out to the sanctuary for the evening prayers. Again he silently invoked the prayer to "David", to cloud the senses of his enemies. After the prayers were concluded, he was taken to a room, where a stern man in police uniform, with the rank of a colonel, pointed to a packed bag and a full set of documents sitting on a table in the middle of the room saying," You are to be sent to Algiers, where your services in the name of Jihad are needed.

Your new identity documents and funds are on the table and in the travel bag are new clothes for you to wear. When you reach your destination you will be greeted by our people who will direct you in your new task, providing for all of your needs. Remember this from this day forward. You will answer only to the Muslim Brotherhood. No one else. You are an agent for the Imam and thus the Prophet, be he ever merciful. Never forget that until you are called to join him in eternity"!

As Yaakov was driven to the airport for his flight to Rome, he thought caustically, 'Apparently I passed muster. So much for celebrations'. Yaakov wasn't much for celebrations anyway. He was at last deep inside the belly of the beast. Nothing he'd intended, but fate often has an interesting way of providing for one's purpose. It had taken ten long and eventful years to get to this point. Many had met their death along the way. The Gates of Hell must've been quite busy during his rites of passage. No one ever had come so close and if not done right, no one ever again would be afforded this opportunity. Even greater care must be undertaken to shield his true identity, from prying eyes. So he went completely to ground, especially from the Mossad who after repeated attempts to discretely contact Yaakov, quietly dropped him from their roster as "Missing".

Three months later, while in Milan Italy, Yaakov made contact with an old friend of his fathers on a trade mission to Italy and explained what he was up to during his absence. He wanted his father to know that he was alive and well and that as soon as his business would permit, he would make arrangements for a rendezvous. But even more important he impressed to his father's life-long friend and a committed Zionist, to tell only one person in the Mossad that he was still alive and functioning in the behalf of "The Brotherhood", in Cairo and nothing more. That one person would know precisely what to do and when.

Mordecai Richter had risen through the ranks to become a General in the IDF over the years and then transferred to the Mossad where he successfully ran a group of deep cover agents throughout Europe and the Mediterranean.

Two weeks later he flew to Florence Italy, to have a casual meeting with someone he'd never met but had heard of as a member of the Israeli trade mission to the Continent. During a late evening meal Richter asked, "Thank you for this invitation and wonderful dinner, but why am I here"?

"I encountered an old friend of yours several weeks ago and thought it prudent to tell you this directly as per his wish"!

"So you're going to keep me in suspense all evening, eh minister"? "The friend was probably thought to be dead, but due to his new responsibilities decided It better to be out of touch for a time, before contacting someone he could absolutely trust above all else in this world. Even his father long engaged in the most sensitive aspects of our government's efforts is unaware of his activities"!

"And that person is", questioned Richter casually eating his salad? "Kitterman. Yaakov Kitterman is still in the land of the living and he wanted you alone to know that"!

"Kitterman hasn't been seen or heard from for the last six months. He's about to be dropped from the rolls"! "That's because he's involved in something of supreme importance to the State of Israel"!

"And that thing is"?

"In his words, he deep within the belly of the beast"!

"Israel is surrounded by beasts which would readily see us all driven into the Mediterranean Sea in a heartbeat if they could. So which particular beast are you referring to"? "The Muslim Brotherhood in Cairo. That particular beast. Yaakov said to reveal this to you alone and no one else.

That you would know what to do"!

Very few things brought Mordecai Richter to a halt. But as he sat back in his chair with his back to the wall he sat silent for several minutes, scanning the room and watching the busy waiters scurry back and forth, his eyes opened in wonder. The 'Belly of the Beast' meant that he was deep inside the Muslim Brotherhood in Cairo of all places. However did this come to pass, he wondered?

"So what are you to do Richter"?

"Nothing. Not a damn thing. The message is received and will be stored for future retrieval. When it is time he will contact us. Only one other will be told and certainly no politician or bureaucrat will hear of this. No record will be made. I'll see to it that he's still carried on the books as missing. I was never here and we have not met. Are we understood"?

"Completely Richter, but what of his father"?

"You can tell his father, with the utmost discretion upon your return in person. But do this in your own time as we are doing now"!

As Kitterman and Magellan sat in the rooftop apartment looking at the three monitors that reported the comings and goings of the all those who attended prayers at the Grand Mosque in the heart of old Cairo, Nestor asked, "When was the last time you ever attended a Hebrew service Yaakov"?

"I really can't remember, said Kitterman trying to think back. "Probably before my twentieth year I think"!

"Do you miss it"?

"Yes, I suppose in a way. But I was never that good a Jew anyway.

Except maybe for the dietary requirements. The Moslems have kosher laws that are almost a carbon copy our kosher laws. So being in their midst for the longest time was almost like being in a Jewish environment, except for these "Wahhabi's", its far stricter. Screw up and it'll go hard on you"!

"So after this will you do. Return to duty or rejoin the family of man", asked Magellan?

"Tell you the truth, I don't really know? After we send these bastards on their way, someone will step into the void and the show will continue on.

I'd like to walk away and go somewhere far away. But what would I do? Been involved in trade craft all my life and know little else. I'd like to meet a girl, fall in love, have kids, but what kind of father would I be"?

"I would think that would depend upon the woman my friend. The right woman could settle you down. I met one and we have a nontrade agreement between us"!

"Yet here you are with me Nestor, in the tall grass waiting for the prey to walk casually by"!

"I'm here because of an old friend. My presence here is not what I usually do. Most of the time I'm involved with electronic security for business's in Europe. In fact should you ever think of leaving this, come look me up in Paris and I'll make room for you in a far less onerous capacity and in Paris there are women who would take your breath away while you're still young enough to appreciate the feminine form"! "I'll give it some thought", said Yaakov.

"Then there's always scholarship. You could go to some European University and teach Islamic history, or perhaps the refinements of Sharia Law. I hear there's an old Jewish man that has written many books on

Islam and all of its attributes both pro and con. Bernard Lewis is his name I think"!

"My formal educational experience doesn't qualify me at any level to teach higher education, Nestor"!

"Then either become a writer, or join me in Paris and become a merchant, or stay mired in what you are currently doing. But should you opt for the latter, you run the risk of missing out in what is best in life. You've done your service for your homeland. With luck, soon the Brotherhood will be no more, or at the very least setting their cause back quite a bit. The beasts will mill about for some period of time, before regrouping. By then, perhaps a new generation of Yaakov's will surface to take up the sword"!

"Tell me how you came to know this man Jaeger"!

"I owe him my life", said Magellan, "In almost every way, but since that is a long story we shall have wait until another time". Then Magellan looking at his watch said, "Our two American Delta operatives should be landing in Madrid shortly. What about our two friends with the Egyptian National Police"?

"On holiday in Mallorca as of yesterday, with special drawing accounts on a bank in Barcelona. It's just you and me sitting here waiting for Gigot"! "If you know about Gigot, then you must be a Frenchman at heart", said Magellan bringing a smile to the face of Kitterman.

The explosives in place all around the Mosque, their manner of extraction well in place, all they could do now was wait. The meeting between the heads of the various factions of middle-eastern terrorist groups was one of the worst kept secrets anyone could remember.

All the Mossad did was act as an enabling agent for the operation, providing the monetary and the implements in which to effect the operation.

All of the planning was on the shoulders of Yaakov Kitterman. It was his show all the way, since he had intimate firsthand knowledge of the long overdue gathering. It was to be during the evening hours, an hour after the last call to prayer shortly after sundown. Guards would be posted, the entire premises would be electronically swept for explosives, cars would arrive and deposit their guests and then the internal meeting would commence far into the night, or that's what was planned.

As usual, Kitterman's information was spot on, with the secret dignitaries arriving after dark. Waiting patiently for an hour, until they were as certain as they could be that all had arrived and were deep into discussion, or derision with each other, whichever the case may Be, they both agreed to signal the trigger switch that would electronically 'turn on' and engage the firing mechanism's carefully placed at every support column in the older Structure. The explosives were a product of Israeli manufacture, designed for maximum impact leaving scant trace of an explosive signature and the triggers were designed to be undetectable while 'turned off'. Only when the signaling device received the electronic command to 'turn on' and stand ready were they able to be detected.

The day before, Yaakov left a bag behind in the dark recesses of the sanctuary that had some of the identifiable markers that "Omar Farouk" had been in attendance. Soon Farouk would be no more and Yaakov could possibly resume a normal existence.

The firing signal given all of the explosives went off exactly on que, with the walls caving in exactly as planned and the entire roof descending upon those below with unrelenting force. If all went as planned, the Egyptian media and general gossip would blame several of the rogue factions that exhibited displeasure at the meeting, especially those of the Sunni and the Shiite factions that has scant regard for each other.

Since the explosion took out some of the electric infrastructure in the area, part of Cairo went dark for the remainder of the night allowing two men dressed in the garb of Bedouin tribesmen to casually depart the area, along with a hoard of others, to make way for the authorities.

Ninety minutes after Magellan and Kitterman departed, the entire top floor of the building they were staying at exploded, showering the streets below crowded with police, a fire brigade, some civilian onlookers and ambulances, with all manner of debris, adding to the carnage in the Mosque. The very signature of a Shiite operation.

34

The following morning every news service in the world had a story about the explosion of a Mosque in the older section of Cairo. News surfaced that most of the terrorist political leaders in the Middle East were hosted by the Moslem Brotherhood, in order to plan a course of action to deal a mortal blow to the State of Israel.

That a few Islamic factions were dead set against this meeting for reasons of their own was revealed, thus confusing the direction of culpability. In every Egyptians heart they suspected the Israeli government as wearing the mantle of responsibility, but the proof of the after action directed eyes and minds elsewhere.

"They'll mill about like a herd of Wildebeests for a while, then in each group a leader or a group of leaders will emerge", said Bollinger reading the Washington Post, "perhaps a political merger for a while until some throats are slit, then thing's will be back to normal. Nature abhors a vacuum, unless it's in outer space"!

Orval Goodwin was starting to enjoy the company of the formal Marine Corps, General, during their early morning working breakfasts. The man was a far cry from the endless parade of lobbyists and politicos he was compelled to deal with on a daily basis. Straight as an arrow no nonsense, wall to wall common sense, suffering fools and incompetents not at all and yet when called for, a Machiavellian capacity for intrigue. It was a wonder he ever made it to the rank of Brigadier. Goodwin had read the file on the man, annual ER's far to the right, with high marks in tactical as well as strategic thinking, planning and execution. Graduated in the top ten percentile from the Naval Academy and yet he should have been on the fast track for promotions. Always opting for the high risk line level assignments, never once taking a staff level assignment during his active duty career. The answer was clear. His endless unheralded successes made some feel uneasy. His ramrod presence made lesser men feel inferior and lesser men do not want to be out of their zone of comfort. So they limit his accolades, much the way some Roman Emperors of old, greeted victorious returning Generals laden with slaves and booty, with Ovations through the streets of Rome rather than the Triumphs they richly deserved. Goodwin had seen them come and go for years, preening sycophants in many cases, wearing the mantle of an Alpha, yet without the heft to carry things off.

Bollinger's brilliance was in his ability to select those with the operational skills to plan, organize and execute, while facilitating their operation, then get out of the way. The man's people picker was fully operational. The Cairo operation, the action in the Balkans, as well as Jaegers presence locally was proof positive of his capabilities.

"Well General, Jaeger said that this Magellan told him to read the papers as a sign of the Cairo operation and it appears that he was right. Do we know anything about this Nestor Magellan"? "Only that he and Jaeger go way back together. Somehow their paths crossed after I lost touch with him and after his incarceration. I know that Magellan is a former French Legionnaire which means he has something in his past than best not be revealed. He has an electronic security company outside of Paris and apparently is doing quite well. But the man clearly has connections in a host of places that he keeps to himself. Better to have him working with us than otherwise. The fact that he was able to get into Cairo tells me that he must have a connection with the Mossad, but after that is anyone's guess and a guy like that makes certain that others keep guessing wrongThe secondary explosion was a masterstroke. My guess is that covered their tracks as well as make things look like it was a local job. They didn't care about collateral damage. Too many people in Cairo anyway and few of them friendly to us"!

"The President gives his speech the day after tomorrow. Any word from Jaeger and this Duke Vultee about the local surveillances"?

"Ten residences currently are surveilled in the greater DC area. Inside the district, Silver Springs, Chevy Chase, Arlington and two in Baltimore. No one fitting the profiles in any of the areas Hotels or Motels. Molly and Harvanian have done an excellent job selling the local media on keeping a lid on for the time being. Yet I'm concerned about the outlaying media.

Since we've personally contacted the various law enforcement agencies regarding our concerns about our recent visitors, we've gotten feedback about their former lives. Every one of them burned their bridges by murdering their family members, before heading to Washington. Thus far the local media's haven't connected the dots, but any day now someone will make the connection and then the jig will be up and we'll have to act. The reason we're holding on so long is that we haven't gotten a handle on where the shooters are. The FBI wants to wrap them all up at once and I have to agree, thus far. Now the roof tops have been all covered out to fifteen hundred yards and we've secretly met with building management on every building and have gone through every vacant space with a firing position of the President's address with a fine tooth comb. The evening before the speech we'll infiltrate the buildings cleaning staff and have someone in every vacant space. The Bureau has called in agents from other areas to handle the manpower constraints"!

"Sounds like you have all the bases covered General", said Goodwin! "And yet something is missing and I'm damned if I know what it is.

Now that the Cairo mission has been completed, we'll have Bergdorf back full time to focus on our local problem. I'm meeting with him and the rest at ten this morning to finally decide whether or not to pull the plug and have a coordinated raid on all the residences. Where we can we have directional mikes on all the homes to see if we can pick up bits and pieces of conversations. All of the land lines are tapped and monitored round the clock, with linguistic operatives. Thus far nothing of any use regarding the locus of the shooting team. My guess is that what with the news of the Cairo operation hitting the papers, that'll force some chatter amongst the hostiles, which hopefully will generate some information. If not we may have to force their hand. Anyway I'll know more by noon and give you a heads up right after"!

"I'll let the President know of our discussion and thanks General"! "Heard from Hondo yet", asked Vultee as they sat waiting for the others in an obscure office in Quantico?

"Talked to him last night at Rafferty's office. He just returned from

Canada, where he snagged the runner he was chasing. A rapist and murderer. Real hard case to hear him tell. Likes to fillet his victims then eat em. Anyway, he turned them into the RCMP in Winnipeg, got the paperwork executed and flew back to town. The Mounties are good at holding and transporting, so the rest is just paperwork, between nations. At least Rafferty is off the hook for the bail. So I told him to relax and stay put"!

"You know, with that Cairo thing hitting all the papers, it just might get the rag heads to talking"!

"Yeah Duke, I'm just hoping the ten houses under surveillance are putting a roof over the heads of our shooters, including this Salaam. The St.

Louis thing is about to wrap and go away. More fish food into the Mississippi and a lot of information for the DEA to work with. That oughtta cost the Cartels a lotta money"! "Yeah, nut you know they'll recover and sooner than we think"! Just then Bollinger entered the room followed by Rex Wallace, Preston Bergdorf, and a dozen others representing team leaders of the various inter agency and jurisdictional task force members. Bollinger took charge from the onset giving them all a current report on the surveillance of the various homes thus far and adding, "Gentlemen this will be a short meeting. Recent intercepts from our directional microphones have indicated a good chance that we think we have located the location of the shooting team imported to hit the President. Jaeger, you and Vultee will have the task of attaching yourselves to Sergeant Greenlee of the Arlington Virginia SWAT team.

As for the rest of you gentlemen get your men ready for a full on assault of their target locations"! Then Bollinger looked at his watch as he said, "We will synchronize our watches on my mark", as he waited then said, "Coming up on 1015 hours, Mark! The go time is at 1230 hours. Tell your men to be careful and capture where possible but not as to risk life and limb unnecessarily. Gentlemen good Luck"!

As the various unit commanders split up to go to their assignment areas, Jaeger and Vultee, walked out of the building with Sergeant Greenlee as Jaeger said, "How do you want us to deploy Sarge"?

"Mister Jaeger, you and Vultee have sat in on all the strategy meetings and from what I can understand about your background, I'm not about to give you any orders on how to deploy. Now I know the area like the back of my hand, it's where I live and work, so I ask that you follow my lead where you see fit. We all have the same comm devices keyed into the same frequency. I'll probably need some help at the back of the property. It's an exclusive neighborhood, full of retired and current governmental employees and politicians, so here above all we need to be cognizant of collateral damage because almost all of the residents are lawyers of some sort"!

As they got into the black Federal SUV Greenlee said, "That's some kind of hog leg you've got on your belt Jaeger. You sure that's enough firepower"?

"This? It just an old single action Colt converted to fire the .45 long Colt ammo. Brought fifty rounds with me stashed in my jacket. I'll let you guys throw the important lead and if all goes well I'll just pick up the pieces"!

As Greenlee drove them across the Potomac River be brought them up to date on the location of the assault. "The residence is at the end of a long cul de sac and sits on three acres of property that slopes upward towards the back of the property. That's where I'd like the both of you. There's plenty of trees at the back of the property to provide cover and there'll be two snipers flanking you with scoped M-16's. You'll approach from, the adjoining neighbor's property in the rear, now they have this guard dog on a chain in the rear of the property, who'll no doubt bark like hell at your approach, but we don't think that'll alert the target. It's almost winter outside, all the windows are closed, there's a hill and much tree cover behind them and the property in the rear so any sound should be absorbed or deflected"!

"Three days ago, we sent a Satellite Repair truck to repair a neighbor's home with good line of sight of the subject's property. Fortunately the property is owned by a consenting Federal Judge who consented to allow us to attach a directional mike on a portion of his roof. The collector dish looks like any other Satellite dish except it is pointed right at the 'front picture window. Took two days and a direct request from someone up top with clout Before the Judge gave his go ahead. Can only pick up what's discussed in their living room with any clarity and it was early this morning when we heard the current occupants arguing in the living room. Picked up on the African sounding accents. Plus there are two vehicles parked behind the house in front of the large garage with Missouri license plates. The former residents haven't been seen by the neighbors for the better part of a week and there is no one entering or exiting this house. So since two and two make four, we think this is where the shooting team is holed up. Oh before I forget, there's what appears to be a wooden storage shed about twenty yards from the rear of the house. We're guessing it's the standard structure that houses lawn and garden implements"!

"Once you guys signal that you're in place at the rear of the property, we'll make ourselves known at the front and the sides of the property. Since there's a good twenty yards between the adjacent properties and reasonably good cover, we should be able to set up in good cross fire positions. We'll signal you on the comm line when we get ready to commence operations"!

"How many occupants are in the house do you reckon Sarge", asked Vultee?

"One black with a Chicago accent, three with definite West African accents, which should be the imported shooting team and three other males with pronounced Middle Eastern accents"!

"Did you remember to bring cotton to stuff into your ears after the firing started", asked Jaeger of Vultee?

"Of course. Right here in my jacket pocket"!

"So the chances that they'll all still be there when we arrive are still good, eh Sarge", asked Jaeger"?

"Arlington PD has had a loose cordon of patrol cars at every intersection in the neighborhood, ever since midnight. Every intersection except that which is visible from the front of their house. As of an hour ago, conversations were still occurring in the house and the two visible cars in the driveway haven't moved. The Judges home has been informed of our plans and the family has left the premises leaving two of our people there"!

Ten minutes later, Sergeant Greenlee pulled up his SUV at the property behind the target property and joined up with the two snipers from the Arlington SWAT unit and two others and introduced Jaeger and Vultee saying, "Misters Jaeger and Vultee work for the White House and their going to join in the party gents. The snipers will each occupy a position at the rear edge of the property, Borger and Fanning will each take up a position at the neighbor's property on either side and our friends will plug up the middle between the snipers. Gentlemen keep your ears on and good luck"!

As the six made their way towards their target locations from the street to the back of the adjoining rear of the property a large Alsatian dog lunged from his dog house and started barking at the intruders. Everyone was aware of the dogs presence beforehand yet immediately brought their weapons to bear upon the dog. Jaeger immediately put his hands up silently as a signal to the others to hold back and got down on all fours staring right at the dog and made sounds which brought the charging dog to a halt just short of the length of his chain attached to the dog house. The dog gradually stopped his barking and looked at Jaeger who started to rise to a kneeling position. The others watched in amazement as Jaeger made a series of guttural noises and moved his hands in a horizontal position. Then the Alsatian slowly lay down prone and eventually rolled over on his back making allowing Jaeger to slowly approach and start to gradually rub his belly as Jaeger motioned to the others to move ahead slowly while he was occupying the animals attention. Once the othersdisappeared into the trees at the rear of the property, Jaeger snorted once then slowly stood up and joined the others never looking back. The Alsatian then stood up, shook once and returned to his warm dog house and his bowl.

Once Jaeger crested the ridge behind the subject's property he joined Vultee saying, "That must be the storage shed Greenlee was talking about"!

Vultee looked at Jaeger saying, "Man, I've known you for a long time but never knew you had the ability to settle the critters"!

"Legend has it that one of my people who came to Texas, back in the days of the Republic learned it from Davy Crockett. Been passed down from generation to generation and my daddy taught me how. Comes in handy every once in a while"!

Just then the comm units came to life with Greenlee saying, "Unit two are you in position". The lead sniper responded, "In position Sarge. Let er rip"! Greenlee drove the lead SUV down the street towards the property followed by one other SUV, as two Arlington patrol units took up position behind them blocking an escape from the subdivision. He drove the lead unit to the end of the Cul de Sac and parked it horizontally blocking the front driveway as the second unit passed him and took up position by the other driveway, both vehicles with the right side facing the target property as four men piled out of the left side of their respective vehicles taking up firing positions. Greenlee took up the microphone and punched the button saying, "This is the Arlington Police. Everyone in the house come out with your hands up and unarmed. You have one minute in which to comply"!

Ten seconds later, everyone heard over their comm units, "Sergeant Greenlee. This is Lookout One. A lot of yelling is going on in the house and it sounds like they're going for their guns"!

Greenlee then punched the button on his PA mike and said, "Inside the house, you have thirty seconds in which to comply"! Within seconds of his announcement, the front picture window exploded outward as a result of a chair being thrown through it and a form briefly appeared holding what appeared to be a Soviet RPG launcher. He took quick aim at the Task Force members in the street launching his missile. His hurried shot missed the SUV by inches landing curbside some forty yards behind Greenlee and his group, while his men fired at the front of the home when a target presented itself intermittently. Greenlee got on the comm and yelled, "Unit two, unit two, Hold your fire until a target presents itself.

Thirty seconds later, the front door quickly opened as the RPG launcher again made himself visible and this time took his time aiming at the other SUV and once again the bullets from the task force and the RPG passed each other in flight, both claiming full possession of their targets. The shooter of the RPG was knocked back inside as a dozen bullets laced his torso, never seeing his RPG hit his target full on exploding with such force it knocked the vehicle on its side. Automatic fire was coming from both the first and second floors of the house, at the Task Force in front of them, focusing on those lying in the street, knocked back by force of their cover being obliterated. Yet one of them laying in the street wounded, kept a steady fire of his M-16 on full auto on the house as bullets ricocheted all around him in the street, one of which found a home in his upper leg.

Those in the rear and the two flanking the property held their fire, in spite of what was going on in front of the property until one of Task Force located near the adjoining home saw a man peeking out of the upstairs window right in front of him and opened fire. Then the rear door opened and two of the dark skinned Africans stepped out and sprayed automatic weapon fire, to their left and right, firing at random, as a light skinned African wearing a red baseball cap ran out and towards the wooden storage shed, firing a round at the lock that secured the door and ran inside, quickly followed by another dark skinned African and one of mixed descent. The dark one made it to the innards of the shed while the other was cut down in midstride by one of the snipers at the rear of the property. As two of the Africans quickly reloaded their Kalashnikov's opening fire towards the rear of the property, both fell together as two bullets from the snipers each found a home on their target simultaneously, then a second and then a third as each one crumpled to the earth, with a death grip on the trigger which fired their weapons into the air until empty.

As they started to fall Jaeger and Vultee rose up and charged the storage shed, with weapons drawn and Jaeger yelling, "Fire into the Shed". The snipers each zeroed in on the storage shed and fired a steady stream of bullets into the structure, until their clips were empty, then quickly reloaded as Jaeger and Vultee raced to the shed fifty yards away down range stopping at the sheds rear in a crouch. Then they both rose up and advanced cautiously.

The front door of the shed was partially open as Vultee motioned to Jaeger to enter while he opened the door. As the door swung open they both heard sporadic fire coming from the front of the house and then stop, as Jaeger dove through the opening quickly, tumbled and came to his knees in firing position. Since the shed was a crowded place full of lawn care implements, measuring 10 by 20 feet, there was no place to hide. He quickly saw the bullet holes in the structure but no one was there. He yelled, "Clear" as Vultee came in. As he made his way towards the rear of the shed, he saw a trail of blood and then a trail in the floor dust ending behind a large wooden work table. 'Clearly the table was recently moved covering something up, then set quickly back', he thought as he swung the table forward and there was their manner of escape. The shed had for some reason been built around a manhole cover, which was slightly ajar, with evidence of blood splatter disappearing into a storm sewer drain. Jaeger then yelled behind him to the others, "Tell the others that several have escaped into the sewer system and one of them is wounded. You guys, give up your metal flashlights, to me and Vultee, we're goin' down after em"!

Jaeger and Vultee then descended into the cramped quarters of the sewer. Thoughts raced through Jaeger's mind of what he feared the most, doing HALO's out of perfectly good aircraft, fanged snakes of every kind, being alone surrounded by those who were there to end your life with the absolute knowledge that no help was coming, or being in a closet with a larger and stronger man knowing that only one of you were to emerge alive.

Of all of those possibilities, Jaeger knew why he feared what he did. But sewers? Just an instinctive fear, he supposed but as real as it got in his mind. Soon enough, he reckoned, he'd be able to hang clothes on that fear.

As both shined their flashlights around the tunnel, they discovered it went in two directions with a trail of blood leading towards the rear of the property and under the hill that separated the properties, with Jaeger quickly deciding, "Duke, you follow the blood trail and I'll take the other". Then a giant explosion rumbled overhead as the entire house exploded. Both Jaeger and Vultee had the cotton in their ears which was the only thing that saved their ear drums, still the sewer and the shed being in close proximity to the home, threw them to the concave bottom of the sewer. He was about to climb back up to the top and see if anyone in the shed was in need of help, but shook that thought off. He helped

Vultee to his feet, starting off in the direction down the street towards the intersection. His quarry must have a big lead on him by now. He thought about using his flashlight as he crouched uncomfortably forward, but oddly enough once his eyes got used to the darkness, he saw that he could make his way forward by the little swatches of light that filtered down through the curb side openings. 'No good telling this guy that you were coming and the flashlight would be a great, "Here we come"!

Up ahead, having scurried past the intersection where the police road block was stationed, Salaam was angry that all of his meticulous plans had been overturned. Only Blood Alpha has made it to the sewer with him, wounded as he was, with both Killer and the Chameleon going down. The rumble he felt from the homes explosion was the only good news he was likely to experience this day. Hopefully the home was full of the infidels celebrating their victory and the heavens would be full of the true believers before this day was done. He'd gone to the trouble of having the homeowner, himself a believer and one having taken part in the conflagration over the previous summer, having provided a schematic of the sewer system in this part of Arlington. His guess as to where the roadblocks would be, having been proven correct thus far, gave him a little comfort.

He'd taken several daylight excursions within the last week through the sewers on a reconnoitering expedition and had charted the way out in both directions, in anticipation of the worst case scenario. That only left Blood Alpha and him left to make their way to safety and Blood Alpha was wounded. All bets being off now and everyone for themselves. As he moved through the four foot in diameter tunnel he was grateful that it had not rained for a week, as the light from his trail lantern illuminated the way ahead clearly.

He wondered about the other believers and had they also been compromised. If so he was certain they'd find their way to glory in the bosom of the Prophet, may he be ever so beneficent. As he passed each intersection in the tunnel he saw the red chalk markers he'd left on the concrete walls just days before, showing the way ahead. He'd already gone about three quarters of a mile already and was almost half way towards his destination, a manhole cover that would easily be able to be muscled out of its niche on a sparsely traveled side street. He'd left an iron crow bar at the location just in case it was needed. The early morning news report was that the temperature was to go down to below freezing during the night so he was glad he'd worn dark colored boots, woolen socks, gloves and a hat. The plan was to wait until almost midnight before emerging then make his way towards the bus station. There in a locker, was everything he'd need to make his way west again, to St. Louis and hit the reset button. He should be quite satisfied as to the way his life had turned out. With what he had to originally work with back in Gary Indiana, he'd come quite far and had accomplished a great deal, from his point of view.

Yesterday's newscasts revealing the destruction of the Muslim Brotherhood, should've told him that something was amiss. Quickly followed by the disaster he'd just been a part of. Yet he was unable to connect the dots, focused entirely on the task at hand. As he moved forward through the sewer he was determined to shake things off and continue the struggle in different ways. For now, skill and patience was what's needed. He'd many accomplishments under his belt and really no longer needed the help from abroad any more. He'd soon rejoin, The Blade and others to continue his work.

Jaeger stopped and removed the cotton from his ears. He looked at his watch, the dim light revealing that he'd had but just a few hours of daylight left. He was coming up to an intersection and now realized that his quarry could go in a number of directions and he'd lose him. He closed his eyes and went to that far off place in his mind asking the question, 'If I were him what would I do'? The answer was simple when one thought about it a certain way. His quarry Salaam had never put one foot wrong as far as he knew, covering his tracks very well. Always having a plan and a backup. Why did he make a bee line for the sewers? Because he knew his way around somehow. He knew how to get out. He had the time. He'd prepared his ground well. Nothing wrong with this guy, he was great at what he did, planning things down to the very last dot. He'd have a light source and what with the explosion of the house, would have every reason to believe that no one would be following him. That he was all alone, yet something must be showing him the way out.

Jaeger took a risk and turned his flashlight, slowly shining it against the concrete sides of the sewer, up and down finally seeing a red chalk arrow pointing straight ahead. With renewed confidence and vigor Jaeger turned off his light, allowing his eyes to adjust a few minutes and scrambled ahead. As he moved ahead, he thought about the weather. In his rush early this morning he'd not bothered to watch the weather report as he grabbed his coffee, kissed Mel and ran out the door. He knew it was going to be cold tonight and was dressed appropriately but what if it rained? He'd certainly be up shits creek and now he knew why he feared the storm sewer he was in? But so was his quarry Salaam. As he came to the next intersection he stopped, turning on his flashlight careful to shield the light in a narrow path with his hands as he shown the light slowly up and down the walls, eventually coming across another red chalk arrow, this time the horizontal shaft of the arrow pointed in a downward direction. He assumed that if it pointed upward that the direction would be to the right so Jaeger turned left and continued on. Eventually he came to another intersection and shined the light carefully on the walls and saw the red arrow pointing straight ahead horizontally. He's guessed correctly.

A half hour later he came to another intersection and stopped to rest a bit. Every so often he heard the sound of a vehicle going by overhead, but since it was infrequent he supposed he was still in a subdivision and not on the main road. He heard the rumble of what appeared to sound like a school bus rumbling by then stop, as the muted sounds of children filtered down into the sewers. He checked his watch and saw that it was about the time school usually let out.

He shown his light again on the walls of the sewer, this time the red arrow pointed upward which meant to turn right as he turned the light off and scurried onward.

Salaam turned on his hunting lantern and saw the manhole cover overhead and as he traversed the light downward saw the iron crowbar laying right below as he moved forward to his last position before freedom. He needed some energy so he opened up a package of chewing gum removing several sticks and popped them into his mouth. There was a street culvert opening ten yards away and he could make it out by the dimming light below, as heheard less and less the sounds of children playing and more and more sounds of automobiles moving into their driveways after a long day at the office. He was now several miles away from the scene of his disaster and he could relax and wait for dark and his freedom. He pulled out a pack of cigarettes and withdrew one slowly from the pack and put flame to its end, slowly inhaling its warmth deep into his lungs. He was grateful this was a storm sewer and not a wastewater sewer. He could at least emerge without the everlasting stench of the infidels excreta inexorably in every crack and crevasse of his being. Allah be praised.

Jaeger moved slowly ahead step by step as he came again to another sewer intersection. He was about to turn on his flashlight again to gain his bearings, when something stopped him. He sniffed the air. He sniffed again and yet again. Something was wrong The odor of a cigarette in a storm sewer in early winter? He sniffed the air again and there it was. Definitely a cigarette was nearby. He slowly peered around the corner. Behind him all was darkness and just around the corner was the shadow of a single figure taking the last puff of a cigarette before putting it out. Above him was an ever so faint light from the round holes of an iron manhole cover, filtering down on a dark form.

He drew back into the shadows deciding to play this one by the book and slowly crawled back a hundred yards down the sewer to a place where another manhole cover was. He tried to lift the cover so he could emerge and call the others on his comm unit but the iron cover wouldn't budge as often was the case. Then he scurried back to one of the street culvert openings, pulling out his comm unit from his jacket and inserting his ear piece and said, "Unit one, Sergeant Greenlee come in"! Hearing no reply he repeated his call several more times on the two channels allotted for this operation. After some five minutes of patient trying he concluded that the designer of this unit hadn't considered sewer combat as a possible usage.

'So it's gonna be this way or nothing', he thought as he secured the comm unit back in his jacket, checked his weapon and started back from where he came. As he stopped at the intersection the lights from above were all but extinguished. He was thankful that Salaam, if that was who was ahead was into smoking for the smell of the cigarette drifted down the tunnel like a roadmap. As he hugged the opposite wall of the tunnel from its intersect with one eye peering out from the edge, he could barely make out softly glowing ash moving up and down with every inhalation. He could see nothing else, yet was able to gage his approximate form by the way the glowing ash traveled in an oblique pathway. He slowly put down his Colt revolver on his lap and reached inside his jacket pocket, reaching for his cotton plugs and slowly put them into his ears, ever watching the glowing ash of the freshly lit cigarette traverse up and down. The cotton well in place, his hand slowly folded around the handle of his single action Colt, as both hands came together in firing position and he waited, taking in each breath slowly and deeply and slowly and silently releasing each breath and waiting for his heart rate to diminish. He reckoned roughly that Salaam was about forty some odd yards away and if done right, just one shot in the dark from the big Colt would be sufficient to end things. He decided upon the head shot even though he couldn't see his target, he'd follow the path of the glowing ash. As the glowing ash moved upward, Jaeger lightly put pressure on the trigger and lightly squeezed.

Perhaps Salaam was coming down with a cold, but as he lifted the cigarette to his lips, he felt a sneeze overwhelm him in an instant, his head moving forward uncontrollably just as Jaeger pulled the trigger, the bullet barely grazing the back of Salaams. As Salaam was briefly deafened by the sound of the gunshot in the confines of the dark sewer, he'd the presence of mind to roll forward and bring his short barreled AK-47 to his right and press the trigger releasing some ten rounds quickly in a wide pattern. Then a light came on and he felt a bullet slam into his leg as he pulled the trigger of his weapon and release another short burst of rounds at the light source.

Holding the large metal flashlight in his left hand far out horizontally and shooting one handed with his right Jaeger slowly fired off a single round into the target. As bullets whizzed missing his arm by inches, he fired two shots in succession at where he thought Salaam was, as one of the errant rounds knocked the flashlight from his hand, coming to rest on the floor of the tunnel shining at the wall downrange. Jaeger quickly dashed across the sewer intersection as Salaam fired off a quick burst at moving shadows.

The flash light was still lit; its light casting an oblique shadow across the tunnel that was of little help to either man as Jaeger saw an arm quickly reach across the tunnel and another light come on facing in his direction.

Both men knew exactly why they were there, as well as knowing that words between them would be a wasted effort as they went about the business of summoning death. In every way Salaam relished the summons, for this is what a true warrior for the cause of Jihad was about. That he would live or die in the next few moments was of complete indifference. His accomplishments would live on as he entered that other dimension of Eternity, embraced by the Prophet himself and held up for all time as an example of a true warrior. His only concern was that the other one would join him part way in his journey, eternal grace causing the gravity of the damned to take hold and drag the wretched infidel down into the abyss of eternal hellfire. He said a quick prayer to Allah to guide his hand as he pressed the trigger.

He aimed a short burst from his full clip at the bottom of the concrete sewer hoping for an errant ricochet to find a home. When they hit, malformed as they were, they did far more damage to the target than a straight on shot. He fired high a short burst from the shadows, then he fired low, another short burst.

Jaeger cringed as the ricochets bracketed all around him. He quickly fumbled about his jacket pocket and reloaded his weapon the only rap against an old Colt revolver was the slow time of reloads. Surviving the onslaught of rapid indirect fire, he took several of the spent shells and tossed them into the partially lit intersection as they drew another short burst from Salaam.

'God only knows how many clips of ammo this guy has', thought Jaeger. He knew he'd knicked him on the first shot, then he'd caught a round in the leg, usually prompting someone with a grunt of some kind. But this one was a hard case. He'd go down without a word. Jaeger decided to risk playing the man's own game and sidled up close to the intersection of the sewer trying a bank shot of his own. With the light shining in his direction he squeezed off two rounds at a point at the sewer wall he thought was twenty yards away, then quickly ran across to the other side as several single shots followed in his wake. Then he did the opposite firing off two more bank shots, far down the sewer wall, hearing an involuntary grunt as one of the shells hit home.

Jaeger quickly as he could reloaded additional shells and took a deep breath and leaped into the tunnel crouching, weaving and firing as he went. In the process he caught two rounds in his front Kevlar vest, but given that it was from a .25 caliber back up automatic and that Jaeger's blood was up, he missed not a stride, as two more of his big rounds slammed into Salaams torso. As he arrived Jaeger kicked Salaams empty gun away, pistol whipping him with his gun barrel. With his free hand Salaam withdrew a flick knife, bringing it into play and making one last desperate swipe at his aggressor. Jaeger parried the slow swipe with his boot, bringing the full weight of his body down on his enemy with a crushing blow.

Jaeger could feel the bones of Salaams face buckle as he brought his elbow crushing into his face. The breath left Salaams body in a rush as Jaeger rolled back against the far wall in the dim light, from the lantern. He now lit one of his own cigarettes and waited, looking at the one who had caused so much death and misery for so many. Wondering why? He knew he would never know the answer. He surmised it was Salaam, because of the lighter color of his skin as opposed to the imported shooters and then because of the tenacity of his fight. This was the kind of man with a deep unyielding hatred, very intelligent, clever and driven. The kind that words will never reach. Bargains made while under a state of duress can be broken with or without cause or reason, as well as reasons crafted out of thin air.

No this man must never again see the light of day. Yet he had to respect the toughness of the guy as he started to come around rejoining the world. He rolled his head over and looked at Jaeger in the dim light of the sewer as he said, with great effort through crushed teeth, "You musta run across Da Blade, before. I see you got his mark"!

Jaeger then straddled him and placed the old Colt's barrel right into Salaams mouth and said, "Yeah, The Blade and I crossed paths not too long ago and he was the one who gave you up to me sport and when I was done with him he joined the fishes in the Mississippi. I was also the guy that caught up with your boy Beslan Bujovic and now I've caught up with you. It's check out time"!' Jaeger slowly pulled back the hammer and barely touched the trigger as the big Colt bucked in his hand. He would have to clean his weapon completely before the night was through, what with the detria that came with the blowback from such a short range shot.

He then looked up and said, "I hope you'll give me a pass on this one, but I think we both know where he's going"!

Then seeing the crowbar nearby he reached over for it and pried the iron man hole cover from the opening and stood up reaching for Salaams lantern and hoisted himself wearily onto the street. His weapon in his holster he pulled out the comm unit pressed the button saying, "Unit One Commander please come in. He repeated the command a second time before his comm unit came alive, "Unit One Sergeant Greenlee here. Who is this"?

"It's Jaeger Sergeant and Salaam is dead. So you can come get me"!

"Where are you Jaeger"?

"Damn if I know Sarge. Somewhere in the subdivision. Just emerged from the storm sewers on some back street. It's starting to get cold out here and Salaam is gonna get stiff real quick if you guys don't saddle up. How'd Vultee come out Sarge"?

"Just a moment while I round up somebody to home into you". A minute later Greenlee came back on saying, "He caught up with one of the imports an hour ago. They had a shootout in the sewers, Vultee caught a scratch, but the import is dead. The medics are tending to him as we speak. How about you"?

"Just need a shot or three of Old Overshoes and I oughtta be fine. Tell your boys to look for some son of a bitch sitting by an open manhole with a flash light and hustle up"!

Five minutes later two Arlington patrol cars rolled up with Greenlee in one of them as they saw Jaeger sitting on the curb smoking a cigarette. As Greenlee rolled out of the patrol car he yelled over to Jaeger saying, "Those things are going to be the death of you", as he walked up to Jaeger with a pint of 'Old Guckenheimer'. "This is as close as the corner liquor store could come to Old Overshoes pal"!

"You catch anything", asked Greenlee his arm in a sling from the bombing?

"Just a couple of small caliber rounds in the Kevlar. It'll bruise up before midnight. Tell your boys that Salaam's down in the sewer. So any reports on the other sites"?

"The nine other sites had the very same thing we had. A fire fight once the various places were surrounded. Bullets flying everywhere and they got the worst of it in every case, but as the first guys went in to clean up, they all walked into a trap because every home was wired to blow and they all did. The bad news is that seventeen of the task forces are gone and another eighteen in the hospital"!

As neighbors started to emerge from their houses to see what all the commotion was about an ambulance pulled up with all of its lights flashing as Jaeger asked, "How about our unit"?

"Caught an RPG round early on in one of the SUV's, three of our guys bit the dust right away. Luckily none of our guys went into the house when it blew but two others bit the dust from the explosion. The two snipers you were with that joined you inside the shed only had superficial damage and I was just getting up from the curb, was the only thing that saved my ass.

Everyone else went to the emergency room. All of them went away in a blaze of glory so no taxpayer dollars are gonna have to be spent taking them to trial. That's the good news. The bad news is that local funeral homes just might be very busy"!

"So I guess we all can read all about in the papers tomorrow and on the tube" said Jaeger.

"Departmental procedure says I gotta take you to the hospital to have you checked out. Do ya mind"?

"Anything to get warm, as long as I can get some shut eye this evening.

Besides, procedure is procedure, so after they haul up Salaam for the post mortem I might as well ride along with them"! "I'll follow you in the unit that brought me here. Others will be here shortly to take command of the crime scene.

While Jaeger and Greenlee were each being tended to for their injuries in the ER the Presidential Limousine with General Bollinger and Orval Goodwin arrived. Both men made a cursory visit to see Jaeger, Greenlee and Vultee, and then made their way into the mortuary where the autopsies were currently being performed on Salaam. As the coroner made a fuss about their presence mentioning something about County procedure, Orval Goodwin interjected himself saying, "We're from the White House and this is a matter of National Security. Were here as observers. You will conduct the autopsy in our presence. Are we understood? Now go to work"!

The county coroner went immediately to work on the cadaver formerly known as Salaam. As he worked swiftly the coroner duly noted the various gunshot wounds and injuries suffered by the deceased. Then as he turned the body over he noted the large hole in the back of the subjects head indicating the appearance of a gunshot wound at close range. He turned the body over again and opened the crushed mouth of the subject declaring, "I see powder in the victim's mouth indicative of an inter-oral shooting"!

"Turn off all tapes Gentlemen" said Bollinger, "And give them to me immediately". The Secret Service agents in attendance made certain the tapes were removed as the Coroner protested saying, "What is going on here? You gentlemen are my guests as a courtesy only taking part as observers"! Just then Jaeger, Greenlee and Vultee entered the morgue as the Coroner grew anxious saying, "What is going on here? These people aren't authorized to be here"! Then Bollinger took over and turned the Coroner toward him saying, "As we mentioned before we're from the White House acting in behalf of the President and these gentlemen are with us in fact they had an active role in the demise of your subject in that god damned table who has been responsible for the death of thousands and was plotting the death of the President. Now here is what you will do. You will perform your autopsy of this man omitting you final discovery in your report. When completed you will have it immediately transcribed in our presence and hand the report to us. Then you may go home to your family. Failure to do precisely as I say will find you in a faraway place by noon tomorrow. I trust we are now completely understood"?

"You're asking me to falsify my findings" said the Coroner!

"I'm not asking you to do anything. I'm telling you to correct your findings immediately old man or suffer the consequences which will be immediate and rather unpleasant"!

Just before two AM Jaeger opened the door to Mel's town house and silently let himself in. He was loathe to wake her so he went to the liquor cabinet and poured himself a double shot of whiskey and flicked on the Television to one of the all night news channels. As he flicked through the channels he discovered they were still telling the story of the completed operation not quite twelve hours old. Technically it all went off like clockwork. The initial assaults all started on time and proceeded along predictable lines, except that no one could know that all of the homes assaulted would be booby trapped. Jaeger and Vultee's target was the first to explode, followed quickly by three others as they were quickly overwhelmed by the assault teams trapping all in the residences in the subsequent explosions and fiery aftermath.

Many of the other assault units were quickly notified to lay back as they did, answering the withering fire coming from the respective homes in kind. Yet as each of the homes ran short of ammunition a decision was made to ignite the charges, with all of them exploding into flames. All except one. A lucky mistake in wiring had prevented the ignition of the charges as the assault team breached their defenses, killing all within except one, who was whisked away to a hospital in Silver Springs under guard. His bullet riddled body never made it to the local emergency room dying en route.

By five PM, the bomb disposal unit disarmed all of the charges after discovering the bodies of the former residents stuffed in the attic. As Jaeger grew sleepy from his day's exertions, lack of food and the liquor he fell asleep on Mel's couch with the Television on low volume as not to wake the mistress of the house. At five in the morning Mel awoke and went to relieve herself on her way back to bed she noticed through the half open doorway a faintly flickering light coming from the first floor. As she gathered a shawl around her she tip toed down the stairs and saw what the matter was. There on her couch was Jaeger asleep with a mostly consumed glass of liquor and the television turned on to one of the all night news channels. She gently removed the glass from his hand, then removed the boots from his feet, placing the other leg on the couch.

Normally, she discovered, the man was a very light sleeper. No doubt a trait born out of necessity, given the life he'd grown accustomed to. She tiptoed to the hall closet and removed a comforter and went back to place it over him. She briefly considered removing the Colt revolver from his waist holster, but thought better of it, deciding to quit while she was ahead as she gently placed the comforter over him, then turned off the television and tiptoed back up the stairs. She'd anguished all through the day knowing full well that Jaeger was an integral part of the assault operation and was no doubt far too busy with other things to call her and tell her that he was safe. He'd told her that he would be back and he was a man of his word. As she climbed back into bed she silently thanked the eternal for answering her prayers.

At 0800 hours Jaegers eyes opened, to find the television turned off, a warm comforter laid over him and his boots on the floor. He smelled fresh coffee, turned on the TV and padded into the kitchen where he saw a note by the coffee maker that read; "Thanks for returning in one piece. Enjoy your coffee and call me when things settle down".

Two days later at a hastily called news conference at the White House, televised during Prime time, The President approached the podium this time without his usual folder Containing his prepared remarks, this time with but a few three by five cards hand written for the occasion as he said, "I wish to thank all of you and the Media Networks for allowing me to make a few remarks. First, I'd like to welcome back to the fold Vannevar Harvanian to resume his responsibilities as the Executive Offices Press Secretary. The Doctors have given him a clean bill of health. All I ask is that the members of the Press Corps. Be gentle with him for a short time, so he can get his sea legs back"!

At that, everyone rose and gave him a brief round of welcoming applause. When that had concluded the President resumed by saying, "Now no doubt some of you may be wondering what will become of Van's replacement, Molly Pringle who by all accounts filled in admirably during his absence? She's been called to a far more important task, which is keeping track of me. For you see, as of nine PM last night she became Molly Magnusson, here in the White House. Neither of us wished to make a fuss over it. She'd become an integral part of my life and like two magnets we just came together. So Molly please come up here to be formally introduced to the nation. Ladies and Gentlemen, the First Lady"!

Everyone immediately stood up and applauded with a look of wonderment and shock in their eyes, for not even the savviest of them saw this one coming. As the applause died down Magnusson said, "I hope the network cameras caught the look of utter astonishment in each of your faces that I see. Priceless. Just priceless. Oh, in case any of you are wondering where our honeymoon will be? Forget about it. And now to the reason I've called you all together"!

"By now everyone has heard, read about and have seen on the network news programs, the various reports regarding the assaults on the homes in the DC area. This was the culmination of an ongoing investigation and operation as to those involved in first the Urban bombing in Houston and then the forest and urban fires that consumed our nation during the summer heat wave that destroyed billions of dollars' worth of property as well as taking literally the lives of thousands of people. Those involved were traced back to dissident foreign terrorist organizations in the Middle East. The manner of their demise was indicative of the fact that none of them were going to allow themselves to be taken alive. The good news is we believe that we've gotten all of them. They were summoned from all over the nation to the DC area, to provide a distraction for those imported from abroad to assassinate me during my speech two days from now; similar to the conflagration we all endured. I wanted to publicly introduce all that were involved in the heroic assaults, but at their insistence to a man, decided to honor their wishes to respect their privacy. Besides, there are so many of them to honor it would fill up most of this room. Instead, the celebration at the Lincoln Memorial two days hence will be dedicated to each member of the task force that perished in the operation and the remarks I'll make at that time will be in homage to their bravery and sacrifice"!

"And now I'll be happy to take questions"!

"Mandy Cosgrove, LA Times Mister President. What our readers may like to know is why you and the First Lady decided to become man and wife behind closed doors? Is she pregnant"?

"Ms. Cosgrove. Are you certain you work for the LA Times? I'd think a question like that would be more appropriate from someone in the employ of the National Enquirer"?

"Ah yes, Mr. Johnson"!

"Harold Johnson Mister President, the Washington Times. The timing of this attack on homes owned by Muslims seems curiously scheduled to occur just after the bombing of the Moslem Mosque in Cairo several days ago, that has reportedly slain most if not all of the Moslem Brotherhood"! "Is there a question in your statement, Mister Johnson"?

"Do you know anything about it sir"?

"As a matter of fact I do. I read excerpts from your newspaper every day, along with a host of others and by all reports it looks like an internecine struggle between the various terrorist elements"!

As Magnusson went on, Harvanian turned to the newly minted First Lady whispering, "Your husband is on a roll. Call 911 for I smell blood and it's not his"!

Standing in the back of the large room next to Jaeger and Mel, was the Countess Fabiola Hargraves holding on to the other arm of Duke Vultee.

Wounded during the post assault chase, his left arm was in a sling. It took her just eight hours after she was summoned by Molly for her to pack and fly down to Washington on her private Jet, book a suite of rooms and appear at the White House during the appointed hour to serve as Maid of Honor for Molly, in which she performed exceedingly well, the preceding evening.

After the "I do's", as the entire White House staff milled past the President and the new First Lady, Countess Hargraves saw Mel and Jaeger standing together along with Vultee. As she approached Mel whispered to both men, Hold on to your butts boys, we're about to be confronted by faux royalty"!

"Mel darling, it's been too long", drawled Fabiola as she came near! "Gentlemen, may I introduce the Countess Fabiola Hargraves! Fabiola this is Jaeger and his good friend Duke Vultee"! As both men nodded Fabiola said, looking Jaeger up and down, "So this is the legendary Jaeger, I've heard so much about. That dueling scar looks ominous"!

"Good things I hope"!

"Exemplary things to be sure". After a pause she added, I trust I'll be invited to perform a similar ceremony for Mel"? Mel immediately looked at the Countess embarrassed and before she could say anything, Jaeger said, "I was waiting to pop the question after the ring I was having made in Houston was finished, but since the questions now out there, how about it babe", he asked turning towards Mel?

The ice now being broken Mel thought a second then said, "Only if the Countess gives me away a throws the party"!

"I take it that's a yes"? Mel nodded her head in agreement!

"Well that's settled and thanks Countess. First time I ever asked someone to marry me and was concerned I'd screw things up"!

Then the Countess turned her attention to Duke Vultee, saying "And you must be Duke Vultee another of the heroes of the assault"!

Turning to Mel and Jaeger, Vultee said, "Damn, this woman is direct ain't she"? Then he turned to the Countess responding, "That I am Mamm. Happy to make your acquaintance"!

"And what precisely is it that you do Mister Vultee"?

"A little bit of this and a little bit of that, but mostly one might say that I'm in the ah, entertainment business"!

"Entertainment business eh, very well then", she said slipping her arm under Vultee's good arm. "Come with me so we can chat awhile", she said leading him away.

"So that's what Vultee does", said Mel! "You might put it that way. You see Duke is the owner of a string of Men's Clubs", said Jaeger!

"Men's Clubs? You mean Titty Bars don't you"!

"Exactly"!

"Isn't the Countess in for a surprise", smiled Mel.

Then General Bollinger joined them with Mel telling him the good news of their impending marriage. His face beamed with joy as he said,

"Of course your son will have to be there to give away the bride. Tell me when and hopefully it'll coincide with his schedule at the Naval Academy and I'll make the arrangements. Where will the ceremony be held"?

"I'm thinking about the ranch I'm restoring in Waco. My gift to Mel for waiting so long"!

35

The next several days were a whirlwind of activity. The President's speech in front of the Lincoln Monument went off as planned. All of the precautions by the security teams were still in effect. The area mortuaries were busier than ever, with a minor fluff raised in certain circles regarding the less than timely burial of the Moslem terrorists, given their religious affiliation. Of course the Americans slain during the assault were given preference, but since each of the families of the terrorists were in fact slain themselves massive confusion as to the next of kin occurred. The government then reached out to various Moslem groups around the nation to help with mixed results.

The Delta operatives were debriefed by the Defense Department as a matter of course after their return, the results of which immediately were placed in Deep Security Classification for the next generation. Their significant contribution silently noted by the Secretary of Defense in a private ceremony.

The heart and soul of the Moslem Brotherhood was, for the time being rendered inoperable, yet as almost everyone knew this was but a temporary setback, for the cause of Jihad.

After the festivities, the Countess Fabiola and Duke Vultee made a hasty departure to the Big Apple in her private jet as she made it a point to trot her new man out for Nueva York's society. New blood would surface eventually for the face of evil never sleeps.

Yaakov Kitterman drifted quietly back towards Tel Aviv, offering himself up to the Mossad for the requisite debriefings, before reuniting with his father. Most all of the demons chasing him were over the years were exorcised during that evening with Nestor Magellan. There we're several very capable others in Cairo ready to fill in the void of being the eyes and ears of the Mossad. For now it was a quiet time for Yaakov and his father.

Rex Wallace had received a full promotion as Agent in Charge of the FBI's Houston office and was busy with that task, as a reward for his contribution as part of the DC task force receiving a minor wound in the conflict and a letter of commendation in his file.

Nestor Magellan made his way to Tel Aviv with Kitterman and in a few days boarded a flight back to Paris to resume his life as a quiet family man and a Security Expert, with no regrets.

General Bollinger resumed his retirement, confident that he would be attending many events in the future in behalf of his non paternal extended family.

After the Christmas and New Year's holidays Jaeger flew back to Houston to go through his mail, pay bills and spend time at the ranch preparing it for the June wedding to Melanie.

Every other day they called each other like teenagers eager to hear the others voice. Early in February he flew to DC to present her with the engagement ring this time formally on bended knee. Her duties at the White House being especially important during this time, whereas the President was busy clearing the way via legislation to embark on the first phase of a Transcontinental Mag Lev people carrier, secretly in behalf of the consortium headed by Dax Sonntag and Pierre Duquesne. The solar and wind power initiatives were on track and on schedule. Somehow one by one the political obstructions evaporated into thin air as revelations and scandals hit those who stood in the way of progress and jobs.

After one especially grueling day of negotiating with the current congressional leaders regarding legislation effecting the Presidents overall jobs bill, namely for Congress and many regulatory agencies to simply get out of the way of progress, Magnusson, Goodwin and Harvanian sat down in the Oval Office for an afterhours drink, with the President musing offhandedly, "Somebody up there must like me"!

"How so Mr. President", asked Goodwin?

"When I look back at the last two and a half years, things initially looked about as bleak as could be. The nation in turmoil, spiritually, economically and in just about every way imaginable. President Dobbins and his entire family obliterated. Almost as if they never existed. My family gone and me in the hospital with one foot in the grave. Fortunately

Hiram Mulvahill stepped in and filled the gap admirably. I just want to thank the both of you for standing at my side, through everything. When I look back it was like I was on auto pilot just getting through each day as best I could. Then in the aftermath of your heart attack Van, here was Molly hitting the ground running interference every bit as well as you finally resulting in my being smitten with her and our marriage. Finally, when we embarked on this seemingly over ambitious plan of starting the Mag Lev System and the Wind and Solar electricity efforts, I just didn't know how we were going to get through the maze of regulatory hurdles that faced us. Then one by one the hurdles faded away. It seemed that many of our politicians and key bureaucrats were leading double lives all along. The media was thankfully busy with all of the scandals that faced them giving us time to maneuver and accomplish things. It was like the hand of God parting the seas for us"!

Harvanian quickly glanced at Goodwin over his drink as Magnusson nusson looked out of the Oval office window wistfully saying, "Hand of God Mister President? That seems to explain it, don't you think Orval"? "God's mighty hand seems appropriate to me Mister President", said Goodwin. "By the way how did your conference call go with Sonntag and Duquesne go this afternoon"?

"Their putting up a mile of overhead pathway each day, following the original railways with minimal interruption, on every one of their projects, adding additional bridging as needed, employing an army of workers and subcontractors in the process. They've tested the viability of the wind and solar power generators along the pathway dedicated to their needs, with no work stoppages by the unions. Of course they're just waiting in the wings for completion before they rear their heads. Something we'll have to come to grips with eventually but that's for another time. Those on Wall Street are happy with the progress for they're banking on the new Consortium IPO's started by Sonntag and Duquesne to make them a boat load. People are just happy to get back to work on something meaningful that will last and endure for the benefit of all. Everything's being made in the US and the prices and quality are just what is needed, without one single dollar of taxpayer's money. Yes sir, the hand of God is upon us it seems"! "The hand of God", echoed Goodwin and Harvanian knowingly!

Spring was just around the corner and within the month, what was left of the newly resurrected ranch started by Henry Jaeger long ago, came into its final stage of completion. Of course everything was in a different location, but the cavernous barn, the main house, the newly constructed guest house and the residences for the two newly hired vaqueros and their small families from Mexico were almost completed. Twenty mustang horses and another twenty long horn cattle inexpensively acquired made up the starting of a new herd. In time Jaeger would improve on his herd, with cross breeding with other herds from neighbors, finally glad to see the Jaegers return to this part of the country. Invitations to selected people were sent with, Molly and the Countess handling all of the necessities and logistics visiting the new home as needed keeping, Melanie inWashington as not to ruin her surprise as the future Madam of the Texas Prairie. Molly secretly flew in the Countess's private jet for her various trips, making a side trip to Houston with the Countess, to personally deliver invitations to Elizabeth Beauvior and old Boyd Parmalee, partner emeritus of the law firm started by Leo Swartzwald long ago. After an introduction of the Countess to Buffy, at her office downtown, Molly presented the invitation to the wedding personally to Buffy saying, "Both Jaeger and Mel would dearly like you and Mister Parmalee to attend"!

"Why of course I'll be there along with Boyd", said Buffy. "A modest soiree of his closest friends to see old Jaeger bite the dust at long last"!

Buffy had remembered her from long ago reporting at Jaegers abortion of a trial. "You've appeared to have done well over the years Molly", referring to her garnering a sitting President as a life mate"!

"I've been fortunate, beyond measure Ms. Beauvior"!

"My friends call me Buffy and I do hope we'll be friends and that goes for you also Countess"!

"My friends call me Fabiola, and I've decided we will be friends, for I hear you're a fabulous lawyer and one never knows when one will need a great lawyer"!

"It's settled then everyone here are friends till the bitter end. But

Fabiola what ever happened to Jaegers friend Duke Vultee, the gossip rags were saying you two were an inseparable item. He was in prison with Jaeger and I got them both out at the same time. Why I'll bet you didn't know he was a former bank robber"!

"A bank robber? Well that explains it. He always grew very nervous when the Paparazzi swirled. Besides he misinformed me, when we first met. I asked him what he did and he said 'Entertainment', failing to add that he owned a string of Gentlemen's Clubs. We both decided to go our separate ways and remain friends"!

As they all got up to depart, Buffy drew Molly aside and said, "Since she's in a Texican mood I think I'll have another old friend of Jaegers come up with me if it's OK with you. His name is 'Hondo' and he is a dyed in the wool bounty hunter"!

"Consider it done Buffy", said Molly. Of course Vultee will be there"!

"They'll be good. I guarantee it"!

A week later Jaeger received a call from overseas from Nestor Magellan thanking him for the invitation to his wedding but declining claiming a conflict with some important contracts he was working on, yet he added, "None the less you shall be the beneficiary of two gifts that are on the way to your home, one consumable and the other from our dissolute past endeavors. The latter, I'd almost forgotten about and that knowing you're a substantial man of honor, I am confident that you'll know what to do with it. Now when you've a mind please bring your new wife to Paris so I may house and entertain you both and introduce you to my family"!

Jaeger agreed as they rang off. The following day two parcels were delivered from abroad, both from Magellan. The larger of which he put aside for the day of the wedding and the smaller a letter. It was from Magellan reminding him indeed of past endeavors in behalf of someone they both worked for. Ortega. Jaeger remembered that terrible night and the slaughter in Menard County. Nestor briefly reminded him of the source, the laboratory long ago destroyed in the Andes Mountains and the valuable narco product that came from it, "Crystalline". On a separate sheet of paper, he drew a map of where the remaining tonnage of the concentrate lay buried along with the approximate GPS coordinates.

Years ago in an abandoned barn off an old country road in Val Verde County Texas. Of course he knew what to do with it and picked up the phone and called Rex Wallace in Houston, for an appointment the following day. They both met for lunch at the Silver Dollar Café in Houston. Served personally by Rae the printer, who received his formal invitation to the wedding along with Wallace. After he left while they were waiting for their order to arrive, Jaeger asked, "Ever hear the old saw about never looking a gift horse in the mouth"!

"Sure, What about it"!

"Do you believe it"?

"Depends on the source"!

"You're looking' at the source"!

"Then I believe it. What's the skinny"?

Jaeger then shoved the single sheet of paper that Magellan sent to him with the map and the GPS coordinates of the location of the remainder of the Crystalline and gave him an edited version of how it got there and why.

Wallace usually went through a disciplined procedure of confirming information given to him, but since he'd come to know Jaeger and remembering the commitment he just made decided to forgo his discipline just this one time.

"I suppose we could contact the San Antonio office and get some people together and drift on down to Val Verde County and see what develops in the next few days. I'll thank you after we see whether or not it's of value"!

"Oh it'll be of value, ye of little faith"!

"Sorry sport, but its habits born out of training"!

Three days later he received a phone call from Wallace, asking him what he wanted for a wedding gift and then saying, "Thanks"!

"Just bring you and your family to the wedding, nothing more.

"The details will be on the evening news and in most of the papers and thanks again", said Wallace as he rang off. Jaeger knew that information of a massive haul like that would be a career builder within the bureau. Yet another chapter in his life closed.

36

Two o'clock in the morning was far too early for the Countess to rise but if she was to be on board of her Gulf Stream Jet in time to arrive at Andrews Air Base and pick up the First Lady and Jaegers soon to be bride Melanie for the trip to Waco, she'd better get her ass in gear. Many reasons that Molly was to be the only one in attendance from the Oval Office, starting with the President's schedule with foreign dignitaries that couldn't be ignored or rescheduled. Then there was Jaegers penchant for keeping everything in his life low key. Plus where ever the President went, it was a media event. Habits of a life time are often hard to break, especially when they work.

Mel's son was to give his mother away at the ceremony as well as serve as best man, flew into Waco with General Bollinger, to stay at the guest house. This was to be Melanie's first glimpse of where she would spend the rest of her life. Pleasant surprises were to be the order of the day.

As the aircraft topped off its tanks for the trip to the Waco Airport, the executive limousine pulled up alongside disgorging the First Lady as well as Melanie who boarded the plane followed by two members of the White House detail of the Secret Service who dutifully loaded the luggage for the trip. They were the last to board the aircraft each lifting a pet carrier with them to be transported inside for the trip. The inhabitants of the pet carriers were sound asleep as the Gulf Stream lifted off into the predawn skies in a southwesterly direction.

As soon as the jet gained cruising altitude, Molly exclaimed to Fabiola, "You were wondering why we were transporting animals. Well they're not just any pair of animals but Canadian Timber Wolves. The story behind them is that their mother was killed by some hunters who came upon their lair. They're not a month old. The hunter was a retired Minnesota politician who thought they'd make an excellent present for the President. Of course when he saw them he fell in love with them straight away and so did I. However I recalled in researching Jaegers background for his trial long ago, the legend of his families penchant for Wolves and the role they played in guarding the early Jaeger herds. From generation to generation Wolves have somehow always stood guard on a Jaeger herd, so I thought it more than fitting the President forgo this present and give the new Jaeger family something of meaning. Now as to the female or, bitch, I've given her the name of the original female wolf and the name is "Chani". The little dark male is to be named "Akila", which was the name of the original ancestors. So Mel you are to be the one who presents these two adorable critters to Jaeger right after the ceremony. What do you think"?

"If anything will bring that man to tears of joy it will be the Wolves", she said, her eyes starting to mist up!

Molly went to the pet carriers and extracted the baby wolves as they were waking up and handed one of them to the Countess who had never held a wolf in her arms as she extracted the other saying, "Their still in the weaning stage, so milk right from the cow is necessary for them to grow. In a few weeks I'm told, they'll be ready for raw meat or at least pet food from the store"!

Over the years as Jaeger, with Buffy running legal interference for him had taken back or purchased much of the land that was his inheritance, even going as far as purchasing the home that abutted the old Jaeger burial grounds and building the family a similar home a short distance away. Over time he'd located the burial locations of his immediate family murdered long ago and had them re-interred at the Jaeger family burial grounds as well as having new grave stones placed at the head of each of his ancestors. In as much as the wolves were an integral part of the family proper, he went to the effort to reidentify as much as possible, each of the wolves grave markers as well, with the proper headstone. All was in readiness for the coming day.

The Countess had gone to the trouble of contracting with a full Mariachi band and Caterer from San Antonio to provide the appropriate music refreshments for the wedding ceremony as well as the reception afterwards.

Of course the site of the wedding ceremony was to be adjacent to the burial site of his ancestors outside the now well—manicured copse of old trees that had served the family well for over a hundred and fifty years.

The Gulf Stream landed and was met by Hondo, Rafferty and Duke Vultee who hustled them as well as their two Secret Service handlers to the House adjacent to the wedding site to prepare for the One PM ceremony conducted by a priest carefully selected from the same San Antonio parish that served their ancestors long ago.

At the appointed time the Mariachi band commenced their playing a signal for the ladies to join the others near the copse of trees, as the Countess said, "Ladies, it's show time in Texas"!

Rory gave his mother away to Jaeger and provided the ring and earrings Jaeger had crafted by the Houston Jeweler as well as any best son could, as the Mariachi musicians played softly in the background.

As those in attendance filed past and paid their respects to both bride and groom, Buffy was the last to pay her respects drawing Melanie aside saying, "Jaeger may tell you this one day or maybe not, but we've known each other for quite a while. I was his original lawyer who screwed things up in his trial long ago. Took me some time but I finally made things right for him and now since I'm his family lawyer, now that he has a family at long last, I do hope we can be friends and invite you to come and spend some time with me in my home in Houston so I can fill in the blanks somewhat regarding his life. It's been a long dark ride for that man, but since you're the focal point of his life from here on out I believe you're owed that. Also, he'll probably tell you this himself, he came to me last month and had me prepare his will. You and your son are the single beneficiaries of his estate. Just so you know"!

"Thank you Buffy. I'll take the best of care. And soon as things settle down I'll take you up on that offer to come and see you"!

Just then the Mariachi's horns signaled everyone to draw near as they went towards the burial site of the Jaeger family. Somehow the Countess Fabiola had become attached to Hondo as they followed the grouping saying, "They tell me that you're a real live Bounty Hunter, Mister Hondo. Is that true"?

"Funny that's what they tell me too. Yup I chase the bandito's Countess.

But I thought you were runnin' with Vultee? He's a friend of mine and I wouldn't want to cross his trail none"!

"A passing fancy for the moment Hondo. Besides you will note the youngster on his arm currently, part of his endless retinue no doubt. But enough of him. It's you I'm interested in. You must tell me about all of your adventures. Is what you do dangerous"?

"Dangerous? Is the Pope Catholic? Of course it's dangerous. A guy could get killed"!

"Then we shall be friends Hondo. Very good friends", she said as she drew him near, "And you shall call me Fabiola from now on Hondo"! Then she shivered slightly saying his name over "Hondo. Oh how I like that name Hondo. What is your first name"?

"Been Hondo all my life. Just Hondo"!

"Like Jaeger, a man with no first name, just a cognomen"!

"Cognomen? What's that"? Fabiola smiled and with a slow wink, she whispered in his ear, "Stay close to me and I shall enlighten you to the mysteries of the universe"!

As everyone gathered around the copse of trees, Molly hung back and summoned the two Secret Service Agents to bring forward the pet carriers and deposit them in front of Jaeger. Molly and Mel each opened a carrier bringing forth one of the little wolves as Molly, now acting as the First Lady recounted the story of how Henry Jaeger was presented with two similar wolves when he was but a small boy by an Indian Shaman and the role they played throughout the years.

"The President would like you to raise Chani and Akila as your own, to complete the circle of life"! Both she and Mel then placed the baby wolves on the ground as they both ran to Jaeger as if by natural instinct. He kneeled down and scooped them up with tears in his eyes as they wiggled in his grasp, feverishly licking his face, instinctually imprinting his scent as their new master. Then as if on que they both grew restless as everyone recognized the emotional significance of the gift as Jaeger gently placed them on the ground saying, "I didn't think anything in the world could top my marriage", as he looked at Mel, "but I was wrong".

The little wolves then made for the grave sites sniffing each one in turn stopping at the grave markers of Henry and Melanie, giving off tiny plaintive howls, and then moved on finally stopping at the grave markers of the original Chani and Akila, giving out their tiny howls as somehow an inexplicable recognition of an ancestor.

One by one the guests peeled away to allow the bride and groom time alone with their new family, as the Mariachi's began playing softly in the background, Mel joined her husband kneeling at the restored grave sites of Henry and Melanie and then his father and mother as he said to them, "I hope you all approve"! Only Rory and General Bollinger stood at some distance to drink in the full meaning of the sight before them.

"I suppose I'm going to have to call him Dad from now on General"!

"The finest man that ever served under my command, young man is now your father. You couldn't do much better"!

As they turned to join the others, Mel asked Jaeger, amidst the tiny howls, "I didn't know that your original ancestor was named Melanie"?

"It's a long story and we've enough time for me to tell the tale as it was told to me", said Jaeger as they joined Chani and Akila.

"Tomorrow we'll spend the day looking over your new home"!

* 9 7 8 1 9 6 4 7 4 4 0 0 1 *